SAUL and RIZPAH

Liam Dunne 1960

a novel

RIZPAH

by Charles E. Israel

Simon and Schuster • New York

· *to Verna* ·

contents

book one

TORASH

prologue

I SUPPOSE the most vivid memory I have of Rizpah involves a situation
in which I never actually saw her. In fact, our paths were not destined
to cross for the first time until nearly two days later.

It seems strange that of all the images of her my eyes have seen,
my mind has chosen to enshrine the one which did not even exist for
me. Certainly other moments in the long years of our knowledge of
each other are equally clear. Without difficulty I can remember her as
she was at the height of her beauty—her chestnut hair catching the
glint of a dying sun as she sat in the garden of Saul's house at Gibeah
or picked her way among the wagons and cook fires of his encampments; high cheekbones guarding those eyes of deep and troubling
green; body supple and softly provocative. Or later, when the fury
worked in her as strongly and bitterly as it did in Saul, matching his
despair, when her eyes grew haggard and hopeless, and she cried out
desperately from shallow sleep beside a guttering lamp. I can see her
in the sand-blown provincial town of exile across the Jordan, Abner
beside her, where life coursed in quiet, melancholy rhythms and conveyed a faint promise of peace. And finally, beside the blasted tree
where she kept her terrible vigil . . . the silky hair I had combed
so often disheveled and caked with grime, her skin festering with sun

sores, lips parched and cracked . . . yet somehow still beautiful, with a loveliness which transcends time and fear and suffering.

Certainly these moments are clear, imprinted deeply on the tablet of my heart. Clear, and probably much more significant than the one I first spoke of. Yet are they?

Perhaps, if I am permitted to live a few more years this side of the Land of the Dead, if my brain begins to shrivel like the skin of my body . . . perhaps I will come to believe I was really with her on this particular day. In the pathetic blurring of time and space which afflicts those of us who have lived longer than we should, I might begin to dream many things that are not true.

That is why I am determined to set down this record now, while I can still write with some objectivity of events, both the joyous and the gloomy, as they happened. Before my love for Rizpah and, if I am truly honest, the long-harbored shreds of resentment against her, combine to create some pretty little cloud of fiction which would obscure verdant hill and stark crag alike.

Rizpah herself would never write down these things. Not that she lacks the gift. On occasion her words can be as pointed as the filed tip of a javelin, her insights as probing as torchlight in a tomb. But she is impatient. Even now, when she has long since proved her capacity for acceptance and endurance. She can talk for an entire night, her husky voice calling up memories, comparing personalities, speculating about meanings. But to spend even a few moments taming reed and scroll to mirror thought is for her unmitigated drudgery.

Nor will the scribes of her own people ever do her justice. They have already woven the fabric of the chronicle of all those years: the time of Samuel's ascendancy and uncompromising grip on king and commoner, of Saul's troubled reign, of David's ambivalent dance between ambition and compassion. They have paid great attention to detail. They have recorded with pedantic care the names and some of the deeds of mere tribal captains. But *her* they have only mentioned twice. Once they spoke of her slightingly, backhandedly paying tribute to her influence and beauty. The second mention they could scarcely avoid, endowing it with a measure of grudging admiration. But to set down her name only twice, she who placed her mark on the very foundations of the kingdom . . .

However, why not? The scribes eat at David's table, drink his wine, and when they retire to dusty chambers to ponder the profusion of legend and record, can one expect them to forget where they eat and drink? And if in their zeal to serve they neglect Rizpah, have they not also perverted the might of Saul? How clever they are, to leave intact

the story of his rescue of beleaguered Jabesh-Gilead, to recall faith-
fully his cry for union of the tribes, which reverberated throughout
Israel . . . and yet to color everything with the sly brush of conde-
scension. To give agile interpretation of incidents, to omit, to endow a
casual encounter with heroic value . . . and so to make possible a
comparison of the tragic strength of Saul with machinations of an
ambitious shepherd . . .

But I am wandering. They say old women do this. It is true that I
am old. And with vanity of the aging, I resent hearing about it. Only
Rizpah was ever able to call attention to my years with impunity. "Old
woman . . ." she would say, leaning her elbows on the table, chin between her hands, looking into my eyes with that intriguing mixture of
candor and guile which belongs to her alone. And I would wait. For
if she said it a second time, it meant the beginning of a confidence.
Something which had happened that day, her reactions, what she had
said and felt.

I welcomed this. The uses of love are manifold and subtle. And
one of the touchstones is the nature of the gifts we bestow on those
we love. She gave her heart to me, placed it trustingly in my hands
through long nights of reminiscence, of pride and remorse, of joy and
suffering. And I, aged and spent, what could I offer in return? I gave
her what I could: acceptance, suspension of judgment, a degree of
understanding. She accepted the exchange as fair. And it was a signal
between us, her pausing, then saying a second time in her low, husky
voice, "Old woman . . ."

That is why, even though I was not physically present on the day
of which I speak, still I feel I was. I never saw the territory of
Simeon, where she was born, until some years later, but she has a
talent for description, and I was able to picture the gaunt wilderness
of sand and rock, erupting irregularly into low savage hills which
looked as though they had been flung across the desert by some great
contemptuous hand. She made me feel the burning emptiness of the
wasteland, punctuated here and there, for no apparent reason, by a
spring or natural well. Around the watering place would grow an oasis.
And if a man were enterprising, he would extend the cool boundaries
of the oasis, make the soil fertile and productive. Such a man was
Rizpah's father, Aiah.

So it was that I could see her father's house, and Rizpah herself,
and understand something of what happened that day. At this moment she was completely innocent, untouched by knowledge, sophistication, avarice . . . any of the virtues or vices by which we live. For
every one of us there is this time of perfection, when we are untroubled

and unspoiled. Some of us lose it early, others are sheltered longer from the withering, eroding winds of the world. And once we have been exposed, we wax maudlin for the rest of our lives and mourn whatever it is we believe we have lost. But I often wonder if, instead of mourning, we should not bless the gods who rob us so cruelly of innocence and turn us out into the vale of suffering.

For Rizpah this was the beginning.

chapter one

As ALWAYS in the late afternoon, a vagrant breeze touched the top leaves of the palms, whispering the approach of evening. But the sun was still warm on her back as she slipped through the seldom-used rear gate of the garden. She hesitated in the narrow space between the wall and a slender tamarisk, aware, in the sudden coolness that was like silence, of the pounding of her heart. She stood motionless, straining to hear the conversation of the men at the other end of the garden. Their voices rose and died away, mingling with the drone of bees hovering above clustered flowers.

Someone said, ". . . the wedding," and Rizpah allowed herself the luxury of a small, delicious shiver. They were coming to the point. She had to get closer. To hear each word they spoke about her, to glimpse for the first time the face of the man she was to marry.

In the house a dish shattered on the floor. Rizpah stiffened as her mother's rebuke cut across the whining apology of a servant. Then all was quiet except for the sound of the men's voices. She crept forward cautiously.

The lilies were fresh and sweet, cool to the touch. She threaded her way through the tall, fragrant stalks, searching for a place where she could eavesdrop safely, found it between two closely twined climbing roses.

From just beyond her father's laughter rose sharply, hearty but measured, responding carefully to some jest from the lips of her prospective father-in-law.

There was a lull in the conversation. She could hear her mother in the house, giving orders concerning the betrothal feast. Her father said deliberately, "Now then." He cleared his throat and spoke again. "Now then. The matter of a dowry."

"If you wish, Aiah." The reply was smooth, deprecating. "If you wish. But between you and me such talk is not necessary. It is generous enough of my friend Aiah to give his only daughter in marriage. This gift alone will enrich our house beyond description."

Aiah's voice and manner were well suited to the formal bargaining ritual. "It is kind of my friend to speak so graciously. His words refresh the ears as the sound of a mountain spring heals the weariness of a traveler. But the life of my daughter Rizpah would be indeed unfulfilled if she went forth empty-handed to the son of my friend. My daughter is young, having lived barely sixteen summers. And while she displays a certain amount of promise . . ."

"She's lovely!" A new voice interrupting: gentle, charged with fervor. Rizpah caught her breath.

For once, surprise shook the measured quality out of Aiah's laugh. "Now then," he said, and without being able to see, Rizpah knew he had placed his hand on his round stomach. "Now then. And where did the son of my friend set eyes on my daughter, seeing this is the first time we have had the honor of his presence in our house?"

The young man did not answer immediately. Trembling a little, Rizpah raised her hand, carefully separated two rose branches, and peered through.

"Shiphri, tell Aiah where you saw his daughter."

The voice of the boy's father was stern, but he and Aiah exchanged a quick, amused glance. Rizpah shifted her position to see more clearly.

The boy's face was like his voice: gentle, still unformed. Rizpah guessed he could not be much older than she, eighteen at the most. He had a small silky beard which quivered tremulously as a shy smile grew on his lips.

"Where, Shiphri?" The boy's father was insistent. "Where did you see her?"

The smile ripened to sweetness but still remained shy, flickering. Rizpah waited, curious as the men to know where he could possibly have seen her.

"This morning," said Shiphri, looking from his father to Aiah, "when we first reached the house of Aiah, I went for a walk."

"I don't recall that." The father, mock-cross, again exchanging the amused, knowing glance with his host.

"My father was inspecting one of Aiah's vineyards. He and Aiah were greatly absorbed. So was I."

His smile flickered again, and Rizpah felt her heart contract, suddenly, inexplicably. "So was I," Shiphri repeated, "until I saw a girl in the distance, walking toward the pool where one draws water."

"So you followed her," said Aiah, rubbing his belly.

"Yes." Softly, "I hid behind a rock and watched her while she filled the pitchers with water."

How was I, wondered Rizpah, doubt fluttering through her mind like an anxious bird, how did I look? My hair not properly combed, my face still swollen with sleep, my robe thrown about me like a sack over a camel. How did I look?

"She's the most beautiful girl in the whole tribe of Simeon," said Shiphri.

Aiah cleared his throat. "So the son of my friend has had so much experience with women that he is personally able to crown the queen of Simeon."

The two men laughed. Shiphri flushed; his beard trembled.

"I know it was not mannerly of me to follow the daughter of Aiah." He spread out his hands, and Rizpah saw that they were slender and graceful. "But now that I have seen her . . ."

"You want to get on with the wedding as quickly as possible." Aiah raised his eyebrows.

"If it pleases Aiah." He smiled again and suddenly seemed to have no control over the cascade of words that poured from his lips. "With Rizpah by my side I shall be the happiest man in all Israel. And I will prosper. The vineyards my father has given me will grow rich and heavy. The sheep will multiply and become fat. Everything will blossom and grow fruitful under the touch of your daughter Rizpah."

"And perhaps my daughter Rizpah will grow fruitful under the touch of Shiphri."

The men nudged each other and laughed, slapping their thighs. Shiphri turned crimson. In her hiding place Rizpah chewed her lower lip, half in annoyance, half in excitement.

"Now then," said Aiah gruffly, to cover his amusement. "The matter of the dowry."

Shiphri raised a slender hand. His beard trembled, but this time with earnestness. "If it please Aiah and my father, let us talk no more of dowries. My heart sickens with fear that my father and Aiah might stumble over some disagreement in this matter, and each will retire to consider, and I will not be permitted to marry Rizpah until another year has passed."

"So eager, this one," said Aiah.

"You must learn to be patient, Shiphri," said his father smoothly. "If the loveliness of Rizpah is but one quarter that of Zia, the wife of my friend Aiah, it will not spoil for many years. And certainly," he added with a smile, "not before you take her to the marriage bed."

Aiah coughed and said, "Now then."

Shiphri relaxed, fingering his beard, while the men resumed their lengthy bargaining.

Rizpah's hand had grown tired from holding the rose branches apart, but she scarcely felt the fatigue. She nibbled at her lower lip and continued to watch Shiphri. As she watched, her breathing quickened, sweetly, in a transport of innocence, so there was no pain in her eagerness, only the simple pleasure of yearning. She was so engrossed she failed to hear the light, firm step behind her. A hand touched her shoulder. She wheeled, stifling a cry, and looked full into the impassive eyes of her mother.

Zia placed a finger to her lips and motioned Rizpah to follow her. It was only when the girl tried to move that she discovered her robe was caught on a thorn. She twisted around and hooked a second thorn through the material, looked at her mother with the helplessness of a baby lamb. Deftly Zia freed her from the thorns and motioned again, more impatiently now.

Her mother did not speak until they were near the house. Then her low, flat voice rushed out, enveloped Rizpah with scorn. "So! Now you spy on men, seek them out in their privacy, like some skulking Bedouin whore."

Rizpah was frightened. What she had done was wrong, but nothing so bad that her mother should curse her. "Mother . . ." she began.

Zia raised her hand quickly, peremptorily, as she did everything. Rizpah's words died, lost in apprehension. She felt tears starting into her eyes.

They drew near the spit, just outside the house, where a servant was roasting the kid for the betrothal feast. He was a squat, swarthy man, with a lonely light in his eyes like most of the inhabitants of the land of Edom, which lies even deeper in the wilderness than Simeon. He had come to them recently, brought by a caravan at the end of the winter rains. As Rizpah and her mother passed, the Edomite looked up from his work and smiled shyly at the girl. She glanced at her mother and was afraid to return the smile.

"Shameless," said Zia harshly, but too low for the servant to hear. "Absolutely shameless. One would think you had been born the daughter of a camel driver."

"Mother . . ." Rizpah said again, but her tears would not let her go on. She shrugged and was silent. They entered the house.

Aiah was not a wealthy man. At least he would not have been called so among tribes to the north of Simeon, Judah or Benjamin, for instance. There more rain fell, from clouds trapped by the rolling hills. Fertile soil soaked up moisture and produced lush fields of grain, rich grass where fat sheep grazed. But Aiah had done well. No one could conquer the sandy sparseness or the blistering heat of Simeon. Aiah had done the next best thing. He had made his peace with it. And because he was patient and persevering, able to bend with disappointment, his flocks multiplied and his vineyards defied the blazing sun. Long ago Rizpah's great-grandfather, being a third son and not entitled to more than a meager parcel of land from his father, had found this spot and settled down beside the tiny trickle of water which spelled life. He and his wife had lived alone in a crude hair tent, had themselves broken the hard ground, planted, nursed tender fruits to maturity.

Those times were forgotten. Aiah had inherited a spacious house, built of straw brick reinforced with wooden beams purchased at great expense from itinerant traders. To attend the needs of land and family, Aiah possessed a score of servants.

Some of these were busy now, preparing dishes for the feast. It was not exactly gourmet's fare. In the great cities of Philistia, where palates are jaded, they would have sneered at the simplicity and called it fit only for peasants. But sometimes the very lack of variety in peasant food gives it a certain charm. And whatever is served is always fresh. In Aiah's house on this day the long table next to the hearth boasted great glazed bowls in which green and purple grapes banked bright pomegranates and peaches with the tint of dawn. Honeycombs lay on beds of leaves. Pots of leeks and lentils were simmering over the fire. Bread still warm from the day's baking was heaped in careless profusion next to the hearth oven.

Through her tears Rizpah caught a glimpse of a large basket of almond cakes resting on a corner of the table and at once forgot that her mother was standing next to her, stiff and angry. She took a step toward the cakes, her mouth watering, before she remembered and paused. Her mother was watching her.

Zia said reflectively, "Sometimes I forget . . ."

Rizpah looked at her. "Forget what, Mother?"

Laughter gleamed in Zia's eyes and was gone so swiftly Rizpah was not sure it had been there at all.

"Forget what, Mother?"

"Looking at you," Zia said in her flat voice, "one would almost believe you were a woman."

Rizpah smoothed her robe, preening as much as her mother's gaze would allow. "I am a woman."

Zia snorted. "And what did you think of your husband-to-be?"

Rizpah felt herself blushing. "I don't know."

"Staring at him as if you wanted to eat him and you say you don't . . ."

"Can I have an almond cake?"

"They're for the feast."

"Just one."

"You'd better go and fetch some water."

Rizpah cast a fleeting glance at the almond cakes, then started for a pitcher which stood in a corner of the room. Her mother put out her hand. "Wait . . ."

She turned, prepared for some fresh reproach, surprised to see a tenderness she had never known in her mother's face. They stared at each other, then, "You're very lovely," said Zia. And in that instant Rizpah knew how her mother had looked as a young girl.

The tenderness fled, giving way to the customary flat, derisive voice. "And how did you really like Shiphri? Did you find him handsome?"

Rizpah could not think of an answer.

"Never mind then," said her mother. "I know what I want to know. It is good to feel this way about your husband. When Aiah married me, I thought there was not another girl in all Israel so happy, so filled . . ." She stopped, turned to the table, and with her quick, deft movements began arranging fruit in a silver bowl. "Go fetch the water," she said, without looking at Rizpah, and added, "Your uncle Amaziah is on guard duty. Tell him a servant will relieve him as soon as the feast is ready to begin."

Rizpah walked slowly over to the pitcher and picked it up. Then, seeing her mother busy, she darted to the table, snatched an almond cake from the top of the pile and ran out the door.

"Rizpah!"

Zia's flat voice pursued her. She smiled and, as she walked quickly away from the house, took a huge bite of the cake.

chapter two

RIZPAH CHEWED slowly, trying to make the cake last, but it was gone before she reached the old well. Once there had been water here, and two fine fig trees, but the well had dried up, suddenly and without reason, while she was still a small child. This, of course, could have been disastrous, and Aiah, with his customary flexibility and levelheadedness, at once made plans to move the entire household north, where they would find temporary refuge with distant relatives. Jahveh was good to him, though, and at the very moment of departure a servant rushed up with news that a spring was gushing from rocks a little way beyond the old well. From that time forth they had more water than ever, and Aiah was able to increase his holdings of arable land.

Rizpah set the pitcher down and rested, watching puffs of wind pick up sand and swirl it in little eddies across the face of the abandoned well. She turned to watch the sun burn red just before it plummeted behind the low mountains to the west. Purple fingers of shadow reached toward her across the flatland.

As she often did, she wondered now what lay beyond the mountains. She knew very little. She had been told that Simeon was the southernmost of Israel's tribal territories, that it was ringed about with strange peoples who worshiped outlandish gods and were sometimes hostile, sometimes grudgingly respectful, but never to be completely trusted. She had seen their caravans and knew how they were called: Moab, Edom, Amalek, and the powerful nation hugging the Great Sea, Philistia. When she was very young, Zia had recounted tales of the Hebrew heroes. Rizpah had cherished their names: Joshua, Gideon, Jephtha, Samson, men who had fought for Israel and acted as judges of the people. But her mother's accounts of warfare and high adventure were, after all, only stories, and she half disbelieved them. Reality for her was the sun's warmth in the vineyards, the hot wind causing a lamb to bleat. She was content with what she knew and what she had and, beyond that, what she knew would be hers. Yet there were times when contentment stretched thin, when the sight of a new moon balanced poignantly above the dark mystery of the mountains could stir in her a restlessness she could neither quell nor fathom.

Rizpah sighed and picked up the water pitcher.

She saw Amaziah at the top of the hill. He stood silhouetted against the evening sky, head tilted back, drinking from the small skin of wine he always carried with him. Rizpah felt a pleasant glow of anticipation as she climbed toward him. Amaziah was young, not at all like an uncle. In fact, strangers often took them for brother and sister. They had the same chestnut hair, the same high cheekbones. Even their voices were alike, low and husky. Listening to Amaziah was like hearing herself talk. With him there was never need for restraint or pretense. She said what she felt. He answered her in kind, carelessly and with affection.

He lowered the wineskin as she reached him, hung it on the spear stuck in the ground beside him.

"Hold, Little One," he said. "Nobody passes here without paying proper tribute to the house of Amaziah."

He circled her waist with his arm and swept her to him. A pleasant odor of wine surrounded her. She laughed as he planted a gusty kiss on her lips.

"Almond cake," he said, releasing her. "You taste of almond cake."

She asked with a touch of coquetry, "Does it displease my uncle?"

His laugh was as gusty as his kiss had been. "If only all women were so sweet." He placed his hand under her chin, surveyed her critically. "You still have a crumb on the corner of your mouth."

Delighted, she flicked out her tongue, captured the morsel and savored it. After a moment she told him, "My mother says she'll send a servant to relieve you when the feast is ready."

He groaned. "That won't be for hours yet." He retrieved the wineskin, opened his mouth and squirted a fine stream far back into his throat. "Philistines," he grumbled, making the words sound like an oath.

"Amaziah," she asked, "where I'm going after I'm married, will the men there also have to guard againt the Philistines?"

"Always," he replied casually. "Until we conquer them or they conquer us." The downward twist of his mouth belied the lightness of his tone. She saw in his eyes the restless apprehension all the men she knew, even the imperturbable Aiah, seemed to emanate when they mentioned the Philistines. "There has been talk," Amaziah continued, "of choosing a king over Israel, a man who would unite the tribes and conquer the idol worshipers." He grimaced and for an instant turned into a stranger before her eyes. "It would never work. Judah distrusts Benjamin. Benjamin looks on the men of Dan as outlanders. Each tribe keeps its own counsel, and single words of wisdom flow together to form a river of fear." He shook his head as if bothered by a fly, then smiled at her, inquired teasingly, "Are you not curious to see the man you will marry?"

"I've seen him." She looked at her uncle, eyes full of mirth, saw the response spring into his as she added, "I hid behind the roses in the garden and watched."

"He can't be worth much looking. Otherwise you would still be there."

"I didn't want to leave. Mother found me."

He threw back his head and roared with laughter, relishing the situation. "And what did Zia say?"

"That I behaved as though I were the daughter of a camel driver." She grinned. "And that I was like a Bedouin whore."

"Your mother," Amaziah observed mildly, "would not know a Bedouin or any other kind of whore if she stumbled over one in the act of entertaining."

Rizpah wrinkled her forehead. "Amaziah . . . I know if you call someone a whore it's a curse. But what does it mean?"

He directed a stream of wine into his mouth, swallowed and took a deep breath. "A whore, my darling, is an enigma, a paradox. Men seek her out eagerly, then later revile her. And in order to be worthy of these curses, she must possess singular virtues . . . patience, charm, skill, learning. Her life is fashioned only for the delight of men like myself, her conduct shaped to our whims and desires."

"Is that not what a wife does?"

Amaziah laughed. "Your young bridegroom is a lucky man." He brushed a strand of hair off her forehead. "I have never been so fortunate. Every woman into whose eyes I have looked has given me back a reflection of my own selfishness." He paused, then added, looking at Rizpah, "With one exception."

"Who is she, Amaziah? You've never told me about her."

"No I haven't," he said flatly, taking another swallow of wine. "What did you think of your young man?"

"He has beautiful hands. And a gentle voice."

"That's a good beginning for respecting a husband. I'll have a long talk with him when I've fortified myself with a new skin of wine."

"The old skin," she said boldly, noticing how he was beginning to sway, "the skin that keeps your belly from falling out, seems to be very well fortified already."

She found it disquieting when he did not laugh as she had expected.

"Rizpah, my darling," he said, "I have watched you since the days when you were an infant, when I myself was only a runny-nosed boy.

I remember the morning you took your first steps, and the impression your tiny feet made in the sand is still one of my best-loved memories. I have observed the sharpness of the child-spirit softening and mellowing within your woman's body." He sighed. "It has been a lovely experience. And a painful one."

She shook her head, not understanding. He smiled, yawned, and patted her shoulder.

"Leave me now, so I can consider the vagaries of fate that have made you the daughter of my sister."

He kissed her once more and she set off for the pool, the smell of his wine pungent and yet somehow pleasing in her nostrils.

Daylight was fading when she reached the water. But the air was still warm, so she decided to bathe. She removed her robe and sandals, then cast a swift glance in the direction of the rocks behind the pool, remembering that Shiphri had watched her from there. The thought gave her pleasure. She pretended he was still there, observing her as she moved slowly to the water's edge. His eyes gentle as those of a newborn kid, and his hands . . . she placed her own hands under her breasts, stirring fantasy to savor already the long life of mingled excitement and peace she would know with Shiphri. Lovely, he had said she was, the most beautiful girl in the whole tribe of Simeon. She smiled, thinking how one day she would tell him she had stood behind the intertwining rose bushes, listening and yearning.

Rizpah stooped beside the water, dangled her hand in its coolness, reveling in the soft splashing sound, the gleam of dying light against the ruffled surface of the pool. She filled the pitcher and shivered as she poured water over her body. For a time she amused herself by drawing designs on the wetness of her thigh. Even as I saw her do on occasion years later. Some remnant of the child one often finds in beautiful women. A privilege perhaps, an admiring and sometimes charming obsession with self. Or perhaps simply a puzzled response to that discomfort akin to fear beauty generates in people, even in the person who possesses it.

She began dreaming. She pictured the vineyards Shiphri's father had given him, heard the soft, plaintive calls of his sheep. She tasted the quality of joy she would know when she ran forth from their house in the red glow of evening to welcome Shiphri after his day's labor among the vines and trees. She considered the children she would bear him, the shape of their hands and feet, the innocent stare of eyes reflecting her own love. They would be happy together. She was as sure of it as he had been that afternoon, pouring out the tenderness of his young hope before the leveling amusement of the men. She would be proud to be his wife. . . .

She turned, feeling clean and refreshed, toward the rocks, as if to offer herself to the man who had followed her and looked at her with love.

She was surprised to see how dark it had become. The outline of the rocks was barely visible, a black imposing mass crouching above the water. They would be wondering at the house what was keeping her. She picked up her robe and quickly rubbed the rest of the moisture from her body, slipped into the garment and found her sandals. A moment later she was on her way, a full pitcher of water on her shoulder.

As she climbed the hill where Amaziah stood guard she heard a distant cry: shrill, hollow, desperate. Some animal, she thought, and it made her feel lonely, some small animal in the desert, fleeing the jaws of the mountain lion. She walked a few steps further, and as the cry was repeated, Rizpah stumbled over something soft, yielding. She fell heavily to the ground, losing her pitcher and coming to rest with her face almost touching that of her uncle.

Amaziah's open mouth grinned at her. His eyes, wild and vacant, looked through her. She decided he was drunk and had fallen down the hill in his stupor. She had often seen men drink themselves into insensibility. At harvest time, when the work was done, the servants lay beside the wine press like felled oxen. She accepted this as easily as she accepted the ripening of the grapes. But whenever she saw Amaziah lying among the snoring men, her indifference sharpened to an indefinable sense of pain. She felt the pain rising in her now and was concerned with her mother's fury if Amaziah's negligence were discovered.

Then she saw that the hairs of her uncle's beard were wet, matted. His throat was slashed, a deep uneven cut running from his left ear to his right shoulder. She wanted to cry, to be sick, to get up and run, to scream. But she could only lie facing him, held motionless by the power of his sightless eyes, listening to the water from the pitcher she had dropped running onto the hard dry ground.

The cry came again, full of fear. Gradually, using all her strength, she was able to move away from Amaziah, until finally she could no longer see his face and was free to rise. She ran without looking back and without thinking. And because she did not think, she found herself mounting the hill leading toward the house.

As she came over the rise she saw the flames leaping from the roof. Rizpah stood, holding her robe close about her, watching the fire destroy her father's house. She wanted to turn, to run off into the blackness of the desert. But the thought of her parents drew her forward. As she walked, trancelike, she could see the shadowy forms of men scurrying about outside the garden wall, piling cloth, goblets, silver pitchers and bowls in a great heap. Their voices came to her over what seemed an infinite distance. She tried to pick out some familiar figure: her mother, her father, a servant. But there was only the ragged double line of alien shapes, moving like ants to and from the heap of booty.

She heard a sheep moan somewhere behind her, then another answering. Turning, she saw a man herding them toward the house. He spied her in the same instant and started for her. She screamed, and the sound of her voice released her from the shock which had held her since she found Amaziah dead on the hill. For the first time she understood what had happened. The Philistines had come. They had killed Amaziah, stolen her father's property, set fire to the house. And now one of them was pursuing her, only a few steps away, coming on swiftly. She saw the gleam of his teeth as he approached, open-mouthed and laughing.

Rizpah turned and fled. The departure of shock left terror, brought fresh strength. She could hear the raider's steps coming closer. She tried to run faster, but her lungs were bursting, her legs suddenly numb. Her foot caught in the hem of her robe. She tripped and sprawled forward onto the ground.

He was on top of her at once, the sound of his low, harsh laughter grating in her ear. Rizpah struggled, but he held her arms fast. She twisted around, caught a glimpse of flashing white teeth, managed to sink her own teeth in the soft flesh of his neck.

The laughter ceased abruptly.

"Hebrew bitch!" snarled the man and struck her under the chin with the heel of his hand.

Dazed from the blow, she allowed him to pull her to her feet. Holding her arm tightly, he led her toward the house. "Bitch," he said again, but with the epithet his laughter returned: low, empty, harsh.

When they reached the garden wall, the sense of unreality again descended. She saw the bodies of the servants scattered grotesquely on the ground, a nightmarish pattern of death. The Edomite who earlier in the day had smiled at her while tending the roasting kid lay in the fire pit, his face charred almost beyond recognition.

Rizpah caught sight of Aiah's body, his mouth frozen open in a grimace of fear. And nearby, next to the body of Shiphri's father, lay her mother, robe pulled up above her waist, naked limbs distorted and somehow pitifully small in the glare of the fire. Rizpah closed her eyes, stumbled and fell. Her captor pulled her up roughly.

"Bakesh!" he called, and led her to a tall gray-haired man who was directing the raiders. Bakesh turned and surveyed her coldly.

The man who had caught her was still holding her arm. He laughed. "A bitch," he said, displaying her teeth marks on his neck. "A true bitch."

Bakesh touched his gray hair with a delicate gesture.

"Well?" asked the man who was holding her, and after a pause again, "Well?"

"We shall take her along." Bakesh spoke in the clipped, precise Philistine accent. His voice held a note of weariness.

Rizpah's captor put his arm around her. She struggled as his hand groped for her breast.

"Dintor!"

It was Bakesh again, his eyes burning with passion. But his gaze was directed at Dintor, not her. She watched his rage evaporate as he looked at the younger man, dissolve slowly into a kind of yearning. He smiled at Dintor sweetly, winningly. "What did I tell you?" he asked softly, like a mother chiding an errant child.

Dintor released Rizpah and hung his head. Bakesh continued to look at him, the trace of a smile still hovering about his lips. Dintor returned his gaze and Rizpah, forgotten, thought of running, but the ache in her legs made even the thought exhausting.

There was a disturbance around the corner of the garden wall. Two men came in sight dragging Shiphri. His clothes were torn, his face swollen and bleeding. Rizpah uttered a cry and tried to run to him, but Dintor's grip on her arm was quick and crushing.

The men pulled Shiphri to his feet in front of Bakesh, looked inquiringly at their leader. Bakesh barely glanced at the bedraggled young man, made a weary, abortive gesture in the air. One of the men drew his sword.

Shiphri, uncomprehending, half turned and saw Rizpah. He opened his mouth, but no words came out. The man with the sword ran his thumb cautiously along the blade.

Rizpah cried out to Bakesh, "Please . . . no!"

Bakesh turned away. The raider hefted his sword, spun Shiphri around to face him.

"Rizpah!" Shiphri's tiny beard was trembling with anguish. Rizpah wanted to close her eyes, but she could not.

Shiphri's hand reached out to her just as the sword descended, striking deep between his shoulder and neck. The boy's blood spouted purple in the light of the fire. He sank to the ground, his hand still extended, an expression of surprise transfixing his gentle features.

Bakesh motioned wearily into the darkness. "Take her to the camels and wait," he said to Dintor, who led her, unresisting, away from Shiphri's body.

The shadowy forms of the camels loomed ahead of them. Without warning, Rizpah felt her stomach turn over. She retched and was sick on the ground. Dintor began to laugh harshly, emptily. Her tears flowed now, and the taste of almond was bitter in her throat.

chapter three

THE WARM tears welling from her eyes were comforting, a soft veil drawn mercifully against the image of horror. But after only a few moments Rizpah could cry no more. And with the tears gone, her eyes felt dry and swollen. Pain throbbed slowly in her chest, like a second heart. She heard someone sob, a terrible strangled sound, raised her head in alarm before she realized dully she had made the sound herself.

Dintor sat cross-legged on the ground and watched her. Now and then his laughter would weave itself into the fabric of her pain. Her instinct for people was clean and true then, as it is now. Even stunned as she was, confused and bereft, she began to understand that Dintor's laughter was no indication of mirth but rather some private supportive communication with himself. It reminded her of the call of the jackal, circling the flocks at night, voicing his anger against the thwarting presence of the shepherd.

She turned toward the house and saw the flames, no longer high now, sending long streamers of sparks into the air.

Bakesh came with the other men and gave her only a cursory glance as he supervised the loading of the camels. There were about twenty men. They worked quietly, efficiently, packing the riches of her father's house into large bags, which they slung across the backs of the animals. One man paused frequently to cough; another hummed softly as he worked. Rizpah felt that if she were seeing these men for the first time she could believe them to be members of any peaceful caravan stopping briefly for refreshment at her father's house. But the illusion could not survive her recognition of a carved goblet from which her father was accustomed to drink his evening wine, the mantle of smooth, multicolored cloth, purchased by Zia only a month before from a trader bringing wares out of Egypt.

She caught sight of the man who had killed Shiphri. He stood watching her, holding a handful of dates, pensively popping them one after the other into his mouth, spitting the stones over his shoulder with an abrupt twisting motion. Rizpah was surprised that she was not afraid of him. She returned his stare evenly until he looked away.

The loading was finally finished. Bakesh tested the ropes lashing the bulging sacks to the camels. Satisfied, he walked slowly over to Rizpah. Dintor, who had remained sitting on the ground until now, rose and stepped close to Bakesh. With an indolent movement he allowed his shoulder to brush against the older man's arm, peered into his face. Bakesh stared back at him in silence, but, as before, the sternness drained from his eyes and the tight lines around his mouth softened.

At length he said, "Pick out two men. Make them responsible for the sheep and goats."

Dintor nodded, then glanced at Rizpah.

"I shall take care of her," the older man said sharply.

Dintor's teeth flashed, and as he walked away, Bakesh touched his forehead with a delicate gesture, sighed and turned wearily to Rizpah. "Come," he said.

She followed him to the lead camel. Bakesh made it kneel. Then he grasped Rizpah under the arms and swung her onto its back with an ease which surprised her. She had not expected him to possess so much strength. He climbed up behind her, shouted an order. The caravan moved off slowly into the darkness, striking a course for the low mountains to the west. Rizpah turned for a last glimpse of her father's house. The garden wall was silhouetted, shattered and stark, in the glow from the dying fire. Suddenly she strained forward, thinking she heard once more the hollow, desperate cry which had risen earlier. But there was only the thud of camels' hoofs, a quiet aftermath to carnage. She closed her eyes, knowing she had been mistaken. . . .

It has been said that grief is like some varieties of poison. A small amount performs its terrible work, but a massive dose does little more than shock, before the body rejects it.

Like many metaphors, this is true to a point, but only to a point. When two people love each other and death takes one of them, the survivor dreads grief, but he also welcomes it. For only after the cruel passage of grief can there be even a measure of peace.

But if the loss is sweeping, if a person is robbed of several he loves in a single catastrophic stroke, grief approaches at once because it is summoned by death. Then often it must wait, hovering in abeyance, before it is allowed to move in and perform its grim service.

I have seen a village, laid waste only an hour before by Israelite marauders, the houses fired, the inhabitants put to the sword. I have seen a single surviving child, miraculously spared by haste or over-sight, playing beside a still-smoldering ruin, drawing pictures in the dust with the broken haft of a spear. When I knelt beside him, he spoke to me calmly, looking into my face with a clear, untroubled gaze, as he told me his parents and two sisters were dead. Over there, he said, pointing to some bodies which lay beside the scorched and twisted wall of a house, then returned to the picture he was drawing.

For many nights after that my sleep was broken by the vision of this child. I was young and I wondered what kind of a race we were breeding, children without feeling who would grow into men without hope.

Until I gradually realized how foolish I was, how shabby my un-derstanding of love. And many months later, passing the shepherd's hut where I had taken the boy for safekeeping, I inquired and learned that only then was he beginning to rest an entire night without fits of violent weeping.

So it was that I understood how Rizpah could be fully aware of what had happened to those she loved, could feel loss and even pain, and could still reject grief in a preoccupation with the sensations of the moment: the sharpness of the night air, the rocking motion of the camel, Bakesh's breath on the back of her neck.

The camel craned its head around, stared at her with wild, white-rimmed eyes, emitted a low complaining whinny. And at the same instant Bakesh spoke to her.

"You have not asked where we are taking you."

His voice with its precise accents, so alien to her ears, was not un-kind, but Rizpah felt a growing sense of apprehension.

He waited, then continued. "Our home is in Askelon, the city by the sea. A lovely place. It is said that once a person has breathed its air he forgets he has ever lived before." When she still did not reply, he went on, "You think it tactless of me to speak to you in this fashion. Your mind and your heart are with those who lie beside the walls of your father's garden. That is as it should be. But it is done." He sighed. "I speak as a man who has seen much of death. I have killed many among the Israelites. And in turn I have watched my two brothers die in battle at the hands of the circumcised.

"For a time you will hate us, for you will believe we have killed joy and hope in your life. But understand what I say. You are young, and for you life is only now beginning."

Rizpah shuddered, partly because his words seemed callous, partly because she felt only dimly the emotions of which he spoke. Bakesh breathed deeply.

"The youth," he inquired gently, "the one who was slain last, was he your husband?"

Pain throbbed inside her, intense, the more startling in its return because she had not been aware of its absence. She knew Bakesh expected an answer and managed to shake her head.

"You are not married then."

Again, not trusting her voice, she shook her head.

He paused, then spoke so softly she barely heard him. "Have you ever lain with a man?" His voice rose. "Have you?"

She turned and cried, "Leave me alone!"

Bakesh leaned forward until his lips were close to her ear. She felt his fury through the precise, clicking accents. "Do you think I ask because I lust after you?" Then, less angrily, he repeated, "Have you ever lain with a man?"

She cleared her throat and said, "No . . . never."

"It is good," he observed simply and was silent.

The sky was beginning to lighten when they stopped to rest. Ahead of them the hills loomed gray and somber. Bakesh helped her off the camel, offered her food: some fruit and a slab of greasy meat. She took a handful of figs and dates. Bakesh made no effort to stop her as she carried them behind a low dune.

Rizpah sat on the sand, the fruit in her lap. She considered it dully. The sight of it made her ill, but she forced herself to nibble at one of the figs, discovered with surprise that she was hungry. She crammed her mouth full, chewed greedily, guiltily, as though she were being watched by familiar, reproachful eyes. From beyond the crest of the dune she could hear the murmured conversation of the men. Once she heard the soft cry of one of her father's goats drifting through the still morning air. She hesitated, then stolidly picked up another piece of fruit. After she had eaten she felt sleepy. She stretched out and closed her eyes.

She sensed the man's presence before she saw him. Then she caught a glimpse of white teeth flashing and knew it was Dintor. She tried to get up, but he pushed her back onto the sand, threw his body across hers. His lips stifled her outcry; his hand fumbled frantically beneath her robe. Rizpah felt the edges of consciousness slowly dissolving, folding in about her. She freed one hand, began to beat a frenzied, futile tattoo on Dintor's back.

She heard a hoarse shout, and the man lying across her was lifted into the air. Rizpah sat up quickly, in time to see Bakesh, rage distorting his features, holding the thrashing Dintor high off the ground. For a moment she thought the older man would dash him against a rock. Then Dintor ceased struggling. His body went limp. Concerned, Bakesh lowered him to the ground, set him carefully on his feet.

Dintor was undismayed, fully composed.

Bakesh said, "She is a virgin. If she is not defiled, she will bring a better price in the market at Askelon."

Dintor stepped out of Bakesh's reach, turned and spoke mockingly. "Is this the only reason my lord Bakesh does not wish me to lie with the Hebrew bitch?"

When Bakesh did not answer, Dintor moved closer and said, "My lord Bakesh should be careful how he handles me. I am sturdily built. But my lord's anger gives him an uncommon strength. In the face of it my body becomes fragile. I can be destroyed. Then Bakesh would be lonely."

He walked around the curve of the dune, laughing to himself. Bakesh's eyes followed him until he was out of sight.

Rizpah got to her feet and straightened her robe. She approached Bakesh and said, "I must thank you."

Calmly Bakesh drew back his hand and slapped her across the mouth. She gasped. He stood regarding her for a moment, the skin drawn tight across the bones of his face. Then he turned and walked away.

chapter four

SHE REMAINED where she was, her lips tingling from Bakesh's blow. From the other side of the dune she could hear him giving orders to the men, his voice even and calm, as though nothing had happened.

The last shreds of darkness were being sucked into the lightening sky. And in the moment between night and day her family was alive again, the perfect entity it had been only a few hours before. She could hear her father's slow, measured voice, could see the deft, impatient fingers of her mother busy with some household task. Amaziah's kiss, heavy with wine, touched her lips. Then she tried to recall Shiphri as she had seen him through the rose branches, strained to restore the memory of the shy smile, the soft eyes, and the small silky trembling beard. But the image of Shiphri only contained the moment of his death, the whistling cruelty of the Philistine sword, the slender hand stretched out to her, helpless, imploring.

And in place of the sporadic pain of the night before a new sensation grew in her breast. Not yet grief, but more alive than pain, softer, more eager to make itself felt. Like a pair of gentle wings fluttering slowly beneath her heart, caressing, and at the same time brushing her with the knowledge of loneliness. She knew the only way she could assuage the feeling was to cry again. Her lips quivered; her eyes called for tears. But none came.

Bakesh appeared at the crest of the dune and stood looking at her. A shaft of dawn light descending through a broken cloud surrounded his gray hair, made it appear white. He blinked and made a delicate beckoning gesture. Slowly she walked after him.

He waited for her beside the lead camel. The other men were mounted and ready to leave. In the morning light they were unkempt, hollow-eyed from lack of sleep, the desert grime crusted deep in the lines of their faces. Rizpah put her fingers to her own forehead. They came away filmed with dirt. She regarded them distastefully.

"There is not much more of the desert," said Bakesh. "Soon you will be able to wash yourself." He seemed to have forgotten his anger.

He swung her onto the camel's back and again mounted behind her.

The sun drove steadily toward its zenith, burning the coolness from the air. Dust rose from their passage, settled over them, making the men grumble and curse. The camel's skin gave off a pervasive fetid odor. At first Rizpah feared she would be ill, but after a while she grew accustomed to the smell.

As the caravan started over the low hills, Rizpah looked back frequently. There was nothing friendly in the grim barrens behind her, but they had contained her home. She wondered if the newly dead were already watching from Sheol, the nether land, and if their sorrow was as great as hers.

The morning wore on. Rizpah grew sleepy. She slumped forward, dozing, onto the neck of the camel and would have fallen had Bakesh not reached out and caught her.

"Stay awake," he said curtly, impersonally.

She tried to keep her head from nodding, her eyes from growing heavy. Perhaps if she talked to Bakesh . . .

She twisted around. His expression was blank. He became aware of her slowly, reluctantly.

"Last night," she began, casting about for something to say, "I heard you tell Dintor you were taking me to the market at Askelon."

"The slave market," he replied absently.

She said softly, "I wish you had killed me too."

"I could no more have destroyed you than one of the silver goblets belonging to your father."

He glanced away, and she thought he had finished speaking. Then he turned his eyes full on her, said bitterly, "I wish I *had* killed you." After a pause, more quietly, "What good would it have done?" He reached forward, touched her shoulder gently. "Forgive me, child. It is not your fault. It is not anyone's fault."

The girl was unable to understand, even dimly, what he was talking about. But she knew he was unhappy and felt an urge to comfort him. Turning as far as she could toward him, she ventured a smile, but it was lost. His eyes were again withdrawn and distant.

She brought her attention back to the trail. They were among the hills now, sometimes crossing them when the way was not too difficult, sometimes threading a path through wild gorges. The sun beat down angrily against dry red rocks, making the air shimmer with reflected heat. The men were silent, and the only sounds were made by the hoofs of the camels striking stone and the occasional moan of a thirsty sheep.

Toward noon they topped a ridge less forbidding than the rest and began a gradual descent to the Philistine plain. As they rounded a curve in the track, Rizpah caught her breath in wonderment.

I wish I could actually have seen her face then. Often enough in my youth, returning with my man from some dusty campaign in the eastern hills, I too have drawn in my breath sharply, involuntarily, at the sight of the endless green fields of grain, bright ribbons of water, bordered by trees, winding leisurely through the verdure.

To the young girl who had all her life known only a fearful dependency on a tiny spring of water, who had lived in defiance of the desert's encroachment, the first glimpse of such abundance must have come as an ecstatic shock. Exhausted now, suffering more than she even knew, she could only waver briefly between delight and despair, before surrendering inevitably to the peace of the plain.

The men revived and began to talk animatedly, shouting jests back and forth. Even the camels seemed refreshed by the sudden change, raising their heads and sniffing the fragrant air.

Only Bakesh was unmoved. The closer they came to the fields, the older and more lined his face appeared.

Dintor rode up alongside them. He grinned at Bakesh and said, "You haven't forgotten your promise."

Bakesh looked at him wearily and passed his tongue over his lips. "I have not forgotten."

"If we hurry, we can be there in time. The men are looking forward to it."

"And you?"

Dintor laughed. "I too. It was mostly for myself that I asked."

Bakesh raised his hand to his forehead but said nothing. Dintor waved airily and dropped back into line. Glancing over her shoulder at Bakesh, Rizpah saw that his face glistened with perspiration.

A little later they stopped to eat beside a gurgling stream. Rizpah bathed her face and hands. When she returned to Bakesh, she saw that he had spread out food for them. There was dried corn and more of the greasy meat. This time Rizpah did not go off by herself but sat next to Bakesh while she ate. When she finished the corn she was still hungry. She tasted a piece of the meat. It was salty, but she found it delicious.

Bakesh watched her, a faint smile on his lips. "Do you like it?"

She nodded, her mouth full.

There was an edge of malice in his voice. "It is the salted meat of a pig."

Rizpah gagged, spat out the meat and regarded it with disgust.

"You Hebrews," Bakesh said amiably. "Your foolish laws, the stiff-necked way you observe them. What good does it do you? What good does it do anybody?"

Rizpah's stomach was too queasy for her to risk a reply, and even if she had been able to speak, she would not have known what to answer. She put her hand to her mouth, felt the grease around her lips and wiped it off vigorously with her sleeve.

"Go drink some water," said Bakesh, relenting. "It will make you feel better."

He was right. When she returned from the stream, she was feeling relaxed and even a little content. She sat down beside him, closed her eyes.

"Do not sleep!" Bakesh spoke sharply, forcing aside the veil of her drowsiness.

"Please," she murmured. "Only until you're ready to go."

"We are ready now," he said brusquely, getting to his feet. "I made the men a promise. If you were the cause of their missing . . ." He broke off, regarding her speculatively, a bitter smile playing about the corners of his mouth. Then he shook his head. "Come," he said and helped her up.

Reluctantly she followed him and waited while he took the reins of the lead camel and made it kneel.

chapter five

ALL AFTERNOON they rode along a raised highway of crushed stone cutting through ripening fields of grain. The people working near the road waved and shouted greetings as they passed. To Rizpah they appeared not unlike the men who had worked in her father's vineyards. The comparison brought on a despondency which could no longer be dispelled by the fresh greenness she saw about her.

But mingled with it was a puzzling thought. The Philistines had taken away all she loved. The men who held her captive, the people who labored in the fields, were Philistines. Ever since she could remember she had been taught to fear them as evil, unclean men. And now she had greater reason than ever before. But while she still felt fear, there was no hatred. These farmers in the fields, they had wives and children. They looked to sun and water for their livelihood, just as her parents had done. And when death parted them from someone they loved, surely they experienced the same sharp sense of loss she was feeling now. She remembered Bakesh speaking of his two brothers who had been killed by her people.

She looked around at the gray-haired man. He was again preoccupied with his thoughts, lost in the unhappy contemplation which seemed to consume so much of his life. He had led the raid on her father's house, had given the order to kill her parents, Amaziah, the servants, Shiphri's father, Shiphri himself. The guilt for their murders was clearly on his head. She should despise him. She wanted to, yet she could not.

Hearing this later from her lips, I spoke to her roughly and told her that philosophizing in a young woman was as much out of place as a wart on the end of her nose. And all the while, remembering my own unceasing struggle to attain maturity, I only wanted to weep. . . .

The day was waning, and the sun swung low, shining directly into their eyes. As it neared the horizon, its rays grew coppery, endowing even the foolish, bobbing head of the camel with a calm, graven dignity.

Just before the sun went down they reached a village, a few squat mud houses, clinging to the banks of a small river. They passed through the village without stopping, ignoring the excited cries of the naked children who danced alongside the caravan, now and then darting dangerously close to the forehoofs of the lead camel. Without knowing why, Rizpah had a feeling something was about to happen. She wanted to ask Bakesh, but his set expression discouraged conversation.

A little past the village the river veered away from the highway. Abruptly Bakesh reined in the camel and made it follow the stream. Some distance ahead, half-concealed in a grove of trees, Rizpah saw a stately marble building.

A wave of excitement swept over the men. Their weariness forgotten, they broke ranks and urged their camels ahead, speeding toward the building. Only those charged with the care of the goats and sheep remained grudgingly behind, shouting curses at the tired and lagging animals.

Rizpah watched the men who hurried ahead, wondering at the reason for their haste. Behind her Bakesh said in a low voice, "Now they are satisfied." He leaned to one side and spat on the ground.

Dintor rode by, calling, "Hurry! They're going to begin soon."

Bakesh looked after him sadly, allowing their camel to continue at its own pace. As they drew closer to the building, Rizpah heard the notes of a flute rising in a shrill, fervent melody, like the tunes her father's shepherds had played on feast nights, only wilder, more exotic.

They reached the grove. Bakesh helped her dismount and tethered the camel near the others. He led Rizpah to a large tree near the end of the grove.

"Sit here," he said, "and do not move. Whatever happens, you are not to move." She thought he was going to leave her, but he sat beside her, his back against the trunk of the tree.

I have witnessed the rites many times in my life. I have seen them performed on hilltops, on jutting bluffs overlooking the sea, in wooded groves like the one where Rizpah sat. I have become familiar with the significance of the basic ritual and the meaning behind the variations. Over the years I have evolved my own personal feelings about the gods. But I have, after all, known of these rites and accepted them since the sign of womanhood first appeared to me.

Rizpah knew nothing of them. She came from a people who worshiped an invisible god. And if there were times when some of the children of Israel deserted their gods to follow the ways of my people, secretly, on hidden hilltops, neither was this known to her. Not then, at any rate.

I shall try to relate her experience as she told it to me, for it was important to her. As she told it to me, not exactly as she saw and felt it. For even by the time she was able to put it into words, the rawness of her reaction had already been subtly seasoned by subsequent events. None of us can see a thing with the eyes of a child more than once. . . .

The grove was rapidly filling with men. On two long tables under the trees stood hundreds of flagons brimful of red wine. Groups of men clustered around the tables drinking quickly, copiously. Attendants with shaven heads refilled the flagons as they were emptied, from huge jars which stood at the ends of the tables. Other attendants made their way to and from the temple, carrying away the empty jars, returning bowed under the weight of new ones. The flute player sat next to the temple entrance, oblivious of the activity around him, intent only on the ceaseless wild melody he coaxed from his instrument.

There was not much talk. The milling groups of men seemed to have only one object: to down as much wine as they could hold. Rizpah saw the man who had killed Shiphri stagger and fall, pull himself up by the edge of the table and reach for more wine. Dintor, holding a flagon in both hands, drank and did not remove the vessel from his lips until it was empty. Then he dropped it to the ground, where it was immediately snatched up by a shaven-headed man and taken off to be refilled. Dintor looked over to where she and Bakesh were sitting, threw back his head and, baring his teeth in an animal grin, laughed loudly, harshly. Rizpah thought she heard Bakesh moan, but when she glanced at him he was staring straight ahead, grim-faced and silent.

The wine was beginning to have its effect on the men. They shrieked with laughter, shouted and danced in crazy circles, falling over their feet and rising to dance again.

The music ceased, and in the same instant the crowd fell silent. It was as if the whole assemblage had been magically, suddenly stricken dumb. No one even moved. Those who had goblets of wine in their hands held them without drinking. There was no sound but the soft rustle of the evening breeze through the leaves overhead. The men in the grove stood motionless as stones, eyes fixed expectantly on the dark, yawning door of the temple, waiting.

The flute player rose, peered into the temple, then stepped aside. From the entrance emerged four men, their heads shaved like those of the other attendants, but wearing richly embroidered ephods in contrast to the simple cotton garments of the wine servers. The quartet was struggling beneath the weight of an enormous statue they bore on their shoulders. It had the head and torso of a man, the tail of a fish. Immediately after them followed four more men, wearing ephods identical to those in the first group. These carried the statue of a woman, naked, with broad hips and heavy breasts. The bearers made their way to the center of the grove, reverently placed the statues side by side on the ground.

The figure of a man appeared in the temple entrance, moved slowly through the twilight. In the stillness his unhurried progress among the trees of the grove was somehow disturbing. Yet his demeanor was that of someone who feels himself completely alone. As he drew near, Rizpah realized he was old, more ancient than she had thought it possible for anyone to be, but still he moved with grace and certainty. He was completely bald, and his skin, a dead, translucent yellow, was stretched tightly over the bones of his head. His eyes were deep-set, almost invisible in the failing light, but she could feel their power as he gazed about him. He wore a snow-white ephod which accentuated the yellowish cast of his skin. On the front of the garment was emblazoned an intricate design, an oddly distorted variation on the two figures beside which he now paused.

He bowed deeply before each of the statues, turned his eyes upward and began to chant, "O Dagon, O Astarte!" His voice was surprisingly resonant. Its rich tones rose and fell on the quiet evening air. "O Dagon, father of the sea. O Astarte, mother of the earth and all it brings forth. O Dagon, O Astarte, grant the blessing of fertility to your children. O Dagon, cause thy seed to brighten the works of creation through thy sons. O Astarte, implant the gift of a fruitful womb within all thy daughters. And as your sons and daughters hallow your coupled names, cause the earth and the waters through which they live to yield in abundance. Bestow on us the fish of the sea, the birds and beasts of the field, the grain which springs from the soil. Dagon, Astarte . . . grant us life!"

The ringing words died away, and the listening men, released from their transfixion, began to murmur and stir restlessly. The flute player began a melody, different from the one before: low, languorous, rising gradually in intensity. The old priest who had called on the god and goddess made his way back to the temple door, disappeared inside. The noise of the crowd was joyous now, expectant.

Out of the entrance marched young women, at least six score, their breasts uncovered, wearing only brightly colored skirts of filmy material. They moved in time to the music, bodies undulating, until they reached the statues. The men pressed forward eagerly, calling to the women, but the shaven-headed priests formed a phalanx and kept them back. The women, still moving their bodies in time to the music, turned slowly toward the temple door.

After a moment a young man and a girl came out, hand in hand, and walked toward the statues. They were completely naked. The man's head was shaven, like those of the attendant priests. His companion's eyebrows were plucked, her lips and cheeks brightly rouged. Looking at her, Rizpah decided the girl was not much older than she. But there was a hard, bold cast to her face. Only her eyes, soft and a little bewildered as they scanned the grove, gave her expression life.

The couple reached the statues and separated. "I am for Dagon!" shouted the girl in a shrill voice above the sound of the flute. "I am for Dagon!"

"I am for Astarte!" shrieked the man. "I am for Astarte!" He leaped onto the pedestal holding the female figure and embraced it. The girl imitated his action with the figure of the fish-man.

The tempo of the music increased. Rizpah watched, hypnotized and frightened by what the young man and the girl were doing. Finally the girl screamed, sprang into the air and sank quivering to the ground. The man turned from the figure of the woman and ran to her.

It was a signal. Men and women immediately seized each other, laughing, shouting, embracing, rolling together on the ground. Their riotous cries drowned out the music.

Rizpah felt sick. Without knowledge she had thought much about what happened between men and women. She had dreamed of the day when a man would come to her, gently, by a quiet pool or in the deep shade of the vineyard house. It would be a sacred thing of solitude, of choice, of delicious yielding, a joy such as she could have experienced with Shiphri. This was ugly, outlandish, an abomination. She felt terror mingling with her nausea.

In her fear she reached out to Bakesh, grasped his arm. He did not respond. She followed the direction of his gaze and saw Dintor, arms around a tall girl, body pressed tight against hers. They swayed back and forth a moment, then toppled together to the ground. Bakesh shuddered.

A man broke from the crowd and staggered toward Rizpah, put a hand under her arm and tried to pull her up. She screamed and Bakesh turned slowly, as though emerging from a trance. He rose to his feet, picked the man off the ground and flung him through the air. The man struck a tree, rolled over once and lay still. Bakesh sat down again and looked for Dintor.

Night fell. The priests brought torches and stuck them in the earth. The revelers continued dancing, drinking, shouting, laughing and embracing. Now the priests joined in, some taking women, some coupling with other men. Shadows moved, weird and misshapen, against the trees, the temple building and the people themselves.

A giant of a man, laughing wildly, thrust his hand into the flame of a torch, held it there until the skin cracked and sizzled, then, still roaring with laughter, staggered away, seized a woman by the hair, dragged her to the ground.

A priest, spying Bakesh, disengaged himself from the arms of a second priest. He came toward Bakesh, stood without speaking, looking down at the gray-haired man, then shook his head and walked back to the crowd.

Gradually couples began to fall asleep where they lay, stupefied with wine, exhausted with love-making. The noise waned. It was once more possible to hear the sound of the flute. Now, too, Rizpah could hear Dintor's laughter. She saw him, his arms about two girls at once, reeling toward a wine table.

Rizpah ached with weariness, but she was afraid to sleep. She bit her lips, pressed her nails into her palms. Finally she knew she could no longer stay awake. She moved closer to Bakesh, lay down on her side. The last thing she remembered was the sight of his face: taut, drawn, eyes straining toward the center of the grove.

chapter six

WHEN RIZPAH woke, the grove was rose-colored with dawn. Birds circled above, glided to resting places on the trees and called clear in the crisp chill air.

Bakesh still sat beside her, head sunk forward on his chest, eyes closed in sleep. She studied him: thatch of gray hair, high forehead, eyelids delicately veined, proud, elegant nose. The deep lines of his face had softened, leaving it untroubled and vulnerable.

Under the trees men and women lay sprawled as they had fallen the night before, limbs askew, faces swollen with drink, hands still reaching out in pursuit of pleasure. Dintor rested on his back, mouth open, snoring heavily. Next to him slept a plump woman, lips curved in the ghost of a smile, filmy red skirt ripped to the waist, revealing fat thighs.

The marble walls of the temple gleamed pink and clean. A priest came out of the entrance, rubbing his eyes and looking around. He hawked, spat on the ground, and walked back into the temple.

The torches were no longer flaming, but a few still smoldered, giving off thin lines of rising smoke which dissolved in the foliage above the grove.

A man sat up, yawned, and became violently sick, his expression reflecting surprise and confusion.

A young girl lay in the embrace of a stubby, pock-marked priest. Her eyes fluttered open. She looked fearfully around, then down at her own nakedness under the priest's hairy hand. She extricated herself with some difficulty from the sleeping man's grasp, wandered desolately to a tree and leaned against it, sobbing quietly.

People began to awaken, coughing, grimacing at the taste in their mouths. One by one, they stood up and crept away through the trees. Few spoke, and none looked back.

Over all, brooding and expressionless, the dead eyes of the two figures, Dagon and Astarte, extended their silent welcome to morning. . . .

Perhaps I am unduly harsh in my opinion of the rites as they are practiced today. Certainly I am not an irreligious woman. I feel deep devotion for Dagon and Astarte, the father and mother of the world. They are constantly with me, dwelling in the two exquisitely carved figurines which always stand close to my bed. I pray to them, commune with them in joy and sorrow. My respect extends to the moon and stars, who are obedient servants of the god and goddess.

Nor am I particularly priggish. I have no sympathy for those who speak slightingly, fearfully, of lust. There is a purity to savage, animal desire, and even those who deny its pleasure must still of necessity pay the price for its existence. I also know that lust by itself is incomplete, a wind howling down from the mountaintops without the following blessing of rain. Lust which lacks love is empty and grinding. Yet love without lust is often barren, a refined retreat from the human condition.

So I have had great reverence for the rites of my people as they have been practiced over the years. They pay homage to the secret of

the universe, fertility, and acknowledge the presence of all its ingredi-
ents, including lust. Therefore I do not feel I am carping when I say
that even in my lifetime the ritual has undergone certain corrosive per-
versions. Once it was honorable to be a temple maiden. The offering
of one's body to the god was more than a careless prelude to orgiastic
excess, and what followed in those days was an honest, dignified symbol, as well as a pleasure for the participants. There was none of the
ferocious assault on the senses with strong wine, little of the brutal,
desperate promiscuity which exists today. In the morning after each
Dark of the Moon festival there was no shame or regret, and one
could greet the dawn with a sense of lightheartedness and even fulfillment.

All things change, and an old woman with a weakness for discur-
siveness should not deplore the passage of time. Today things are different for the average man in my land. The nations around us have
grown increasingly strong. Armies must be raised against them, armies
which need men, food, weapons and equipment. Nobles charged with
defending the country have adopted ruthless methods for obtaining
what they need. Because there is no other source, they have squeezed
the small man: the farmer, the artisan, the hewer of wood and the
drawer of water. They have demanded the blood from his veins, the
marrow of his bones. For such demands there must be periodic com-
pensation. And if the rites attract an undue share of scum and rabble,
they also give a semblance of relief to those who are too hard pressed
by authority and poverty.

Still, knowing this, I am unhappy about the changes which have
taken place. And I suspect that I am not alone. I would guess that
even the old priest Vontela (for it was he who officiated at the ceremony Rizpah witnessed) privately regrets the new shape of the festival. I have no doubt that, even if the ritual did not require him to
leave the grove after invoking the deities, he would do so in any case.

But again I am indulging my tendency to wander. For Rizpah such
distinctions could hardly exist, nor would they have mattered if she
knew of them. The events she had witnessed the night before had
affected her deeply, but she had no time to consider them at length.
Evaluation of experience is an essential quality of man, but I consider it fortunate that it must often wait on the simple demands of
the physical being.

Just now she was hungry. She was reluctant to wake Bakesh, but
she knew there was food in one of the sacks strapped to the camel
they had ridden. As she started to get up, Bakesh opened his eyes.
His gaze first sought Dintor, who still slept in the center of the grove.

Slowly the lines and wrinkles gathered on the face of the older man, resumed their accustomed position. He ran his fingers through his hair and turned to Rizpah.

"You are hungry, child," he said. "I intended to feed you last night, but when I was able to remember, you were asleep."

"I didn't mind. But I am hungry now."

He smiled and helped her to her feet. She was stiff from sleeping on the hard ground. Bakesh took her arm as they walked toward the camel.

"I am sorry you were frightened last night," he said. His precise accent had become familiar to her, reassuring. "Dagon and Astarte would have this effect on one who has known only Jahveh. There was a time when I was tempted to follow your Jahveh. I studied his ways and found them satisfying. Jahveh leaves a human being his dignity and the pride of his soul. Unless a man is extraordinarily strong, these are the very things Dagon and Astarte take from him." He took a deep breath. "But after much consideration I decided against following Jahveh. Perhaps I was afraid of the vengeance of the only gods I had ever known. Perhaps it was because your Jahveh knows too much of a man's inner thoughts."

Bakesh unstrapped the provision sack from their camel, gave her dried corn, some figs and a chunk of strong dark cheese. While she ate, he went away to pay the offering expected from those present at the rites.

Dintor stood beside her, laughing and stretching. She wondered how he could look so fresh.

"I watched you last night," he said. "My heart leaped at the sight of you, sitting there, cool and innocent, your eyes wide with the wonder of the celebration."

She was no longer afraid of him. "My eyes were only wide with loathing," she said acidly. "And as for the rest of what you said, I don't believe you were watching me or anyone else. You saw only the ugly image of your own lust."

"That is where you are wrong, my lovely. I saw *you*. And I wished you beside me, your breasts uncovered and your long limbs masked only by a bit of thin cloth to make them even more enticing."

Rizpah felt herself coloring but could think of no reply to cut off his bold mouthings. And despite her disgust something stirred within her, responding. She felt helpless, like someone balanced precariously on slimy stones at the edge of a murky pool, whose depths both attracted and frightened her. She drew away, gathering the folds of her robe close about her.

His eyes did not leave her face. "Before long there will be a man. Someone strong who will master your innocence, make you delight in his manhood, persuade your heart and body to cry out to him." He moved closer and said in a low voice, "I could be such a man. I could awaken in you . . ."

He stopped, suddenly conscious of Bakesh, who had come up behind them. The older man's lips were white with anger. Dintor stepped away from Rizpah, bowed his head as though he expected a blow. After a moment he glanced up and, realizing Bakesh was not going to strike him, laughed.

"Sometimes," said Bakesh, evenly and precisely, "you make me weary. Weary and sick to the depths of my soul. So filled with loathing that I could crush you as one puts his foot on a scorpion."

"Then why don't you?" asked Dintor. "Why?" When Bakesh did not answer, he grinned and strode toward his camel.

"One day," Bakesh muttered to himself. "One day . . ." He touched his forehead, then turned to Rizpah. "Come, child."

Askelon was not far from the temple. The ride through a vista of vineyards and olive trees was pleasant. Rizpah found comfort in the sight of the twisted, gnarled olive branches, the sun touching their leaves with silver. But now, even as morning spun its slender filaments of beauty in the clear air, the spirit of death rose beside her, mocking, chiding, reminding her that on the night the nether world had claimed those dear to her she had shed only a few paltry tears. And she had not wept since. She bowed her head over the camel's neck and sobbed, but her eyes remained dry.

Bakesh placed a hand on her shoulder, made her straighten up and turn to him. "In time," he murmured. It was all he said, but the words soothed her, salved her heart with restoring balm. He had given her some of his strength, a strength born of his own suffering, and she was grateful for his generosity. If peace had forsaken her, perhaps forever, at least for now there was quiet.

Soon after, they saw the walls of the city rising pure white in the distance. The wind shifted abruptly, bringing to Rizpah's nostrils an odor she could not recognize, a fresh smell, tangy and bracing. She sniffed the air.

"The sea," Bakesh said behind her. "I never tire of its breath in my face. If I could be a young man again, I would journey to the land of the Phoenicians and learn from them the knowledge of the oceans of the world. I would cross the broad sweep of waters and call at far-off cities, where the people wear strange garb and follow bizarre customs and worship exotic gods. I would return to Caphtor, the island of the sky, from which our forefathers set sail many years ago. I would visit the ruined palaces crumbling among green hills. I would search for the meaning of my life before the altar of my ancestors. I would seek the truth which hovers forgotten between past and present. And always, in all my wanderings, I would hear the voice of the sea."

She turned at the eagerness in his tone. His eyes were bright, radiant, filled with the glory of a dream. But even as she watched, the light faded from them.

"We shall be at the city gates before the sun is high," he said matter-of-factly. "Perhaps we shall even reach the slave market before the morning transactions are over."

Rizpah felt herself beginning to tremble. Until now she had not allowed herself to think too much about what would happen when they arrived in Askelon. And until a short time ago she had not realized how she had come to depend on Bakesh for protection, even for friendship.

He must have read her thoughts, because he leaned close and said, "Do not be afraid, child."

She blurted out, "What else can I feel but fear?"

"No great harm will come to you. This I know somehow. The quality you possess is unique. No man will be able to destroy you. He may claim your body, but there is something—" He paused, groping for words. "Something I felt the first night I saw you, when you were overwhelmed with fear and yet . . ." He broke off again, thoughtfully, then, "It is difficult to describe. Perhaps it is a quality you have received from your Jahveh. More likely it comes from your own spirit. . . ."

He stopped speaking. She turned his words over in her mind, trying to extract solace from them. But the closer they drew to the walls of Askelon, the more fearful she became.

The gates were open, but as always the passage through was clogged by the horde of idlers who made the entrance to the city their headquarters during daylight hours. Like a flock of carrion birds they rose from their haunches at the approach of the caravan, swarmed thickly around the camels. Beggars, their filthy garments flapping, clutched at the legs of the riders, displaying sores and infirmities, beseeching alms in tearful voices. Acrobats sprang, danced, leaped back and forth with the nimbleness of gazelles, turning handsprings and somersaults, never losing through the most intricate maneuvers the forced brightness of their smiles. Birds fluttered at the ends of strings held by hawkers who, with more dignity to preserve than their companions, did not run about but stood in select spots and filled the air with shrill, monotonous cries.

Bakesh shoved the beggars away with his feet, ignored the acrobats and hawkers as he urged the lead camel forward. The caravan moved into the city without stopping, pursued by a trio of mangy dogs which shortly turned aside to investigate a melon rind rotting in a doorway. The crushed rock of the open road gave way to uneven stone paving, and the sound of the camels' hoofs echoed sharply from the walls of the houses bordering the narrow thoroughfare.

Part of the city of Askelon is built on a broad, flat ridge, which curves gracefully, like the lines of the new moon. The edges of the inner curve slant off abruptly down a steep slope, ending in the crescent-shaped harbor. Thus Askelon has the feeling and appearance of an amphitheater, with the waterfront as the focal point.

On the flat ridge, high above the sea, are the homes of the nobles, the gardens and dwellings cool and impregnable behind thick walls topped with razor-sharp slivers of flint. Between the homes runs a wide street, curving the entire length of the ridge. It was along this avenue that the caravan now rode, moving slowly because of the crowds. Rizpah gaped at the women carrying baskets of olives and grapes on their heads, threading their way so skillfully through the mass of people that they never missed a step. The wives and concubines of nobles and rich merchants, gorgeously arrayed in gowns of brightly colored linen and silk, interrupted their casual pre-noon strolls to survey the caravan with studied arrogance. An officer of the Askelon Legion, purple plumes flying from his helmet, shouted as he dashed by in a chariot, making the camels whinny nervously. The sound of voices rose from everywhere, merging in the general confusion: the cries of vendors in the market place, calling from where they sat cross-legged before heaps of fruit, vegetables, bread, and chunks of blood-encrusted, fly-rimmed meat; men and women laughing and arguing; greetings and farewells of soldiers. And from every cross street the smell of the sea drifted up to them, pungent and pervasive.

Despite her apprehensions, Rizpah felt a keen edge of excitement, which lasted until the caravan turned off the thoroughfare to reach a deserted square. In the center stood a fountain. Water gushed out of the mouth of a man's head carved from stone, splashed into a basin below. In the comparative silence the sound of the fountain was loud and a little ominous. Bakesh stopped the camel.

"The slave market is close by," he said brusquely. "Wash yourself, so they will know how lovely you are."

Her heart was heavy again. She laved the clear water over her face and hands. When Bakesh helped her remount the camel, she glanced pleadingly at him, but he appeared not to notice.

The square was one of several lining the edge of the curved ridge. A narrow opening in the pitted walls of mud houses let them into a gloomy, down-slanting alley, with scarcely enough room on either side for the camels to pass. Yet, unbelievably, it was almost as crowded as the fashionable thoroughfare. The atmosphere, however, was quite different.

The passage was lined with hovel dwellings, tiny warrens hollowed out of the mud walls. Scrofulous children, naked except for scanty loincloths, played among the dung and garbage which was strewn in front of each doorway. Women, some quarreling loudly and viciously, glanced up with thinly veiled hostility as the caravan passed. One man, his face battered, his ear oozing blood, lay in the shallow gutter, moaning quietly. No one paid any attention to him. The stench was overpowering, compounded of urine and feces, stale wine and decaying garbage.

This was the Lower Town, or Quarter, repeated almost identically in each of the five great fortress cities of the plain. It was a side of Philistia unknown to most Israelites, for whom our nation was contained in a myth of proud armies with plumed helmets and shining armor. Rizpah never forgot her first sight of it.

She breathed deeply, shaken and grateful for relief, as the caravan emerged from the Lower Town onto the waterfront.

Bakesh, apparently unmoved by the squalor through which they had just passed, swept the harbor with a joyful, possessive glance.

"This is where my heart lives," he said, his voice taking on overtones of the eagerness he had displayed earlier in the day. "I would rather gaze on the harbor of Askelon than on a sparkling river in the arid wastes of the desert."

Ships were moored along the whole curve of the crescent, rising and falling on the gentle swell which rolled in from the open sea. Bakesh pointed past her shoulder to a long slim craft with bright purple sails, furled now as a score of sweating, chanting black men worked with frenzied zeal under the lash of an overseer, dragging huge logs from the deck onto the wharf. "Phoenician," said Bakesh with the crisp pride of the expert. "Bringing a cargo of cedars from the slopes of Lebanon. You can always pick out their vessels. Trim, spotless. Not like that one." His finger stabbed contemptuously in the direction of a rime-streaked, stubby ship whose prow was crowned by the cracked and faded carved wooden head of a woman. Bakesh spat. "That one," he said, "is out of one of the coast cities of the Lubim. Look at her.

Blotches of pitch hardened on the decks, rigging fouled. The crews no better than the ships. You would think they were like those animals who live in the Quarter, not sailors at all. Stinking, covered with lice . . ." He spat again, then after a moment of silence, "What is it, I wonder," he mused, "that forges one nation into a breed of seafarers, proud and capable . . . and another, whose people also live by the sea, exist merely as scum on its surface . . ." His voice trailed away. Then Rizpah heard him humming the chant of the black men who were unloading the Phoenician ship.

They were moving past other vessels now, galleys, sailing craft, combinations of the two, some large and ornate, others tiny beside them, looking like miniature replicas. The smell of the sea mingled with other odors: the fragrance of spice and incense, wine and the acrid fumes rising from stacks of animal skins. Gray and white gulls circled overhead, their cries raucous and lonely, occasionally swooping down to perch briefly on the mast of a ship, a bale of cloth, a cask of wine.

The caravan had to stop frequently to allow right of way to the cargo handlers who shuttled between the ships and rows of long, low warehouses. The slave market was situated in an open space between two of these warehouses, near the center of the crescent.

The inhabitants of any large city are familiar with these marts which deal in human flesh. They have seen those who come there to do business: entrepreneurs, middlemen, house stewards looking for a new kitchen slave, galley chiefs seeking to refill a ship's complement oft-depleted by death. And they also know the less savory habitués: the lechers, perverts, panders and, often enough, the citizen who is all of these but conceals his prurience behind a mask of righteous respectability.

To Rizpah it was all strange and, quite understandably, frightening.

Forty or fifty men were lounging around the raised stone platform which served as an auction block. A sale was in progress when the caravan arrived. The auctioneer, a little wizened man whose clicking accents rattled from his lips so rapidly that Rizpah could scarcely understand them, was extolling the capabilities of an enormous Cushite. He pushed and prodded the captive, who regarded him stolidly, the sun catching golden lights on his smooth black skin. Once he moved his arms, testing the strength of the chains that bound him, and muscles rippled in his back and shoulders. The bidding was lethargic, and the auctioneer's voice rose constantly higher as he deplored the low price at which he would be forced to sell.

Bakesh left Rizpah alone while he went to speak to the auction manager. For an instant she considered trying to run, perhaps slipping into one of the warehouses and hiding there. But when she looked around, she saw some of the men from the caravan watching her.

A man turned disinterestedly from the auction block, stopped short when he saw Rizpah. He was a Bedouin, filthy with desert grime. His eyes lighted as he appraised her, circling round her and talking to himself with exaggerated movements of his loose, flabby lips. A sour, fetid odor rose from his garments. Rizpah shrank from his gaze. She had seen Bedouins before, when they had wandered past her father's house and had stopped to claim the hospitality to strangers which is law in Israel. They seemed to come from nowhere, to be going nowhere, as they drifted across the face of the wilderness, driving a few scruffy sheep or goats before them. She had once heard her uncle Amaziah say that the Bedouins possessed a proud history and that in the past they had been valorous warriors, eagerly sought after as mercenaries by the nations of Canaan. Now they were furtive, shiftless nomads, living on what they stole or begged. Rizpah's mother had always despised them, and Rizpah had inherited a measure of fear along with contempt.

Bakesh returned and the Bedouin slunk off, pushed his way through the crowd until he was able to lean his elbows on the auction block. Now and then he cast a glance at Rizpah over his shoulder, moistening his flabby lips.

"I have made all the arrangements," said Bakesh. "You are to be the next sale." His words were devoid of emotion, but he regarded her kindly, touched his hair with a sad, languid gesture and continued, "Now that the time has come to leave you, I find myself filled with regret. I have grown fond of you, child. Do you know . . . I was even thinking I might keep you for myself."

Hope widened her eyes. "Would you?" she asked. "Oh, please . . . would you?"

He looked at her a long moment before he spoke. "It could be a good thing," he said. "Perhaps it would even . . ."

Bakesh stopped as someone brushed past him. Rizpah saw his expression change even before she heard Dintor's low, empty laughter.

"Please," she said desperately. "I would do anything you want. Anything . . ."

He smiled sadly and stroked her hair. "I wish I could. I would give anything if I could."

He turned away from her. She could feel the Bedouin's eyes, watching. Her stomach churned with fear and nausea.

The Cushite was sold. He walked behind his new master, his shoulder muscles rippling as he kept testing the strength of his bonds.

Bakesh led Rizpah through the crowd and helped her climb onto the auction block. Then he was gone, melting back into the group of men milling around the stone platform. Rizpah stood, helpless and frightened, while the auctioneer ran a peremptory, inquiring hand over her body. Everywhere she looked she saw only the staring, lascivious eyes of the spectators. But the Bedouin's eyes were the worst. In them was the gleam of possession.

The auctioneer addressed his audience as though he were confering a favor. "Here," he said, "is a rare prize. A Hebrew maid, beautiful, healthy, fresh from the vineyards of Simeon. And"—he paused for effect—"a virgin. Untainted by the breath of a man's lust. Sweet, unspoiled. A virgin."

The Bedouin's lips hung loose with longing. Rizpah tried to turn away from him, but the auctioneer's claw held her firmly.

"If I were buying today, I would pay no less than one hundred pieces of silver for this bit of loveliness. And it would be a bargain. Now who will give me a hundred pieces of silver? Who?"

"Thirty pieces." The words were out of the Bedouin's mouth almost before the auctioneer had finished speaking.

"Thirty?" The auctioneer's voice was scornful. He squeezed Rizpah's arm. "For a Hebrew virgin? For a girl who will warm your bed and bring you comfort in your old age? Thirty indeed."

A beefy, pleasant-looking man at one corner of the block called, "Thirty-five."

"Forty," said the Bedouin, licking his lips.

"Forty," echoed the auctioneer. "Who'll say fifty? Come now, who'll say fifty?"

The fringes of the crowd stirred and the spectators stepped back, forming a cleared path to the auction block. A man moved forward, his eyes fixed on Rizpah. She was trembling with fear, but she found herself compelled to look at the newcomer. He was young, perhaps twenty-five. He wore a simple tunic of fine linen and carried himself with an air of authority. His features were strong, perfectly molded, as though some master craftsman had made their creation a life's work. But there was a coldness emanating from him, a withdrawn, cruel quality that made Rizpah shiver without knowing why. He reached the auction block and continued to study her, fondling a cone-shaped gold pendant which hung about his neck. A hush fell over the crowd.

"How much is the bidding?" His thin, finely chiseled lips moved carefully, with just a hint of disdain.

The auctioneer grew suddenly obsequious. "Forty pieces of silver, my lord." He bowed slightly.

"I offer fifty," said the man, glancing about him, his manner challenging, imperious, but still reserved.

"Sold to Torash, the Seren of Askelon, for fifty pieces of silver," the auctioneer announced quickly.

Inchoate sounds of distress came from the Bedouin's flabby lips. Tears started in his eyes. He snuffled and turned away.

Rizpah's purchaser continued to look at her, his cold glance holding hers. She felt a chill start at the base of her spine and spread into her arms and legs.

Had she obeyed her intuitive feeling about Torash, she would have fled from the auction block, taking a wild chance on escaping with her life. Instead she stared back at him, immobile, in an odd suspension of thought and will. The spectators looked on silently, conscious that they were witnessing a curious scene, but none of them could have explained why the exchange of glances between a slave girl and the first noble of Askelon was strange.

"Why are you waiting?" asked the Seren finally. "Come. Come quickly."

"You're lucky," the auctioneer whispered to Rizpah, his clicking syllables falling on her ears like pebbles against a roof. "Torash is a rich man. The ruler of Askelon. A good man. You're lucky."

Rizpah took her time climbing off the stone platform, futilely delaying like a moth in its passage to flame the inevitability of Torash claiming her. She had expected his fingers to be icy like his voice. So when he took her arm she was surprised at their warmth and strength.

"How are you called?" he inquired with a politeness which further confused her.

She told him her name and he rolled it on his tongue several times, testing its sound with his cold voice. Then he sniffed. "You smell of the desert," he observed calmly.

Anger coursed through her, momentarily erasing fear. "I did not ask to come with you. If the odor of my journey from Simeon offends you, let me go."

A fleeting smile touched his lips but did little to soften the coldness of his expression. "And where would you go?" When she did not reply, he said casually, "I could let the Bedouin have you. Did you not notice how he coveted you? He was heartbroken when I snatched you away from him. He would thank me forever for such a generous gift."

Her heart turned over. She took a step closer to him.

Torash smiled again. "Do not worry, my dear." The affectionate form of address carried little reassurance. He regarded her critically. "I have no intention of giving you up. The desert odor is easily remedied. And," he added, his hand rising to the gold pendant around his neck, "I have always wondered what the Hebrew women are like. Their men I know from battle. They have spirit. I would think you have too."

He moved with her to where the auction manager, a greasy man in a food-spotted cloak, sat fingering the scales on the table before him. From a leather bag at his waist Torash extracted some circles and wedges of silver, dropped them carelessly onto the table. The auction manager picked them up, wanting to weigh them, but not wishing to show disrespect to the Seren. When they left, he was still holding the silver in one hand, impatiently fingering the scales with the other.

Torash conducted Rizpah through the crowd. She saw a huge man rise from where he had been sitting, his back against the wall of one of the warehouses. His body was burdened with fat, his features bloated, ruined. He watched their approach out of vacant, staring eyes. There was a lifeless indifference about him: in the slackness of his mouth; his careless grasp on a heavy, sheathed, jewel-studded sword, as though he were not even aware he carried it; his ignoring of the fly which crept up his cheek toward the corner of his eye. But when he began walking toward them, the indifference dropped away, like cloud vanishing before the morning sun. His movements possessed all the wary agility of a young mountain lion.

Torash's cold voice was saying, "This is Shishak. He is a foreigner like yourself, an Egyptian. I have some business to transact. Shishak will see you to my house." To the giant he said simply, "Guard her well."

The Egyptian buckled the sword about his waist. "Yes, my lord." His voice was high, flutish.

Torash turned and strode away without looking back. Shishak stood watching her. Rizpah was distressed by the mingled malevolence and frustration, tinged with melancholy, which she saw in his eyes. She looked away briefly, and when their glances met again, his was as it had been at first, vacant and staring. He motioned for her to accompany him.

As they left the auction area she caught a glimpse of Bakesh. He was walking arm in arm with Dintor, his face composed and serene. She thought she heard Dintor's laughter as they left the slave market.

chapter seven

THE SUN hung directly above them. Rizpah felt the brilliant reflection of light from the white buildings burning into her eyes, passing through them to pound against the back of her skull.

Beside her Shishak strode along, seemingly oblivious of her presence. She found she could not keep up with him and said tentatively, "Please . . ." The Egyptian did not slacken his pace. The layer of fat covering his body, ill-contained by the flimsy tunic with its short leather apron, trembled with each step, but his movements were easy, fluid. Rizpah stopped short.

Abruptly, with no apparent effort, Shishak also stopped and swung about to face her, the shadow of a challenge in his flat eyes. Rizpah stared at him reproachfully. They exchanged no words, but when they continued in their way Shishak matched his pace to hers.

They passed along the waterfront, quiet and almost deserted now in the oppressive noonday heat. The boats creaked gently, rubbing against the stone wharves. If I could get onto one of them, she thought, I would hide. I would sail to one of the distant cities about which Bakesh spoke, and there I would be safe. But even before her mind could explore the idea, Shishak's measured tread beside her drew her back to reality.

He selected one of the narrow alleys leading upward from the harbor and motioned her to go ahead of him. She realized that she would again have to traverse the Quarter and shrank from the passage momentarily before his gaze compelled her to enter.

To Rizpah the street seemed identical with the one the caravan had descended an hour before. The children with swollen bodies and misshapen limbs still played among scattered filth. The women in the doorways quarreled endlessly, viciously. Only now, not viewed from the vantage height of a camel's back, the squalor of the alleyway reached her with greater force and immediacy. The inhabitants had gazed at the caravan with hostile indifference. Now they regarded the two pedestrian figures with a venom which seemed to hang in the air, so acrid and intense that it could almost be smelled through the foul odors of the street. Children plucked at her robe with grimy fingers, made obscene clucking sounds to each other. A woman suck-

ling a baby at her withered breast brushed back greasy strands of hair
from her face and shouted imprecations against foreign whores. Others
thrust themselves close to Rizpah, gathering spittle in their mouths,
hawking it to the ground in her footsteps. Yet, where before she had
felt disgust and a distant, congealing sense of horror, now, seeing the
Quarter at closer range, she was oddly enough less disturbed. Instead
she found herself becoming conscious of a curious vitality surging the
length of the wretched street, emanating, though she scarcely understood it at the time, from a hopelessness which called out to her own.

She had little opportunity to reflect on this. Behind her Shishak's
unfaltering stride urged her onward. They came out of the dank passageway into a square resembling the one where the caravan had
stopped earlier. But at the end of this square stood a wall, higher
than any she had seen in the city, its smooth expanse of white stone
broken by an ornately trimmed metal door. Shishak, beside her again,
conducted her to the door, lifted a heavy bronze ring attached to it,
let it fall resoundingly.

Rizpah heard a bolt being withdrawn, and they were admitted to
a garden many times the size of the one she had known at home.
The soldier who had let them in barred the door behind them. Shishak
led Rizpah past a circle of great palms swaying majestically above a
marble fountain, along a path threading an artful profusion of roses,
lilies, iris and cyclamen, toward the Seren's house, whose cold and
imposing lines were half concealed by foliage.

Just before they reached the house they encountered a slim, fair
young man. His name was Manim, and it was the bane of his fop-
pishness to be afflicted with a constant excess of perspiration on his
temples and upper lip. He was a member of the nobility, serving
Torash as a special adjutant, but he neither identified himself to Rizpah nor questioned her, and Shishak took no notice of him. Manim
stood aside to let them pass, dabbing at his upper lip with a scented
white kerchief, watching the girl speculatively. Only when Rizpah and
Shishak disappeared into the entry hall of the house did he turn and
walk slowly toward the bolted door at the end of the garden.

In the foyer Shishak picked up a cushioned hammer, struck a brass
gong in a measured pattern of strokes and pauses. The tones died
away, echoing into the house, and after a few moments a servant
appeared. He and Shishak conferred briefly, the Egyptian's high-
pitched voice mingling with the bass of the servant, but though she
strained to understand what they were saying, she could not catch
a single word. Shishak led her along a wide hall, dimly lighted by
spaced torches which illuminated the rich, hanging tapestries. They

crossed a courtyard where sunlight filtered gently through fig branches onto a gravel path, entered another hall, narrower than the one they had left. Shishak stopped and opened a door.

Rizpah had no way of knowing that the room in which she found herself was one reserved for the concubines of visiting notables. She was only aware that it was the most luxurious she had ever seen. The walls were softly gleaming sandalwood, exuding a subtle, elusive fragrance. In corners of the room stood large, intricately carved wooden chests. Silken pillows piled on the floor surrounded a low table on which there was a silver bowl of fruit and a decanter of wine. Commanding one end of the chamber was an enormous bed, with the soft white sheets turned back invitingly.

Shishak stood at the door, watching her while she surveyed the room. He stepped aside as the servant who had met them entered quietly, bearing a tray of food, which he placed on the table, then departed without even looking at Rizpah. Shishak closed the door from the outside, and for the first time since she had been taken captive, Rizpah was alone.

She sat on one of the pillows and continued to look around the room, conscious only now in the silence of isolation how truly frightened and confused she had been during the past few days. But now, even more than in the course of her journey to Philistia, memory lacked the sharpness of reality. It was as though she were viewing all that had taken place from some vast, remote height. And there were two Rizpahs. The one who sat in this room of a house belonging to a Philistine noble was different from the one who had bathed by a pool in the quiet of the evening, imagining the gaze of her betrothed upon her. Between the two lay the stark cataclysm of death, still uncomprehended. Between the two also lay the remembrance of Dintor's lust, the orgiastic celebration at the Philistine temple, the sickness of fear.

Now, childishly, without knowledge of odds or price, she contemplated escape. The hope had never left her mind, had only been numbed by the swift and brutal passage of events. Somehow she would have to make her way out of the house of Torash, flee this great city of the heathen and pick up the broken thread of her life. A persistent voice grew inside her, mocking, inquiring: and where will you go? She could not answer, but back of her wish to be free hovered a vision of vineyards heavy with fruit, animals grazing peacefully, a house with a quiet garden where at will she could taste privacy. You're thinking of your father's house, she reflected and laughed aloud, her voice sharp and bitter in the silence. Your father's house and there is no house. Yet her mind clung obstinately to the image of freedom, and the very childishness of her tenacity sustained her, when another, more sophisticated, might have abandoned hope.

She found she was hungry. The tray of food contained a dish of curds and something else she had never seen before, morsels of amber-colored meat attached to the insides of round shells. She ate the curds, poured some wine from the decanter. It tasted faintly spicy, lighter than the full-bodied wine of Simeon.

She was finishing her second cup when she heard, muted, a series of strokes on the gong. A babble of voices rose somewhere in the distance and died away. There was a muffled sound of steps whispering along the corridor outside, then quiet. . . .

She must have dozed, still sitting on the cushion next to the table. When I entered the room, she remained motionless, her back to me, for a long moment, then she turned slowly, her glance startled and unfocused.

At that particular time of my life I was no longer easily moved. Or rather, I made it a practice not to be. I felt I was too old to allow myself to be touched by disturbing emotions; I found them far too exhausting. I guarded myself carefully, often rewarded even the simplest advances with a kind of sharp-tongued cynicism. It did not make me many friends, but it left me my equilibrium and preserved the remnants of my energy. And, so I reasoned, what else does an old woman possess to help her stave off the insistent visits of the messenger of death?

The sight of Rizpah caught me unawares. I was not prepared for the full impact of those green eyes, the clean lines of that face so exquisite in its innocence, so tender in its expression of anxiety. As she faced me, her glance like that of a fawn, I felt my heart move within me as it had not done for many years. This one, I remember thinking, can inspire love, and the knowledge frightened me. I could not let her know it, though, and my step was firm as I approached her, but I had to bury my hands in the folds of my robe to conceal their trembling.

I sought for some glib, ironic phrase and, less than half successful, was only able to say, "The Seren told me you were lovely. I had to see for myself. Men are so foolish when they speak of beauty. A pretty face, a softly curved shoulder, and they are blinded forever. But I should have known he would not be deceived."

She got to her feet, appraising me covertly, and in that instant I discovered behind the limpid innocence of her eyes a latent boldness, a stubbornness and resiliency, perhaps even a willfulness. Only a glimpse, but it was enough. And, strangely, it was this that won me completely, this evidence of human frailty, something to like as well as love. Straw to mix with the brick, so to speak.

The beating of my heart had calmed. I stepped closer and sniffed ostentatiously. "The Seren was also right about the desert smell. You need a bath, girl. And some fresh clothes."

I waited for her reaction. She looked at me gravely, anger rising to her eyes from somewhere deep inside. I held my breath, released it in quick relief when she began to laugh. I could tell it was the last thing she wanted to do, and this distressed her. But her mirth was honest and infectious, and we laughed together. I said finally, "My name is Egrep. The Seren has asked me to look after you." I added, intending to impress her, "The stars tell me it will be a pleasure."

She looked blank, and I felt a twinge of annoyance. Who was she, this ignorant daughter of the desert, to enter my life so disturbingly, to pierce the armor of my heart with her beauty? I was beginning to feel like some prurient temple priestess eying a luscious neophyte, and the admission dismayed me. I strode to the door, flung it open, called loudly down the hall for bath water. When I returned to the room, Shishak followed me in and stood leaning against the wall, watching us with his flat, expressionless eyes.

I noticed the food on the tray. "Are you not hungry?" I asked challengingly.

She replied, "I've eaten the curds. That other . . . it's unclean."

It was the answer I was hoping for. The sight of her, slim and lovely, regarding the tray with disdain and a trace of arrogance, inflamed me, gave me strength to vent my irritation. "You'll be here for years," I said, then added cruelly, for I had heard what happened at the slave market, "For the rest of your life, if Torash doesn't decide to sell you to a passing Bedouin. The curds today were a concession to your uneducated peasant palate. Tomorrow you begin to eat what we eat or starve."

She sat down meekly and picked up one of the shells, tasted the meat. "It's like the breath of the sea," she said in wonderment, smiling at me.

Again I felt that absurd fluttering of my heart. "They're called mussels," I said gruffly. And stiffly, trying to atone for my outburst, I changed the subject.

"You impressed the Seren. Never before has he brought a woman to this house. His council of nobles will dine with him tonight. And so will you. This is a great honor. You should feel pride in your beauty."

She turned away without answering. I said to her, believing I understood, "The sadness is still new. No one becomes a slave happily. And there has been no time to mourn whatever it is you have lost. But the young heal quickly. Soon the sharp lines of sorrow will fade into forgetfulness."

She replied thoughtfully, "This is the second time today someone has tried to comfort me with such words. I thank you, but I know I will never forget."

I felt she wanted to say more, but at that moment five servants entered the room, bringing a wooden tub and the large pitchers of hot and cold water I had ordered. They placed them on the floor and departed, but Shishak remained.

I went to one of the chests, took out a vial of crystallized rose essence, another of sweet oil, and a towel. Rizpah watched curiously as I mixed the bath water and poured in some of the crystals. I knew from her expression as the delicate odor reached her nostrils that she had never bathed in scented water, and the anticipation of her pleasure pleased me. "Now, girl," I said, "take off those rags."

She looked from me to Shishak, who was still leaning against the wall.

I had forgotten he was there. "He won't hurt you."

She chewed her lip in embarrassment. "I do not care to have men watch me when I am unclothed."

I could not help laughing. "This is no man. He's a eunuch." She continued to nibble her lip, not understanding. "He can do you no harm. His manhood has been taken away."

Rizpah glanced again at Shishak, considering. He leaned against the wall, seemingly unaware of what was going on. But in his eyes was the cloudy expression I had sometimes observed, a compounded malevolence and frustration. And, deeper, some great sadness transcending both.

"I don't care," said Rizpah. "Make him go."

"You're even more innocent than I thought." I turned to the Egyptian. "Leave us, Shishak."

He moved to the door. I was surprised to see a spasm of something like relief touch his bloated features. Then he was gone.

Rizpah slipped out of her robe and sandals, stepped into the tub. I could see the warm water starting immediately to relax her. I poured more over her hair, scrubbed out the gritty dust. Then, while she washed, I went to the chest and brought back a graceful white robe of heavy linen. I caught myself feeling ashamed of watching her. Angrily I asked myself: will you turn admiration into something evil?

I said, aware of a certain jealousy in my voice, "Once I was like you.

When I was a young girl, I was straight and tall, with firm breasts like yours. Men marveled at my hair, which was black as night, and at the beauty of my eyes. Now"—I sighed, permitting myself a small taste of self-pity—"all that remains is the brightness of my eyes. Many is the time I have wished them faded, for the sight of them in a mirror is a goad to memory."

She studied me. "Is your husband dead?"

"I never had a husband. At least not in the true sense of the word. My father had offers from many men, but I threatened to drown myself in the sea before I would accept one of them. The man I loved was the Seren before Torash, his uncle. My family was not noble enough for him to take me as his lawful wife, so he married another. And so strong was our love that I ran away from my father's house to become his concubine." I paused, remembering. "There are no regrets. Our life together was full and rich. But when he died I had no rights in the household. Torash, who was fond of his uncle, lets me live on here. On the whole," I concluded primly, "it's not a bad life for an old woman."

She asked softly, "Why do you speak words you don't believe?"

"About what?"

"About being satisfied. About being old."

I smiled, knowing we would understand each other. "Make Torash marry you. He's a strong-minded man who cares little for the old conventions of nobility. Already you intrigue him. Turn this to your advantage."

"And if I have no wish to marry him . . ."

I laughed outright. "I thought such innocence only existed before birth. You will learn about Torash." I picked up the towel. "Now come. It is growing late. Time always marches quickly on women's talk."

She climbed out of the tub and allowed me to dry her. I rubbed her body with fragrant oil until it glistened, worked some of the oil into her hair and combed it. Suddenly, looking at her, it occurred to me. I put down the comb. "You were born in the fifth month."

"No," she said wonderingly, "the third."

I snorted. "Don't contradict me. Do they keep such good track of time in Simeon that you would know the difference between the third and the fifth month? The stars never lie."

"It was the third month," she said stubbornly. "I know because my mother always complained that while she was pregnant with me the winter rains made the house so damp that . . ."

I interrupted her crossly. "Never mind all that. You will have to learn that no one enjoys hearing boring details from beautiful lips. A woman should speak as tersely as a general in battle and still clothe the clarity of her words in delightful vagueness. Details breed tedium, and tedium spawns neglect." I hesitated, looking at her. "I see it now. You are indeed a child of the third month." I peered closely at her eyes, added triumphantly, "The fourteenth day."

"Sixth," said Rizpah laconically.

I felt myself growing angry, unused as I was to being challenged on my knowledge of the heavens. "Naturally the sixth. I meant the sixth all along."

"But you said the fourteenth."

"Don't be tiresome. It's just as I said. You were born on the sixth day of the third month. In the hour before noon."

"I don't really know about the hour. Is it important?"

I felt more comfortable. "Every grain of time is important in the study of the stars. The hour of your birth can set the pattern for your whole life."

Rizpah chewed her lip. "Can you tell the future?"

"Of course."

"Will you tell mine?"

"Perhaps. I must get to know you better. The stars are reluctant to give up knowledge about everyone. But it's possible they will tell me about you."

I helped her into the robe, looked at her critically and thought: now, unless the heart of Torash is even colder than I believe it to be . . . I fetched a polished silver mirror for her, watched, amused, while she preened without a trace of self-consciousness.

The muted notes of the gong echoed faintly through the house. I listened to their pattern. "There now," I said when the sound stopped. "We are ready just in time."

Shishak was waiting in the hall and walked behind us. We crossed the courtyard, branched off the main hall and made our way through torchlighted passages. I was so occupied with looking at my favorite tapestry, a scene depicting my man in battle against the Amorites, that for a while I failed to notice Rizpah's stealthy concern with where we were going. Finally I realized she was taking note of the twists and turns of each corridor we traversed. At first I was puzzled. Then it dawned on me. The little rabbit was planning to escape and going about it in quite a businesslike manner at that, attempting to memorize the plan of the house. Half from some obscure sense of duty, half from a kind of taunting malice, I deliberately led her in a great circle through the labyrinth of passages, doubling back twice on our path.

When I was sure I had been successful in confusing her, I was almost remorseful. "Don't worry," I whispered. "There'll be time to learn."

She looked at me openmouthed, as if I were a thought-reading soothsayer. I let her think what she wished, still chagrined as I was over the near fiasco with her birth month.

We reached the broad double door of the banquet hall, with its figure of Dagon carved in bold relief. On the other side of the door men's voices were raised in laughter.

"I'll leave you here," I said casually.

Panic started in her eyes. "Come with me. Please." She clung to my arm.

Carefully I loosened the grip of her fingers. "This you must do alone. Tonight, in particular, the Seren would not welcome a vision of age. My presence would remind him that we are all mortal, that beauty is too soon consigned to dust." It was a pretty little speech of renunciation, one I did not mean for a single moment. I longed to sit once again at a banquet table, to sip rare wines, to revel in the bantering talk, the attentive eyes of men. I embraced Rizpah, said in her ear, "Go in. And may the stars be with you."

chapter eight

RIZPAH PAUSED just inside the door, between two braziers burning Torash's favorite incense, stacte, a fragrant gum of myrrh. After her trip through dim corridors the sudden brilliance of so much lamplight was confusing, and the incense smoke was getting in her eyes. She smoothed her robe with nervous fingers, uncertain as to what she should do.

In the center of the room, at a long table covered with a white damask cloth, some thirty men were seated, Torash at their head. Their talk was punctuated by brief bursts of laughter which rebounded from the walls and ceiling with a peculiar hollow quality. Servants moved briskly between the table and a door at the far end of the hall, bearing trays of food, decanters of wine, fresh wicks and oil for the lamps.

One by one the men at the table became aware of Rizpah's presence and fell silent, raising their eyebrows in mute inquiry of each other, glancing obliquely at Torash. Finally there was only the rustle of the servants' sandals against the stone floor. Torash sat motionless, a smile on his finely chiseled lips, coldly amused at the perplexity of his nobles.

When he had their complete attention he spoke. "I told you we were expecting a guest of honor. She stands before you."

He looked about him, waiting confidently for a reaction. It came in the form of a subdued murmur sweeping along the table as the nobles shifted uneasily in their chairs. From the end of the table a sour-looking man called Kraseg spoke up. "Surely my lord Torash does not intend to seat an Israelite slave as a guest in our midst." He shaped his lips into a painful travesty of a smile. "Surely my lord makes a jest, a sign that we are to begin our feast with special levity."

Torash fixed the speaker with his imperious glance. "Am I in the habit of appearing before my nobles in the guise of jester? Does my friend Kraseg consider me a painted acrobat who turns handsprings for his amusement?" He brushed aside Kraseg's demurral, his voice suddenly assuming the dangerous silky texture which had made it feared throughout Askelon. "And how does my friend know so much about our guest? How can he be sure she is not the daughter of some noble house of the land of Tyre? Does she wear the garb of a slave? Has she the raven locks and dusky complexion of the Hebrew women?" He paused and projected a cold smile the length of the table. "How then does my friend possess so much information?"

Kraseg straightened up. Hatred of Torash sat in his belly like a wad of undigestible food, but he attempted to smooth the sour lines of his face into a conciliatory expression. "My lord the Seren will forgive me if I am mistaken. But it is rumored that my lord made a certain purchase at the slave market this morning. I assumed . . ." His voice trailed off. He took a swallow of wine.

Torash spoke so softly Rizpah could scarcely hear him. "My friend Kraseg has assumed correctly. And Torash will remember the concern of his friend which prompts him to display such interest in the Seren's every action."

Kraseg colored and coughed unhappily. Torash, turning to Rizpah, called, "Come to the table, my dear."

As before, the sound of his voice touched off a chill response deep inside her. She moved forward obediently, only now noticing the empty place at his right hand. The men murmured again as Torash beckoned a servant to seat Rizpah and give her wine.

He raised his own goblet and said, "Drink with me." He watched her over the rim of his cup. "To your happiness."

She ignored the pointed mockery of his words and drank deeply. The wine was light and strong. She felt its warmth spread through her, easing her discomfort.

He was no longer looking at her. His attention was on his chief pastime, goading his company of nobles. He had no illusions about their allegiance. The Serenship was hereditary, but intrigue was rife in Askelon, as in our other cities, and the position was acquired as often by assassination as by inheritance. When my man was alive, he ruled with a firm hand, but he also employed a blend of diplomacy, cajolery and flattery to achieve what he wanted. Torash had no patience with such methods. Instead of suppressing hostility he ferreted it out, constantly testing its limits in the men who surrounded him. He trusted no one, and his mistrust was frequently well-founded. But he had never given an unjust decision, even to the extent of personal sacrifice, and if he failed to inspire loyalty, there was no lack of respect. It was a narrow path he trod, and the effort kept him taut and watchful.

The conversation and laughter in the banquet hall had never quite resumed its former level since Rizpah joined them. "Perhaps," Torash said softly, "my friends take no pleasure in the sight of our guest. Perhaps they feel I have brought her here to satisfy a passing whim, and to demonstrate a lack of regard for my friends."

The men looked at each other, then fastened their glances each on the section of table directly before him. Torash turned to his left, addressed Manim, his slim, fair adjutant. "And what do you say?"

Manim considered, glancing at Rizpah speculatively, dabbing at his upper lip with the ever-present white kerchief. "My lord . . ." he began, his manner lazy, words drawled out indolently. "It is well known in Askelon that your wisdom is supreme. For myself, I can think of no evening more pleasant than one spent in the company of the Seren and an object of his admiration. My lord's taste is my own."

"Thank you, Manim." Torash's words were gracious, but his voice still held its smooth, dangerous quality. "I knew I could rely on the service of your lips, even if my claim on your heart is somewhat more doubtful."

"My lord . . ." Manim objected lazily, then shrugged and was silent. He knotted the kerchief round his fingers, stared past Torash at Rizpah.

Torash turned to her. "Jackals," he said, speaking to Rizpah, but making sure his voice would carry to the end of the table. "Jackals and dogs' heads, every one of them. Not one would hesitate to kill me this very evening if he thought it would be to his advantage. Jackals and dogs' heads, feeding on my power and waiting patiently to devour my body once its strength is sapped. They should take care," he went on, his expression cold, compassionless, "for the well of my authority is deep, and the stirring of the waters it contains can only bring up vengeance."

Rizpah had the uneasy feeling that the Seren's words had been directed at her. And indeed, Torash leaned close to her, placed a hand on her shoulder and spoke quietly in her ear.

"You will do well to remember what I have just said, little Hebrew. Lest one day you want too much of me and use your beauty to seek it." He was smiling, but the coldness of his expression was unrelieved.

The wine Rizpah had drunk gave her courage to reply evenly, "I want nothing from you. Nothing except to be left in peace."

The answer seemed to please him. He chuckled soundlessly. "Good," he said. "Very good."

He was still chuckling when he sat up in his chair and clapped his hands sharply. Two servants immediately came forward with a silver platter on which there lay a whole roasted lamb. Torash carved it quickly, expertly. He helped Rizpah first to the choicest bits of meat, then turned over the duties of serving the nobles to a steward. In addition to the lamb there were tiny pearl onions marinated in wine and oil, spiced black olives, a lentil dish so highly seasoned that each mouthful had to be followed by a sip of wine, which heightened appreciation of the flavor. Finally there were fruits and cakes of all varieties and a heavy, musky liquor.

Under the influence of food and drink the conversation at the table regained some of its ease. Only the sour-visaged Kraseg neither spoke nor ate. He stared morosely about at the other nobles. After the dishes were cleared away, he moistened his lips and directed his voice up the table to Torash.

"My lord," he said, "I have heard reports that the Israelites are massing their armies at Ebenezer near the plain of Aphek."

"It is true," replied Torash.

"And will we be permitted to march against them with the armed might of Askelon?"

Torash glanced around the table. "It is good that you ask. Only yesterday the Council of Serens met to discuss the matter."

Kraseg leaned forward eagerly. "We march then."

The quality of the Seren's cold smile remained constant. "It has been decided that only part of our Philistine armies will go forth to meet the Hebrews. Askelon is not included."

The room had grown very still, each man listening carefully to the exchange between Torash and Kraseg. Even Manim sat quiet and tense, the kerchief crumpled in a ball in his hand, heedless of the perspiration beading his temples and upper lip.

Kraseg's voice contained the barest trace of a sneer. "And is my lord free to tell his nobles why we are to be denied a privilege we have always enjoyed?"

"My friend Kraseg is so adept at gathering reports he should already know the reason for the decision." A brief gleam of triumph showed in the Seren's cold eyes. "But since I see he does not know, I shall tell him. The Israelites who are gathered near Aphek number only eight thousand men. Their strength has been decimated by quarrels between their tribes. Their weapons are few and inadequate. The Council of Serens has agreed they can be defeated with a division of chariots and a few companies of bowmen."

Kraseg stared directly at Rizpah. "I should like to be there," he said slowly and savagely. "I should like to crush each Israelite, man, woman and child, with my bare hands."

The food Rizpah had eaten lay heavy in her stomach. Torash looked at her face and leaned forward. "Do not be troubled," he said casually. "Kraseg always feels it necessary to speak in this fashion. One of his ancestors was among those murdered by your Samson when he pulled down the pillars of the temple at Gaza."

Kraseg, never taking his eyes off Rizpah's face, continued venomously. "I should like to see each Hebrew impaled on the spiked walls of our towns, their bodies rotting in the sun, their . . ."

Torash said sharply, "Enough!"

And at the same moment a servant held a basket of almond cakes before Rizpah. She rose quickly, stifling a scream, upsetting the basket and scattering the cakes over the floor. She took two steps toward the door before she felt Torash's hand close on her arm. He led her back to the table, helped her into the chair. The servant, muttering apologies, was picking up the cakes.

Torash spoke to the group of nobles, who had been watching silently. "I think," he said, the mockery clear in his voice, "our guest of honor is not well. Perhaps . . ." He made a gesture, dismissing them.

They rose and left the room, whispering among themselves. Manim was the last to go. At the door he turned, casting his lazy, speculative glance back at Rizpah.

The servants withdrew. Rizpah and Torash were alone in the great hall. His hand groped for the gold pendant around his neck while he looked at her.

"I apologize," he said at last, his cold voice echoing oddly in the empty room. "It was rude of me to allow one of my nobles to insult my guest of honor."

She said fiercely, "Don't make fun of me!"

He rose, grasped her shoulder and pulled her to her feet. His cold, smiling face was close to hers. "And if I choose to make fun of you, who is to stop me?" He put his arm around her, held her to him. "Who?" he asked again. And a third time, until the word lost its meaning and was close to being an endearment, "Who . . ."

She felt his lips against hers, surprisingly warm and soft. She pushed him away and started to run. He caught her easily, pinned her arms to her sides and held her against the edge of the table. She made a furious effort and got one hand free but only succeeded in knocking over a decanter of wine before he gathered her in his arms and carried her toward a couch in the far corner of the room.

Rizpah screamed, and the sound was tripled in her ears as it reverberated from the walls and ceiling. Torash smiled mockingly and placed her on the couch.

His hands on her body were swift, sure, knowing, unlike the mad, fumbling lust of Dintor. She knew somehow it would be useless to resist further. She closed her eyes.

And the darkness was the night outside her father's house. The pain was the moment when the Philistine sword slashed into Shiphri's body. And the bottomless sense of loss was an image: Shiphri's hand stretched out to her, helpless, imploring. . . .

She heard the sound of his breathing next to her ear. Quieter now. The pain seared through her again, sharp and intense, as he raised himself on his elbow and looked at her. His eyes were moody, troubled.

"Rizpah . . ." he began, and the single word had a warm, caressing quality. Then his voice was as before: icy, faintly mocking. "You have much to learn, my dear."

She turned her head. Across the room, wine from the decanter she had knocked over was dripping onto the floor, expanding slowly across the smooth gray stone in a bright crimson pool.

chapter nine

HAD I known what lay in store for Rizpah as she walked through the dark halls of the Seren's house, back to her own room, I would have come to her, late as it was, and let her speak then, encouraged her to open her heart. I would have made her rest on the great bed, and seated close by in the flickering half-light of the lamp, I would have listened, or not listened, for in such moments it is more a human presence we desire than a pair of ears.

In truth, I was still awake when she left the banquet hall, perhaps dozing a little as I sat beside the beautifully carved god and goddess in the room the Seren had provided for me. Dozing and toying with old memories, as a dog will fondly nudge a bone from which meat and marrow have long since been picked clean.

Also in truth, I was guilty of gross misjudgment. I had been sure what would take place after the nobles had departed, and I had guessed where it would happen. I had gauged Torash's impatience and Rizpah's reluctance which could only inflame him and make refinements impractical and unnecessary. I had divined the nature of the melancholy which would take hold of her, the sense of disorientation, like that of a person who goes to sleep in one room and wakes in another, with no remembrance of how he came from place to place. All this painful prelude to knowledge, all this I knew. For a man's introduction to this particular aspect of the root matter of living may leave him still mystified and even untouched by its meaning. He may, and often does, go smugly on his way, secure in the feeling of this I know, when in reality he knows nothing. But a woman, being the receptor, the bearer, is never allowed to escape so lightly. Her initiation is both loss and gain, and no matter how she may harden her heart, knowledge is there with a barbed scepter to probe its core. And it matters not whether there is curiosity, passion, cupidity, love, or any combination of these, the ultimate effect is the same.

If I seem delicate in my consideration of these matters, and even somewhat mystical and obscure, it is because retrospect often encourages such a manner of web spinning. Events when they happen are nearly always received in their full carnal impact, and only later do we endow them with gossamer. That night my thoughts were simple and direct. Rizpah has lain with a man for the first time. She has mingled her breath with his, willingly, unwillingly, has felt his intrusion into her body.

Being aware of her innocence, I thought she would return to her room, guarded by Shishak, to fling herself on the bed and weep quietly until exhaustion overtook her. Then in the morning I would come to her and we would talk. Words of comfort would pass between us, the shared burden which is at the same time the solace of womanhood.

This is where I erred. Through not knowing at that time all that had happened to her since the raiders invaded her home. Through not taking full measure of Rizpah herself.

She did return to her room. Shishak escorted her through the corridors with its spaced torches, which seemed sinister now, like flaming outthrust hands.

And as soon as the door closed behind her she did fling herself across the bed, where she remained for some time, eyes wide open, staring without thought at the single lamp making wall shadows of the bedposts, the low table in the center of the room, the chests in the corners.

Then, without warning or volition, she began to weep. Only it was not the soft, almost soundless, weeping I had anticipated, which would terminate in the enfolding oblivion of sleep. Rather it was the voice of a bereft desert animal: loud, desperate, verging madness. It came from her throat first in a low keening which grew in volume and violence until it was almost a shriek, then died away and began again.

Now, finally, Rizpah's heart stood open to grief.

She wept for her father, her mother, her betrothed. She cried out, beyond the boundaries of living man, into the vast, remote reaches of the Land of the Dead. She raked her nails across the skin of her arms and smeared the blood on her lips, her eyes, her throat. Tears poured down her cheeks, mingled with the blood and dropped, unheeded, to the floor.

The door opened. Shishak entered the room and stood immobile, watching her, his fingers clenched around the jeweled hilt of his sword. Rizpah's keening stopped. She rose to her feet and faced the impassive Egyptian. They stared at each other without speaking, each a victim of loss, their mutual voiceless suffering more intensely communicative than any words.

Rizpah took hold of the robe she was wearing and tore at it. The heavy linen gave first at the top, ripped with an obscene sound somehow more disturbing than the deprived and desperate keening. Her bare shoulder appeared through the sundered edges of the garment.

She turned her head to regard the smooth skin with a look of fascinated revulsion, then bared her teeth and constricted her throat muscles in what would have been a monstrous, blood-congealing scream. But no sound passed her lips.

Shishak watched her solemnly, making no effort to go to her. He seemed to be waiting for something.

Rizpah's legs gave way. She sank to the floor, still sobbing, but more quietly now. The Egyptian's expression did not change. But he inclined his massive body forward in a small, tight bow, almost as if he were making formal obeisance before a god. Then he backed out of the room.

Rizpah sat up, her fingers clutching at her robe. Deliberately, in the fashion of mourning observed by the people of Israel, she began ripping it to shreds and continued until she sat half-naked amid a wreckage of material. She moaned softly, once, and fell over, senseless. . . .

When she opened her eyes, the lamp had burned out and the room was in darkness. But through the two small windows high on one wall crept a gray hint of dawn.

Rizpah got to her feet, feeling refreshed as after a long sleep. She recollected the agony of her grief, but only its essence, its releasing violence. For the moment her mind had blotted out the details. So, as her eyes grew accustomed to the dim light, and she saw the scratches on her arms, became aware of the rent garment which still hung about her body, she felt first surprise, then distaste. She took off the robe and looked around for something to put on in its place. It was then that she saw her old robe lying discarded in the corner where I had flung it, having intended and forgotten to ask a servant to burn it.

Whether it was the sight of the robe that prompted her decision or the knowledge that Shishak slept, or both coming together, she still does not know. She picked up the garment, smelled the odors of camel and dust and sweat rising from it. And in the same instant there was the unmistakable sound of Shishak snoring outside the door.

She drew on the robe and tiptoed to the door, opening it cautiously. A torch burned fitfully above the eunuch's head. He sat with his back against the wall, the jeweled sword beside him, head slumped forward in sleep, his breathing stirring the cloth of his tunic with a pathetic, incongruous movement.

Rizpah's heart beat more quickly, but with a strong, steady rhythm. It was beginning to be light now. She would have to hurry. But she would need strength. She closed the door softly and went to the table, forced herself to eat some grapes and swallow a little wine. Then she was ready.

To call what she was about to attempt courageous would be a mistake. Courage demands a certain awareness of both chance and penalty. Rizpah knew almost nothing of either. But there was something to inspire admiration in the way she was willing to set out: planless, defenseless, inexperienced. One might also say it was foolhardy, except that the foolish seldom know fear. Rizpah was desperately afraid.

Once again she opened the door. Shishak was still asleep. She considered which way she should flee. To her right the passage led, she knew, to the enclosed courtyard and thence to the main part of the house. In the other direction lay darkness and the unknown. She decided in favor of the latter.

Having made up her mind, she knew she would need light and would have to risk getting the torch above Shishak's head. She took a step toward him. The Egyptian's eyes opened and looked at her. Rizpah felt an eternity of time rush by in the space of a heartbeat. Then the eyes, having seen nothing, closed again in sleep. Gritting her teeth to keep them from chattering, she took another step forward, hearing her sandal scrape much too loudly on the stone floor. The hem of her robe had become like an extension of her body, possessed of life and feeling. She recoiled when it brushed against the hand of the sleeping eunuch. She reached for the torch, and at the same time he moaned. Rizpah heard him say in a clear voice, "My love . . ." and follow it with a flow of Egyptian words, subsiding to a whimper.

She had the torch now and plunged into the black passageway, fleeing past doorways spanned by gleaming patterns of cobwebs, swerving once just in time to avoid falling over a heap of clay kitchen pots. Two ornate council chairs sat side by side, dust-covered, facing the opposite wall like a pair of sightless eyes. She realized she must have reached a storage section of the house. But would there be an exit?

Suddenly the torch she was carrying sputtered and went out. She stopped dead in the clammy darkness and in a moment of hopelessness let the torch handle fall, clattering loudly, to the floor. A few red sparks shot out from the charred end. Rizpah pressed on blindly, bumping into the walls of the passage, stumbling over cracks between the stones of the floor.

Then, from a distance, above the sound of her own steps, she heard them: Shishak's flutish voice calling out in anger and distress; farther away, an answering cry, rising to inquiry . . . all reaching her hollowly, funneled toward her down the narrow passage. The gong began to sound, beating out a frenzied pattern of strokes. It woke a chorus of shouts and curses, but above them all she could hear Shishak's inarticulate bleating. In a matter of moments they would figure out the direction she had taken, would discover the burnt-out remnants of the torch. She would be retaken.

But the momentum of her flight carried her on, through a maze of filmy, clinging cobwebs, past a jagged edge of stone grazing her shoulder. Turning a corner, she felt her heart leap as she saw daylight seeping through the bars of a door at the end of the corridor. Rizpah hurried toward it, conscious of the concert of pursuit gathering behind her.

The door was bolted on the inside. She tugged at the metal crossbar, felt it give, then slide free resoundingly. There was a sense of the sudden brief cessation of shouts from the bowels of the house as she leaned her weight against the door. It creaked outward on metal hinges. She saw the garden, a glimpse of dark tree trunks and gentle blur of iris in a dawn still cold and dim. Too late she realized there was a short drop from the doorsill to the ground. She lost her balance and fell heavily, twisting her ankle.

The grass, luxuriant and untended here, was sweet-smelling, soothingly damp. Tiny beads of dew clung to each blade. She wanted to lie back in it and sleep. Her head spun, dragging the garden out of focus, the stab of pain in her ankle swirling it in again.

Without truly knowing what she was doing, she crawled toward a thick clump of young willows not far from the doorway. Only when she heard the approaching babble of her pursuers did she understand she had attained some kind of precarious safety. She trembled then as they charged through the open door, paused to debate which way she had fled.

The band of guards and servants rushed on. She parted the branches, feeling with disquiet through fear the knowledge of repeating experience, remembered her father's garden and winced with the pain in her ankle, all in a single instant. She saw Shishak running ahead of the others, sword unsheathed, the flesh of his fat arms and legs jiggling with each agile stride. She was about to come out when she noticed a soldier, half-dressed, yawning, his eyes fixed on the spot where she was concealed.

She did not even dare lower her hand. The soldier leaned over to fasten the thongs of his sandals, still looking idly in the direction of the willows.

Something crawled across the back of her other hand, which was pressed against the ground, supporting her weight. She glanced down, saw the reddish-brown body, the wavering pincers of a scorpion. Horrified, she watched and felt its slow progress across each knuckle, waiting for the tail to rise, the poisonous sting to enter her flesh. Suddenly she had to fight down a wave of mirth. It seemed excruciatingly funny that after all that had happened to her she should be threatened with pain, perhaps death, by an insect no larger than her thumb. The scorpion paused, seeming to peer up at her. She was sure it was also amused. Warmth surged through her, dispelling fear, neutralizing the throb in her ankle. She wanted to bend close to the ground, exchange secrets with the scorpion. There was so much to tell and to hear. But the scorpion resumed its journey across her hand, gained the earth and scurried away among the blades of grass.

When she looked out again, through the space between the branches, the sleepy soldier was gone.

She cried, a short burst of sobs, tears gushing from her eyes. A bird called, clear and joyous, and her tears stopped.

Then she was able to rise and hobble through the trees and flowers, until she reached the garden wall. She leaned her face against the rough, crumbling stone and listened to the voices of her pursuers, far away now . . . in what she thought must be the other end of the garden.

Jahveh help me, she whispered and stopped, shocked. Could Jahveh triumph here, in the land of the fish-god and the naked goddess? Had they heard her prayer, and if they had, would she soon feel the lash of their displeasure?

She moved cautiously along the wall, without plan, but knowing that her hope of freedom lay in finding some exit through the solid stone.

Before she realized it, she had almost reached the main entrance.

The guard stood next to it, eating a peach. It was this unconscious admission of human weakness that gave her the presence of mind to do what she did. If he could be hungry and enjoy a piece of fruit in the morning air, he could also be deceived.

She searched for a stone, found it in one of the crevices of the wall. Moving as close to the soldier as she could without being discovered, she used all her strength to throw the stone away from the entrance.

It struck one of the date palms near the fountain, fell and slithered through a bed of flowers. The guard stiffened at the sound, hesitated, then moved away from the metal door to investigate. He disappeared into the circle of trees.

She rushed forward to tear at the bolt, heard the guard cry out from somewhere behind her.

But now she was outside, running across the square, the pain in her ankle forgotten. Two passages led out of the open space. She selected one and plunged into the labyrinth of the Quarter.

Daylight had barely begun to touch the twisting, malodorous streets. She stumbled along, ignoring the filth underfoot, turning corners at random, not knowing or caring where she ran. A rat sitting on its haunches beside a mound of offal questioned her approach out of bold, shining eyes, waited until she almost reached him before he scuttled away into the shadows.

Gradually, the sense sifting through the pressure of flight, Rizpah became aware that she was being watched. There was no one abroad in the passages, but she felt eyes observing her, heard the soft, furtive rustle of voices rising and falling.

This was not the raucous daytime Quarter. Night still ruled, and under cover of darkness the Quarter was accustomed to jetsam of all varieties, castoffs and pariahs from the Upper Town, thieves and runaway slaves, fugitives from the blood feuds of the desert seeking sanctuary in the anonymity of the fetid hovels. Here within its vague boundaries there was a strict basic morality. A man did not rob another resident of his possessions, whether it be his woman or a scrap of food. If he did, there was justice, administered at once by the wronged person, and no third party interfered. But outsiders confused them. They could not fathom the complex system of wrongdoing and punishment prevailing elsewhere. Their reaction to it was unpredictable.

Rizpah knew she could not keep running much longer. She had no idea where she was, understood only that she must rest. Through the haze of fatigue she made out the shape of a doorway, lurched through it.

She found herself in a tiny, low-ceilinged room. A scrawny woman was sitting on a straw mat; next to her lay a man clad in a filthy loincloth. Four or five children rose from the mud floor at Rizpah's entrance, fled chattering like frightened birds and huddled in a corner of the room.

The woman looked at Rizpah, her mouth working with little fish-like motions. "There's trouble," she whispered. "I knew there was trouble."

The man reached up a scaly hand, scratched meditatively under his arm, said nothing.

"Last week I could feel trouble coming," said the woman, her unnaturally bright eyes fixed on Rizpah, unblinking. "Look, there's blood. Blood on her face."

The man echoed lazily, "Blood . . ."

Rizpah felt her face. It was not hurt. She remembered that somewhere her arms had been scratched. It didn't matter now. Nothing mattered. "Hide me," she murmured, her voice dreamy and detached.

"Trouble . . ." The woman's voice died away. One of the children in the corner began coughing.

"Who are you?" asked the man.

"Please hide me!" Rizpah begged, fear returning.

"I dreamed of blood," whined the woman. "I saw the whole ocean turn to blood."

"Hide her," ordered the man.

The woman turned a glance, suddenly clear and inquiring, on the man. "What's she to you?"

"She's in trouble, that's enough."

"Trouble," said the woman, lapsing back into her whining lament. "I dreamed of blood."

The man got to his feet. "I'll hide you," he said, speaking past Rizpah to the wall. "In the warehouse where I work there are places. . . . Sometimes when the overseer . . ."

A voice spoke from the doorway in urgent shrill tones. "Torash! She belongs to him!"

Rizpah never saw who spoke. The woman leaped to her feet, her eyes blazing. "I told you!" she cried. "You wouldn't listen . . ."

The man looked confused, then frightened. Rizpah felt a pair of hands scrabbling at her body, turned to see the woman propelling her toward the doorway. "Get out!" she rasped. "We'll all die!"

Once more she stood in the dank alleyway. Now there was complete silence. Then there was the sound of approaching steps. Two soldiers turned a corner, unhurriedly came toward her. She allowed them to take her by the arms, lead her through the maze of passages out of the Quarter. Her ankle began to throb again.

Torash was waiting for her beside the fountain under the great circle of palms, smiling coldly. Beside him stood Shishak, his sword still unsheathed, observing her approach out of vacant eyes. The sun was beginning to rise. The waters of the fountain caught its pale gold rays.

"When slaves run away," the Seren said without preamble, "they are captured and killed."

Rizpah bowed her head. There was no reply she could make to the chill, even voice speaking of death. Nor did she greatly care.

"Should I do it, my lord?" asked Shishak softly. He made a single swift carving motion in the air.

Torash turned slowly to look at the eunuch. "You would enjoy that, wouldn't you? I can imagine how you would kill her." He paused, then, "She deserves it."

Shishak waited, his eyes fixed on the Seren, holding his sword in a loose, careless grip.

Torash said to Rizpah, "Raise your head and look at me."

She obeyed.

"Where did you think you would go?"

She could not tell him because she did not know.

Torash did not speak for some moments. He looked at Rizpah's face, pulled back the folds of her robe and stared at the scratches on her arms. Finally, "You will not be killed," he said and added casually, "Perhaps you will wish you had been."

chapter ten

I could tell she knew something was amiss the moment I entered the room. Dissembling has never been one of my talents. I set the tray of food down on the table and said, too brightly, "It's a lovely evening. I heard a dove calling from the fig tree in the courtyard. I never saw one there before."

She ignored my prattling and asked, sullenly, "Why do you bring my food? Are all the servants asleep?"

My reply was angrier than even her ungracious questions warranted. "Perhaps you would be happier swilling your food in the Quarter. That is the life you seem to prefer. Perhaps I can find you a piece of fish crawling with maggots. Or a few grains of moldy corn. Is this what you wish?"

"Egrep . . ."

It was impossible to be angry for long with those green eyes when they were turned full on one, commanding and pleading in the same glance.

"Eat, girl."

She approached the table indifferently. In the two days since her attempted flight and recapture she had scarcely touched a morsel of food. Torash had ordered her confined to her room, except for brief strolls in the garden which she took in my company, always followed by Shishak. She spoke little. Once she placed her hand on my arm and motioned toward a clump of young willows. "I hid there," she said, "and laughed together with a scorpion." I looked at her sharply, believing she had gone mad, but the demon of the mad ones was not in her eyes. I shrugged and led her away from the spot. On each of our walks she had wanted to tarry interminably by the fountain among the palms, looking for long, silent moments into its waters.

"Eat," I said now. "Please, Rizpah."

She smiled at me sadly. "Old woman," she said, "you fret too much." It was the first time she used the expression which was to become her term of endearment toward me, and also the first spark of life she had displayed since the soldiers found her standing listlessly in the streets of the Quarter.

I was struck by how much older, and more beautiful, she seemed than when I had seen her first, only a few days before. Surer of herself, yet lacking spirit. More mature. Is maturity then the withdrawal of fire from the human soul? One must always distinguish between wisdom, which is the slow accumulation of earthly experience and the ability to discern its weight and worth, and wisdom's companion, maturity. We often say one becomes mature only when he learns to accept what he cannot struggle against.

If this be so, and I believe it is in part, what a terrible price the gods demand of us who serve them.

Yet if they did not, men would become immortal and outlive the gods themselves. And, in truth, the human fire is never really quenched, only banked, and this is probably a blessing. The shooting star burns brightly and fiercely and expires in an instant, and when it has gone and the murmured admiration it excites has died away, the star of the north still shines steadily in the heavens.

While I was reflecting on these matters I was grumbling to Rizpah. "Old woman indeed," I was saying. "The world is truly turned on end today when a slip of a girl is permitted to be insolent to her elders . . ." I let my words trail off, for Rizpah was only half listening and my heart was not in them. "Eat," I commanded, and the sudden urgency of my tone made her look at me.

"Why is it so important that I eat?"

"Because if you don't you'll make yourself sick," I lied, taking her arm and making her sit down before the tray.

She looked at the succulent stew made from the tenderest flesh of young carp, flavored with spicy herbs. "Did you prepare it yourself?"

My heart skipped a beat. "Why do you ask?"

"I thought since you brought it . . ."

"I helped prepare it," I replied, hoping she would not look at my eyes.

She began to eat. I relaxed a little. "Egrep," she said, "you promised to tell my future. Would you do it now?"

I coughed and mumbled something about not having my charts. She went on eating, but I sensed she was waiting for me to begin.

And suddenly, not knowing where the words came from, I found myself speaking in the measured cadences I have heard rolling from the lips of prophets in the market place. "I see birds," I said, and it seemed that in a chamber of my brain someone was pounding with a great hammer. "Birds with dark and somber wings, hovering between earth and sky, blotting out the sun, obscuring the moon. And beasts of prey, circling with bold and greedy eyes about a blasted tree . . ."

I stopped, breathing heavily. The pounding in my skull had ceased. I was frightened, for the vision had been clear and terrible, and its abrupt departure was as unnerving as its onset.

"And . . . ?"

I looked at her, unbelieving. Her expression was as it had been, lethargic and unconcerned. Then I understood. She thought I had been extemporizing, fabricating for her the sort of tale a mother spins for her child. "And nothing," I said quickly. "This is what happens. A star-teller must have her charts. Otherwise the prediction cannot help but be false."

"And also sinister?"

"What does a desert girl know of words like sinister?"

"I learn them from old women who hoard them like precious stones and dole them out to believing young women."

"Young women," I repeated scornfully. "When you've learned a bit more of the world, you can take on a title. Until then you're only an urchin who needs her nose wiped. When you truly become a woman . . ."

I broke off again, not having realized what I was saying. She glanced obliquely at me and said, "This food has an odd taste."

I waited until she began eating again before I replied, "Only because you're not accustomed to it." Then, before I could stop myself, I blurted out, "My dear . . ."

She said, "Egrep, what is it?"

"Nothing."

I started to chatter about the clothes I was going to ask Torash to let me have made for her, the cloth from which they would be sewn: shining silk from Damascus; the pure, long-stapled cotton of Egypt;

linen woven from the finest flax of our own land, out of the carefully tended fields of Dagon. I spoke about the jewelry we would purchase on the broad street of the Upper Town: the bracelets of hammered gold; the girdles of filigreed silver, so delicate that the waist seemed encircled with laced webs spun by enchanted spiders; the graceful earrings whose stones caught fire from sun and lamplight alike.

Rizpah got up and began to move restlessly about the room.

"Are you all right, girl?"

"Of course."

She returned to the table to pour some wine. Her back was toward me, but I could see her passing her hand across her forehead. She turned. "It's so warm in here."

"Yes."

"Egrep . . . I feel . . ."

Her face was pale, filmed with perspiration. She was beginning to breathe rapidly, tremblingly. In her eyes was a melting confusion . . . and the beginning of something else. I knew I could wait no longer. I took a step toward the door, saying, "I must go now."

"Don't . . ."

I fled from the room, my heart sick at what I knew would soon happen.

In the corridor Shishak stood stiffly beside the door, his glance fixed vacantly on the opposite wall. I knew Torash must be near and turned to see him entering the hall from the courtyard. He looked cool and fresh, and the pleated folds of his tunic were spotless and crisp. I came very close to hating him at that moment.

"You have done what I asked?"

I nodded curtly. "Not because I wanted to."

"Would you rather see her die?" His tone was light, but I knew from his eyes that he meant what he said.

"Why?" I asked. "What has she done to deserve this?"

"You know what is written concerning runaway slaves."

"The law says nothing of this. The law only speaks of death."

"And for her I have myself broken the law."

Something about the way he spoke the words made me peer closely at him. The clean, chiseled lines of his face appeared blurred. His fingers, resting on the broad leather girdle about his waist, moved with a nervous life of their own.

"This was not necessary," I said softly. "She would have been yours in time without this."

"Do you think I mean to go to her?"

I felt the pulse in my throat throb heavily. "You are from the same flesh and blood as the man I loved all my life," I said, shaping each word carefully. "How is it possible for you to become like some loathsome, repulsive . . ."

He laughed coarsely, cutting me off. "My uncle should have made a practice of beating you. Failing that, he should have carved out your tongue. I always wondered how he tolerated your ceaseless chatter."

My reply was frozen on my lips by the sounds which began in Rizpah's room. Had I not known differently, I would never have believed the voice was hers. Swift, faltering footsteps moved to the door. The handle was seized and rattled with insane violence. But Shishak, having anticipated this, easily held the door closed with one hand.

Torash and I stood motionless, scarcely breathing, while the strangled cries from the room grew louder, more urgent. When I could bear it no longer, "Go to her," I said hoarsely.

He shook his head morosely, then turned and walked away toward the courtyard. He did not look back.

Standing helplessly in the coolness of the corridor, I thought how grief-stricken the voice coming from the room seemed. Grief and passion, I wondered, in the end are they so different?

Shishak barred my way as I moved toward the door. "The Seren's orders . . ." he began.

"Will you stop me?" My defiance must have stirred something in him. He hesitated, then, without another word, stepped aside.

I entered the room and, with the greatest patience and tenderness of which I was capable, offered her relief.

chapter eleven

I sat beside her through the night. At first she slept restlessly, toward dawn fell into a stunned, motionless slumber, so deep that at one point I became alarmed. But she was breathing easily now, regularly. Beyond the few tiny marks on her lips where she had bitten them, her face showed no signs of the ordeal she had undergone.

The two windows high above the bed were brightening with the promise of morning. I sighed, knowing it was possible that when she woke she would hate me. Perhaps for the fact that I had drugged her food, but more for the help I had extended her later. It is a rare human being who can cope with the knowledge that another has witnessed the agony of his soul. Help freely rendered is the greatest threat to friendship. If a relationship survives this, it will live through the lesser dangers of greed, envy and even deception.

I knew when she awoke she would be plagued with raging hunger and thirst. The least I could do would be to have food and water ready for her.

When I opened the door into the corridor, Shishak was just coming to relieve the guard who, since Rizpah had tried to escape, now stood the night watch. He glowered at me. I smiled, pleased to see that this disconcerted him. In the complex hierarchy of the Seren's house I moved with familiarity, like a temple priest among relics, scarcely needing to think to maintain my privileged status. I walked quickly on toward the kitchen.

Rizpah opened her eyes to find the Egyptian staring at her from the doorway. When he saw she was awake, he moved slowly toward her bed. The wheel of memory spun slowly, turning up fragments and scraps, so that the eunuch was halfway across the room before recollection was complete. She huddled under the bedclothes, watching Shishak's advance with a sense of foreboding. He reached her side, stood silently, looking down at her.

Then, very gently, he stretched out his hand to stroke her hair. She looked up at him, wide-eyed.

He drew back his hand. "There has been enough pain," he said cryptically. "Too much. And now you are no stranger to it."

He shifted his weight from one foot to the other, and the overlayer of fat on his huge body quivered, fell into new position.

"To be a foreigner," he said, his high-pitched voice lending the words an oddly insistent quality. "To be alone . . ." He stopped, raising his great head to stare vacantly at the wall for a time. Gradually his eyes slid back into focus. There was no malevolence in them now, only the sadness she had occasionally noticed. But as she watched, bitterness crept in to crown the melancholy. "I was a prince in Egypt," he went on, as if he were reciting a lesson. "I say that not to boast but because it was true. I lived the life of a prince, and in the course of time a marriage was arranged for me to Nephir-Amon, the royal daughter of the sun. The wedding plans were complete. Nephir-Amon and I . . ." He paused again, continued almost in a whisper, "Never had I known such happiness. The great river, the god of waters beside whom I had lived since childhood, made himself constantly more pleasing in my eyes. In the mock fights with sword and spear I was an invariable victor. There was only one duty

I had to perform before my marriage—a small punitive expedition north to the borders of the Negev, to wipe out a band of wilderness rats, bandits who were scourging the land of Sinai. It was nothing, a holiday, to last perhaps a month."

When he stopped speaking this time, Rizpah could see, imbedded in the bloated, ruined features, the face of the man who, as a lean, rugged young officer, had led his company lightheartedly into the desert.

"Our expedition did not last a month," said Shishak. "It lasted exactly one week. The bandits had followed each step of our approach. They retreated to the mountains. I was inexperienced. I marched my men into an ambush. I was the only one left alive. They wanted to hold me for ransom. If there had been time for their messenger to return from negotiations, I would be free now. . . ." His voice went flat. "One night they got drunk. They danced and reeled around the fire like savages from the Upper River. Already they had learned that I was to be married. One of them thought it would be a great joke if . . ." He broke off, his eyes once again vacant and lifeless. "After that I could not let them send me back. For a time I wanted to die. They would not do me the kindness of killing me. Eventually they sold me to some travelers from Amalek, who resold me in Askelon."

He turned abruptly and walked toward the door. Only when he had gone a few steps did Rizpah realize she had not spoken a single word. And only much later did she understand the effort it had cost the Egyptian to speak to her in words he knew would bring comfort.

I entered the room just as he was leaving, so preoccupied with how Rizpah would receive me that for a moment it did not occur to me to wonder about the eunuch's presence.

I set down the tray containing curds and eggs poached in oil, poured a cupful of water from a cruse.

She drank thirstily while I waited, unsure of what would happen. When she set down the cup she looked at me calmly and said rather than asked, "You put whatever it was in my food because you had to."

I nodded. She thought a little, then said, "It was cruel of him."

I almost smiled at the understatement. "In many ways he is a cruel man. But remember, he could have had you killed."

She was silent for so long I began to be uneasy again. Avoiding my eyes, she said quietly, "Thank you."

Feeling gay and relieved, I brought her the curds and eggs. I heard myself chirping, "And what did that clod of an Egyptian want?"

"Want?" She seemed puzzled. "I don't know." Then, "He has known sorrow, Egrep."

The stilted, almost pompous way she said it brought a quip to my mind. I was about to give it voice when I happened to look at her eyes. They were filled with a tenderness I had rarely seen anywhere. She knows compassion, I thought. Even without understanding, she has plumbed its depths. And I turned away, not wanting her to see the tears in my own eyes. For even at my advanced age I had not yet learned that the greatest strength love possesses is vulnerability and that, in fact, without it there can be no love.

"He was a prince," she said irrelevantly. "A prince of Egypt."

The childish utterance gave me a chance to recover. I snorted. "Truly," I said, "nowadays every slave has some long, sad tale about his royal antecedents. If we could believe it, there are more kings than commoners."

"Old woman," she said, laughing, "you have lived too long. You have a stone where your heart should be."

"Then you can be sure," I replied, "that it is a precious stone."

Sunlight flooded in through the windows. I heard the dove calling from the courtyard. We decided to walk in the garden. I sent for bath water.

While she was combing her hair, she suddenly turned on me a glance hard with suspicion. "You've tricked me again," she snapped. "The food . . ."

"There was nothing in the food," I protested in surprise.

"No," she agreed. "No . . . it's not the same."

I saw her color deepening. She looked idly at the comb in her hand. She said hesitantly, but with great dignity, "Would you please send a message to my lord the Seren? Would you tell him . . ."

She stopped speaking. I got to my feet, smiling. "Yes, girl," I said, "I'll tell him."

chapter twelve

THE PRIEST Vontela arranged incense pellets in the flat bronze pan. With a pair of delicate tongs he lifted a coal from the brazier and applied it to each pellet in turn. Wisps of smoke curled lazily up into the still air of the temple chamber. "I have found," he said, gazing at Rizpah out of his deep-set, luminous eyes, "that incense is a stimulus to thought."

"It tickles my nose and gets in my eyes," she said.

"That will do," he replied. "You will speak only when you are asked a question. Consider that to be the first lesson."

They were seated in a corner of the main room of the temple, which was situated just outside the walls of Askelon, a jewel of a building almost hidden by the great oak trees which towered over its white marble grace. In the center of the chamber stood an altar flanked by gold-encrusted figures of the god and goddess. The merchants and nobles of Askelon were well off and had contributed handsomely to making their place of worship an adequate reflection of their prosperity. The walls and ceilings were of cedar and fir, inlaid with designs of thyine, a dark fragrant wood capable of taking a high polish. Great marble pillars guarded the entrances to the worship chamber, and at the foot of each column stood smaller representations of Dagon and Astarte, studded liberally and cleverly with precious stones.

Vontela inhaled the incense fumes deeply, with obvious pleasure, and was about to speak when a dozen temple maidens entered the colonnaded area. Under the tutelage of a fat priestess they began to practice antiphonal singing. The girls wore chaste white gowns and kept their hands clasped demurely in front of them as they sang the responses.

Vontela tried several times to speak, but the shrill voices of the maidens drowned each effort. Finally, his patience worn thin, he clapped his hands together.

The priestess stopped her charges in the middle of a song describing a victorious Philistine campaign against the foot soldiers of Egypt and looked inquiringly over at Vontela.

"I have been requested," the old priest said testily, "by Torash, Seren of Askelon, to give the benefit of my personal instruction to this—" he paused and cleared his throat, glancing at Rizpah—"this young lady."

The priestess laughed richly. "Then let my colleague Vontela take his . . . young lady . . . out on the hillside and instruct her properly. That is, if his age will permit him more than a nostalgic recollection of the proper methods of teaching."

The temple maidens tittered, and Vontela shook with fury. "Dagon, Astarte," he cried, "put a curse upon the head of this ignorant one. Call down your wrath from the skies and . . ."

"Now, now, Vontela," interrupted the priestess uneasily. "There's no point in taking offense. All I meant was that singing sounds better when it rebounds from walls and pillars. However . . . we can practice later. Come, girls," she called, and herded them hastily before her.

Vontela's eyes gleamed triumphantly. The slow encroachment of age had increasingly threatened his authority of late, and consequently he had been compelled to exert it more and more jealously. For many years he had been senior priest for the district of Askelon. The temple of the city was his chief domain, but he was also responsible for places of worship scattered throughout the province and often journeyed to conduct their ceremonies. It was in one of these provincial temples that Rizpah had seen him her first night in Philistia.

Torash had asked me to bring Rizpah to Vontela. Despite his age the priest was the best versed of anyone, certainly in Askelon, and perhaps in all Philistia, in the lore and learning of our people.

"Now," the old man was saying, "we shall begin."

His voice, full and resonant when he was invoking the gods, was inclined to be quavery in more intimate conversation and to crack when he became excited. But there was still something about the egg-bald head, the yellowish, translucent skin, the deep-set eyes, which gave one a feeling of ample power held carefully in reserve.

"The first point you must bear in mind is that the worship of Dagon and Astarte is a religion of joy."

"What I have seen of it is not joyous."

"You're impertinent," retorted Vontela angrily. "What have you seen?"

Rizpah told him about the night in the grove.

The old priest grew thoughtful. "All very true. But you must not be misled by what you have seen. Human beings are often given to excesses. Being men, we regard mankind as the highest form of development next to the gods. But it is possible that we may be deluding ourselves, that what we really are is the product of an accident of creation, a cynical experiment by the deities which got out of hand. Have you ever observed a display of excess among the so-called lower animals?"

He waited for Rizpah to reply. She shook her head.

"Of course not. Other animals lead sensible lives. Their appetites and passions are well ordered. Man, being less responsible, needs religion to keep him in check. And our gods are wise. They require men and women to do openly what other peoples do in secret. Naturally there are times, like the occasion you witnessed, when our worship rushes beyond its intended bonds. But, after all, does this not occur in any religion? I have seen the prophets of Jahveh foaming at the mouth and committing what we would term depraved acts, all in the name of their god. Our worship of Dagon and Astarte, in its purest sense, is an ode to life."

"Egrep says the festival as it's practiced today is intended only to pacify the rabble."

"Egrep is a snob. Of course it's intended to pacify. The word pacify implies peace. What greater benefit could we hope to derive from any human activity than peace? But by describing the participants in worship as rabble, Egrep has disqualified herself as a judge. However, to be perfectly fair, some of what she says is true. It becomes constantly more difficult to preserve our worship in its purest form. Which, I suppose, is merely a logical extension of the original bitter joke perpetrated by the gods."

He sighed, leaning toward the incense pan, then looked sternly at Rizpah. "Enough of your prattle now. You are here to be instructed. We shall teach you the holy lore and the sacred words. You will learn the secrets of fertility and the significance of the phases of the moon. And though you are not to be a temple maiden, you will study at the feet of our Astarte priestesses. When you have completed your instruction, you will know many things you only guess at now. Torash will not regret having sent you here."

"I will not worship your Astarte. Or Dagon either, for that matter."

Vontela studied her face. "You are headstrong," he said. "And obviously you are favored by the gods as well. I have seen men struck down for a far milder display of blasphemy. I suppose you wish to worship Jahveh."

"Jahveh is the only God. There is no other god before him," said Rizpah, reaching far back into her childhood and dredging up words she had heard her father speak.

"We shall see," said the priest. He spoke pleasantly, but two spots of color appeared on the tight-stretched, translucent skin beneath his cheekbones. "We shall see," he repeated.

chapter thirteen

THE MORNING of which I shall speak next began uneventfully enough. Perhaps the sun was a little more brilliant than usual, pouring down on the white walls of Askelon, flooding the broad avenue which curved along the upper ridge of the amphitheater-city. Perhaps the bird song was a trifle purer, the sea where it could be glimpsed from the heights a more intense shade of blue-violet.

But these would be subtle portents, not in the same class with the cock crowing at midnight or the kettle refusing to boil. Certainly neither Rizpah nor I was prepared for anything momentous. Though I might have been, if I had given the matter sufficient thought.

I had gone with Rizpah, as I did now three or four times a week, to the temple where she was receiving her instruction. By midmorning we returned to the city, passing through the gates where the idlers were already gathered in full force, gabbling among themselves as they squatted on their haunches, the beggars, hawkers and acrobats, eternally waiting for fortune to smile on them with a shower of alms, a substantial purchase, the favor of some visiting noble who would laugh at a clever handspring and toss a bit of silver.

We made our way to the avenue, where we joined other idlers of a different sort, became part of their company—the exquisitely gowned and plumed who whiled away the morning hours with looking at each other and composing pointed comments about their respective appearances.

Rizpah stopped to inspect a pair of earrings which the merchant swore had been imported from the land of the Hittites. I was about to interrupt and tell the fellow I knew exactly where in the Lower Town of Askelon such things were made and that he was presumptuous to try to foist trash on the consort of the Seren. Firmly, but so sweetly that he could not take offense, Rizpah imparted the information herself and, laughing good-naturedly, drew me along to the next booth.

I stole a glance at her. She was wearing a robe of pale turquoise, a color which often makes the complexion of a woman appear sickly and sallow, but in Rizpah's case merely accentuated the rich chestnut of her hair and the green of her eyes. Tiny earrings of beaten gold, each suspending a perfect emerald, and three copper bracelets on each arm were all the jewelry she wore, yet her elegance put to shame some of the proud ladies who walked the avenue burdened down with as much metal as a royal chariot.

Her beauty had ripened in the three months she had lived in Philistia. When I first saw her, she had carried herself with natural grace. At the temple she had been taught how to improve the provocativeness of her walk, how to display without vulgarity the confidence of her approach to lovely womanhood.

Yet there was something about her—how shall I express it—something unfulfilled. Like a fig hanging on a tree, inviting to the eye, but still requiring the mellowing influence of sun and time to make it ready. And even as my mind played with the simile, discarding it as not quite adequate, I wondered: ready for what?

Since that terrible night shortly after her attempted escape she had accepted without question her role in the Seren's house. She did not share his bed unwillingly. In fact, when she awaited his visits, or went to him when he summoned her, she seemed pleased at the prospect of his company. Torash, for his part, was courteous and attentive. I suspected that some much deeper feeling for Rizpah was growing in him, perhaps without his knowledge. But on the surface his pattern of behavior was unchanged. He still badgered his council of nobles, kept them at bay with probing, venomous remarks. The coldness of his smile had not lessened, nor had the reserve of his bearing. Only now and then, when I saw him watching her, there was a tenderness in his eyes that was like pain. In truth, for Torash it must have been more painful than for many other men to feel even an intimation of softness.

I do not believe Rizpah was aware of his feeling for her. No doubt he went to some trouble to conceal it. And her personality was still too mercurial a blend of naïveté and sophistication, impertinence and sweetness, for her to know what she herself felt.

She no longer contemplated escape. Torash, understanding this, had relieved Shishak of his guard duties. It is true that I was still required to accompany her whenever she went out into the city. But now that she was familiar with every section of Askelon, she could have evaded me at any time and disappeared into any one of a hundred streets. Both she and I knew this, yet I never felt she would be inclined to try it.

If I had not come to know her so well, I might have believed she was content. Many women would have been, and Rizpah gave no overt indication that she was not. She spoke rarely now of her family, of the life she had lived before her capture. But I was sure her dreams were still troubled and that she lived in a state of suspension, waiting for something. I was equally sure she had no idea what she was waiting for.

We walked slowly along the avenue, enjoying the sunlight, the crowds, discussing where we should go next. A voice behind us said, "My lady Rizpah is exceptionally charming this morning."

We turned to see Manim, touching his kerchief to his upper lip, regarding us with the speculative glance his courtier's manners could never quite disguise.

Rizpah said, "My friend Manim has perhaps used the wrong expression. A woman is beautiful or ugly. She is dressed in the height of fashion or she is dowdy. As for charm, this can only be ascertained by a judicious evaluation of both appearance and conversation."

I was constantly being surprised, and disturbed, by her agile use of court language, which she seemed to be able to employ at will.

Manim bowed his fair head. "It is as I said. My lady is exceptionally charming this morning."

"And," Rizpah asked, "have you no suitable compliments for the lady Egrep?"

This, the art of the taunting query, which she had picked up from Torash, I found far more disquieting. Her eyes hardened, reflected a mocking light, and the Seren's cold smile played about her lips.

For just an instant Manim looked uncomfortable. Then he said smoothly, "My lady Egrep's beauty has long been fabled in Askelon. The years have dimmed neither the beauty nor its fame."

"My friend Manim's tongue is coated with honey," I said tartly, "and his lips with oil. But as it is written, the words of the flatterer are like rain in midsummer—welcome, but not to be trusted."

Manim looked sulky. "My lady Egrep does me an injustice."

And so I did. But he could not know, though I disliked him, that my irritation had nothing to do with him.

"Egrep, look!" Rizpah suddenly clapped her hands with delight, pointed at some candied dates a vendor had arranged on his tray. "Don't they look lovely? Do you think I could have some?"

I almost laughed with relief. As long as she could change, rapidly, unpredictably, without self-consciousness, from elegant bored woman to enthusiastic child, I would know the living spirit I had first admired in her was not being stifled. I hoped it never would be, but I was not fool enough to do more than hope.

Manim was staring at her, puzzled, his carefully constructed opinion of her abruptly crumbling, like a breached wall. "Allow me," he murmured, and went away to return bearing a handful of sticky dates, which he regarded with distaste. She let him hold them while she ate, chewing each one with obvious enjoyment.

Finally he said, wiping his hands vigorously with his kerchief, "It was not merely the pleasure of greeting my ladies that gave me reason to seek them out this morning."

He paused, waiting for a sign of curiosity from us, touching his kerchief lightly to his forehead, forgetting that he had used it to wipe the sticky date sugar from his hands. I snickered, somewhat audibly, I'm afraid, at his expression. He ignored me and went on. "My ladies have doubtless heard of the chariot races planned for this afternoon outside the city walls. The most skilled drivers in Askelon will be pitted against a group of newly arrived Hittite charioteers. If my ladies would care to accompany me, I am sure they would find it diverting."

I replied coldly, "Surely my friend Manim is aware that if the Seren wished the lady Rizpah to witness the chariot races, he would escort her himself."

Manim turned to me with a look of indolent but ill-concealed triumph. "The Seren will be occupied for the rest of the day. He has asked his trusted friend Manim to act in his place. If my ladies would do me the honor . . ."

A disturbance at the end of the avenue nearest the city gates interrupted him. We turned, as did most of those around us, to see a path being cleared through the crowd by soldiers from the watchtower. Following on their heels came a runner, stumbling along in the last stages of exhaustion. As he drew near us, we could see the glazed expression of his eyes, the crust of dried foam about his lips, the caked dust on his body. He passed us and turned in the direction of the Seren's house. Silence descended over the whole length of the avenue.

It did not last long. Through the crowd burst the band of painted acrobats who frequented the gates. At that time in Askelon it was customary for them to double as town criers, to convey to the populace word of singular happenings. Turning cartwheels and somersaults, wearing their unchanging professional smiles, they scattered and took up positions at intervals along the thoroughfare. "Victory!" they called. "Draw near and hear news of the great victory at Aphek!"

We were carried along by the crowd, found ourselves close to one of the acrobats, who was waiting until the ranks of curious, excited people swelled to proper proportion. Then he cried, "The legions of Philistia have triumphed over the forces of Israel!" His knowledge of the victory could only have been gained from a muttered word cast aside by the runner as he staggered through the gates, but so skillful was he in his embroidery of details that he made his audience see it as it very well might have happened. "The armies of the circumcised lay by Ebenezer, menacing our borders, gathering strength through the months, boasting of the devastation they would inflict on our sacred land. Fierce and treacherous were the men of Israel. But the holy legions of Dagon were undaunted, the sons of Astarte fearless. They marched with flying plumes to the open plain of Aphek, their spears shiny-tipped, the light of the gods glinting on the strings of their bows.

"There the armies clashed; there the battle was joined. The archers of Ashdod loosed their shafts; the chariots of Gaza rolled forward like thunder. Onto the fertile fields flowed the blood of Israel. Their captains of hundreds lay torn by the relentless teeth of the chariots; yea, their leaders perished under the singing flight of arrows. The sun of Aphek was clouded with blood. From dawn until nightfall Dagon smote them. In the heat of the day Astarte sang her mighty song of battle.

"Shrouds of darkness claimed the fallen of Israel; their dead cannot be numbered. Their strength has melted like the snows of Lebanon beneath the summer sun. But the glory of Philistia is undimmed, the power of our people without equal.

"Israel is crushed! Philistia is victorious!"

The acrobat's harangue ended on a piercing note. He leaped skyward, executed a double somersault, landed on his feet and stood, waiting. Not since he began had his incandescent smile faded from his crimsoned lips.

From all along the avenue we could hear the hoarse shouts of the other acrobats completing simultaneously, as if by prearranged timing, their descriptions of the victory.

The crowded street vibrated with a single jubilant roar. Soldiers and women seized each other, began wild dances, careening off the walls bordering the street, joining hands to form snakelike processions which wound sinuously through the heaps of vendors' wares.

In their excitement they did not forget the acrobats, whose words had touched off the celebration. Pieces of silver and copper bracelets fell about them where they waited. Nimbly, with greedy efficiency, they gathered up the money, their professional smiles only now broadening to grins of genuine delight.

Onto the avenue, a hundred strong, marched the white-robed temple maidens. Tradition ruled that they must swell the sound of any victory celebration with their antiphonal songs.

"Israel is dead!" sang one group.

"The might of Philistia lives forever!" responded the other.

I looked around for Rizpah. She was standing nearby, her fists clenched, tears streaming from her eyes.

I went to her. Together we forced a path through the shouting, dancing throng and made our way toward the sanctuary of the Seren's house.

chapter fourteen

SHE SAW him finish the wine in the bowl. Her sandals made a soft sibilance on the stone tiles as she moved quickly to the decanter, placed a gentle restraining hand on his shoulder.

"No, my lord. Let me refill it."

Torash leaned back in his chair and watched as she poured the wine. "None for you?"

She smiled and tilted the decanter over a second bowl. The fading rays of the sun, reaching the rooftop where they sat, touched her hair with copper, reminding him of the burnished helmets worn in battle by Damascan warriors.

They sipped the wine in silence. After a while Torash rose and walked to the parapet. She joined him and they watched the descent of night over the city. The shadows were deepening, pinks dissolving into purples, purple blending to black. And far beyond the softening lines of the houses a patch of sea shone like molten gold.

"My lord is melancholy tonight."

"Melancholy?" He turned questioning eyes on her, considering. "I suppose you could call it that."

"What are you thinking?"

He smiled. It was the characteristic of his which had changed most since he had known Rizpah. His features in repose, finely chiseled as they were, would never completely lose the cast of austerity, but often now his smile was almost warm. "Why is it that women always want to know what a man is thinking?"

"Curiosity."

"Curiosity is a name women invent to hide a far deeper instinct."

"Deeper? What could be deeper than the well of a woman's curiosity?"

"Her possessiveness, of course. A woman pretends an interest in many things, but all that really concerns her is how to possess a man completely . . . body, brain and soul. The man himself is her most dangerous rival for his affections. In her own mind she suffers a defeat each time she hears her man express to someone else a thought she has not helped him formulate, for this is an indication that at least one spark of his life burns independent of her careful ministration."

"Is this not unfair?"

"Unfair. Another female refuge. A woman can commit the most blatant predatory act and, like the holy prophets when the madness is upon them, believe herself invisible. But let a man say, no, you are not invisible; I have seen you do thus and thus . . . and immediately she raises the cry of 'unfair.'"

Rizpah turned to him, asked softly, "Does my lord believe I try to possess him?"

He shrugged his shoulders with a trace of irritation.

Laughter lurked behind her eyes. "Men speak so bitterly of being possessed by women. Yet I wonder if those who object most violently are not those who wish it most."

He asked sharply, "Where have you learned such foolishness?"

"Egrep and I have often discussed . . ."

"The old woman talks too much."

She felt no fear of him now, even when his voice recaptured some of its old brittleness. "Is my lord angry?" she asked tauntingly. "Does he begrudge women the privilege of discussion?" Then seeing he was truly displeased with the turn of the conversation, she inquired more seriously, "Will you tell me what you were thinking?"

He replied slowly, "I was remembering that it has been three years since you came to my house."

She repeated, her voice trailing off, "Three years . . ."

"You are not unhappy, not the way you once were."

She felt the plea behind his words, strove to please him with her reply. "My lord knows how fortunate I consider myself, how content . . ."

"Contentment is not happiness."

"Happiness," she said in a low voice, "is not a hare or an antelope, to be snared and devoured. It is more like a cool wandering breeze in the heat of the day. One prays for it, waits for it, but one cannot make it come near except in its own time."

"That old woman," he grumbled, "has taught you her bad habit of talking in figures of speech."

"It is with Vontela that I have most discussed happiness."

"Then you've charmed that dry old bag of bones as well. I've never known him to talk about anything but the proper placement of sacrifice at the altar of the gods."

She put her hand on his arm affectionately. "Let us not speak of happiness now. If it is destined to come, it will come."

They were silent again, looking out over the city. Often in the evenings they came here to the roof, enjoying the coolness, letting the twilight gather about them. Only when the bitter wind of midwinter swept in from the sea, driving before it the great gray clouds, did they remain below in the Seren's chamber, hearing above their talk the rain flung like handfuls of stones against the shuttered windows.

I had watched Rizpah change during the three years. After the announcement of the Philistine victory at Aphek she had wept unconsolably for more than a week. Then one day she had asked me to go with her into the city, and she resumed the pattern of her life: instruction at the temple, strolling on the avenue and inspecting the wares of the vendors. But soon the life of idleness began to pall. She made no secret of her contempt for the empty existence led by the wives and concubines of the city's nobility. Consequently they bore her no love, yet because of the Seren they had to make a show of respect. When they would meet her on the street, they would bow gracefully, their faces frozen in overfriendly smiles. It made me uncomfortable to watch Rizpah return their greetings with malicious mimicry, but so accurate was her performance that I could also not help being amused.

She became interested in the operation of the great house in which she lived. With little effort she made a friend of Basro, the Seren's chief steward, and from him learned of the procurement and preparation of foods, the purchase of cloth and household implements, the intricate administration required to control a staff of nearly two hundred servants and soldiers. Gradually, in imperceptible stages, Basro began to consult her, to refer matters to her for decision. And she had accomplished this with such smoothness, such patience and tact, that I know he never felt his authority threatened. I observed all this with admiration, but there was more than a trace of jealousy as well, for a nineteen-year-old girl, a foreigner, had succeeded in doing in a few months what I had failed to do all the years my man was alive.

But, with all her activity, there was a deadness about her. Somehow the defeat of Israel at Aphek seemed to have killed her spirit, as even the death of her own parents had not. Nothing dismayed her now, but nothing gave her joy. I found myself playing the fool, jesting to make her laugh. She joined in readily enough, but there was no spontaneity, little of the impulsive small-child quality which had lent her wit such charm. I made the mistake of trying to protect her, to guard against her hearing talk of the crushing occupation of the land of Israel: how a heavy tribute of grain and livestock had been levied against the country, leaving them barely enough for subsistence; how their blacksmiths had been deported or put to death, so there would be no one to forge new weapons. I might have saved myself the trouble. She was clever and tireless in ferreting out information from officers and civil officials who visited the house.

She seemed to want to torture herself by hearing about the desperate plight of her people. Her people I say, and yet by now they were no more hers than they were mine. She was becoming a product of the country in which she lived . . . in dress, in manner, in taste for food. Still, she always referred to herself as a daughter of Israel and persisted in pursuing her odd, self-punishing patriotism.

It was during this period that the Seren's love for her approached open expression. She became aware of it and of the subtle change it effected: master became slave and slave master. It saddened her, for she had not sought this power. She was fond of him, and between them tenderness was ripening, but she could not love him. To compensate for what she felt was a lack in herself, she grew solicitous, learned to anticipate his wishes, doing for him many of the small menial tasks servants had once performed.

She stood beside him now at the parapet, her hand still resting lightly on his arm. The last vestiges of light were vanishing from the sky, drawn upward into the night.

Someone coughed discreetly behind them. They turned to see the fair head and slim body of Manim, clothed in the golden light of the lamp he carried, mounting the stairs.

"My lord," he said, "could I speak with you?"

Torash's manner changed. The warmth and tenderness dropped away from him like a cloak being cast aside. "My friend Manim leaves me little choice, since he is already in my presence and silence is not one of his virtues."

Manim's eyes narrowed at the unwarranted attack, but his voice remained lazy and smooth. "I would not have come to interrupt my lord in his hour of leisure if he had not instructed me to act with all possible speed."

"Very well. What is it?"

"The count is complete. Chariots, spears, bows, arrows, swords, daggers, armor, shields. Complete."

"Then there is enough to equip our divisions?"

"Enough. But no more than that." He handed Torash a scroll.

"You will inform the head smith to begin work at once."

"I have already taken the liberty of doing so."

"We shall have to depart with what we have. But I shall want you to remain behind and supervise the building up of reserve arms."

Manim set down the lamp, removed a kerchief from his belt, crumpled it in his hand before he spoke. "I trust my lord intends for me to join his forces . . ."

Torash smiled coldly and said, "My friend Manim has not always been so anxious to engage in battle."

"I have felt myself growing sluggish of late, my lord, too steeped in the life of the city. Perhaps a taste of action . . ."

"Or perhaps," Torash interjected softly, "you feel your power is sufficient now, so that if I should fall under the sword of the enemy, leaving no heir, you would be on hand to assume the Serenship."

For a moment the two men stood motionless, probing each other with hostile eyes. A little puff of wind bent the flame of the lamp. Manim said, "My lord . . ."

"We understand each other," said Torash, still speaking softly, then more briskly, "as soon as the reserve stocks have been acquired, you will accompany them to our encampment. And I promise you there will be enough action."

"Thank you, my lord."

He turned to go. Torash said peremptorily, "Wait."

Manim wiped the perspiration from his temples and upper lip while Torash unrolled and studied the scroll. The adjutant's glance shifted, found Rizpah. She had seen the same expression in the eyes of Dintor and many since him. It no longer disturbed or frightened her. She looked back at him until he turned away.

The parchment crackled between Torash's fingers as he rolled it up, handed it back to Manim. "You have done well."

"My lord is kind."

He made his indolent little bow and walked to the stairs. Just before he descended he turned once more to look at Rizpah. She moved close to Torash, took his arm, her glance still challenging Manim's. He shrugged and left the rooftop.

"You are going away?"

Her warm, husky voice fell on Torash's ears with a peculiar gentleness. He looked at her face. Her lips were slightly parted, her expression one of yearning.

"Why do you ask?"

"Because if you are, even if it is only for a few days, I shall miss my lord."

Suddenly he was angry. It was the unreasoning, baffled anger of a man who loves and is frustrated, not by rejection but by tantalizing half-acceptance. "I shall miss my lord," he echoed, mocking her. "And why will you miss your lord? Does your heart ache with love for him? Do you even know what love is?"

He turned away, trying unsuccessfully to conceal the anguish distorting his features. "Never before," he said evenly, "has any human being touched my soul . . ." The lamplight flickered. He concentrated his gaze on it as if he expected it to convey to him some long-hidden secret, some oracular reply to all his questions. He continued, his voice fully under control now, "Yes, I am going away. The Hebrew clowns have chosen a king. He has gathered a few hundred men about him and turned them into insolent gnats buzzing about the heads of our garrisons . . ."

"A king," she said wonderingly, not really knowing why she spoke.

"So they call him. Saul, King of Israel. He has slain a few Ammonite bandits who menaced one of their dirty little border towns, and the feat has made him drunk with arrogance. Now, with a few sharpened plowshares and pruning hooks, he wishes to challenge the power of his governors." He made a savage gesture with his thumb and forefinger. "We will crush him like this." He looked at her sourly. "They have been growing restive, your Hebrews. Very well. They have been hungry. We shall see how they react to starvation. We will sell their eldest sons into slavery, their daughters into harlotry . . ."

Rizpah shuddered and turned away. Torash was silent for a moment. Then he put his hands on her arms, looked into her eyes. "Forgive me," he said very gently. "I have never asked anyone before now to forgive me, because I have never had cause to regret anything I said or did."

"My lord spoke in anger."

"Anger is no excuse for inflicting pain."

"I have already forgotten it."

He smiled, but not coldly now. "You speak most regally yourself, my dear. Are all Hebrews victims of the delusion that they are kings and queens?"

He held her close. "Rizpah . . ." His lips sought hers.

She hesitated only an instant before she put her arms around him, but long enough for him to notice. She heard him sigh. Then he led her toward the stairs.

chapter fifteen

I GLANCED around my room. It did not seem any more bare than before I had begun my packing. The old can travel lightly, I thought.

A robe or two, an extra cloak to ward off dust or cold, a few mementos to ward off loneliness, and the old are ready to go anywhere.

I closed the cover of the single chest I was going to take along and summoned a servant to carry it to the wagons. He preceded me through the halls, balancing the chest on one shoulder. We passed the great kitchen, dark now except for one corner where a baker was busy preparing bread for the journey, and left the house by the supply door.

The four-wheeled carts were lined up, three of them beside one another. By the glaring light of half a dozen torches a tanner was fitting new leather tires onto the wagon wheels. I stood admiring the nimble movements of his stained fingers handling the needle and thongs. Basro, the steward, came up beside me to inquire, "Are the lady Rizpah's belongings ready to place on the wagons?"

"Has she still not sent them out?" I clucked my tongue and was both amused and annoyed to see reproach enter Basro's normally suave and careful eyes.

"A young lady has so much to pack."

"She's had the whole day and half the night to do it," I replied, turning away toward the house.

I made my way back through the corridors to Rizpah's room. Near the banquet hall I passed Shishak talking to one of the guards. He laughed, and I stared at him in surprise, never having seen him even smile before. Perhaps he was excited by the prospect of the journey. He had not left Askelon since the Seren purchased him.

The message had come from Torash that morning. The armies had not been successful in tracking down Saul and his followers, but of course they would in time. The Israelite who called himself a king (I could see the mocking expression Torash must have worn as he wrote these words) was waging a cowardly guerrilla action, striking unexpectedly at a garrison, a granary, a headquarters town, then disappearing into the hills without a trace.

Torash had been away for six weeks. He was lonely for Rizpah and wanted her with him.

I found her in her room, standing among a litter of robes, banquet gowns, jewelry, vials of perfume and scented salts. I opened my mouth to scold, then forgave her without speaking. It seemed to me I had never seen her so beautiful. Her cheeks, pale for so long, were now softly colored, her eyes wide and bright. I had seen the change occur almost immediately after the arrival of Torash's message. Perhaps, I thought, love for him is growing at last. Perhaps the separation has made her realize . . . and on and on in this fashion. Those who buttress their feelings with cynicism are probably the only true romantics.

"Old woman," she said after a few moments of silence, "what am I ever to do?"

"You might try packing."

She shook her head in childlike confusion. I was pleased to see her alive again, so pleased that it did not occur to me to suspect there was something unnatural about her excitement. "I came here with nothing," she said, "and now look."

"The Seren has been generous," I said stiffly. It was not like her to make insensitive remarks. But in truth I was the one who was being insensitive.

She had not heard me. "I came here with nothing," she said again, "and now when I'm ready to return . . ."

"Return?"

I must have spoken more sharply than I intended. She turned toward me quickly, startled. "Am I not going back to the land of my people?"

"Rizpah . . ." I went to her, feeling that my face must have gone ashen. I took her by the arms, shook her gently. "Do you not understand?"

"Understand what?"

"That you are going back to Israel . . ."

"Of course. That I'm going back . . ."

My words came slowly, stumblingly. "The Seren . . . his expedition to Israel . . . the Philistine armies with their chariots . . . enemies of the land where you were born . . . and you . . ."

I stopped. There was no need to go on. Her shoulders had begun to slump; the brightness was leaving her eyes. "Oh, Egrep, what is the matter with me? Am I mad? When I received the message this morning, I could only believe . . . What *is* the matter with me?"

I asked bluntly, "Did you intend to escape?"

Her voice was faint and far away. "No . . ." She sat on the bed. "You must think . . ."

"I think we should pack your clothes," I said gently.

She was not much help. I filled the chests, marking them so we would know where everything was. When I finished, she was still sitting listlessly on the bed. I helped her change to her nightdress, gave her a mild sleeping draught. "We shall be leaving early. Otherwise I should give you enough of this to make you sleep till noon." I kissed her on the cheek. "Tomorrow, while we are traveling, if you like we shall talk about it."

I called servants and accompanied them as they carried the chests out to the wagons.

As I passed the entry hall, Manim was just coming in. We had seen little of him since the Seren's departure. He was taking his responsibilities seriously, and on the few occasions when I had encountered him, I found myself liking him better. I knew from gossip that he was constantly occupied, making the rounds of the forges, urging on the smiths, inspecting the completed weapons and armor. It was not unusual now in Askelon to hear the full-bodied sound of hammers against metal far into the night.

He passed me with a nod and walked briskly on. I remember wondering vaguely why he was visiting the house at this hour, but just then one of the servants bumped a chest against the wall, and my attention was taken up with reprimanding him.

Manim made his way purposefully to the walled courtyard, strode through without pausing into the corridor on the other side, knocked at Rizpah's door. When he received no answer, he entered.

I had left a lamp burning by her bedside. She had not troubled to put it out. Now, almost asleep, she became aware of Manim's figure in the doorway.

"Egrep?"

There was no answer. He came toward the bed. She sat upright, saw who it was, but surprise prevented her speaking.

He came and stood beside her, his glance flicking over the lines of her body, clearly visible through her flimsy nightdress.

"I only heard now," he said, "that you will be leaving in the morning." He sat down on the bed, smiling. "Are you pleased to be joining the Seren?"

He took her hand. "Such a lovely slender hand," he said, the lazy, speculative note returning to his voice. "I have always wondered why you wore no rings. Now I know." He stroked her fingers lightly, almost absently. "The work of the most skilled craftsmen could never improve the beauty of these fingers."

She withdrew her hand from his. "Why are you here?"

"Women ask such unnecessary questions." He laughed. "Who knows how long you'll be away? I couldn't let you go without accepting your invitation."

"Invitation?"

He moved close to her. "Come now," he said. "Surely you have known of my feeling for you. I knew you could do little about it until the opportunity presented itself. Then that night on the roof, the way you looked at me while Torash was reading my report. The way you took his arm when I left, telling me with your hands and eyes that thus and thus would you do to me. . . . I have waited, Rizpah, for the shyness to burn away from your heart, for longing to break through the barrier of hesitancy. Now there is no more time for waiting. . . ."

Her mind was still fuddled with the disturbing events of the day, with the effect of the sleeping draught I had given her. Manim mistook her silence for compliance. He pulled her to him.

She thought: if I am not able to stop him now, he will take me. She thought: and what if he does, will it mean so much? Is my body so precious? Does it belong to Torash or even to me? The night I writhed in agony on the floor of this room, and Torash did not come, I would have belonged to whoever appeared. This one now, his hands tearing at my nightdress, could I stop him, do I really want to stop him . . . ?

His mouth was on hers. She could feel the perspiration which always beaded his upper lip adhering moistly to her own. She found herself calm, unresisting, only waiting for it to be over.

Suddenly, with such clarity that it seemed to be a re-enactment, the death of Shiphri was once more taking place before her eyes. She saw the fitful firelight, the extended, pleading hand, heard the sickening sound made by the sword as it entered Shiphri's body.

She twisted her mouth away from Manim's and screamed. After the first scream she could not stop.

He released her abruptly, looking at her out of astonished, frightened eyes. Then his hand groped frantically for her mouth, trying to stifle her outcries. He succeeded, took his hand away when she stopped.

They sat facing each other, neither able to move, both horror-stricken at what she had done, both fully aware of the only thing that could happen, neither capable of preventing it.

He said thickly, "Why did you . . . ?"

"Please go! Quickly!"

"It's too late." His eyes stared at her, helpless, accusing. "If you hadn't screamed, I would have gone," he said plaintively. She was sure this was untrue, but it made little difference now.

The sound of running footsteps approaching drew him to his feet. She knew she should hurry past him to the door, tell whoever was coming that she had had a nightmare, but her legs refused to respond. She was no longer certain that what was happening was not a nightmare.

Manim was still standing in the center of the room when the door was flung open and Shishak entered. The eunuch's eyes took in the situation swiftly: Rizpah's torn nightdress, her face set in a horrible staring expression, Manim frozen where he stood in fear and guilt. He took his sword from its sheath.

It was over in an instant. Shishak moved to Manim's side with one agile bounding motion, plunged the sword into his body, pulled it out as the adjutant sank to the floor.

She was not fully aware that it had really happened until the Egyptian bent down and calmly wiped his sword blade on Manim's white tunic. Then she covered her face and began to cry.

She was still sobbing when I arrived. No explanation was needed. Shishak was dragging Manim's body unceremoniously from the room. In our country such offenses bring swift, merciless punishment. The rank of the offender is never considered. I could hear the captain of the guard in the corridor, asking questions in his flat voice, Shishak replying without emotion.

I went to her, put my arms about her and rocked her as if she were a baby. After a while I felt her relax, but only a little. "Egrep," she said finally, her voice unsteady, "Egrep, will it always be?"

"Will what always be?"

"My whole life . . . is it to be lived in violence?"

I spoke to her soothingly, assuring her it would not be so. If the stars had given me even a hint of the future then, my reply could not have contained this grain of comfort.

chapter sixteen

OUR LITTLE caravan of three wagons pulled by pairs of gelding horses, and one chariot escort, rolled through the city gates shortly after dawn. In the first wagon were three servants. Shishak drove the second conveyance in which Rizpah and I were riding. The third was reserved for baggage. It had been intended for us to have an escort of two chariots, but the captain of the guard in the Seren's house had commandeered one to ride ahead and inform Torash of Manim's death.

Since the gates were normally locked until a full hour after dawn, it was necessary for one of the soldiers from the watchtower to open them especially for us. The great wooden doors, reinforced with metal, swung back gratingly on their hinges, thudded together again as soon as we were outside the walls.

It was too early for the usual habitués to be present at their posts by the gate. Only one old beggar with a scraggly, gray-streaked beard hobbled along beside our wagon, defiling the quiet air with his screeching voice. Rizpah took off one of her copper bracelets and, before I could stop her, handed it to the old man. Nothing like this had ever happened to him. At first he was as stunned as if someone had hit him. He stared at the bracelet, bit it disbelievingly, then tucked it away in his rags and ran after the wagon. He was unable to kiss the hem of Rizpah's robe, so he contented himself with touching his lips repeatedly to whatever part of the wagon he could reach. Eventually he found it difficult to keep up, but we could hear his voice for some time, calling down the blessings of Dagon, Astarte, and even the Hittite, Phoenician and Egyptian gods on Rizpah's head.

Her expression was itself like that one sees on the graven visage of a temple figure: masklike, brooding, devoid of any spark of life. She had spoken little since Manim's death a few hours before. When I gave her food just before our departure, she had eaten it meekly on my command, had allowed herself to be led to the wagon and installed there on cushions beneath the canopy. Giving away the bracelet was the first voluntary move she had made that morning, and even this almost seemed as if her hands had moved independently of her brain. She gave no sign of having really seen the beggar or of having heard his pathetic cries of gratitude.

I knew what I had to do if I wanted to help her. "That was most generous of you," I said. "The old man will be able to drink for a month on the proceeds of your gift."

"Did it never occur to you," she asked coldly, "that he might have a family, and perhaps the bracelet will give them a little food for a few days?"

"I have seen him at the city gate since the time when I was a young woman. His only family is the wine cruse. He is known as a drunkard and a thief and, though it has never been proven, as a murderer."

"Am I so much better?"

I had been waiting for this. "Do you think you can ever purchase freedom from remorse?"

"Will it come any other way?"

I put my hand on hers. "It was not your fault."

"Manim told me he only came to my room because he felt I wished it."

I smiled bleakly. "That frayed and ancient gambit . . ."

"Perhaps I did."

"I doubt it. But even if you did, Manim knew the chance he took and the penalty."

"I should not have screamed. I could have made him go."

"Do you really believe that?"

She looked me full in the face, her eyes hard. "And if I had not been able to, is my body worth a man's life?"

"It's not that simple."

We were passing the temple where she had received instruction from Vontela and the priestesses. She looked at it moodily. The great oak trees overhanging the marble building were alive with sparrows. The sound of our horses and the creaking of the wagons set them in flight, sent them chattering into the gray dawnlight.

"When I lived in Simeon," said Rizpah, "I would often hear my father referring to my beauty. Even my mother, who was not given to praise, told me on the day she was killed that I was lovely. My uncle worshiped me. I know now how my appearance must have tortured him. Since I was taken from my father's house . . ." She stopped, set her lips in a thin, bitter line. Then, after a moment, "You have just reminded me that money cannot buy freedom from remorse. I believe this. It was a stupid gesture, giving the bracelet to the beggar. But tell me, old woman, since money has no value in matters of the spirit, what can beauty buy?"

"Why do you think of life only in terms of the market place?"

"Is it not the only way of looking at it? You sell what you have, you buy at a price."

"To be a cynic without having achieved wisdom," I said tartly, "is like offering someone unripe fruit."

She leaned toward me, sneering. "Tell me, old woman, what did your beauty earn for you? A position of charity in a noble's house, with not even a respectable widowhood to show for the years you devoted to your lord's bed."

I slapped her across the face as hard as I could. Shishak turned from the driver's seat to look at us, but I did not care. I heard myself shouting, "You rude, venomous, spoiled little bitch!" I used the vernacular of Askelon's Lower Town, the oaths of whores and their pimps. "Your mother's milk was dog piss; your father cast his seed into a fouled vessel and you were born . . ." And more in this vein, until my anger began to cool. She winced under each word, as I meant her to do.

When I stopped cursing her, she sat watching me, touching her face where I had slapped her. Then she said, "I'm sorry, Egrep."

"Any time you want some more of the same," I grumbled. "Any time at all . . ."

She began to laugh. After a moment I joined in, and the two of us fell into each other's arms, laughing and weeping.

A little later her sober mood returned. "Yesterday," she said, "I lived the whole day in an illusion. I thought that now that I was returning to my native land, I would somehow find things as they were before . . . my father's house still standing, my family alive. Perhaps I *was* mad. Only not truly. It might have been better if I had gone mad. Because now I'm only frightened. Each time the wheels of this wagon turn over and bring us closer to Israel I think, I'm going home. And each time I realize who I am, what has happened to me, I want to shout: no, take me back, I don't want to go. . . ."

She sank back into a corner of the wagon. There was nothing I could say. When I put some extra cushions behind her, I could feel her trembling.

The wagons rolled smoothly along the highway of crushed rock. I knew that before the day was done we should look back on this part of the journey with longing and that even the cushions on which we sat would do little to ease the unceasing, monotonous pounding our bones would absorb. Knowing this, I found myself looking forward to a cool garden and the sweetness of twilight, to the welcome sight of servants bringing water in which we could bathe our feet. I called to Shishak, asking, "Has it been decided where we are to rest for the night?"

"At the home of one Naarai the son of Abiel," he replied.

I hoped this Naarai possessed well-padded beds free of insects and at least a passable table. In journeys with my man into the hills of Judah I had found the country considerably lacking in amenities. I smiled, realizing how quickly I had taken on again the concern of the campaigning soldier for creature comforts.

We stopped for the noon meal at a well near the frontier. In the distance we could see the Judean mountains, hot and sinister-looking under the midday sun. The servants unhitched and watered the horses. We slept under some trees during the two hours when the heat was intolerable, then resumed our journey.

We came to a fork in the highway. The southerly road led to Gath, one of the five royal cities, but neither as prosperous nor as populous as our own. However, it was noted for its skilled swordsmen and its lovely women, the latter possibly a result of the mingling of Philistine and Hebrew blood strains which had been taking place here over a long period of time. Gath was the last city of any consequence we would encounter in Philistia, and it might have been pleasant to stay the night. But there were still several hours left before the sun would set, and Torash's camp lay far to the northeast, near the spot where the tribal boundaries of Judah, Ephraim and Benjamin joined. If we wished to reach it by the following night, we could not afford an early halt.

Therefore we took the northerly fork. The road, though not paved, was still relatively flat, and our wagons moved over it easily. Far to the south we could see walled Gath, perched on the cliff which gave its watchtowers a commanding view of the land beyond the border.

The frontier station consisted of a crumbling mud hut built to house a dozen soldiers. Only four or five were on hand when we reached it, the rest being, as we learned later, on leave in Gath.

The soldiers were squatting on their haunches in the dust in front of the hut, absorbed in a game of dice with triangular black-and-white pieces. One of them looked up as we approached and, seeing Rizpah and me, began to make coarse jests which doubled up his companions with laughter, until one of them noticed the Seren's standards fluttering from poles on each wagon. Then there was an abrupt silence. One of the men went to get their officer, while the others remained, kicking at the dust like small boys.

The commander had obviously just been awakened. He emerged from the hut yawning but trying to convey an impression of smartness, fitting a tarnished helmet with bedraggled plume over his balding head. He stumbled once and almost fell as he marched toward our wagon, and one of his men snickered. When he drew near to tender his compliments, there was a strong odor of garlic and the kind of wine smell which results from liberal and continuous tippling. I was reminded for the first time in years of the corrosive monotony which eats into the lives of those who serve in small, nondescript stations. My man had once sponsored a measure in the Council of Serens restricting the service of border patrols in any one location to a maximum of three months, but it had died through lack of interest.

The commander conferred with the soldier who was serving as our chariot escort, warning him in our hearing that the way ahead might be dangerous. There was no telling where Saul and his ragged band of rebels might appear, and (with an eye-rolling glance at Rizpah and me) the atrocities they had committed were too evil to discuss. He and his men had lately seen some strange flashings of torches across the border—signals, no doubt—in the hours between sunset and dawn. Would it not be wise for the two ladies to remain at his station, at least overnight, until some of his men returned from leave and he could provide us with a proper escort through the hills. The accommodations, as we could see, were not fit for royalty, but he would do his utmost to make us comfortable.

Our escort looked uncertain, glanced askance at me.

I found myself increasingly embarrassed by the naked display of his loneliness and his pitiful attempt to magnify the prospect of danger and so increase the importance of his post in our eyes. "We are most grateful to the captain for his courtesy and concern," I said. "Nothing would give us greater pleasure than to remain and partake of both his hospitality and his generous offer of protection. But the journey ahead of us is a long one, and we are being anxiously awaited by the Seren himself."

His disappointment was evident, but a few additional words of flattery cost me nothing and helped preserve what was left of his self-respect. When we left, he mustered his listless charges into a semblance of formation and sent us on our way with an exaggerated salute.

I had been fairly sure there would be no danger, and the commander's warning had in no way distressed me, but I had forgotten the ominous character of the terrain we had to traverse. The arid, eroded hills rose somberly in our path. The sparse bits of vegetation were somehow more forbidding than none at all. Vultures, perched on yellow and red rocks overhanging the road, rose screaming and flapping their wings noisily at our approach. Among the burrows and tumbled boulders was ample hiding place for any number of armed men.

I looked at Rizpah, wondering whether any of the nameless apprehensions I had begun to experience were communicating themselves to her. I was surprised to see her appearance much the same as it had been all the day before, when she was living her unreal, excited dream of a return to her home. Her eyes sparkled. She seemed to be enjoying every breath of the acrid, dust-laden air.

I said tentatively, "You're not frightened any more."

"No."

"Rizpah . . . are you . . . ?"

She smiled and patted my knee. "Don't worry. I'm all right. But, Egrep . . ." She looked around, and I could feel her excitement. "It *is* my land, is it not? No matter how I return to it. I know who I am, what I am. I know I have never seen this part of my country. It's far less my home than Askelon. And yet . . ." She spread out her hands, unable to articulate her feelings further.

I grunted and resumed my careful survey of the hills and crags. When I saw a man standing motionless, observing us from a point high above the road, my heart leaped convulsively. But it turned out to be only a shepherd watching over a score of sad-looking sheep.

We were deep in the hills, climbing all the while. The road was bad now, sharply rutted and studded with rocks. The wagons bounced and jolted and more than once seemed in danger of capsizing.

As we rounded a bend, an enormous boulder crashed down onto the trail just ahead of us, then went careening on down the side of the hill. Our escort rode forward quickly but could see no one. Since the way was strewn with chunks of rock every bit as large as the one we had seen fall, I was satisfied that no human agent had caused the near-calamity. But I could not get over the feeling that our progress was the subject of constant scrutiny.

Now the land began to assume a more fertile aspect. The hillsides were covered with grass, brown and withered, to be sure, but still more pleasant to look at than the thorny clumps of scrub brush.

Ahead of us the rugged range of hills appeared to split, one section swinging north, the second, more spiny and barren, taking a sharp turn to the south. Between the two lay a rich plateau of cultivated fields. Our escort drove up alongside and pointed to a sizable village some distance away. "We shall rest there overnight."

The news came none too soon. Behind us the sun was already beginning to sink among the hills.

The fields were thick with grain nearly ready for harvesting. Most of the people working in them ignored us. The few who glanced our way did so sullenly. I was struck by the evidence of hunger I saw on their faces—the sunken cheeks and cavernous eye sockets. I had known that our occupation was severe; I had not realized it was so cruelly efficient. The collectors of tribute would have to be capable, ruthless men, able to judge both the potential of the land and the nature of the people themselves. Otherwise they could not have maintained in a defeated land the skillful balance between starvation and a bare subsistence minimum.

Since I knew none of the people I saw as individuals, I felt no great outpouring of sympathy. On the rare occasions when the Israelites had conquered segments of our country they had proved themselves equally merciless. While the two nations strove together, neither possessing the power to absorb the other completely, death and suffering would be the only clear victors. I hated the struggle. My heart ached with wishing for its end. But as long as there could not be a lasting peace, no one could expect a genteel war.

As we drew near the village, our escort called out to a group of field workers, asking where we would find the home of Naarai son of Abiel. Some of them looked at us blankly; others shook their heads. One grizzled, emaciated elder leaned on the shaft of his mattock and said, "Naarai, son of Abiel . . . did he not die just after the battle of Aphek?" Grim smiles touched the lips of the others as they turned back to their work.

At the outskirts of the village we encountered a Philistine officer and two of his soldiers riding in from a patrol. The officer sniffed loudly when we said no one had been able to tell us where to find Naarai. "These swine, these filthy goat heads, this is their idea of a joke. There . . ." He pointed to a cluster of buildings not far away. "There lives Naarai. He's the only civilized person in this den of jackals."

The village itself was unwalled, but Naarai's house had a high barrier around it, appearing to be newer than the buildings it surrounded, a mud and stone affair topped with jagged bits of broken pottery imbedded in the mortar.

Naarai's house was constructed of stone and wood, contrasting markedly with the shabbiness of the rest of the dwellings in the village. They were of mud brick, and there was a peculiar desolated air about them, as though they were not completely lived in. An old man sitting outside one of the houses got up when he saw us and disappeared through a doorway.

Across from Naarai's gate was the village well. A group of women filling their pitchers looked at us curiously, whispering among themselves.

Shishak got down from his wagon and thumped with the hilt of his sword on the gate. It was opened by a servant, who closed it hurriedly as soon as we had entered, but not before I caught a last glimpse of the women, knotted together in a tight little circle by the well, talking and gesticulating animatedly.

Naarai son of Abiel came out of the house as we descended from our wagon. He was a thin, graceful man, with a pleasant, wistful smile that kept starting and disappearing at the corners of his mouth. He prostrated himself and kissed the hems of our robes, as the ceremonial custom demanded. "Welcome to my home, good ladies," he said, rising then and brushing the dust from his knees. "The captain of the guard of the household of the Seren of Askelon informed me this morning on his way to the camp of the Seren of Askelon that your gracious ladyships would honor my house . . ." He paused for breath. I was amused by his formal insistence on full formal titles, which gave this little introductory speech an odd rambling quality.

He clapped his hands, gave orders for the horses to be stabled, for water to be brought so that we could bathe our feet at once. It was then that I realized I had been in danger of misjudging the mettle of our host. When he spoke to the servants his voice took on a steely, vibrating timbre. He expected instant obedience from those who served him, and he received it. But when he turned to us again the wistful smile was back, starting shyly across his face. Not a simple man, one who operated with awareness on a number of different levels.

The chamber to which I was shown was cool and well-appointed. Rizpah had the adjoining room. She had been unusually quiet since we entered Naarai's house, but I was too weary and hungry to inquire if anything in particular was troubling her. I instructed our servants which chests to bring from the wagon, and I made Rizpah change into one of her loveliest gowns. She looked most charming in the soft mauve, with a slim circlet of gold crowning her chestnut hair and the graceful copper bracelets on her bare arms. I did the best I could with my own appearance, and together we descended to the evening meal.

Naarai was properly complimentary to us both, and I began to agree with the officer's estimate of him as a civilized man. His wife, a small, nervous woman with a slight stammer, sat at table with us. Had we been male guests, she probably would not have been so privileged, and she acted as if she were overcome with the honor, at first speaking only when addressed, and then in halting, inept phrases. Rizpah began to chat softly with her, and the woman warmed to the girl, fixing adoring eyes on her, gradually growing more talkative. Naarai's expression hardened, and he seemed ready to close off his wife's chatter, but when he saw we were not displeased, he also relaxed, then became expansive.

The fare was better than I had hoped for. In fact, I found it astonishing. There were the inevitable curds, but they were lighter and more flavorful than any I had ever tasted. Two kinds of roast meat—kid and lamb—were served from great silver platters, and I complimented Naarai on the seasoning.

He favored me with his wistful smile. "When the Seren of Ashdod journeyed through our land a year ago, he was gracious enough to seek hospitality in my house. His cook, who I understand accompanies him even to the army encampments, instructed my servants." I nodded, thinking of the fat, epicurean Seren of Ashdod, who was so fearful of being poisoned that he would taste no morsel not prepared and then sampled by his cook, who was also an expert swordsman.

There were green and ripe olives stuffed with several varieties of cheeses, loaves of flaky bread and, just before the fruits were served, a delicious sweet concocted of eggs and raisins.

I thought about the people we had seen in the fields that day, their gaunt faces and bodies clearly evincing the ravages of hunger.

Collaborators were no novelty to me. Warfare being what it is, there will always be those who choose, through principle or greed, to side with the enemies of their people. We have had our share in Philistia, and many of the children of Israel have served our cause to their own ends. In my youth I looked on such men and women with the definiteness of the young. I called them turncoats and went out of my way to register disgust with the whole breed. In the course of time my man taught me that the tangled web of human motive takes on many lights as it turns in the sun. "Pursue your own path," he used to say after I had concluded some particularly virulent discourse on the subject. "But question not too piously the actions of others, lest your own be held up close to the critical eye. When it seems necessary to destroy those who oppose the things you believe in, do so, but do not compose psalms to your own righteousness. For in a day or a year you may be forced to retreat in shame along the same path you now travel in pride."

Even so, though I could now tolerate the presence (and, as on this occasion, the hospitality) of collaborators, deep inside me I still thought of them as birds who fouled their own nests.

The way of the collaborator is at best a lonely one. It has its advantages and its perils. For Naarai the benefits were apparent. But I had seen the faces of the people among whom he lived. I wondered how he paid for his position, and when the meal was over I made a discreet inquiry.

"I act as assistant to the district collector of tributes," he replied coolly.

I raised my eyebrows. This, of course, explained the sumptuous board. If I had lived in Israel, I would have done my best to kill Naarai. But I was not a Hebrew.

Rizpah, hearing his reply, sat up straight in her chair. "How can you do it?"

"Do what, my lady?" Naarai asked pleasantly, turning to her.

"Inform against your own people. Feast while they starve." Spots of color appeared on her cheeks. "Have you no shame?"

Naarai smiled shyly, wistfully. "And you, my lady?" he asked, very quietly.

The captain of the guard must have told him about Rizpah. I waited for the storm to break, hoping she would rise and challenge his impudence. Instead she bowed her head and said nothing. In her eyes was the haunted expression I had so often observed.

Naarai said, "I meant no offense. It is only that I believe so fervently in peace between the Hebrew and Philistine nations."

"As do I," I said lightly. "And doubtless you have considered the terms of such peace."

"I have," he answered. "The Philistine nation is strong and well armed. If Israel continues to struggle against Philistia, we will destroy ourselves. See what has happened even now. Because we have resisted, and continue to resist, the price we must pay in lives and livelihood is heavy. If we accept the rule of your country, only good can come of it. The tribute which is now crushing would diminish until it becomes a mere token. There would be commerce between our lands, and Israel would have the use of Philistine seaports. In addition, we could expect protection from Philistia against enemies who threaten our land from all sides."

It was a reasonable speech, even with its flaws of logic. If we had been served a meal of dry bread and thin gruel, I might have been able to admire the sentiments which lay behind it. I watched the servants clearing away the remains of our feast, then turned again to Naarai. "My friend is indeed a gracious and generous host. Seldom have I enjoyed a repast so completely. Even in Askelon, where we pride ourselves on the abundance of delicacies, the board of Naarai would be sure to achieve a distinctive reputation."

My insinuations stung him deeper than Rizpah's outright accusation. I had not meant to commit myself to this extent. His conduct was his own concern. I was only angry because he had included Rizpah in his rationalization. Naarai's eyes narrowed, but his voice reflected only a trace of the steely vibrations I had heard when we first met. "Would my lady have me and my family endure hardship for the sake of a struggle in which we cannot believe?"

His wife laughed nervously, breaking the silence which followed his question. I decided to retreat. "It was not my intention to criticize the hospitality of Naarai. I simply meant that the misunderstanding of his countrymen must be a great burden to him."

It was a shoddy apology, but he chose to accept it. He sighed. "Conditions were on the way to improving. If it had not been for the hotheads who stirred up talk of a king, and the mad prophet Samuel who acceded to their requests . . ."

"What of Saul?" I asked, glad to return to safer ground.

"What is there to say?" He attempted his wistful smile without much success. "He is an ignorant farmer with a flair for drama and a measure of insane courage. When the Ammonites came up against the town of Jabesh-Gilead, as they do each year, Saul saw an opportunity to capitalize on it. He carved up a yoke of oxen and sent a grisly relic to each tribe, with the message that they would endure a similar fate unless they rallied to his leadership. Some were deceived into joining him—the indolent, the malcontents, the lunatics one finds idling at every city gate. They helped him drive off the Ammonites. Saul became drunk with power and turned against the Philistines." He sighed again, the lament of a man who had been made weary from dealing with stupidity. "This adventure can only end badly. Already the demand for tribute has increased, and more stringent laws against my people are being considered. Fortunately only a few have been asinine enough to follow Saul, and I have heard that even the majority of those have deserted him. Soon he will be caught and executed. Then we shall be able to progress once more toward a lasting peace between our countries."

He was able to smile now. Rising from his place, he regretted in polished phrases that he had no garden to offer us, but he recommended the cool breeze of evening one could enjoy on the rooftop.

I kept watching Rizpah as we walked from the spacious common room toward the stairs leading to the roof. I need not have worried about her ability to carry off a situation like this. Without seeming to snub Naarai she conversed easily with his wife, and when we were settled in chairs on the rooftop, she seemed the picture of composure. Only someone who knew her as well as I would be able to detect any signs of strain.

Naarai tried only once to engage her in talk. "I understand my lady Rizpah formerly made her home in the territory of Simeon."

It was an unfortunate blunder. Rizpah fixed him with an icy stare. Her voice was low and musical. The combination was devastating. "Then my friend Naarai must also understand that I was removed from my home by force after my parents were slaughtered. That I was transported against my will to live in Philistia. One does not always have the freedom to choose the course of one's life. Freedom of choice is a gift worthy of man's highest respect. Does my friend Naarai not agree?"

Naarai replied with a sickly half-smile, then began an animated discussion with me about the beauties of the city of Askelon, which he professed interest in seeing one day. He must have been more discomfited than even his manner admitted, for when darkness closed in about us he neglected to call for lamps. I smiled to myself, holding up my end of the conversation, wondering how long it would be before he noticed his negligence. We continued to talk. Naarai's wife signified her participation with an occasional nervous laugh. Finally I decided it was time to get some rest. We were to set out again at dawn. I smothered an audible yawn, and Naarai was at once all apologies.

"I fear I have been boring your ladyships," he said. "If you would care to retire . . ."

"Lamps, Naarai," said his wife, stammering slightly, following her reminder with a small, mirthless giggle.

Naarai was furious. "Why did you wait until now to speak? My guests will believe me to be a dull clod, no better than those who live in the village hovels."

All his arrogance was unleashed now. He clapped his hands loudly, shouted in a shrill voice for servants to bring lamps. They came, and he cursed their slowness. I had the feeling he was venting, perhaps for the first time, fears and frustrations that he had managed to keep in check for too long.

It was then that I noticed that Rizpah's chair was empty.

I was not greatly concerned. I thought she had slipped away to her chamber, not trusting herself to bid Naarai a civil good night. It was not like her to be this rude, but Naarai, not she, had drawn the line of battle.

She had actually left as soon as darkness descended. She found the stairs, groped her way down. It had been her intention to go to her room, for Naarai's voice was indeed grating on her nerves. But as she approached the sleeping quarters she felt suddenly oppressed. She believed if she did not have some fresh air she would faint.

The thought of returning to the roof was distasteful, so she continued down the stairs, stumbling once or twice, until a glow from the kitchen where the servants were still busy gave her light to find her way through the common room and out into the courtyard.

Her eyes soon became accustomed to the darkness again. When she saw the door in the wall, not far from the gate, she had no thought of escape and only the glimmering of an idea that she would simply like to walk around the village. She crossed the courtyard, quietly eased the wooden crossbar from its metal pinions, opened the door and let herself out.

She heard voices and, instead of avoiding them, moved in their direction. The blackness of night was more intense in the shadows cast by the village houses.

Two women were talking. She could not make them out in the gloom but heard one saying, "The son of Shammoth is worse," and the other replying irritably, "He will soon be dead." The word "dead" lay in the silence of the street like the corpse itself.

Rizpah bumped into a hard stone surface, realized she had reached the edge of the well and tried to back away. Her foot dislodged a pebble. One of the women asked sharply, "What . . . ?" The other drew in breath between her teeth. "There . . ."

She could see them now and knew they saw her. The movements

of their loose, shroudlike robes gave them the appearance of great birds as they came toward her.

"It's the Philistine woman," said one.

"The younger," replied the other. "Look at her bare arms."

"Whore!" cried the first. "A torch! Bring a torch!"

Rizpah was not afraid. Were these not her people? She had only to tell them . . .

A man came running with a torch, and before she understood what was happening, Rizpah was surrounded by at least a score of men and women, peering at her, looking at each other, uncertain of why they were there and what they were going to do. In the light of the torch Rizpah could see the hollow eyes, the gaunt lines of their faces, and the sight moved her deeply. She put out her hand toward them in an involuntary gesture of sympathy. The woman nearest drew her black robe closer about her shoulders, inched away. "Harlot . . ."

One of the men spat into the dust and muttered, "Philistine bitch."

"No." Rizpah looked around the circle, pleading with her eyes. "You don't understand. I'm not a Philistine. I'm an Israelite. Don't you see? —a Hebrew, like the rest of you."

For a moment there was silence. Then the hatred gathered and thickened in the throats of the people. They pressed in about her, uttering little angry cries which soon coagulated to become a roar of mob rage.

It was the fact that they were so many and she alone which gave her fleeting protection. They milled about, trying to reach her, succeeding only in getting in the way of one another. Someone jostled the man with the torch, and it fell to the ground. The darkness and confusion only increased the crowd's frenzy.

I was just entering Rizpah's room in search of her when I heard the shouts of anger from the street. I moved hurriedly to the bed, saw she was not there, and understood somehow that she must be the cause of the hubbub outside the house.

Shielding the lamp flame with my hand, I ran down the stairs and out into the courtyard, calling for Shishak as I went. He came quickly, sleepy-eyed, but moving with that terrible catlike agility, buckling on his sword as he rushed past me.

Two of Naarai's servants followed, bearing torches. I traveled in their wake through the door in the wall into the street, in time to see Shishak laying about him among the massed bodies with the flat of his sword.

The crowd parted then and I saw Rizpah, her hands raised to ward off the frantic but ill-aimed blows. I gained her side and dragged her back toward Naarai's house. She was sobbing loudly, and when we passed through the door I stopped and slapped her several times, half to stop her sobbing, half in anger.

"You fool!" I said bitterly. "You senseless little fool!"

The courtyard was filling with light as servants with lamps and torches poured out of the house. Naarai appeared, followed by his wife. When she saw Rizpah's disheveled state she shrank back against the side of the house, wringing her hands in a washing gesture, which in its desperation was almost comical.

Naarai came forward, trembling. "You won't report this to the Seren? You won't . . ."

Even in my anger and concern I felt a little sorry for him. This night, in so many ways, had shaken and threatened his security. His life could never again be the same as it had been before our arrival. I nodded, letting him interpret this as he would, and led Rizpah into the house. In the background the noise was dying away.

She was regaining her composure quickly. I had not been mistaken the first day I met her when I thought I detected the toughness and resiliency beneath her soft, feminine exterior.

We entered her chamber. She turned to me. "I'm sorry, Egrep," she said. "Truly and deeply sorry."

I was not quite ready to relent. "You're still a little fool."

"I will not—" her eyes became hard and opaque—"ever be so foolish again."

She was wrong. Vows can be broken. And sometimes quickly.

chapter seventeen

I ALLOWED Rizpah to sleep until an hour past dawn. After she had breakfasted in her room we went together to the courtyard, where the wagons had been brought out and were waiting. The soldier escort was leaning against his chariot, chewing on a piece of bread, his expression reflecting some of the mortification he must have felt at having slept through the disturbance of the night before.

Naarai came to see us off, his face gray with lack of sleep, eyes wavering between anxiety and hostility. Rizpah turned to him before being helped up into the wagon.

"My friend Naarai has indeed exceeded the duties of hospitality."

There was no irony in her manner. "Your handmaiden Rizpah wishes to express her gratitude. If my tongue spoke words displeasing to my friend, I beg that you forget them, or if this is not possible, that you attribute them to a heart overflowing with confused emotions. May the blessings of Jahveh follow you all the days of your life."

Tears filled Naarai's eyes. The wistful half-smile came and went several times in quick succession. His voice choked up as he said, "The Lord God of our fathers . . . protect the lady Rizpah . . . forever."

We drove out of the courtyard, the horses' hoofs kicking up a cloud of dust, the creak and clatter of the wagons resounding through the oddly silent village. A woman stood at the well, filling a pitcher, regarding us with an emotionless, detached gaze. Nearby lay what was left of a torch, broken in several pieces by trampling feet. Otherwise there was no sign that the open space before the well had a few hours before been a dark arena of violence.

We left the village behind, and the horses settled into their monotonous traveling rhythm. I leaned over and kissed Rizpah on the cheek and was pleased when she did not make a coy inquiry into the reason for my display of affection. There was often a man's directness about her, woven strongly into the threads of her female intuitiveness. "What use to hate Naarai?" she asked. "A man can only answer to Jahveh and himself for what he does. . . ." Then she smiled at me. "Tell me, old woman, is the acquiring of wisdom always accompanied by so much pain?"

"You should ask someone much older. I still ache more often than I care to admit."

"Why trouble to seek it then?"

"Few seek wisdom. It finds you."

"Can you not flee from it?"

"Can you flee death?"

"Everyone dies," she said, "but many grow older without becoming wiser."

"This is not because they run away. Wisdom comes and stands before us, like a silent and unobtrusive stranger. If we ignore him, he may leave of his own accord. But once we have taken notice, we are obliged to strive with him and suffer the pain of struggle."

"My mother used to tell me a story of the patriarch Jacob as a young man, how an angel came to him as he slept and woke Jacob and made him wrestle the whole night. And in the morning they were both weary and bruised, but neither had won. And after the angel had gone, Jacob realized that he had really wrestled with God."

"There is a great deal to think about in the old stories."

She seemed to be considering this for a time. Then suddenly her eyes came alive and a puckish grin brightened her face. "We're much too somber, old woman. Speculating like crones on the meaning of the world."

"I am a crone."

"You have the heart of a young virgin and the voice of a bird. Come, old woman. Sing me a song."

I sang to her in my cracked and aging voice of Caphtor, the island home of our fathers, of how the god and goddess met there in a secluded grove and their offspring was man, how the child even at a tender age built palaces and temples for his immortal parents, and how when he was grown a mighty storm raged over the island one night, the waves sweeping up into the hills and nearly drowning the man. In the morning the storm was over. And walking into the sunlight from a glistening bower came the woman who was to be the man's mate. And neither ever saw the god or goddess again, but the man fashioned images of his mother and father to preserve his memory of them.

She sang a touching little song taught her long ago by her father's shepherd, about a lamb who strayed from the flock and became lost in the wilderness. But Jahveh protected the lamb and led it out of peril into a green pasture beside still waters and watched over it until the shepherd found it.

The day was passing quickly. When we stopped at midday, our escort told us we were traveling along the division between the territories of Judah and Ephraim and that tiny Benjamin, home of the rebel Saul, lay not too far ahead. If nothing delayed us, we should sight Torash's camp long before sundown.

I found myself eagerly anticipating our arrival. Some of my fondest memories center about an encampment at evening, with the fires sending fragrant smoke into the air, and the striped tents of the Serens and the division commanders, and the rough jests shouted back and forth between companies, everyone relaxed and laughing, listening to the nostalgic songs rising from various corners of the camp. I have heard many words spoken about the horrors of war, and they are all true. I also remember encampments at evening when the wounded were brought from the field of battle and laid out on the ground, row by dreary row. I have watched the surgeons, their arms crimson to the shoulders with blood, their eyes glazed from prolonged traffic with pain, moving wearily among those who had fallen, working by torchlight, cutting, slicing, removing an arrow, touching a hot iron to a spear wound, turning aside from those already dead. I have heard the cries of the dying, have knelt beside many to ease their last moments. I have smelled the sweet, cloying odor of new death and the ripe putrefaction of old death. I have seen headless bodies and bodyless heads. A man remembers these horrors. Often he is so brutalized by having lived through them that his soul never completely heals. But men also remember other things about war: the deep cameraderie, the fear before battle, the relief that is almost an ache when it is over and they have survived. Men remember many things about war that they cannot speak of to those who have never shared the experience. This is why they are often moody and inarticulate when they return to the women they love. And this is why I have always considered myself fortunate in having been able to accompany my man on his campaigns.

We entered the camp just as the sun was setting. Torash and the Serens with him had chosen the location well: an open plain with a long, unobstructed view of the surrounding country.

The outpost sentries watched our approach suspiciously, then, seeing Torash's standard, waved us on.

Everything was as I remembered it: the enclosure containing livestock; the supply wagons drawn up in a great circle; the spears knotted together like bundles of firewood, but showing gleaming lethal tips; the neat rows of helmets, shields and cuirasses. An odor of roasting meat rose tantalizingly from a hundred campfires.

An officer showed us to our tent. He informed us that Torash wished to see Rizpah the moment we arrived, but I sent him on his way with the message that she would first bathe and scent herself, since surely the Seren was more interested in his lady than in the dust of the country through which she had traveled.

Rizpah had grown quiet again. I helped her bathe and change her clothes. She prepared to go to the Seren willingly but with no great show of eagerness.

I brought her to his tent. We stood outside, and for a moment her expression was that of the child who had stood with me three years before, outside the banquet hall in the house at Askelon, lonely and frightened. "It is always like this after an absence," I said to her. "It will pass."

She walked on alone. Just before she entered the tent she turned and smiled at me over her shoulder.

Kraseg was with Torash. He scowled at the sight of Rizpah. The anger and resentment he felt toward her that first night had only increased with time. His mouth twisted with a silent oath. Then he quickly turned to see if Torash were watching him. He might have spared himself the trouble. Torash had no more interest in his presence. Kraseg gathered up the scrolls he and the Seren had been discussing and left the tent, making an exaggerated detour around the spot where Rizpah stood.

She walked to Torash. He remained silent, touching the gold pendant at his throat, while she bowed gravely.

Then, "Your journey was a pleasant one?"

"As pleasant as could be expected, my lord."

He tried to continue with the formal words of greeting, failed. Suddenly his reserve left him. He took her in his arms, held her close, murmuring over and over, "My dear, my dear . . ."

She felt a difference in him. It was not only that he was leaner, more fine-drawn, burned deep brown by the sun. She had expected the change in his appearance. But there was something else, something she found it difficult to define. It was, in a way, as if a stranger were holding her in his arms, a stranger performing the intimate and delicate offices of love. She was just now beginning to be aware of the many different levels on which each human being lives, of the multitude of personalities lying mingled in each spirit. A man and woman who live together and believe they know each other usually know only the small portions of each other forced into exposure by habit and environment. Occasionally the shadows of new dimensions are revealed: through joy or sorrow or passion shared, or sometimes through venturing into new surroundings together.

When this happens, there is a shifting and shuffling of their personalities in terms of each other; for a time, at least, they are different people. Where there is love between them, this newness is welcomed and becomes an absorbed part of the man's and woman's deepening knowledge of each other. Where there is no love, the newness means only a temporary mystification, even an irritation, until these unfamiliar facets can be expunged, rubbed clean and relegated to the limbo from which they emerged. For while love is an adventurer, an intrepid and zestful explorer, no love is a meager and timorous thing, risking little and daring to take only what the eye can see and the hand can touch.

It was dark in the tent now. Lying beside Torash, aware of his body close to hers, his breath touching her cheek, Rizpah wanted to remain in the safe warm darkness without ever moving.

He said quietly, "There have been times during all these weeks away from you when I thought I would never see you again. I would awaken in the night and feel the emptiness beside me calling out to the emptiness within me. And I would rise and walk through the camp, among the smoldering campfires and sleeping men. And the stars would mock me with their thin light, asking me how it was that I, who have existed all these years without you, could now not bear a few days away from your presence."

"I am here now, my lord."

"You are here now." There was a trace of sadness in the repetition. He ran his fingers lightly along the line of her jaw, down over her shoulder and breast, let them rest on the curve of her hip. "The captain of my house guard informed me about Manim."

She shivered, mostly from remembering, but a little from the memory of Manim returning while Torash's hand was on her body.

"If I had been there," the Seren said slowly and heavily, "I would have carved the jackal into many pieces and sent a portion of his dismembered body to each of my nobles."

There was something about the cruel image, not its cruelty alone, but a sense of having encountered it before. Then she remembered. Naarai's description of the message Saul had sent to the tribes of Israel: the yoke of oxen and the admonition.

"I would be happier to forget . . ."

He drew his head away. She could feel his eyes searching for hers through the darkness. "Did he . . ."

"No, my lord. I screamed and he was terrified. Nothing happened to me." She had to add with a touch of recrimination, "And still he had to be killed."

"And still he had to be killed. Just as you would have had to be killed if you had lain willingly with him."

She knew he meant what he said, and a sharp pulsing terror began in her innards, refusing to spread, turning back into the pit of her stomach to become a small hard knot. The gloom in the tent threw up shadows of fear: great threatening wings moving slowly and ominously, the forms of hideous animals crouching ready to spring, a misshapen dwarf with stubby arms held high in malediction . . . She stifled a cry and buried her head in the pillows.

Torash stroked her hair and spoke soothingly to her. "Forgive me, my dear. I should not have frightened you. In my anger . . ."

She turned over and took his hand in both of hers, wanting to speak affectionately to him, but the terror still stirred too strongly in her bowels. He waited a moment, then rose and threw a cloak about him. He went to the entrance and asked the guard outside for a torch, then lighted lamps until the inside of the tent was brighter than day.

Rizpah saw the apparitions disappear: the ominous wings becoming rich tapestried hangings, the crouching animals and the evil dwarf carved chests and a dining table and ornate chairs. She lay still on the couch, letting her eyes wander over the luxurious furnishings of the tent, laughing a little at having been afraid.

He watched her uncertainly, as if there were some joke he did not understand and he was waiting for her to explain it. When she said nothing, he let his eyes caress her body and moved toward the couch.

She sat up, reaching for her robe. "Please," she said in a small voice, "could I have something to eat?"

Torash laughed, too loudly. "Of course." He went again to the entrance of the tent, gave brisk orders, seeming relieved to be involved once more with matters over which he had firm control.

Later that night she clung to him, grateful for his kindness, trying to make up somehow for pain she had caused him without exactly understanding how she had done it.

She was awakened by someone calling to the Seren from outside the tent. He stirred beside her, yawning, recognizing the voice and replying, "What is it, Kraseg?"

"A prisoner. One of Saul's men. The outpost sentries found him prowling near the camp. Will you question him, my lord?"

It was still dark. "How long until morning?"

"Three hours until daylight. But I would suggest that my lord question him now. If there are others nearby . . ."

Torash got up, grumbling, dressing as he called to Kraseg that he would interrogate the man outside the tent, asking him to have torches brought so there would be a good light, leaning over to kiss Rizpah before he left.

She could hear Torash's voice, grown cold once more, then Kraseg's, first responding obsequiously to the Seren, in the next moment barking a command to the prisoner. She rose and put on her clothes, slipped through the entrance of the tent and stood by the flaps, unnoticed, blinking in the bright light.

The prisoner was in his forties, a sallow man with unkempt beard and hair. He wore a stained and faded black cloak, open in the front to reveal a tuniclike garment of dirty sheepskin. He was on his knees before Torash, hands tied behind him, eyes raised pleadingly and fearfully to the Seren's face. Two guards stood by, studying the captive with contemptuous interest.

Torash asked his name. The reply came in slurred syllables. "Akkub, son of Sacra."

"Are Saul and his men also in the vicinity of our camp?"

Akkub said nothing, but the fear deepened in his eyes. Kraseg took a slim dagger from his girdle, thrust the point expertly under one of the man's fingernails. Akkub screamed.

"Answer the Seren when he speaks. Are Saul and his herd of swine in the area?"

The prisoner breathed out an anguished negative. Kraseg, his normally sour and unexpressive face alight with animation, used his dagger again, hissed, "Next time don't be so long in answering."

"Where is Saul?"

The reply came quickly. "Michmas."

Torash and Kraseg looked blankly at each other. One of the guards spoke up. "If it please my lord, Michmas is the name they give to a wild gorge a half day's journey from here."

The Seren looked down at the prisoner. "How many men are with Saul?"

"Two thousand with Saul. Another thousand with his son Jonathan."

"You lie," said Kraseg. "Even in Israel there are not three thousand mad dogs."

"I speak the truth. In Jahveh's name . . ."

"How are they armed?"

"As I was. With whatever farm tools that can be sharpened to serve as weapons. Mattocks and colters and oxgoads . . ."

Torash began to laugh. "And bits of chaff to throw in our eyes."

"And slings with stones," said Akkub with a sudden show of boldness.

Kraseg cuffed him sharply on the mouth. A spot of blood appeared between his lips, trickled down his chin.

"What are Saul's plans?" asked Torash quietly, his voice assuming its silky, dangerous texture.

Akkub shook his head. Kraseg compressed his lips and went to work with dagger. The prisoner shrieked, "I don't know!" And again, beginning to blubber, "I don't know . . ."

Kraseg calmly selected another finger. Rizpah started forward, managed to check herself. "Not now," said Torash, placing a restraining hand on his officer's arm. Kraseg's eyes were furious, but he dropped Akkub's hand and stood, waiting.

"Think about it," Torash said to the prisoner. "If you tell us what Saul is planning next, we shall deal fairly with you."

Akkub bent forward until his forehead touched the ground. "How can I tell more?" he mumbled. "I've told you all I know."

Kraseg said, his lips barely moving, "If my lord would allow me to . . ."

The Seren raised his hand in a simple, commanding gesture. Kraseg stopped speaking. Torash said to the guards, "Tie him to one of the wagons." They led him away. "I believe he speaks the truth," continued Torash, adding without emotion, "We shall question him once more in the morning, then kill him."

A spasm of pleasure crossed Kraseg's face, ended abruptly as he saw Rizpah standing in the doorway of the tent. He regarded her intently until Torash turned. Then, smiling evilly past Torash's shoulder, Kraseg called, "Good night, my lord," and was gone.

Torash held the tent flap open for Rizpah to enter, then followed her inside. "I'm sorry you witnessed that," he said. "It was no concern of yours."

She looked down at the rug covering the floor of the tent and said nothing. He came to her and lifted her chin with his finger tips. "So often I have no idea what you are thinking."

Her mind was occupied with what she had just seen outside the tent and the words she had heard between Torash and Kraseg. But she managed a smile, vaguely unhappy over her deception, as she said, "Now my lord knows that women are not the only ones who inquire into the thoughts of others."

Her reply softened his features, which had been hardening into the old cast of watchful reserve. "I wish you were less charming. Do you know there are times when I would sacrifice half my wealth if you were bitter and ugly, instead of the way you are."

"Why is my lord so unkind?"

"Because your lord is not a god, and the heart of mortal man can only endure a certain amount of punishment. Come to bed."

Rizpah lay beside him in the soft, thick darkness, waiting until his regular breathing would tell her he slept. She did not know why she must do the thing that had sprung to her mind while she watched the prisoner kneeling before Torash; she knew only that she had to do it. It was her hope that she could accomplish what she planned and return before Torash woke.

He was asleep now. She touched his shoulder, and for one instant her resolve wavered. There is something so naked about a man's sleep. A woman's strength is in her softness, her waitingness. The aura of the womb is upon her, and the passage between waking and sleep is an open one, involving no loss, expressing the logical balance of life. But a man, with his obligation of aggressiveness, his need to stir and thrust, must always die a little each time he yields to sleep. So Rizpah touched the slumbering Torash's shoulder and felt a prescience of death and came close to settling back beside him, to shield his spirit from its dark visit.

But the compulsion was strong upon her to complete what her mind had begun. She got up from the couch and made her way cautiously to the table in the center of the tent. There she knew she would find the knife she and Torash had used that evening to peel and slice the fruit they had eaten. It was not really sharp enough for her purpose, but it would have to do.

Her hand groped across the table like a small blind animal. The fingers found what they sought, but as she grasped the handle there was a sharp click of metal against wood and Torash's breathing halted, hung suspended for a desperate moment before it resumed its deep and regular rhythm. She took a few more steps and picked up her robe, which she had dropped with careful forethought across a chest near the entrance.

She emerged from the tent into the cool night air. Panic gripped her as she realized she had forgotten about the sentry who was supposed to be stationed just outside the entrance. But he was not there, and she remembered that he had gone with the other guard to secure the prisoner Akkub for the night. She breathed more easily.

Now she had to find the place where Akkub was being held. Torash had instructed the guards to tie him to one of the wagons, but which one? She stood thinking, listening to the silence which always hovers like sound itself around any large group of sleeping men. Far away in the hills an owl called, the throaty notes borne faintly but clearly to her on the breast of the night wind.

There was no moon, but in the star glow she could easily see the beginning of the great graceful sweep of wagons which formed the perimeter of the camp. She reasoned that, if the Seren intended to resume his questioning of Akkub in the morning, the guards would not have taken him too far away.

Rizpah began walking toward the wagon closest to her and had nearly reached it when she was confronted by the silhouette of the two guards leaning on their spears. She had taken them to be part of the baggage piled near the wagons and had almost brushed past them. Fortunately their backs were to her. Now she could hear their low-voiced conversation, casual and heedless. They had not noticed her presence then.

She circled around, choosing a new approach to the wagon where she believed she would find Akkub. He was there, lying on the ground between the wheels, lashed to the axle. He must have been dozing, for he started and almost cried out when she placed her hand on his arm, then was so astonished at seeing a woman that the cry was frozen in his throat.

She worked as quickly as she could, sawing at the leather thongs with the dull blade. Akkub's breathing grew ragged with excitement and fear. Rizpah kept watching the guards anxiously, certain they would hear and come to investigate. But they seemed too engrossed in their talk, and she continued to saw steadily at the prisoner's bonds. She became conscious of small, inconsequential details about him: the starlit gleam of spittle on his lower lip, a deep cut in one of his sandals, the way the tangled hairs of his beard seemed to grow more thickly on the right side of his face. And something else: the smell of stale sweat from his garments mingling with the subtle and pervasive odor of fear.

He sat for a short time after he was free, chafing his wrists where the thongs had cut into them. He turned to her, trembling lips soundlessly shaping words of gratitude. She, impatient for him to be gone, sat with her face congealed into the mask of strained listening one assumes in the presence of a bore. And still his voluble, silent message of thanks poured out, until she grasped his arm and shook it roughly, indicating that he should go.

Beyond the wagon was an open field. It contained ripening grain, long since trampled by the feet of many soldiers. Beyond, at the edge of the field, was a small thicket which would give him temporary refuge until he could gather strength and courage to evade the outpost sentries and cross the rest of the plain to the safety of the hills. She tried with sign language to convey to him what he should do. He nodded, got to his feet noiselessly and began to run across the field.

Rizpah watched his flight, remembering her own long ago in tasting the bitterness of his terror in her mouth. Then, as he seemed certain of reaching the thicket, she allowed a tiny flame of triumph to rise within her, out of not yet dead ashes of fear.

She was never quite sure what happened after that. One moment she had succeeded in rescuing a man with only a few hours to live, had opened before him a vista of freedom. In the next she was witnessing the collapse of the whole structure she had laboriously built up. The guard's spear was flying through the air, a lethal shaft propelled to its target by a sure arm and a deft hand. Akkub's limbs flew akimbo as the spear struck him in the center of the back and raised him off the ground. The cry she heard was as much air being forcibly expelled from his lungs as it was fear or pain. He fell, and in the same calamitous instant the other guard spied her crouching beneath the wagon. He crossed hurriedly, unsheathing his sword, stopping in confusion as he recognized her. Then, with heavy, silent movements he pulled her up from the ground and, holding her arm tightly, began walking with her toward the Seren's tent. She said, "Let me go. I won't run away," and became aware, in an odd burst of retrospection, that these were her first words since she had bidden the Seren good night.

The other guard came running up, and the baffled look which passed between the two soldiers infuriated her. She strode along, consumed with a cold anger which gave her strength.

When they reached the tent, one of the guards went in to wake the Seren. She could not hear what was being said, but the inactivity of waiting made her apprehensive. She began to pace, guiding her steps in a rough circle, avoiding the second guard's embarrassed glance.

Torash came to the entrance and stood, holding the tent flap open, looking at her out of eyes still pouched with sleep. The guard who had been inside passed them with a clumsy bow and hastened off, as if on some errand. Torash motioned for her to come into the tent.

They sat looking at each other in the pale yellow lamplight, neither speaking, neither glancing away from the other. Rizpah could not be sure whether his eyes reflected disappointment, hatred, admiration or sorrow. It is likely that all of these emotions, and more, were passing through his heart without his being clearly aware of any of them.

A soldier entered the tent and stood respectfully by. It was only then that Rizpah looked away from Torash. She gave a quick involuntary gasp when she saw that the waiting soldier carried a heavy leather whip.

Slowly, with a tenderness as terrible as violence, Torash removed Rizpah's robe from her shoulders, knotted the sleeves about her waist so the upper part of her body was naked. He stood facing her and seized her wrists tightly, then nodded curtly to the soldier, who uncoiled the whip.

The lash bit into her back ten times. She writhed in Torash's grasp but did not once cry out. After the tenth stroke he released her and held up his hand for the soldier to stop. Rizpah sank to the floor of the tent, dimly conscious through her pain that she had seen tears streaming from the Seren's eyes. He was still weeping when I came to fetch Rizpah and had her carried, half fainting now, to her tent.

I gave her as strong a sleeping draught as I dared, and when she had fallen into uneasy slumber I washed her wounds and sent for a surgeon to apply a poultice of herbs blended into a paste with thickened oil.

I sat and watched her as she slept, trying to divine from the expression on her face her motive for committing such a foolhardy act. At length I believed I knew and admitted to myself that in her position I might have done the same thing. But I spent a long time reflecting on the manner in which human beings torment themselves.

I walked to the tent entrance, lifted the flap. Dawn was staining the night sky. All around me rose the sound of an army encampment returning to life.

chapter eighteen

RIZPAH SLEPT most of the next day. Torash came several times to the tent and stood looking down at her still form, a slight frown of melancholy deepening with each visit. Toward sunset the surgeon returned and announced after examining her that her back would heal nicely, though of course she would always bear scars.

Torash dispatched scouts early in the day, and they returned with the exciting news that Saul was indeed encamped at Michmas. After a brief council it was decided that a third of the army, under the personal command of Torash, would advance to engage the rebel chief.

The Seren came again to the tent, and now Rizpah was awake. She was sitting on the edge of the bed, sipping some broth I had made. I found myself the vertex of an odd triangle of communication. There was no rancor between them, but they were somehow incapable of addressing each other except through me.

"Tell my lady Rizpah that, until she is completely well, traveling is out of the question. Moreover, tell her that we shall undoubtedly be engaged in battle, and while it will probably be no more than a skirmish, still it would be wiser for her to remain here in the safety of the main camp."

She was pale and must have been suffering, though she gave no indication of it. Since she could not lean back against anything, I was supporting her by holding her arm. However, she had no fever, and her eyes were clear. "Tell my lord the Seren that I shall travel wherever he travels. Inform him that I have neither the slightest interest in remaining behind nor the intention of doing so."

I had never known her to address the Seren with such assurance in someone else's presence. Her speech might have been termed defiant, except that there was no truculence in her tone. Torash looked at her

closely, appearing to consider her words. Then he smiled, and there
was not the slightest vestige in his manner of the cold reserve which
had once ruled him.

"Tell my lady Rizpah that I have encountered strong wills both on
the field of battle and in civil life and I have rarely admitted defeat.
This is one of the occasions, and you might also tell her I am not
displeased."

So it was that when the divisions under Torash departed from the
encampment the next day Rizpah and I traveled with them, riding in
the cushion-lined wagon which had brought us from Askelon. Shishak
was again driving. He did his best to keep the vehicle from jolting,
but the roads of Benjamin were not the highways of Philistia, and I
knew the girl was in constant pain. I would have been happy to hear
her complain, but she pressed her lips together obstinately and kept
silent.

An army on the march is always a formidable and stirring sight.
The legions under Torash were no exception. The Hebrew scribes
later recorded that the main Philistine camp consisted of thirty thousand chariots, six thousand horsemen, and foot soldiers "as sand which
is on the seashore in multitude." Actually this was something of an
exaggeration. Chariots, with their armored cowls and the murderous
battle knives extending from their wheels, pulled at awesome speed by
foam-spattered horses, seem to be everywhere in a fray. Anyone who
has watched even a single chariot performing in an encounter can well
be forgiven if he believes there are at least a score at work. The total
number of chariots accompanying the Philistines on this expedition
was no more than three thousand, and a third of these were now with
Torash. He also commanded about seven hundred horsemen and four
thousand foot soldiers. An impressive force, to be sure, but hardly to
be described as a multitude.

There was a set marching order. First came the heavily muscled
spearmen, who also carried wicked-looking swords, which they employed for close fighting. These spear throwers were proud of their
skill and were fond of demonstrating it by spitting a pigeon or other
small bird at a hundred paces. Behind them traveled the archers and
back of them another group of swordsmen, just in front of the supply
wagons. The logic was simple. If there were an ambush, the spear
corps would receive the first shock of attack, and the archers could
release arrows over the heads of their own vanguard into the body of
the enemy advance. The swordsmen would then be a reserve line of
defense, protecting the supply wagons. Chariots and horsemen, being
more mobile, usually rode to the rear but also ranged up and down the

flanks of the marching divisions. All of the soldiers, mounted and on foot, were equipped with armor suitable to their rank and task.

I must admit that when we set out that morning I was thrilled by the sight of the sea of plumed helmets and the sun glinting from polished shields and the jaunty standards floating above the heads of the marching men. The sound of an army on the move is musical, expressed in a threatening, faintly ominous mode, as martial music should be: the cadenced tread of the foot soldiers, the irregular muffled thunder of cavalry, the dull roar of chariot wheels in ceaseless rumbling friction between axle and ground. Sometimes there is singing, mostly in the morning, before heat and dust and flies work their attrition on the spirits.

It was estimated that we would arrive at Michmas around midafternoon. Scouting parties hastened ahead to bring back an accurate, detailed report on the situation of Saul's camp. In the meantime, though Torash was sure his army vastly outnumbered the Israelites, he was careful to dispatch patrols to fan out into the hills on either side of our route, knowing that one man, even badly armed, who fights on familiar ground is worth five who have no knowledge of the country. Torash had no intention of allowing his superior force to march blithely into a trap.

I did not expect to see him during the trip, but early in the afternoon the chariot in which he and his armor-bearer rode pulled alongside our wagon. He tossed the reins to the armor-bearer and, leaping nimbly from chariot to wagon, climbed up beside Shishak, then made his way back to where Rizpah and I were sitting. I went through diplomatic motions of withdrawing, but it is difficult to isolate oneself in a small conveyance. Besides, after their strange conversation of the night before, addressed through me, I was curious to see how they would behave with each other.

They took no more notice of me than they did of Shishak, who was also obviously able to hear everything that was said. Rizpah was sitting hunched forward, cushions under her elbows, so she would be spared the additional pain of having anything touch her back. The Seren watched her for a moment without speaking. His expression frightened me a little until I realized what it was. Then I came close to weeping. I had rarely seen such dedicated, unprotected love shining from the eyes of a human being.

"I suppose you hate me."

He spoke with that peculiar mixture of petulance, hope and yearning taken on by lovers who feel their suit threatened. Love, having an unpredictable nature, is necessarily full of paradoxes. One of these is that it heightens the sensibilities generally but dulls the lover's perception of the person he loves. By this I do not mean the trite observation we have all made at one time or another, that a person in love is blinded to the faults of the one he loves. No, it is too often other qualities in our loved ones to which we become blind: their strengths, their capabilities, their needs. Particularly their needs.

If Torash had only realized it, his decision the night before to have Rizpah whipped for what she had done brought her very close to loving him. Not the act itself, for alone it would have been brutal, and only deeply troubled or insensitive women respond to undiluted brutality. The thing that made it possible, merely possible at this point, for her to love him was the strength he had displayed. She had known she would have to be punished for her misdeed. If he had allowed her to escape retribution, she would have despised him. When, to the contrary, he did what he did, even though it was apparent that his spiritual pain matched her physical suffering, something awakened in her. She was standing on the threshold of love, waiting for him to lead her firmly and surely into the haven she desired as much as he.

Torash did not lack experience with women, but this was the first time he had ever loved, and like any neophyte, he was unsure of himself. His moment of opportunity had arrived. He had only to reach out and take it. Instead he peered at Rizpah anxiously, compounding his initial error, asking, "Do you hate me?"

She hesitated just an instant before she replied, but it was an instant pregnant with loss. "How can I hate justice?" She was temporizing, trying to give him another chance.

"I did what I had to do," he said in a low voice.

She looked up at him hopefully. "Yes . . ."

He took her hand. "Before you came into my life," he said, "I lived in emptiness. My spirit was like seed in a dried gourd, rattling about in captive barrenness. You opened my heart, Rizpah. You taught me the meaning of compassion, a word and an emotion I had always feared. I want to thank you for making me live."

Everything he said was true. It was a tender, marvelously pure expression of the way he felt.

Only it had been spoken too soon.

Once love has begun to grow between a man and a woman, it can be nourished infinitely or it can even withstand a certain amount of the blight of neglect. But while love is still a seedling, and one does not know if it will flourish or wither, it makes peculiar demands on those who tend it. Often it can be destroyed by ignorance, by fear, by excessive care prematurely lavished. Rizpah's love required the impact of strength before it could become susceptible to tenderness. Torash had offered her this kind of strength, but he had withdrawn and vitiated it before it had a chance to achieve its purpose. He had made what is perhaps the most common mistake in love.

She listened to what he had to say with cast-down eyes. When she finally looked up, I saw the beginnings of pity in her expression, and I knew then that he would fail.

He must have also sensed something, though no visible change had taken place in whatever was between them. He fumbled nervously with the pendant at his throat. "After this expedition is over," he said, "when the rebellion is crushed and we return to Askelon, the Council of Serens will meet again. We have long discussed the advisability of setting a king over Philistia, someone to unite the five great districts of our country and give us the power of speaking with a single voice. I am the youngest of the Serens and the only one not completely distrusted by each of the others. I have every reason to believe they will choose me as the first monarch."

Rizpah said warmly, "It would be nothing my lord does not deserve."

"Would you be pleased?"

"I should be pleased and proud."

He flushed like a young boy. "I would want you to be my queen," he said softly. "Our son would rule after us and his son after him."

"My lord flatters me greatly."

"If I chose to flatter," he said, exerting some of his considerable charm, "I could do so in much more flowery language than that I have used now. I would compare your eyes to precious stones, your lips to rose petals, your breasts . . . but then, you have been entertained by poets before. I speak to you in the language of my heart."

A touch of mischief entered her eyes. "Would my lord wish to make me his queen even with the stripes I display on my back?"

"Perhaps because of them," he replied soberly.

She said, "I am sure my lord will make a wise and powerful king." And somehow it was as if she had closed a door in his face.

I decided it was time to intervene. "I trust my lord will forgive my intrusion, but my lady Rizpah is tired, with her wounds and the rigors of the journey. Perhaps it would be better if she refrained for a time from speaking."

"Of course," he said, a little glumly.

My words did not spring entirely from subterfuge. The wagon was rocking and bumping, and the strain was truly beginning to show in Rizpah's face. We were traveling through curious country: rocks and

gorges, alternating suddenly with brief stretches of cultivated fields
and rolling pasture land. It was as though when the gods created this
part of Israel they had either not been able to make up their minds
about its character or had used it as a repository for bits and pieces
left over from the creation of other lands.

The Seren's chariot came alongside and his armor-bearer shouted,
"My lord, one of the scouting parties has returned. There is something
very strange . . ."

Torash's glumness dropped from him. He was at once all energy
and decisiveness, rising and bidding us a courteous farewell, leaping
from wagon to ground to chariot in one flowing motion, giving curt
orders to his armor-bearer. I thought: if he could only be like that with
her. . . .

In a few moments a halt was called. The mass of men, horses and
chariots came to a stop. In the comparative stillness which ensued we
could hear the twittering of birds and the shrill drone of cicadas. The
foot soldiers shifted uneasily, speculating to each other in quiet voices
over the reason for the halt. Horses nickered and pawed at the dusty
earth.

The rest was brief. Soon we were again under way. An hour later
we were approaching Michmas.

Two gigantic crags towered on either side of a deep, rock-strewn
pass. On the north side of the gorge, which seemed to be our destination, the crag sloped off to become a plateau, which ran for some
distance until it ended in a round-topped rise. A wild and desolate
feeling pervaded rocks, sky, earth.

Wondering why we continued on without hesitation, I climbed up
beside Shishak and shielded my eyes to look ahead. Between the edge
of the pass and the hill was an excellent site for an army encampment,
commanding a view of the surrounding countryside.

An army had indeed camped there, and recently. Threads of smoke
still rose from several of more than fifty campfires. Carrion birds
picked at bits of food among the ashes. I began to notice a few rags,
a broken waterskin, assorted debris one always sees around an encampment.

But that was all. Along the plateau and over the lip of the gorge
into its depths, on the other side where a smaller plateau retreated
from the edge of the chasm . . . in all that evil stretch of wasteland
there was not another living sign of Saul's army.

book two

SAUL

chapter one

TORASH ORDERED his camp set up on the north side of the Pass of Michmas, on the site evacuated by the Hebrews. Patrols were sent out, but no trace could be found of Saul and his men. There was something uncanny about the way the rebels had vanished so quickly and completely.

During the next seven days Rizpah and I spent many of the daylight hours walking on the plateau, always taking care to remain within the ring of outpost sentries. Her back was healing well, and she was restless. Our strolls sometimes took us to the crest of the rounded hill, where we had a good view of the archers practicing, wagering bits of silver on their prowess. But she was particularly fascinated by the gorge, spending much time sitting near the edge of the great fissure, gazing dreamily into its depths. I was content to keep her company. There was something hypnotic about the wild throbbing silence emanating upward from the floor of the pass. Early in the morning and late in the afternoon the rocks cast grotesque shadows on the cliff walls, populating the abyss with a swollen galley ship, a fish-headed pig, a wine goblet split down the center and pouring out its contents in an absurd sidewise stream.

One day toward noon, when there were no shadows, Rizpah turned to me, startled. "I saw someone moving down there." I stood up to see better, squinting into the glare. I could make out nothing but the sun-baked rocks, shimmering in the heat. One of the outpost sentries, chafing under the burden of idleness, joined us to inquire what we were looking for. He shrugged when I told him. "Probably a bird. Or some animal. We saw a hyena yesterday, not forty cubits away." He grimaced and rubbed his chin reflectively. "I wish Saul were as bold."

During these seven days Rizpah went to the Seren's tent whenever he summoned her, but I guessed from his expression on occasions when I saw them together that things were not going well between them. I wanted to speak to him and tell him what I felt was wrong, but I refrained. A man committing an error in love does not welcome being told about it. Nor could I trust him to use good judgment in rectifying it. I recalled too well what Torash had been before Rizpah came to him. If I hinted to him about strength, he could very well misunderstand and apply cruelty.

Moreover, he had enough problems to occupy his mind. A series of odd and worrisome events was taking place in the camp, keeping the men in a state of barely subdued turmoil.

On the evening of our arrival the sun turned blood-red and appeared to hang in the sky long after it should have set. When darkness came the stars were so brilliant, and seemed so close to the earth, that the camp was bathed in a kind of eerie half-light. Even their arrangement in the heavens seemed different, though when I studied them more carefully I found this to be illusory.

In the second hour of the night a raucous blast of sound shattered the air, seeming to come from the very center of the camp. I had not heard this sound for many years, but I was able to identify it at once. The Hebrews, when going into battle, are given the signal to charge by a trumpeter blowing on a ram's horn. There could be no doubt that this was what we heard. The harsh, complaining notes rose clearly in the stillness.

We could see, almost too well, by the unusual amount of starlight, but torches were ignited and officers shouted commands for battle formation. It took some time for the milling, fearful men to shape themselves into companies, but eventually out of the chaos grew some sort of orderly alertness. Then, as the entire camp waited, nerves taut, weapons at the ready, a second trumpet call sounded, this time from far to the south, lingering, and in some peculiar way more terrifying than the first, closer, blast.

Torash acted with crisp efficiency. He divided the force into two parts, leaving one group on the commanding height of the campsite, sending the second section out under Kraseg to form a long but tightly knit defense ring. He tripled the number of men comprising a normal patrol and sent a score or more of these parties out from various points on Kraseg's line, so their coverage would roughly resemble spokes running from the hub of a giant wheel.

At dawn the men were still scouring the countryside. By midmorning they had all returned, having found no living soul in the entire area. Torash recalled the outer line of soldiers, and the camp settled back uncomfortably into its ordinary routine.

Then came the matter of the horses. On the third day several of the horsemen reported that their animals had suddenly died and that their bodies were covered with strange, erupting boils, the like of which no one had ever seen. By evening over two hundred of the beasts had expired in the same fashion. Torash ordered the carcasses hauled away to a distance of at least five hundred cubits from the camp. The task was completed toward sundown, and the twilight sky became black with vultures. The noise of their greedy, predatory cries was sickening, but they picked the bones of the dead horses clean and saved the soldiers the necessity of burying them.

By the fourth day the men had begun to quarrel among themselves. They had not minded the idleness at the main camp, but there was something about the desolation of this spot which seemed to creep into the innards and pick at the nerves. Nor was the incident of the trumpet blasts forgotten. There was much discussion of it around the fires, and sentries standing guard in the hours from dusk till daylight became edgy, declaring they heard the movement of many men around them in the darkness.

On the eighth day after our arrival the Hebrews were sighted.

Torash had come to visit Rizpah in the hour before noon. They were sitting in the sunlight before her tent, chatting more easily than at any time since their reunion. I stood nearby, making conversation with Torash's armor-bearer.

We saw Kraseg running toward us, heard him bellowing like a bull long before he reached us. He could scarcely contain his excitement. The Israelite army, he said, was on the other side of the pass, not a thousand cubits away, drawn up beside a great clump of pomegranate trees. He begged the Seren's permission to take half the Philistine force and engage the enemy at once.

Torash asked, considering, "How many men would you estimate are with them?"

"Not more than six hundred, my lord."

"Then we shall remain where we are and await further developments."

"But, my lord, we have already waited too long. In another hour . . ."

"Have you lost your power of hearing?" Torash's voice was hard and cold. "The report we had of the Israelite army was that it consisted of three thousand men. If there are no more than six hundred across the pass, where are the others? Waiting, no doubt, until we split our forces. Has it not occurred to you that the reason the small group of Hebrews stands so plainly revealed is that they intend us to do exactly as you suggest?"

The blood rose in Kraseg's face. He said thickly, "Yes, my lord," and turned away. Torash placed a hand on his shoulder. "Come. I shall need your help in planning our next step." Somewhat mollified, Kraseg walked away with the Seren, followed by the armor-bearer.

When they had gone Rizpah said, "I should like to see for myself. Can we go to the crag?" She spoke in a matter-of-fact tone, but I could sense a gathering tension beneath her calm expression. However, I could see no harm in our going, since the crag overlooking the pass was well within the borders of the camp.

The sentries were staring out across the gorge. We selected a position a little distance from them, out of their way, and caught our first glimpse of Saul's army. Army is not really the word to describe them. Even seeing them from afar, I could tell they were badly armed and equipped. They wore no armor, and I could make out neither shields nor spears. In truth, they might well have been some exceptionally large band of Bedouin nomads. I wondered, studying them, how they had the effrontery to show themselves to the well-equipped, battle-wise Philistines. Unless Torash's surmise were correct and they were acting as decoys.

Suddenly one of the sentries laughed loudly and pointed down into the gorge. The others crowded around him, also laughing and gesticulating. For a moment I could see nothing. Then I was able to discern two figures picking their way laboriously over the boulders. The men were young and unhelmeted. Both wore the sheepskin tunics common to Hebrew shepherds, and one, who had bright blond unruly hair, carried a small sword. The other was not even this well armed. His weapon was a mattock of the kind that farmers use to cultivate their fields. Yet on they came, clambering over rocks, trudging through the open spaces between, evidently intending to ascend the Philistine side of the gorge. It was unbelievable. I found myself holding my breath, hoping they would not be struck down for their

stupid display of bravado. Then they stopped and seemed to be waiting. I wanted to shout: go back, fools, go back before you die.

One of the sentries cupped his hands to his mouth and called out,
"Look . . . the Hebrews come forth out of the holes where they have
hidden themselves!"

Still the two youths below waited. They were close enough so I
could see them breathing heavily from their exertions. The fair-haired
one wiped the perspiration from his forehead, but his upward glance
never swerved from the knot of sentries on the lip of the gorge.

"What are they doing?"

I had almost forgotten Rizpah was beside me. She was staring, her
mouth slightly open, down into the pass. One of her hands clasped
the other, and she was nervously rubbing a knuckle with her thumb.
I shook my head and looked back at the two Israelites.

The sentry shouted again, tauntingly, "Come up to us, and we'll
show you a thing."

It was like a signal. The fair-haired youth said something to his
companion, and together they started to climb up.

My heart sank. Surely they would be killed, and to what purpose?
The sentries first fell silent, admiring in spite of themselves the alacrity
with which their unfair challenge was accepted. But soon they were
laughing again, tossing insults down the side of the cliff, sneering at
the efforts of the two Hebrews.

When they were only a few cubits below the spot where the sentries
stood, so close that they could have been killed by spears cast even
with indifferent skill, the fair-haired youth took something from the
girdle round his waist and, after making a few rapid, mysterious motions with his hands, began whirling whatever it was around in the
air. There was a blurred vision of some kind of pouchlike affair made
of leather, with two leather thongs. I should have known what it was,
having seen similar objects before, but at that precise instant my
powers of reasoning and recognition were paralyzed by what was happening.

The sentries were apparently taking no notice of what the Hebrew
youth was doing. The ragged tide of their jeers rolled unabated down
the steep incline all the while the leather pouch was whirling on its
thongs above the earnest fair head. Until suddenly one of them broke
off his laughter with a strangled cry and crumpled to the ground.

There was no time for those with him even to register surprise,
for now a second pouch was spinning in its orbit above the head of
the fair one's companion, and before the laughter had died away com-

pletely a second sentry fell, toppling over the edge of the cliff and tumbling past the two Hebrews.

I understood then what the weapon was. Many shepherds in Israel carry them as protection against marauding beasts. I had never until now seen one put to use, but I had heard that with these slings and smooth stones to fit into the pouches the shepherds were able to achieve a lethal accuracy at incredible distances.

The taunting insults had ceased with the fall of the two sentries, leaving those who remained alive in the grip of a kind of open-mouthed vacuity. I believe they understood only dimly what it was that had struck down two of their number, but they were well aware that the flying death had come from the Israelites.

If one of them had had presence of mind even then to cast his spear or rush down the slope to murder the two youths with a sword, the events which followed might never have occurred. Instead all of them, about fifteen in number, milled and circled about the edge of the cliff like blind oxen. And the two Hebrews continued to climb toward them, silently and inexorably.

The panic did not strike until the youths were actually among the men. Then the fair-haired one drove his sword deep into the side of his nearest adversary, who collapsed with an audible sighing grunt like the sudden release of air from an inflated water bag. The fair one's companion began with great dexterity to use his mattock, the points of which, I could see now, had been filed to needle sharpness. Three more men fell before the others had time to find their wits . . . or rather, before they gathered them up so they could lose them more disastrously.

They took to their heels with wild cries, shouting that the Hebrews were coming up through the pass, hundreds of them, armed with terrible new weapons. The two youths, having snatched a pair of long Philistine swords from the hands of two men they had already killed, pursued the fleeing sentries with grim coolness, overtaking and slaughtering one after another.

Rizpah and I had remained motionless all this time, dumfounded by the boldness and suddenness of the attack, not knowing what to do next. When the sentries fled, I took her arm and pulled her toward the crag, where we shrank into a shallow recess in the rock wall.

It was fortunate that we retired even this far from sight. For now we were watching the beginning of the most amazing and frightening debacle I have ever witnessed.

Attracted by the cries of the terrified sentries, about a hundred soldiers from the main body of the camp began running toward them.

But instead of aiding their fellows and converging on the two Hebrews, the new arrivals mistook the approaching sentries for the vanguard of the invaders and cut them down with swift savagery, somehow managing to spare only the two genuine enemies.

The same tragically ludicrous error was repeated almost immediately on a larger scale. Two companies of swordsmen, hastily assembled by their officers, bore down on the mass of struggling men and
began to slaughter them indiscriminately. Soon this section of the
camp, which but an hour before had been shrouded in the silence of
boredom, had become a battlefield of screaming, blood-crazed killers,
each using whatever weapon was in his hand to attack the man nearest
him.

To this day I find it difficult to give cogent reasons for the appalling
melee taking place before our eyes. Perhaps it was the release of ferocity which had been generated and pent up over weeks of inactivity.
Perhaps it had something to do with the troubling and mysterious incidents which had occurred during the time the army had been encamped at Michmas.

Whatever the explanation, the undeniably brave but still minor ex-
ploit of the two Israelites had spread out its initial impact so that now
half the Philistine encampment was embroiled in a demented struggle, each against his fellow.

I realized that before long Rizpah and I would probably not be
safe in our relatively exposed position. I held on to her hand tightly,
and together, keeping as far from the fray as possible, we began working our way back toward the Seren's tent.

The noise was indescribable. I am no stranger to the sounds of
battle. I have often heard the din raised by countless swords and
spears striking against helmets and shields. I know the cries of rage
and fear which rise, unbidden, into the throats of warriors. But this
was like nothing I had ever heard. The shrieking and screaming were
as if all the beasts of prey in the world had been starved for weeks
and then locked together in a giant cage. And, in truth, the soldiers
had become like infuriated animals. A swordsman was not content to
run another through or cut him down. He hacked and beat at the
body of the man he had killed, strewing his entrails on the ground,
dismembering his torso with demonic energy, until he in turn was
felled by another. And the eyes of all the warriors, even seen from a
distance, were filled with the light of unbridled bestiality.

We saw the Seren ahead of us, and I began to breathe easier. He
was acting with his customary calm, marshaling the unengaged remnants of his army to intervene and put an end to the fray within his

camp. But as we drew closer, I saw he was having difficulties. For though the men who were not yet involved in the incestuous massacre appeared shocked and revolted by what was taking place, still the atmosphere of bedlam and blood lust cast an evil contagion. Even as they formed ranks, some of the soldiers ignored the commands of their officers and plunged forward, to kill and be killed.

Still, Torash might have been able to avert complete disaster if a new element had not been introduced into the situation at this moment. The Hebrews who had been waiting across the pass, hearing the sounds of slaughter, had advanced, unnoticed, toward the Philistine camp. Now, pouring in upon the already demoralized warriors of Dagon, they attacked to the repeated, terrifying trumpeting of the ram's horn. They burst into the ranks Torash had so laboriously assembled, slashing and thrusting with mattock and oxgoad, shrilling their battle cry: *For God and Israel!*

Brutally, incredibly, the proud, well-trained Philistine force was being demolished. Even those still capable of perceiving who the true enemy was had little chance to use their skills. Chariots had no value in such close quarters except for flight. The archers lacked the space needed to draw their bows, and those who were able to loose a shaft usually saw it fly harmlessly over the top of the battle and arc into the pass.

Rizpah and I were trapped now in the crushing mass of dead and living bodies, riderless chariots and rearing horses. Each of us tripped frequently over discarded swords and broken spears and only with great difficulty kept our footing on ground grown sodden and slimy with blood. Several times we narrowly missed being struck down by both Israelites and Philistines.

I saw Shishak, fighting by the side of Torash, fall, an oxgoad piercing his back and protruding from his chest. As he sank to the earth, his expression changed suddenly from the savage malevolence of a warrior to the peaceful, almost holy, look of a very young child.

I was still holding tightly to Rizpah's hand. Her mouth was opened wide and I realized she was screaming, though I could not hear her voice. Then I became conscious, with a terrible sense of shock, that I was also screaming.

A Hebrew in a rough hairy mantle caught Torash in the side with the point of his mattock. Blood gushed at once from the wound, but Torash managed to kill the man with his sword before he went down on his knees. His armor-bearer slashed a path to the Seren, picked him up and slung him over his shoulder.

Rizpah had also seen Torash fall. She pulled her hand free of mine, fighting and clawing now through the massed men, heedless of danger, to reach Torash. I was not trying to get anywhere except to some point of safety where I would run less risk of being beheaded. But in one of those strange eddies which often sweep through mobs, it was I who was carried along toward the Seren, while Rizpah, separated from me now, was borne farther away. I tried to get back to her, but it was useless.

She watched helplessly as I was flung by the human current almost to the side of the armor-bearer, who was carrying his royal burden like a sack of grain. There was little choice of movement. A rout was developing, and I fled with the others.

Rizpah continued to struggle, trying to break through the barrier of human flesh and overtake us. Then the butt of a spear grazed her head, stunning her. She found herself close to the Seren's tent and was able to stumble inside. The cool semidarkness revived her a little. She was vaguely aware that it would be necessary to conceal herself, so she darted into the first available hiding-place, a space between a chest and a tapestried hanging.

How long she remained there she did not know. Her head was aching from the blow she had received, and she felt lassitudinous, all at once indifferent. She heard the noise of battle abating, dimly understanding that the Philistines were in flight and the Hebrews pursuing them.

Then she saw the tent flap opening and flattened herself against the floor in an agony of terror. But when there was no further sound she ventured to raise her head.

A huge man with heavy, sloping shoulders stood in the center of the tent. He was dressed in a mantle of goat's hair, but unlike the other Hebrews she had seen that day, he possessed fragments of armor: a crudely fashioned, ill-fitting breastplate and a helmet, which he was holding in powerful, stubby fingers. He had a rich black beard which only partially hid a full, almost voluptuous, mouth. Even though he was standing motionless, Rizpah sensed the radiation of strength from his presence. Only his eyes, mildly baffled and a little distant as he glanced about him, marred the impression of great power carefully held in check.

Her caution began to dull. She shifted her position slightly to be able to see better. The man sank to his knees and spoke in a hoarse whisper. "Lord God of Israel, I thank thee this day for having delivered the enemy into the hands of thy people. Though they were many and we were but a few faltering souls, yet thou hast discomfited them. I thank thee for the gift of victory, and I swear to thee that the oath which I set upon the people shall be law for this day. Hear, O Israel, the Lord our God, the Lord is one."

The last bit of his prayer, recalling to Rizpah words she had heard her father speak many times, brought quick tears to her eyes. A sob escaped her lips, and her heart beat heavily, for she feared that now she would be discovered.

But the man kneeling so near had heard nothing. He remained where he was for a few moments, eyes closed, lips moving soundlessly. Then he got to his feet and began hesitatingly to explore the interior of the tent.

And it seemed to Rizpah that through the gaze of those soft, baffled eyes, so incongruous in the rugged face, she was seeing everything as he saw it. She too felt wonderment at the richness of the tapestries, the satin curtains, the damask cloth on the table, still laid for the noonday meal. When he picked up a silver goblet, caressed it with callused hands, she was also touching the cool metal, allowing the graceful carved relief of the naked goddess to make a delicate impression on her palm. He walked to the couch, gathered up an armful of silken cushions and held them to his cheek.

But now the memory of Torash flooded back, the way he had moved about the tent, graceful, courteous, so unlike this clumsy interloper who crushed lovely cloth in his hand, breathing heavily with vulgar enjoyment.

Where was Torash now? Was he alive, or had the crimson stain spreading so swiftly over the white tunic become his banner of death? Would she ever again watch the cold features blur and soften as his eyes met hers?

But even as she thought of him the outline of his image faded, obliterated by the presence of the hulking man shuffling around the tent. He paused now to sniff at the vestige of incense odor which always hung about the curtains and tapestries. What was there to attract her in the way his nostrils, large and laced with stiff black hairs, flared even wider with audible inhalation? Why did her heart begin to flutter and the slender filaments of desire begin to tighten deep inside her? Could she be so quickly faithless to a man . . . ?

"Saul!" A grating voice called loudly from outside the tent. This then was the farmer proclaimed king, the rebel whose hands had carved the oxen into pieces and sent the reeking summons through the land. Why then were those hands suddenly hanging slack at his sides? Why were the stooped shoulders hunching forward even farther, as if he were expecting a blow? Did it have something to do with the rasping voice outside the tent, which was now calling again, "Saul! Why do you not answer?"

Saul cast away the cushions he was holding with a guilty, small-child gesture. Triple furrows grew on his face, troubled lines between his eyes and on either side of his mouth. "I am here, Samuel." Though he raised his voice to call, it somehow sounded more subdued than when he was praying.

The tent flap lifted abruptly and a tall, angular man wearing a dust-streaked brown cloak strode through the entrance. His long gray beard was mottled with yellow, and it wagged foolishly as he turned his head quickly from side to side, glancing around him with distaste. But there was nothing foolish about the pale, compelling eyes fixing themselves now on Saul.

"What are you doing here?"

"I came to pray and give thanks to Jahveh."

"In a house where idols are worshiped? In a dwelling where abomination is rampant?"

Samuel picked up the goblet bearing the figure of Astarte. He spat on it and dashed it to the floor of the tent. It bounced up almost jauntily from the carpet. Saul watched the other man's show of violence without visible reaction, but Rizpah saw his sandal begin a slow, furtive flirtation with the pile of the rug. Whether Samuel noticed it or not she could not tell. But the prophet suddenly brought down his foot with reckless force onto the goblet. An edge of metal, curling up with the impact, scraped his instep. A thin trickle of blood appeared, but Samuel paid it no heed.

"Is it for this I anointed you king? So that you could continually disobey my orders . . ."

Saul asked mildly but firmly, "Your orders or the Lord's?"

For a moment Rizpah thought Samuel would strike the king. The flesh of his sunken cheeks swelled and became suffused with color. A tic beneath his right eye pulsed convulsively. Saul stood waiting, looking a little sheepish as he faced the older man, the triple furrows on his face intensifying his baffled expression.

The prophet gained control of himself. Gradually his color returned to normal, and the fluttering rhythm of the tic steadied itself to an almost regular beat. He said in his rasping voice, "I have no orders of my own. The commands I pass on come from the Lord."

Saul bowed his head assentingly as Samuel continued. "Did I not warn you with the Lord's voice that the Philistines were marching toward Michmas, so that you could gather the people together and retire to Gilgal? Did I not admonish you to remain in Gilgal until the

Lord instructed you to depart?" His voice filled again with anger. "And you, what did you do? When I was absent from the camp of Israel on the Lord's work for only a few days, I returned to find you offering the battle sacrifice without the blessing of God, without the permission you knew only I could grant."

"You had been gone seven days, Samuel. My army was melting away, deserting our camp for the safety of hills and caves. Only six hundred remained of our original three thousand. We feared that the enemy would come down on us at Gilgal. It seemed important to march at once."

"It seemed important . . ." Samuel's scorn was naked. The pulsing of the tic grew more rapid.

"Surely the Lord was not displeased. He gave us victory . . ."

"The Lord gave you victory in spite of your foolish action. He protected his people Israel even though the oaf he set over them as king could not keep his commandment."

Suddenly Saul's ingratiating manner dropped away. The troubled lines still furrowed his face, but his eyes were no longer baffled. They were fiery, exuding power. "Why did you anoint me then? Why did you take me from my land and pour the holy oil over my head?" He grasped the prophet's robe and shook him so vigorously that the older man's head snapped back and forth with each movement. "Did I ask to be king? Why did you not anoint one of your own sons? Is this not what you really wanted?" He stopped shaking Samuel, but his hand, white-knuckled, still held on to the dust-streaked robe. "Will you hate me forever, Samuel, because you cannot be the father of a king? Because your own sons are too corrupt to serve the people, much less the Lord? I may be an oaf, a clumsy tiller of the soil who knows the change of seasons better than the order of sacrifice. But I have never dealt falsely with people who trust me. Nor will I ever!"

Again Rizpah, watching and listening from her post of concealment, felt the tiny thrill of desire flowing into her blood. It frightened her even more than the dead silence lying between the two men.

Finally Samuel spoke, very quietly. "My son, you will tear my robe."

Saul released the prophet, who calmly smoothed out the crumpled fabric of the cloak and asked, "Have you informed the men of the Lord's wish that they taste no food until sundown?"

"I have. I spoke to them while we sat by the pomegranate trees, waiting for word to attack."

"It is good." Samuel made a gesture taking in the tent. "Burn this filth and go after your men, to encourage them in their pursuit of the Philistines."

Saul asked slowly, "Could the spoils of battle not include . . ." He broke off, looking at Samuel, who returned his gaze without replying. Then Saul said, "I will set the torch to it myself."

Rizpah, abruptly aware of her predicament, waited impatiently, hoping to make her escape when the men left the tent. But Samuel remained behind. She hardly dared move while he was there. He seemed to be watching the corner where she was hiding. But then she realized that the pale eyes were not focused. She heard him say in a low, weary voice, "Lord God of hosts . . ." and she tugged frantically at the pegs securing the inner cloth of the tent, managed to pull one out of the ground. There was enough space now for her to squirm through and cope successfully with the maze of thongs and pegs keeping the outer cloth taut.

She crawled along the ground, threading her way among the sprawled corpses of those who had died in the battle, lying very still whenever she heard voices. Once she looked back to see smoke and flames rising from the Seren's tent.

She reached a dry stream bed and collapsed, unable to crawl any farther. As she lay on the hot, rock-studded ground, the clear, reasoning thoughts that sometimes come with exhaustion rose in her mind.

This is what I have wanted for so long, she reflected with irony. To be in Israel, free, among my own people. But if I had the strength, I know I would use it to hasten after the fleeing Philistines. She admitted slowly, feeling herself smothered by the thought: I am afraid of my people.

She wept a little, first for herself, then for Torash, and finally for me.

After that she fell asleep.

chapter two

WHEN SHE awakened it was late afternoon. She lay in a strip of coolness shadowed by one bank of the stream bed. Though she had slept heavily, her mind was at once very clear, as if it had continued to grapple with the problems of her plight while her body rested. She remembered everything that had taken place during the day. She was even able to associate the distant voices and the occasional metallic clinking sounds with the collectors of booty, men from Saul's army gathering up the weapons of those who had fallen in battle.

Despite, or perhaps because of, the lucidity of her thoughts, she had no desire to move from where she was. She was hungry, but who would give her food? She was lonely, but where would she find someone with whom she could speak, or even with whom she could sit in companionable silence? She had returned to the land of Israel as she had left it, vulnerable and bereft, but now she had a reservoir of experience on which to draw, and the possession of it was somehow disheartening. Innocence is often its own best protector.

She reflected that she might very easily have died during the battle that day. The spear butt which grazed her head might just as well have been reversed, the point piercing to her brain and sending her at once to the fathomless gloom of Sheol. How frail and inadequate the vessels which contain our lives and evade the cynical touch of death. And yet how insistent life itself . . .

Tomorrow, she thought, tomorrow I shall do something.

What?

She heard a flapping sound close beside her and turned with mild curiosity to see what it was. The vulture was perched not quite a cubit from her head, on the rim of the stream bed. Its wings were fanning the air gently as it regarded her from somber, unblinking eyes, as if trying to decide whether she was legitimate prey. She found herself hypnotized by the bright scarlet and ocher coloring of the naked head, the twisted beak shaped for the tearing of flesh. The wings kept gently fanning, fanning, wafting to her nostrils an odor so foul that it was, oddly enough, not unpleasant.

The bird folded its wings and took a tentative waddling step toward her. She screamed, and the creature rose awkwardly into the air, the unblinking eyes reproachful, to hover with furious effort for an instant before flying away to seek less troublesome fare.

As when the scorpion had crawled across her hand long before in the Seren's garden at Askelon, she felt an impulse to laugh. This time she surrendered to it, sitting in the dusty stream bed and chuckling to herself.

This was how the man found her, and in this desolate spot the sight of a young woman, beautiful despite her dirt-smudged face and bedraggled robe, laughing in the presence of carnage, must have disturbed him deeply.

He was a small man, no longer young, scrawny and predominantly gray. He had a gray fringe of beard and a thin gray fringe of hair haloing a bald head. Even his skin had a grayish cast, which probably accentuated the red-brown stain on the bandage circling his arm and drew Rizpah's eyes to it rather than to the man himself.

Her first words must have confused him still more. She stopped laughing and said, redundantly but warmly, "You've been hurt."

He nodded dumbly. Rizpah's sympathy, expressed in that low, husky voice, could always melt the stoniest reserve. The man standing before her was neither stony nor reserved. He was a gentle person, far too old to have participated in battle, still frightened by what he had seen that day. And he possessed a warmth of his own, which responded readily and naturally to Rizpah's.

He allowed her to remove the filthy dressing from his arm and replace it with a strip of cloth, only slightly cleaner, torn from her robe. He could feel the genuine concern in her touch and watched closely, his lower lip protruding a little in his absorption, as she ministered to him.

He had not yet spoken a word, and she had said nothing beyond her first remark. Yet in the failing light over Michmas, surrounded by the hush which is the inevitable aftermath of violent death, these two were establishing an intensely alive human bond. Whether it lasted a few moments, a day, or for the rest of time was unimportant. The simple beauty of its having happened would be forever.

When she had finished bandaging his arm, she sat down on the ground and began to cry.

At first he made no effort to comfort her, merely looking on and allowing her, even in his presence, privacy for her tears. Only when her sobbing became ragged and he sensed the imminence of hysteria did he sit beside her and take her hand in his. He had the self-effacing strength of the truly gentle, and soon she stopped weeping.

They began to talk then, and because of the bond which had been forged between them without words, they were able to tell each other all that was important in a very short time.

His name was Zaccur, and he came from a village far to the north in the territory of Dan. He was a widower and had been one of the first to respond to Saul's call for fighting men. Saul and his general, Abner, had been reluctant to accept him, because of his age and slight physique, but he had insisted. He participated in the rescue of Jabesh-Gilead and then had been assigned by Abner to be in charge of weapons. Only until today there had been no conventional arms, and his duties had consisted of overseeing the conversion of farm tools to implements of war.

After Rizpah had told him about herself, he sat thinking, then said abruptly, "Wait here."

While Zaccur was gone, dusk began to settle over the plateau. Rizpah could barely discern the outlines of the two sharp crags on either side of the pass by the time he returned. He handed her a sheepskin tunic and a cloak with a hood. "Dress yourself in these," he said, and added with casual impersonality, "Tear some cloth from the robe you have on now and bind your breasts tightly."

She retired a little distance from him and changed into the clothes he had brought. When she came back, he pulled the hood up over her head and subjected her to a careful appraisal. "It will do," he decided. "A trifle delicate, but not much more so than some of the youths we have with us out of Judah. And it would be a pity to make you cut off your hair."

His plan was somewhat risky but not complex. News of the victory had probably already spread quickly. Those who had deserted Saul's army to hide in hills and caves would undoubtedly flock back to the ranks now, and they would be joined by many others anxious to partake of the new glory. None of the veterans would object to this openly, whatever their private opinions. There were many battles yet to be fought, and the need for manpower was desperate. Rizpah would remain in the camp until Zaccur could make arrangements for her to travel to his village in Dan, where he had relatives who would care for her. If she refrained from speaking in the presence of the soldiers and exercised a certain amount of caution in other matters, her disguise would probably serve for a few days.

She rode with Zaccur to the site of Saul's new camp in a wagon heaped with spears, swords and armor. She became aware with mingled sorrow and wry amusement that it was the same wagon, stripped now of its cushions and canopy, which had brought her from Askelon.

The camp was being set up not far from the clump of pomegranate trees where the Israelite army had paused that morning. Zaccur told her that the location had been selected because it was only two hours' journey from Saul's home in Gibeah . . . close enough so he could travel there when he wished, but far enough away so his family would not be troubled by the presence of the army. Rizpah was dismayed to find that Zaccur's mention of Ahinoam, Saul's wife, stirred in her a nagging feeling of jealousy which she could not dispel. She questioned him more closely and learned that there were four children, three of whom—Jonathan, Merab and Michal—were about Rizpah's age and a fourth, Ishbaal, was in his twelfth year.

"He must have married very young," she said, conscious of the banality of her words, but anxious to keep Zaccur speaking of Saul.

The gray little man needed scant encouragement. Gossip was one of his few indulgences. Like many mild, unprepossessing men, he was an acute observer of people but seldom enjoyed an audience for his comments. He was too truly gentle to be malicious, but his remarks were spiced with shrewdness and, as Rizpah later learned, contained sharply accurate insights. "Yes," he said, picking up her statement, "Saul was young when he married. His father Kish owned some fertile fields, but he was not wealthy and could only give his son one or two servants. Ahinoam helped Saul with sowing and harvesting until their son Jonathan was old enough to take her place in the fields."

"Is she very beautiful?"

"Beautiful . . . Ahinoam?" He pondered this for a moment. "I suppose you would describe her as serene rather than beautiful. She has a quality of peace about her, but I have a feeling she is not entirely happy with the new life that has been thrust upon her. She still wears the garb of a peasant woman, even though I understand Saul has presented her with garments captured from Ammon and cloth taken from the Philistine garrisons we have raided."

Rizpah wanted to hear more about Ahinoam, but Zaccur had begun speaking of the children. She learned that Jonathan was fast gaining a reputation for valor, that the men worshiped him for his bravery and his open nature; that Merab was a homebody like Ahinoam but was too fond of eating and was already plumper than a girl of her years should be; that Michal was the one member of the family who was taking naturally to her new royal status. She, so Zaccur said, was beautiful, but she had a sharp tongue and a somewhat imperious manner which would have discouraged suitors had it not been for her elevation, overnight as it were, to the rank of princess.

He was discussing Abner, who was Saul's uncle as well as his general, as they were drawing near the fires of the new camp. "There," he said, "is a man. Brave, modest, capable. A born soldier, though he never knew the feel of a sword in his hand until a year ago. Abner may not possess Saul's daring, but when the king is indisposed . . ."

"Indisposed?" She had not meant to interrupt, but she was startled by the possibility of having to revise her impression of Saul's strength and vitality.

"There are times . . ." began Zaccur, then stopped, for their wagon had arrived in the camp.

Over a score of fires meat was roasting, some of the livestock supplies captured from the Michmas encampment. The main force had not yet returned from its pursuit of the Philistines, but as Zaccur had predicted, there were many newcomers.

Two tents of black goat's hair were being set up, one for Saul and

the other for Abner. Everywhere there was singing and laughter. The
atmosphere was that of a feast day. Even the wounded, some of whom
were obviously in great pain, hobbled about, making jokes about their
injuries, displaying their bloody bandages like decorations of honor.

A group of men were rolling a great stone into the space between
Saul's and Abner's tents. Zaccur saw Rizpah preparing to ask what it
was for and placed a finger to his lips, cautioning her to silence. She
glanced at the men standing nearby, having forgotten that her voice
would give her away, and signaled her apology to Zaccur. "It's an
altar," he whispered. "After a battle, no matter what the outcome, an
offering is made to God, a complement to the sacrifice before." Rizpah
thought warmly about being once again so close to the living soul of
Jahveh, but, used as she was to the elaborate temple of Dagon and
Astarte, she considered the unadorned stone a little plain, not really
quite worthy of the God who had that day granted Israel such tre-
mendous success.

Zaccur took Rizpah to one of the fires. "It is dark now, so we are
permitted to eat." Men crowded around as a whole sheep was removed
on its spit from the bed of flaming coals, not waiting for it to cool
before hacking off pieces of flesh with their knives. Zaccur procured a
section of the haunch for himself and Rizpah, cursing the impatience
of the men that caused him to burn his fingers in order not to go hungry. "I suppose they must be forgiven, though," he said. "For so long
we have had little to eat. The Hebrew farmers and shepherds have
been so closely controlled by the Philistine tribute officials that they
could give us next to nothing. We lived on what we could steal from
the Philistine garrisons. There were weeks at a stretch when we ate
grass and the bark of trees and what few berries we could find in the
hills."

Rizpah ate hungrily, but she wondered why the meat tasted somewhat flat, until she realized with a flush of shame that this was because it lacked the herbs and spices to which she had become accustomed in the Seren's household.

When they had eaten, Zaccur began to supervise the sorting of
weapons taken from the field. There were at least a thousand spears
and swords, several hundred bows together with quivers of arrows, and
countless assorted pieces of armor. Best of all, fourteen chariots had
been captured, complete with battle knives to be attached to the
wheels. The little man was jubilant. "Now when we fight we shall
not be like a gazelle facing a lion. Saul will be pleased."

But he was not to know for some time if the king was pleased or
not.

While the arms were still being sorted, the distant sound of the ram's horn announced the return of the rest of the army. The encampment rose as one man, singing and shouting, to greet them.

Saul marched at their head, followed closely by a stocky, serious-looking man (Abner, whispered Zaccur, pointing to him). The soldiers of the victorious army were exhausted. They straggled along behind their two leaders, garments stained with blood, faces drawn, eyes staring blankly into the darkness beyond the fires of the camp. Abner turned and called to the captains of hundreds to dismiss their companies, and even before the order was relayed, many of the men dropped to the ground and lay like stones.

Rizpah kept her gaze fastened on Saul. He also showed the strain of the day's effort, but his stride was unfaltering and there was a proud lift to his head. He stood in the center of the camp after the men had been dismissed, talking to Abner, his hand fondling the haft of the spear he carried, looking about him with a quick appraising glance at the fires, the roasting meat, the tents and the altar.

His eyes probed the rim of darkness surrounding the camp, and suddenly he stiffened. Samuel was approaching the king, picking his way carefully among the prostrate forms of the soldiers. Saul waited restlessly, shifting about, until the prophet reached his side. Abner retired a few paces, allowing the two men to confer privately. After a moment Saul nodded, and to Rizpah he appeared relieved as Samuel strode to the altar, where brush was being piled for a fire.

Wagons were beginning to roll into the camp now, filled with more weapons and armor. Zaccur could hardly contain his joy, but he decided to wait until morning to unload the fresh additions to his newly created arsenal, since it would soon be time for the sacrifice. The driver of one of the wagons recounted what had happened after the rout at Michmas. The Hebrews had followed the retreating Philistine army, overtaking and slaughtering many of them, until at a distance they saw a great multitude of men drawn up in battle formation. They had been frightened then, for they saw they had blundered onto a force even greater than the one they had encountered at Michmas. They had slowed their headlong pursuit and formed into ranks at the commands of their officers. Surely, they thought, Saul will give us the order to retreat. Our victory at the pass was great, and it would be folly to risk another encounter against superior numbers. But Saul, at their head with Abner beside him, continued to advance toward the waiting Philistine troops.

The fleeing remnants of the defeated Michmas units reached their main force, which opened ranks to receive them. For a few moments the great mass of men blocking the Hebrew advance seemed to stand absolutely motionless. Then there was a furious stir of activity. At first the Israelites thought the enemy was attacking, and many hearts were faint with fear, for each felt: surely the setting of the sun will find me in Sheol. But to their amazement, Saul's army saw the Philistines moving *away* from them. Not only moving, but running, throwing down their arms and leaping over those who fell in their path. As many of the enemy were trampled to death in that terrified retreat as were killed in the whole battle of Michmas. The Israelite army followed hard on the heels of those who escaped. If Saul's men had not been weak from hunger, adjured by the king's order against touching food before sundown, they might have pursued the Philistines even to the borders of their own land. As it was, some of the men of Israel, commandeering abandoned chariots, drove furiously after the enemy, only leaving off the chase at Aijalon, far to the west. Truly the hand of the Lord had lifted up Israel that day. . . .

Everyone was now waiting expectantly for the sacrifice, for until it had been performed there could be no real rest. Some of those who returned with Saul had revived somewhat, enough to crowd around the spits and clamor for bits of roast meat, but even they glanced more and more often at the altar.

Rizpah noticed that a fair-haired young man had joined Saul, embracing the king affectionately. He turned his face in Rizpah's direction, and she recognized him as the one who earlier in the day had climbed the side of the cliff to begin the attack on the Philistines. She touched the arm of Zaccur, who was laughing at something one of the drivers had said, motioned toward the young man and framed silently with her lips the question: Jonathan? Zaccur nodded and said something she could not hear, because she was already turning again to watch the king and his son. Observing the warmth between the two men, she felt somehow lost and excluded.

A Levite priest was bringing the animal for sacrifice to the altar. It was a proud young male goat, prancing and tossing its horns until it drew near the great stone, then suddenly sensing the imminence of its death and bleating loudly, struggling to free itself from the leather lead.

Saul walked toward the altar, followed by Samuel, who snapped his fingers at a second Levite and bade him add more brush to the sacrificial fire.

One priest held the goat firmly by the horns, while the other, drawing a long thin knife from his girdle, expertly slit the animal's throat. The goat gave one long agitated shudder and collapsed beside the altar. A murmur ran through the assemblage, the soft, sibilant release of a thousand breaths. Then there was silence while the first priest dipped his finger in the blood of the goat and smeared it on the stone altar. Reverently the two Levites lifted the animal's body onto the closely packed wood, which they then ignited with a pair of torches. The flames leaped high. Rizpah smelled the acrid odor of burning hair and heard the sputter of burning fat.

Saul knelt before the altar, head bowed, sloping shoulders hunched forward, remaining there for some time. When he rose and turned slowly to face his assembled army, Rizpah saw with a sense of shock that there was fear in the king's eyes. He glanced at Samuel, as if seeking instructions, but the prophet looked away.

Saul let his eyes travel over the faces of those who stood before him. He began to speak, his powerful voice carrying out into the night air. "I have prayed to the Lord, who this day blessed us with deliverance from our enemy. I have called out to him, asking, Shall I go down after the Philistines? Wilt thou deliver them wholly into the hand of Israel?" He waited, and when he spoke again there was something hollow, sepulchral, in his tone. "The Lord answered me not."

He looked around, his expression challenging, as though he expected men to answer him where God did not. A soldier near Rizpah coughed nervously. Otherwise there was no sound. Saul clenched his fists and thundered, "One of our number has sinned. A man among us has transgressed. If this were not so, the Lord would answer his servant Saul." Another pause, then more quietly, almost casually, "Whoever that man is, he shall die." The furrows appeared on his face. He was silent, thinking. After a few moments he cried out suddenly, pleadingly, "Who is the man who has tasted food before sundown this day? Let him come forward." He waited, the anger gathering on his brow, in the hands, clenching and unclenching. "Who has eaten food while there was light in the sky? Who? Answer!"

Someone moved toward the altar. Rizpah felt Zaccur stiffen at her side. With a kind of fascinated horror she saw Jonathan reach his father, stand before him with a trusting, guileless expression. An anguished cry escaped Saul's lips.

Jonathan shook his head, not understanding. "What is it, Father?"

Saul was trembling like a man with a violent fever. "You ate food during the day?"

The youth ran his hand through his unruly hair. In the simple gesture Rizpah felt his lack of complexity, the candor of a soul so open to the world that it contained no dark places. Surely he has not sinned, she thought. Surely he will tell his father that he misunderstood, that he has come forward by mistake. Jonathan smiled bewilderedly and said, "I tasted a little honey, yes. While we were pursuing the enemy, my way led through a thicket. There was a honeycomb, perfect and untouched, just within reach of the staff I had picked up earlier. I stretched out the staff . . ."

"Stop!"

Saul's shout awoke a wailing moan in the throats of all those close enough to have heard Jonathan speak. The youth looked about him, uncomprehending, his clear eyes suddenly filling with tears which glistened in the firelight.

"My son, did you not hear the admonition I put upon the people of Israel this day? Did you not hear my words, Cursed be the man that eateth any food until evening?"

"I did not hear."

"I spoke not of my own will. The words came from the Lord."

Jonathan looked steadily at Saul and said with unpretentious dignity, "Then I must die."

Saul's shoulders slumped. He tried several times to speak before he was able to say, "Yes, my son. For the sake of Israel you must die."

The light from the campfires flickered on the faces of those assembled around father and son. Smoke still rose from the burnt offering before the altar. These were the only signs of life in the camp. But among the soldiers who stood without stirring one could feel the tension growing, like a bow being stretched with intolerable slowness toward the limits of its resistance. And if there were an arrow fitted in the string, who knew when it would be released or where its flight would carry it?

A voice shouted from the ranks, "Shall Jonathan die? Shall the prince who brought salvation to Israel be murdered?" The massed bodies separated to let the one who had spoken out of their midst. It was Jonathan's companion in the initial attack on the Philistines. He spoke half to Saul, half to his fellow soldiers. "God forbid. As the Lord lives, not one hair of his head shall fall to the ground. For if it had not been for what Jonathan did this day, all of us would lie tonight on the earth, our lives destroyed by the spears of the enemy."

Then he told in stirring words the story Rizpah already knew, the account of the ascent from the pass. When he had finished, he cried with great feeling, "Who kills Jonathan must first kill us!"

It was the signal the men had been waiting for. A roar shook the camp. The ground seemed to tremble. There were no words, only the many-tongued, single-voiced howl of sustained rage.

Saul looked helplessly toward Samuel. The prophet's pale eyes

glinted, but he said nothing. He turned abruptly and strode away into
the darkness.

The king raised his hands high above his head, commanding silence.
One by one the men of his army quietened, until there was silence.
Saul said, dropping each word heavily into the charged stillness, "Jona-
than will live."

There was no rejoicing. A sigh as restrained as a whisper circled the
multitude. Then the crowd was a crowd no longer, but a group of
weary soldiers, each going about whatever task he had been performing before the offering was burned at the altar. Only now there was
very little talk.

Saul clasped Jonathan to his breast. The two men stood holding on
to each other, weeping, while the soldiers of Israel moved about them,
eyes carefully averted from father and son.

chapter three

IN THE night, sleeping on the hard ground, she dreamed, as she had
not for many months, of her father's house in Simeon. She was walking across the trampled sandy stretch which led past the juncture of
the house and garden walls. In the corner, growing out of an indentation in the soil, were three anemones, the blossoms purple, white and
pink. Memory began to argue with her dream. No, said memory, there
were no flowers near the house except those in the garden; if there
had been, particularly such lovely little things, I would certainly have
noticed and recorded them. They were there, said the dream with
calm surety. And memory was finally forced to admit then that they
were, adding in sulky defense, but only one spring. Every spring, replied the dream; is it my fault you were blind?

Once having triumphed, the dream explored other details forgotten
by memory: a large nodule on one of the grape vines, the potter's
thumbprint near the base of a favorite water pitcher, a stain that
looked like the head of a sheep on the whitewashed side of the house.
And memory became acquiescent. Yes, yes, it said, all of this is true.
I'm sure it just temporarily slipped my mind.

Then the dream, pressing its newly acquired advantage, became
capricious, treading heavily on memory, to create a father Aiah who

sat rubbing his stomach and saying: my daughter Rizpah, my daughter
Rizpah, what does she do with the Philistine lord, what does she do
in the dead of night; what does she do when the sheep come home,
what indeed does she dooo . . . and a mother Zia whose deft fingers
rapidly plucked one hair after another out of Uncle Amaziah's beard
. . . and when his face was hairless as a boy's, Amaziah became
Shiphri, who said in Aiah's voice: come to me now, beloved girl, come
to me now from Askelon. And all—Aiah, Zia, Amaziah, Shiphri—
joined hands and danced, and sometimes Rizpah was with them, sometimes not, as they floated through the vineyards, touching vines which
then lost their fruit; among the flocks, where each animal they passed
became either Bakesh or Dintor; and finally to the terrible spot beside
the garden wall, where they all lay down and assumed the grotesque
postures of their deaths. And out of Aiah's grimacing mouth came
the words: what did you do in Askelon, why did you ride away, what
mean you now in Benjamin . . .

She woke, shivering and perspiring at the same time. A chill little
wind moaned faintly through the camp. Hanging from the top of a
spear stuck in the ground, blown about by the wind, was a water bag
which slapped against the spear handle, saying clearly: what mean you
now in Benjamin?

She breathed deeply, and the message of the water bag lost its meaning, became a random rhythm of leather against wood. Even swathed
as she was in the cloak Zaccur had procured for her, she was very
cold. Zaccur lay on his back, snoring softly. Still drowsy, not entirely
conscious of what she was doing, she snuggled closer to the little man,
fancying she felt the warmth from his body flowing into her own.
Then she slept.

Or thought she slept. When the hand touched her shoulder, she
rolled away from Zaccur to look into the eyes of the man bending over
her. Only it was not a pair of eyes, but one. The other was an empty
socket, which looked into and through her, seeing everything, seeing
nothing. She was prepared to accept it as a continuation of her dream,
and when he beckoned her to go with him she rose docilely, for she
had learned even that night that one does not, with any success, contradict a dream.

He walked ahead of her, past sleeping men, around the gently
glowing embers of many fires, into the deep darkness where only starlight ruled. And still she followed him without question, thinking that
she felt warmer now, wondering what shape the new dream would
take when it changed, as dreams always do, wondering then how she
was able to wonder.

When they were well clear of the camp, the man turned to her. His face is still the same, she thought. But I don't know anyone who has only one eye.

He pursed his lips before speaking, then said, "Do you not know that sort of thing is forbidden in Saul's army?"

Muddled now, for the dream was far out of hand even for a nightmare, she could only repeat in a whisper, "Forbidden . . ."

He said flatly, wearily, "You young shepherd lads . . . where is it you're from . . . out of Judah, is it? Or perhaps Reuben, where you learned your habits from the Moabites." He came closer to her. "Listen. What you do with other lads when you're herding sheep in your native hills is none of my concern. But I warn you . . . now that you have enlisted in the army of Saul, leave your Moabite habits aside. This is a camp of Jahveh, and the sin of one brings punishment for all. I have no wish to die in battle because you and some of your pretty shepherd friends defy the laws of God."

She looked at him, speechless. The single eye narrowed, but the socket remained round and wide, giving her the feeling she was being watched by two people at once.

"Also," he went on, "you're wrong about the old man. I've watched you with him all evening, not leaving his side, touching him sweetly. And now, when you think everyone is asleep . . . I tell you, he's lonely, and a little peculiar, but not . . ." He shrugged.

She was thoroughly awake now, indignant at his ponderous accusation. She should have been fearful of what might happen to her, but she was so angry over this affront to her female vanity that she did not care. Much later the irony of the situation whenever she remembered it would appeal to her and she would be amused: at the man's error, at her own reaction. Now, forsaking caution, she stared haughtily at him, then turned and started walking back in the direction of the camp. She had only taken a couple of steps before he seized her roughly, intending to spin her about to face him again. His hand, reaching over her shoulder, pressed against her breast, and he drew back with a startled oath. Then he reached out and tore the hood back from her head.

They looked at each other for several long moments, Rizpah not moving because flight was useless, the soldier because his warrior's world was suddenly shattered and he had to piece together the fragments to restore his notion of order. Then, "That old head of a ram," he said. "That ancient head of a goat. That sly head of a pariah dog . . ."

It became apparent even to him that his portraiture of Zaccur was not only repetitious but also strikingly inept for his purpose. He gave up and continued to stare at her, his good eye now as round as the socket. Then he shook his head. "He'll have to be punished, of course. He knows as well as I that lying with a woman makes a man unclean for battle. Who knows when he shall have to fight again? Does he think he can defile himself and all his fellow warriors?" He mumbled on, almost to himself, "The law of Jahveh expressly states that for three days before battle . . . and it makes no difference if the woman is a Philistine or . . . He'll have to be punished, of course."

She had remained quiet through all his tiresome diatribe, holding back her anger. But finally she could listen no longer. "He will not be punished," she said, using the imperious manner she had learned from Torash. "All he did was try to help me when I had nowhere to turn. Furthermore, I am not a Philistine woman . . ." She stopped, wishing she had not added the last bit of information, sensing that somehow it was wrong to tell him this.

He pursed his lips, trying to sort out what he had seen and heard. He lived by his belief that people and their actions belong in clearly defined categories. Since he could not classify Rizpah, he was anxious to reiterate his own role—good soldier, loyal servant of Jahveh—and leave the problem of the unknown to someone else. "The general must deal with this," he said tentatively, then, having decided definitely that he was pursuing the correct course, more decisively, "The general himself."

He made her pull the hood back over her head and hustled her through the camp with a furtive, conspiratorial air, choosing a course which avoided as much as possible the groups of sleeping men. Even so, they encountered a sentry, who glanced sharply at Rizpah, then turned away as he recognized her escort. It was still dark, but there was a feel of approaching dawn in the air.

Outside Abner's tent he hesitated again, launched into one of his mumbled, rambling discourses. "If I wake the general now, and he weary from fighting beside us like any good soldier, perhaps he will be angry, not at this hussy or that head of a serpent Zaccur, but at me. A captain over a hundred he promised to make me, and I would rather die in the next battle than take a chance on losing . . . on the other hand, am I to stay with this woman until daylight, and if someone sees me and learns . . . and if I turn her over to my own captain, he will receive the credit for my zeal. . . ."

He sighed, and Rizpah sighed with him. She was cold and weary of waiting to know what would happen to her. They stood alone before the darkened tent. At that time it was not yet the custom for the Israelite king or his general to post personal sentries to guard them while they slept. She shivered with the cold and glanced away, past the stone altar, to the other tent. She felt an unreasoning desire to look on Saul's face as he slept, speculating on what would happen if the king opened his eyes and saw her standing over him.

The soldier's speech had run down. He took a deep breath, lifted the tent flap and called into the darkness, "My lord Abner, it is I, Bela. A thing of importance, my lord Abner."

He was at the entrance almost immediately, his eyes alert and questioning. Rizpah's first impression was that he had not been sleeping at all, until he yawned. Bela removed the hood covering Rizpah's head and made an elaborate gesture, like a vendor displaying his wares. She waited calmly, smoothing her hair. "I found her here in the camp of Jahveh, my lord. She . . ."

Rizpah felt he was about to say something to implicate Zaccur. She turned on him with such a sudden, savage movement that he recoiled and even Abner looked startled. Bela concluded lamely, "I thought it best to bring her to you at once, my lord."

"You have acted wisely." Abner's voice was well modulated, courtly like the gesture which accompanied his words: a graceful raising of the hand calculated both to praise Bela and conciliate Rizpah. It was effective. Even in the half-light Rizpah could see the expression of pleasure on the soldier's face, and she herself felt at once she would be dealt with justly. "Bring a torch for the lamps," Abner said to Bela.

The general and she spoke little while they waited for Bela to return, yet she felt no sense of constraint. "You are cold," he said, and when she nodded, he brought a heavy mantle from the tent. He himself was clad only in the sheepskin tunic which was standard dress in Israel for both warriors and shepherds. She looked askance when he sought to place the mantle about her shoulders. "I am used to the cold," he said. At this moment Bela brought the torch and, when Abner nodded, passed them to light two lamps inside the tent.

After he had gone, Abner held the tent flap open and courteously motioned for Rizpah to go in ahead of him. The tent was bare except for some boughs spread on the ground to serve as a bed and the general's implements of war neatly arranged beside it: sword, spear, helmet and cuirass.

"Bela is a loyal soldier," he said abruptly, breaking the silence. "He lost his eye in a foray against the Philistines half a year ago. You have probably already discovered he is a little tedious, and he is more ambitious than his abilities warrant. Yet I could do worse than make him a captain over a . . ." He broke off, a look of surprise and amusement crossing his face, then stammered slightly as he said, "Now why am I telling you this?"

She smiled, feeling at ease with him, studying him more closely now. He was stocky, as she had noticed the night before when he and Saul entered the camp, but his hands, which he used constantly and expressively as he talked, were slender and graceful. It was difficult to imagine them wielding a sword or spear, more difficult to think of this courtly, hesitant man killing anyone, even an enemy. Yet he was Saul's general and had the respect of the men who served under him in battle.

He responded to her smile, returned it with a shy, gentle movement of his features, appraising her covertly all the while. "I apologize for not being able to offer you anything but the ground to sit on." He waited until she sat down, then did so himself, drawing up his knees and circling them with his arms. He looked almost youthful as he sat facing her, and the gray hairs of his chest, visible above the top of his tunic, seemed strangely incongruous.

"Now why did I tell you what I did about Bela? I am not given to gossip, and for all I know you might be a Philistine spy."

"Do you believe I am?"

"Tell me who you are."

For the second time in only a few hours she found herself telling her story. She heard the phrases rolling out, the recounting of events glib and easy now. When she had spoken of these things to Zaccur on the field at Michmas, the telling had seemed natural and honest. Now she felt she sounded like a false soothsayer she had once heard in the market place at Askelon, speaking the same formula words to each person who consulted her. Yet everything she said was true. She wondered why she should be so reluctant in speaking to Abner, who so far had shown her nothing but kindness.

Then, as she happened to glance up unexpectedly in the middle of a sentence, she saw in his eyes the unmistakable signs of adoration. She tried to frame in her mind a less intense description, but no other word would do. His expression as he looked at her was adoring. Like most beautiful women, she was accustomed to admiration and had almost come to accept it as a matter of course. But she found herself withdrawing from what she now saw in Abner: from its too-rapid materialization, from something else about it she felt rather than knew with any certainty.

Women have a way of evaluating a man's feelings, often long before he himself is aware of them. A woman can sense in a man's smile, in some small alteration of expression, in an almost imperceptible tensing or relaxing, exactly how he is reacting to her.

Rizpah knew in that moment that Abner was a sensual man and that he was deeply stirred by her presence. But she was also aware of his shyness, and while women often feel an attraction, mostly maternal in nature, toward a shy man who is not sensual, they are sometimes repelled by a shy man who is. For sensuality filtered through shyness asserts itself mostly as a sort of refined lust, bordering on lechery.

A healthy woman will usually react positively, frequently against her will, to a man who is unabashedly carnal. And even if nothing overt occurs, the potential is there, and the atmosphere of their simplest conversation is charged with the possibility that something *could* happen.

But a shy man's sensuality is a burden, both to him and the woman he encounters. Only if she feels she can care deeply for him can she bring herself to ignore the shyness. Then in time, if she is any kind of a woman at all, her man's shyness will dissipate itself and he will become, with her, what both of them want him to be. If she is not able to care for him almost at once, she might find contempt for him gathering in her, and she will deal cruelly with him, using her perceptiveness like a whip, inflicting a thousand tiny cuts and abrasions on his sensitivity before he has time to escape. She does not mean to be heartless; she is, in truth, flinging a challenge at him, trying to make him assert himself and earn what she wants to give him: respect.

So it was that while Rizpah was speaking to Abner a subtle change was taking place in their relationship, which was only a few moments old. She sensed that behind the courtly manners and the genuine kindness this was a man who harbored desire without being able to express it, for his shyness dreaded rebuff. And his lack of courage gave her a power over him she did not really want.

Having decided this about him, she was prepared for a certain predictability in his behavior toward her. She was fairly sure when she stopped speaking that he would look at her silently for a time and then say, as he did, stammering a little, "You're a very beautiful woman."

And she found herself replying, as if it had been ordained, "I wish you hadn't said that."

"If I feel it . . ."

She shrugged, knowing it would hurt him, unable not to hurt him, also knowing he would absorb the pain without rebuking her. She wished fervently she had not liked him so much at the instant of their meeting, for then she might not feel so guilty about being cruel. She asked flatly, "What will you do with me?"

He got up and went to the entrance of the tent, threw back the flap. The sky was graying. Past him she could see the forms of sleeping men, like sacks of grain flung carelessly off a threshing floor. "Do you see the silhouette of that hill which looks like a camel's hump? An hour's journey beyond it is my home. Since I have no family, a man and his wife from a nearby village care for the land when I am away. The vineyards and orchards are not those of a rich man, but they are pleasant." He paused and turned to her, letting the tent flap close. "In a week or a month we shall have to fight again. In the meantime we must build our army, train the recruits. Who knows when I shall be able to live on my land again and enjoy the sight of fruit ripening on my own vines and trees? But if you wish, you may live there, and when finally there is peace in Israel, you may stay or go where you like."

She said, meaning it completely, "You are very kind."

"I do not offer this out of kindness."

She was grateful for his honesty. "In that case I will make a bargain. I am no stranger to vineyards and orchards. I would want to work."

"If you wish."

"Thank you, my lord Abner."

"Then as far as you and I are concerned, it is settled. I shall consult Saul this morning."

She asked, her heart leaping at the mention of the king's name, "Consult Saul about what, my lord?"

"To tell him of you and my plans for you. To obtain his permission."

"His permission?"

"He is the king. You were found in the camp of Israel. Whatever transpires within the camp must have his approval."

"But you are Saul's uncle. And his general. Surely . . ."

"He is the king."

She looked at him steadily, wanting him to take her to Saul, but also hoping he would not. "Could we not go to your home now, at once? If you could not take me yourself, could you not send someone with me? The soldier Bela, perhaps . . ."

From his eyes she could tell he was aware of the urgency of her plea, though he could not know what it meant. She saw him consider. Then he moved his hands in his conciliatory gesture. "If it were possible, of course I would, but . . ." His hands fluttered, fell to his sides.

She said coldly, "You are of course right, my lord Abner. You must consult the king. It was wrong of me to suggest that it was even possible for you not to do so."

She sighed and averted her eyes from his, so she would not have to see the pain in them.

chapter four

ABNER BROUGHT her some dried corn and a bit of cheese, then left her with instructions to remain in the tent until he returned. She obeyed for a while, but time passed slowly and she found the canopy of goatskin first confining, then stifling. She arranged the hood of her cloak carefully, to cover her hair, pulled back the flap of the tent and stepped out into bright sunlight.

All around her rose the cacophony of an awakening camp: the chorus of coughing, hawking and spitting; the complaints of the wounded, whose injuries had stiffened during the night; the curses, growls, laughter and occasional snatch of song from the soldiers who stood around waiting for the pots of lentil soup to finish cooking.

Rizpah guessed from the stares cast in her direction that word of her presence had already spread through the camp. She caught sight of Bela watching her from a distance. When she nodded to him he blinked his single eye rapidly and turned away.

Most of the men bold enough to look at her at all did so fleetingly, trying to satisfy their curiosity in a series of hasty glances. Others were not so discreet. They whispered and snickered behind their hands, and some made obscene gestures which they took no trouble to conceal. Rizpah was annoyed but not afraid. While she lived in Torash's household, such behavior would never have been tolerated. She knew she could end the lascivious appraisal at once by sending for Abner, but she had no intention of stirring up enmity against herself in the camp of Israel. Instead she gazed steadily back at the grinning soldiers, her lips curved in an enigmatic smile. Soon their gestures ceased and they began shuffling their feet and mumbling uneasily to each other. She bowed graciously in their direction to show there was no ill-feeling and was rewarded with a sudden burst of amiable laughter. Some of the men waved to her as they moved away toward their morning tasks, whooping and calling to each other like small boys.

She felt warmed by the sun. Her eyes were growing a little heavy with lack of sleep, and she was on the verge of retiring to the tent to stretch out on the bed of boughs when she noticed three riders mounted on donkeys entering a far corner of the camp. The man in the lead, evidently a servant, halted his mount and deferred courteously to the two women riding with him. They advanced slowly, allowing the donkeys to find their own path among the men and campfires.

Rizpah saw Jonathan rush toward the two women, arms outstretched, unruly hair flying in the breeze. He helped them dismount and embraced each one in turn. Rizpah was caught up again by the feeling of being excluded, as she had been the night before when she had watched Jonathan greet Saul. At the same time she was waiting anxiously for a closer glimpse of the women, for there could be no doubt that they were Saul's wife and one of his daughters.

They came toward the spot where she stood, engrossed in their conversation. Jonathan was explaining something to the older woman, who was nodding solemnly, now and then cupping her hand to her ear in the manner of one who has trouble hearing.

Ahinoam, as Zaccur had indicated, was not beautiful. Her forehead was too broad, her cheeks too flat, her lips too thin. Her figure was ungainly, and the old brown robe of rough-spun wool which hung down in a straight line from her shoulders to her ankles heightened the impression of shapelessness.

Then Rizpah saw Ahinoam's eyes. They were large and luminous, almond-shaped, and they regarded the world with such calm and (Zaccur had named it) serenity that there could be no doubt as to the nature of the woman herself. It has been said that the eyes are the gateway to the soul. Ahinoam's eyes *were* her soul, and before them all the defects of her face and figure faded to irrelevance.

They stopped near Rizpah. Jonathan continued to speak excitedly, in his simple, blunt fashion, of the victory, of Saul's courage in battle, of all the events of the day before which had freed Israel from the grip of the oppressor. Ahinoam listened, her hand straying now and then to her ear, her eyes watching Jonathan's face with obvious and unaffected adoration.

"Please, my mother, can we not break our fast now?"

The girl who stood a little apart from Ahinoam and Jonathan was plump, drab in appearance. Rizpah had no difficulty, remembering Zaccur's description of the family, in recognizing Merab. She was like a fat brown mouse. Even her voice was mouselike. She squeaked a little as she called to her mother and brother, who were paying her no attention. "Mother, Jonathan . . . I'm famished."

"We shall wait and break bread with your father." Ahinoam's tone was firm, but her glance, turned on her daughter now, was warm and loving.

Merab pouted, a little rodent pout, and strangely the expression lent her otherwise dull features a certain piquancy. "I shall want cheese," she announced. "Some of those dark brown little cheeses made of sheep's milk. And dates, and honey, and if the pomegranates are ripe . . ."

"You shall have all of those, darling," said Ahinoam, interrupting her. "I know how hungry you are, and we shall eat soon."

To Rizpah, Ahinoam's attitude toward her daughter was so cloying that it could not possibly be genuine. She waited for some sort of negative reaction from Merab. Instead the girl moved close to her mother, kissed her moistly on the cheek. Jonathan took Ahinoam's hand, patted it and said, "I shall go now and tell my father you are here."

Just then Saul emerged from his tent and, seeing his family, hurried toward them. Rizpah waited, holding her breath, to see how he would greet his wife. He approached her unsmilingly, with his plodding, hunching gait, kissed her formally on each cheek. Rizpah's heart leaped up exultantly, sank as quickly when she saw Saul's hand lingering affectionately on Ahinoam's shoulder.

One must remember that Rizpah, despite her sharp intuition and the surface sophistication she had gained in Askelon, was still basically inexperienced. She was unable to distinguish between the passion she had occasionally felt for Torash and this new sensation, which by far transcended any response Torash had ever been able to evoke in her. Not understanding it, she feared it. The envy she felt was not the general type, common to most of us, when in our loneliness we may resent the sight of lovers embracing, any lovers. Rizpah's envy was specific and unreasoning, with Saul as its only concern. Yet she had never exchanged a single word with him, and he had never seen her.

She found all this painfully confusing, and she tried to turn away from watching Saul and Ahinoam. She could not.

She wished Abner would come and tell her he had changed his plans, that they would leave at once without consulting the king. Where was Abner?

"Our uncle Abner will be occupied with his duties for a time," Saul was saying in unconscious reply to her question. "He is aware that your visit will be short, and he has asked me, if he does not return before you leave, to convey his greetings." He looked around. "Did Michal not come with you?"

"Our daughter Michal has begged to be excused. The way of women is upon her, and she asks me to assure my lord Saul of her continued love and regard and to inform him that she will visit him as soon as she is able."

Their conversation was stilted, like words between diplomatic envoys, but their manner with each other was easy, as though talk were only a form with them, neither mirroring nor affecting their feeling. As they strolled toward the king's tent, Rizpah was seized with apprehension. Please, Jahveh, she breathed, let them not be alone together now, not even for a few moments. She was relieved when she saw Jonathan and Merab follow their parents into the tent.

Zaccur was coming toward her, his face creased with concern. She realized as he drew near that he was angry and at once began to apologize. "Forgive me," she said. "I know I should have come to find you or at least sent word of what had happened . . ."

"So you should have," he replied shortly. "When I awakened this morning and you were gone, I was afraid for your life. I feared someone had dragged you away while I slept and dealt brutally with you. I berated myself for not having taken better care of you. It was only when I learned that you had contrived to be taken to Abner that . . ."

"Zaccur," she said, "I did not ask to be taken to Abner."

He stared at her, sucking in his lip, letting it out again. "This is the truth?"

"The truth."

After a moment his features relaxed in a smile. "You should hear what they have been saying about you in the camp."

"It demands no gifted imagination."

"They have called you both a Philistine queen and a harlot of the pagan god."

She said candidly, "Both are to some extent true."

"For a time there was even talk of your being a witch and a soothsayer. That was earlier. Now the men who saw you this morning vie with each other in praising your charm."

"I said nothing to them."

"Since when must a beautiful woman employ speech? Loveliness is a master of pantomime. Once you had won them over, they could scarcely wait to ask me what I knew."

"You told them?"

"I spoke only the truth. I said you were stolen by the Philistines from the house of your father, whose wealth was fabled throughout Israel."

"Surely they know this is not . . ."

"Surely they know nothing. In my native territory of Dan we have a saying—if a story is worth telling, it is worth embroidering. Besides, would you have them believe they have succumbed to the charms of a poor shepherd's daughter?"

"My father was not a poor shepherd," she said indignantly. "He had vineyards and orchards . . ."

Zaccur was laughing delightedly. "You see? I did not speak falsely. And if, as I say, I have embroidered slightly, well then, you are on the way to becoming a myth. There is nothing men like to worship so much as a living myth." His laughter faded and he asked, "What is going to happen to you?"

She told him and he said reflectively, "It is good. You will live a better life here in Benjamin."

"Perhaps I shall still need your help in journeying to Dan. Perhaps I shall not be able to stay here in the south. Abner says he must consult Saul. If the king does not give his approval . . ."

Zaccur glanced at her quickly, shrewdly. "You sound almost as if you wish he will not."

"Did I say that?"

"There was no need."

"I want to go away from this camp. I *must*," she said fervently, too fervently, for the little man stared at her in silence, his lower lip protruding, then retracting as he took it between his teeth.

"The king will insist on seeing you," he said at last.

She replied with studied indifference, "Possibly . . ."

He turned from her swiftly, but not before she had caught the sound of his dry laughter. She was about to speak to him angrily when he called out to a young soldier lounging nearby, "Bring what I asked you to keep aside."

In a few moments the soldier was back, carrying a chest on his shoulder. She recognized it immediately as one of those which had come with her from Askelon. Zaccur said, "It was in my mind when I came to you just now, first to vent my anger for the concern you caused me, then to surprise you with this. Now I find it is you who have surprised me."

She avoided asking what he meant, for she did not wish to discuss what she was sure he sensed.

"Open it," he said.

She did and saw inside several of her finest robes and two pairs of graceful Askelon sandals.

"I sent men back to Michmas at daybreak," Zaccur was saying, "to gather up any weapons we might have overlooked. There was this. It belongs to you?"

She nodded.

He reached into the girdle about his waist, brought out four copper bracelets and a pair of turquoise earrings. "Then these must also be yours." He handed them to her, then stepped close and spoke in a low voice. "I wish for you whatever it is you wish for yourself."

Tears filled her eyes. Before she could trust her voice enough to thank him he was gone. She watched him stride briskly over to where the weapons were still being sorted. He did not look back.

Female voices were coming from the direction of Saul's tent. She glanced over quickly and saw Ahinoam and Merab leaving. The servant was bringing up the little donkeys on which they had come. Rizpah thought: surely they have scarcely had time to break bread together. If I were his wife . . . She paused, feeling mingled exhilaration and shame at the idea, then letting it continue. If I were his wife, and I had not seen him for a month or a week, or even a day, I would not leave him so quickly. . . .

Saul kissed Ahinoam, as formally as before, then helped her to climb up on the donkey. He remained watching until the women were out of sight before he turned and entered the tent. Rizpah was surprised to find that she was trembling. If I were his wife . . . She said it aloud this time, but now the supposition was only depressing.

She sat down on the chest, waiting for Abner to return. When he did, he failed to notice the chest. We are given to believe that shy men are infallibly observant, but most of the time they see no more than anyone else. And Abner was only concerned at the moment with the sight of Rizpah, shrouded in her cloak, more enticing for the knowledge that beneath the concealing hood lay the soft mass of her chestnut hair, which a simple gesture could liberate and send tumbling into the brilliant sunlight. Then he remembered that he had told her to stay in the tent. He smothered his irritation and said mildly, courteously, "It would have been safer for you to remain inside."

She said, unable to keep the willful note out of her voice, "I wanted to sit in the fresh air."

He hesitated, then bowed his head slightly. "Of course." After another moment, "I shall go now to see the king."

She felt herself trembling again. "Perhaps it would be wiser not to make trouble. There are other places I can go. It was selfish of me even to think of accepting your hospitality. I would only be a burden, and the king . . ."

Her teeth began to chatter violently, and she could not continue. Abner stared at her in amazement, then came to her and placed his hand on her shoulder.

"There is nothing to fear. My speaking to Saul is a courtesy, nothing more."

He went on talking to her soothingly, reassuringly. She was aware that his hand had slipped down onto her arm, and the pressure of his fingers was not as impersonally benevolent as his voice, but she pretended not to notice. Gradually her trembling subsided.

"I shall go now."

She nodded, her face expressionless. Abner waited, peering at her anxiously. He asked, stammering slightly, "Are you feeling better?"

"Yes!"

The vehemence of her reply surprised and embarrassed them both. She said, at once contrite, "My lord Abner, please forgive me . . ."

"There is nothing to forgive."

"You are much too kind."

"Can one ever be too kind?"

She said, falling into a pattern of speech she had learned from me, "Kindness is like a newborn lamb, naked and unprotected."

He smiled. "The lamb grows older, becomes a ram."

"Then it can no longer bear the name of kindness."

"The ram does not forget the day he was born, nor what he was in the hour of his birth."

He started to leave, and she caught his hand impulsively. He turned, first pleased, then puzzled by what he saw in her eyes.

"My lord Abner," she said, "you must not consider me ungrateful, nor think ill of me . . ."

He repeated, stumbling over the words, "Ungrateful . . . think ill . . ."

She shrugged, the slightly arrogant movement of her shoulders which she knew hurt him, and turned from him impatiently. "I shall be here," she said, "when you return from seeing the king."

Abner left her then, looking back several times as he crossed the space between the two tents. Rizpah waited until the goatskin flap of Saul's tent had closed after him. Then she rose, icy calm, and opened the chest. She selected the most diaphanous of the robes, the more frivolous of the two pairs of sandals, and entered Abner's tent. She would have liked to bathe, using the scented crystals to which she had become accustomed, and to anoint her body with perfumed oil, for she wanted to make herself as lovely as she knew how.

She discarded the warrior's mantle and cloak, dressed herself in the robe and sandals, looked around automatically for a mirror and of course did not find one. She tried to resign herself to patient waiting, but the tension was too great. She paced back and forth across the tent, started wildly at the dull metallic sound given off by Abner's helmet when her lightly shod foot grazed it in passing.

Abner came into the tent, stopping short when he saw her. Cruelly she turned to face him, took a tentative step in his direction. His expression told her she looked the way she wished to look.

"Where . . ."

"The chest outside the tent belongs to me," she said casually. "One of the men found it at Michmas and brought it here. I thought you had noticed it before."

He shook his head. Then, stammering badly, he said, "The king wishes to speak with you."

"Yes." She had never doubted for an instant that this was the way it would be, though even now, if the news had been different, if Abner had returned to say that Saul had given his consent for her to travel to his general's house, she would have been relieved.

"We are to wait until he sends for us. I do not think it will be long."

She managed a thin smile but said nothing. He gave her a piercing look, then for a time remained silent, his head bowed in thought. When he glanced up again, she saw a shrewd, bitter light in his eyes.

"Is it because he is king and I only his general?" There was an edge to his voice. "I know I am no longer young, and often I find it difficult to speak without stammering." He attempted a smile. "Our leader from ancient times, Moses of Egypt, also had an affliction of speech. Yet he was able . . ."

His voice trailed off; his hand made a vague gesture in the air. Then he said, "You have eaten nothing since dawn. Forgive me for having been so thoughtless . . ."

He went away and came back with fresh fruit and more of the dried corn. She tried to eat, but her throat muscles kept constricting and she found it almost impossible to swallow.

"How did you know the king would ask to . . . ?" He waited, and when she did not reply, he said wonderingly, "But you have not yet met him."

"I have seen him."

He laughed unpleasantly. "Yes, you have seen him. You have watched him return victorious from battle. You have seen one image —the proud, restless, invincible warrior. But Saul has many facets. How do you know what he is like when . . ." He stopped, regarding her sadly. "You are only a child. He will destroy you."

A pulse beat unevenly in her throat. "You know I am not a child."

He said, hope surging into his voice, "Perhaps he will receive us and only speak with us for a few moments, then give me permission to travel with you to my home."

"If my lord Abner would go to him now and convince him that seeing me would only waste his time . . ."

"Do not mock me, Rizpah. You have no more wish for me to do what you say . . ."

"I do!" She was suddenly close to tears.

"I thought I understood. Now . . ."

"Will you do it? Will you?"

He hesitated. She watched him, biting her lip with nervousness, waiting. Then he shook his head. "It would not do," he said. Then, softly, "I have never seen anyone so beautiful as you."

She stamped her foot exasperatedly just as a soldier called from outside the tent, "My lord Abner, the king awaits you."

The eyes of the soldier who had summoned Abner widened when he saw Rizpah, in her fine linen robe, emerge from the general's tent. In the time it took Abner and her to walk past the stone altar and approach the king's tent several score of the warriors of Israel pressed as close as they dared to the pair, gaping, muttering to each other. Had she not been so preoccupied, it is certain Rizpah would have appreciated the moment for the comic thing it was. However, though she was aware of the presence of the men, her chief concern lay in negotiating the clearing between the tents without fainting.

Nor was Abner amused by the gathering throng of soldiers. He turned and shouted at them abusively, a thing he had never done before, bidding them disperse at once.

He took Rizpah's arm, looked at her anxiously. "You're so pale. Are you sure . . ."

She turned to him with an expression so contemptuous that he shrank from it. He removed his hand from her arm and walked on in dignified silence at her side.

He held the tent flap open for her, and she entered. In the instant it took Abner to follow she was alone with Saul.

Many months later, when Abner was describing the moment to me, he was still filled with wonder and bitterness. "I followed Rizpah into the tent," he said, "and neither of them seemed to know I was there. It was as though they had been alone with each other for hours.

"The king was sitting on a rough-hewn bench. It was one of his better days. He was clear-eyed and vigorous-looking, and even as I watched, he seemed to grow younger, more vital, until he resembled the youth who had tilled his father's fields, full of a dark, restless power not yet burdened with the knowledge of his destiny. Rizpah stood before him, those lovely green eyes steady on Saul's, the only movement of her body a soft, rapid rise and fall of her breast.

"They looked at each other, the man I loved more than any other in the world and the woman whose beauty had already begun to make me suffer. I think if someone could have extracted the exquisite pain present in the air of that tent and turned it into some visible, stable substance, so that it could be preserved and administered to others, it could have filled the inhabitants of a whole city with a nameless, intolerable ache.

"I believe I must have sighed. Perhaps I sobbed. I only know that some deep, inarticulate sound rose from the bottom of my soul, and the moment was over. The king tore his gaze from Rizpah and turned to me."

Saul did not look at Rizpah again during his discussion with Abner. For her part, she watched the king as if no one else existed for her, and in truth, no one did.

Saul said, in a very ordinary tone, considering the tension permeating the tent, "This is the woman of whom you spoke?"

Abner wanted to smile at the unnecessary question. But he was only able to move his hands in a gesture somehow self-deprecatory. "It is, my lord Saul."

"And you wish to send her to your home."

"To send her or escort her myself."

"How can you be sure she is neither a witch nor soothsayer, or a spy sent by the Philistines to report our plans and the strength of our army?"

"My nephew Saul, she is but a child . . ."

"It is a matter of record that the woman Delilah was also young. Did this prevent her from dealing treacherously with the hero Samson?"

"My lord Saul," said Rizpah in a very low voice, "I am no spy. Nor am I a subject of the Philistine nation. There is no treachery in my heart. I ask only to be allowed to live peacefully in the land of my birth."

The king did not even glance at her. He said to Abner, "Did you not tell me she had lived in the land of the enemy? That she had come with the invaders to Israel?"

"I did, my nephew. But if you will recall, I also told you the circumstances of . . ."

Saul held up his hand and Abner stopped speaking. Again there was silence in the tent. The sound of one of Zaccur's men hammering on a piece of armor far across the camp was clearly audible.

Saul said, "I shall question her myself."

"As you like, my nephew."

"Alone."

"Saul . . ."

The king rose from the bench. "When I command," he said angrily, "I am neither Saul nor nephew to you. I am the king of Israel."

For a moment it seemed that Abner would defy Saul. His eyes blazed; his hands clenched to fists, and he took a threatening step forward.

The king watched him with an air of detachment, as though Abner's rage were but the foible of an otherwise tractable child. He said quietly, "Leave us, uncle."

Abner's hands relaxed, slowly turned palms upward in a gesture of resignation. The anger drained from his eyes, leaving a pitiable expression, half-pleading, half-stricken. Without another word he turned and left the tent.

Now that they were truly alone, both Rizpah and Saul felt constrained and ill at ease, as they had not while Abner was present. After a long moment of silence Saul asked with diffidence, "You are called Rizpah?"

"I am, my lord."

Another pause, then, "I do not deem it advisable for you to journey to the home of my uncle."

Rizpah felt herself beginning to smile, but she said soberly, "I shall do whatever finds favor in the eyes of the king."

"You are smiling. Do I amuse you?"

She searched for words to answer him, but all her natural wit, her practice in courtly discourse, deserted her, and she could only stare at him. And still she could feel the smile fastened to her lips, ineradicable as one of her features. Saul came to her, repeated irritably, "Do I amuse you?"

She found her voice at last to say, "No, my lord," then, afraid he would misunderstand, she tried to go on, but speech had fled again.

And between them once more was the vibrant, compelling excitement of their first moment together in the tent.

She could sense the passion growing in him, keeping pace with her own yearning. To her what was happening was neither strange nor frightening. At this moment she could not remember a single day of her life when she had not wanted the man who stood before her, and though one small rational corner of her mind knew this was absurd, it was the most pleasurable absurdity she had ever indulged in.

She wondered how long he would stand there, not moving, looking into her eyes. She wanted to cry out to him, take me, and feel the strength of his powerful arms holding her close, the crushing pressure of the hunched, sloping shoulders. And yet she wanted this moment to last forever.

But it could not last even a little longer, for the yearning was unbearable, and she was sure that before the next throb of the pulse in her throat she would scream and fall senseless to the ground. And then her heart beat again, and yet once more, and still neither of them moved.

Until, just before she knew she would die, he took her shoulders between his hands and pulled her to him. She reached up to his face, touched his lips, trailed her fingers across his cheek, wanting now in the surety of what would happen to savor the experience slowly, deeply. He brushed her hand aside with savage impatience, so fiercely that she gasped, first with pain, then with the sudden surfacing of imprisoned passion whose fervor she had never suspected. Their lips caught and held, and they sank to the earthen floor of the tent. She seized his hands, held them for an instant to her breasts, then in the time that followed no longer knew what was her body or his, lips, shoulders, limbs or heart.

And suddenly out of the darkness there appeared, clear and dispiriting, the vision of Shiphri, quivering and helpless before the Philistine sword. But as the blade arced toward him, the cruelty of its entrance was into her own body, and it was her own death and soaring rebirth, and Shiphri was gone, never to reappear, and Saul was warm and alive within the circle of her arms and she in his. Life grew and waned, rose and fell, successive waves of aliveness.

In the quiet that followed she looked at his face, grown so quickly dear and beloved, his eyes brimming with gentleness, and breathed his name, less to him than for the sake of hearing it herself. And experienced the joy of watching his lips as they formed her name, feeling her name again through her fingers pressed against his body.

His hands, hard and callused but so tender, moved slowly, sweetly, up her arms to her shoulders, to her breasts, to her shoulders again. She saw his expression change and was fearful until she realized that what she saw was concern. His fingers were touching the ridges, so recently healed, left by the whip on her back. She shook her head in response to the question in his eyes.

"Tell me how it happened."

"One day. Not now."

"The Philistines?"

She hesitated, troubled by the memory of Torash, then barely nodded.

He said grimly, "They will pay." The furrows were beginning to form about his eyes and mouth. Rizpah pulled his head down to her, kissed him, feeling childishly pleased when she was able to smooth out the lines, leaving his face relaxed and almost boyish looking.

Saul closed his eyes, and when he opened them they were filled with something beyond gentleness, something beyond even tenderness, and she knew she was looking back at him in the same way. She began to feel the stirring of happiness within her, the first faint revival of capacities long withered. She laughed aloud. Saul watched her fondly but with perplexity bringing a return of the furrows to his face. She thought with a touch of sadness: my poor Saul, my dear lord, you do not know how to laugh, but I will teach you. In the confidence of burgeoning joy her mind repeated: I will teach you. . . .

chapter five

THE SENSE of unreality, which should have been present all during the day, did not actually find her until evening, when she and Saul were partaking of a meal brought by two of the soldiers of Israel.

Lamps had been lighted, and between Saul and Rizpah on the boards of the makeshift table lay the platter containing the haunch of roast kid, the flat gray loaf of bread baked on a stone at one of the campfires. Sounds filtered into the tent, evening sounds of men in an army camp, perfectly ordinary, reassuring sounds. Saul sat across from her, carving the meat, speaking to her of the first days after he had formed his army when he and his men had hidden in the hills and from their shadow bases harassed the Philistine garrisons. He described the courage of his son Jonathan, who had led a small party of Hebrew warriors against one of the mightiest forts of the enemy, had set it afire in the hours before dawn, slaughtering the Philistines to the last man. Rizpah then told Saul of witnessing the incident at Michmas, where Jonathan's valor had bordered on foolhardiness and yet had struck the spark which was to kindle victory. Saul's eyes filmed with tears, and he said softly, "Jonathan, my son, the fruit of my loins, to think I might have killed you . . ."

There was ease between them now, the comforting sweetness, gentle as twilight, which surrounds those who stand together on the threshold of love, passions momentarily slaked, spirits reaching out toward each other, tentative, exploring.

But it was then, paradoxically, that the aura of unreality settled round her. Rizpah had been sure the king would wish to see her; she had never taken time to doubt that he would want her when he did see her. The only conflict had taken place in her own mind, whether to pursue what she wanted or to flee from it. Then the decision was removed from her hands, and what followed had seemed preordained.

Only now that it had all happened did she wonder how it was that she was here in his tent, how he could regard her affectionately and speak to her with a familiarity which bore the mark of long years of shared experience.

Reality. Was not reality her life with Torash: the house in Askelon, the gardens, the city? But it was only with some difficulty that she could recall this life at all. When she tried, her mind reverted to sharp, clear memories of childhood. The form of the Seren's face was vague, obscured by the same kind of yellowish mist which sometimes rolls in from the sea to shroud the city of Askelon.

Yet it was not even two days since she had sat with the Seren at Michmas. And it had been only a matter of an hour or so later that she had first seen Saul and felt the knowledge of desire that in the beginning frightened her and then consumed her. Was her allegiance so fickle, so easily exchanged?

She stretched her hand across the table to Saul. He touched her fingers, and in the instant of contact her faith was reborn, the checked flow of happiness once more free to take its course.

Someone coughed outside the entrance to the tent and said, "My lord the king . . ." Saul called out permission to enter. The tent flap lifted and Abner stood before them.

She was shocked by his appearance. His eyes were puffy and redrimmed, and for the first time she noticed the stringy flesh of his throat, the flesh of an aging man.

In the flush of her love for Saul she felt a sudden warmth for Abner, regretting her earlier behavior toward him. She wanted to put her arms around him, smooth his gray hair, speak sweetly to him. Thus do lovers, with their cups of kindness running over, wreak more cruel damage than the indifferent and the uncaring.

But Abner was protecting himself. He had come only to see Rizpah, yet now it was his turn not to look at her. He fastened his glance on Saul and said crisply, "My lord, I did not wish to disturb you . . ."

Saul's response was unduly effusive. "My uncle disturb us? Nonsense. How could my uncle even think his presence could be an intrusion?" Saul's use of "us" instead of "me" confirmed what Abner had already assumed to be true. Even so, he was unprepared to have it shown him so blatantly. He had expected his nephew's customary brusqueness, had been depending on it to carry him through his visit to the tent. Devoted as he was to Saul, he could muster no abiding anger against him. He could only suffer.

Saul went blithely on. "Please, my uncle, sit down and join us at our meal."

Abner thanked him stammeringly, protesting that he had already eaten with Jonathan and some of the men. "That is why I have come, my lord," he said, gathering about him again the shreds of painfully concocted subterfuge. "The men are anxious to know where we shall march now, whether we shall arm our host and go up against the Philistines in their own country or turn our attention first to the other enemies of Israel."

"My good uncle," Saul said gently, "only one day has elapsed since the Lord gave the Philistines into our hands. Are the men already so hungry for further battle that they cannot rest? Our ranks have increased tenfold, and most of those who have joined us are raw and untrained. They must be taught the disciplines of fighting men, and all of the warriors of Israel must be schooled in the use of the weapons we have captured from the men of Dagon. Then we can consider our next campaign."

It was sensibly spoken, a speech Abner himself might have made to an overzealous captain of a hundred. Rizpah understood this and turned away as Abner colored and looked abashed. But Saul did not appear to notice anything out of the ordinary. Abner had asked a question and he had answered. Again, pleasantly, he enjoined his general to sit down with them, and when the offer was again refused he said casually, "My uncle, do me a kindness and ask some of the men to set up a tent for the lady Rizpah. She will remain in our camp for the time being."

Rizpah's hand fluttered to her mouth. The color in Abner's face, heightened by his previous embarrassment, drained away. His skin took on the appearance of parchment. And still Saul remained unaware of the drama being played about him, with himself as a principal character. Rizpah wondered how he could be so insensitive. Her mind worked rapidly, inventing excuses. But none would do, and in the end none were necessary. For a woman, once she has committed herself in love, is prepared to accept the shortcomings of her man far more readily than he will accept hers.

Nonetheless she was shaken, and she tried desperately to catch Abner's eye to inform him of her sympathy. It was just as well she could not, for aside from providing her with a measure of self-vindication, it would have done more harm than good.

Abner, stunned, was still able to stammer, "It shall be done, my lord," and if he had been allowed to leave then, he might have been able to preserve a semblance of composure. But Saul, eating unconcernedly, called out to him, "I have heard nothing today from the prophet Samuel. It is unlike him to remain silent for so long." Abner replied, "He is not in the camp of Israel, my lord. He left word that he intended to journey to his home in Ramah to rest and meditate."

Saul nodded, and Abner was able to make his escape. But not before Rizpah had seen in his eyes a reflection of such agony as she had never dreamed could exist. And knowing that she was causing this pain both repelled her and gave her an uncomfortable, unwanted sense of exhilaration.

Lovers protect each other, for in doing so they are really protecting themselves. When Abner had gone, Rizpah felt a sudden, urgent need to touch Saul, and he responded as she hoped he would, so that in the circle of lamplight they drew close together again. Now it needed only some word from Saul which would convince her that he was neither cold nor unfeeling, and the new breach in her love would be swiftly healed.

It came sooner than she expected. Without preamble Saul began to talk of his life as a farmer. He described the green fields of Benjamin, nestling in small pockets between forbidding hills. He spoke of the sounds of morning, the bird calls, sharp and quiveringly alive; the pulsating fullness of the earth at noon; the entwined joy and sadness of fading sunlight over plowed earth.

"And now," he said, all at once melancholy, "it is past. The earth is no longer what it once was to me . . . a lovely woman waiting to be made fruitful. Now the land is a shrieking hussy, crying out for my blood and the blood of those who follow me. There can be no rest until she is assuaged."

She hastily took his head in her hands, brought it to her breast. "You will know peace," she said.

He twisted around until he could see her face. "Will you bring me peace, Rizpah?"

If Torash had asked the same question, his voice would have contained an ironic edge and she would have answered in kind. But there was no room for irony in Saul's make-up. She replied, "We shall find it together," and held him closer to her.

"When I was seeking the asses which strayed from my father's land," Saul said after a moment, "I had a strange premonition that after that journey my life would never again be the same. But I did not know what it meant, and it was only important to find the animals belonging to my father, for they were our wealth and our future."

She was learning that his manner of speech often sounded abrupt and dislocated, but that if she let him speak on without questions he would eventually explain what he meant.

"My servant and I set out early one morning, carrying with us only a few loaves of bread, a cruse of water, and stout staves with which to ward off beasts of prey."

They had searched at random, traveling through the hilly country just south of Benjamin, circling among the crags of Shalisha and the parched wasteland of Shalim. The asses were nowhere to be found.

They had reached a spot not far from the town of Ramah when Saul declared himself ready to give up. The asses, it was plain, were irrevocably lost. He had said to the servant, "Come let us return. We have been gone three days, and my father is old. Soon he will cease caring about the animals and will become concerned about us."

But the servant said, "Are we not close by Ramah? There lives in the town a man of God. He is renowned for predicting the future. Perhaps he can tell us where we should go to seek the lost animals."

Saul was reluctant. "What have we to give a prophet for his services? Our bread is long since gone, and if we bring him a question and say we have no payment he will laugh at us."

The servant had produced some silver, a quarter of a shekel-weight, and Saul had sighed and said, "It will do no harm. Let us go."

They had found the prophet at the altar on the town's high place, for it was a feast day in Ramah and he had climbed the hill just outside the town to bless the sacrifice. Saul had been impressed, and a little fearful, at the sight of the tall man with the long gray beard and the pale, knowing eyes. His voice was rasping, authoritative, and when Saul had approached him hesitantly with his problem, he had said at once, "I have been expecting you. Set your mind at ease. The asses you seek have been found." Saul thanked him and turned to go, but the prophet called him back and said without any graciousness, "You will eat at my table tonight." When Saul protested that he wished to begin the homeward journey as quickly as possible, the prophet had grown angry. A frightening tic had begun to throb under his right eye, and he shouted, "Is the prophet Samuel required by his God to traffic with idiots? You shall stay!"

He had, of course, remained. Samuel had given him no reason for commanding his presence, but at table that night, in a company of about thirty people, he had placed the choicest portions of the roast on Saul's plate and had urged him, still without much show of grace, to eat and drink his fill.

When the meal was over, he had asked Saul to follow him up to the rooftop of the house. Dusk surrounded them. Samuel looked about carefully to be sure they were alone, then said abruptly, "The Lord has chosen you to rule over Israel as king."

Saul had been first astonished, then deeply disturbed. He believed the prophet was mad, but when he backed away Samuel pursued him, the tic pulsing under his eye, rasping, "You will do what is required of you. The Lord has called you to his service. Will you reject the word of the Lord?"

In the end, trembling and anxious to escape the demented attention of the old man, he had done as Samuel ordered and knelt before him. The prophet took a vial of oil from his cloak and poured it over Saul's head, saying, "With this holy oil and the blessing of the Lord God of Israel I anoint thee king over his people." The oil had a slightly rancid odor, and it ran into his eyes and mouth and down the back of his neck under his mantle. It had been all Saul could do to remain still while the prophet continued to intone a meaningless jumble of prayers.

Finally he allowed Saul to rise and said, "Tomorrow, when you leave, you will encounter two men by Rachel's grave at the border of Benjamin, and they will tell you the asses you seek have been found and that your father is concerned for your safety. Then, on the plain of Tabor, you will meet three men, one carrying three kids, another three loaves of bread, and a third a bottle of wine. And they will salute you and give you two of the loaves of bread, which you must accept. Then, as you pass onward toward the Philistine garrison, you will be met by a band of prophets. Afterward you will return to your home."

Saul had slept badly, believing he heard the old man's footsteps through the house the entire night, fearing that in his madness Samuel would enter the chamber where Saul lay and make some violent attempt on his life. Once, in fact, after he had dozed off, he woke suddenly, sure that someone was indeed standing by his bed. He was petrified but ready to gather his strength and leap into the darkness, to kill the prophet if it became necessary. But after a few moments he heard a gentle sighing sound, like the wind through grain. Then all was quiet. He had gotten out of bed and searched the room, but no one was there.

The next day everything happened just as Samuel had predicted. There were the two men, then the three, one of whom gave him bread. Instead of allaying Saul's fears, this confirmation of the old man's words only agitated him. When, close by the Philistine garrison, the band of prophets hastened toward him, singing to the accompaniment of the harps and pipes they carried, Saul had grown light-headed, then nauseated. Without knowing why he did it, he had leaped into the midst of the group and begun to dance wildly, shouting in a tongue he himself could not understand. Then he had fallen unconscious to the ground, and when he regained his senses his servant was bending over him anxiously. They were quite alone. The noonday sun beat down on them. Saul had a violent headache and there was a crust of dried foam about his lips.

"When I rose from the ground," he told Rizpah, "I felt I was no longer the same man. I knew who I was, but I had to keep repeating to myself, 'You are Saul, son of Kish, a farmer,' for a voice kept droning in my ear, 'Hail, King of Israel, hail, Saul, ruler of the people of God.' It ceased only when I reached the house of my father, greeted him, and returned to my own house."

Then, nearly a year later, a messenger had come from Ramah and told Saul that the prophet Samuel required his presence at Mizpeh, a small village on the border between Benjamin and Judah, about an hour's journey from Saul's home. He was unwilling to go, since it was the time of the wheat harvest and he was busy in his fields. The messenger, a gaunt man with thin twisted lips, interrupted Saul's protests and, putting his misshapen mouth close to Saul's ear, had said dourly, "The prophet has commanded me to tell you that if you do not obey his summons the Lord will blast you and your family with a virulent sickness, so that neither you nor any of your flesh and blood will ever again walk upright in the sun from this day on."

Saul had accompanied him, riding on the donkey which the messenger provided.

Mizpeh was perched on a height of land overlooking fields heavy with ripe grain. As they approached the clump of houses that made up the town, Saul saw several hundred men milling about an open space just north of the dwellings. In their midst stood Samuel, holding himself stonily aloof from the crowd. The messenger brought Saul to the edge of the throng and left him abruptly.

The prophet clapped his hands for silence. As the people quieted and waited, Samuel's eyes moved slowly over their faces. Then he began to speak. "You, the representatives of the children of Israel, have journeyed from Dan and Simeon, from Asher and Reuben. Many months ago you came to me where I dwelled in the peace of my home in Ramah. You asked me to give you a king. I told you then that your demand was a rejection of the Lord God of Israel. I warned you that a king would take your children, your fields, your servants and your flocks and put them to his own use.

"Now I have sent for you and you have gathered before me again. And once more I ask you, will you persist in your foolish desire?"

And the voices of the assembled men had risen on the air. "A king! Give us a king!"

Samuel's pale eyes had again surveyed the people. There was a hint of a sneer about his mobile lips, his elegant aquiline nose. He said, "You have spoken. Bring the lots."

The day was hot and sultry. Saul's mouth was dry. He felt a return of the same feeling of lightheadedness and nausea he had experienced when the band of prophets approached him months before. Samuel and the congregation were watching the messenger as he entered their midst with the Urim and Thummim, the sacred stones which served as an oracle for the transmission of God's word. Saul slipped away from the crowd and went to the well on the other side of the village. He drank deeply, intending then to return to the assemblage. Instead his legs grew weak and his vision blurred. He sank to the ground, resting his back against the edge of the well, and for a time he knew nothing.

Someone was shaking him by the shoulder. He opened his eyes to see the messenger bending over him, twisted lips working furiously. "What are you doing here? Hurry. Come at once. You are wanted!"

Saul had mumbled, "Wanted . . ." and got to his feet. There was absolute silence in the village, and Saul had thought the crowd was no longer there. Then he saw them, standing in the same open place, all their eyes turned in his direction. Samuel stood among the people, hands outstretched, holding the sacred stones. A pigeon in the village began to call foolishly, repeatedly. Saul advanced toward the congregation of Israel.

The people in his path stepped hastily aside as he approached, allowing him free access to the spot where Samuel stood. When Saul reached his side, the prophet lowered his hands and looked at Saul for a long moment with an expression that made him tremble. Finally Samuel turned to the people.

"You have learned the wish of the Lord. He has despised your clamor for a king, but you are his people. He will set a king over you. From all the tribes you have seen him select the smallest—Benjamin. And of the families of Benjamin, the house of Matri. And of the house of Matri, the son of Kish."

He turned to Saul. "Behold your king—Saul, the son of Kish."

For a moment there was no sound except the soft persistent cry of the pigeon. Then from hundreds of throats burst a great cheer. The people crowded around Saul, fondling his hands, prostrating themselves to kiss his sandals and the hem of his robe. The press of humanity about him was so thick that it seemed certain someone would be trampled. Saul had shaken off the lethargy which had gripped him and raised his hands above the heads of the people. They fell back, gradually becoming silent again. He had looked about him, suddenly conscious of his height, which was greater than any of the men who surrounded him. When they had grown still, he had said simply, "I will serve you."

They had opened their mouths to cheer him again, but before there were any more than a few ragged cries the prophet Samuel was speaking in his deep, rasping voice.

"Hear the words of the Lord. If you will fear him, and serve him, and not rebel against his commandments, then both you and the king who reigns over you will find favor in the eyes of the God of hosts. But if you do not obey . . ."

He stopped speaking and looked past them, down from the height onto the fields of amber grain far below. The people turned, and as they did a dark cloud appeared on the horizon, at first no bigger than a man's hand, but growing steadily larger as it moved toward them, until it was directly overhead, ballooning, ominously black-fringed, with tongues of flame darting over its surface.

The sound of the first drops of rain combined with the cry of distress rising from the assembly. A shaft of fire crackled past them, and the earth trembled, and all the people, including Saul, had turned pale and fallen to the ground, pressing their faces into the wet earth. They had remained where they fell, heedless of the deluge soaking their garments, terrified by the constant, deafening roar of thunder. Until, as suddenly as it had begun, the storm was over. The representatives of the people of Israel got to their knees, disregarding the mud caked on their garments, and gazed at the prophet still standing in their midst, beard sodden, robe plastered to his spare body, pale eyes wide and staring into space. Samuel had raised his hand and pointed down to one of the broad fields below the village.

Where only a few moments before had stood myriad stalks of grain, bursting with ripeness, there was now a scarred and stubbled stretch of ground.

The prophet's voice mingled with the distant rumble of thunder. "So shall the Lord do to you if you disobey him. Do wickedly, and you shall be consumed, both you and your king!"

Then he turned and strode away, never once looking back at the assembly he had summoned.

Not having received any specific instruction from Samuel, Saul had returned to the only existence he knew: his farm and his home. He had made an effort to erase from his mind everything surrounding his contact with the prophet, and for a time he had nearly succeeded. Then one afternoon, several months after the events at Mizpeh, when he was plowing his fields for the spring planting, he had looked over the backs of his oxen to see the messenger with the twisted mouth standing at the end of a furrow.

"When I saw him," Saul told Rizpah, "I wanted to run and hide. I turned my oxen about and started for the other end of the field. Then the same voice I had heard after being anointed by Samuel at Ramah spoke in my ear. 'Saul, King of Israel, thy people need thee, Saul.' My heart grew heavy as a stone, but I retraced my steps to meet Samuel's messenger, to hear word that Nahash, King of Ammon, had laid siege to the city of Jabesh-Gilead."

Two of the lamps in the tent had burned out. The third and last was beginning to fail. Rizpah rose and crossed the tent to fetch the cruse of oil. She poured some into the dish containing the sputtering wick and waited until the clear yellow light flamed up again. Then she returned to Saul's side. There was no sound from outside the tent now. The laughter and sporadic singing which had reached their ears earlier in the evening had ceased. Rizpah leaned her head against Saul's chest, then slowly, caressingly, moved her hand up across the rough fabric of his mantle and inside to let her fingers touch his naked shoulder. He took her in his arms and pressed his lips to hers.

Their love-making lacked the furious splendor of the first time, but it was deeper, more complete, and there was a tender awareness of each other. As she lay in his arms afterward, Rizpah felt that surely her joy must burst from her heart and soar out of the tent to fill the night with music.

She had no idea how long she had been asleep—a few moments, an hour. The lamp was still burning when she awoke. Saul was lying beside her, leaning on his elbow, watching her. She checked the word of endearment even as it was on her tongue, for there was a strange light in his eyes. She recognized the baffled expression she had noticed the first time she saw him, but there was something else . . . pain?

He shifted his position slightly and asked, "Who are you?"

She made an involuntary solicitous movement. He withdrew, holding himself stiffly away from her.

"Who are you, to come to me with guile, to lay bare the secret places of my heart? Who are you?" His voice was harsh, devoid of gentleness, passion, all she had found in it such a short time ago.

She said, beginning to be frightened, "My lord Saul . . ."

His eyes grew hard. His full lips tightened to a cruel line. She watched him, unable to speak or move.

Then, just as the tension between them became intolerable, his whole body went limp, his elbow spun out from under him and he lay stretched out beside her, scarcely breathing. She touched his cheek. He did not move. She was afraid, but she moved close to him, pressing her body against his, not in passion, but all the same yearningly, as if by covering his nakedness with her own she could take some of his pain to herself. Over and over, not really hearing the words, she was murmuring, "My love, my dearest darling . . ."

Until finally she felt his body stirring, responding to hers. It was as though he had been dead and was returning to life.

"Rizpah . . ."

She stroked his hair, his throat, his shoulders. Her lips brushed his eyes. He was weeping. She felt tears in her own eyes. They clung together.

Only when she was sure he was asleep did she allow herself to relax. Just before her eyes closed, the lamp flamed high, then went out.

chapter six

IN THE morning Saul was not beside her.

She emerged through successively thinning layers of drowsiness to become conscious of the empty space at her side, and to put out her hand, first in languorous exploration, then in a frantic fumbling search.

Just as panic was beginning to descend, she heard his voice outside the tent, speaking to someone in a vigorous, authoritative tone.

She rose and dressed, smiling at the random sight of various objects in the tent, which recalled moments of the night before: the three lamps, their wicks lying dry and spent in the saucers; the empty dishes standing beside the platter still holding the remnants of the roast kid; Saul's outer cloak, lying crumpled in the corner where he had thrown it.

Then another segment of memory took hold of her: the vision of the troubled time before sleep had ultimately claimed them. She fastened her robe with fingers that trembled a little and went to the entrance.

Saul's back was to her. He was speaking to Zaccur, who was scowling and nodding vehemently, his lower lip stuck out at a ridiculous angle in an attitude of fierce concentration. Then the little man saw Rizpah, and his face lighted up with a congratulatory smile of such radiance and good will that she immediately forgave its obvious insinuation.

Saul turned, and seeing Rizpah, at once dismissed Zaccur, who touched his brow in a respectful salute and walked away with a dignity befitting his position. But when he had gone only a few steps, he gave a little skipping jump and threw an impish glance over his shoulder at Rizpah.

She laughed aloud, and Saul, who had swung around just in time to witness the bit of byplay, knit his brow. "You know this man?"

"He rescued me from the battlefield at Michmas."

"I shall see that he is suitably rewarded," Saul said gravely.

She felt a return of the pity she had known the day before, when she had first discovered his lack of humor. But it was only for an instant. She had already recognized the qualities in him which had inspired devotion from so many others: strength, warmth, unflinching honesty. Even at this point she was too much of a realist to expect, or in truth to seek, perfection. She would have her man as he was.

Or so she thought then.

But she had no time to dwell on such thoughts, or even to remember how in a transport of tenderness she had promised to teach Saul laughter.

He had her by the hand and was leading her into the tent. He let the flap fall, shutting out the morning sunlight, and turned to her. They stood looking at each other, and in his eyes she saw no trace of the unpleasantness which had marred the last part of their night together.

Saul took her face in his hands. She was still surprised at how gentle his touch could be. "I have ordered it proclaimed in the camp of Israel," he said, "that you are to be my wife."

She was grateful to him for employing the word "wife" rather than "concubine," though the latter could be her only official title in the community of Israel.

"What are you thinking?" asked Saul.

(A fleeting memory of an evening with Torash on the rooftop of the house in Askelon. The bittersweet banter, and the exchange of ironic comment on the foibles of men and women.)

"I was thinking," she said teasingly, "that my lord did not consult me before he issued his proclamation."

She had forgotten for a moment how literally he would be bound to take her words. He stared at her in puzzlement. "But I thought that would be what you wished."

She put her arms around him. "It is," she said fervently. "It is what I wish. I am happier than I have ever been in my life."

And she was, especially when he looked at her with an expression that was as close to a smile as she had yet seen on his face. "I shall have to learn," he said, "that not everything you say is to be taken seriously."

She kissed him. Perhaps there *was* hope. "I shall never again joke with my lord about important matters."

"I hope you will joke with me about unimportant matters," he said soberly. "I like to hear you laugh. I should regret it forever if you forsook laughter on my account."

He was so earnest, so intensely serious, that she found him particularly appealing. She burst into laughter and kissed him again.

"What have I said?"

"Only something to endear you more to me."

"If this is true, I am happy. They have already begun to refer to me as the lightning out of Benjamin, the slayer of the enemies of Israel. But before you are done with me, I shall laugh like a jackal the better part of each day, and what will happen to my reputation?"

"My lord," she said slowly, "I shall indeed be glad to become your concubine."

He started to protest, but she placed her fingers over his lips. "I know you used the word wife to please me, and I am grateful. But I would be happy to be called anything, or nothing, as long as I can be near you. So, my lord, I am glad to become your concubine."

He nodded unsmilingly, and they held each other close for a moment. Then he said, "There are many things I must do today."

"I shall await my lord's hour of leisure."

"It cannot arrive too soon."

They went out into the sunlight. Four or five officers were standing about waiting with matters for the king's consideration. Saul looked beyond them to one of the fires, where the one-eyed Bela was engaged in conversation with another soldier. The king called to him, and instructed him to escort the lady Rizpah to the tent which had been erected for her.

She walked at Bela's side, waiting a trifle defensively for him to make some sly allusion to the last time they had been together. There was none. Rizpah had been classified. She was now a concubine of the king. This was enough for him. It was ordered and it was understandable. He derived the same pleasure from order that some men took from a goblet of old wine or a night with a woman. To him, order was an organic part of life, to be savored and enjoyed.

He spoke only once on the short walk. "My lady has visitors."

"Visitors? Who?"

But he would say no more.

Her tent was not far from Saul's and Abner's, but it was pitched just beyond a slight downward slope leading away from the camp, so that there was an illusion of isolation.

She thanked Bela, who backed away, bowing several times as he took his leave. Then she went into the tent.

There was a bed in the corner, covered with a mantle of snowy-white sheepskin. There was a bench and a small table on which stood two bowls, one containing dried corn, the other dates. In the center of the tent was the chest containing her clothes.

The chest was open, and a girl was kneeling beside it, her back to Rizpah. A young man stood next to the girl, shifting uncomfortably from one foot to the other as he watched the girl delve into the chest with curious fingers, snatching up a robe, only to drop it after an instant in her eagerness to examine the next object.

They had not heard her enter. Rizpah said evenly, "I am quite capable of unpacking my own belongings."

The man swung around quickly. It was Jonathan. He began to blush. "I told you, Michal . . ."

The girl rose slowly to her feet before she turned to face Rizpah, her manner perfectly composed. She looked strikingly like her mother. It was as though they were two nearly identical pitchers fashioned by the same potter. She had Ahinoam's broad forehead and enormous eyes. But what in Ahinoam was gentle and serene, in Michal was startlingly carnal. Everything about her bespoke sensuality: the movements of her hands, the way she moistened her lips with the very tip of her tongue, the definite carriage of her body which made her small high breasts achieve generous prominence. She reminded Rizpah of the tiny, spirited horses bred with such pride by the nobles of Askelon. The total effect was one of vital and captivating beauty.

She said to Rizpah, "I did not know you would be coming so soon." Her voice was strident, and there was no shame in her eyes. "I had thought you would be longer with my father. From tales I have heard, the harlots of Philistia are able to make a man dally at their sides forever."

"Michal . . ." Jonathan's manner was full of gentle reproach. He turned to Rizpah. "You must not be distressed by my sister's words. She has gained some renown for having a sharp tongue, and she loses no opportunity to give it play."

Michal's eyes narrowed. "So speaks the valiant warrior of Israel. The darling of the host of God. Will you not welcome this intruder, Jonathan? Why have you not already offered her in your name the freedom of the encampment of Israel?"

Jonathan gave Michal a pitying glance. Then he said to Rizpah, "I bid you welcome to the community of Israel."

The girl's laugh was nervous, filled with a neighing bitterness. "We both bid you welcome, dear lady, in our names and the name of our mother. With so many men here deprived of the company of their wives, you should be able to ply your trade with profit."

Rizpah controlled her temper with an effort. She chose to ignore Michal's remark and smiled sweetly at Jonathan. "Thank you. I understand that for a time it might be difficult for us to regard each other as friends. I hope these difficulties will not be of long duration."

Michal laughed her bitter laugh and said, "My brother is known for the simplicity of his soul. But part of the price of simplicity is a refusal to recognize evil. Perhaps you can teach him something of its nature." She knelt again and put her hand into the chest, fingering the cloth of one of the gowns. "See, dear brother, the first lesson. The raiment of evil."

She had made the error Rizpah had been watching for. Swiftly, before Michal could be aware of her intention, she moved forward and slammed the lid of the chest shut. Michal just managed to pull her hand out in time.

The girl's eyes widened with fear. Her composure had vanished. "You could have hurt me," she whimpered.

"Not badly," said Rizpah laconically. "Not nearly as much as you deserve."

"I will not forget this."

"It is not my intention that you shall." She stepped close to Michal.

"I did not ask to be your enemy. I am still willing that we should treat each other kindly. The decision must be yours."

Michal opened and closed her mouth several times like a stranded fish gasping for air. Rizpah laughed.

"Dear child," she said, "do not be so distressed. One day, if you are able to control a certain sourness in your virgin spirit, you will have a man of your own. Then perhaps we can speak to one another of those things precious to women. In the meantime, please remember that children who meddle must always be punished."

Michal flicked out her tongue, moistened her lips. Her fright had passed, but so had her initial advantage over Rizpah. She was wise enough to keep silent until she gained the doorway of the tent. Then she could not resist a parting epithet. "Harlot!" she cried, and flounced out.

Jonathan, who had been standing by in the acute unease most men feel in the presence of a woman's quarrel, now came to Rizpah's side. "I'm sorry," he said.

"She is not to blame."

"She was rude."

"And I was cruel. Both acts were intentional. But it is possible that both may be forgotten."

He brushed back the hair from his forehead. "I must tell you. When my father spoke to me earlier this morning and informed me . . ." He groped for words. Rizpah's first feeling about him was being confirmed: here was a man without guile, possessing an integrity almost painful in its purity. "My father has every right to take a concubine. But I had hoped for my mother's sake . . ." He paused again, surveying her out of clear blue eyes. "It is no fault of yours."

"I love your father." Her statement sounded clumsy, false in her ears.

Jonathan put out his hand to touch her shoulder. "You're weeping," he said bewilderedly. "Is it because of what Michal . . . ?"

She shook her head.

"I wish my sister were happier. She becomes restless, and when she does . . ."

"There is no need to apologize. Michal and I understand each other."

He smiled suddenly, charmingly, and she knew then that the nature of this man was by no means as simple as her first impression had indicated. "I could see that," he said. His smile faded. "Michal is not used to being thwarted. She will not forgive you easily." He waited for her reply, and when it did not come, he sighed. "I wish I could

understand women. I know they say of me that I am simple and un-
complicated. Perhaps they are right. I have heard that only the simple
ones make good warriors, and I am a good warrior. In battle I feel
. . ." He stopped and smiled again. "All this is nothing to you. Can
I help you in any way?"

She hesitated. "If I could have some water for bathing . . ."

"There's a stream nearby. I'll go with you and stand guard. If you
wish, that is," he added shyly.

On their way back from the stream they met Abner. He was more
in control of himself than he had been the night before. His manner
was somewhat distant as he inquired if the arrangement of her tent
was to her satisfaction. She thanked him too cordially, trying to disregard the pain she could still see in his eyes, welling through his calm
exterior like blood through a newly reopened wound. Men and women
never seem to learn what to do about unwanted love. It hangs about
like spoiling meat in a market place at the end of the day, a bane
to the vendor, an object of the buyer's scorn, but impossible for either
to ignore.

After the noon meal, the camp of Israel began to lose its easy lassitude. Since there was no chance of the men returning to their families
at this time, even on short furloughs, they were happy to be active
again. The captains of hundreds organized their companies of veterans and new recruits into training units. One group practiced with
javelins, another with swords, a third with bows and arrows. No one
was very proficient with the new weapons in the beginning. Some objected to using them at all, protesting that all they needed was a good
sharp mattock or an oxgoad. But even in the course of one afternoon,
much of their reluctance and some of their clumsiness wore off.

Rizpah sat watching, chiefly so she could look at Saul. He practiced
along with the men. He was wearing the Israelite battle tunic of sheepskin, which left his arms bare. His shoulder muscles rippled as he
cast a spear again and again, driving it from greater and greater distances through the stook of barley which served as a target. She was
filled with pride at the spontaneous cheers of the men as they witnessed the growing prowess of their king. She wished he would come
and sit with her for a moment, but she knew he could not, nor did
she really expect that he would.

But she did wait eagerly for either his visit or his summons in the
evening. Zaccur brought her some food: slices from a leg of lamb,
pieces of the unleavened bread of the camp, and fresh fruit. He remained to eat with her, and to pass on some exciting gossip. Word
had reached the encampment just before the evening meal that the

remnants of the Philistine army had retreated beyond their own borders. The garrisons of the enemy had been abandoned. Israel was free.

All over the land there was awakening joy as the people realized they no longer lived under the hand of their oppressor. Food and wine, long requisitioned by the occupying forces, belonged again to those who grew it. It was a time of celebration, but also a moment for settling accounts. The collaborators (and there were many) who had worked with the Philistine military administration had either fled or been hanged by the angry Hebrews. Rizpah wondered what had happened to Naarai and his unhappy wife. Had the villagers unleashed on them the brunt of violence held in check for years? She remembered the murky darkness of the clearing before the well, the clawing fury of her own countrymen directed against her, and she shivered.

Then, after Zaccur had left, she began thinking about me. It was in her mind that I had been killed. She sat in the tent, remembering words we had spoken to each other, experiences we had shared, and a terrible loneliness possessed her. When she told me about this later, I laughed and informed her that her concern was not really about me at that point, but rather about Saul's absence. She smiled, and with the beautiful, cruel candor of which she is sometimes capable, she admitted this was so.

The hour grew late, and still he did not come. She thought of going to his tent, but she knew that if she did, and found him busy with Abner or some of the other officers, he would be justifiably angry. Men sometimes say that women are born to wait patiently, and that since this is their lot they do not mind it as much as men. I wonder if they ever realize just how much agony is contained in that patent misconception.

She sat motionless on the bench in the center of the tent, her ears attuned to every slight sound outside. When a couple of soldiers, talking and laughing loudly, paused nearby, she cursed them in a frenzied whisper, for while they were there she could hear nothing but their voices.

At length all talk and laughter ceased; the silence roared in her ears. She was beginning to be sick with longing. Then she heard footsteps.

She was afraid they would pass the tent and held her breath, waiting. The steps paused just outside the entrance. She got to her feet, heart beating wildly, the laughter of relief trembling in her throat, ready to leap out as soon as she saw him.

The tent flap stirred, lifted, and Samuel strode into the lamplight.

As he stood there, staring at her without speaking, she knew what it was Saul feared in him.

He raised a bony hand, slowly, ponderously, until the extended first finger pointed directly at her. "What have you done?" he rasped.

His bearing and the words he spoke had overtones of the ludicrous. But in the person of Samuel, the potentially comic became sinister.

"What have you done?" he repeated.

She could not answer. Apparently he did not expect her to. He walked toward her, his beard wagging gently, finger still stabbing the air, stopped less than two paces away from her. She was fascinated by the mottled yellow stains streaking the gray of his beard.

He let his hand fall, waited an instant, then said in a thundering voice, "You have sinned against the anointed of God."

Spittle, flung from his lips by the force of his speech, hit her cheek. She wanted to wipe it away but did not dare. She shook her head fearfully.

The tic began to beat under his eye. "I have labored to preserve the power of the man the Lord chose to lead Israel. I have prodded him out of lethargy. I have channeled his spirit with great effort into the way of Jahveh. Why have you come here to disrupt my work? Why do you stay?"

She found her voice. "I love him." The words sounded even more naïve than when she had spoken them to Jonathan earlier in the day, but she gathered her courage and said again, more firmly, "I love Saul."

"*Love!*" The prophet's scorn was magnificent: his lips curled, the single syllable rolled out sonorously. "Do you have even the faintest idea of what your *love* will do to him? Do you know what kind of a man Saul is? Have you seen him when he is immobilized by despair, or when he is in the grip of one of his bootless rages?" He stepped closer to her. The tic under his eye pulsed furiously. "Saul has been chosen to lead Israel against her enemies. You will prevent him from doing so."

"How?" The word burst out of her on a rising petulant note. She felt like a tiny child.

He ignored her question. "Leave him to the task for which he has been chosen. The only woman he needs is his lawful wife."

She said stubbornly, desperately, "It is not unlawful for a man to have a second wife. The patriarchs . . ."

His words brushed hers aside as if they were chaff. "You cannot help him. You can only do him and the people of Israel harm by staying. Will you heed my warning and go?"

She felt as if she were choking to death. Streaks of fire danced behind her eyeballs, making her wince with pain. The prophet towered over her, waiting. "Will you go?" he asked again.

She took a deep breath. Her vision cleared. Slowly she shook her head.

Samuel did not seem surprised by her reply. He said, much more quietly now, "Then you must be prepared to share the tragedy which will surely be his."

She tried to understand the meaning of his words, but they made no sense.

The prophet stood looking at her for a few more moments, his pale eyes half closed and expressionless. Then he left the tent.

Saul did not come to her at all that night.

chapter seven

NOR DID he come the next day, or the day after that.

Zaccur, understanding better than she knew the nature of her suffering, took on himself the task of providing her with food. He would bring enough for Rizpah and himself to eat. Often they would not speak a single word to each other during the meal, but the bond which had been established between them on the battlefield of Michmas sufficed. In the silence his sympathy was still apparent.

On the evening of the second day she felt she could bear it no longer. She asked aloud the question they were both aware she had been thinking, "Why does he not come to me?"

His sigh contained a whispering sadness. "The king is indisposed."

She pushed aside the plate of lentils she had been eating. "Is he ill?"

Zaccur took another mouthful of food. His jaws worked steadily, ruminatively. "Indisposed," he said, avoiding her eyes.

Rizpah got up, knocking over the bench on which she had been sitting. Her voice rose toward hysteria. "Why didn't you tell me? Why did you let me sit here, wondering what had happened? I should be with him. If there's something wrong . . ." She started to leave the tent.

He moved swiftly to intercept her. "No, Rizpah."

She tried to remove his hand from her shoulder. "He needs me!"

"Have you seen him at all these past two days?"

Something in his tone made her feel chill. She shook her head.

"When he is like this," said Zaccur, "no one can help him. He sits without moving. He neither eats nor sleeps. Nor does he hear when someone speaks to him."

His words were tearing great chunks out of her heart. She tried again to pass him. He clung to her, his scrawny arms straining. "You must not go to him now."

She was struggling in his grasp, hating him. "I will!"

He said, effort giving his utterance a spasmodic quality, "The prophet Samuel is with him."

Zaccur released her, knowing she would not attempt to leave now. She returned to the table, picked up the bench she had overturned, calmly and precisely set it in place, sat down on it. Zaccur also came back, suspicious of her sudden calm.

"What will happen now?"

The little man shrugged. "The spell will pass, just as it has on other occasions."

"Will he want me then?"

"If he wanted you before . . ."

"Zaccur, help me."

"I wish I could," he said moodily. "How I wish I could. But I am neither prophet nor soothsayer . . ." He broke off, staring at her eyes.

She was watching him oddly, with strange, rapt attention. "In Askelon," she said, "if I were in Askelon now, I would know where to go to learn of the future."

"The future is in the hands of Jahveh."

"There are those who can foretell . . ."

"Their way is black and evil."

"Only because they are feared. Are there none in Israel?"

"The prophets of God . . ."

"I hate the prophets. They twist the future to their own device. Are there no conjurers or sorcerers, are there no soothsayers who will speak the truth for a piece of silver?"

"It would be better if . . ."

"Zaccur, please do not preach to me."

"What else can I do?"

"Find me a soothsayer."

He had never seen her in one of her willful, stubborn moods. It made him unhappy, but he was entranced by the steely strength he could sense rising in her. "The village of Parah is not far away. Perhaps there . . ."

"Please . . . go as quickly as you can."

"There are many charlatans who claim . . ."

"Ask each one you meet to tell you in whose name you approach to seek word of events to come."

"There will be no one who can say this."

"Ask!"

He got to his feet unwillingly, and as he did, the force left her. She put out her hand in a tentative, trembling gesture. "You are right. It would be better if I knew nothing of what will come . . ."

"Do you want to know?"

"Yes," she breathed. "I must know!"

It was just past sundown when Zaccur rode out of the camp. More than five hours later he returned.

Rizpah was sitting where he had left her. She barely raised her head when he entered the tent. Alarmed, he went to her and took hold of her hand. Her skin was clammy. There were blue-tinged circles under her eyes.

"You found her?"

He nodded.

"I knew she was coming. I felt it."

"She did not know your name. But she spoke of the king and said you were close to him."

Rizpah said in a flat, dry, recitative voice, "She has a brown wart on the left side of her nose and a cast in one eye."

He shrank from her. "You've seen her. How . . ."

"I have not seen her. But I know now she can tell me what I must hear."

"I would have returned sooner, but she would not come until she found the things she said she needed—a frog, some hair from a yearling goat, and a freshly hatched pigeon."

"Is she outside?"

"I shall bring her in." He hesitated. "If you need me . . ."

For a moment she gazed at him as if she did not understand. Then she rose from the bench. The attitude of detachment dropped from her, and she looked at him warmly, almost gaily. "I shall not forget you, Zaccur."

The woman came in an instant after Zaccur left. She and Rizpah stood for a time, taking each other's measure. Then the woman set the bag she was carrying down on the earthen floor. She squatted beside it and took from it a tiny squab, which cried once or twice in a piteous, peeping voice, then was still, regarding the woman with bright, frightened eyes.

"We shall not require the other things I have brought," she said matter-of-factly. She took a small knife from her bag and with one dexterous motion decapitated the little bird, with another laid its chest open. The heart continued to pulse for a moment. The soothsayer watched it critically. A drop of blood slid off her fingers onto the ground. Rizpah shuddered convulsively.

Suddenly the woman looked around her frantically. "You will pay me nothing," she said harshly.

"I can only give you copper bracelets. But they are pure . . ."

"Nothing. You will pay me nothing."

She wrapped the remains of the pigeon in a bit of cloth and tucked it into the bag along with the bloodstained knife. Her unfocused eye rolled wildly. "I knew I should not have come."

"Tell me," begged Rizpah. "Tell me what you saw."

"The owl brayed and lay down beside a lion that barked like a dog."

"Tell me!"

"The trees spoke to me. She knows, they told me. Beware of one who knows."

"I know nothing."

The woman came close to Rizpah and spoke in a terrified, wheedling voice. "He'll kill me. Don't let him kill me."

"Who wants to kill you?"

"Him!" She plucked at Rizpah's sleeve. "He's outside now!" Her voice sank to a whisper. "Now . . ."

The woman trembled. A ripe, cheesy odor rose from her body. Rizpah looked toward the entrance with mounting horror. She felt the presence outside: foreign, menacing.

Saul came into the tent.

His face was pale, his eyes bloodshot and staring. He raised the sword in his hand, his gaze intent on the woman. "Unclean," he said, his voice strained and grating. "An abomination before the Lord . . ."

Rizpah screamed and snatched at the sword. Saul seemed to see her for the first time. His glance wavered, and the soothsayer took the opportunity to dart out of the tent. Saul dropped the sword to the ground.

"Thus speaks the King of Israel . . ." His voice grew rich and resonant. "From this time forth they will no longer befoul my kingdom with their filth. From this time forth on pain of death . . ."

He stopped speaking and closed his eyes. His shoulders slumped and he appeared all at once very weary. Rizpah put her arm around him and led him to the bed. He opened his eyes and looked at her.

"Rizpah," he said wonderingly. "How did I get here?" He took her hand, brought it to his lips. "I have been lonely without you."

"And I without you."

"Don't leave me again."

For just an instant there was a grim twist to her smile before it softened and she said, "I'll not leave you, my darling."

chapter eight

THE SUNLIGHT was clear and liquid, the kind that often pours out of the heavens in such abundance during the last days of harvest. It was a morning without blemish, the early hour untarnished by the memory of the night before: the visit of the soothsayer and Saul's violence.

As Rizpah walked back to her tent from the stream where she had bathed, her heart sang, a continuation of the simple, almost bumptious, melody of water burbling over rocks. Nothing could mar her happiness now, not even her perception of a small stain on the earthen floor of the tent, the mark made by the drop of pigeon blood falling from the soothsayer's hand. She ground it from sight with the heel of her sandal and walked to the bed where Saul lay, watching her approach from half-closed eyes in which there gleamed the pride of possession.

She sat beside him. It was a moment of peace for them both, when each was beginning to understand for the first time the subtle, exquisite demands love makes on its acolytes: the necessity to give of one's self, which many are a lifetime learning and some never learn; and even more exacting, the obligation to take from the person one loves, completely but without exploitation.

It occurs to me now as I write of love that I might appear to employ the word indiscriminately, without first constructing the pedestal on which we are accustomed to envision it. I have spoken of Abner's love for Rizpah and the unbearable pain it inflicted on him, after he had known her but a few hours . . . in truth, when it could be said he did not know her at all. I have described Rizpah's confusion after her first sight of Saul, have accepted her swift certainty upon meeting him that what she felt was love.

I might be tempted to question the genuineness and depth of these feelings. But if there is one thing I have learned about love, it is that no one can predict its emergence or the exact path it will follow.

The writings of the Hebrew scribes contain in more than one place the laconic comment: "And he saw her, and she was fair in his eyes. And his heart cleaved to her, and he loved her." This flat acceptance seems to me infinitely wiser than niggling speculation.

By this I do not mean that love cannot undergo change. Abner's love for Rizpah was unrequited, yet it was to deepen over the years until the course of events lent it an almost startling significance. Saul's and Rizpah's love, having found a certain fulfillment almost from the beginning, was still to change its shape many times, as the shadow of a tree on a garden wall assumes many forms between dawn and dusk.

The love between them was growing, and in the growth there was exultant happiness for Rizpah. Yet the nature of happiness is such that it sometimes contains the seeds of its own destruction.

For Rizpah the frightening experience with the soothsayer was already relegated to the past. Her mind closed it off, and in the next few days she became more and more convinced that Saul had also forgotten it, if in fact he had even been aware of what had happened at the time.

Yet, on the fourth day after the woman had come to Rizpah's tent, Zaccur showed her a proclamation he had been ordered to dispatch to all the tribes of Israel. She read its text over several times. "A decree of Saul, King of Israel. From this time forth, with the exception of those known to be authentic prophets or priests of Jahveh, no soothsayer, wizard, witch, conjurer, sorcerer, or others professing to predict the course of the future, shall be permitted to practice their pagan art within the borders of Israel. Those apprehended in violation of this decree shall be put to death by the sword, and their heads displayed on public view as a warning."

She felt numb at first, somehow betrayed, as if her love had been deliberately and brutally flouted. It was not the fact that he had outlawed soothsayers from the land; this was his prerogative as king. But she had been directly involved in the generating incident. And he had nurtured his intention in secret, without sharing it with her, without even informing her of its imminence, as though he numbered her among the offenders.

She held herself back from Saul that night in self-righteous resentment, trying to retaliate by hurting him. But when she succeeded, when he regarded her with the baffled, frustrated expression she was coming to know so well, her heart melted and she flung herself into his arms.

The matter of the soothsayer and the ensuing proclamation taught her an important lesson. A man and woman who profess love for each other may come to know each other's bodies as they do their own. They not only may but must share a certain community of spirit. But in the spirit of each lies a forbidden area which the other cannot invade.

Rizpah did not speak to Saul about the decree he had issued. It was consigned to a place among other matters which they could not discuss freely. Ahinoam, for example. Saul had never so much as mentioned her name to Rizpah. There were many things she wished to know. Things a woman is always desperately anxious to learn about another who has a claim on her man: the way she spoke to him when they were alone, the endearments she used, how they quarreled—in short, the fabric of their life together. But she was wise enough not to reveal this avid curiosity to Saul. Questioning could only anger him, and sooner or later she was sure she would learn what was important for her to know.

Now it only seemed of consequence that he wanted her, that since Michmas he had not once returned to his family home in Gibeah.

There were many official matters to occupy his attention in the camp of Israel. The army, now numbering over six thousand warriors, was rapidly turning into a disciplined, efficient fighting force. Saul and Abner knew their respite from battle was only temporary. They pressed the training program on at an accelerated rate. Saul sent spies to reconnoiter the Philistine border, to filter into the coastal plain itself and learn the state of the enemy's recovery from his recent defeat. He dispatched patrol units to investigate rumors that the Ammonites were again becoming bold enough to raid the eastern fringes of Gad, across the Jordan. He sifted and evaluated reports which reached him from the south, that the Amalekites were casting envious eyes on flocks and produce in the southern tip of Judah.

Very soon the army would have to test its newly forged strength.

In the meantime there were some hours of leisure, which Saul invariably spent with Rizpah. They would ride together into the countryside surrounding the campsite, through fields from which grain had already been cut. They would watch the gleaners—mostly impoverished widows and their children—gathering the stalks which law prescribed should be left for them in the corners of the fields. They would pass threshing floors and see dust-covered harvesters tossing grain high in the air to let the wind winnow off the chaff. They stopped at vineyards in the heat of the day to receive the hospitality of fresh-baked cakes and a bowl of new wine.

There was a blue tinge to the hills of Benjamin these days. The air was still warm, and there was no hint of the rains to come, but winter lay, waiting, in the morning haze over the olive trees.

Only one factor impaired the sweet progress of the idyll: the presence of the prophet Samuel. He had not spoken to her since the night he visited her and made his pronouncement, but his silence was eloquent. He would watch Saul and Rizpah riding from the camp, and long after they had vanished from his line of vision, she could feel the pale eyes boring into her back. The matter of Samuel was another of which she refrained from speaking to Saul. And usually, once they had passed the first line of hills beyond the camp of Israel, she could manage to forget the prophet.

One morning, after a night when the king had worked late with Abner and Zaccur and the six captains over thousands, he sent Bela to bring Rizpah to the place where the donkeys were tethered. Saul was waiting for her, and they rode together into the blue-tinged hills.

He was in high spirits. He was never talkative, except by occasional spurts of what amounted to monologue, and she was used to the unsmiling line of his lips. But now she could sense the lightness of his heart by the lift of his shoulders, the way his expression softened as he breathed deeply of the clean air.

They reached a vineyard nestling in a sun-warmed hollow at the base of a hill. The fruit had been stripped from the vines, but the foliage was still rich and glossy, thick enough around and overhead to provide shelter from the direct rays of the sun.

Saul helped her dismount and led her through the cool labyrinth of latticed branches to the vineyard house. They sat on a bench and drank the wine and ate the figs they had brought. The vineyard had an air of gentle abandonment, as if it were slowly preparing to sink into the repose of winter.

She sat quietly for a time, absorbing the silence. Then she said, "This might be our vineyard."

He replied, "It belongs to us. Not that I mean it is my property. But . . ." He made a gesture to include both the vineyard and the surrounding hills. "All of this belongs to those who love."

It was the first time he had told her, even obliquely, that he loved her. She remained very still, scarcely breathing. He got up and took her hand, and at his touch she rose to her feet. He helped her remove her robe. Then he took off his cloak and the sheepskin tunic.

His body reminded her of one of the oaks outside the temple at Askelon: stalwart, with just a suggestion of gnarl in the bunched muscles of his shoulders, hips and thighs. The whiteness of his loins contrasted beautifully with the weathered darkness of his arms and lower legs.

His gaze moved over her. She felt herself beginning to glow under its caress.

He said slowly, "I wish I had a poet's gift. I would be able to tell you then how the sight of you refreshes my soul."

She said, "Your eyes on me are poetry enough."

He came close to her. She felt the full length of his body against hers. His ardor started an answering chord of desire deep inside her. He buried his fingers in her hair, drew her gently with him to the ground.

The leaves above her flashed from silver to green and back to silver. And the little cries she uttered rose like birds to flutter through the dappled canopy of the arbor.

They rode slowly back toward the camp, in no hurry to reach it, letting the donkeys amble along close together at their own speed. They touched each other's hands often, with a kind of wonder, as if each wanted to be sure the other was really there.

Before they crossed the last hill, when they could just make out the sentry on top of the ridge, Saul turned to her. "My love . . ." was all he said. It was enough.

The men of Israel were beginning their afternoon weapons practice. Until now they had not paid much attention to the chariots. The vehicles had sat idle, drawn up in a neat row behind the altar of God, while the horses had been herded into a special pasture area beyond where the close-cropping sheep and goats grazed. Now they were harnessed to the rigs they had been trained to pull, and a score of sweating warriors maneuvered the chariots about an open space: cursing, shouting, getting the reins hopelessly tangled, jamming the wheels of one vehicle into those of another. Fortunately, they had not attached the battle knives, or the exercise might quickly have become more of a shambles.

Saul and Rizpah separated at the outskirts of the camp. He watched the desperate jockeying of the fledgling charioteers for a few moments, then moved on. Rizpah looked after him until she saw him enter his tent.

Feeling warm and relaxed, not yet wishing to go to her own tent, she sought out Zaccur. The little man was busy polishing two shields, one for Saul, the other for Abner. She helped him. For a time he said nothing. His lower lip emerged farther and farther as he frowned over his task. Then he looked at her, an impish light dancing in his eyes. "The general of the host would swoon with delight if he knew your hands were brightening his shield." He added, more soberly, "You have not been kind to him, Rizpah."

"Would it help if I gave him only kindness?"

He nodded glumly, agreeing. "You could not do otherwise. The other night I was watching him when he did not know he was being observed. Do you know, his expression wounded me more painfully than the spear that laid open my arm at Michmas. I spoke to him, as tactfully as I could. 'My lord Abner,' I said, 'it is not proper for a valiant man of battle to remain too long celibate. It dulls his reflexes and sours his judgment.' Then I suggested, very gently, that he come with me to Parah, where I know some wenches who would be overjoyed to entertain the general of the army. He only looked at me, his eyes as sad as a pariah dog's, and turned away. I would have been better pleased if he had flung an oath at me or struck me."

She made no comment. He put down the sheepskin polisher and looked at her. "My heart aches for Abner, but there is nothing anyone can do for him. You, the king, I . . . least of all he himself. But he bears his pain well. And I am glad that you and Saul . . ." He reached over and patted her hand. Then, after peering into her face, he began to blink his eyes exaggeratedly. "Something joyous has happened to you today. Your beauty is starting to blind even me."

She laughed and tossed her head. "Since my friend Zaccur is so perceptive, he will know well enough what has happened to me. And since he is so tactful, he will surely refrain from further discussion of the matter."

"I assure you, I can scarcely wait to catalogue each detail to the captains of hundreds. But first you must make the picture absolutely clear for me. I am after all a man of limited imagination."

"Then you should go and gain experience. I find it tedious to converse with the uninitiated."

He heaved a large mock-sigh. "If the lady Rizpah would only be charitable enough to supervise personally . . ."

She cut him off with a hoot of laughter. He hung his head, peeped up at her with a ribald grin. Then his expression grew serious and he said, "I have never seen the king so untroubled as he has been these last few weeks."

Rizpah looked back at him gratefully. At that moment Zaccur was called away by one of the new charioteers, who told him that a chariot had been damaged and would require repairs. "I am not surprised," he said wryly as he got to his feet. "What amazes me is that you have not destroyed the entire encampment."

He tousled Rizpah's hair and left her. She sank into a pleasant reverie, allowing her mind to float back through the hours and touch the bench in the vineyard house, linger on the silver and green leaves, soar to the blue hills.

Someone tapped her on the shoulder. At first she thought it was Zaccur returning, and turned to greet him.

The boy who stood next to her was about twelve years old. He had a sly, foxlike face which made his large, unblinking eyes seem out of place. His mouth was stained purple with the juice of the grapes he was eating. He popped one after another past his lips, never removing his gaze from Rizpah's face.

"You're to come with me," he said.

"And who are you?"

He gave no sign of having heard her. "You're to come with me," he repeated.

Half amused, half curious, she went with the boy. He walked ahead of her with a kind of mincing dignity, without once looking back to see if she was following.

When they were halfway across the camp he stopped abruptly, turned over a stone with the toe of his sandal and stared fascinated at a pair of beetle grubs. While Rizpah watched, horrified, he picked up a small pointed stick and with a skill which appeared practiced he impaled the larger of the grubs. The insect writhed; the boy bent close over it and observed its death agony with intense engrossment.

Rizpah snatched the stick from his hand, dropped it to the ground and stepped on the squirming grub. The boy turned a glance of hatred on her. "You had no right to do that."

"Nor did you." She had the feeling that she was not conversing with a child.

"I wanted to watch it die."

"You saw it die."

"Slowly. You killed it too fast."

The child's unblinking eyes were making her uncomfortable. She started to turn away. He leaped ahead of her, blocking her path. "You're to come with me."

Rizpah shrugged and followed him again, surprised, then uneasy, when she realized he was leading her toward her own tent.

He stopped outside the entrance and, reaching into the folds of his tunic, brought out a handful of bruised, dripping grapes which he began to eat with noisy smacking movements of his lips. Rizpah looked at him questioningly; he returned a blank stare. "You're to go inside," he said.

She entered the tent. Ahinoam rose from the bench, her expression as serene as if she had been welcoming Rizpah into her own home.

"I am sorry to have sent the child after you, but I thought it better for us to have our first conversation away from the eyes of the men."

Rizpah walked to the table, displaying a composure she did not feel. She had been tricked into a disadvantageous meeting, and there was nothing she could do about it. To assert proprietorship in the tent, to offer Ahinoam fruit or water to bathe her feet, or any of the other offices of hospitality, would appear gauche. To ask her what she wanted would be worse.

She decided to rely on a rule I had taught her: when in doubt, say nothing. There are few human beings, particularly in an atmosphere of tension, who can survive an ordeal of silence.

Rizpah smiled and walked to the bed, on which lay one of Saul's cloaks. She turned to Ahinoam, waiting.

Her performance was effective. Ahinoam's serene expression clouded; her enormous eyes grew wider; she seemed about to weep. Then she said in a rush, "I've come to ask you to go away."

Rizpah raised her eyebrows. Her heart was beating furiously, but the exterior she presented to Ahinoam was cool, inquiring. She still said nothing.

Ahinoam said, "I have no right under the laws of our people to ask this of you . . ."

She stopped, and Rizpah's expression said clearly: then why did you?

"If Saul were not king . . ." She paused again as Rizpah looked pointedly at her rough-spun robe. "I am no queen," she continued quietly. "But Saul is king over Israel. He must be allowed to do the task for which he has been anointed."

Rizpah took a deep breath. "Do you believe I have any intention of hindering him?"

Ahinoam replied falteringly. "You must understand . . . I have known Saul since we were both children. There is no finer man in the land of Israel. He is strong and honest. But his spirit . . . there are times, weeks on end, when the demons inhabit his soul. Surely you have seen already how—"

Rizpah interrupted her brusquely. "I would like to put one question to my lady Ahinoam. This thing she asks of me—that I go away —does she request it for herself or in the name of Israel?"

Ahinoam hesitated, then said faintly, "For Israel. I ask it for Israel."

"How could my presence as Saul's concubine interfere with his obligation to Israel?"

"When the demons invade his soul, he feels only despair. As long as he has around him only those who know him, who understand how to combat . . ." Her voice trailed off. She stared at Rizpah, her great eyes misty. "You are so young. And beautiful. The demons that rage in Saul . . . you would try, but you could not help cast them out."

Rizpah moved toward her. "The prophet Samuel sent you to me."

Ahinoam glanced desperately around the tent. Her lips opened and closed soundlessly. Just then the boy who had summoned Rizpah appeared in the entrance and stood watching them.

Ahinoam's desperation vanished. Her face resumed its accustomed serenity. She went to the boy and smoothed his hair, made an effort to wipe the grape stains from his cheeks. The boy's manner changed at once. A faint smile touched his lips, softening the sly, foxlike features. He reached out hesitantly, groping for his mother's hand. She said in a crooning tone, "Now then, Ishbaal. You will wait for me outside."

The boy turned obediently and left the tent. Ahinoam came back toward Rizpah and said, "Is it always the youngest who gives us most concern? When he was born I wondered . . ." She broke off, looking at Rizpah's face. "I'm sorry. For a moment I forgot who . . ." Again the instant of silence. Then, "You were right. I came here because Samuel asked me to come."

"Then it is not your own wish that I leave."

"I would not dare ask it for myself."

Rizpah knew now she could never dismiss Ahinoam lightly. In many ways she was like her son Jonathan, direct, without guile. But often a lack of guile is more surprising and dangerous than the most elaborate subterfuge.

Ahinoam confirmed this now. "You are wondering how deeply I love Saul. I have sometimes asked myself the same question. But I have never concerned myself with it for long. Our marriage was arranged. I have lived with him for over twenty years and borne his children. When he was a farmer I worked beside him, sharing his labor. Now that he is king I can no longer help him in the way I once did, but I will come to him whenever he needs me. I have never known any man besides Saul." She looked steadily at Rizpah. "Nor have I wanted to."

Rizpah waited a moment before she said, "I will not leave Saul."

Ahinoam bowed her head. "I did not think you would. When you came into the tent and I saw your face, it was not even necessary for me to ask. But I had promised Samuel . . ."

"Why does he hate me?" She could have bitten her tongue as soon as the words were out.

Ahinoam's eyes were fathomless. "Do not condemn Samuel. He hates no one. But his love for Israel is more possessive than hate could ever be."

Now Rizpah was able to say, "Can I offer you some fruit? Some water to refresh yourself?"

Saul's wife shook her head. She gathered her robe more closely about her. "I have done what I wished to do. I have seen you. I have spoken with Saul. Now I shall return to Gibeah."

Rizpah walked out of the tent with Ahinoam, the last words she had heard spinning frantically in her mind. What had Ahinoam said to Saul? What had he replied? She was scarcely aware that Ahinoam was making her a simple, gracious speech of thanks. She replied in kind without thinking, only half hearing her part of the formal exchange.

Ishbaal plucked at his mother's sleeve, and when she leaned down, whispered something in her ear. Ahinoam smiled and pressed him close to her side. Together they turned to face Rizpah. Despite her preoccupation, she noticed the resemblance now. Just as Michal was a replica of her mother charged with sensuality, so Ishbaal was also identical, but the stamp of slyness on his features was disfiguring, misleading.

She walked with Ahinoam to where the donkeys were waiting, conscious of the surreptitious glances of the soldiers of Israel. Ahinoam said, "We shall surely see each other again, when next I come to visit Saul."

Rizpah waited only long enough for the animals bearing Ahinoam and Ishbaal to leave the confines of the camp before she hurried to Saul's tent. She did not care that the tongues of the soldiers would wag, that covert jests would be passed in whispers around the campfires that night. She did not even care that she was breaking an unspoken rule by going to Saul without being summoned. She knew only that she had to see him at once.

He was alone. His back was to the entrance, and he did not turn when she came in.

She called softly, then went to him. Now he turned, and she saw that he was pale and distraught. The furrows had returned to his face and his eyes had lost the softness she had seen in them only a few hours before.

She spoke his name again and he put his arms around her. His embrace was disconsolate, devoid of passion. She moved her hand soothingly over his back, careful not to let the gesture imply provocativeness, seeking only to comfort him. In a little while she felt his body relax. Then she dared make him look at her.

"Each time she visits me," he said, speaking as was his wont without preamble, "I find myself wishing more fervently I had never been made king."

Rizpah thought about Ahinoam's plea to her and reflected with a rising sense of irony: for Israel indeed.

"She was so weary when she came to me today," Saul was saying. "I recalled how she had looked as a young girl. She was never beautiful, but there was a fresh eagerness about her, a quiet joy . . ."

Rizpah listened, knowing she must not in any way reveal the impatience or resentment stirring in her. Men create many roles for the women they love. They expect a chameleon receptivity, an ability to change from paramour to daughter to mother of the world without perceptible effort. A man will often speak to his woman of another, quite unconscious of the pain he might be causing. When a woman speaks of another man, she nearly always does it deliberately, with a full awareness of the effect of her words.

Saul went on. "When I first returned from Ramah and told her of my experience with Samuel, she wept. I also wept. I had known when I came to my senses after dancing with the prophets that my life would never be the same. In Ahinoam's eyes I saw the proof. I saw it again today."

If there had been any commiseration for Ahinoam in Rizpah's heart, any thought of granting quarter, it disappeared now. She saw the older woman only as a formidable rival using every weapon at her disposal: the years she and Saul had spent together, their children and the shared experience of youth, the sanction of the prophet. Rizpah knew better than to believe her beauty alone could win and hold Saul. If she wanted this man, she would have to defeat Ahinoam.

Until now, Rizpah had not cared deeply for any man. So she had been prodigal with her natural gifts: her beauty, her wit and charm, her intuitive ability to anticipate the male mood. Now she knew she would have to co-ordinate these gifts, to use them sparingly and with effect. She would have to conserve her power as a woman, understand how to assert it in competition for the man she wanted.

So, even with Saul's arms about her, Rizpah considered what she had to do. She thought of Ahinoam's dowdiness, of the almost ascetic life the king had led. She remembered Saul's rapt expression as he contemplated the luxurious furnishings of Torash's tent. And in her mind a plan was beginning to take shape.

But once having decided, even tentatively, on a course of action, she put it out of her thoughts and was aware only of Saul's nearness, his need for her love and support. She gave freely of both her body and spirit to help restore his equilibrium. And for an hour or two she and her man forgot that anyone existed besides themselves. By the time night fell Saul was as he had been earlier in the day, and Rizpah's apprehensiveness retreated.

It was just after the last lingering trace of light left the sky that I was escorted into the camp by the patrol to which I had surrendered myself. By then I had learned what I wanted to know and asked to be taken to the lady Rizpah. One of the soldiers who were crowding curiously around informed me that she was with the king, that they had just begun their evening meal and could not be disturbed by anyone, certainly not by a wrinkled old hag like myself.

"Take me there at once!" I snapped. I had not lived for years in a house of nobility without learning the effectiveness of a brisk command, and the rule of thumb: the more unsure of yourself you are, the brisker the order.

I must admit that as I approached the tent where I knew Rizpah was, my heart pounded considerably more heavily than is good for someone of my age. Nor did it slow appreciably as I waited for the soldier to announce my presence. I had purposely avoided giving my name—why, I am not quite sure, unless it was through a desire to see for myself how my arrival would affect her.

She and Saul were sitting across from each other at the table. When I came into the lamplight, she drew in her breath sharply and the color drained from her face. There was an instant while both of us were absolutely immobile. Then she sprang up and we fell into each other's arms, weeping copiously.

It was some time before we separated, sniffling, to gaze at each other with speechless regard. Saul was watching us, a little jealous perhaps, more than a little puzzled, but obviously somehow pleased by Rizpah's extravagant outburst of emotion.

With a babbling rush of words she told Saul who I was. I prostrated myself on the earthen floor before the king.

Rizpah spoke sternly to me. "Get up, old woman. The king of Israel has no wish to see dead bodies lying before him."

"Then perhaps," I said, the sudden joy of reunion robbing my tongue of caution, "my lord the king will allow me to taste a little food with his servants, lest he truly have a dead old hag in his camp."

A single harsh note of laughter rose from deep in the king's throat. Rizpah wheeled about, startled.

Saul got up from his place and with simple courtesy invited me to join them at table. I ate ravenously, having touched no food since morning, and Saul kept urging me to eat more, slicing choice bits from the roast with the air of a benevolent father. I liked him immediately, and I believe our mutual love for Rizpah accelerated our understanding of each other.

She sat by, shaking her head in wonderment, saying over and over, "I was sure I would never see you again."

I said between mouthfuls, "Two things you can be sure will always turn up—the new moon and an old ewe."

Again I was rewarded by that short sharp burst of laughter from the king. And again Rizpah looked startled. Not knowing that she had never heard Saul laugh, I was only pleased that my bits of ponderous humor were amusing him.

Zaccur called from outside, requesting permission to enter. The little man and I had each other's measure at once and knew we would get along, even before Rizpah had finished presenting me.

Saul called for another cruse of wine, and the four of us sat comfortably about the table. Rizpah avoided asking me questions that I knew were in her mind, and I of course volunteered no information beyond the fact that I had been walking for two days before I encountered the Israelite patrol. Zaccur, with his customary sensitivity, forestalled any questions from Saul by regaling us with stories of the villagers in his native Dan.

Saul consented readily when Rizpah asked if I could remain in the camp as her companion, and since Zaccur and the king planned to go over a final weapons inventory and allocation, she and I left.

When we were settled in her tent, I told Rizpah of the things that had happened since we were separated during the holocaust at Michmas. How the terror generated by Jonathan's bold attack and furthered by the horrible confusion we witnessed had spread into the main Philistine camp. How we had fled far to the west before Saul's army. How that night Torash, who had been growing steadily weaker throughout the retreat, had died in the Valley of Aijalon.

When I spoke of his death, Rizpah was silent for some moments. Then she looked at me and said, "What is wrong with me, old woman? Am I some evil demon, a monster? Should I not be stricken with grief, should I not weep bitterly for a man with whom I lived? I know, I did not love him, but he had my respect, and there was warmth in my heart for him. . . ."

I said quietly, "You have found love. Grief must wait."

"I mourn him," she said, almost desperately. "I do mourn him. I wish I could have loved him."

"You wish nothing of the kind," I said sharply. "Torash did not need your pity when he was alive. He needs it even less now."

She raised her head angrily. I returned her gaze in stony silence. And finally tears glistened in her eyes. "You are right," she said. "I wish him peace wherever he is."

"You brought him closer to peace than he had ever been. You were not dishonest with him. For these things his soul will thank you."

We spoke no more of Torash. There was nothing else we could say.

I told her how I found refuge with a farming family near the Philistine border, how they had accepted me even though they must have known I was not an Israelite, how I had remained with them for the past month, intending each day to journey westward, back to Askelon, each day putting off my departure. Somehow I had not been able to return to a life I suddenly considered sterile and useless. "Until just two days ago, the stars told me you were not dead and it was time to seek you out."

Rizpah smiled. "The stars, old woman?"

"In a manner of speaking," I said. "It was dusk. I had just finished helping the woman of the house with the evening meal. I stepped outside and heard two villagers gossiping with the farmer, telling him that King Saul had taken a beautiful young concubine to his bed. I looked out through the valley, and the star of Astarte was shining clear and bright on the horizon. I was sure then it was you they were talking about. I began walking eastward at dawn the next morning."

Rizpah told me of the things that had happened to her. When she recounted the story of her meeting with Saul her face softened and the color of her eyes seemed to deepen. I went to her, and we wept again in each other's arms. I cannot be sure, because neither of us spoke of it, but I think her tears were part her love for Saul, part her lament for Torash. Sometimes it is better not to inquire too closely into the reason for tears.

Then we talked of other things, and before long it was as though we had never been apart.

We stepped out of the tent to breathe some fresh air just as the false dawn was fixing its faint aurora on the near hills. We stood looking over the sleeping camp.

Rizpah said softly, "Old woman, I have never known such happiness."

chapter nine

BUT HAPPINESS is, after all, only a word, a vague trisyllable most inadequate for capturing an elusive and unstable quintessence.

Three days after I arrived in the camp of Israel, Saul departed for his home in Gibeah. His daughter Merab, the plump mouse transformed into a princess, was marrying Barzillai the Meholathite, a grave, middle-aged, prosperous farmer from the tribe of Ephraim. Saul would be away four days, to attend the ceremony and participate in the celebration.

I watched Rizpah's face the morning he and Jonathan rode out of the camp to the accompaniment of affectionate shouts from the host of Israel. There had been rain during the night, and the air was perfumed with the musky odors of late autumn. Rizpah stood by Saul's tent, clad in a simple white robe. Her hair gleamed richly in the brilliant sunlight. And as she waved gaily after the departing figure of Saul, her mouth stretched in the shape of laughter, I could see what was in her eyes. And my heart ached as if it were being crushed between two grinding stones.

This is happiness, I asked myself . . . to love so deeply that there is no life without the one you love? Then I remembered the suffering that had been mingled with my own joy, and I was able to repeat with a kind of sad certainty: this is happiness.

For a few days Rizpah was able to keep herself so busy that she scarcely had time to think. Her activity was in connection with her plan, which she had conceived on the afternoon of my arrival and now set about executing.

Had Samuel remained in the camp, Rizpah might have had to postpone what she had in mind. But only an hour after Saul's departure, the prophet was seen riding out of the camp. He left no word where he was going, and it was supposed at first that he was returning to his home at Ramah. However, a sentry whose post was on one of the hilltops reported that he had seen Samuel proceeding in a southeasterly direction, toward the somber cliffs enclosing the Dead Sea.

As soon as he had gone, Rizpah sought out Zaccur, who as usual was delighted to see her. She came quickly to the point. "The kingdom of Israel has not yet provided a throne for its king," she said. "Nor does he wear a crown as a symbol of his authority."

Zaccur gave her a shrewd glance. "Saul's crown is the word of God," he observed mildly. "As for thrones, an ornate resting place for a man's backside does not make him a king."

"The people of Israel demanded a monarch. If they had wished for something less, they would have requested a general, or nothing at all."

Saul's supply chief looked around at the familiar morning scene: the usual weapons practice; the charioteers, growing more skillful now, putting their vehicles through simple maneuvers; off-duty sentries competing in a game of chance played with sticks and smooth round stones. He turned back to Rizpah and asked gruffly, "What is it you want?"

She could be as curt as he. "The throne first. And the crown. A proper cloak for the king. A tent of cloth so the ruler of Israel will no longer be forced to breathe the odor of goatskin. Silk and satin hangings for the tent. A wooden floor and a carpet to cover it . . ."

Zaccur held up his hand, stemming the flow of her words. His expression was troubled, a little frightened. "Do you know what you are asking me to do? Does it not occur to you . . ."

"Let it be clearly understood, Zaccur. The responsibility will be mine."

"All very well for you to say . . ."

"Would I suggest something I did not feel would please the king?"

"With Saul one never knows."

She smiled at him, radiantly. "I think I know. It means a great deal to me. And to Saul."

He avoided her eyes. "There is a saying in Dan—whoever does not crave the lion's claw should not dislodge the stone before his lair."

"I have thought about what I ask, Zaccur. Very carefully."

"Have you also considered the reaction of the prophet Samuel?"

"Saul is king."

"Rizpah . . ."

"Saul is king," she repeated firmly. "Besides, will any of this violate even one of Jahveh's commandments?"

He sighed, retreating. "And who will pay the price of the things you ask?"

"You have charge of the gold and silver taken at Michmas. What better use for it?"

In the end, of course, she got her way, as both she and Zaccur had known from the beginning she would. Abner's permission had to be obtained. He had declined his invitation to Merab's wedding, preferring to remain in camp to cope with any emergency.

When Zaccur and Rizpah approached him to state her request, he only asked, "You truly wish this, Rizpah?"

"I do, my lord Abner."

He moved his hand in a weary gesture. "Then it shall be done," he said, turning away from them.

Emissaries were sent to nearby towns to seek out merchant caravans and divert them from village market places to the camp of Israel. A special detail was dispatched into the hills to select the wood for the throne.

The soldiers, who had been growing bored with the monotony of camp life, entered enthusiastically into the scheme. Some, who had been tentmakers in civilian life, helped pick out the cloth and set to work sewing the pieces together into a tent three times the size of the one in which Saul had been living. Although carpentry was not a craft at which the Hebrews usually excelled, there were in the camp two brothers from the territory of Asher, which adjoins the land of the Phoenicians. They had absorbed enough knowledge from their neighbors to be able to design and begin to fashion a handsomely carved throne, with a high back and broad armrests.

Rizpah herself worked feverishly, hemming the curtains for the tent, making silken cushions, cutting and sewing with intricate needlework the finespun wool for Saul's cloak. I helped her as much as I could, but I was not able to maintain her punishing work schedule.

The whole camp began to exude a holiday atmosphere. Morale was high, and even those not directly involved in any of the operations took a bright interest in all that was going on.

By the fourth day, when Saul was expected to return, the throne was far from being completed, but the tent had been sewn and placed in position, and enough of the hangings and cushions installed inside to give an idea of how it would finally look.

Rizpah's eyes were shining. Despite the fact that she had been sleeping only a few hours each night, she was vibrantly lovely. Her supply of energy seemed inexhaustible.

During the afternoon, between bouts of frenzied sewing, she supervised the roasting of a kid seasoned with herbs she had purchased from one of the caravans. A tantalizing odor, unknown around the cooking fires of Israel, rose from the spit.

Toward sundown she bathed in the stream and changed into the filmy gown she had worn the day Abner had first taken her to Saul.

As she stood outside the gaily striped tent, looking eagerly in the direction of Gibeah, I saw more than one soldier gape at her and swallow hard before turning away. In this womanless society, her beauty might easily have bred resentment merely by its presence. There is little doubt that almost any of the warriors of Israel, even if they had not been living under enforced deprivation, would have given a great deal to take Rizpah to bed.

Nor was it fear of Saul alone that made them keep a deferential distance. Rizpah respected their situation. She could not conceal her sensual attractiveness, but she took care not to flaunt it any more than she could help. And in the few days she had been working with the tentmakers, they had found her a cheerful, unaffected companion. They had learned she could trade bawdy jests with them and still preserve her dignity. Her repartee was duly reported and circulated around the campfires. The men were beginning to adore her.

I have said she did not make a brazen show of her beauty. But as she stood in the sunset before Saul's tent, her guard was down. She was a woman waiting for her man, and nothing else mattered. The evening breeze pressed her gown tight against the swell of her breasts, outlined the long curve of her flank. Her lips were parted, her eyes softly yearning. It was a vision that could hardly fail to inflame even the most unresponsive male.

Yet, oddly enough, even the sight of her as she was did not seem to incite anger or lust or envy or any of the unpleasant reactions it might have aroused. She was so intent on catching a first glimpse of Saul, so oblivious of everything else, and it was as though each man who looked at her hoped this would be the way his own woman would await his home-coming. They shared her excitement. They gazed with her down the long valley toward Gibeah. They were in truth like fond brothers anticipating the arrival of their sister's bridegroom: jealous, fiercely protective, filled with sentimental concern.

The sun sank lower. Shadows were beginning to expand across the camp. The breeze billowed the cloth of the new tent. I brought a cloak for Rizpah, but she waved it aside impatiently.

One of the men cried out and pointed. A solitary figure was riding along the valley toward the camp. The dust spurting up from the donkey's hoofs shone gold in the remnants of sunlight.

The rider reached the outskirts of the camp. Even at this distance we could see it was not the king. Rizpah remained motionless, waiting.

The man spurred his donkey through the camp and dismounted before Rizpah. It was the servant who had accompanied Ahinoam and Merab on their visit to the camp the day after Michmas. "My lady Rizpah," he said, bowing low, "the king has commanded me to inform you that the lady Ahinoam is unwell. He finds it necessary to remain at Gibeah until she has recovered sufficiently for him to leave her side. He sends his deepest regrets and assurances of his fondest esteem."

A hush had fallen over the men who stood near. The servant's words rose clearly above the slight moaning sound of the wind.

Rizpah thanked the messenger courteously, in a voice that did not once falter. She called out to Bela, "Please see that this man has water to wash away the dust of his journey. Let him also be given refreshment." Then, calmly, she turned and walked into the tent.

I hesitated a moment, then followed her. One lamp was already lighted. Rizpah's back was to me. She held a wooden taper in the flame, brought it over to the wick of a second lamp. The yellow glow touched the satin hangings, imparting a soft luster. I waited.

When she turned around, I saw what I had expected. Her face was a mask of despair. The skin was tight across her cheekbones, and even in the few moments since the messenger's arrival, dark splotches had settled beneath her eyes. It was as though all the nights of too little sleep had suddenly collected their toxic force and flung it at her. Without the protection of expectancy she was defenseless.

"She has won," Rizpah said tonelessly. "How naïve I was to think that this—" she waved a listless hand to include the tent and its furnishings—"could help me. I believed I was so clever. I knew he cherished a secret longing for luxury. I thought if I provided . . ." She stopped speaking and shrugged. There was more despondency in that small motion of her shoulders even than in her expression or the dreariness of her voice.

I said casually, "Perhaps Ahinoam is truly ill."

"And if she is?"

"She is his wife." Now I made no attempt to soften the brutality of my words. There was a time to be gentle with Rizpah and a time to be savagely honest. "His responsibility to her is older than his love for you. Could you have any respect for him if he neglected his obligation?"

It was as if I had not spoken. "He promised he would come today," she said, tears filling her eyes.

I saw then that I was no longer dealing with a mature woman. She had reverted to a hurt, petulant childishness. One neither reasons with a child nor scolds him for being what he is. I took her in my arms and rocked her, as I had done on other occasions long ago. After a few moments she put her hands on my shoulders and held me at arm's length away from her.

"Egrep, do you think he will come?"

"He will come."

"I love him so. I want him so."

The way she spoke these words was also childish, but in their wake the woman was beginning to emerge again: uncertain, desperate, but deeply, eternally feminine.

At first her weeping was wild and unrestrained. There was nothing I could do except stay with her and by my presence hold off some of the black despair.

As her sobbing grew quieter, I knew she was beginning to think about what had happened and her reaction to it. I knew she was realizing now how foolishly she had acted, but I said nothing, either by way of comfort or censure.

Then I sensed another change. I could see it in the rise of dark anger to her expression, then in the anger giving way to a kind of holy agony one sees in the eyes of a market-place prophet. I guessed that the jealousy which had roiled in her even before she met Saul was finally rising to the surface.

I did not know until later the actual shape of her thoughts, but I had also been a concubine. I remembered how I had felt when it was necessary for my man to be with his lawful wife. When you loved and were sure he loved you, but he was not with you, where was surety? When all the doubts and anxieties you had shuffled off in the satisfaction of his company now returned in his absence like a parade of little viperous creatures crawling into your spirit, probing for your heart.

She thought of the hands that had caressed her body now touching Ahinoam. She saw his face at the moment of climax, heard Ahinoam's cries as the ecstasy filled her body, her soul.

It did not matter that Ahinoam was reported to be ill. She did not believe this. Nor did it matter that Ahinoam's claim on Saul was true and just, and that she, Rizpah, was the intruder. The fire of jealousy burns away any such reasonable considerations. It did not even matter that Saul had told her repeatedly in the last few days before his departure that he loved and cherished her. If he truly loved her, why was he not with her when she needed him?

She began to hate her body, to think of it as inadequate and ugly. But even in her depression she knew she was not ugly. Then Saul had used her only as a release, a vessel for his passion. Why should he be content with passion when he could find peace with Ahinoam?

Inevitably, she began to hate Saul, and the ferocity of her resentment flushed out the core of the fester.

I saw the muscles of her jaw tighten. I heard the words coming from between her clenched teeth: ripe, anger-excreting oaths that even I was not aware she knew.

In the middle of one of them she fell asleep. The tortured lines of her face relaxed. Her breathing was as gentle as a baby's.

When she awoke in the morning, she apologized to me almost before the sleep was out of her eyes. Then she looked around the tent and said simply, "I shall have time now to finish the arrangements for the king's home-coming." And I felt that, for a time at any rate, she had purged herself of anger.

I was not entirely correct in this feeling. When we came out of the tent, we saw Abner regarding it with an expression of disdain. Then he saw Rizpah, and his eyes brightened with that light of adoration which, on the face of an unrequited lover, is so beautiful and so hopeless.

He came toward her saying, "I trust you slept well," and from him the cliché politeness was like every endearment known to man.

Rizpah was having none of it. Her lip did not curl with scorn, but it might as well have. "You hate the sight of this tent, don't you, my lord Abner?"

Taken aback, he made a deprecatory gesture, then recovered himself and said with dignity, "The king of Israel was still a king when he lived in a goatskin shelter. Should I pretend to be pleased by something of which I do not approve?"

She said venomously, "Then why did you grant permission to have it set up?" Before he could answer she strode away.

Abner looked at me sadly. I was angry with Rizpah, but almost as angry with him. I wanted to tell him he should have slapped her face hard enough to make her teeth rattle. But it was none of my business, and, looking at his face, I was sure he would not have known what I was talking about.

"Egrep," he said, "you understand the meaning of the word devotion very well, don't you?"

"I understand," I replied tautly, still angry at them both.

"I have watched your devotion to her. I feel I am not being presumptuous when I say it makes for a bond between us. I am devastated when I know she is unhappy." He spread out his hands, quickly retracted them, and added in his quiet, melodious voice, "You can always rely on my help."

And now it was I who wanted to slap *him*, or shake him, or commit some violence against his impossible goodness. But, as he had said, I understood the meaning of devotion, and so I bowed my head and

answered, "Yes, my lord Abner." There are times when I wish I understood less.

During the rest of the time Saul was away Rizpah no longer worked
as she had during the first fever of her enthusiasm. However, she was
calmly efficient, and soon all the additions to the camp she had requested of Zaccur were installed. There were no more displays of
childishness or overt jealousy. She was quiet and self-contained. More
than anything she seemed to be waiting to see what would happen.

Nine days after he and Saul had left, Jonathan returned to the
camp. He brought Rizpah affectionate greetings from his father.
Ahinoam had indeed been ill—a bout of the recurrent fever to which
she had first fallen prey some years before. She was growing stronger
again, and Saul would leave Gibeah very shortly.

We were never to know how much longer Saul would have remained away. On the eleventh morning of his absence, Abner sent
for him. The reports from Gad had been verified. The Ammonites
had been making repeated incursions on Hebrew territory and had
laid waste several border towns. Israel would have to march against
the invaders.

Bela rode from camp at midmorning, his good eye flashing with
pride at having been selected to fetch the king.

It was the start of controlled turmoil in the camp. Weapons were
checked over. Little Zaccur, who could be so mild and self-effacing,
became a giant of authority, exhorting, praising and cursing by turns.
Shields, helmets and breastplates gleamed in the sunlight. Swords
and spears were retested for sharpness. Archers tried the tension of
their bows.

Excitement was running high. Men called to each other in loud
voices, describing what they would do to the warriors of Ammon, making pointless jokes at which everyone laughed uproariously.

Jonathan moved through the camp, waving to a group here, stopping to talk with another there. Everywhere he went the soldiers
crowded around to touch him, to receive his smile. They looked on
him as their talisman, their symbol of confidence. He was as brave or
braver than any of them, yet like them he was pathetically mortal. The
blood that flowed in his veins could also be shed. But while Jonathan
lived, they could disregard the specter of death that hovered, waiting
for them, on some desert battlefield far to the east.

Rizpah was not obviously affected by the preparations for the campaign. She continued to make last-moment changes in the arrangement of furnishings in Saul's tent, and the calm which had settled over
her in the past several days did not leave her now.

But as the afternoon wore on, I saw her glancing with increasing frequency down the valley along which Saul must ride to reach the camp.

There was an increased stir of excitement in the camp as the prophet Samuel entered from the eastern hills. His robe was stiff with grime, his hair and beard unkempt. The donkey on which he was mounted appeared to be in equally sorry condition. Its eyes were red and the rims were encrusted with sores. The bones of its rib cage stood out in sharp relief, and it appeared to be on the verge of collapse. Samuel dismounted and gave one of the men brusque instructions to care for the beast.

Rizpah was just coming out of her own tent as the prophet arrived. She walked unhurriedly over to the king's tent and stood beside it, waiting for the prophet's attention to turn in her direction. Her attitude said clearly: this is my doing; if there are objections, let them be spoken to me. She displayed no sign of nervousness, but I was aware of the tension which must have been mounting in her.

She waited, just a trace of defiance showing in her eyes, as Samuel moved majestically over to the new tent. The flap was thrown back, and I was sure he could see the throne occupying its position of splendor inside.

He stood without speaking, his pale eyes expressionless, looking from the tent to Rizpah and back again. The men of Israel watched curiously, ready to slink away at the first indication of prophetic rage.

There was nothing. Samuel's lips moved, but no one was close enough to hear what he was saying. Then he walked on. He was not seen again for the rest of the day.

Saul arrived just before sundown. He looked tired, but there was no weariness in the hearty greetings he tossed to the soldiers who jostled about him, shouting cries of welcome.

When he reached the tent, he first kissed Rizpah, who was standing as before just outside the entrance. The onlooking warriors were pleased. Their king had come home. He was according proper deference to the woman who had become their beloved as well as his.

They were keenly aware that, since Saul would be going forth to battle the following day, Hebrew law would prohibit his sharing his bed with Rizpah that night. A man was strictly forbidden to lie with a woman for a period of three days prior to combat. But as far as they were concerned, no law could preclude the warm embrace of reunion.

Saul seemed to notice the tent for the first time. His eyes brightened with pleasure, then abruptly grew fearful as he cast a quick, searching glance around him. He entered the tent. Rizpah followed, stopping to unfasten the flap and let it fall behind them across the doorway.

She watched him carefully as he inspected the interior of the tent. As once before, in similar surroundings, his experience became hers, but much more intensely felt than on the earlier occasion. We sometimes become a sensory extension of those we love. So Rizpah's eyes reflected wonder at the richness of the satin hangings, the luxuriousness of the profusely cushioned couch. Her face flushed with pride at the sight of the throne of ash and oak. Her nostrils flared at the odor of incense rising from the brazier at the rear of the tent.

She brought him the cloak she had made—the fine wool dyed deep purple, with a lining of flame-colored satin. He took it from her hands, gazed as it in rapt admiration.

"Put it on!" she cried, unable to contain her excitement any longer.

He continued to hold the cloak in both hands, caressing the material. Then without warning he let it fall. It made a quiet purring sound as it crumpled in a heap on the carpeted floor. Saul raised his eyes to look at Rizpah. "Is this what they taught you among the harlots of Philistia?"

He had spoken mildly, without rancor. She was so surprised she could not reply at first. Then she managed to say, "I thought my lord would be pleased."

"Pleased?" The furrows were deepening around his eyes and mouth. "Would I be pleased if all the Serens of the coastal cities entered my camp with their unclean legions? Would I be pleased if Israel were conquered again and I were forced to defile myself?"

Disappointment triumphed over caution. "Will my lord remain a brigand chief all his days? Will he sit in judgment over his shepherd army, a peasant father at the head of a country table?"

"I am not ashamed of being a farmer," he said stiffly. "My father and his father before him tilled the soil. . . ."

Her lips drew back from her teeth. Anger came and went in her eyes. "The farmer king," she said, endowing each word with the full weight of her derision. "The monarch with earth still clotted beneath his fingernails. The ruler of the children of God, still dreaming that his hands grip a plowshare instead of a spear."

He took a step toward her, heavily, his fury both inflamed and vitiated by her beauty. He trembled and said thickly, "The whores of the heathen . . ."

She laughed. "Am I a whore? Very well then, I am a whore. Do you want my body? Do you, my lord?" She brushed past him on nimble feet, allowing her breast to graze his arm before she danced out of his reach.

He lunged after her, stumbling against the throne, gripping the arm-rest to keep from falling, glaring at her with a face gone wild-eyed, glistening with perspiration.

Again she whispered past him, a willow possessed of magic frenzy, weaving, pirouetting, bending her body voluptuously to evade his seek-ing arms, all the while laughing her mad laugh compounded of hurt and love and tantalization. "Come and get me, my lord. Come and get your Philistine whore. Catch me and feel my harlot's breast against your hand. Let your lips taste the evil honeyed mouth of Askelon . . ."

Until finally with a baffled roar he charged at her and found her in his arms, limp and yielding, her face turned up to his. He released her and stepped away. She sank to the floor, her head thrown back, her mouth open and her eyes gleaming . . . a tableau of brazen desire. She moved toward him on her knees, her hands outstretched. He mum-bled, "The law . . ." but did not try to retreat when her arms en-circled his thighs. "What of the law?" Her voice had the texture of the silk and satin which surrounded them.

She had been scrupulously schooled in the temple of Askelon, where the body's susceptibility to passion is revered, where the knowl-edge of enticement is an art. Nor did she forget now the things she had learned.

The hatred that lurks beneath each act of love drove them together in furious consummation. But out of the violence, out of the turbu-lence that gripped them and swept them about like dead leaves caught by the whirlwind, emerged the sweet afterstorm essence of love. And they were once again a man and his woman, one and yet two, a little awed by the intensity of the emotions which had shaken them.

He took a strand of her hair between his fingers with a touch as gentle as if he were handling the petals of a delicate flower. And the very lightness of the pressure brought her to life again and rekindled desire in them both, but differently this time, softly, as the rising sun imparts dawn flame to a mountain peak. . . .

He was quiet a long time, so long that she thought he was asleep. But his eyes were only half closed, and through the lashes she could see in them a peculiar, withdrawn alertness.

"My lord . . ."

"I am afraid." His words had a dead, hopeless sound.

"Of what, dearest one?"

"Of Jahveh. How can I go forth to fight his battle when I have broken his commandment?"

"You will go forth," she said, the sudden resounding fervor of her voice surprising her. "You will go forth and smite the enemies of Israel.

You will lead the host of God to glory and victory. And Jahveh will look with favor on his servant Saul."

His eyes were wide open now, staring at her. She felt that the words she spoke had moved him deeply. He sat up and put on the tunic he had cast aside earlier, began to pace restlessly about the tent. When he looked at her at all now, it was with the absent, tender glance one bestows on a favorite child who has wandered unbidden into a workroom. An hour before this would have distressed her. Now she was pleased.

He picked up the purple cloak from the floor and idly, almost as if he were not conscious of his movements, he wrapped it about himself. Then he approached the throne slowly, a trifle suspiciously, like a hart advancing through concealing trees toward an unexplored glade. He sat in the chair which had been fashioned for him.

Carefully, so as not to distract him, she got up from the couch and dressed. Then she went to a corner of the tent and returned with the heavy circlet of gold which had been lying on an embroidered cushion. She placed the crown on his head and stepped back.

"Hail, Saul, King of Israel," she said softly.

His lips were moving, but it took an instant before sound passed them.

"Lord God," he was saying, "give me the power to do what thou requirest of me."

There was humility in his voice, but it was not the obsequious pleading of a supplicant. He was talking to his God in the way a capable servant addresses his master: quietly, confidently, with full knowledge of his own value.

He rose to his feet and Rizpah's eyes met his. In them she saw a clear, unwavering strength, and back of that, his love for her.

"I shall leave you now, my lord," she said. "You will have many things to do before you lead the host of Israel forth tomorrow."

chapter ten

WE WAITED impatiently, along with the several hundred warriors who had been left behind when the Hebrews marched out to meet Ammon. We went about small menial tasks, but all the while we were watching the crest of the camel-humped ridge to the east, searching for the first sign of the army's return.

The runner had arrived at dawn, bringing news of the battle.

Nahash, King of Ammon, had dredged his wilderness domain and collected a legion of greater size than anyone had expected. It was reported that nearly four thousand followers of Baal-of-the-desert, the serpent-headed god of Ammon, were waiting for the Israelites in the barren mountains far to the east of the Jordan.

Saul's army had forded the river and crossed the fertile western portion of Gad. Even with winter threatening the land, the rolling pastures and quiet forests were pleasant to the eye. But here and there a clump of charred foundations, blackened fields, the bleached bones of sheep and goats, gave evidence that Ammon had indeed been active.

On the first evening of their march a deputation from Jabesh-Gilead joined Saul's forces. Tall, saturnine men who spoke a dialect containing many Ammonite words, they offered their services as scouts and interpreters. Their love for Saul was almost idolatrous. To the end of time, said their leader, Jabesh-Gilead would remember the valiant deeds of the warrior-king who had freed their city from oppression. The very least they could do would be to assist him in smashing forever the threat of their traditional enemy.

The vistas of fertility gave way to sparseness, the sparseness in turn to a wasteland where the wind howled ceaselessly. To the east lay the sandstone mountains, and deep among the eroded pockets of those mountains Ammon had its chief city.

Saul and Abner led the troops through Beth-nimrah, a desiccated settlement at the southern edge of Gad. From here it was only a half day's quick march to Rabbah, the Ammonite capital.

As the wagons and chariots rolled past the sand-blown huts of Beth-nimrah, there was a sudden commotion among the silent ranks of the villagers lined up to watch them pass. An old man was struggling with five or six younger men. Finally, screaming and gibbering with rage, he tore himself from their grasp and ran with extraordinary alacrity after one of the companies of foot soldiers, with which the men from Jabesh-Gilead were marching. He clawed his way to the sides of two brothers and greeted them excitedly as flesh of his flesh, blood of his blood. He had recognized them immediately, he said, in spite of long years away from Jabesh, as the sons of his nephew. The brothers dropped out of the march, and, after questioning the old man, learned that he was indeed their great-uncle. A moment later one of the brothers hastened forward and asked Saul to call a rest stop. If what the old man said was true, the Hebrew army was advancing into a trap.

Not an hour from Beth-nimrah the Ammonite legions were concealed on either side of a valley through which the Israelites would have to pass. The inhabitants of the village knew, of course, about the ambush, but they had lived too long in the shadow of Ammon to risk informing Saul now. The vengeance of the desert tribesmen was known to be swift and savage.

The king and his general called a hasty council. Under the blazing noonday sun, with the sand flies buzzing about their heads, they conferred with the men of Jabesh, drawing maps of the region in the powdery dust of the road.

Knowing now what lay ahead, their strategy was simple. One of the captains of thousands would take his troops along the intended route, so as not to make the Ammonites suspicious. The bulk of the army would be split into two flanking units, which would wait until the decoy division had almost reached the valley, then fall upon the enemy from either side.

It was a classic maneuver, and eminently successful. The troops of Nahash had been so confident that they had not even troubled to place sentries at the vulnerable wings of their army. Their entire attention was concentrated on the approach of the thousand men of Saul toward the center of the valley. Because of the dust which rose round the marching Hebrews, their force appeared much larger than it was, which was exactly what Saul and Abner were depending upon. The timing of the counterambush was perfect.

By sundown, the armies of Ammon had been crushed, and before the sun set the next day, Saul's men had razed Rabbah and were retracing their steps westward, laden with booty.

As is depressingly usual, on their return trip through Beth-nimrah, they found the formerly reluctant villagers changed into a cheering mob. Young women rushed out into the path of the vanguard, hysterical with joy, and threw their arms around the first soldiers they could reach. The elders had ordered each *baal-habayis*, or head of a household, to slaughter an animal from his flock and roast it to help feed the victorious Israelites. There seemed to be no memory of the reticence which could have resulted in the annihilation of the host of God. But then, who can sit in judgment when the only true culprit is fear?

Now, having heard the news brought by the runner, we at Saul's base camp waited to extend our own welcome.

At noon they came, singing and shouting, over the ridge and down into the camp. The charioteers were especially jubilant. They had acquitted themselves beautifully, and as Zaccur later noted dryly, the only real danger they had encountered was a near collision of four chariots converging on a knot of Ammonite swordsmen. But, he added, the screaming curses of the four drivers had discomfited the enemy nearly as much as the sight of the gleaming battle knives. In fact, he mused, he was seriously considering requesting Abner to place an extra man in each chariot who would be taught the most virulent oaths known in every tongue, and whose only function in battle would be to curse at the top of his voice.

There were, naturally, other more somber reminders of the campaign. Israel had left over three hundred dead in the valley east of Beth-nimrah. And there were the walking and riding wounded: whey-faced, still dazed from the blows or thrusts which had opened their bodies and poured their blood onto the dust of Gad. Some of these would soon die. The stench of corrupt flesh surrounded the wagons that bore them, and the eyes that peered out at the camp they had left only a few days before were already haunted by the knowledge of death.

But the soldier who has come through battle unscathed exudes a contagious, very personal, joy. He does not forget the dead and wounded. It is because he remembers them so well that he sings more loudly and shouts more robustly than he might have otherwise.

Saul marched as usual just behind the vanguard, at the head of the main body of his troops. He walked with his head high, looking neither right nor left as he entered the camp. Lightly balanced in his hand was the massive spear which had become his special weapon.

Rizpah waited with me, a little apart from the welcoming soldiers, doing nothing to attract Saul's attention. This was his moment of triumph, not hers, and she had no wish to force him to share it before he was ready to do so. But the love in her eyes was so open, so compellingly dazzling, that I knew it would not be too long before he turned to her.

When he did, it was a moment I shall never forget. Abner had just given the order to break ranks, and the foremost soldiers were milling about, beginning to seek out their former resting places in the camp, looking for companions who had not gone on the expedition. Saul was talking to one of his captains. All at once he seemed to break off in the middle of a sentence and as he turned away from the captain, his eyes found Rizpah immediately.

I have seen men with a pride of possession—of a house, a vineyard, precious jewels—that bordered on obsession. This same quality was in Saul's eyes, but it was pride burned clean of avarice. And because the assertion of his possessiveness was so intense, so unabashed, Rizpah

responded to it with an equal lack of reserve. Such a personal exchange, better suited to the bedchamber, might have been only embarrassing to those who saw it. This was not so. It was a very beautiful thing to watch.

Unfortunately, it was short-lived. The prophet Samuel came forward to stand at Saul's side. The king did not notice him at first.
But he must have perceived some subtle change in Rizpah's attitude,
and it was through her eyes that he became aware of Samuel's presence.

The prophet spoke a few words to Saul, then left him. The king
came to Rizpah. Their greeting was warm, but it was not what it might
have been only moments before. Perhaps that was just as well. The
kind of intensity I had witnessed was too brilliant a flame to burn long.

Shortly after midnight it began to rain. Until now, we had been
exposed only to showers, furious deluges which came and went in an
hour. This was a steady, pelting downpour. Winter was upon us.

There is nothing quite so bedraggled as an army camp in the rain.
Many of the men of Israel were shepherds, accustomed to sleeping out
in all kinds of weather. And there is a certain satisfaction in knowing
discomfort is shared. But this bit of satisfaction is apt to wear thin
among thousands of men huddling under sodden mantles, crowding
around steaming, ill-protected fires. I lay on my bed in Rizpah's tent,
listening to the drum of rain on the goatskin, feeling only passing
guilt that I was one of the three people in the camp sheltered from the
downpour.

Saul left Rizpah sleeping in his tent soon after the rain began, and
for the rest of the night he moved about the camp, talking with the
men, assuring them they would not have to endure this unfortunate
situation much longer.

There was a story behind this. It had been decided even before
Michmas that winter quarters would be established at Gilgal. Though
it was only a comparatively short march to the east, it lay behind a
protecting range of hills, close to the Jordan, and received only a
small portion of the cold rain driving out of the west.

Saul had wanted to bring the army to Gilgal when they were returning from Gad. It was practically on the way, and he had almost
given the order. But Samuel had said they should remain in their present camp until the new moon, which was two weeks away. No reason,
for Samuel seldom presented reasons for his decisions, and then only
to say it was the will of God. Saul had respected the prophet's command.

Now, however, with the rain teeming from the soggy dawn sky and showing every likelihood of continuing, Saul sought out the seer and said bluntly, "We shall move our camp this day to Gilgal."

Samuel was soaked to the skin like every soldier of Israel. He stood for an instant, moisture dripping from his hair, his beard, his mantle, before he said in a low voice, "If you wish." He was always able to create the feeling when he granted a request of which he did not approve that some terrible calamity would follow at once.

As a matter of fact, what followed was far from calamitous. The men, after a night with very little sleep and no hot food, were beginning to grumble. Their complaints were not directed against Saul. This kind of discontent is endemic in an army camp. Their muttering was their own protection against the prospect of two more weeks of misery. Few expected Saul to keep his promise of moving them at once to winter quarters. They knew what Samuel had ordered, and no one defied a prophet of God, not even a king.

Thus it was when the command to break camp came later that morning, there was a short period of shocked disbelief. But when they actually began to carry out the command and saw Samuel, glum-visaged but not objecting, their spirits rose and they sloshed cheerfully through the mud, going about the business of packing weapons and supplies. One of them began to sing; another took it up, and soon most of the camp was chanting the paean someone had composed on the march back from Gad:

> "Saul, our beloved king.
> Like an oak he stands fast
> In the blast of battle.
> The enemy rages, the blood
> Is dark in his face.
> But the hand of our king is sure;
> His eye strikes terror in their hearts.
> He slays a thousand of the foe
> Between dawn and sunset.
> Saul, our beloved king."

When we reached Gilgal, the rain stopped, and the sky was as it had been in midsummer.

Gilgal was not a town, or even a village. It was situated on a stretch of headland overlooking the sweep of the Jordan Valley. Twelve great stones set in a circle occupied the highest point of the headland. Tradition had it that these were the stones the leader Joshua had set in the river in ancient times so the priests carrying the words of the law could cross on dry land. Now they were regarded as sacred to Jahveh, and in the center of the circle an altar had been erected.

The men were delighted to be in Gilgal. For the veterans it was in the nature of a home-coming. For the more recent recruits there was promise of leisure, a few days or even weeks under the peaceful sun before they would again have to think of battle.

But the new campsite had been set up for exactly one hour when Samuel summoned Saul and informed him that he must march at once against the Amalekites.

chapter eleven

As USUAL, the order was peremptory, delivered with no grace and little reason.

The Amalekites were a group of desert tribes, springing in some dim past from the same origins as the Bedouins, now occupying the torrid wilderness south of Simeon. They had been hated by the Hebrews since the exodus from Egypt, when they had harried the northward-migrating Israelites, cutting off stragglers from the main group and brutally murdering them. For over two centuries there had been intermittent warfare between Amalek and Israel, but of late the conflict had lain dormant. Even reports of Amalekite invasions into southern Judah had proved on investigation to be mostly false: exaggerated accounts of sporadic bandit raids.

Edom, Amalek's neighbor in the south, was a more potent menace to the new Hebrew monarchy. Even Moab, touching the territory of Reuben on two sides, could be considered a greater threat than Amalek. And of course, though Philistia lay smarting under her recent defeat, she was far from being rendered harmless.

Yet it was against Amalek that Samuel insisted Saul should lead his army.

He said to Saul as soon as the king appeared before him, "The Lord sent me to anoint you king over his people, over Israel."

Saul waited, saying nothing, not wishing at this moment to challenge the sneer implicit in Samuel's words.

The prophet fixed his gaze on Saul's face and continued in his rasping voice, "Now hear the words of the Lord: I remember that which

Amalek did to Israel, how he laid wait for him on the way when he came up from Egypt. Now go and smite Amalek . . ."

Saul was incredulous. "Amalek?"

The tic began to pulse under Samuel's eye. "Is it not enough that you consistently defy the word of God, that you disobey his commandments? Must you also interrupt when he speaks?"

"I only asked a question." Saul's voice was offhand. He studied the twitching muscle on Samuel's face with interest, even with some concern. Rizpah's love had strengthened him to the point where he could now converse with the prophet without fear.

Samuel must have sensed this. The tic pulsed more rapidly, but his voice softened. "Thus saith the Lord: Go and smite Amalek, and utterly destroy all that they have, and spare them not, but slay both man and woman, infant and suckling, ox and sheep, camel and ass. Slay every living thing that belongs to Amalek."

It would have been better if the words had come roaring forth in a torrent of prophetic wrath. The softness with which Samuel voiced them only served to increase their intrinsic horror.

Saul looked up at the clear afternoon sky. He narrowed his eyes against the glare of the sun and focused his glance on the bright ribbon of the Jordan in the distance. He thought of Rizpah dying by the sword, visualized her lovely body mutilated, lifeless. He closed his eyes to blot out the vision and opened them again quickly, for darkness made it worse.

"Would it not be enough," he asked, choosing his words carefully, "to slaughter the warriors of Amalek? Does the Lord also require the death of women and children?"

Samuel smiled bleakly. It was almost as though he had read Saul's thoughts. "Every living thing," he said. "What is innocent in the eyes of men is not necessarily guiltless in the sight of the Lord." He paused, then repeated, "Every living thing."

"When shall we depart?"

"At once."

"The hour is late. We shall leave in the morning."

Samuel bowed his head. "As you wish." His pale eyes were stony with reproach.

The king turned abruptly and walked away from the prophet. An odor of carnage seemed to hover about Samuel. Saul had never recoiled from violence when he believed it was necessary. He had hewn his favorite oxen to death and sent the reeking pieces to the tribes of his kingdom. He had been savage and merciless in battle, slaying without quarter. He would kill again, and lie down to sleep with the blood of the enemy still spattered on his garments.

But there was something about the way that Samuel had instructed him to go out against Amalek . . . Not for the first time, he wondered if the prophet's decisions truly originated with the Lord.

Fearful before his doubts, he hurried toward his tent, which had been set up just below the circle of sacred stones. The gaily striped cloth of its covering appeared particularly brave and inviting. He knew Rizpah would be waiting for him. The disquiet still worked within him, but his spirits rose a little.

He told her of Samuel's orders, of the harsh admonition. She said nothing, for she could tell he was troubled, but she was suddenly afraid without knowing why. They sat for a long time, not speaking, not even touching each other. But each took comfort from the other's presence, so that when she rose to leave him, there was between them a peace they had never quite attained before. Yet her nameless fear had not stilled itself.

It was just past dusk when she left the tent. She intended to bathe and change her gown, then return to Saul in time for the evening meal.

A wan moon lent faint light to the evening sky. Above her towered the twelve stones, each roughhewn in an odd, distinctive design, every one more than three times her height. She felt drawn toward them. She did not want to go, but she knew she had to enter the circle and do something. Exactly what she was not sure.

She climbed the stony path, hesitated between two of the stones, then walked past them into the circle.

Twelve monoliths. Twelve tribes. Twelve sons of the patriarch Jacob, who had thereby fathered all of Israel. In the uncertain light the stones seemed to be moving, coming to life.

The air within the circle was thick and clammy. She could distinguish the outlines of the altar. She stumbled toward it, propelled by some invisible force, fell to her knees before the altar. Now she knew why she had come.

"Lord God!" she cried. "Lord God of hosts, help him. He needs thee. He needs thy strength. He . . ." She stopped, not knowing what to say next. The pebbles digging into the flesh of her knees were beginning to hurt. She got up and groped for the cold stone of the altar.

A sound behind her made her turn. She stifled a scream. The prophet Samuel was standing before her, moonlight illuminating his features. His hands were rising slowly from his sides. Now they stretched above his head, fingers curved like talons. But he made no other move toward her, and in a moment his hands fell again to his sides.

They stared at each other, neither speaking, neither moving. She wanted to flee, but she knew somehow that she had to remain and continue to face those pale eyes. Above the circle some presence waited, an implacable master, judging the struggle between two of his servants.

The silence became painful, then intolerable. An owl hooted close by. She turned, half in fear, half in relief, and made out its silhouette atop one of the stones. When she looked back, Samuel was gone.

His abrupt disappearance shredded the remnants of her reserve. She ran out of the circle, down the path, just managing to hold back her tears until she reached Saul's tent.

He did not ask questions. His arms were warm and strong about her. When she had cried herself out, he moistened a cloth from a cruse of water and wiped the tearstains from her face. She had known he could be gentle and tender, but until now she had been the one to comfort him, to drive the darkness from his soul. Now she felt he was giving all of himself to her, with nothing held back. His strength was restoring hers.

She said, her voice barely audible, "Take me with you. Please take me."

Then she waited, and life stood completely still. For if he questioned, or debated, or even hesitated . . .

He looked at her gravely. "I shall take you," he said.

chapter twelve

It was somewhere in the eastern wilderness of Judah that the idea of booty began to obsess the men.

No one knew exactly how it happened. First there was only talk around the fires of the gold and silver and precious stones that would be taken from Amalek. There was nothing out of the ordinary in this. Any army marching to war so occupies itself. They speak of treasure, of the women of the enemy, of the plunder which is due the victor. Warriors thrive on such talk, and spike their courage with boasting of their feats in previous campaigns.

Now, for no apparent reason, the men began to speak of capturing the flocks and herds of Amalek and bringing them back to Gilgal. It is true that the livestock supplies of the army had been gradually depleted since Michmas, and the expedition against Ammon had yielded no appreciable replenishment. But the tireless Zaccur had already expressed his intention of acquiring livestock from landowners in the vicinity of Gilgal.

No, the talk of bringing animals back from the south was something new, and distinctly odd. The soldiers of Israel were aware of Samuel's instructions concerning Amalek, that every living thing be put to the sword. This made their obsession even more peculiar, for they feared the prophet nearly as much as they dreaded death in battle.

In the beginning, only the common soldiers spoke of it, and then in whispers. But soon the fever spread to the captains of hundreds, and finally even the elite captains of thousands considered it around their own exclusive campfire. And in the end, it was almost the only topic of conversation.

They sent Jonathan to discuss the matter with Saul. He came before the king on an evening when they had pitched camp early. The day had been excessively warm, even for this inhospitable section of Judah, which is noted for having an oppressive climate.

Saul was sitting outside his tent with Rizpah, enjoying what there was of an evening breeze. The scarred Judean hills, just beginning to soften now in the fading light, brooded over the camp. Far off to the east they could see the miasmic haze which rises nearly always off the torpid waters of the Dead Sea.

Rizpah was once again lighthearted and content. She took easily to the routine of the campaign. Also, she had her man to herself; the dual threat of Ahinoam and Samuel had been left behind in Benjamin. I had not accompanied her on the journey; it was enough of a concession on Saul's part to take Rizpah with him.

She saw Jonathan first and smiled her welcome. They had established a rapport. Jonathan believed in her love for his father and respected it; she understood the young man's feeling for Ahinoam and avoided presuming on it.

The king greeted his son pleasantly and made place for him on the bench where he was sitting.

Jonathan said immediately what was in his mind. "Father, the men want permission to take spoils from Amalek."

"It is their right. Half of any treasure goes into the coffers of Israel. The rest belongs to the soldiers. Surely you know this, my son."

"I have not made my words clear to my father. The men refer to the flocks and herds of Amalek."

Saul started, recovered himself and began to investigate a cut on one of his knuckles. Rizpah, who had been looking off toward a gold-tipped hill, shifted uneasily and turned so she could see Saul's face. He said, "Amalek is still three days' march from here."

"The men of the south are reputed to be uncommonly good herds-men," said Jonathan. "It is said that even in the desert they have raised sheep whose fleece is pure white as the snows of Lebanon."

"You know that the prophet Samuel has commanded me to slay every living thing belonging to Amalek."

"Surely he meant only the warriors of Amalek."

"Every living thing."

To Rizpah it seemed that Saul's words had taken on the very accents of the prophet. With an effort, she kept herself from shivering.

It was not in Jonathan's nature to argue. He inclined his head grace-fully toward the king. "I have heard my father's words. If he wishes me to—"

"Will my son stay and take his evening meal with us?"

Jonathan looked at Saul, bewilderment deepening in his eyes. It was obvious that his father did not wish to discuss the matter about which he had approached him. Yet nothing was settled. And he had to take an answer back to the men. With the persistence of the guileless he began again. "About the flocks and herds . . ."

"Rizpah has given the cook some of those priceless herbs she hoards. The haunch of lamb will be particularly savory this evening."

Jonathan smiled his sweet smile and accepted his father's invitation. But he looked askance at Rizpah. She warned him with a barely per-ceptible shake of her head not to bring up the subject again.

Nor did Saul himself refer to it, even after they had crossed from Judah into Simeon. They were veering southwestward now, leaving the Dead Sea behind and trekking through the magnificent barrenness which marks the approaches to the wild Negev.

Late one afternoon, Rizpah noticed that the surroundings of their route were taking on a sharp familiarity. She knew that the razor-backed hill on their right would be succeeded by a round rise with a great jagged *wadi* cutting a widening track from summit to base. And beyond that a gentle grade which climbed for some distance. Then . . .

She called one of the charioteers over to the wagon in which she was riding and asked him to take her to Saul. As she clung to the sides of the chariot, she could see the slope where grapevines had once brought forth fruit. Even now, there were a few sere and twisted shoots snaking out of the sandy earth. Her excitement grew . . .

Saul was reluctant to grant her request. It was growing late; the well where they intended to camp was still two hours away; they would have to hurry to reach it before dark.

"There is water here, my lord."

He looked at her quizzically, then gave the order to halt. He dismounted from the donkey he was riding and took over the chariot which had brought Rizpah up to the forward columns. While the soldiers of Israel stood watching curiously, he flicked the whip over the horse's back, urging it up the long grade.

Rizpah put her hand on his arm. Perhaps he could feel the excitement in the pressure of her fingers, perhaps not. He glanced around at her once, then gave all his attention to driving. They came to the crest of the grade and started down.

She did not realize she had gasped aloud until Saul stopped the chariot and turned to her. For what was probably the first time since she had known him, she was indifferent to his presence. She stared past him, straining her eyes toward what was left of her father's house.

She had forgotten the starkness of the shattered foundation, the wounding ugliness of the breached garden wall. When she had been taken away, darkness shrouded some of the desolation. Now, in the full glare of sunlight, even after the passage of years, the sense of destruction, of life abruptly choked off, was painfully apparent.

"Shall we go closer?"

She shook her head savagely, angry for once at his lack of sensitivity.

He shrugged and said, "The water of which you spoke . . ."

Rizpah pointed up the rise on the other side of the house. Saul flicked the reins, and they moved on, up to the plateau where Amaziah had stood guard, down into the little gully where he had lain dead. She tapped Saul's shoulder, and he reined in the horse. She made a careless gesture. "Over there."

He peered in the direction she was pointing, then turned to her, a question in his eyes. It was only then that she really looked . . . and saw a smooth expanse of sand where the pool should be.

"The water?"

She was resentful, and at the same time frightened. Not of Saul, but of the confounding of her memory. "It's right there. I know it is."

She jumped from the chariot. The sand ground aridly under her sandals. This was not the land her father had cultivated so perseveringly. Saul followed her, caught up to her as she paused, looking about wildly. A lock of hair had fallen over her eyes. He brushed it back. "Rizpah . . ."

She pushed his hand away. "It's here! The water's right here!"

For a moment a kind of madness infected both of them. They stared at the forbidding ground, hands clenched, breathing rapidly. Then Saul's shoulders slumped. He turned to go, heavily, as if even the effort of walking back to the chariot were too much for him.

As she was starting to follow him, she caught sight of a tip of black rock protruding from the sand. She called after him calmly, "Here, my lord. If you will have men dig here, there will be water."

He did not reply, but left her standing where she was and drove the chariot to the top of the ridge. She heard him shouting to Abner to send some men with spades. She felt a flutter of panic. Suppose she was mistaken after all. Suppose the stream under the sand cover had dried up. . . .

The men dug steadily, their shovels grating against the parched earth. As they worked, the shape of the pool as it had been began to emerge. She watched them uncover the full body of the black rocks, fancied suddenly she could hear the bleating of her father's sheep in the distance.

A soldier's shovel scrunched with the special sound metal makes when it drives into moist sand. The man gave a grunt of satisfaction. Others began digging at the same spot. Rizpah went closer, just in time to see the tiny trickle of living water oozing out of the ground.

She turned. Saul was standing next to her. She whispered, "My lord . . ." He smiled. It was the first time she had seen him smile. She had heard him laugh, twice, when I had played the clown before him, but his laughter had been harsh, almost desperate. His smile was fragile, tentative, and very beautiful.

She took his hand and held it to her cheek for a long moment.

Now she felt she could venture into the house where she had once lived.

After she and Saul had eaten, and he had gone to inspect the camp, she walked toward the ruins. The moon was waning but was still full enough to limn what was left of the walls in dazzling whiteness.

She passed the spot where the bodies of her family and betrothed had rested in death. She had been afraid that the bones would still be there, but there was no sign of them. Perhaps some passing trader who had known her father had interred the remains out of respect. Perhaps Bakesh had directed his raiders to bury the dead while she sat waiting by the camels.

She stood for a while, her head bowed. There was sadness, but she was detached from it. There was pain, but it took a serpentine course inside her, winding a long and devious path to her heart; when it arrived, it was somehow oddly akin to pleasure.

She walked toward the house itself, made a detour to seek out the place where her dream had reminded her anemones grew. But it was not spring, and the corner where they had bloomed was bare.

Moonlight poured into the common room, mellowing the brutal shape of objects left over from violence: a charred table leg, the twisted scrap of a wall, the hole where the oven had been, gaping like a toothless mouth.

A voice behind her said softly, "And still to come home . . ."

Abner was standing in the doorway, his face in partial shadow.

"Is there something in the soil of the place where we were born that cries out to us, calling us back from wherever we wander? We are restless to go, restless to return . . ."

He took a step forward. She could see his features clearly now as he glanced around the room.

He said, stammering slightly, "And someday there will be home, with its peace, and the end of strife, and all loneliness vanished."

He was looking at her now. Then, without speaking again, he left the house.

She wanted to go after him, but she knew she should not.

And suddenly she understood what Zaccur had meant when he said of Abner, "There is a man."

chapter thirteen

THE LAND of Amalek possessed a fierce and inhospitable climate. A blistering wind roared up from the Sinai wilderness, scorching everything in its path. The earth was cracked and crumbling, poorer even than the semidesert soil of Simeon. Yet, where one least expected them, there were verdant fields and groves of living trees. Sometimes the men of Saul would round a curve in the caravan trail, which wound between grim buttes and towering crags, and would come upon a hill whose slopes were carpeted with tender green pasturage.

The progress of the Hebrew army toward the heart of the country was unchallenged. In fact, they did not encounter one single person on the route of their march. There were no farmers in the fields, no shepherds tending flocks. The villages through which they passed were completely deserted. There was evidence that the inhabitants had fled hastily, sometimes in the middle of a meal.

This went on for two days. On the third morning, the Israelite encampment was awakened by a strange moaning sound which reached them over the wail of the wind. Abner quickly mustered the soldiers, who stood in formation, listening nervously as the moaning increased in volume. It seemed to be coming from an evil-looking ridge, which was pockmarked with caves and recesses.

A sentry rode breathlessly into camp to report that a great multitude was advancing toward the opposite side of the spiny hill.

The moaning grew louder. Some of the older Israelites remembered having heard that the Amalekite battle cry resembled the sound of mourning. An uneasy tension began to flicker and spread among the ranks of Israel.

Abner surveyed their position. Since they had entered the land of Amalek, they had tried as a matter of course to set up camp in an easily defensible location. This was not the best they had been able to select, but neither was it the worst. They had camped on open ground, near a well, far enough from the ridge to be out of range of the spears and arrows of any force that might attempt to scale its height. If the attacking force proved too powerful, the Israelites could always fall back to a height of land some thousand cubits distant, and there make a stand.

The general deployed his troops for a defensive operation. Then he and Saul climbed the ridge to reconnoiter the situation, taking with them a newly elevated captain of a thousand, a snub-nosed lad named Paltiel son of Laish. By this time, judging from the sound of the keening cries, the multitude reported by the sentry had arrived at the base of the ridge, directly opposite the Israelite position.

The three men made a cautious ascent of the escarpment. As Saul was advancing along one of the ledges, a great reddish-brown serpent struck at him from a recess near the king's head. The snake's first thrust narrowly missed Saul's shoulder, and as it coiled to strike again, Paltiel, coming up quickly, beheaded it with a single stroke of his sword and pressed on toward the top of the ridge without even looking back.

When they reached the crown of the escarpment, which was a level shelf of rock about three cubits in width, they looked down on an awesome sight. On the plain below, filling a vast area, were perhaps ten thousand people, all completely clothed in black. They did not seem to be armed. In fact, on second glance, Saul and his companions were able to distinguish many women and children among them.

Here on the height of the ridge, the groaning of the wind was even louder than at ground level. And still the choral wail of the throng below filled the ears of the three men.

As they watched, they saw one of the black-clad figures detach himself from the others and start up the steep slope. When he was some ten paces below the summit, he stopped, opened his cloak and spread out his hands to show that he carried no weapons. He was a vigorous-looking man about Saul's age, with a neatly trimmed, graying beard and flashing black eyes. Saul motioned for him to advance, and in a moment he was beside them, his bright eyes appraising each in turn. Then he wheeled about to face those he had left behind him on the plain and raised his arms high in the air, as if he were about to pronounce a benediction.

Immediately the moaning ceased. The wind whistled ominously in the suddenly created void.

The man's voice was a trifle high-pitched, trembling with tension. "Do I greet Saul, King of Israel?"

Saul inclined his head but said nothing.

"I and my people have come to seek clemency at your hands."

Saul admired the honesty implied in the omission of the long, oily, flattering overture which usually preceded any diplomatic negotiation. But he said coldly, "The Lord God of Israel has commanded us to destroy utterly the nation of Amalek."

"My people have lived in Amalek since time was young. We have married their daughters and they have married ours. Their people and mine occupy the land together in peace. But always my people have retained their own identity. You will appreciate this when I tell you how we are called." He paused dramatically, assuring himself that he had their full attention. "We are the Kenites."

Abner and Saul exchanged a swift glance. The king touched his sword with an uncertain gesture. Only Paltiel looked blank and uncomprehending.

The Kenite leader continued. "When Amalek made war on Israel as the Hebrews came up out of Egypt, we refrained from any hostile act. Moreover—"

"We are aware of the deeds of the Kenites," Saul said hastily, uneasily.

The Kenite was not to be put off. "Moreover," he went on, "the father-in-law of Moses, who led the children of Israel out of Egypt, was of our people . . ."

"We know . . ." interjected Saul, but it was all he was able to say.

"Moreover," said the Kenite, rushing ahead in a high-pitched sing-song, "Jael . . . she who hammered a tent pin through the temple of the evil Sisera, whose chariots created such havoc in Israel . . . this same Jael was the wife of Heber the Kenite. Moreover—"

"Enough!" shouted Saul. "You are making my ears ring with all your moreovers."

"Each one is true," observed the Kenite, with a little pious inclination of his head.

As so often happens in moments of strained seriousness, a strange comic overtone was developing. The Kenite, with all his dignity of appearance and manner, was terribly nervous. He knew that, after an impressive start, his speech had run on too long. In his anxiety, seeing that he had begun to annoy Saul, he reached out pleadingly and took the edge of the king's mantle between his thumb and forefinger. Saul, affronted, slapped the hand of the Kenite, who drew back so hurriedly that he lost his balance and almost tumbled over the edge of the incline. Abner looked on impassively, revealing only by a slight twitching of his lips a certain grim amusement. Paltiel's eyes, which tended to bulge even when he was relaxed, nearly bugged out of his head.

"I and my people throw ourselves on your mercy," said the Kenite, attempting to recover his dignity.

Saul said slowly, "The command of the Lord God—"

"We are not Amalekites!" interrupted the Kenite, anticipating Saul's words, again placing himself at a disadvantage. His voice, already pitched too high, had risen until it was almost a screech.

This time Saul did not respond with anger. He stepped close to the edge of the flat space on which they were standing and looked out over the thousands of men, women and children congregated below, silent and waiting. Samuel's command had been unequivocal—every living thing that belongs to Amalek. The Kenites were not of Amalek, but they belonged to the country. If Amalek was to be destroyed, the Kenites must also die: men and women, infant and suckling. This was Saul's responsibility as king.

The wind fell momentarily, rose again. The brassy desert sun was climbing higher in the sky, heating up the already suffocating atmosphere.

Saul turned to the Kenite and, speaking very distinctly, said, "Go, depart, get out from among the Amalekites, lest I destroy you with them. For you showed kindness to all the children of Israel, when they came up out of Egypt." Then he put his hands on the Kenite's shoulders and embraced him.

For a moment after Saul released him, the man seemed incapable of motion. His face was chalk-white, his black eyes glassy. Then he turned slowly until he faced his people, and raised his arms high over his head. The roar which answered the gesture made the ground shudder. After that for an instant there was silence, followed by a new sound, unlike the moaning before, not in any way similar to the great cry of relief which had just ascended into the air. It took the men standing on the summit a few moments to realize that below them on the plain, thousands of people were weeping with joy.

There were also tears in Abner's eyes. When the Kenite had departed down the slope, Abner said to Saul, "My nephew, I am proud to serve you."

Saul took his uncle's hands and held them so tightly that when he let them go the flesh showed white marks.

He turned to Paltiel. "There has been no opportunity until now to thank you for saving me from the fangs of the serpent."

The young captain blushed and said, "Would that I shall always be permitted to help my lord the king, with my own life if need be."

Saul's eyes grew suddenly cloudy. "For what purpose?" he said in a dull voice. He gazed moodily down at the throng of black-robed Kenites, who had turned and were flowing like the waters of some dark sea away from the base of the ridge. Then he took a deep breath. "Come. We have talked enough. We must set about doing what we came to do."

chapter fourteen

ON THE day after Saul granted dispensation to the Kenites, the Israelite army reached the valley which contained the capital of Amalek. There they were greeted with an incredible situation.

The valley had a peculiar shape. At its northern end, where the Hebrews entered, the bordering mountains were widely separated, encompassing a great plain. But from this point, they ran sharply inward, like the legs of a triangle, converging in apex on the southern extremity, where the city was located.

Saul's army advanced carefully, watching the mountains on either side to forestall the possibility of ambush. As the sun began climbing above the heights on the east, a scouting party sent out earlier raced back to the marching Israelites and conferred excitedly with Saul. The king was seen to nod gravely, and the army continued its advance.

Saul distrusted the chariot as an implement of war. For himself, that is. He was well aware of its destructive capabilities, but he preferred to fight on foot. When the army was on the move, he either rode on a donkey or walked with the men. This day he was marching at the head of the vanguard. Suddenly he gave the order to halt. Those in the foremost columns gazed unbelievingly at what they saw.

Far ahead, the floor of the valley slanted upward toward the city walls, so that the capital possessed a commanding view of the entire vast canyon. On this approach to the city, closed in by the cliffs on either side, was massed the host of Amalek: about fifteen thousand men, drawn up in stiff formation, row on row, the backs of the rear guard seeming from this perspective to be pressed up against the very walls of the city.

Saul and Abner considered the situation in hasty council with their captains. Abner was perplexed. "Why should they choose to fight here? Look at those cliffs. There is no escape for them."

The king said gloomily, "The Lord has given us a bitter victory."

"The Lord is all-powerful," said one of the captains, "but I doubt he can make fools of that many fighting men. I believe it's some kind of trick."

"The Lord has given them into our hands," said Saul. There was resignation in his voice.

The captains looked at their leader with some puzzlement. He stood a full head taller than any of them, and in the captured Philistine armor—helmet, breastplate, greaves—he was an impressive figure of a man. Around his waist was buckled a heavy, two-edged sword; in his hand was his massive, metal-tipped spear, which had been filed to gleaming sharpness. His armor-bearer, a young Reubenite, carried his polished shield. To the officers their king epitomized the valiant man of battle. Why then this doleful attitude?

Another captain spoke up. "Perhaps some of their force is hiding just behind the edges of the cliffs. When we march in against the warriors we can see, the others will have us in their power, and we shall be slaughtered."

A third captain said thoughtfully, "If we split our force in three, and send a unit to either side of the cliffs, as we did against Ammon, then even if there are no Amalekite soldiers waiting above—"

Saul cut him off. "We shall advance in one body," he said.

The officers looked at each other, then at Abner, who said, "You have heard the king's order. Obey it."

Paltiel, who had not spoken until now, said, "But surely, if there is no treachery, they would have sent an envoy to us by now. They have no more wish to die than we."

The others shrank into themselves, waiting for Saul's rage to flare out and consume this young upstart who questioned his order. Instead, the king placed his hand on Paltiel's shoulder and spoke kindly to him. "Do not be concerned, lad. Today you shall lead your division to such glory as it has never known."

The words should have been inspiring, should have sent the captains off with the fire of battle in their hearts. But they came from the king's lips in such accents of sadness that all they stimulated was uncertainty. The captains returned to their men stirred by a deep uneasiness.

Abner rode back along the ranks, checking the formations to be sure all was in readiness for the advance. When he saw the wagon in which Rizpah was riding, he pulled over to instruct the driver to remain a safe distance back from the fighting.

"What is it?" asked Rizpah. "What is happening?"

"I'm not sure," replied Abner. "I'm not at all sure. Something altogether strange . . ."

He turned away abruptly and rode back to where Saul was waiting.

The sun was almost overhead. In the distance the city of Amalek shimmered with the dazzling whiteness of a desert mirage. The host of the enemy had not moved.

Israel advanced at the pace set by Saul—such a slow, measured headway that the charioteers had difficulty holding their fidgety steeds in check. The valley narrowed. The mountains on either side seemed to be closing in. Still there was no sign of movement among the Amalekite legions.

The Hebrews were near enough now to see the faces of the enemy. The men of Amalek waited, immobile, helmeted and armored in leather, long spears and wicked-looking swords at the ready. The silence grew oppressive. Even far back in the ranks the Israelite warriors could hear clearly the squeaking noise made by the wheel-and-axle friction of the advancing chariots.

Saul raised his hand. The order to halt was passed down the line. The two armies faced each other.

Abner could now see the full strength of Amalek. Not only did their soldiers outnumber his by more than two to one; they were heavily armed; the ranks of spearmen, swordsmen and archers seemed endless. He felt a sudden chill fear touch his heart. What if Saul's curious and gloomy confidence were misplaced? Perhaps the tactics of the foe were not as suicidal as they appeared. With their overwhelming man power . . .

The only logical maneuver for Israel at this point was to launch a quick, aggressive attack. Abner waited for the king to give the order. But Saul seemed to be paralyzed by some strange reluctance. He stood motionless, staring at the enemy's front lines as if he were searching for something. What?

Then he heard Saul raise his voice and call out, "Men of Amalek! Will you not strike the first blow? You who snapped like jackals at Israel when he came up out of Egypt . . . are you now afraid?"

A low angry murmur ran through the Amalekite ranks, but not one of their soldiers moved. Abner wondered if everyone was mad: Saul, the whole army of Amalek . . .

Saul's powerful voice went forth again, taunting. "Dogs' heads! Spawn of scorpions! Is there not one of you man enough to lift a hand for his country?"

An archer in the second rank drew an arrow from his quiver, fitted it into his bow. In that ocean of immobility the simple movement stood out like the charge of a whole division. But no sooner had the Amalekite drawn the bowstring taut than, unbelievably, the two men on either side of him seized him and tried to restrain him.

For a moment the three remained locked in weird struggle. Then with a strangled cry the first archer flung off the hands of his companions and managed to send an arrow across the stretch of neutral ground into the Israelite ranks. Abner heard the whistling sound of its flight, saw it find a mark in the shoulder of a horse-faced swordsman from Naphtali.

Now at last Saul sprang forward. His order to advance was more inhuman shriek than command. The two armies met head on with a smashing impact that echoed from the walls of the cliffs.

From the beginning, the Israelites fought with an insane fury uncommon to them. The trumpet-blast signal for the charge was lost in the concerted scream of rage which seemed to shake the entire host. And Saul was more possessed than any of his followers. He plunged into the living barrier of the enemy, lips drawn back from his teeth in a bestial snarl, impaling the nearest Amalekite on his spear, flaying about with his sword to kill three others in the first instant of attack.

The Amalekites, on the other hand, seemed victims of an odd lassitude. They fought mechanically, falling back slowly past the bodies of their dead and wounded, toward the walls of their city. Only occasionally would a small company of them make the kind of angry stand that might have slowed the Hebrew juggernaut. Soon the earth over which the battle seethed was stained crimson, strewn with mounting heaps of corpses.

Rizpah, watching from the wagon which had been pulled over close to the base of the palisade, tried to keep track of Saul, but he disappeared very soon into the welter of struggling warriors. She spoke to the driver, a shepherd from Judah who had recently joined the army and had never seen men die in war, urging him to move the wagon in closer to the line of battle. But the man was so terrified that he would neither obey her nor allow her to touch the reins.

She felt quite ill, but the insanity which had hold of the Israelites was also affecting her. She was no longer able to regard even those she had come to know well in any individual perspective. She ground her teeth, feeling the blood lust boil inside her. Had she been able, she would have seized a sword and dashed into the fray. And still, at the back of her brain, the sick horror of war was leaving its indelible imprint: the sight of the chariot knives slashing a gory path through tangles of arms and legs; a warrior clutching his middle with both hands, staring dumbly at his entrails swelling out around them; the fishlike mouth movements of a young soldier dying on the blood-soaked turf, calling out vainly . . . to a mother, a sweetheart, a god?

The sun reached its zenith, began its descent toward the western escarpment. The tide of battle roared on up the valley, rolling ever closer to the walls of the city. Already some of the Israelite units had slashed their way to the gates and were setting fire to them. Smoke rose in a heavy cloud, blew down over the slope where the remnants of the Amalekites were making a token rear-guard stand.

Then, in one of the curious lulls that often settle over a long battle, a small flock of white sheep darted through the still-smoldering entrance to the city. Like tiny clouds fleeing across the vastness of the sky they raced down the hill toward the oncoming Israelites. Terror-stricken, they ran back and forth among the soldiers, some of them brushing against the legs of Saul himself.

One of the Hebrews, bolder than his companions, seized a ram by the horns. The others, remembering Samuel's admonition and the fact that Saul had given no reply to their request for booty, held back, waiting. The king was standing no more than five cubits from the man who had caught the ram. He looked directly at the soldier. Then he turned away almost indifferently and trudged up the hill to join the Israelites who were beginning to enter the city.

There was a shout from the soldiers as they quickly rounded up the rest of the sheep and assigned one of their number to guard them.

The word spread quickly. Saul was allowing Israel to take living spoils from Amalek.

chapter fifteen

SAUL CAME into the tent, which had been set up back at the wide northern entrance to the valley, away from the battlefield where the inevitable vultures were already flocking to their grisly task, away also from the worst of the smoke still rising from the blackened ruins of the city.

His armor was dented in several places and smeared with dried blood. He stripped it off and flung it into a corner. Then he tore at the grimy tunic and let it fall to the floor.

Rizpah brought water and began to sponge the filth from his body. He was breathing heavily, wearily. His eyes were bloodshot and listless. Once he tried to raise his hand to touch her, but the effort was too great. She put her lips to his hair, which was spiky with dried sweat.

Suddenly he stood up, snatched a cloak and wrapped it around himself, reeled out of the tent. She followed, alarmed, and saw him on the ground on all fours, vomiting. Two or three soldiers stood nearby, watching him with the openmouthed intensity of complete exhaustion. She decided she could not go to him while they were present, and waited helplessly, listening to his pathetic retching, until he was able to clamber to his feet and return with her to the tent.

She gave him a cruse of wine. He took a long swallow, then sat very still and let her finish washing him. For a time he did not speak. Then he said, "Every living thing. I have killed every living thing."

She was frightened by the deadness of his voice. It was a sound from the burial caves, from the distant reaches of Sheol. She stroked his cheek, and the contact brightened his eyes briefly, but then they slid back into apathy.

He began to speak again. "We pursued them through the streets of the city. They were all crowded within the walls, all the inhabitants of Amalek. We carved paths with our swords. We killed and slew and murdered. We carried out the commandment of the Lord." His face hardened into desperate lines. She thought for a moment he would weep. "I saw children disemboweled, old men sliced in half. I myself killed a woman big with child."

She felt her own innards contract, but continued to face him, fighting down nausea.

"What does the Lord require of his people?" There were tears in his eyes now. "Is this his loving-kindness we have seen today?" He looked at her, through her. "Rizpah . . . Rizpah . . ." Her name on his lips was pure anguish, at once a plea for help and a warning to her not to help.

She said coolly, impersonally, "My lord Saul, you must rest now."

He shook his head. "Do you know . . . we suffered fewer losses here than we did against Ammon."

He began to laugh, a repetition of the harsh mirth she had heard on only one other occasion, but ragged now, hopeless. She tried to stop him, but the discordant sound grew, rising until its misery filled the tent. He looked at her imploringly. She made a fist and hit him as hard as she could in the face. The laughter ceased.

He rubbed his jaw where her knuckles had struck him. It was all she could do to refrain from gathering his head to her breast, covering his face with kisses.

"Every living thing," he said again, then lapsed into silence.

Through the silence came a sound of bleating and lowing. Saul looked up. For the first time since he had returned from battle, there was a trace of eagerness in his eyes. "I had forgotten," he said, and got quickly to his feet.

Once more she followed him out of the tent. Passing before them was a flock of several hundred sheep, and after these a few score of oxen. Soldiers of Israel crowded in on the animals, jostling each other for the privilege of touching them.

Formerly, many of these same warriors had been shepherds and farmers, prone to chuckle over the immemorial lewd jokes concerning the conduct of lonely men and the flocks they tended. In time they would be again what they once had been.

But now, there was neither coarse comment nor snickering over the sight of men following after the animals with such terrible urgency. All self-consciousness had disappeared in the immediate aftermath of the slaughter they had wrought that day. Most of the men were crying, the tears rolling unheeded down their cheeks. One grizzled Benjaminite, his bare arms still brown with caked blood, pressed his head against the shoulder of an ox, saying over and over again in an awful monotone, "Alive . . ."

Now at last Saul was able to weep, and beside him Rizpah also wept.

They still had tears in their eyes when Abner came to them. Behind him walked two Israelite archers, and between them a fragile, birdlike man.

The archers, Abner explained, had been returning from pursuit of the few Amalekites who had escaped from the corpse-choked alleys and passageways of the city. They had been passing a part of the rock wall which bounded the south rim of the capital when their attention had been caught by the sound of sobbing. Searching for the source of the sound, they discovered an empty cistern in the wall. Hiding inside was the man whom they now had in custody. They had been about to kill him—for they had their instructions: death was the order of the day—when he blurted out his identity.

Abner signaled the archers to release their captive. He came forward slowly. Saul's general said, "This is Agag, King of Amalek."

The over-all impression Agag created was one of dryness. There was dryness in his delicate, slightly shriveled appearance, in his nervous little cough, in the fastidious precision of his movements. Even before he spoke, one knew his voice would be light and brittle, his wit ironic.

For a long moment the two rulers gazed at each other without speaking. Then Agag said, "When I lay in the darkness of the cistern, I was afraid. I am no longer afraid, Saul. Do with me what you will."

Saul said, raising his head defiantly, "The Lord has commanded me to destroy all that lives in Amalek."

The Amalekite king breathed a weary sigh. "Gods," he murmured, making a small gesture of contempt. "They are like capricious women, demanding whatever comes into their minds at a given moment, changing their wishes like gowns, constantly contradicting themselves, but always speaking with that strident, imperious certainness which defies opposition." He sighed again. "My gods told me you were coming. They conferred among themselves and spoke through Avila, the head of the bull. He roared and thundered when I proposed to challenge you at our borders. 'No,' he said, with that terrible air of rightness I was speaking about. 'No. You will draw up your host before the city dedicated to me, before the city of Amalek.' When I suggested in the mildest possible fashion that this might be poor strategy and my army would be bottled up like a beetle in a basin, to use an expression a silly nurse taught me in my childhood, this head of a bull became absolutely furious. He covered my whole body with boils. Look . . ." Agag pulled back the sleeve of his cloak to reveal several ugly sores, just beginning to heal.

He pulled down his sleeve. "What choice did I have? The god Avila said, 'Meet Israel in your own valley, but be sure you are not the one to strike the first blow.'"

"You were, though," said Saul. "Jahveh instructed me to provoke Amalek. One of your archers began the battle."

"So I heard. I must admit that until now I hardly believed it. However, when one thinks about it, what could one expect? All my valiant, loyal warriors . . ." His voice choked up, and he had difficulty continuing. "All my devoted soldiers forced into a space between piles of rock where a city never should have been built in the first place. Why should they not strike first when an invader threatened the land they loved? And then, knowing they had disobeyed the command of Avila, all spirit left them and they were easy prey for the enemy. Gods," he said again. "First they issue a ridiculous, incomprehensible order. Then they attach impossible conditions, so that when the inevitable disaster follows, they have a perfect excuse. I can hear Avila now. 'You did not obey my commandments,' he will bellow in that egotistical voice of his, and I will have no answer, because what he says is true. Tell me, my good colleague from Israel, do you have the same trouble with yours gods?"

"Our God is one," said Saul stiffly.

"So I have heard. Ah well, that's probably a better system in the long run. At least you don't have twenty or thirty to deal with." All at once he closed his eyes and stood quietly for a moment. When he opened them, his expression was haggard. "I have done nothing but talk since they brought me before you. I might tell you the reason is because it is unlikely you will slay me while I am still speaking. The truth is, I am a sorrowing man. I cannot even comprehend the depth of my sorrow. There is a limit to the amount of misery the human spirit can accept, and I have long since passed that point. Draw your sword, and let me join my people."

Saul glanced about the little semicircle of those who surrounded him: Rizpah, Abner, Agag, and a few paces back, the two archers looking on with wide eyes. "There has been enough killing today," he said gently.

"Am I not to die?" asked Agag after a pause.

Saul shook his head.

"Very well." The Amalekite king's smile was twisted and a little melancholy. "Then I must become an impolite guest and ask for food. If I am not to die, I must live. How easily we are bribed into breaking our convenant with the dead. They can no longer feel hunger, and they gaze on us who remain alive with funereal eyes, reproaching us for our rumbling bellies and our watering mouths. But so it is with life, and for the nonce I must turn my back on the dead."

Agag waited for Saul and Rizpah to precede him into the tent. After an instant's hesitation, Abner followed them.

chapter sixteen

The journey back to Gilgal was uneventful, and its pleasantness was enhanced by the company of Agag.

He traveled in the wagon with Rizpah, guarded by a charioteer who rode alongside. It was purely a token security measure. The Amalekite had absolutely no thought of escaping. As he said to Rizpah, "This is my escape. Can you imagine what it would be like for me in that barren kingdom of mine, with the south wind moaning over the bones of the dead, and the fields and pastures parching under the brutal sun, without a living soul to pour water on them? Can you conceive of the wretched loneliness, the self-reproach?"

No one had decided what was to be done with him once they returned to Israel. Abner thought there might be a place for him in the army. Saul was more inclined to the idea of sending him to Ammon to act as governor over the newly conquered land. Agag himself had other plans. "You have spared my life," he said. "Surely that is enough and gives me no prerogative to beg another favor. But . . ." He paused, looking out at the oxen and sheep the Israelites had taken in Amalek. It was evening, and having finished their meal, he, Saul and Rizpah were sitting outside the king's tent enjoying the soft approach of darkness. "There is one thing I have always wanted to do. When I was a child, I used to run away from the palace of my father the king and join the herdsmen on a sheltered slope. All my life I have wanted to care for animals, and instead I was carefully trained to become a shepherd of people. You, my lord," he went on, glancing shrewdly at Saul, "you have been a farmer. Do you never wish to return to the land and deal with growing things rather than the stale and stagnant intrigues of human beings? If you will but allow me a few of the sheep from Amalek and a small portion of ground in some remote province . . ." The smile of pleasure which had been growing on his lips faded. "I have many things to think about. While

I live, I know I can never be free of the presence of those who died before me. If I can face them on a green hillside with my hands holding a shepherd's staff instead of a scepter, perhaps the dead and I can make our peace."

He was seldom openly as somber as this. Most of the time he was an amusing companion who entertained them at every meal with his dry, ironic conversation. Beside him, Saul's lack of humor became even more apparent. But when Agag retired tactfully in the early part of each evening, and Rizpah was alone with Saul, she came to his arms with renewed ardor. For despite Agag's light, bright chatter, his civilized acceptance of human frailty, he seemed to lack some vital ingredient of life. His fragile exterior, so delicately fashioned, yet as she had seen, so tough and unyielding, seemed to be a shell housing . . . nothing. He spoke fervently of searching, but he did not know what it was he sought. He spun words into delightful stories, but his own laughter which followed was mocking. He was a man who understood compassion and feeling, and was sadly aware that he possessed no capacity for them. He was, in the last analysis, a deeply despairing man.

Saul—humorless, often insensitive, given to fits of weakness and bouts of brooding—was still a man, with a man's warmth and tenderness and an abundance of the fantastic male ego that both delights and dismays women. And so, partly because of Agag's presence, Rizpah's love for Saul developed new dimensions and grew even stronger during the march back to Gilgal.

However, she could not help becoming fond of the Amalekite. As the host of Israel crossed from Judah into Benjamin, and the familiar hills took shape in the distance, she told him of her regret that they would not be together much longer.

"Let us have no excessive show of distress, dear lady," he said in his dry voice. "On occasion, you and your king can come to visit me at my hillside retreat. And I shall kill one of my tenderest lambs—no, not kill. I shall never permit that word again in my presence. But we shall eat and drink and look upon the moon and laugh about the freakish animals who walk painfully upright on two legs instead of sensibly on four. No, not laugh. I forget that your king does not laugh. But he is a fine fellow, and I have a high regard for him. And for his land."

So saying, he gazed about him in open admiration of the winter-tinged landscape of Saul's native territory.

It was afternoon when they arrived at Gilgal. There had been rain the night before, but it was clear now, and the breeze that blew from the western hills was refreshing for them after the long trek through the southland.

I greeted Rizpah and asked her to tell Saul that the prophet Samuel was waiting for him. From her startled expression I knew that neither she nor Saul had given the old seer much thought for some time. Therefore, I refrained from telling her what else I knew. The king would learn of it soon enough, and I saw no point in disturbing Rizpah.

Samuel was standing in the center of the circle of stones, his eyes fixed on the altar of God. If he heard Saul's approach, he gave no sign, not turning until the king stood directly behind him. His speech of greeting was deceptively gentle.

Saul said abruptly, in his straightforward fashion, "I have performed the commandment of the Lord."

The prophet looked at him for a long time. And gradually, even with his lack of sensitivity, Saul perceived that Samuel was violently angry.

And he knew in that moment that he had been spinning, all unawares, the threads of his own peril. So, often we move from day to day, closing our eyes and minds to gathering clouds of crisis, reckoning neither profit nor penalty, until the ability to reckon is lost.

Samuel's voice was still quiet. "If you have performed the Lord's commandment, what means this bleating of sheep in my ears, and the lowing of oxen which I hear?"

Saul moistened his lips and said with an attempt at casualness, "My soldiers have brought them from the Amalekites. They spared the best of the sheep and oxen, to sacrifice to the Lord God. And the rest we have utterly destroyed."

The prophet's anger was beginning to show. He mastered it with an effort, but the telltale pulsing materialized under his eye and began its convulsive rhythm. "I will tell you what the Lord said to me."

Saul leaned forward deferentially. "Yes?"

"The Lord sent you on a journey and said: Go and utterly destroy the Amalekite sinners, and fight against them until they are consumed." Now he could control himself no longer. His pale eyes burned. His voice rasped and crackled. "Why then did you not obey the voice of the Lord, but flew upon the spoil, and did evil in the sight of God?"

With the tediousness of a small boy accused of a misdeed who believes that if he repeats a thing often enough and with a wealth of detail, he will develop a logic of innocence, Saul said, "Yes, I have obeyed the voice of the Lord, and have gone the way which the Lord sent me and have utterly destroyed the Amalekites. But my soldiers took some of the spoil . . . sheep and oxen . . . the chief of the things that should have been utterly destroyed, to sacrifice to the Lord God here on this altar in Gilgal."

Samuel drew himself up and thundered, "Does the Lord have as great delight in burnt offerings and sacrifices as in obeying the voice of the Lord? Behold, to obey is better than sacrifice, and to hearken is better than the fat of rams. For rebellion is as the sin of witchcraft, and stubbornness is as iniquity and idolatry." He paused briefly, quivering with rage, then went on more quietly, but venom still dripped from his voice. "Because you have rejected the word of the Lord, he has rejected you from being king."

Saul turned pale and had to take hold of the altar to keep from falling. But he still retained a measure of his strength and dignity as he replied, "True, I have sinned. I have transgressed the commandment of the Lord, because I obeyed the voice of the people instead of God's words." He put out his hand toward the prophet. "Pardon my sin, and help me, so I may again worship the Lord."

"I can neither pardon nor help you."

Samuel turned away and started to leave the sacred circle. With a cry Saul sprang after him and caught hold of the prophet's robe. There was a sickening sound of rending material. Saul released his grasp, horrified.

Samuel's bony shoulder lay bare to the afternoon sunlight. He made no effort to gather the folds of his torn robe about him. With great solemnity he intoned, "As you have torn my robe, so will the Lord tear the kingdom of Israel from you, and give it to a neighbor of yours, a better man than you."

There was a long silence. Then Saul said, conversationally, as if nothing had happened, "Will we prepare the sacrifice now?"

The prophet's tone matched Saul's for unconcern. "Bring me Agag, King of the Amalekites."

Saul, stumbling in his haste to obey, ran to the boundary of the circle and called down into the camp, "Bring Agag here."

Abner brought him. The Amalekite entered the circle of stones, looking around curiously. When he saw Samuel, he stopped dead and said in a restrained voice, "Surely the bitterness of death is at hand." Then he walked calmly forward to stand before the prophet.

Saul looked anxiously from Samuel to Agag, not appearing to understand what was happening. Abner understood. His expression was stricken, helpless.

The prophet stepped to Saul's side. With a quick movement he laid hold of the king's sword, pulled it out of the scabbard. Then returning to Agag, he said, "As your sword has made women childless, so shall your mother be childless among women." And as he spoke, he raised the sword above his head, brought it down with all his force. The blade bit through Agag's skull with a dull crunching sound. The Amalekite crumpled and fell against the altar. Blood spurted onto the rough stones, filled the crevices, flowed onto the ground at the base of the altar. Agag collapsed slowly and lay face down on the earth.

Samuel dropped the sword beside Agag's body. The prophet's color had gone greenish-gray. He turned to Saul, who was standing by, rigid with horror. "I have done what was required of *you* by the Lord. While I live you shall not look on me again."

Having spoken, he turned and strode away without looking back.

chapter seventeen

THE NIGHT began no differently than any of the fourteen they had passed together since Agag's death.

Rizpah was sitting on the couch, cushions piled behind her back, working over a piece of embroidery. She did not have to bend toward the lamp. There was plenty of light in the tent. Nowadays Saul insisted at the first sign of dusk that a score of lamps be set blazing, and even these he complained were not enough.

He sat in the great wooden throne-chair the brothers from Asher had fashioned for him. He was wearing his resplendent purple cloak. He had taken to wearing it most of the time. A month ago she would have been happy about this. Now it depressed her.

As usual, he was mumbling to himself. He would go over campaign plans which even Rizpah knew sounded grandiose. Or he would recite bits from the day's litigations he had heard. This latter was an innovation since the departure of Samuel. Saul was now the sole judge in both military and civil disputes. He took his position seriously, listening patiently to rambling accounts of grievances, handing down decisions. It was while he was acting as mediator that he presented his best face, both to strangers and those who knew him well. Rizpah would sit by, admiring the logic of his questions, which pierced subterfuge and turned up untruth. But when darkness fell and they were left alone, his muttered repetitions made a mockery of the day's brilliant performance.

She was so accustomed by now to the incoherent mouthings that she had succeeded in shutting them out of her consciousness. Saul would sit babbling of extending the kingdom of Israel from the northern mountains of Ararat to the dark kingdom of Cush, far to the south of Mizraim, land of the Pharaohs. Or he would speak of disputed sheep or contested ground, assuming the roles of both judge and litigants. Until finally it was late enough for her to suggest retiring. Then, beside him on the silken couch, she would touch him and soothe him to silence, so they were both able to sleep with some degree of tranquillity.

This night, not having listened to the words he had been speaking, she did not notice their absence. It was more the feeling of his eyes on her that drew her gaze away from the lulling comfort of fingers, needle and cloth.

He was watching her thoughtfully, almost tenderly. Her heart skipped in sudden joy. She thought: he is coming out of it; the worst of the shock from Agag's death is over; he will be himself again.

"Rizpah," he said. "My love . . ."

"Yes, my lord?" Wait. Do not go to him yet. Let him ask you to come. Then go and let the healing benison of lips and hands do their work, let love place balm on terror . . .

"I wish to speak with the prophet Samuel. Tell the guard outside the tent to seek him and request him to come here."

She could do nothing about the bitter little sigh that fluttered out of her and lay resigned between them. "Samuel is not here."

"Not here?" The piteous incomprehension of a child.

She forced herself to be patient. "He is no longer in the camp of Israel."

His bafflement began to dissolve with a return of memory. "No," he said. "Samuel has deserted me. He has abandoned the king and his people." He raised his hand to his mouth, nibbled at the thumbnail. "Agag was not an evil man. It was his forefathers who dealt wickedly with Israel. But Samuel killed him. He struck him down with my sword." He waited, then said in a cold, spiteful voice, "The sword I should have used when they brought him to my tent in Amalek."

"Saul . . ."

"What is the matter with you? Why are you wailing at me?"

"I'm not wailing . . ."

They would quarrel. There was nothing she could do to prevent it.

Nor was she sure she wanted to avert what was coming. The past couple of weeks had worn her nerves too thin for tact.

His expression grew crafty. "I shall go to Gibeah soon."

"Why?"

"Are you an idiot? My wife is there. I have not seen her for too long."

"She seems to have survived without you."

"She is a patient woman. She understands that someone has poisoned me with wickedness. She will help me purge the evil from my heart."

"She does not love you. She doesn't know how to love you."

He got up from the throne chair and came over to her, slowly and deliberately. "And you call the things you do love." His laughter was harsh, frightening. "Love. The soft fingers. The tip of a tongue. The lips that know how to provoke a man until he loses his senses. Things someone can find behind the curtained doorways of any city, as long as he has a piece of silver to spend."

"Can your Ahinoam give as much?"

"She gives herself honestly. She does not come sneaking into a man's life with thieving hands, stealing his heart, pretending . . ."

Tears of rage were hot in her eyes. "Your Ahinoam is a prissy bitch. She would give her soul to be able to charm just one man. Or even a young boy. She would play the wanton with every male in Israel if—"

"She does not pretend to love in order to provide luxury for herself." He reached past her, tore down one of the satin hangings, and with unhurried thoroughness ripped it to shreds. "Does that turn your love cold? If I tear up another, will your body turn to ice? What will it take to thaw you then? One satin cushion? Two silk gowns? If some rich merchant promises you three jingling bracelets, will you spread your legs for him? The way you did for the Philistine pigs? Will you?"

She was on her feet now, grinding her teeth, her eyes narrow slits. Her voice was low, scathing. "The Seren of Askelon was a man. He was no infant, bawling and whining at every unkind word. He was not like you. He was a man." She threw back her head and screamed at him. "He was a man!"

His hands were on her arms, pinning them to her sides, crushing her. He lifted her, held her in the air and began to shake her. Her head snapped back and forth.

"Whore! Dirty filthy lying whore! You've taken my kingdom from me! You've stolen my life!"

He threw her onto the couch. Her head thudded into one of the cushions and she bit her tongue. The pain was unbearable. She tried to get up and strike out at him, but he was too quick. The flat of his hand caught her across the face, then the knuckles on the return swing. Consciousness fled, returned, then faded again.

It was quiet in the tent now.

She blinked her eyes to focus them. He was standing before her, hands at his sides, mouth hanging loose.

She sat up gingerly. Her whole body was aching, and she would be covered with bruises. But nothing was broken. At least nothing seemed to be.

Saul sank to his knees. His lips barely moved as he said, "What have I done? What have I done?"

The anger was gone out of her now. She made a wry face. "You very nearly killed me."

Her words acted on him like an astringent. His eyes cleared. "I don't know what happened. All at once . . . Rizpah, are you all right?"

"I think I will be."

She was glad that he did not fawn on her, or become effusive with remorse.

He said simply, "I'm sorry."

"I should not have said the things I did. They were not true."

"Nor was what I said."

"You *are* a man. My man. The only one I've loved. The only one I want to love."

The language of reconciliation, ritualistic, patterned as a prayer.

They dared to touch each other now. She winced when his fingers brushed her jaw. He drew them away hastily. She reached out and brought them back, bracing herself against the pain.

"Something is happening to me," he said. "Something I cannot understand. The demons have taken possession of my soul."

"You have been struggling against the demons for a long time, my lord."

He shook his head. "It's different now. I can't explain. Sometimes it's black, so black I can scarcely see. Then the red. Also blinding, but choking as well. There is nothing I can do. Nothing." He was quiet for an instant. Then he said, his words bitter and malignant, "I wish I had never been made king."

"The people want you to be king. They respect and love you. They are grateful for what you have done for them."

He repeated obstinately, "I wish I had never been made king."

She hesitated. Then, "Will you go away with me, my lord?"

He looked at her without replying. But she could tell he was weighing her words, waiting for her to continue.

"Zaccur has told me a great deal about the territory of Dan. How the mountains rise to the north, placid and snow-capped. How in the spring the snows melt and bring cascades of clear water off the slopes, down to fertile fields and rich orchards. We could go there, my lord. You and I could go there. We could work together on the land. We could have our vineyards and our flocks . . ."

She stopped speaking. He was frowning.

He said, "Ahinoam . . ."

"Of course, my lord. She is your wife."

"There is nothing in the law of Israel," he said musingly, "that forbids a man to have two houses. One could be close by the other . . ."

"Not too close," she said, laughing, at the same time watching him carefully.

But he was no longer thinking about Ahinoam. "I have heard much of Dan. I have heard of its beauty, and the richness of its soil."

She saw in his eyes a reflection of the idyll she had conjured up for them. How beautiful it would be to have him to herself. To wake in the morning and to know that the day belonged to them. Not to Israel. Not to battle or strife or uncertainty. To them alone. She envisioned a quiet river flowing through a fruitful valley, the waters giving back the image of lacy clouds. The old shepherd's song she had learned in childhood: He leadeth me beside still waters . . .

Saul shook his head, a man emerging from a dream. Her dream. She followed him out of it, listened to the words he was saying. "No, my love. Jahveh has anointed me king. Even though Samuel, who poured the oil over my head and gave me the Lord's blessing . . . even though he has gone . . . even though he has said the kingdom will be taken from me . . . I am still king. No matter where I fled, no matter where I lived, I would still remember the day of my anointing. The odor of the oil and the memory of the blessing would haunt my life and drive me to a shameful grave."

She smiled, surprised at the sudden relief flooding through her. "So be it, my lord."

He sighed. She knew she should tell him now. "I am going to have your child."

She had not meant to phrase it quite so bluntly, but when she saw his response she knew it would not have mattered how she told him. His face was radiant, transfigured as it had not been even during their fantasy of flight.

There was no necessity for them to speak.

In the darkness she held him close and breathed, "Let it be a son. I want so much to have your son."

And she fell asleep, happy.

But later she awakened to the sound of muffled sobbing. There was only one lamp still burning, at the far end of the tent. Saul was sitting on the edge of the couch, his face in shadow. She touched his arm.

He turned, and as the wan light fell across his features, she recoiled at what she saw.

His voice was a grating whisper, "Let us tremble. For you carry within you the seed of a madman."

chapter eighteen

SHE THOUGHT she would never be able to stop retching.

Her face was streaming perspiration; she could feel the strands of hair plastered to her forehead, but she had no energy to brush them back.

Another wave of nausea swept over her and she leaned toward the basin, gripping the sides of the stand, powerless to control the convulsive heaving. Her throat was raw; she could taste the bitterness of bile.

At length it was over. She stood in the curtained-off section of the tent, gathering her strength. She had been sick almost every morning since the second month of her pregnancy. I kept assuring her that, now as she was entering her fifth month, the period of illness would soon end. I had no idea if it really would, but my words gave her hope.

She came out of the cubicle into the main part of the tent, intending to lie down for a while. When she saw the figure of a woman facing away from her into a corner, she thought I had returned sooner than expected from fetching water, and she said wearily, "It seems to get worse."

The woman turned. Rizpah saw with a sense of shock that it was Ahinoam. Saul's wife was smiling. "It will not last," she said. "Now that you are in the fifth month, all this will soon end."

She used almost exactly the same words I had spoken to Rizpah, but far from giving her any comfort, they sent her into a blind rage. She was mortified that Ahinoam had heard the sound of her retching, resentful that her disheveled appearance should be exposed to the older woman's cool gaze. And as often happened with Rizpah, anger drove her naturally low voice even lower, gave it a cruel edge. "You and your daughter," she said, "seem to regard my privacy as a mat on which you can trample at will."

Ahinoam said, "I apologize for trespassing. It is only the urgency of my visit which makes me bold enough to intrude."

"If your purpose in coming is the same as it was before, my answer has not changed."

"Has it not, Rizpah? Then I am glad."

Ahinoam had not spoken ironically. Rizpah stared at her, confused. At the same time she was becoming conscious that something about Ahinoam's appearance had changed since she had seen her last. Her hair was more liberally streaked with gray, but it was not only this. Nor was it the dark circles under her eyes, which had the effect of making the eyes themselves seem larger, more luminous. Rather it was some sense of unsureness communicating itself from her whole person. Her serenity of manner was still present, but beneath it was a tentativeness, an uncertainty verging on fear.

Ahinoam continued speaking. "I have not come now to ask you to give up Saul. And this time no one has sent me."

Puzzled, and unable to maintain anger in the face of Ahinoam's calm, Rizpah was also mistrustful. She probed for an advantage. "I understand you've not been well. It's dreadful the way some illnesses leave a person drawn and tired-looking for months afterward."

Ahinoam brushed this aside. "I'm well enough again. It's not myself I've come to talk about. Saul . . ." She paused. Again the impression of uncertainty emanated from her, so strongly that Rizpah could feel its physical presence. "Since Samuel left . . ."

"Saul was unsettled by the killing of Agag," Rizpah said hastily. "He had fought two arduous campaigns immediately before, and the senseless execution sickened him. He will recover soon enough."

"Will he?"

The woman's quiet sadness was maddening. Perhaps this was because Ahinoam was giving voice to doubts Rizpah herself had felt for so long. She waited before replying, finding a mirror and peering into it critically as she arranged her hair. She decided there was no profit in the pretense that all was well with Saul. Possession was both her weapon and her security, and she set about using it. "I have seen his illness grow. I know its nature, and I shall battle it in my own way."

"You are wrong, my dear, about at least one thing. *I* have seen Saul's illness grow. You have only watched its evil flowering. This has been, I am sure, a terrible thing for you. I have been to see Saul this morning, and my heart wept at what I witnessed. But I believe that together we can help the king and free him of the demons which have invaded his soul and threatened the welfare of Israel."

"How would you help?"

Ahinoam's hand had wandered to her ear in her habitual gesture of strained attentiveness. She ignored the brusqueness in Rizpah's question and said, "Long ago, before the Lord elected Saul to his heavy responsibility, when he was still able to delight in the tender shoots of a furrowed field, even then the blackness would descend on him and send him plunging beyond reach of every human voice. But always without fail a few days of ease among his own vineyards and orchards . . ."

"You want to take him to Gibeah?"

"Would it not be wiser? You could both come. Here in the shadow of the stones of Joshua, tormented by constant reminders of Samuel's rejection, he has little chance of regaining the strength he needs. In Gibeah . . ."

"Can he rule Israel from Gibeah?"

"Can he rule Israel here in his present condition?"

Ahinoam had logic on her side, of course. Rizpah realized this, and in desperation began, "You think a few days in Gibeah would cure him. You speak of knowing how he is. How can you know?" What she had intended as a simple refutation was rapidly slipping toward tirade. "Have you seen him rise up in his bed and converse with the dead? Have you heard him speaking with Agag and the pregnant woman he killed in Amalek? Have you seen his face go sly and furtive and heard his lunatic laughter while he hoards and gloats over a bit of dirty cloth, a scrap of leather found in the refuse heap? Have you stood over him while he cries for hours without knowing why? Have you watched suspicion corrupt his love for those who serve him, until he feels each sentry is a spy and his young armor-bearer a Philistine general?" She stopped, experiencing a grim satisfaction in having shaken Ahinoam. The older woman's hand fell from her ear in a bereft, unbelieving gesture. Rizpah stepped close to her and, feeling spent and ineffectual, asked quietly, "Have you ever had to struggle against all these things?"

"I would like to."

Ahinoam's serenity was returning. The great almond eyes gazed into Rizpah's with deep sincerity. Rizpah knew she could no longer regard this woman simply as an adversary, someone to be outwitted in an endless tactical conflict for Saul's affection.

She took Ahinoam's hands in hers. "We could never join forces.

Too many things hold us apart. Each of us believes she has a claim on Saul, and each of us is right. But for just this reason we could never agree on what is best for him. We should end by battling over his spirit, and the only victor would be the virulence which is even now overwhelming him. I must do what I can alone."

Ahinoam's eyes filled with tears. "Once I could have spoken those same words. I no longer can. That power is yours now."

Is it? Rizpah wondered. For a second time, she had defeated Ahinoam. To what avail?

Saul's wife embraced her. Together they went out of the tent. The first breath of spring was beginning to stir among the trees of Gilgal. Fresh green grass was growing at the feet of the sacred stones.

Jonathan came running along the path from the camp, his blond hair flying in the wind. He kissed his mother, then looked questioningly at both women.

"He is worse than I have ever seen him," said Ahinoam. "You must help Rizpah to help him."

Jonathan nodded and said to Ahinoam, "I shall walk a little way with you."

Rizpah watched them going toward the place where the donkeys were tethered. She felt lonely and resourceless. Perhaps, after all, she should allow Ahinoam . . .

She shook her head, dispelling the thought, and walked toward Saul's tent.

The air inside was stagnant and foul-smelling. Saul alternated between insisting on excessive air and light, and banishing it altogether.

He was sitting, as he did most of the time, in the carved wooden chair. His spear lay close beside him. She went to him, quelling her uneasiness, and put her hand on his brow. He reached up to touch her fingers, and she felt an absurd surge of hope. It was the first sign of affection he had shown in weeks.

"Rizpah . . ."

"Yes, my lord?"

"I have been thinking."

What to say to this? "Have you?"

"One thinks a great deal, sitting here as I do."

"You should come with me, my darling. Spring is in the hills. We could ride out over the land as we used to do."

His expression was wistful, turning to eagerness. "It would be comforting to see the greenness spreading, to feel the first faint warm breeze, and to know that soon the leaves will emerge, tiny and furled, then glossy and luxuriant . . ."

"Then you'll come?"

"To ride with you across the fields of Benjamin. Perhaps to find another vineyard like the one we once found, another place where we can be peaceful and undisturbed."

"Oh my dearest one, I love you so. Come. Come now. We'll go together and . . ."

He put his fingers over her lips, very gently. "There is too much to think about."

"It can wait. Later you can think. When you're refreshed."

"I must think now. Do you believe he's really the one?"

"Who? Which one?"

"Samuel said my kingdom would be taken from me and given to a neighbor of mine. A better man than I. Do you think he's the one?"

"My lord . . ."

"Answer me, Rizpah. I asked you a question and I demand an answer. Is he the one?"

"But I don't know . . ."

"Abner!"

She stood in shocked silence. The furtive look was stealing over his face again. "So, I was right. He *is* trying to usurp my kingdom."

"My lord, Abner is the most loyal, devoted servant . . ."

"And you're in league with him!" His voice sharpened. "I knew you were. From the moment he brought you here, that's what you both had in mind. Plotting, conniving, meeting each other in the dead of night after I'm asleep." He rose from the throne, towering above her. "You'll never do it! Abner will never be king! I, Saul, will reign forever. And as for you . . ."

She knew the blow was coming, as she had known on other occasions. She was waiting for it. Her head rang with the force of it.

They stared at each other. All recognition had fled from his eyes. He sank back into the chair. Weeping, she leaned over and kissed him. He did not move.

Then, having paid the price of admission to his presence, she turned and left the tent.

chapter nineteen

How SHALL I write of the events that followed?

How can I chronicle a thing so monstrous that even the scribes of David, with their innate prejudice against Saul, have only alluded to it obliquely? I might add that if the matter had actually concerned David they would have described it fully enough, distorting it cleverly in his favor, as is their custom. But my animosity in this case would be only a temporizing, a reluctance on my part to set down what I must. For shame or no, I have vowed to record her story as it happened.

This was a time when I came closest to hating her, yet understood and loved her best.

The day began innocently enough, even hopefully. Two months had passed since Ahinoam's visit to Gilgal, when she and Rizpah reached an understanding. Rizpah was now in the last stages of her pregnancy. Her morning sickness had finally ceased, but I was greatly concerned over a more serious menace to her health. She was pale and tense, with the blue splotches under her eyes that with Rizpah are a sure sign of malaise. Her face was puffy from lack of sleep, and it was all I could do to make her eat even a little food.

The difficulty lay in her fanatic solicitude for Saul.

There had been little or no improvement in the king's condition. He sat day after day in his throne chair, stuporous, malevolent and cringing by turns. Rizpah would lead (and sometimes drag) him from his couch in the morning and put him back to bed at night. She tended him constantly: feeding him, trimming his beard, changing and washing his clothes, which were often as not befouled. She would speak to him soothingly when he raged, hold him close to her when he wept. And for all her pains she would usually receive a cuff or a slap from Saul—or worse, and more frequently, the indifferent stare of insanity.

In spite of this, she insisted on nursing him herself, rejecting offers of assistance from Abner, Jonathan and me.

Abner, however, did take over complete administration of the army and civil affairs. It was he who now sat in the seat of judgment, hearing disputes and rendering decisions. He had little of Saul's flair for interrogating witnesses and ferreting out misstatements, but his word was fair and respected. Saul's general went to great lengths to inform all concerned that he was only acting in a caretaking capacity and that he would immediately surrender all his new functions the moment the king's health was restored.

In truth, he went too far in this direction, at what might be termed the peril of Israel. Moab, lying on the eastern shores of the Dead Sea, had become emboldened by reports of Saul's incapacity and was sending small test forces into Reuben and as far north as Gad. It was long past time to take action. But Abner postponed from week to week the dispatching of a punitive expedition, holding that his temporary authority did not extend to launching a campaign against a foreign state.

So, during that spring, the kingdom of Israel limped along, not sacrificing too much of the progress it had made in consolidating the twelve tribes, but certainly not displaying much evidence of positive activity.

The morning of which I speak dawned clear and warm, giving promise of an unseasonably sultry day.

I had been successful in convincing Rizpah she should rest in her own tent for at least a few hours each night, but she was usually up and on her way to Saul as soon as the sky showed its first streaks of light. This particular morning she was still sleeping at daybreak. So the sun was well up by the time she walked through the long shadows cast by the sacred stones. She entered the king's tent and stopped short.

Saul was pacing back and forth across the carpeted floor, fresh-faced and vigorous. When he saw her he almost ran to take her in his arms.

She could hardly breathe with the suddenness of her joy. "My dearest . . ." was all she could say, murmuring it over and over.

Finally he said, "I was just about to come seek you. I have never been so ravenously hungry."

"And I am just what you had in mind to eat," she said, feeling lighthearted and frivolous.

He regarded her unsmilingly. "I wanted to have my breakfast *with* you."

She burst into laughter. "Oh my lord, you *are* yourself again."

They had fresh figs and curds and lentils and eggs poached in oil. It was more food than either of them had eaten at a single meal for months.

Saul pushed his plate away, sighed with satisfaction and said, "Now tell me, my love, what has happened during all the time I've been away on my journey."

She said "Journey . . ." tonelessly and let her spoon clatter onto the plate, picked it up with a mumbled apology and dropped it again. He was on his feet instantly, around the table and onto the bench beside her before she was aware of what was happening.

"Are you all right, my darling?"

"Are *you* all right?"

"You're so pale. And your eyes. Why have you not been taking care of yourself? Do you want my son to be sickly?"

She felt the color coming back to her face. "Are you so sure it's a son?"

"What man isn't?" He stroked her hair. "I asked you what happened while I was away. That was foolish of me. I should have known that where I was, you were with me. Not all the way. I would not wish any human being the tortures of that land of darkness." He brought her head around until he was looking directly into her eyes. "But there were times . . . when there was blackness all about me, except for a horizon red-rimmed with fire . . . and the voices would shriek in my ear . . . and the shape of the demons, gray-winged and brooding, their eyes burning coals, and their nails sharp as dagger points raking across my heart . . ."

"Saul, stop!"

"I want to tell you. Because I want you to know that I know." He gazed at her fondly. "Through all the darkness, through all the horror, there were times when I could see your face. Not always, but sometimes. And then the pain would cease, and for a little while I could push back the gray-winged monsters." His expression grew suddenly anxious. "You *were* with me . . ."

"I was with you."

"Thank you, my love. I will not ask you about the misery I must have caused you. Not just yet. But I am sorry for it, even if it was slight, and I know it could not have been that."

"It doesn't matter now."

"We shall speak of it again. We must." He kissed her. "Now," he said briskly, "tell me first what month and day it is, then what has been happening. I have a feeling there is much to do."

She told him about Moab.

"We shall deal with them at once," he said. "They are like the crawling things that slither from under rocks at night. We shall turn the rays of the sun on them. Now. Who has been acting as judge in my place?"

The pulse began pounding in her temples. She swallowed, took a breath and said, "Abner."

A shadow crossed his face. She watched him intently, waiting for his eyes to go blank, his lips to become serpentine with rage. But he only nodded curtly. "Splendid. But my uncle already has enough to do as general of the army. I shall also have to make amends to him for the extra burden he has carried for my sake. And the best way to begin is by hearing cases myself. This very morning."

"My lord, do you think . . ."

"I think it is time I showed my face in the camp of Israel. Lest they have forgotten they have a king. Then, if you like, you shall sit and hear me render judgment."

The first case was a dispute between a merchant from the village of Adummim and a shepherd who had been bringing some of his flock to market. The merchant claimed the sheep had run untended among his wares and had broken a number of pieces of expensive pottery. The shepherd, who was not very bright and was also frightened by the merchant's use of words he did not understand, could only look around vacuously at those assembled for the hearing and mumble a few words in broad Judahite dialect. Saul questioned him patiently, and it became apparent that his sheep had indeed damaged the merchant's property. It seemed a fairly clear case in favor of the merchant. But Saul was not satisfied. He quizzed the merchant relentlessly, and eventually discovered that the man had borne a grudge against the shepherd since the previous year, when they had squabbled over the favors of a serving-wench in the village. He forced the merchant to admit that perhaps he had frightened the sheep with overloud shouting and violent gestures as they came abreast of his stall.

Saul dismissed the case amid hearty acclaim from the company. Ordinarily only a few persons attended the litigations, mainly friends and relatives of the disputants. Today, Abner and all of Saul's captains of thousands were present, and as many of the captains of hundreds as could crowd into the tent of judgment. Word of Saul's recovery had spread rapidly through the encampment, and the joy of the men almost equaled Rizpah's happiness. They had come to the judging chiefly for the pleasure of seeing their leader miraculously in repossession of his vitality and acumen.

Now, watching him dispose so efficiently of the matter of the merchant and the shepherd, even those who had doubted the good news were filled with gladness. They called out words of praise and tried to catch Rizpah's eye, seeking by ridiculous winking grimaces to show her how delighted they were. Every one of them was aware of the price her long vigil had extracted from her, and each wanted to add some little tribute to her moment of victory. She smiled back at them, sitting glowing and placid, at the edge of the crowd, her hands crossed composedly and resting on the swelling curve of her belly.

She was thinking: how remarkable it is that a man like Saul, devoid of two of the most necessary components of life, sensitivity and humor, should be able with such economy of effort to strip falsehood from human intention. Then, watching the merchant slink from the judgment tent, babbling incoherently, his expression compounded of cunning and wrath, she came to a disturbing conclusion. Saul's gift for uncovering motive stemmed from his madness. Having himself sojourned in darkness, he possessed an uncanny knowledge of the darkness in others. For does not most chicanery ferment and reach maturity in the fetid, lightless corners of the mind? As it is written: madness cries out to the insane, and the words of the deceitful confound all but the demented.

She looked at Saul now. He was calling for the next case in the firm, authoritative voice she had waited so long to hear again. She breathed a prayer of thanks to Jahveh that her man had returned from the land of the living dead.

A Gibeonite and a farmer from the territory of Ephraim came forward to stand before the king. Their contention was a question of boundaries. The Ephraimite claimed that, while he was observing the Lord's sabbath by rest as is prescribed, the man of Gibeon had moved the piles of stones dividing their farms a distance of some eight cubits to his own advantage. The defendant denied this in a loud, complaining voice.

The Gibeonites were not of the tribes of Israel. Joshua had found them living in Canaan when the Hebrews arrived after their historic exodus from Egypt. It is recorded that they negotiated a treaty with Israel by questionable means: pretending to Joshua that they came from a distant land, when in reality their settlement was just a short distance north of Mizpeh, the village where generations later Saul was formally chosen king. They obtained their treaty, but as payment for their trickery, they were committed eternally to the task of hewing wood and drawing water in the service of the Lord. However, the ancient edict had long since been relaxed, and most of the Gibeonites earned their livelihood side by side with the people of Israel as merchants, shepherds and farmers. They were a peaceable group, predominantly fair haired and hazel eyed, and their only claim to distinction was a love for protracted debate on any subject. It is said that a Gibeonite will take either side of an argument, pursue it at length, and if he finds he is winning, switch without the slip of a word to the opposite side.

The Gibeonite now standing before Saul was an eager exponent of the art of dispute. He could scarcely wait for the Ephraimite to finish a sentence before he burst out with a long-winded refutation. Several times Saul cautioned him to respect the decorum of the court, but the Gibeonite was irrepressible. It was clear that he either believed passionately in his case or was efficiently pursuing the maxim about an offense being the strongest defense.

After more than an hour of wrangling, during which Saul grew increasingly irritated, the Ephraimite said, "If it please my lord the king, I can give positive evidence that this person moved the boundary stones, as I have stated."

Saul leaned forward and addressed the plaintiff formally. "Say on."

"At the edge of my property is an ash tree. It is of ancient origin. My father's father cut from it a staff which my son still uses today in herding our few sheep and goats. That tree was a full cubit within the line of my land. Yet now it stands well beyond the stones this person moved."

The Gibeonite could not contain himself. He jumped up and down, first on one foot, then the other, shouting, "This is a patent, outrageous lie. Which ash tree? There are many such in our region. I can prove without a shadow of doubt that this tree to which he refers is the same under which my father wooed my mother many years ago."

There was a round of snickering from the captains, then outright laughter as the Gibeonite turned on them with an affronted expression.

Saul, as usual unaffected by any note of levity, pointed his finger at the Gibeonite and boomed, "You will be silent until you are asked to speak!"

"My lord," said the Gibeonite, "you have given this prevaricator the privilege of speaking whenever he wishes. I demand for myself the same right, in the name of justice, which so far has not been dispensed."

A shocked silence greeted this impertinent outburst. The captains moved about uneasily. Even the Gibeonite, realizing he had gone too far, made an abortive gesture of apology. Everyone waited for the storm which was certain to burst over the man's head.

But Saul did not even reprimand him. Instead, while the audience looked on in horror, the king's jaw grew suddenly slack. Rizpah saw his eyes slide back and forth between anger and the dreadful vacancy she now knew so well. She half rose from her seat, sank back again, waiting, hoping. Saul opened his mouth to speak, but no words came out. A pitiful cry, abject as the howl of a pariah dog, flew over the heads of the assemblage.

The captains averted their eyes from Saul's face. Two of the subordinate officers made for the doorway of the tent, upsetting a bench in their haste. The Ephraimite and his Gibeonite opponent drew close together, until their trembling hands were almost touching.

Just as Rizpah was getting up to go to Saul, Abner moved forward. In his melodious, courteous voice, speaking as calmly as if nothing untoward had happened, he said, "This case will require the king's further attention at his leisure. Judgment will be reserved until tomorrow or the following day. There will be no more cases heard this morning."

The spectators filed out of the tent, too dismayed by what they had seen and heard even to murmur among themselves. Abner and Rizpah were left alone with Saul. No words passed between them. After a moment Abner also departed.

Rizpah led Saul to his own tent. It was not an easy task. The king stumbled and almost fell several times, whimpering as he lurched against Rizpah. Some of the officers who had attended the judgment session were still standing by and sprang forward to assist her, but she warned them away with her eyes. She and Saul continued their painful trip unaided.

Eventually they reached the tent. Rizpah helped him to the couch, where he lay, weeping inconsolably. She sat beside him, remembering her delirious happiness of a few hours before. Her eyes were hard and hopeless now. Soon he would stop crying. Then he would either sit staring at nothing until nightfall, or fly into his customary rage and strike her. Everything would be just as it had been.

Saul sat up. Rizpah went to get a cloth to wipe his face. When she returned to the couch, she stood absolutely still, feeling all at once that she would faint.

His face was still flabby and frightened, but his eyes were not dead. They looked at her imploringly. He stretched out his hand to her.

She sat down beside him carefully, so as not to frighten him more. For a moment she wished he had gone directly into a stupor. She did not know how to cope with this shell of a man whose soul was pouring out before her.

She took his hand in hers. The contact seemed to reassure him. His lips quivered a little less.

"What is happening to me, Rizpah? What have I become?"

The words struck aside the skimpy armor she had so laboriously set around her, and pierced her heart. It was all she could do to keep from bursting into tears. "You will be well again, my love. We shall destroy the demons together."

"But what shall I do? I could not even hear a dispute without . . . What shall I do?"

All the strain, all the impotence, suddenly focused in a flash of anger. She cried, "He should be punished! The Gibeonite swine should be severely chastised! He was insolent to the king of Israel, and he should pay for it!"

She knew the instant she had spoken that it was the wrong thing to say. Why, she was not sure, but there was something odd about the way Saul's face was turned toward her, seeming to drink in every syllable she uttered. She watched with a fascination which sent a chill along her backbone as the king rose slowly to his feet. She saw the resolve come back to his eyes, his mouth, the lines of his body.

"You are right," he said. "You are absolutely right. He and his tribe have always been a thorn in the side of Israel. They are treacherous. They came to Joshua in old garments, carrying moldy bread, pretending to come from afar. So they won their deceitful peace. And now they do the same with us. . . ."

He strode to the door of the tent. She followed him, asking anxiously, "What, my lord? What are you going to do?"

Saul did not answer her. He said to the guard outside, "Send me the soldier Bela."

When the one-eyed man arrived, glancing curiously around the tent with his peculiar, flickering gaze, Saul said at once, "You will go and find the Gibeonite who pleaded in judgment this morning. You will place him under arrest."

"Very good, my lord."

"When you have done this, you will speak to Paltiel, son of Laish, and ask him to give you a hundred men. You will leave at once and proceed by quick march to the city of Gibeon. How long do you estimate it will take you to reach there?"

"Let me see, my lord . . ." Bela launched into one of the rambling discourses to which he was addicted. "Some of the country between here and Gibeon is over quite rough terrain. But other parts of the road are passably smooth and level. If we go . . ."

"How long?"

Bela snapped to attention. "By quick march, no more than four hours."

"Good. You will be there by midafternoon. You will round up as many Gibeonite males as you can find before nightfall. You will return with them at once."

Bela raised his hand, nervously fingered the flesh around his gaping eye socket. "Begging your pardon, my lord, but it would be wiser not to march with captives at night."

"Of course. Take them far enough from the city so you will not be plagued with the presence of their women and children. At dawn begin your march back to Gilgal."

"Yes, my lord." He hesitated. "They will ask why they are being . . ."

The crafty look stole across Saul's face, but now there was strength behind it. "If you do not know, you will not be able to tell them. This is the way I prefer it."

"And I am to be in charge of the hundred soldiers?"

"In complete charge."

Bela repressed a smile of pleasure and repeated, "In complete charge."

"That is all. Do everything exactly as I have ordered."

When Bela had gone, Saul paced back and forth for a few moments, then sat down in the throne chair. Even early in the day, when he first emerged so vigorously from the labyrinth of his illness, he had not appeared so regal, so fully in command of himself and his surroundings.

Rizpah went to him. She had to know. "Saul . . ."

"They will be here by noon tomorrow."

There was no way of asking subtly. "What will you do?"

"An example. An example must be made. The authority of the king cannot be challenged."

"The Gibeonites . . ."

"Will be executed."

She stared at him, not sure for an instant that she had heard correctly. But then she knew it was the reply she had been expecting.

Her silence disturbed him. His feet began to move in a curious shuffling motion on the carpeted floor. "It is necessary to do this." A pause, and again, "It is necessary."

His newly gained assurance was slipping. She watched his mouth starting to work, the distant look gathering in his eyes. The pleading voice. "Rizpah . . ."

It was a moment of balance. She knew Saul would listen to her, heed what she said. In effect, the decision had passed from his hands to hers.

There should have been no question about her reply. Under ordinary circumstances there would not have been. But under ordinary circumstances there would have been no decision to make.

"Rizpah . . ."

His voice was growing more insistent. She would have to answer. *Now.*

If she reasoned with him, there would still be time to countermand the order to Bela.

But if she did this, she was certain what would happen. Saul would slip back to what he had become these past few months: a blob, a vegetating organism, a dying mass of flesh. To live again? . . .

It is always difficult to dissect the thought processes which operate during moments of stress. Uppermost in Rizpah's mind was her love for Saul. Aside from this, nothing seemed significant.

"Should I, Rizpah? Should I?"

There was agony in the furrowed brow, the outstretched hand, the wheedling tone of the direct question.

Perhaps it was already too late. Perhaps the moment of balance had passed. Perhaps no matter what she said now, she would not be able to prevent his return to the terrible half-life which had claimed him for so long. At least then she would be released from her dilemma.

But she could not let him go. She could not.

She said, "You are the king. You have spoken," and waited breathlessly, watching his face with the intensity of an anxious parent keeping vigil over a sick child.

And she saw the strength flood back across his features, bringing life, like water flowing onto parched earth. "I have spoken. It will be done."

She clung desperately to him all through that long night. Once she thought she heard the tramping of many feet outside the tent, but when she rose from the couch in terror there was no sound but the wind soughing through the olive trees.

At dawn Saul got up and threw back the tent flap. A light the color of thin gruel crept in through the doorway. Rizpah gazed at Saul, sure that the metallic glitter in his eyes must be reflected in her own.

She discovered she was enormously hungry, but before the food arrived the morning soured, and the sunlight outside was a travesty of past joy.

She became suddenly convinced that the child she was carrying was dead, made Saul place his ear to her belly to listen for signs of life.

For her the hours were interminable, but Saul waited calmly, passing the time by speaking of his early life in the house of Kish, his father. He was warm and tender with her, and she drew sustenance from his growing strength.

At least there is this, she told herself. Saul is Saul again. The pride of Israel is once more alive. Is not the life of the king worth . . . But she could not even complete the question, much less venture a reply. She only knew she had made a decision from which she could not retreat.

They came just after noon, marching in from the west, the hundred soldiers under Bela and the captive Gibeonites. She was appalled at the size of the group, among whom were old men with long beards, young men in their prime, boys with down on their cheeks. She turned away from the mute questions on their faces, the confusion in their eyes.

Bela reported that there were four hundred and ninety persons, by actual count.

"They are to be lined up," said Saul, "and brought by sevens to the circle of sacred stones. There they will be executed."

Bela's expression did not change. "All of them, my lord?"

"All of them. Will you serve as one of the executioners?"

"If my lord wishes."

"Select six volunteers from among your hundred. If no man will come forward, impress six into service."

"You shall have them, my lord."

I heard about what was going to happen at the same time as most of the rest of the camp, and went immediately to seek Rizpah. She was standing outside the circle, leaning against one of the stones. I stepped close to her, whispered urgently, "You must stop him. You must stop him now, before it begins."

She turned on me a look so frigid and full of hatred that I moved away, leaving her to gaze morosely at the long lines of Gibeonites, who were obviously still not sure what was happening to them.

Abner came running up the path. Undoubtedly he had just heard, and was rushing to obtain a denial from Saul. He stopped when he saw the captives. Something in the way he stood there informed me that it would be useless to approach him in the name of action.

Saul was waiting at the stone altar in the center of the circle. Ranged around him were Bela and six grim-visaged Israelite soldiers.

The king made a sign, and the Gibeonite who had pleaded his case in court the day before was led toward Saul, who now drew his sword.

The man had no time to be frightened. Saul cried, "Death to those who defy Israel!" He decapitated the Gibeonite with a single swift sword stroke. While the body was still spouting blood, seven more captives were led in, and the executioners took over.

Now the other Gibeonites saw what their fate would be. Some wept. A few vented long shuddering cries of rage and fright, and tried to burst through the retaining ring of Hebrew soldiers. These were slain on the spot. The others had to wait, and reflect on their impending death. After a time, most of them fell silent and stood, their eyes unseeing, moving forward step by step toward the altar, without any urging from the guards.

The pile of bodies inside the circle grew too large to permit the soldiers to move freely. There was a short respite while a detail worked to carry them away. Then the slaughter was resumed.

On Rizpah's face was one of the most horrible expressions I have ever seen. There was nausea, and fear . . . and something else, strongly akin to sexual passion.

Suddenly Abner groaned aloud, so heart-rendingly that an Israelite soldier standing near fell to his knees and buried his face in his hands.

Rizpah rushed to Abner, seized his arm and tried to pull him toward the circle. "Then stop him!" she shrieked. "Stop him!"

He disengaged her clutching fingers. "Saul is the king," he said coldly. How much he had guessed of her part in the butchery she did not know, but she backed away from his accusing stare.

Then without warning she screamed and toppled over, senseless. Abner's icy demeanor melted abruptly. He helped me lift her and carry her to our tent.

Her scream must have infected the rest of the Gibeonites. Until now the executions had been proceeding in silence, broken only by the gruesome mechanical sounds of slaughter.

Now, as Abner and I worked to revive Rizpah, we could hear from human throats the kind of bawling fear one usually associates with an abattoir.

Gradually Rizpah began to stir, and to breathe more normally. She opened her eyes, and was at once rackingly ill. I motioned for Abner to leave us, which he did reluctantly.

I nursed her for the rest of the afternoon with cold proficiency, which became even colder when she insisted on telling me all that had happened. Her dead voice sliced away sections of my heart, bit by bit, leaving me in the end as empty of feeling as she was.

Evening fell. The executions were over. For a time the camp was filled with the creaking noises of carts bearing away the victims for burial. After that there was no sound. Even the insects, usually so voluble on spring nights, were still now.

Then it was that Rizpah came to life. She screamed and tore her hair. She cried out over and over, "I killed them! I killed them . . ."

Once when she tried to pummel her belly with her fists, I restrained her and slapped her several times with all my strength until she stopped. Otherwise I left her severely alone.

Toward midnight, exhausted from her fury, she crawled to the bed. "Egrep . . ." she called in a small voice.

I went to her, suddenly sick of my self-righteousness. What she had done, she had done. It could neither be blotted out nor ignored. But who was I to dictate the limits of despair?

She was speaking now, shaping the words painfully. "Saul was mad," she said. "This is his forgiveness. Samuel was consumed by prophetic zeal. But what have I, Egrep?" Her tortured eyes looked up at me. "What have I?"

I thought: You have love, child. Madness is its own escape. The zeal of a prophet is a form of madness, and so absolves itself. But love is too aware. Too beautiful and too terrible. Too selfless and too selfish. And from its demands there is neither escape nor absolution.

All this I thought. But to Rizpah I said only, "Sleep, girl," for who but the gods can answer the questions of one who loves?

chapter twenty

EIGHT DAYS later Saul led his army forth to meet Moab.

The camp of Israel had quickly returned to normal after the brutal slaying of the Gibeonites. By that I mean there was no lengthy self-recrimination or expression of mass guilt, such as there might have been had the executions taken place in a civilian community. For one thing, combat warriors under arms develop a different perspective in their dealings with death. They fear it as much as any man, but they have had to school themselves to expect it, for themselves and for others. The massacre of nearly five hundred Gibeonites was a frightful event for the soldiers of Israel while it was actually taking place. But so were the sights and sounds of every battle in which they had ever participated. And the memory of Amalek, where they had followed orders in murdering even women and children, was too fresh in their minds for them to suffer unduly over the incident of Gibeon, in which few of them had been directly involved.

To suffer as a group, that is. As individuals the men would prob-ably feel the influence of Amalek and Gibeon in their lives long after they returned to their farms and villages. And so would their wives and children, who perhaps would never understand the reasons behind a sudden burst of rage or a bout of savage moodiness.

For the warrior in his unit, death does not lend itself to the subtle classifications accorded it by those poets and philosophers who have never known war. The soldier divides death into two rough but iron-clad categories: "we" and "they," and subdivides it more secretly into "I" and "they." He learns not to press beyond these rudimentary dis-tinctions, for to do so could very well decrease his chance for survival in battle.

So the army of Israel rapidly "forgot" the shameful afternoon when the sacred stones of Joshua were stained with Gibeonite blood.

If they discussed it among themselves at all, it was only to remark that since that day their leader seemed to be purged of the demons which had plagued him in the months after the departure of Samuel.

In truth, Saul's manner had undergone a striking change. He was energetic and decisive as he had not been since the days of the rescue of Jabesh-Gilead. He seemed to be everywhere in the camp at once. No sooner had he completed a tour of weapons inspection with Zaccur than he would turn up at an outpost to chat with the sentries. Or he would be seen having a bowl of wine with two or three of his captains of thousands. It became a standing source of wonder and sly amuse-ment in the camp that each night at least four or five different com-panies claimed the king had broken bread with them around their fire. And so ubiquitous had he become that I am not sure any of them was mistaken.

It would have been regrettable if his new burst of activity had led him to neglect Rizpah. She had recovered enough after her frantic dis-play of remorse to present the stereotyped tranquil exterior of a woman in the last month of pregnancy. She could even laugh at Zac-cur's frequent reference to her size and his suggestive speculation over which of the chariot stallions had been her companion the autumn before. But there were times when, even in the middle of a jest, her expression would turn inward, and I would sense that some ominous rite of memory was being renewed. Just as she would always bear the scars of the Philistine lash on her back, so would she always carry her share of the burden of Gibeon. But (and this made the nature of the burden complex) there was always the feeling that she and her man had fought a perilous, costly battle for his spirit . . . and they had won.

Even with his self-imposed preoccupation with his army's welfare, Saul managed to spend a portion of each day with Rizpah. And at night, long after the camp had settled into slumber, they would sit talking in his tent.

It was a period of new facets in their relationship. He spoke to her now of his plans, not only for the campaign against Moab, but also of his aspirations for a definitive conquest of Philistia, of his desire to establish a trading relationship with Phoenicia, of his hope of drawing the newly consolidated Israelite territories even more closely together.

Neither of them mentioned the Gibeonite episode, but it was as though through it Rizpah had come to play an even deeper role in Saul's life than ever before.

The tenderness between them was like the earth's soft flowering in the wake of winter's rampage. I once caught a glimpse of tears in Zaccur's eyes when I saw him watching them. And I myself, remembering how it was long ago for me, went off and sat through an entire afternoon dreaming and gazing at the distant river.

Too soon it was time for Saul to march forth with his troops to repel the Moabite invaders.

When the army had gone, and the camp took on its customary deserted-city aspect, I expected Rizpah to become depressed, for her life to enter a sort of desolate suspension until Saul's return. Instead, she was peaceful almost to the point of lethargy.

On an evening three weeks after the army's departure from Gilgal, Rizpah's labor pains began.

They were more than an hour apart at first, and during the night became gradually more frequent. It was not until the next morning that I began to suspect something was amiss.

Not having had children myself, I could not draw on personal experience. But I had several times assisted with the delivery of women in the Seren's household, and I knew what was happening was not normal.

The pains were coming quite close together now, but instead of reaching culmination, they maintained the same interval throughout the morning and early afternoon.

I could see Rizpah's weariness increasing. And when finally I saw a great quantity of fluid burst from her, I knew I could no longer deal with the situation alone. I sent one of the soldiers who had remained in camp to the nearby village of Naaran, instructing him to find a midwife, or if there were none, one of the village women.

At dusk, two of them came: the stout, middle-aged wife of a potter, and her daughter, a buxom girl of nineteen, who had already borne three children. They took over immediately, and after giving me the tongue-lashing I deserved for not having sent for them sooner, they set about their task with the offhand gusto of professionals.

The daughter put a leather thong between Rizpah's teeth, while the mother rubbed her belly and thighs with oil. "To make him pop out just like a pea from a pod, dear," she said. "Now when the next pain comes, you set your teeth on the leather and push."

"And don't be afraid to scream," said the daughter with an air of lugubrious pleasure. "They say the louder you scream, the more fright you put into the angel of death."

"You're not pushing hard enough, dear," said the mother when the pain came again. "Why, for all the effort you put into it, you'd think you were giving birth to a flea."

"If what's in that belly is a flea," said the daughter with a great guffaw, "I'll not stay around to be bitten by it."

Together they succeeded in both calming Rizpah and exhorting her to greater effort. They treated me with a kind of gentle contempt, ignoring me most of the time, until finally the mother took pity on my concern and assigned me to wiping Rizpah's face with a damp cloth.

An hour later she gave birth to her son. The younger woman pounded him on the back, and before handing him to Rizpah, held him up to the lamplight. "Ten each for holding and walking," she said. "And the proper number of all else he'll need."

"He has a head like a bull, dear," said the mother. "No wonder he was so stubborn."

And the two women roared with laughter, bending over double and slapping their thighs.

Rizpah smiled at them, then looked at me over the baby's head. Her lips shaped soundless words I could not make out. Only now did I begin to tremble with accumulated fear and joy.

The women were still there half an hour later when we all heard the distant blast of a ram's horn. They looked startled until I explained with mounting excitement that this meant the host were returning, victorious, from their campaign.

The potter's wife beamed at Rizpah. "There now, dear. Isn't it like a sabbath blessing to have the king marching home, and him all dusty and manlike from his journey, and soon to come and stand beside your bed and look down on what he and you made together."

"And her looking so beautiful," said the daughter with a lewd grin, "that it'll be all we can do to keep him from falling to and starting another one."

"Hold your tongue," said her mother sternly. "Have you no respect for the King of Israel?"

"King or common man, they all itch in the same place."

"And if you could keep your brain above your waist for one night, there wouldn't be such a brood for your poor husband to feed."

They went on in this vein for some time, while we continued to await the arrival of the troops.

Rizpah was indeed beautiful. Her hair spread out on the pillow gleamed like copper in the lamplight. Color was returning to her cheeks, and her gaze on the infant in her arms was soft and unguarded.

Soldiers were entering the camp now. We could hear the rumble of chariot wheels, the muffled cadence of marching feet. The potter's wife and daughter could no longer contain their curiosity. They rushed out of the tent, but not before the girl had smoothed her hair with a few quick coquettish movements of her hands. Rizpah smiled to me to follow them.

In the glow of torchlight I saw Zaccur and Jonathan and wondered why their faces looked so drawn and miserable. Then it occurred to me that the men were neither singing nor shouting, an odd omission in view of the earlier trumpeted report of victory. Nor, as had been customary until now, had a runner preceded the army to bring the tidings to those who had remained in camp.

Then I saw him. He was lying on a litter, his eyes closed, his great body jostling back and forth in spite of the excruciating gentleness of the four men who carried him.

I ran to Zaccur. "A spear wound," he said, poking out his lower lip until he looked like a child about to cry. "It happened three days ago, and he has not regained consciousness."

"What does the surgeon say?"

"The surgeon has prayed to Jahveh." He glanced around. "Where is she?"

I told him about the baby.

"You will not let her learn about Saul."

I smiled bleakly, and he sighed, his small frame seeming to shrink and become even more diminutive.

"Why can she never have a moment of joy unseasoned by sorrow?"

I left him and returned reluctantly to Rizpah, knowing very well what would happen. She had already sensed something wrong.

"Why is there no singing?"

"The men are weary, and the victory itself was inconclusive." I am not really a very good liar.

Her eyes grew flinty. "Saul?"

I nodded wretchedly.

"Is he dead?"

I had never seen such hardness in a woman, or even a man for that matter. I had a momentary, frantic flight of fancy in which I envisioned a sword striking her and careening off with a clang and a shower of sparks. It seemed impossible that only a short while before she had presented such a touching portrait of maternal gentleness.

"*Is he dead?*"

"Wounded," I said, and that was all there was time to say.

She rose unsteadily from the bed and seemed about to fall, but when I went toward her she straightened up forbiddingly. I knew there was nothing short of violence that would prevent her leaving, so I brought her a cloak. She picked up the baby and held his cheek to hers for an instant, then handed him to me. "Take care of him, old woman." And in those six words I felt the full ache of her heart.

When she reached Saul's tent, the surgeon was changing the dressing on the king's wound. Jonathan was hovering about the bed. When he saw Rizpah, he went to her and put his arms about her. Then he led her gently to his father.

The spear had pierced Saul's side, and he had lost a great deal of blood before his armor-bearer had been able to carry him from the battlefield. For a time they had thought he would die there in the sandy barren lands of southern Reuben. But toward evening of that first day his pulse had become stronger. However, the surgeon was puzzled and concerned over Saul's continuing unconsciousness.

"I have done all I can," he said, repeating the immemorial formula of doctors. Then, too weary to complete it with the usual reference to Jahveh, he merely shrugged. "I shall come again in the morning."

Jonathan stayed with her for the first while, but it soon became apparent that he could scarcely stay awake. Rizpah sent him away with the promise that she would call him if his father's condition worsened.

She took Saul's hand in hers, distressed at the feeling of dead weight. Her own strength was beginning to wane, but she preserved the remnants with grim stubbornness. Until even this was no longer effective, and she fell asleep.

She was awakened by the pressure of fingers against her hand. Daylight was filtering into the tent, and Saul was gazing at her intently. She was afraid to speak.

"You're very beautiful," he said. "Even more beautiful than you were when I left for Moab. Why? What has changed about you?"

She laughed with sheer relief. "My lord, you have a new son."

"I have? Since when?"

"Since last night. At least I think it was last night." She was babbling now without caring what she said. "He's strong and healthy. The women say he has a head like a bull. All I know is he took his own good time arriving." Her voice softened, and she touched his shoulder. "Like his father. Does the wound hurt?"

"Is that what it is?" He tried to raise himself off the couch and sank back, grimacing with pain. "I remember seeing the Moabite spearman bearing down on me while I was engaged with another . . ." He looked up at her. "A son?"

She nodded happily. "I have decided to call him Armoni. I hope this pleases my lord."

He tried it out. "Armoni son of Saul."

"I will bring him to you."

"Not now. Stay awhile. Are you well?"

"Tired, I think."

"How long have you been sitting here?"

"Not long."

"I don't believe you."

"It only matters that you are going to be well again, my lord."

"You must rest. You . . ."

And he was asleep again, his eyes closing in the middle of his sentence.

She also slept, and did not know whether she dreamed that I came into the tent and put the baby to her breast. As a matter of fact, I had done this twice during the night as well, and she had stirred, holding him close, but had not awakened. She was also aware, half in her dream, of the intermittent intrusions of the surgeon and Jonathan. She knew someone tried to take her from the tent, and that she resisted vigorously.

When she woke this time, she and Saul were alone, and he was also awake, staring at her. But she knew at once, even before he spoke, that it was not like before. He was quite mad.

"The prophet Samuel warned me. Thus saith the Lord: Stand upon thy own two feet and plunge thy head in oil . . ."

The laughter, aimless and grating.

The voice raised to a shout. "Whoever does not come forth to Jabesh after Saul and after Samuel . . ." Again the laughter, trailing off in a small, plaintive cry. "Samuel . . . Samuel, why have you forsaken me? Why? Why do you not . . ."

Rizpah speaking out of her own anguish, interrupting, "My lord . . ."

And the dead, tense silence, while he stared at her, his lips tightening in anticipation of the rage she knew would follow.

"You have stolen my kingdom!"

The old, stale, meaningless accusation. For this, she reflected wearily and bitterly, for this I have brought down the blood of Gibeon on his head and mine.

"You plot, you plan, you whisper by night with my enemies!"

He raised himself up in bed and aimed a blow at her. It caught her on the mouth, and though there was little strength behind it, she could taste blood. It is all I deserve, she thought, her own despair seeping through her, mingling with her weariness.

Then she saw that he was writhing in agony. All she could think was that he had broken open the wound, and with a cry she pulled the bedclothes away from his body. No blood showed on the cloth bandage. She waited until she was sure none would appear, ignoring his weak attempts to strike her again.

"Whore! Philistine harlot!" Then, very softly, "Samuel . . . why do you not return, Samuel?"

She could bear it no longer and fled from the tent.

It was late afternoon. She was surprised at the sight of Gilgal basking lazily under the warm sun, the stones of Joshua rising above her, indifferent, eternal.

Out of the corner of her eyes she saw a female figure approaching Saul's tent. It was Michal. Rizpah took a few steps backward, barring the entrance. The guard, a young soldier from Zebulon, turned away tactfully as Michal bore down on Rizpah.

"Your father is very weak. He has been wounded."

The girl's face was more sensual looking than ever in anger. She glared at Rizpah, flicking her tongue over her lips. "Do you not think I know this? Since my mother is not able to take her proper place at his side . . ."

Saul's voice drifted out to them. "Samuel . . . why do you not come? . . ." And the insane laughter.

Michal recoiled from the sounds coming from her father's tent, then spoke to Rizpah, her eyes narrowed and blazing. "You have driven him mad again. You are evil and corrupt!"

Rizpah was able to retort, "Do not think your innocence deceives me . . ." But then she lost track of what she intended to say.

Saul's daughter smiled contemptuously and brushed past Rizpah, who stood without moving, the taste of defeat like gall in her mouth.

She heard Saul begin to weep.

It was then, weary as she was, that she decided what she had to do.

chapter twenty-one

THE DONKEY's jogging gait gave her acute discomfort, which the hot sun and choking dust did nothing to mitigate.

She passed the ruins of Jericho, the ancient Canaanite stronghold destroyed long ago by Joshua, and relegated to perpetual desolation by the curse of the Lord. Little remained of the once-powerful city. Rizpah rested briefly beside a pitted, crumbling segment of masonry. Out of a crack in its side grew a tamarisk: stunted, withered, but still raising slender branches defiantly to the sun. The sight pleased her somehow and gave her courage.

Just past Jericho, there was a choice of two caravan roads. One led sharply northward to Shechem, in the heart of the Ephraimite highland. The southern way led almost due west to Beth-el, where it joined the trunk route running from Egypt all the way up to Aram. She took the southern road and followed it until she could see in the distance the twin crags topping the pass of Michmas. Then she left the road. From here the track leading to her destination across the hills was practically negligible, but it was country through which she and Saul had often ridden, and the terrain was familiar.

I had been very angry with her when she announced her intention of undertaking the journey. "You are too weak," I told her. "You have not rested a moment. Who ever heard of a woman giving birth—a difficult birth at that—and then sitting up all night at a sickbed, and the very next day planning to set off . . ."

"I have heard of women who have their babies in the fields and go back to work immediately as if nothing had happened."

"These are cows, not women. And do you also know what happens to these bovine fools? Most of them die, if not on the spot, then certainly much sooner than they should. Besides if you go away now, who's going to feed Armoni? Me?"

"I'll only be away two days at the most."

"The baby could starve in the meantime. In any event, you're an idiot to think of going alone. At least take one of the men along."

"I will go alone. I must," she said, setting her jaw in that willful, almost nasty way she sometimes has.

And so the argument ran on, for over an hour. But I was determined, and eventually won a compromise, which was the best I could hope for under the circumstances. She would travel alone, as I knew she must do in this case. I would find a wet nurse for Armoni in the village of Naaran. (As the potter's wife had said with an excessively artless glance at her daughter, everyone in Naaran is always having babies, and there's enough extra milk around to feed an army.) Rizpah agreed to rest for two days before starting. It was not nearly long enough, but I knew how anxious she was to set out, and I sympathized with the purpose of her journey.

Now she was well on her way, passing within a few thousand cubits of the old Israelite encampment near the village of Parah.

She stopped for an hour at midday, as I had made her promise she would do, so it was well past the third hour of afternoon when she arrived at Ramah.

It was a market day, and though most of the buying and selling had been done early in the morning, before the heat could spoil the perishable food, there were still vendors hawking pottery, jewelry, cloth and various household items. The streets were crowded, and Rizpah realized for the first time what an insular life she had been leading since the days in Askelon.

She made inquiries and was directed to the house she sought. A manservant admitted her to a great dim common room, which held a welcome coolness after her long hot journey. A few moments later she heard the sound of shuffling footsteps, and the prophet Samuel appeared in the doorway.

He seemed considerably smaller than she remembered. Perhaps this was due in part to his stooped posture. He appeared to have trouble walking, and the stern craggy face was marked with the lines which indicate chronic pain. But the pale eyes were as piercing as ever. They regarded her now with the same chill knowledge that had inspired fearful reverence in all Israel.

After what seemed an eternity, he said, "Has the man not brought you water to bathe your feet?"

She had just decided that his voice sounded old and tired when he raised it to shout for the servant. Then it was as it had been before, rasping and imperious.

He upbraided the servant for his negligence, then abruptly left the common room. After Rizpah had washed away some of the dust of her journey, the servant led her down a long, airless corridor and opened a door for her.

Samuel was waiting, sitting in an austerely fashioned armchair. Two other plain chairs, a wooden table and a narrow couch completed the severe furnishings. Over the chamber hung the faint musty odor sometimes associated with the living quarters of the aged.

After a moment Samuel motioned her to sit in one of the chairs. She did so and began, "I have come to . . ."

"I know why you have come."

There was another silence, during which he continued to watch her. She noticed that he was wearing a spotless white robe, so different from the streaked and faded cloak he had worn in the camp of Israel.

He got painfully to his feet, shuffled to the door, flung it open and stood listening. Then, apparently satisfied, he closed the door, saying, "The man eavesdrops." And further, as he recrossed the room, "My joints ache all the time now. Too many years of sleeping on the cold ground and making journeys in all kinds of weather . . ." He sighed, easing himself into his chair.

Rizpah managed to conceal her confusion. Was this the prophet who had inspired awe and terror, and sometimes hatred, in all who dealt with him? This arthritic old man, who worried about eaves-droppers, who prattled querulously of his ailments. Could this be the same man who had laid down the brutal edict against Amalek, who had murdered Agag with bitter words of vengeance?

Suddenly she was no longer afraid of him. And as often happens when fear of a person retreats, pity moved in to take its place.

But then he said with a gruffness in which she detected a trace of a sneer, "Saul is ill."

And now she could say, "He is ill, and you are responsible."

The tic pulsed under his eye. "Who are you to speak to me of responsibility?"

Rizpah said, "I love him." And the statement contained neither the awkwardness nor the naïveté it had held when she first spoke these words to Samuel.

"I will tell you a thing," he said, his eyes compelling hers to look at him. "When God told me he would send a man to me to be anointed king over Israel in his name, I was resentful. Who is this Saul, I thought, that he should take precedence over my own sons? I was prepared to dislike him, but I did not know I would hate him."

He paused and stared moodily at Rizpah. The word "hate" had struck the still air of the room like a hammer blow.

"I hated Saul on sight with every fiber of my soul. I know now it was, among other things, because he was so honest. Honesty can be like a whip, both injuring and goading. He made me admit, by simply being what he was, that my own sons were devious and venal. But honesty is also outspoken, and Saul was never blessed with tact. He

often reminded me, with blunt and inept words, of the corruption of
my sons.

"A prophet does not have to like a king, nor a king a prophet. I
did what was required of me by the Lord, and despised every moment I had to spend in Saul's company. I begged God to release me
from the task of being the transmitter of his word to Saul. But the
Lord heard me not."

He repeated, "The Lord heard me not," and again pulled himself
out of the chair. He straightened up, and for a moment he was the
Samuel she remembered: stern, unyielding, eyes glittering with pale
fire. He took a step toward her, and she recalled the night they had
faced each other before the altar of God at Gilgal. As he had done
then, Samuel raised his hand in a threatening gesture. Rizpah tensed
to rise and flee from him. But as on the other occasion, suddenly the
hand went limp, and dropped to his side.

"If I had been able to maintain the purity of my hatred, it would
have been better for Saul. But a strange thing began happening." The
glitter departed from his eyes, leaving them oddly, luminously, soft.
"I found that I was growing apprehensive each time he went out to
battle, that I was concerned during each engagement lest he be slain,
or even wounded. I told myself . . ." He broke off with an impatient
shake of his head. "What does it matter what I told myself? It was a
lie. The truth is, I was beginning to love Saul, more than I had ever
loved my own sons. I knew his faults, his frailties. And knowing them,
I wanted to protect him, and chastised him more severely. Yet it was
Saul, with his honesty, his courage . . ."

He stopped speaking. Rizpah sat very still, hardly daring to breathe.
From another part of the house came the sound of voices raised in
some domestic altercation. Then all was still.

Samuel said, "But Saul was disobedient. I fought to keep him in the
path of God. When he spared the Kenites without express orders to
do so, I admired his courage and his mercy. When he allowed the
men to capture the flocks of Amalek, and when he himself refrained
from slaying Agag, I understood. But the commandments of the Lord
are given to be obeyed, and Saul had defied them. I was forced to
kill Agag myself. I had no choice but to abandon Saul. Even when
I knew I would mourn . . ."

Rizpah blurted out angrily, "Your mourning has broken Saul's heart,
not yours!"

He looked at her. She stared back at him, not believing what she
saw. But she was not mistaken. The shadow of a smile was hovering
over the prophet's features.

"Why do you think I have troubled to speak to you as I have? It has been said that only before an adversary do you display what you truly feel. If someone had told me when I first took on the mantle of prophecy that in my latter days I should find myself striving against . . ." He stopped for an instant, shaking his head. "My days of strife are over. Yours are not. But do you believe because a man is a prophet he has no feelings? Do you know what it means to be so lonely that your very soul shrivels, because this is the only way you can commune with God? Do you know what it means to have the power of life and death over other human beings, and to wonder if you are truly translating the word of the Lord in saying who shall live and who shall die? I will tell you, child. There are times when I have loathed my gift of prophecy, when I have thrashed about trying to flee the word of God. I have ridden into the desert. I have climbed to the tops of mountains. I have hidden in dank caves. And still his voice has pursued me."

He fell silent, and after a moment limped to the chair and sank into it. She thought he had forgotten her presence, but after a while he raised his eyes and said, softly but commandingly, "You will stay the night. Later we shall speak of the reason for your visit. Go now."

She left the room, feeling perplexed and filled with a vague depression. The servant who had admitted her to the house was waiting in the common room. Without a word he showed her to an upper bedchamber. She lay down on the bed and began to weep and to her amazement realized it was as much for Samuel as for Saul.

She and the prophet ate their evening meal in silence. There were not nearly enough lamps in the dreary common room, and the shadows of the two men who served them leaped frighteningly on the walls. When the meal was over, she gathered her strength to ask the thing she had come to ask, but before she could, Samuel began to speak.

He told her of his childhood in the sanctuary at Shiloh, under the tutelage of the priest Eli. He spoke of the night he had first heard the word of the Lord, and had run to Eli through the darkened house, along corridors echoing his terror of the Voice. And finally he described the day only a few years before, when tidings of the Battle of Aphek had been brought to Shiloh. His aged mentor Eli had been sitting at the gate of the sanctuary, and when he was told of the Philistine victory and the death of his two sons, the old man had toppled over and broken his neck. Samuel had grieved then as never before, as he had stood looking down at the man who had been like a father to him lying dead in the dust. The spasm under his eye, Samuel said, had first appeared during the stress and sorrow of that day.

It did not seem strange now to Rizpah that this man whom she had feared until today should be speaking to her of such matters. The voice of loneliness is compelling, and calls clearly to a responsive heart.

He had stopped talking, and she saw he was waiting. She said, "Then you will come back with me to Saul."

Samuel said nothing, and in the bad light she could not see his expression. She pressed her point further. "Saul knows he needs your help. And now I know he needs your guidance. I beg you to come before it is too late. Let his spirit walk again in the sun. Restore the strength he must have to lead Israel."

He said, very quietly, "Only the Lord can give Saul back his strength."

"You are the Lord's prophet. Please go to Saul."

He leaned forward, and the lamplight fell across his features, showing them gaunt with sadness. "I cannot. The Lord has already chosen one from the house of Jesse to reign in Saul's stead."

The name meant nothing to her. "But Saul is still king. Surely . . ."

He got up quickly, knocking over his chair. "Woman . . . do you think the word of God can be revoked?"

She said stubbornly, "You love Saul. You told me . . ."

"I also love Israel. And even more than I love Saul or Israel, I love the Lord and hearken to his word."

She knew she had lost, but desperation would not let her surrender. "I know if Saul could look once more on your face and realize that . . ."

He raised his hand, stopping her speech. "Do you not understand, child? I have already anointed the son of Jesse."

In the hush that followed his words she could hear one of the lamps sputtering. Samuel turned and shuffled from the room, his tall frame bending and twisting with pain at each step.

She did not see him again that night, nor in the morning before she departed.

chapter twenty-two

I was frantic, waiting for her return. It was coming on to sunset, and I ran every few moments to the top of the rise overlooking the road from Jericho.

The host of Israel was getting ready to move. All around me was the bustle of preparation: the intermittent clangor of weapons and armor, the whinnying of horses, the shouted orders. Soldiers hurried about the camp, bent on a thousand purposeful errands. Only the area surrounding the tent of Saul seemed unaffected, a dark island of inactivity.

Word had arrived at noon that day that the Philistines were mounting an invasion. Abner had tried to consult Saul, but finding him incapacitated both physically and mentally, had finally taken matters into his own hands. The Philistines were not a band of desert raiders like the Moabites. Against the warriors of the coastal nation one acted quickly and emphatically, or not at all.

The intelligence reports received at the Hebrew camp indicated that the Philistine advance would probably move from Gath into Judah, following a route slightly south of the one Rizpah and I had taken when we journeyed to find Torash. Therefore, Abner decided that the army of Israel would march southwest from Gilgal, cutting through the Judean hill country, and take up a position in the Valley of Elah. The plan was to leave at dawn the next day.

I was forced to tell Abner of Rizpah's whereabouts. He was unconcerned by the possibility of her not returning before the army's departure. "Her condition would not allow her to travel with us in any event," he said.

"If she can make the journey to Ramah on the back of a donkey, she can certainly ride in a wagon . . . all the way to Egypt if needs be."

"It would be better if you took her to Gibeah. She would be far safer."

I became angry. "Safer indeed! Do you think Rizpah thinks of her safety? She is as much a warrior as any of your men." He smiled, and I realized the absurdity of what I had said. I laughed, and continued more quietly, "If you leave without her, she will only follow. Besides, suppose she brings the prophet Samuel?"

"If Samuel wishes to look on Saul again," Abner said soberly, "he will find his own way to the camp in Elah."

But he eventually agreed that Rizpah and I should accompany the army of Israel.

This accomplished, I began to worry about her. The country between Ramah and Gilgal was not exactly a wilderness, but there were dangers enough for a young woman traveling alone. Perhaps, weak as she was, she had been thrown from the donkey and was even now lying in some thicket, calling vainly for help. Perhaps she had been attacked by wild animals or bitten by a serpent.

With these anxieties constantly in my mind, my trips to the top of the rise became more and more frequent, and finally I simply sat down on the ground and waited, my gaze fixed on the farthest reach of the dusty highway.

When I saw her, I nearly wept with relief. She was weary, and unhappy over the failure of her mission. Otherwise, she seemed considerably stronger than she had been the day before when she set out for Ramah.

I told her what had happened, and we made our plans. Rizpah consented reluctantly to let me arrange for her baby to be sent to Gibeah. The wet nurse was a quiet young woman from Naaran whom I had come to trust in the two days I had watched her with Armoni. Her own child had been born sickly, and had died only a few weeks before. Her husband had been slain fighting with Saul's army in the Ammonite campaign. She welcomed both the new responsibility and the means of livelihood. Armoni would be safe with her.

As soon as we had settled this, Rizpah went to visit Saul. Michal had been with him most of the day, but fortunately only Jonathan was at his bedside now. The king was recovering rapidly from his wound, but his eyes were wild and unseeing. He gibbered about the demons who were besieging him, called out for his spear, and once or twice tried to rise from the bed, his arms flailing as he struggled against Jonathan's firm restraint. He did not recognize Rizpah, addressing her as the woman Deborah, who had judged in Israel many years before. After a time, I came to the tent and convinced Rizpah she should rest in preparation for the next day's journey.

It was a weird and unforgettable experience. When Michal learned that Rizpah would be traveling to Elah, she insisted on coming along. The four of us—Michal, the mad king, Rizpah and I—rode together in one wagon. Saul was gorgeously arrayed in his purple cloak and his crown, which he had persisted in wearing. His recuperative powers were unbelievable, and already he could move around freely, which was unfortunate. He resembled a tragic jester more than a king: shrieking with laughter and whining piteously by turns, rising and bowing in all directions, and calling out over and over at frequent intervals, "Bring on the joint. My men must eat meat. Bring on the joint."

Rizpah and Michal were like two lionesses inadvertently trapped by circumstances in the same lair.

Michal would say something like, "I have heard that accomplished harlots have a way of getting rid of their spawn before they are born. It is only the lower-class whores who bear the brats and desert them."

To which Rizpah would reply sweetly, "And some women are unable to attract a man at all, and so cannot know in which category they belong."

"Death!" Saul would shout. "Death to the wizards and soothsayers!"

Now it would be Rizpah's turn. "Did you weave the cloth for that robe yourself?" she would ask Michal. "I have heard that the virgins of Benjamin are uncommonly good weavers when they can spare time from tending their village refuse heaps."

"I bought this robe," Michal would say, thrusting out her chest at Rizpah, "from a Bedouin nomad out of Simeon, who claims descent from the only noble family there."

"Bring on the joint!" cried Saul. "My men must eat meat. Bring on the joint!" And he would rise and bow to the charioteers riding protective escort on either side of the wagon.

When Saul was not shouting, and the two females were not engaging in their childish exchanges, the three of them would sit glowering in a vicious, charged silence.

All in all, at the close of the second day, I was happy to see in the distance the valley which was to be the new campsite for the army of Israel.

chapter twenty-three

THE LYRE player was Abner's idea.

It came about in this way. After the Israelite army arrived at the Valley of Elah, the situation was discovered to be not nearly so urgent as had originally been supposed. True, the Philistine legions were

massing in the frontier vicinity of Gath, a day's march from the Hebrew encampment. But scouting parties quickly brought back information that the size of the enemy host had been greatly exaggerated.

Abner held a long council with the captains of thousands to debate
the advisability of attacking at once. This plan was finally vetoed. The
city of Gath's cliff-top position was virtually impregnable. Any attacking force would automatically set odds against itself, with the chances
for ultimate victory uncertain. Here in the region around Elah, the
Hebrews would have the advantage. They held the high ground, and
if they stayed where they were, they could inflict great damage on an
army even twice their size.

As soon as it had been decided to remain, the next concern was
Saul. Abner's assumption of full control over the troops was readily
acceptable to the men. But the general himself had an almost obsessive aversion to exerting kingly authority. He fretted over decisions;
even after the council of commanders voted to maintain the army's
position at Elah, Abner tried to consult Saul.

This proved difficult. At times the king appeared to be listening intently to his general, nodding his head and grunting as Abner outlined the situation. But when Abner finished talking, Saul would still
be nodding his head and grunting, in exactly the same manner. Abner
would fling out his hands in despair and turn to Rizpah. "There is
very little to be done now," she would say quietly. "Perhaps this
evening."

However, by nightfall, Saul might have sunk even farther into lethargy. Or he might be weeping, or raging back and forth in the tent,
beyond the reach of anyone, including Rizpah.

For her, it was a repetition of the tragic months at Gilgal following
the death of Agag. Only now the situation was complicated by the
presence of Michal. Saul's daughter was willing to let Rizpah perform
all the more menial functions of nursing her father. She hovered
about, not even pretending to help, but making the occasional cutting remark. Rizpah did not want her assistance, but she was too worn-
out and discouraged to drive the girl from the tent. Jonathan tried his
best to keep her away, but his gentle coercion was no match for
Michal's persistence.

One night, Rizpah was taking away the remains of the meal she
had fed Saul. Michal was lounging on a chair, leaning against the
back in one of her usual voluptuous poses. Rizpah had just reached
the doorway when, with a horrible cry, Saul rose from the couch and
tore off his clothing. The sight of her father, stark naked, his body
rigid and trembling, so disturbed Michal that she got to her feet,

screaming to Rizpah, "Do something! Do something!" She tried to run from the tent, but Rizpah blocked the doorway, staring coldly at her.

This steadied the girl's nerves. She set her mouth primly, picked up a cloak and advanced toward Saul. "Put this on, Father," she said. "If that trollop won't take proper care of you . . ."

The flat of Saul's hand caught her squarely on the nose. Blood flew in all directions. Michal's howls of pain and fear mingled with the king's anguished roaring. For a few moments the din was so great it could be heard through the whole camp.

Rizpah calmly set down the tray she was carrying, walked over to the king, took him by the arm and led him back to the couch. When he had subsided, whimpering, she approached Michal. The girl shrank away, her eyes animal with terror.

Rizpah seized Michal's arm and propelled her toward a basin in the corner of the tent. There she washed the blood from the girl's face.

Michal was still sobbing. "He struck me," she kept saying. "My own father struck me."

"Your father is mad. Just be thankful he didn't kill you. Next time he very well might."

Thereafter Michal kept her distance, and was not nearly so quick with her tongue.

Saul's struggle with the demons was more heartbreaking now than it had been at Gilgal. Where before he had been past recall from the onset of his sickness until it ended, he was apt now to emerge into moments of poignant lucidity.

He would raise his head suddenly and look at Rizpah, his eyes tender and yearning where an instant before they had been glassy and withdrawn. Sometimes he would say nothing, only look at her and hold out his arms. On other occasions he would speak. These were the hardest for her to bear. "My love," he would say. "Help me. Help me, my love . . ."

And she would come close to him, put her arms about him, brush her lips against his, try with the pressure of her fingers to communicate the strength of her love. Sometimes they would sit like this for an hour, sometimes longer. But invariably the interlude would end with his flying into a blind, hopeless rage. Often he would strike her. Always he would curse her and cry out that she had stolen his kingdom.

I knew how bad the situation was because Rizpah would discuss it with me. Talking to me was her release, her own protection against going mad. But until Abner had spent futile hours attempting to consult Saul about battle plans, I do not believe he understood the extent to which his nephew had deteriorated. And until he actually saw the king strike Rizpah he refused to become personally involved.

On this day, when he entered the tent, Rizpah was sitting on the couch, close to Saul. Abner, sensing a certain relaxation of tension, was about to speak when Saul began to revile Rizpah in a loud, acrimonious voice. She did not even try to get away as he raised his hand and cuffed her on the side of the head.

Abner's fury was nearly as intense as Saul's. If Rizpah had not restrained him, he would have rushed at his nephew and tried to kill him.

Rizpah made him leave the tent, and followed him into the warm Judean afternoon sunlight. It was some time before he recovered enough from his anger to speak sensibly. Then he said with great determination, "Something must be done."

Men are curious creatures. They are given to sweeping categorical statements at moments of crisis which usually accomplish nothing but are the hallmark of their masculinity. It is ruinous if a female laughs, or even smiles at them after one of these pronouncements. We must conceal our amusement and nod gravely.

Rizpah signified the proper deference and Abner repeated, "Something must be done." He pursed his lips and added, "I will think about it."

In this case he actually did, and the result of his thinking was to exert a singular influence on the course of events in Israel. At least this is what I believe. There are others who feel that when the gods ordain something, it matters little what men do—this thing will come to pass.

Abner was back in an hour. He called Rizpah out of Saul's tent and said, "When Saul was younger, and afflicted with what we then called his 'moods,' I remember that he would often revive noticeably after listening to some traveling musician who happened to be passing through the town."

"Yes," said Rizpah absently, for Abner was being long-winded, and she was concerned with other matters.

"I believe we should try to drive the evil spirit from Saul by finding a lyre player and having him perform before the king."

"No!" said Rizpah, so abruptly and feelingly that Abner stepped away in amazement.

She said later that she had had a sudden dark premonition. Perhaps this was so. Or perhaps, having nursed Saul so long, and nursing having become an integral part of her love, she did not want to share any part of it with another person.

In any event, she was unable to give Abner a reason for her distress. Wisely, he did not press the matter at that moment.

But nearly a week later, on an afternoon when I had persuaded Rizpah to walk with me along the bank of the river a little distance from the camp, we returned to hear music drifting out of the king's tent.

Rizpah grew very pale and began to tremble. I thought she was ill, and reached out to steady her, but she twisted away from my hand and called over her shoulder, "Come . . ."

Outside the tent, she stopped and took several deep breaths to compose herself. Then we entered.

The king was sitting in the throne chair, head bowed in a listening attitude. Abner, Jonathan and Michal were seated nearby. Standing with his back to us, plucking the strings of his lyre with strong slender fingers, was a tall young man. He was sturdily built, but there was something of the grace of a gazelle in his carriage and the way he moved. To the accompaniment of the lyre he was singing:

> "Saul, mighty man of valor,
> The mountains quiver when he passes,
> Yea, the stones revere and rejoice.
> But the enemies of Israel are as morning dew
> Before the sun of his wrath.
> Saul, mighty man of valor."

All my life I have been accustomed to the wiles of sycophants. I have heard courtiers lave out the oil of flattery so plentifully that one could hardly get about the banquet hall or council chamber for fear of sliding on a slippery phrase.

The song the young man was singing, in a not particularly distinguished voice, was no different from a thousand I had heard. Shorter perhaps, and not as elaborately fashioned as some. Yet there was a sincerity about it that moved me strongly. And I could tell that Rizpah had been affected in the same way. Her breathing had quickened, and her gaze was fastened on the back of the singer's head.

When the song was over, Abner called Rizpah forward and said, "This lad is known as David. Three of his brothers are serving with our forces, and we are fortunate that he has come to visit them. Otherwise we should not be favored with the charm of his playing."

David inclined his head graciously toward the king's general. His face was warm and mobile. I was struck by the similarity of his and

Rizpah's coloring. They had the same reddish-brown hair, though David's was perhaps a shade darker, the same rich golden lights glinting from their skin, the same expressive green eyes.

The young singer glanced at Saul, who was still bowed in his listening attitude. Then he looked directly at Rizpah.

I do not know if anyone else present felt it. Perhaps Abner did, but if so, he kept his reactions carefully veiled. But to me, the meeting of those two pairs of eyes crackled with the sudden intensity of lightning on a still, sultry night. And like lightning, it was visible for an instant, then gone.

Rizpah said, "Your music has a rare beauty."

"My lady speaks too kindly. I am only a shepherd, with a shepherd's uncouth ways. But when I return to my lonely hills and sky, I shall bear your compliment with me, and treasure it as one cherishes a priceless jewel."

There was the quality of the courtier in his reply. It was saved from overripeness by a just-perceptible touch of banter. And withal, he was able to convey the same note of sincerity he had achieved in his song.

"You will play more?" This from Michal. I had been so engrossed with watching the quick spark of affinity between Rizpah and David that I had forgotten her presence. Now I looked at her. The habitually bold, carnal expression had softened, and the effect, strangely enough, was not entirely pleasing. It gave the impression somehow of a strong-featured face beginning to spoil and run to flab. But there was no mistaking her fascination with David. Michal was probably one of the most blatantly sexual women I have ever seen, and now she was turning the full force of her desire directly toward the singer. The great Ahinoam-eyes were smoldering. Her breasts were thrust forward, straining at the fabric of her garment, and as I watched, one shoulder began to perform a slow, delicate, circular movement.

But also as I watched, David's glance slid from Michal to her brother. He and Jonathan exchanged a look filled with understanding, irony and mutual admiration.

Thus, in the space of only a few moments, the young shepherd's eyes had obtained him a degree of intimacy with three of the six persons in the tent. He was wise enough to refrain from turning his charm on Abner. The general's shyness would only make him retreat from any conspicuous bid for his favor. It would take time to cultivate Abner. As for me, I felt instinctively that David did not regard me as important enough to impress, and also that he would fear me and avoid me if at all possible.

There remained only Saul.

David spoke to Michal, but his attention was directed toward the king, who had not changed his position since we entered the tent. "I shall play for Saul's daughter a melody long familiar among the shepherds of Judah. It contains, I believe, something of the grandeur of sweeping hills and the simple longing of a herdsman sleeping under the cold beauty of the stars. I hope it will please the king's daughter. Perhaps it will possess enough merit to find some small favor before the king."

He paused, waiting, but Saul did not stir. Still keeping his eyes on the king's face, David plucked the strings of the lyre and began a low-pitched melody which indeed possessed great beauty. I found halfway through that, without knowing it, I had been holding my breath.

Then a marvelous thing happened. Gradually, as if he were struggling against some gigantic invisible force, Saul's head came up, until he was looking straight at David. His eyes glistened with tears. But they were tears of pleasure, of response to the loveliness of the music. I heard Rizpah sigh, saw her lips move in what I was sure was a prayer of thanksgiving. The others in the tent were equally overjoyed.

The last notes of the melody died away. Saul's brow furrowed, quickly cleared. "Who is this young man?"

Abner said, "You are well acquainted, my lord, with three of his brothers—the two archers Eliab and Abinadab, and the swordsman Shammah. David is the youngest of the family of Jesse."

I saw Rizpah stiffen, and could not understand why until I remembered what she had reported concerning the words of Samuel: *I have already anointed the son of Jesse.*

Could this young singer of songs, this tender shepherd boy, be the one Jahveh had chosen to rule in place of Saul?

I watched Rizpah searching his face for some sign of guile. She could not have missed it. Responding to some vibration of suspicion in the tent, his eyes went hard and flat. He appeared years older in a single instant. The mobile features froze in a mask of ruthlessness as he looked about him, suddenly wary and vigilant.

The expression was gone as quickly as it had come, and laughter bubbled from his lips: spontaneous, artless, contagious.

Saul asked, "What amuses you, son of Jesse?"

"My lord the king, I hope my mirth has given you no offense. I am accustomed to being alone, with only my sheep for company. When I think a thing, the emotion it evokes is out of me. And at this moment I was rejoicing that my simple music has apparently given the king pleasure."

Saul grunted, but everyone present could see he was favorably impressed with the reply. "You will play more?" he said, in an odd echo of Michal's words a short time before: half command, half plea.

David played. Time passed, and the light outside the tent began to fail. Saul himself went to the entrance and called for lamps. The young shepherd's repertoire seemed inexhaustible. Occasionally he sang some extemporaneous panegyric to Saul, but not enough to overdo it. Mostly his songs were of the wild beauty of Judah, or of a shepherd's fervent devotion to Jahveh. He seemed to prefer instrumental music to singing, and here he truly excelled. His fingers could call up the molten radiance of sunlight, the cool brilliance of the moon's rays, the savage terror of a storm. And he himself seemed to reflect each mood he exacted from the lyre, so that his face was a study in ever-changing expressions.

Not one of us would have left, even if he could have. I myself would have been content to sit for days, in thrall to those enchanted fingers plucking the strings. But finally he put aside his lyre and said, "If it please my lord the king, I have played enough for today. My lord and his family have been kind with their attention, but now I am empty of music."

The straightforward speech pleased Saul. He clapped Abner on the back and said, "Do you hear that, my uncle? Here is a man who is not only gifted but unafraid to speak his mind. I shall be forever grateful to you for bringing him here."

Abner beamed, and Saul clapped him on the back again, then turned to me, asking me to go fetch supper for us all.

At table the king overflowed with joviality. He ate prodigiously, and urged food and wine on all of us. At one point he put down the lamb shank on which he was gnawing and turned to me. "Well, old woman, what have you been doing to keep yourself busy?"

"Until my lord the king reminded me of my age," I replied, bristling a little, "I was filling my stomach with excellent food. Now it would seem I was only stuffing an old bag with provender."

He threw back his head and gave one of those short sharp bursts of laughter my words seemed to arouse in him. And I was so pleased at seeing him restored that I quickly forgave the injury to my vanity.

Only occasionally would the embers of earlier interplay suddenly glow and emit tiny flickering flames—Michal's lips parting, the tip of her tongue moving slowly over them as she gazed at David; Rizpah's quick glance of annoyance at her then darting to David and searching his face speculatively; Abner's obvious joy at Saul's recovery, mixed with the residue of pain as he allowed his eyes to find Rizpah's face. . . .

When the meal was over, Saul suddenly said to David, "Tell me, shepherd. Are you as skilled in the use of weapons as you are with the lyre?"

"When I guard my flocks, I fear neither the birds of prey nor the beasts of the field. I have caught the lion by his beard and made sport of the claws of the bear."

I was happy to see at least one flaw in the make-up of this otherwise perfectly integrated young man. He was still youthful enough to boast.

This did not seem to disturb Saul. "Then you will help me guard the flocks of Israel." He turned to Abner. "From this moment, David will be my armor-bearer."

Abner stammered, "But my lord already has an armor-bearer."

"Will he serve as such forever? Promote him this very night to be a captain over a hundred, and let David's position be proclaimed."

Michal smiled with secret pleasure. Rizpah glared at her, then at David, then let her eyes go soft and happy as she gazed at Saul and received a tender look in return. And again, Jonathan and David exchanged their ironic, understanding glance.

Soon after, we left Saul and Rizpah alone in the tent.

They held back from each other with a peculiar restraint which neither understood.

At length Saul said, "You must be very weary of wrestling with my demons."

"The victorious are seldom weary, my lord," she said smilingly.

"This time . . . this time perhaps we have vanquished them forever. Your love has sustained me, and David's music . . ."

He broke off, his hand beating time to some melody which still lingered in his mind.

A shadow crossed Rizpah's face and was gone. "My dearest one," she said, "I am so happy you have returned."

Then Saul took her in his arms, and once again their love was strong and pure.

book three

DAVID

chapter one

THE ZENITH of summer came and went, and still the Philistine army did not attempt to invade Israel.

The Hebrew troops remained on their height of ground at Elah, waiting. It was a nervy business, for the rank and file were growing restless. They had been nearly two years under arms and felt if Israel would only launch a single smashing attack against its major enemy, they would then be free to return to their homes. But Abner and the captains maintained their original opinion, and now that Saul had recovered his faculties, he concurred in the position taken by his senior officers.

I say Saul had recovered. This was only true in a sense. He was no longer given to fits of uncontrollable weeping or rage. But he was still subject to periods of depression, when he seemed in danger of regressing into a paralyzing stupor. He fought mightily against these depressions, and Rizpah strove together with him. To see the two of them battling his demons—Saul sitting on the edge of the couch, his face oily with perspiration, the veins of his temples swelling with effort, and Rizpah kneeling before him, her hands gripping his—to see this was to understand to some small degree the nobility of man's continuing struggle for existence.

But now it was David's ministration which was most effective. The young shepherd had adapted quickly and easily to military life, and so great was his personal magnetism that he soon became overwhelmingly popular with the men. It was a common sight to see him sitting at one of the fires, or assisting a weapons-cleaning detail, always the center of attention, always the leader of laughter and raucous raillery. At first his three brothers resented the intrusion of the baby of their family into their military lives. Staunch, solid warriors themselves, they looked on David as too mercurial for the life of an army camp, a butterfly among eagles. However, in view of his favored position as Saul's armor-bearer, they kept their peace and endured his presence.

Saul's affection for the youth was apparent even to the lowest ranks in the camp. Often while David was amusing a throng of soldiers— telling the hilarious and slightly ribald stories of Judean shepherd life, or displaying his shrewd gift for mimicry—Saul would stand unnoticed at the fringe of the crowd, listening and looking on with the fond countenance of a doting parent.

And when Saul's depression would become unbearable, he would ask David to play and sing for him. Seldom did the sound of the shepherd's lyre fail to give the king a measure of relief, at least enough so he and Rizpah could continue the struggle against less crushing odds. And invariably now, when David finished playing, Saul would say to him, "Thank you, my son."

Among the men in the camp of Israel, only Zaccur seemed unresponsive to David's charm. The little man remained unmoved by the bright smile, the ready wit, the warm manner of the youth. He would stare glumly at David whenever he saw him holding forth, and would frequently turn his back and walk away. Curious because this was so unlike Zaccur, I asked him why he seemed to dislike the lad. For a moment he did not reply. Then he shrugged and said, "Call it jealousy. That's what the captains say. I'm envious because he's a better mimic than I." No amount of persuasion could make him say more.

For a variety of reasons, the most important of which was not known to her or anyone else at this time, Rizpah's attitude toward David also displayed a marked coldness. There was one thing she knew she must learn: whether this son of Jesse was the successor to the throne designated by Samuel.

One evening when Saul, worn out by two days of nagging depression, had retired early, Rizpah approached David outside the tent and said bluntly, "I want to talk to you. Come with me."

David looked at her, a corner of his mouth twitching with some private amusement. Then he made a small mock bow and said, "Your servant, my lady."

By tacit mutual agreement, they took care not to be seen together by any of the soldiers of Israel. David let Rizpah go ahead of him, only following when she began to descend the slope leading away from the camp.

He caught up with her at the bank of the river running through the valley. It was a brilliantly clear night, and the moon lighted their way. The waters of the river had dwindled to a midsummer trickle, but the trees lining its course had soaked up enough moisture earlier in the year to retain their rich foliage. Rizpah paused between two willows, and in a moment she and David were surrounded by a swarm of buzzing gnats. They walked on, swatting at the insects, until they reached a gentle rise capped by a mass of rock. There a breeze dispersed the gnats. David and Rizpah stopped and faced each other.

For a time neither spoke. Rizpah was not certain how to begin, and David was content to wait until she did. In the silence that lay between them, the affinity apparent at their first meeting became again apparent, making each stir uneasily. Then, abruptly, it was gone.

She said, "I wish to speak to you honestly."

He made his mock bow. "Honesty is my purest characteristic. It is fabled among the rabbits of the field and the sparrows of the air."

"Do not play the clown with me," she said angrily. "What I have to say is extremely serious."

"Then my lady has yet a thing to learn," he said lightly. "That jest is grave and gravity jest—a truism long known among simple folk."

"You make much of your lowly origin. But your speech is not that of a shepherd."

"Nor yours that of a beautiful woman. Which gives us something in common. Both of us are expected by the law of stereotype to express ourselves like idiots." His teeth showed white in the moonlight. "You tell me where you found your wisdom, and I'll warrant we'll learn we drank from the same fountain."

It had been a long time since she had fenced with a man in this fashion. Sometimes she and Torash had traded ideas disguised as banter, but the Seren, despite his outer sophistication, had lacked the tough inner core she was sure David possessed. To come by the information she wanted would not be easy.

She let her voice become silky and languorous. "Tell me something?"

"My lady commands. I obey."

"Did the oil also stain your garments and fill your nostrils with its rancid odor?"

She saw his face go hard and wary. "The oil?"

"The oil of anointing," she said casually. "The holy oil reserved for the blessing of kings."

"It would seem you have been speaking with knowledgeable people."

She corrected him. "The only knowledgeable person."

"So there is no need for me to answer your question."

"Then answer this!" She flared at him. "Were you born treacherous, or did you acquire the art? How can you dare deal so foully with a man as honest and generous as Saul? A man who loves you and trusts you . . ."

The mask had slipped away from his features. There could be no doubt about the genuineness of the torment in his eyes, the pain twisting his lips. "Do you think I do not love him?"

"So you show your love by worming your way into his heart, all the while knowing you are the one chosen by Samuel to depose him. You allow him to become dependent on you . . ."

He cut her off, also angry now. "I had no intention of even appearing before Saul until Abner approached me . . ."

"But you came quickly enough once he did approach you. After you had allowed yourself to be anointed by Samuel . . ."

"Does one flee from the hand of the prophet? Does one hide from the word of the Lord?"

She had no answer for this. He waited, allowing silence to press his advantage.

Then he said quietly, "I love Saul with all my being. My own parents in Beth-lehem inspire no more affection in me than does this man. He is like a second father. And Jonathan is my brother."

She asked tauntingly, "And Michal your sister?"

He was angry again. "Michal is no concern of yours."

"Saul is my concern."

"Then understand this. I could not escape the blessing of the prophet, any more than Saul could. But while Saul and Jonathan live, I would cut out my heart before I would usurp the throne which belongs to them."

She considered his words. "But," she said slowly, "you would not refuse the crown if it were offered."

"There can be no question of this. My father Saul and my brother Jonathan are king and prince in Israel."

Rizpah waited for him to continue, but apparently he had finished speaking.

She had learned what she wished to know. But she had the feeling that somehow they had both evaded a vital issue between them.

chapter two

LATE ONE night the scouts who had been assigned to keep the area around Gath under surveillance suddenly arrived in the Israelite camp. They brought news that there was an unusual amount of activity across the enemy border. For some reason no one, including Abner, took the report seriously. Autumn was coming on, and I think everyone preferred to believe the Philistines would not be able to muster enough strength to march until spring.

How wrong they had been was soon to become obvious.

At dawn we were all awakened by a sentry's cry of alarm. Rizpah and I dressed hastily and rushed out of our tent. A heavy mist shrouded the camp of Israel. We could make out the forms of the Hebrew soldiers sitting up, rubbing their eyes and yawning. The captains hurried from group to group, calling to the men in low voices, ordering them into battle formation. There was no sense of panic, only the knowledge that somewhere beyond the camp limits, concealed by the fog, trouble was gathering.

The sun climbed over the rim of an eastern hill. Its rays struck the curtain of mist and tinted the droplets red, so that the movement of soldiers to their battle stations became a weird dance performed in an inferno which glowed without giving off heat.

Suddenly the rosy veil disintegrated. The morning burst on us in an extravagance of gold and green and clear blue sky. And across the valley, on a lesser height known as Ephes-dammim, was arrayed the full might of Philistia. Sunlight glinted from the armor of row on row of spearmen, swordsmen and archers. The familiar purple helmet plumes waved in a soft breeze, giving the impression of a hillside field of strange and gaudy wheat. At the flanks of the legions stood the chariots, motionless, imposing, battle knives fixed to the wheels in readiness for attack.

There was consternation in the Israelite ranks as they realized that the Philistine army was not only as large as theirs, but actually exceeded their numbers by at least a thousand men. However, the dismay was momentary. The Hebrew position was far more easily defensible than Ephes-dammim, and it was evident that the Philistines could not mount an immediate attack without suffering heavy losses.

In effect, the opposing hosts were so evenly matched that neither side wished to make the first move. Although both armies remained in battle formation, as the morning wore on there was a perceptible lessening of tension among the warriors of Israel. And across the valley we could see the sharp lines of the Philistine ranks blurring somewhat as food was passed along from one soldier to the next.

I found I had been dreading this moment, and now that there was time to consider it, my anxieties were coagulating. I had voluntarily given up my allegiance to my native land, and through my love for Rizpah, had come to identify my fate with the fortunes of Israel. For long periods at a stretch, I had even forgotten my Philistine origins.

Not forgotten. It is foolish of me even to intimate this. A little leather bag beside my bed still contained the figures of Dagon and Astarte, and if my references to Jahveh were more frequent, I could certainly not bring myself to worship him.

Most of my experience, and whatever wisdom I had distilled from it, had been gained as a Philistine. To deny this would have made me guilty of the same "nest-fouling" I had once attributed to collaborators.

Now, as I looked across to Ephes-dammim, my feelings were peculiarly ambivalent. There were no doubt many on that hillside whose name I could call, whose wives had been among my acquaintances, whose homes held the same familiarity for me as the one where I had spent so many years.

It never occurred to me to leave the camp of Israel and make my way over to the ranks of my compatriots. But I could, and did, feel a sharper sense of the futility of warfare than at any other time in my life until now. And so I did what most of us do at one time or another when we are confronted with conflict. I withdrew. I chose a spot on the hillside where I could be alone . . . or at least removed from immediate human contact.

Consequently, although I was in an excellent position to witness the more sensational aspect of the drama which was about to unfold, I missed some of its most subtle and significant phases. These I learned about later from Rizpah.

The noon hour was approaching. I could see the soldiers of Israel sweating in their encasements of armor, and I remember reflecting vaguely that two armies could not remain much longer in this state of unrelieved ferment. Then I chanced to look across the valley, and my reverie ended abruptly.

Out of the Philistine lines stepped a fully armed warrior. I stared openmouthed as he walked forward until he stood midway between the two armies.

The scribes of David, anxious to give favorable impetus to any story involving their master, have endowed this Philistine soldier with more formidable dimensions than he actually possessed. They need not have exaggerated. The man standing before us was clearly a giant. He was a full two heads taller than Saul, and his shoulders were almost twice as broad. Brass armor covered him from head to foot—helmet, coat of mail, greaves—and the weapons he carried were equally impressive.

The giant planted his feet apart, threw back his head and bellowed at the Hebrew formations: "Why have you set your armies in array in this place? Am I not a Philistine? Is my name not Goliath, of the city of Gath? And are you not all servants of Saul? Choose a champion from among you, and let him come down to me. If he is able to fight with me, and to kill me, then we will be your servants. But if I prevail against him, and kill him, then you shall be our servants, and serve us!"

Dead silence greeted the challenge, as well it might have. My own mind was racing with the irrelevancies which often besiege such moments. From Goliath's accent, I knew he came from the Quarter in Gath, which was almost identical with Askelon's Lower Town. I kept thinking of the low-ceilinged warren which must have been his home from birth, and how he must have grown to maturity baffled and furious at the cramped enclosure in which circumstances forced him to live. Until the army had liberated him, and made his freakish size an object of admiration. Standing here now between the stalemated legions of two nations must have been the proudest instant of his life.

As if underscoring my thoughts, the giant threw back his head again and laughed. The sound mingled contempt and delight.

The Israelite divisions were still silent. I could almost smell the waves of fear rising from the closely massed troops.

Goliath roared again, "I defy the armies of Israel this day! Give me a man, that we may fight together!"

When once more there was no answer, it seemed to goad him to a white rage. His repeated challenges became increasingly abusive, sprinkled liberally with the obscenities one can hear in the Quarters of any of the five cities of Philistia.

The giant's booming voice was clearly audible in Saul's tent. The king was sitting in his great wooden chair, his face impassive as he listened to the vulgar phrases of defiance rolling up from the valley. Rizpah was also there, having run out to see the source of the tumult and returned, shaken and frightened, to Saul's side.

They were quickly joined by Abner, Jonathan and David, all wearing sober expressions. The dilemma was clear to each of them. If a champion went forth from the Hebrew ranks, it was most unlikely that he could defeat Goliath in hand-to-hand combat. His failure would so unnerve the soldiers of Israel that they would fall easy prey to the Philistine attack that would surely follow. Yet if no one went forth, the end result would be the same, for Goliath was striking fear into the hearts of those who heard him. And terror, once generated, can quickly become epidemic among warriors.

So it was better to try and fail than languish and let defeat rush in unimpeded.

But who would be the champion?

Saul was the logical choice. He was mightier than any soldier who served him, and if anyone could vanquish the Philistine, it would be he. Everyone in the tent watched him covertly, not daring to question him with a direct glance.

However, it was soon shockingly apparent that Saul was in the grip of one of his numbing depressions. He was sweating profusely; he ground his teeth and clenched the arms of his chair in an effort to dispel the bitter lassitude. Finally he said in a hollow voice, "I shall go forth."

The others watched with growing horror as he tried to get up. His shoulders shuddered spastically; his huge torso writhed; his feet beat a frustrated tattoo on the carpeted floor.

As if to mock his anguish, Goliath's laughter battered against the cloth walls of the tent. And following it a reiteration of the strident challenge, "Is there no *man* in all of Israel?"

The king's face went gray; his breathing grew ragged. A thwarted, strangled sound burst from his throat.

Rizpah put out her hand, let it fall again. She knew if she touched him now, the last barrier holding off his madness would collapse, and he would be gone from them.

Abner stepped forward. He spoke calmly, but his stammer betrayed his extreme agitation. "It would not be wise for the king to meet the Philistine. If he were to be wounded, who could then direct the forces of Israel? No, my lord, you are more needed as commander than as champion."

The logic of Abner's words was shaky, and everyone knew it. But to Saul it represented sorely needed salvation. He sank back into the throne chair, gasping, grateful for the respite.

And before Abner could take the inevitable next step and volunteer to go himself, Jonathan came to the center of the tent. "I must go, uncle," he said quietly. His eyes looked steadily into Abner's, imploring him not to raise objections.

A demon whose presence she could not explain rose in Rizpah. She heard herself saying, "Is the core of Israel so rotten that a king or his general or the king's son must court death and risk bereaving the people of God? Is there no man with courage to fight for the land of his birth?"

And roaring up from the valley came the giant's voice, echoing, "Is there no man . . ."

She was looking straight at David, her eyes ablaze. Jonathan and Abner stared, shocked speechless by the unabashed directness of her implication. Saul, still exhausted from his own struggle, shook his head, not quite able to understand what was taking place.

David turned until he was looking full into Rizpah's face. Without removing his gaze from her, he spoke past her to Saul. "My lord the king, let no man's heart fail because of the giant. Your servant David will go and fight with this Philistine."

Now at last Saul understood. The color, so recently returned to his face, drained away once more, and he said haltingly, "You are not able to go against this Philistine. You are only a youth, and he a man of war."

The note of concern in Saul's words caused David's expression to relax. He stepped around Rizpah and went to the king. There were tears in his eyes as he said, "Do not fear for me, my father. The Lord, who has saved me in the past from the paw of the bear and the claws of the lion, will deliver me now out of the hand of this Philistine."

Saul looked at David for a few moments, searching his face. Then he said, "Go, and the Lord be with you."

David turned to leave the tent, and suddenly Saul's features constricted. "David, my son!"

The young man came back.

"You will wear my armor and carry my sword when you go forth to meet this beast."

David bowed his head but did not reply. The others in the tent watched solemnly as he walked to the corner where Saul's brightly polished armor lay, strapped on the breastplate and greaves, secured the sheathed sword about his waist and placed the helmet on his head. Everything was too large for him, which gave him a slightly pathetic appearance.

At this moment Michal entered the tent. Her quick appraising glance took in the situation. She uttered a small grieving cry and ran to David's side. "You cannot go!" For once she had forgotten herself. Selflessness lent her beauty an ethereal quality.

David's smile to her was filled with sweetness. "There is no choice."

Anger shook her. "Who has done this? Who would dare?" Again the rapid appraisal, and the sharp intelligence understanding at once. She said nothing to Rizpah, but her face spoke of her unrelenting enmity.

David, still smiling, began to unbuckle the sword. The others looked on as before, puzzlement replacing solemnity. David stripped the metal plates from his body, gently placed the helmet on top of the heap of armor. Now once more he was the lithe and graceful shepherd. To Saul he said, "I cannot go with these. For I have never proved myself with them."

Saul asked sadly, a madman recognizing signs of madness in another, "How will you fight against the giant, my son?"

From the girdle at his waist David extracted a worn leather sling. "With me I have five smooth stones which only last evening I gathered from the brook. I marveled then at their loveliness. Now they will make a bridge between beauty and death."

Jonathan found his voice. "The sling you carry is cracked and frayed. Among my weapons is the sling I used at Michmas. Let me go and fetch it for you."

David shook his head. "If my brother will lend me his love, this is all I will ask of him. The weapons with which I face Goliath must be my own. The sling, pebbles from the earth of Judah, my shepherd's staff, and I am prepared."

True bravery breeds its own special kind of dignity. The brave know fear, and David's hands were trembling. But his step was firm, and his eyes did not waver as he looked around at the four people already so closely bound up with the course of his life. I must admit, even distrusting him, as I always have, that when Rizpah told me of his behavior, I came close to weeping.

David clasped Abner's hand in both of his. Before Saul he knelt and only rose when the king touched his shoulder lightly, benedictively. He embraced Jonathan and kissed Michal on the lips.

But it was in front of Rizpah that he paused the longest. She had steeled herself to expect the same revelation of hatred she had received from Michal. She was therefore startled to observe in David something far more devastating: the unmistakable eyes of compassion.

From the valley the giant Goliath again bawled his abuse of Israel. The light went out of David's eyes, leaving them fathomless, adamantine. He turned and hurried from the tent. After a moment Jonathan and Michal rushed forward to follow him.

David's struggle with Goliath has been so thoroughly chronicled by his scribes that it seems unnecessary for me to rehash it here. I shall only note one correction. He did not make the lengthy speech attributed to him. This I know, because if he had spoken even one word, I would have heard it. But perhaps he thought some of the things he is supposed to have said, and certainly they are eloquent and moving enough to be preserved.

The giant did speak, however. Goliath was as much put out by David's silence as by his youth and his lack of either weapons or armor. And since he had been shouting all day, it was not easy for him to stop now. He glared at the approaching shepherd, and singled out for special disdain the cudgel David carried. "Am I a dog that you come to me with staves? By Dagon, I shall flay your carcass and feed it to the monsters of the sea. Astarte will gnaw your bones and slake her thirst on your blood."

This was all the trio in Saul's tent heard, and their hearts sank. None of them was able to move.

The hush seemed to continue forever. Then, like a sudden torrential rain, the roar of thousands of voices burst over them. For a moment they were not sure whether the sound came from the Israelite or the Philistine camp. But after the first shout there was a lull, and they heard the voice of Jonathan crying out, "The valor of David has saved us! Let us pursue them now . . . for God and for Israel!"

Abner remained motionless, his head bowed. Rizpah fell to her knees and began to sob. And Saul laughed—a rumbling, throaty, empty chuckle.

The din of battle was resounding now across the valley—tumultuous at first, then receding to the north of Ephes-dammim. The Philistines were in flight. Abner, recovering, was torn between his will to join his forces and his concern for Saul. In the end he stayed in the tent. Rizpah rose and went to the king, but at this point neither was able to comfort the other.

In through the doorway strode David, a cocky grin on his lips, bearing the severed head and bloody sword of Goliath. He advanced to the throne, and with the relish of malice thrust the grisly locks of the giant toward Rizpah. She did not back away and once again her eyes met David's, this time in resumption of the battle between them.

Saul was looking quizzically at David. In a perfectly rational tone he said, "Abner, whose son is this youth?"

The general was so startled that he replied, with oddly formal phrasing, "As your soul lives, O King, I cannot tell."

With great dignity Saul turned to David. "Whose son are you, young man?"

Not the least disconcerted, David answered, "I am the son of your servant, Jesse the Beth-lehemite."

With which the king's eyes grew glassy, his lips flaccid, and he mumbled, "Jesse . . . Jesse? . . ."

Even at that period in his life, David was a remarkably complex personality. A scant half hour before, he had been facing almost certain death. He had escaped and bore in his hands the relics of victory.

Now, seeing the distress of the man whose throne he had been anointed to assume, he wept and said aloud, "Will they beset you always, my father?"

He wrapped Goliath's head and sword in a cloth, rinsed the giant's blood from his fingers, found his lyre by Saul's couch and began to play.

He continued until he saw returning reason begin to flicker in the king's eyes. Then he made his little mock bow to Rizpah, took Abner by the arm and walked with him out of the tent.

chapter three

"AND WHY does my love come to me with suspicions concerning my son David?"

"There is nothing so weighty as to merit the name of suspicion, my lord."

She watched him narrowly. In the month since the defeat of the Philistines at Ephes-dammim, there had been no recurrence of Saul's madness. Yet sometimes, in a word, an aimless gesture, an instant of excessive preoccupation, she could feel the hovering presence of the demons. And if for a single day David were prevented from playing and singing for him, Saul would be dangerously disappointed.

"Has David done you some harm?"

"No, my lord."

The flaps of the tent were stretched back, admitting a swath of brilliant sunlight. It was a dry, sparkling day late in the harvest season. A year ago on a morning like this she and Saul had ridden across the hills of Benjamin to the sanctuary of a lonely vineyard house. Amalek and the shame of Gibeon had still been imbedded in the future. And David had been tending his sheep, as yet unaware of the austere prophet who would seek him out with the anointment of destiny.

"Then I see no reason for you even to hint at David's treachery."

"Again, my lord, treachery is much too strong a word."

"He calls me father. He is as dear to me as my own son."

"But he is not your son." She was handling this badly. She knew now she should never have broached the subject without benefit of solid evidence. And there was no evidence.

Outside the tent she could hear the voices of Jonathan and David. The prince of Israel was instructing his father's armor-bearer in the proper use of the sword.

"No, my brother. The riposte is done in this fashion . . ." Here a pause, and several grunts. "If my brother David continues to wield the sword as he did on the last raid we conducted into Philistine territory, he will kill many of the enemy. They will die from laughing."

Saul, listening, chuckled dryly at the bulky jest.

"And if my brother Jonathan would not be so insistent on burdening me with heathen weapons and allow me to use . . ."

"Like this, David. Thrust, parry, thrust. Thrust, parry, thrust . . ."

Could she vilify the devotion that had grown up between the two young men? Could she point out the smallest blemish on the affection of the armor-bearer for his king? But Samuel had anointed the shepherd. The Lord had transferred his blessing from Saul to David. Was God so ironic that he could cause two men, king and incipient pretender, to love each other?

"I am sorry, my lord. I do not know why I spoke as I did. Truly David has done nothing to warrant even a breath of criticism."

Mollified, Saul said, "His heart is pure and innocent as the morning star."

She, bent on mending as much as she could of the breach, "And his courage . . ."

"Who would have thought," said Saul, agreeing with enthusiasm, "that a simple shepherd could perform such feats. . . ."

"My lord was a farmer."

He sighed. "Sometimes I find it difficult to remember when I was ever anything but the ruler of Israel."

"You are weary, my dearest."

"Weary. Have I earned the privilege of weariness? But you are right. Soon it will be winter. You and I will journey to Gibeah . . ."

Once the prospect of dwelling at Gibeah, in the same house with Ahinoam, would have filled her with apprehension. Now she herself was weary, sick of the transient atmosphere of military life. She wanted to see her son, to watch him grow. . . .

Saul was continuing. "Then, after we have refreshed ourselves with rest, when the earth is green again . . ."

He was interrupted by an explosion of laughter from outside the tent. He listened a moment, his expression full of a sad fondness.

"Have you ever thought . . ." he began, then shook his head. "No, of course you haven't. You're still too young. But when the years begin to knit themselves together like threads from some relentless weaver's hand, and the pattern that emerges is age, one thinks sometimes: this and this I shall never be able to do again . . ."

She kissed him quickly, saying, "My lord has proved repeatedly that he is stronger than any callow youth who serves him, and having the benefit of years, more seasoned in his strength." But as she spoke, she was cataloguing carefully the signs of his melancholy, planning how she could subvert their further onset.

He held her close. And as always, his nearness touched off an incandescence of desire in her. No extravagant sunburst of passion, as during their first days together. Rather now a sure steady flame which he could call to intensity by his hands and lips and voice. She thought: how dear he has become to me, how inseparable from the very breath I draw. And then, because love is rooted so deeply in mortality, she also thought: if something should happen to him . . .

"My lord," she said, her voice containing no hint of the chill uncertainty whispering round her heart, "could we not walk together in the sun? The olive leaves in autumn possess a special silver hue that suddenly I feel I should like to see."

He went with her at once, for one of the pleasures he had found in their relationship was acquiescing to her enthusiasms, and through her joy blunting the sharp edge of his sobriety.

They passed David and Jonathan, their swordplay forgotten, wrestling together like half-grown lion cubs on the turf. She and Saul stopped to watch their frantic scrambling, their simulated vehemence, their eventual collapse side by side, shaken by uncontrollable gusts of laughter.

She smiled looking at them and thought: how distrustful I have grown; has David not given me his pledge that he does not covet the throne? And even if he does, how could this boy threaten the might of Saul? Samuel is in his dotage, and he blessed the first likely stripling he saw on one of his aimless wanderings. No harm will come of it.

So thinking, she went with Saul along the Valley of Elah, and touched the olive leaves and basked in the sun, and tasted the sweetness of solitary leisure with the man she loved.

But that evening, when Saul stopped to speak with Abner at the campfire of the captains, she, feeling a little tired, went ahead of him to the tent.

David was there, bending reverently over the king's armor. He did not hear her enter, and she was about to speak to him when she saw that he was holding the crown of Israel in his hand. She gasped, and he turned quickly, making his face smooth and expressionless when he saw her.

chapter four

AHINOAM WAS very ill.

All winter she grappled with the recurrent fever from which she had suffered for years. She had resisted staying abed, had busied herself with running the household at Gibeah. "It is all I have left," she would say with just a trace of bitterness when I or one of her children would remonstrate with her. "Do not take that away from me."

She grew thin. Her garments, never fashionable or attractive, hung on her even more shapelessly than before. Her skin took on an alarming translucence. The servants spoke of her privately as The Spirit, and indeed there was something wraithlike about the way she moved through the rambling farmhouse, so quietly that one rarely heard her approach.

Yet, probably for the first time in her life, she was beautiful. Her enormous eyes, which had always dominated her face, gave off a radiance which was deeply moving. This, combined with her pallor and her sharply defined cheekbones, lent her an altogether arresting quality.

In the last week of the cold weather Doeg, Saul's chief herdsman, on his way to discuss the flocks with the king, found Ahinoam lying unconscious outside the house. He was an excitable Edomite, and believing her dead, he set up a vociferous lament which brought out a throng of family and servants.

Ahinoam was far from dead. She regained consciousness in a few hours, and would have risen to oversee the preparations for the evening meal had Saul finally not been firm with her. I am not sure he should have been, for after he ordered her to stay in bed, the will to struggle seemed to leave her.

Rizpah came to her room. "Spring will soon be here," she said. "The warm weather will bring back your strength."

Ahinoam did not behave resentfully toward the younger woman who had taken her place with Saul. In truth, a strange sort of friendship had matured between them. She had heard, perhaps from Jonathan, of Rizpah's devotion to Saul during the ugliest period of his insanity, and this had made her first respectful, then trusting. "No," she said now. "If I am to be well again, it will not be spring that works the miracle."

"You will see," said Rizpah, arranging the bedclothes about Ahinoam's thin body. "When the trees come to life, and the vineyards turn green . . . you will see."

Ahinoam looked keenly at Rizpah. "You will welcome spring yourself, my dear. Winter has worn you out."

There was nothing feline about the remark, and even if there had been, the words were true. Rizpah did not look well. In some ways, Saul's comparatively peaceful frame of mind was more exhausting for her than his most virulent madness had been. Rizpah was constantly watchful for signs of melancholy, diverting them when they came, protecting him from the nagging doubts she knew could prove disastrous. The strain could hardly help but tell on her.

David, too, was contributing to her concern over Saul.

The greater part of the army had returned to their individual homes for the winter. But about a thousand men, mostly those without family connections, had remained in service, and set up a base near Gallim, a short distance from Gibeah. They were a tough cadre of fighters who thoroughly enjoyed the whirlwind raids they made into Philistine territory. Technically, Jonathan was their chief, but more and more it was David to whom they looked for leadership. And so enamored was Saul's son of the young shepherd-warrior that he was probably not even aware of any switch in allegiance. In fact, he fostered it. He and David would map out their miniature campaigns together. Then Jonathan would say, "You speak to the men, my brother, and give them their assignments. I am going to visit my mother and father until nightfall. We shall depart as soon after that as you are ready."

David thrived on warfare. His shoulders broadened; his face took on the weather-beaten look of the seasoned campaigner. He was now expert in the use of all conventional weapons, and his daredevilry across the enemy border was becoming legendary. So it was that this particular group was no longer known as part of the army of Israel, or Saul's men. The whole countryside spoke of them as the "Legion of David."

On his visits to Gibeah, however, he was the epitome of modesty. He was charming to Ahinoam and even managed to establish a certain rapport with the sly, foxlike boy, Ishbaal. Before Saul he was still the unschooled armor-bearer, the shepherd who played comforting melodies on the lyre.

Which made even more startling the moment when Rizpah again saw the mask of ruthless ambition take possession of his features. I also saw it, so I know she was not mistaken.

It was a fragrant evening in early spring. Buds were starting on the trees. The balmy air was beginning to ease the pain in my bones, which had ached chronically all winter.

Rizpah was pregnant again. She was only now sure, and had intended to tell Saul after the evening meal. But he was in conference with Abner, who had arrived at Gibeah that day, so Rizpah and I were passing time by strolling in the garden.

Twilight was just leaving the sky. We walked without speaking, listening to the calls of night birds, watching the plummeting descent of a bat in pursuit of insect prey.

Suddenly Rizpah gripped my arm. I almost cried out, but her expression warned me to silence.

Then I saw them. They were close, so close that another several steps would have brought us alongside them. But gathering darkness and the thick trunks of two palm trees gave us partial concealment.

David and Michal were locked in an embrace, the length of their bodies pressed tightly together. I could hear the sound of their breathing and Michal's repeated small moaning cries.

I made a motion to leave, but Rizpah's hand held me fast. After a moment Michal twisted away from David. Her lips were curved in a sensual, coquettish smile. "You will speak to him soon?" she whispered.

"I will speak to him."

Then she was gone, with a seductive rustle of her gown and the swift light sound of her footsteps receding toward the house.

But David's gaze as he peered after her was not that of a fond lover sending his heart after his beloved. Rizpah and I remained rooted where we were, stunned by the calculating cruelty we could see in his face.

Then he also left, making his way through the trees like some great lithe cat.

When Rizpah and I returned to her room, she took Armoni from Helah, the young widow from Naaran, whom she had kept on as nurse. Even after Helah had gone, Rizpah did not speak to me. She held Armoni, and rocked him, and sang him the nonsense verses he seemed to love. After a while he fell asleep, and she placed him tenderly in his tiny bed.

Only then did she look at me. "I must tell him, of course."

"Tell him?"

"Saul," she snapped. "I must tell him about David."

I had been thinking about this. "What will you say? What is there to say? That he embraced Michal in the garden and afterward did not faint away with love?"

"Don't be ridiculous. You've heard the songs."

"Songs . . ." I repeated, somewhat inanely.

"The maidens who sing at the well of Gallim."

"Must you trouble Saul with the words of foolish girls who go simpering around an army camp?"

"He should know what the people are saying. He should understand the threat."

"Saul loves David," I said slowly, evenly.

"Will he love him when he learns that it was David who was anointed by Samuel?"

I was shocked. "You cannot tell him that. You must not."

"I must not," she echoed mockingly. "And why must I not? Will we wait until he organizes a rebellion against Saul?"

"Rizpah," I said, "be careful what you say and do. You know better than I how uneasy his spirit is. Do you want to bring back his madness?"

There was a hard glitter in her eyes. "He must know. David must be stopped before it is too late."

I reasoned with her. I grew angry and shouted. It was a waste of effort. I do not believe she heard half of what I was saying.

And then, all at once, my heart grew sick within me. I was beginning to understand the nature of the pattern which was appearing, shaping itself toward inevitable tragedy.

The terrible thing was, I knew I could do nothing to help avert it.

chapter five

SAUL RODE along beside her, looking about him good-naturedly, convinced that the trip was merely another of her quicksilver enthusiasms, prepared to enjoy it thoroughly. She had told him earlier in the morning that she was with child, and he was so pleased that he failed to notice the febrile gleam in her eyes, the brittleness of her manner.

Gallim lay about half an hour's journey east of Gibeah, off the main caravan route, at the base of a range of hills. It was a good-sized, walled village, and some of its inhabitants were distantly related to Saul.

A thousand cubits before Gallim they rounded a bend in the narrow track and saw the camp of Israel. It had the appearance of a permanent garrison. David had insisted that, between engagements, the men make shelters for themselves, and the black goatskin tents they had fashioned were laid out in neat avenues. Sentries patrolled the perimeter of the camp in full armor, pacing and turning with brisk precision.

Saul gazed on all this admiringly. "The army has wintered well. Soon it will be time to call back the rest of the men from leave. Soon, too, it will be time for me to rejoin my host."

"Soon, my lord."

"Perhaps we should stop now. I have not seen David or Jonathan for some days. Come. We shall break our journey. They will give us a cup of wine, and I shall speak with the men."

"Our journey is almost over. But we must hurry if we are to be in time."

"In time for what, my love?"

"Simply . . . in time."

The gate into Gallim was open. There were cisterns within the fortified limits of the village, but the well of fresh water was situated outside the wall, between two giant oaks. Rizpah tethered the donkeys to a sapling a little distance away, then made Saul sit on the ground with his back to one of the oaks, facing away from the village so he would not be visible to anyone coming out of it. He did as he was told, tolerantly, with a bemused expression. She sat down beside him, and they waited.

After a while he said, "This is very lovely, and it is most pleasant to be here with you, but you said there was something you wished me to see."

For an instant, looking at his face, so open and untroubled, she considered relenting. But it was just for an instant, and she replied, "Something I wished you to hear, my lord. If you will be patient . . ."

The maidens of Gallim were coming out of the village now, pitchers on their shoulders, laughing and chattering. One of them broke into song.

Saul leaned forward. "What is it she is singing?"

Rizpah placed her hand over his. "Please, my lord. You must not be seen."

The others joined in the leader's song:

> *"But let the righteous be glad.*
> *Let them rejoice before God,*
> *Yea, let them exceedingly rejoice."*

The last word dissolved in a ripple of laughter as one of the girls pushed another and then stumbled herself. The group reached the well and began drawing water. Saul looked questioningly at Rizpah, who put her finger to her lips.

Then over the rise separating the army encampment from the town came eight or ten soldiers of Israel, laughing and shouting among themselves. As soon as the girls saw them, they giggled self-consciously and then immediately after, as if on cue, began another song.

First the leader lifted her voice, clear and carrying. Saul listened, furrowed his brow, shook his head. He hunched his shoulders forward as the whole group of maidens sang:

> *"Saul has slain his thousands,*
> *And David his ten thousands."*

And the laughter of the girls mingled with the calls of the approaching soldiers.

Then Saul stood up, and revealed himself to the group around the well, and there was a deathly hush, and the soldiers withdrew hastily, and the maidens fled toward the sanctuary of their village.

Rizpah and Saul were alone between the giant oaks that sheltered the well.

He said, speaking with difficulty, "Has my son David then grown so powerful?"

Rizpah did not reply.

Saul said, "The shepherd lad, who plays so sweetly on the lyre, whose voice sings my praise. Into whose hand I have given my armor, my heart and my love . . ."

Still Rizpah kept silent.

"They have ascribed to David ten thousands, and to me they have ascribed only thousands. What more can he have but the kingdom?"

Now Rizpah said, "The kingdom of Israel belongs to Saul . . ."

She stopped speaking on a rising inflection, indicating that she had more to say. He watched her, waiting for her to go on.

Then Rizpah told him how she had gone to Samuel, and how he had refused to return with her, and how he announced that he had anointed a Judahite, a son of Jesse, as king.

"And you are certain that David was the one anointed by Samuel?"

"I am certain, my lord."

Saul gave a great cry and fell headlong into the dust. He rolled and thrashed about, foamed at the mouth, then lay completely still. Rizpah, terrified, knelt and put her ear to his chest. Saul's heart was beating, but erratically.

She ran to the well for water and bathed his face and hands. He did not move. She dragged him deeper into the shade of the oaks and sat beside him, cushioning his head in her lap. Finally he revived.

She expected him to be wild with rage or lost in lethargy. With either of these she was prepared to deal.

What she did not expect was a terrible, cold, resolved calm. He got to his feet. She rose after him, regarding him anxiously. There was a smudge of dirt beside his left eye. She did not now dare wipe it away.

"Come," he said. "We must return to Gibeah. There is a great deal to do."

chapter six

ONE THING David did not lack was sensitivity. He realized something was wrong the moment he entered Saul's room. But excessive self-esteem is a dangerous characteristic. It perverts awareness as a pool of water refracts the sun's rays.

David was sure the king had heard of his conquest of Michal and was merely displaying fatherly protectiveness.

So when Saul said to him, coolly but politely, "We have not had the pleasure of my son David's company for all these many days," he replied, "No, my king and father. I have been away in the region around Ekron, harassing the Philistines for the glory of Saul." And thus he fell squarely into the older man's trap.

"Have you killed many of the enemy during this past winter, my son?"

"I have done my best to uphold the honor of Israel."

"How many have you slain? A thousand? Ten thousand?"

David laughed. "My lord is the mightiest warrior in Israel. He knows better than I how exaggerated are the claims of battle."

"I am sure in your case they are not exaggerated favorably enough. In any event, the winter's campaigns have made it clear that it would be travesty to stifle you longer in the position of armor-bearer to the king."

"I only wish to serve my lord."

"Then serve me best by becoming one of my captains of thousands."

Again the distortion of fact by ego. For now David reasoned that the king had already decided to let him have Michal, and was promoting him in advance to a rank commensurate with a position in the royal family. He was profuse and flattering with his thanks. Nor did he notice that Saul had reached down beside him to pick up his spear, that he was gripping the shaft in a strained and agitated manner.

Saul said, "But it was you who wished to see me about a matter."

"It can wait, my king."

"With warriors such as we, nothing can wait. For who is to say which sunrise might be our last?"

David drew a deep breath. "I love your daughter Michal. I have come to ask that you give her to me in marriage."

Saul raised his spear and heaved it broadside across the room. It clattered off the wall onto the stone floor.

David did not even turn his head. "Have I displeased my father Saul?"

"On the contrary, I am greatly pleased. More so than you can possibly know. What a pity you could not have come to me a year ago when my daughter Merab was still unmarried. For I would have honored you more by giving you my eldest."

David said, "As my soul lives, my lord, it is Michal I love. And she loves me."

The crafty light passed across Saul's face like a sickly moonbeam darting out of thick cloud. "Then my son David and my daughter Michal have agreed beforehand as to what will happen, and my word is only a formality."

"Not at all, my king. I—"

Saul cut David's protest short. "Play for me."

When David had played and sung for an hour, Saul stopped him, saying, "I will give you my daughter on one condition."

David said in a gratified rush, "My king has only to speak . . ."

"You will go forth in yet another foray against the Philistines. And your part of the marriage dowry will be to bring me the foreskins of a hundred of the enemy whom you have personally slain."

For a moment even David lost his aplomb, struck not so much by the stringency of the demand as by its obscenity. Then he recovered himself and said, "It shall be done. My men and I will leave this very evening."

"Your men?"

Now at last David understood that what had gone awry had little or nothing to do with Michal. He said smoothly, "Has not my lord the king even now made me the captain of a thousand?"

"Even now," said Saul.

That evening the king told Rizpah what had transpired between him and David. She listened without comment to the end, then waited, sensing there was more to come. Saul looked at her and said tonelessly, "I have sent my son David to his death."

She was angry at his relapse into what she felt was weakness, but said only, "David has it in his heart to kill you."

Yet both of them, without speaking of it further, fell into the habit of going to the rooftop at sundown and peering westward into the copper light . . . across the broad caravan trail, into the hills toward Kirjath-jearim, the direction from which they knew David must return . . . if he returned.

He did, of course. Twenty-three days after the king had commanded him to go forth, he entered the common room, and in front of all of us he opened the sack he carried and dumped the odorous, repulsive trophies in a heap before Saul.

"My lord may wish to count them," he said, not troubling to conceal the anger in his voice. "I have brought two hundred, so there will be no question that I have fulfilled the conditions of the dowry."

We waited, wondering how the king would react. This was no obsequious shepherd lad standing before him. David had spoken as an equal, as one warrior to another.

Saul grew pale. His eyes burned with a cold, hard flame. Then he closed them and lowered his head. When he looked up again, the flame had died. He stood up, took David by the arm and led him away from the stinking mess on the floor.

"I am deeply ashamed," he said.

"My father . . ." David began, but then he choked up and could not go on.

"The wedding will take place as soon as it can be arranged."

Saul and David embraced. Then David went at once to Michal. I looked at Rizpah. She kept her gaze unwaveringly on Saul. Her face was shining with love, but even as I watched, love was extinguished like a snuffed-out lamp. And into its place crept the haggardness peculiar to suffering.

chapter seven

AHINOAM'S HEALTH was somewhat improved, but she was still not well enough to attend the wedding festivities. Therefore she asked Rizpah to see that the boy Ishbaal was properly washed and dressed. "He is nearly fourteen now," she said, "and he should be able to do these things for himself. This is why I am ashamed to ask the servants . . ."

"Of course," said Rizpah, touching her hand.

Searching for Ishbaal, Rizpah entered one after another of the upper chambers of the house. So it was without thinking that she entered Michal's room. The bride had already left to descend to the great hall, and the wake of her departure contained scattered ornaments, little pots of oils and creams lying open on the table, a jumble of sandals on the floor. Lying across the bed was the everyday robe Michal had discarded when she changed to her wedding dress. There is something about the recently worn gown of a beautiful woman which gives mute testimony to her loveliness—the drape and fall of the cloth—a visual stanza no poet could ever hope to emulate. And no one is quicker to take note of this than another woman.

Where beauty was concerned, Rizpah had no cause to be envious. The nausea which had plagued her during her first pregnancy was passing her by this time. Her hair was smooth and glossy, her complexion unblemished, her body full and firm, with the ripeness of gestation only beginning to assert itself.

She took up a corner of Michal's robe, held it between her thumb and forefinger. How vulnerable it made the girl seem. I had told Rizpah tales of the sorcerers of Cush, the black empire to the south of Egypt, who claim that if you allow an enemy to come into possession of an article of your clothing, you are thenceforth in his power. She could understand this now, yet even as she stood there, recalling all the reasons why she should hate Michal, she felt the hatred leave her heart.

"You love David," she said aloud to the robe, "just as I love Saul. In this there is honesty, and power. And perhaps the sharp-toothed rocks of our enmity will be blunted now and crumble with disuse." Then she added in a rush of words so fervent they were like a spasm, "O Jahveh, make it so!"

A burst of laughter from below reminded her that she had a task to perform before she could go down and join the celebration.

She found Ishbaal on the rooftop pulling the legs off a beetle. She had seen him torturing insects and small reptiles so many times in the period she had lived at Gibeah that she was no longer shocked.

"Get up and come with me," she said.

"What for?" The boy turned an insolent, furtive face up to her but made no effort to rise. As usual his mouth was streaked with a mixture of dirt and juice of the fruit he had eaten. Near him on the stone floor lay a sprinkling of date pits and fig stems.

"I'm going to wash and dress you for your sister's wedding feast."

"My mother washes me."

He turned his attention back to the beetle. All but one of its legs were gone now, and he put it down on the floor. The creature quivered in a frantic effort to move. Ishbaal observed it solemnly. Rizpah brought her sandal down on it. Ishbaal leaped to his feet.

"You killed it!"

"I'll do the same any time I find you torturing something."

"It's not your business."

Suddenly his expression changed. His round unblinking eyes grew secretive, insinuating. She felt his gaze traveling over her body and repressed a feeling of repugnance.

"You're going to have another baby."

"Who told you that?"

"Doeg the herdsman told me it was in your belly. Can I see it?"

She was so stunned she could not reply at once. And he said, malevolence crumpling his features, "I'll pull its arms and legs off!"

She slapped him and he burst into tears. Then, because she was a little afraid of him and wished to keep him in the role of child, she seized him by the ear and pulled him to the stairs. He allowed himself to be led in this fashion with surprising docility.

While she was washing his face and hands, he looked up at her and asked, "Will my mother die?"

"She's getting better every day."

"If she dies, I don't know what I shall do."

He had spoken so simply, without pretense, that her heart went out to him. O Jahveh, she thought, why did you give us love's pleasure without equipping us to deal with its pain? But then, she countered, can there be love without pain?

It was in this frame of mind that she descended to the common room.

The ceremony was over. David and Michal had declared their vows before God. Now the guests were waiting for the feast, circling about the room like ants in search of a clot of honey.

The captains of thousands were there, gathered in a tight excluding group as military men will before they have drunk enough courage to mingle with others. Among them was Joab, David's young cousin, barely grown to manhood, but possessing a bold, questing face which spoke of unlimited self-assurance.

David's seven stolid brothers were present, but not his parents, since they were too old to make the journey from Beth-lehem.

In a corner, surrounded by cushions, sat Merab, attended by her grave, balding husband. The plump mouse had turned into a fat cat. Exactly nine months after her marriage to Barzillai she had given birth to twins, and she was again big with child. One knew simply by looking at her that she was destined to live as long as she was able to conceive in a state of everlasting pregnancy.

David stood next to Michal, his green eyes dancing with excitement, responding with sharp wit to the conventional teasing jests tossed at him from the knot of captains.

Michal was radiant. She was dressed in a white gown which was cleverly contrived to look demure and at the same time reveal all the pertinent features of her sensuous body. The carnal blatancy would never be erased from her face, but now it was so tempered and transmuted by her happiness that one could scarcely recognize her.

Until she saw Rizpah moving toward her through the crowd. Then she was once more the wary, predatory virgin. Her eyes narrowed, and her tongue flicked out over her lips. And in one of the strange lulls that sometimes fall over a large group of people, voices were hushed and heads were turned in the direction of the two young women.

As she reached Michal, Rizpah without hesitation put her arms around the girl and kissed her warmly. "May your joy live forever," she said.

Michal was first taken aback. Then she began to cry. It was the second time that day Rizpah had caused a child of Saul to weep, and now tears sprang to her own eyes.

The assembled guests enjoyed the little exchange immensely. It was, agreed many, just what the wedding needed. In a space of moments everyone was laughing and crying at once, and there was a sudden run on the jars of wine.

Into this chaos came the musicians, adding the shrill sound of pipes, the vibration of plucked strings and the percussive beat of the timbrel to the general din.

The whole roast lambs and kids were brought to the long table and disappeared as fast as the servants could carve them, along with great bowls of spiced vegetables and mounds of candied figs and dates.

Zaccur, forgetting his dislike of David, performed a wild solo dance ending with a handspring which brought him up directly between two huge jars of wine. He seized a cup, and raising it high in the air, called out, "To the bride. May her womb soon be as full as my heart is at this moment!"

And Michal actually blushed.

Weddings often have the power to do this . . . to dissolve old rivalries and fill the being with the joy of living. But there is another, just as common, side to a marriage feast. Nuptials are frequently like a warm day in midwinter: they bring to life things which would be better left sleeping.

Abner had drunk a little too much of Saul's heavy red wine. He said to me, "Does she not look particularly beautiful today?"

There was no point in pretending I did not know who he meant. We both glanced at Rizpah, who was laughing and clapping her hands in time to the music as she watched Zaccur engaging in another of his abandoned dances.

Abner stammered a bit as he went on. "It is spring, and I should be alive and joyous as one of the birds out there in the garden. But what is spring to me? A meaningless muddle of trees and flowers." He paused while he gulped down the rest of the wine in his cup. "She pities me. Pity. It is the most insidious emotion that ever existed. It masquerades under the name of compassion, but it really hides only anger. Why is she angry with me? I love her so much. I shall love her until I die. . . ."

What could I say? It is written in the Hebrew laws that if a man comes before you naked and shivering, you should provide him with a cloak. But nowhere is it written what to do when you are confronted with the nakedness of a soul. I did the only thing I could do.

I led Abner to the table, where we provided ourselves with fresh cups of wine, and I drank with him. I tried to tell him with my eyes that I understood, but there is no understanding yet fashioned which can mend a breaking heart.

Abner was not as alone as he might have thought. Paltiel son of Laish found himself next to Rizpah. He had drunk far more than his general. His bulging eyes were glazed, but his speech was clear, too clear. "You kissed her," he said to Rizpah. "You kissed her, and I was even jealous of you."

It took her a moment to realize he was talking about Michal. "Since I first joined the army of Saul my innards have melted away every time I saw her. Sometimes she would look at me in that way she has, and I would think perhaps she was interested in me. But then I knew . . ." He broke off and peered owlishly at Rizpah. "Do you have any idea what I would give if she would let me touch her, or even kiss the hem of her robe? And now David, this very night . . ."

He began to weep so loudly and violently that one of his fellow captains came and led him out into the garden.

Rizpah felt a sudden desperate need to be with Saul. She found him sitting quietly in a corner of the hall with Jonathan, who smiled at Rizpah and left to join David.

She whispered to Saul, "My love, can we leave now . . . quickly?"

chapter eight

THE HOUSE at Gibeah was charged with tension.

It was late summer. For weeks the sun had been rising blood-red, coursing through a brazen sky and plunging toward the west with its ferocity undiminished. There was no relief from the heat, no customary cool breeze of evening, only the ceaseless torrid wind sighing up from the south. The barley was withering in the fields, and the kernels of wheat atop their sere stalks were hard and shriveled.

The men arrived late one night—Saul, Abner, Jonathan and David —dust-covered and exhausted from their journey across Ephraim.

Rizpah, Michal and I were waiting up to welcome them, though the torchlit reception in the courtyard could scarcely be called a welcome. Even at midnight the air was oppressive. The wind plucked at our garments, rattled a shutter on the house and flattened the flames of the torches.

Neither of the women had accompanied their men on this last campaign. Even if Rizpah had not been in her seventh month of pregnancy, Saul would have refused to take her along. A roving band of Philistines, over a thousand in number, had been terrorizing the Ephraimite countryside from Beth-shan to Shiloh. The army of Israel had been pursuing them for over a month, traveling in forced marches, sleeping only a few hours out of each day or night. They had just succeeded in running the Philistines to earth, destroying most of them, dispersing the rest, when the urgent summons came from Gibeah.

Saul embraced Rizpah perfunctorily. "How is she?"

"Who can know?" Rizpah spread out her hands in a gesture that made her look peculiarly aged. "Two days ago we thought she was gone. Now Egrep says she may live for months."

I was annoyed with her for making me a prophet of hope. Saul looked at me. "She may also die tonight," I said, returning his gaze steadily.

He strode into the house. Rizpah drifted after him. Michal, whose nature defied even the smell of death, tugged at David's arm, bent on taking him at once to the dwelling which had been built for them, separate from the main house. I was left alone with Abner and Jonathan.

"Is she conscious?" asked Abner.

"Sometimes. She babbles. Once today she cried out for Rizpah and me. When we reached her bedside, she smiled sweetly at us and began to talk about a vineyard growing beside a violet sea. Has she ever looked on the ocean?"

They stared at me blankly.

"I must go to her," said Jonathan, but he made no effort to do so.

"Come eat and drink something, both of you."

Jonathan's face took on the simple, guileless expression it assumed in moments of stress. "She was always very good to me."

"I feel old," said Abner. "I feel the weight of years pressing down on my chest. When Ahinoam was a young girl . . ."

"When Ahinoam was a young girl, you were a young man," I said tartly, the heat making me impatient with him. "She no longer has her health. You have. And that gives you the power to feel as old or young as you wish. Now come eat and drink."

"You're a terrible old woman."

"I am alive."

All at once he broke into laughter. "Thank you," he said.

"Come along now," I said. "Both of you."

Ahinoam did not die that night. She rallied enough to recognize Saul and speak cogently to him. He remained constantly by her bedside. But by dawn she had lapsed back into delirium.

The morning sun lent more heat to air that darkness had not cooled, and by noon it was an effort even to move.

Rizpah and I hovered close by the door of the sickroom, in case Saul should call for us. We could hear Ahinoam's voice, rising and falling in a meaningless mumble. Once she said quite clearly, "The plow . . ." but otherwise we could not make out the words.

Ishbaal wandered by, eating grapes from one of the few skimpy bunches the vineyards had yielded. He stopped, turning a disconsolate, purple-stained face toward us, his great eyes questioning. Rizpah spoke to him, but he did not reply, instead resuming his aimless course down the hall.

Saul came out of the room and leaned against the doorjamb. Perspiration beaded his forehead. "She doesn't want to live," he said to no one in particular.

There was nothing we could say in reply.

The gibbering voice inside the room stopped abruptly. Saul turned, quickly alert, and disappeared into the chamber. When he came back, we knew from his expression it had happened.

Rizpah approached him wordlessly, her hand outstretched in the entreaty of sympathy. I saw his face go livid and distorted, but before I could shout a warning, he had seized her and was trying to choke her.

I found my voice and shrieked for help, then rushed at Saul, attempting to disengage his fingers from her throat. He flung me back against the wall.

Rizpah screamed. I have seldom heard a sound of such pure terror. It brought Saul to his senses, at least enough for Rizpah to break free and crawl away from him. Then she collapsed. By the time Abner, Jonathan and some of the servants arrived she was in labor.

Abner stepped up to Saul, who was standing quietly, his hands hanging at his sides. He tried to speak to the king, but his anger was too great, and all he could get out were a few stricken, incoherent noises. He joined Jonathan and me, helping us carry Rizpah to her room.

Helah and I worked desperately over her. Her agony was so intense that she tore the bedclothes to shreds. The servants told me later that her screams were so piercing and held so much horror that two donkeys in the stable broke out of their stalls and fled across the hills.

But all through that long afternoon I cannot remember hearing a single sound.

Just after dark we delivered her of a male child, smaller, more red and wrinkled than was normal, but otherwise well-formed and very much alive.

Only then did I hear the lyre music floating through the house . . . dark and brooding at first, gradually becoming lighter in tone until it ended with a series of sprightly melodies.

An hour after the music stopped, Saul appeared at the door. I was alone with Rizpah now, and the moment I saw him I flew at him, cursing him with all the extensive vocabulary at my command. He merely stood, his head bent forward as if he were walking into a storm, making no effort to reply to my abuse.

I shall never cease to marvel at the miraculous power of love.

As I was catching my breath between curses, a faint voice behind me said, "Saul . . ."

He moved past me with the fumbling steps of a blind man and fell to his knees beside the bed.

She held up the baby. He put out his hand to touch it, drew back hastily.

"Go ahead. He belongs to you, too."

"Rizpah . . ."

"I thought Meribaal."

"You thought . . ."

"Meribaal. His name."

"Oh. Yes."

"It pleases you?"

"It pleases me."

"I'm very glad you came."

"I didn't know . . . My guilt is so great, Rizpah."

"As is mine."

He held up his hands and looked at them. "They should be cut off. What have they ever wrought but evil?"

"They have saved Israel. And they have comforted me."

"And tried to rob you of life. Even as they withheld life from Ahinoam."

"Saul . . ."

"Hear me. I shall swear an oath this night . . ."

"There is no need."

"I swear that except against the enemies of Israel my hand will never again be raised in violence. May the Lord God be witness to my words." He paused, then said again, "Never except against the enemies of Israel."

And by his own standards he kept the covenant.

chapter nine

No ONE knew precisely why it happened just at the moment it did. Certainly even Rizpah had no intimation of what was coming. Yet the forces behind the act must have been gathering for some time, dark and relentless, in Saul's mind.

It was winter. Since the matter of the dowry, when the king had been overcome with shame after sending David on that dangerous and indecent quest, he had not spoken a single word against his son-in-law. To the contrary, he lavished praise and affection on the young man.

The winter camp had again been established at Gallim, with the same cadre of battle-wise veterans. David and Jonathan once more took them out on periodic forays across the Philistine border. However, in contrast to the year before, David was now meticulous about consulting Saul before each campaign, and reporting to him the instant he returned. And as before, David would play his lyre in the king's house. But now it was not so much for the purpose of lightening Saul's melancholy as for pure entertainment.

Though he never actually spoke to her about it, occasionally while he was playing David would catch Rizpah's eye, and it was as though he was trying to convince her that he truly had no designs on the throne of Saul.

I have often wondered about David's innermost feelings during this period. It is difficult for me to divest myself of prejudice in the matter. I had more than once marked the signs of ambition in him. He was clever and competent, and always he must have remembered that Samuel had rejected Saul and chosen him. Yet I believe his professed love for Saul and Jonathan was genuine. He was a man capable of both great generosity and great ruthlessness, and the two qualities must have waged constant war within him.

But during this winter there had been peace in Saul's house. The king was more tranquil in spirit than he had been for a number of months. He had again set up the sessions of judgment and heard litigations each day from early morning until well after noon. He spent a great deal of time playing with his and Rizpah's children. The infant Meribaal received his fair share of attention, but it was Armoni, now a year and a half old, who entranced Saul. He already possessed the king's dark handsomeness, and on fine days when Saul and Rizpah would take him into the garden he would crawl about, scooping up handfuls of dirt and inspecting them with critical attention. "You see!" Saul would cry delightedly. "A born farmer. Look at the way he takes to the soil. When he becomes a man, he will only have to touch the earth to make it green and fruitful." And to Rizpah's amusement, he ordered a miniature plow made for Armoni and presented it to him with a ceremonious little speech. She was even more amused when the child treasured the toy above all others, keeping it by him day and night.

As Saul had withdrawn his anger from David, so Rizpah consolidated her truce with Michal. In truth, the two women were so syrupy with each other that it nearly made my stomach turn to be in their presence. They would praise each other's clothes; they experimented with new hair styles; they giggled together like young girls. I found myself longing for the days when they would not have traded a pair of words unless each was an epithet.

But at least there was peace. And even I allowed myself to be deluded into believing it would be eternal.

One day toward noon we heard the sound of the ram's horn and saw the cadre of Israel's army passing on its way home to Gallim after a raid. David and Jonathan dropped out of the march and approached the house.

Rizpah, Michal and I met them in the courtyard, for Saul was holding judgment in the common room. As usual, Michal wasted not a moment in twining herself around her husband and making motions toward their house.

"Not now, my dove," he said, laughing. "We must first report the results of the campaign to my father Saul."

Michal pouted. "The campaign," she said scornfully. "How can you speak of campaigns when you know how I've been pining for you these past ten days?"

"When she finally gets him home," I whispered to Rizpah, "I'll wager he'll remember the battlefield as a minor paradise." She looked at me blandly, but said nothing.

"You should be proud of your husband, my sister," said Jonathan. "In one encounter he came to my rescue and killed three of the five

Philistines who were surrounding me. Had it not been for David's quick courage, I should now be part of the soil around the town of Ono. Or else resting in some filthy vulture's craw."

Something made me turn. Saul was standing in the doorway, gazing benevolently at the two young men. They swung around and, seeing the king, ran to greet him respectfully. "I did not expect you back quite so soon," he said. "My judgments will take another two hours. After that, we shall have a feast to welcome both my sons home." He looked at Rizpah. "You will see to the arrangements, my love?"

The feast lasted until late afternoon. As was customary when the table was cleared, Saul asked David to play. We all repaired to the end of the common room and seated ourselves around the carved throne.

I should have sensed something amiss when Saul, most courteously to be sure, asked us to move back on either side so David would have ample room for his playing. And the feeling should have been confirmed when I noticed that the king had lifted the spear which was always by the side of the throne and was caressing the handle in an absent, almost dreamy, fashion. But I, along with everyone else, had been lulled by the successive months of tranquillity, and the amount of food we had consumed further dulled our senses.

So it was with deep pleasure that I listened to the notes of the lyre. David had always played well, but his experiences of the past year seemed to have heightened his power of expression. The more serious selections reflected his acquired knowledge of the nature of death, without which there can be no true feeling. And the lighter melodies spoke of this as well, but they also contained the fire and lyrical joy of the lover.

During a pause in the playing Saul sighed and said, "No one in Israel has ever played as you do, my son. Come a few steps closer that I may hear you better."

David approached obediently, but as he took his last step, I saw his expression of pleased devotion undergo a rapid transition. Nothing I can point to even now and say thus and thus did he change. But suddenly he was no longer the shepherd-lyrist. He had again become the warrior, calculating and watchful, balanced for charge or flight.

I do not believe anyone else in the room noticed this. Nor should I have, had I not happened to be watching his face. For after the first lightning rearrangement of his features, David was once more quite at ease. Saul still sat quietly, seemingly lost in the pleasantest of reveries.

David plucked the strings of the lyre. The melody was one I knew well: an ancient marching song from the city of Ashdod which had been taken over by the Hebrews and restyled in a minor mode. This preserved the martial atmosphere of the piece while imparting to it something of the feeling of lostness which stirs in every warrior on the eve of battle. Looking back on it now, I am sure David chose the song deliberately, to bring into the open whatever lay concealed beneath the deceptive calm of the room. And once again I must admire his coolness and courage, his confidence in the face of peril.

I was watching Saul, but he moved so quickly I did not see his grip tighten on the handle of the spear. Later I remembered that I heard the quick shuffling of his sandals on the floor. Then he was on his feet, his body poised in the magnificent arch of the expert spear thrower.

The weapon hurtled through the air directly toward David's chest. He seemed to move only one shoulder in a languid, almost careless motion, but his face was twisted with effort. The spear whispered close by him and imbedded itself with a solid thump in a wooden stanchion halfway across the room.

The two men faced each other. Anger, fear and sadness were mingled in David's expression. Saul was icy calm, his eyes full of the terrible excluding wrath they had contained the day he and Rizpah returned from the well of Gallim.

No one in the room moved. Then from Jonathan came a sudden incongruous titter which was half bewilderment, half heartbreak.

This broke the tableau. David turned from Saul, and the young warrior became once again a boyish, frightened shepherd. He tucked his lyre under his arm and scampered from the hall. Michal followed him with the howling cry of an animal in flight.

During all this Rizpah and I sat motionless as statues. But Jonathan, recovering from his initial shock, walked over to the stanchion in which the spear was still quivering. He wrested the weapon from the wood and returned with it to Saul, who was again sitting in the throne chair. Without a word he handed the spear to his father and turned to go.

Saul's voice stopped him. "Come back, my son."

Jonathan retraced his steps. It was impossible to tell from his face what he was thinking. "My father called?"

"Where are you going?"

"To seek my brother David."

"You will bring him back with you."

"So my father can cast his spear at him again? My father has never been known to miss any target a second time."

There was a studied insolence in the young prince's tone which struck me as disturbingly familiar, and yet somehow strange. Then it came to me that the inflection of Jonathan's voice was not his own, but David's.

Against David, Saul's wrath was cold and terrible, given to silence and chilling calm. But his anger at Jonathan contained some of the more characteristic roaring overtones. "You son of perverse rebellion, you have chosen the son of Jesse to your own shame, and the shame of your mother's nakedness. For as long as the son of Jesse walks on the earth, you shall not inherit the kingdom which the Lord God gave to me." His voice grew waspish. "Now go and fetch David here, for he deserves to die."

Jonathan's expression did not change. "Why should he be put to death? What has he done?"

The veins in Saul's forehead swelled. He raised the spear, drew it back to striking position. Rizpah and I gasped simultaneously, but Jonathan did not even move. And in a moment the rage went out of Saul. The spear clattered to the floor.

But as the anger departed from Saul, it entered the person of his son. I had rarely seen Jonathan even mildly reproachful. Always there had been the open expression, the warmth, the underlying presence of irony which seldom found its way to the surface. I should have known there was some basic connection between the personable youth everyone loved and the bold warrior who had struck the first brave blow at Michmas. The bridge was now apparent in his anger. It gave him stature; it wiped all trace of youth and simplicity from his features. Saul's son had in one instant become a man. And more: Jonathan in this moment was more of a king than either of the men Samuel had anointed. His words rapped out forcefully, each one making Saul wince. "My father has dealt treacherously with the proffered love of David. Therefore he has forfeited his claim on my affections. Let my father henceforth wither alone in the field of his own iniquity!"

He left the hall, his footsteps sounding loud and ominous in the silence. Out of the corner of my eye I could see Rizpah watching Saul, alert for the first signs of weeping or the onset of stupor. But Saul's face hardened, and he called after Jonathan, "So be it!" Then he turned to me. "Bring the captain of the house guard into my presence."

I did as he asked. The captain of the guard listened carefully to the king's instructions. "You will go at once with your men to the house where David dwells. You will bring him to me, by force if necessary. If he attempts to escape, kill him."

The soldier had served with Saul as captain over a hundred against Ammon, Moab and Amalek. He was well acquainted with his king's honesty and bravery, but he had also witnessed his episodes of madness. Therefore he scrutinized Saul's countenance closely. He was neither a subtle nor a tactful man, and his inspection was obvious even to Saul, who said, "Are you looking to see if I am mad?"

The captain took in Saul's cold, regal bearing, the stony resolve of his eyes. "No, my lord," he said, beginning to tremble.

"Then go at once and do as I order."

Neither Rizpah nor I stirred during the time the captain was gone. Tragedy was abroad, and in each of us was the unarticulated feeling: if I do not move, it will pass me by.

The captain returned alone. "My lord, your daughter Michal has informed me that her husband David is sick in his bed and is unable to come before my lord the king."

Saul sneered. "Have I men or infants in my service that they are put off by such flimsy excuses?"

The soldier was ready for this. "Begging your pardon, my lord, the same thought occurred to me. I insisted that the lady Michal bring me to David. She went away, and when she returned she led me to the room, bidding me walk softly, and let me look into the chamber. He was there in bed, covered and so still and lifeless I can only believe he is grievously ill."

The king got up and walked to the window, where he remained deep in thought for a time. Daylight was failing, and a servant slipped into the hall and began lighting the lamps. Saul came back to the throne and spoke to the captain.

"Go again to David's house. Bring him to me in the bed, so I may kill him here."

The cold-bloodedness of the order shook the captain. Soldiers in battle become resistant to the effects of horror, but brutality contemplated in quiet often makes the most seasoned veteran's gorge rise. A trickle of saliva appeared at the corner of the man's mouth and started down his chin. He left the hall hurriedly without replying.

As he went out, Abner entered. The general had been resting at his home, several hours' journey from Gibeah, but it was his custom during winter inactivity to pay frequent, unannounced visits to the king's house. He approached the throne, and as always, his eyes first sought Rizpah. So it was from her expression that he learned something was wrong. He then looked questioningly at Saul.

"You are just in time, my uncle. The next hour will witness the death of a traitor in Israel."

"And who is this traitor?"

"Need you inquire? David will die by my hand."

Abner subjected Saul to the same kind of scrutiny accorded him before by the captain, but he was able to do so without appearing obvious. "What has David done that he should be slain?"

"He is preparing to steal my kingdom."

"I see." He went on with scarcely a break, switching smoothly into speech designed both to humor and divert Saul. "Would it not be better, my nephew, to devise some different method of dealing with treachery? Perhaps to wait and—"

Saul's voice interrupted his temporizing. "We have already waited too long. Will we display our weakness forever?"

"But surely if we delay—"

"Why does my uncle defend the scoundrel? Do you not know this scheming shepherd has been anointed by Samuel to be king in my place?"

I had forgotten that Abner did not know. Saul's overt antagonism toward David had been short-lived, and had taken place the year before while Abner was away. There had been no mention of it since. The general, disbelieving but sensing a ring of truth in Saul's words, cast a desperate glance at Rizpah. She nodded once, almost imperceptibly.

Even convinced as he now was, Abner attempted to reason with Saul, to sway him from his avowed intention of killing David. But he had only managed to utter a few halting sentences when there was a commotion outside the hall, and the captain entered, escorting a fuming Michal.

"Trickery, my lord," he said while he was still approaching the throne. "I made my lady Michal bring me again to the sickroom. And now I began to wonder at the stillness of the form in the bed. So before I ordered my men . . ." He paused, breathless, unused to such involved reportage. "There was nothing in the bed, my lord. By that I mean David was not there. Only an image covered with a cloth, and a quilt of goat's hair at the head. And at the rear of the house there was a rope suspended from an upper window. It is my considered opinion, my lord, that your servant David has fled."

He stopped speaking and knitted his brow earnestly, waiting for commendation on the thoroughness of his investigation. Saul ignored him and turned sadly to Michal. "Why have you deceived me, and let my enemy escape?"

And Michal, opening her eyes wide, said, "Oh my father, he said he would kill me if I did not let him go."

It was such a transparent lie that I feared for the girl's life. Saul's cold fury against David could easily have transferred itself to her. But he only shook his head gravely and said, "So he very well might have."

In my absorption with what had been taking place between Saul and Michal, I had not been noticing Rizpah's reactions. Now as I looked at her, I was startled by the transformation which had taken place in her. She had been as shocked as I at the unexpected attempt on David's life. She also seemed to have been immobilized by Saul's obsessive desire to make good his first failure. But now, after Michal's devious statement, her expression matched Saul's for murderous intent. As I watched, she got up and made an unobtrusive exit from the hall.

Saul was beginning to discuss with Abner a plan for pursuing David. Michal stood by, listening, a wily gleam in her eyes. The captain shifted from one foot to the other, miserable in his exposure to something he did not understand. As soon as I could do so gracefully, I left the hall to look for Rizpah.

I found her in the courtyard, pacing back and forth beneath the dim light of the two torches flanking the doorway. She seemed scarcely conscious of my presence.

After a while the captain of the guard came out, mopping his forehead. Rizpah flew to his side.

"Will you do something for me?"

"Anything my lady commands."

"This must be carried out in complete secrecy. No one must know, not even the king."

The captain sighed. I felt sorry for him. He had just endured one confusing ordeal, and doubtless considered himself fortunate to have survived. Now here was something else which promised to be as bizarre and unpalatable as the king's desire to kill his son-in-law. But he dared not refuse whatever Rizpah asked. "It shall be done as you say, my lady."

"Send one of your men to the camp at Gallim. Tell him to ask Paltiel son of Laish to come to me as soon as he is able."

The captain brightened, relieved that he was not being asked to commit mayhem.

But I found myself growing more and more uneasy.

chapter ten

I HAVE heard of a type of demon which is able to divide itself and inhabit the spirits of two persons simultaneously. It stirs up the same fears and hatreds in each, goads them to the same extremes of attitude, tortures them with the same obsessions. And because there is only one demon at work in both spirits, neither of the afflicted ones finds anything odd in the behavior of the other.

This is what was happening now with Saul and Rizpah. After David's escape from Gibeah, she became as relentless as the king in her attitude toward the fugitive. She echoed Saul's cry that David was a menace to Israel and should be hunted out and slain like a wolf which threatens a shepherd's flocks.

I myself had no great affection for David even then. However, in my most cynical moments I could not believe he seriously intended to usurp Saul's throne. The warring elements within him would give him ceaseless torment, but in the end I felt that love would at least restrain ambition from making any open bid for the kingdom.

Whenever I ventured this opinion to Rizpah, I might as well have shouted it in the empty reaches of the desert. She would appear to listen to me, but the moment I stopped speaking she would be off on some frenetic diatribe of David-denunciation. And there would be no halting her until finally she succumbed to exhaustion.

A few times I heard her discussing David with Saul. These were always chilling experiences. The two of them were like demented antiphonal singers composing a hymn of hatred. Even the tone of their dialogue was liturgical.

"David is a beast of the field," Saul would say.

"His name shall be wiped out forever," she would reply.

"The shepherd has become a serpent, lying in wait for the king."

"He shall be crushed and destroyed forever."

There was only one difference between them in this matter. Saul gave himself over to single-minded plans for the pursuit and capture of David. Rizpah concurred in these and encouraged her man with all the fervor of which she was capable. But she recognized Michal as an additional enemy, and felt a constant threat in the girl's presence at Gibeah.

She possessed far too much insight and flair for intrigue to approach Saul directly about his daughter. She had seen that the king would believe even the most implausible lies from Michal's lips. So Rizpah made a private vendetta of her enmity, and set about a plan which she hoped would culminate in Michal's exile from the king's house.

It is said that a woman's beauty can be increased in equal degrees by love and hatred. I would take exception to this, for beauty born of love is soft and tender, like the first flowering of an almond tree. And what it seems to be it is. But the beauty which springs from hatred is a mask, a deception of greenery over the face of a bitter salt marsh.

Rizpah's beauty at this time was enhanced by both love and hatred. But the latter was gaining ascendancy. Her eyes were bright; the comeliness of her body could weave a provocative spell. Only, the brightness of her eyes was febrile. And too often one of her most graceful gestures would end in the convulsive clenching of her fingers.

But to Paltiel when he came to Gibeah a few hours after David's flight she must have appeared a little like a goddess.

She had dressed and arranged her hair with considerable meticulousness. When the captain of the guard tapped at her door to tell her Paltiel had arrived, she was ready. It was a cool night, and she had lighted two braziers in the room—one with wood coals for warmth, the other containing incense.

The snub-nosed officer entered, blinking his awe at the softly lighted chamber with its profusion of silks and satins.

Rizpah let him take all this in, and when she saw he had observed the two chairs drawn close together at the table, the wine decanter and the two silver goblets, she came forward. She welcomed him warmly, with just a touch of intimacy, taking careful note of his reaction. For if he responded too enthusiastically to her greeting, she would know she had been wrong about him and her plan would have to undergo certain revisions.

But his attitude toward her was both respectful and shy. He seated himself diffidently at her side and accepted a cup of wine.

Through skillful guidance of the conversation she learned what she wanted to know about him. Paltiel was a stone without polish, a poor lad who had grown up in a village nor far from Gallim. As with so many others, the army had meant to Paltiel emancipation from poverty. In the service of Saul he had gained whatever education and experience he possessed. He idolized the king. And the confidence he had poured out to her at the wedding feast of Michal and David had not been merely a mouthing of drunken desire. He loved Michal with every fiber of his being: hopelessly, eternally.

And as he talked of Michal, Rizpah learned another thing. The young man was neither a simpleton nor a weakling. There was strength and integrity in his speech. And gradually as he spoke emerged a sweetness, a generosity of spirit, which transcended his undistinguished features and made him quite attractive.

Rizpah knew better than to reveal anything of her true purpose in summoning him. Instead she alluded to the events which had taken place that afternoon. "The king has discovered to his deep regret that the man he considered his son and trusted servant has become his enemy. Indeed, has been his enemy almost since the moment he first set eyes on the king at Elah."

"David?" Paltiel's eyes bulged slightly as they always did when he was perturbed. Then promptly, with no further question, "Whatever wrong he has done my lord Saul, he shall be punished. I shall go at once and request permission of my king to deal with the traitor."

Rizpah smiled. "Unfortunately, the king will have to make other use of your loyalty. David has fled Gibeah."

He was silent for a moment. "And Michal?"

"Remains here with her father."

She was rewarded by seeing a look of such pure happiness pass across Paltiel's face that she was sure now her plan would work. But she would have to proceed carefully.

"The king will soon be going forth to seek David and bring him to justice."

"Then I shall go with him."

"I knew you would. Did you not wonder at my sending for you?"

"I wondered."

"The king is no longer the young man he was."

"There is no more valiant warrior in all Israel."

"But he is older than when he marched against Ammon and Jabesh. And—" she coughed delicately—"since you are one of his captains, you will know what I mean when I speak of the demons which plague his spirit."

"If I were able, I should flay each one of them with my sword and drive them back to Sheol."

Rizpah, whose own dedication to Saul had on occasion been monumental, found this unbridled devotion touching, and at the same time somewhat unrealistic, but she said only, "The king is fortunate to have an officer on whom he can depend so completely."

"And my lady would also like to depend on me."

She was pleased with this. It told her Paltiel was not lacking in initiative. The pace of the plan would be dictated by her alone, but there would come a time when she would have to count on Paltiel to take matters into his own hands. She continued along the line of thought she had begun. "With some men," she said, "the more years they add to their lives, the more cautious they become. This is not true of Saul. I have a premonition that the search for David will prove dangerous. If David remains a fugitive for any length of time, he will gather men about him . . . malcontents and dissidents who will be desperate and . . ."

"My lady," interrupted Paltiel, "if what you are asking of me is that I take special care of the king's life, you need not have asked. I shall not let my lord out of my sight."

"Thank you," she breathed. "And I hope you will visit Gibeah frequently in the future and honor us by your presence at our table."

The young officer flushed, trying manfully to conceal his embarrassment and pleasure. Rizpah steered the talk into inconsequential channels. Then, as she was bidding him farewell, she remarked casually, "I know you will say nothing of my request to anyone, particularly the king. If he should learn that I am overly concerned for his safety . . ."

She did not have to complete the thought. Paltiel accepted readily the bond of benevolent conspiracy she was tendering him.

Now, she thought when she was once more alone, we have begun. Paltiel will be constantly in the king's eye. There is no doubt that he will acquit himself favorably. And after the first few visits to Gibeah, his presence will be taken as a matter of course. . . .

The news of David's defection (though not its immediate cause) spread rapidly through the army.

But the civilian population was not so quick to understand that there was now open enmity between Saul and David. This led to an incident which brought blame onto the heads of both men, and also gave clear indication of the bitterness gathering between their two houses.

The town of Nob was famous for the sanctuary of Jahveh within its walls. Even before Saul ascended the throne, it had been a center for religious pilgrimages, and now Saul had given it added prestige by sending the sword of the giant Goliath to the temple.

The administrator of the sanctuary was an aged priest named Ahimelech. A few days after David's escape from Gibeah, he appeared at Nob and demanded food and weapons. Ahimelech, who was no fool, grew suspicious because David was alone, and at first refused to give him what he asked. But David lied smoothly, saying he was on a secret mission for the king. So the old priest gave him loaves of holy bread and the sword of Goliath.

It so happened that Doeg, Saul's chief herdsman, was in Nob at the time. He saw David enter the sanctuary with Ahimelech and emerge a few moments later with the bread and the sword. This appeared a bit strange to him, but he thought little of it until he returned to Gibeah and learned what had taken place. At once he informed Saul of what he had witnessed.

David's scribes, perhaps in an effort to minimize David's fault by magnifying Saul's, have written that the king had Ahimelech and eighty-four other priests of Nob put to death and that he also destroyed every living soul in the city as he had done in the land of Amalek.

In point of fact, nothing of the sort happened. What did occur was reprehensible enough, but in this case Saul was not guilty of wholesale murder.

Doeg went to Nob on Saul's order and returned with Ahimelech. The priest was terrified when Saul confronted him with having aided David. He protested with great sincerity that if he had known of the break between the king and his son-in-law, he would have turned from the young man as from a viper. But Saul hardly listened to him. The fact that Ahimelech had helped David at all was enough. He condemned the old man to death and commanded Doeg to execute him in the courtyard of the house at Gibeah.

Doeg never had a chance to carry out the order. He took Ahimelech by the arm with the intention of conducting him from the common room. They had only walked a few steps toward the door when the priest collapsed. He was dead by the time Doeg knelt at his side.

When word of this reached the sanctuary, Ahimelech's three sons at once fled the city. One of them, Abiathar, found his way eventually to David, who, when he heard what had happened, is said to have expressed himself contritely. "I knew it that day," he said, "when Doeg the Edomite was there, that he would surely tell Saul. I have brought about your father's death."

But his knowledge had not prevented him from accepting food and arms in full view of Doeg and thus exposing the old priest without benefit of any warning to certain punishment.

I have no intention of becoming an apologist for Saul in the manner that David's scribes are for him. The king's madness does not excuse his brutal acts. But at least it explains them. Whereas David's career is checkered with the most opportunistic, calculating deeds, followed almost invariably by an eloquent admission of guilt. Again, I believe his warring emotions are responsible for this pattern. And if one is to be absolutely fair, are not two emotions in conflict within a person as terrible as any demon? Or, putting it another way, could they not be called demons in disguise?

All speculation aside, the fact remained that David was in flight. And being a clever, vital man, he could hardly have been expected to wander in solitary aimlessness about the country, waiting for Saul to track him down. The king had declared war, and David picked up the challenge.

He sent word to his cousin Joab at Gallim, where the thousand-odd members of the Israelite cadre were still wintering. During one night Joab, with ability and persuasiveness rare in one so young, was able to convince six hundred of the cadre to follow David into exile. So skillful and intuitive was he that he carried on his recruitment without arousing the suspicions of those he knew would remain loyal to Saul. He wove his way through the camp, speaking to small groups, cornering individuals, but always making his purpose appear casual to anyone who might be watching. As Zaccur said later, "I saw the little beast strutting around, but then he always acted like a ram just returned from rutting, and I thought he was detailing his latest conquest among the maidens of Gallim. I should have used my head for something other than a convenient place to hang a battle helmet. I should have known that David's first move would be to delegate this little crow to stir up trouble. In the morning, when those of us who remained awoke, we could hardly believe what we saw. And worst of all, the little swine made away with over a third of my arsenal."

The men who departed consisted of those who had come to admire David enough to follow him to Sheol if necessary, and those who had grown discontented under Saul and Abner. Among the latter was the one-eyed soldier Bela. Abner, possibly because of the part Bela played in the Gibeonite massacre, had never appointed him to be a captain over a hundred. Joab found the man's bitterness fertile ground for his persuasive talk. And ironically enough, Bela was able, through his own efforts, to swell the ranks of the deserters by almost exactly a hundred men.

Belatedly, the pursuit got under way. Saul had sent out a call to the various tribal territories, where the majority of his soldiers were spending winter in their homes. In the last weeks before spring, the balance of the Israelite host collected at Gallim.

Saul knew it would not be easy to find David. On the other hand, the fugitive could not remain concealed forever. Sooner or later he would have to come out of the cave or forest where he was hiding, to seek food and other basic supplies. And Saul would hear of this.

But there might be a long wait. It would seem that David antici-pated this, and also was taking no chance of Saul's striking at him through his family. From Beth-lehem came word that David's parents, old as they were, had left the city hurriedly one night in the company of two armed men. The rumor was that David had sent them to find sanctuary in the land of Moab.

The winter rains became less frequent, then ceased altogether. Saul waited, chafing with frustration. But never once did he become melan-choly, or lethargic, or give himself over to weeping or undirected rage. His obsession sustained him, clothed him with the cold power of the mountain lion.

At last the report came. David and his band showed themselves near the border town of Keilah, battling the Philistines and capturing large numbers of their cattle. Saul marched westward at once, but even be-fore he reached Keilah, advance parties brought back word that David had vanished.

Saul scoured the countryside, spreading out a network of troops, sending them into cities, remote villages and wasteland. However, for some time after his appearance at Keilah, nothing more was heard of David.

Then, as spring opened out into the fullness of summer, a strange delegation found the camp of Saul. Before the king came a wizened old man, a hunchbacked young man, and a robust, angry-eyed girl. The old man was the girl's father, the hunchback her betrothed. They came from the town of Jeshimon, north of the wilderness of Maon, and they brought welcome news. David had set up a camp somewhere in Maon.

The reason for their coming was this. About six weeks before, Jeshi-mon had received an influx of strangers. It did not take the inhabit-ants of the town long to discover that they were David's men, but no one even considered informing Saul. To a market town clinging to the edge of a wilderness the newcomers with silver to spend brought unexpected prosperity.

And to the maidens of Jeshimon, the soldiers of David brought equally unexpected opportunity: for the romance strangers often bring with them to isolated towns, for trysting, and for the more dar-ing among them even the hope of elopement to set them free from distasteful marriage contracts arranged by their parents.

Such a girl was Sheerah, who now stood before Saul. She had caught the eye of Joab, David's chief aide, and had given herself will-ingly, even fervently, to him. For several weeks they had met each night outside the gate of Jeshimon. Sheerah's father was angrily disapproving, but he could not control his headstrong daughter. Despite his best efforts, she would find a way of slipping out of the house and joining Joab. Her betrothed was heartbroken, but Sheerah treated his plaintive objections with contempt.

Then, as often happens in such encounters, Joab tired of her. He had doubtless had no intention from the beginning of tying himself to some ignorant girl from a country town. And eventually her artless yielding, her limited conversation, must have bored him. One night he was not waiting for her outside the gate. Nor was he there the next night, nor the next. Finally, even to unschooled Sheerah the truth was apparent. Joab was casting her aside.

She retreated to the reclaiming custody of her father. Her betrothed chose to ignore both her indiscretions and the sullenness that had accompanied them. And all three—father, daughter and fiancé—were reunited under the aegis of a more powerful collective emotion than any one of them had ever experienced individually: the desire for revenge.

A classic situation, re-enacted so frequently that its structure sags with the weariness of repetition. Yet how often can such tired, stale elements group themselves into a charged, lethal pattern.

Saul sent the trio ahead of him back to Maon, which is in southern Judah, almost at the border of Simeon. He gave them instructions to spy out the camp of David and report its whereabouts to the advance units of his army.

By the time the troops arrived at Jeshimon, David had left his original encampment, but the vindictive Sheerah had heard of a new site and had herself journeyed there to confirm its location. She had glimpsed Joab, and the sight of him had filled her speech with so much vitriol that even Saul, laden with hatred against David as he was, recoiled from its violence. He had to have her forcibly restrained from accompanying the pursuing army, for she wanted to "tear Joab's flesh from him, ribbon by ribbon, while he yet lives." It is a fiction that all men are warlike and all women peace-loving. Given a host of suitably armed, sufficiently aroused women, any commander could conquer the world. But the feminine warriors would have to be retired after each fray, and a fresh supply of properly motivated replacements sent in. The ferocity of a woman towers over any male anger, but it is intensely personal, and tends to crumble once an immediate objective has been attained.

Saul and Abner led the Hebrew army into the wasteland of Maon, a bewildering terrain of forests, jagged mountains, giant crevasses and boulder-strewn plains. Following the route described by Sheerah, they approached the base of a mountain and saw there evidence of a recently vacated campsite. The fires were still smoking and there was every indication that David's band of rebels had departed in great haste.

The plain stretched vast and empty in three directions from David's camp. If he had fled in any of these directions, his troops would still be visible. Therefore, Saul reasoned, he must either be hiding in caves on the mountain, or else he had crossed to the other side. In any case, he had been delivered into the king's hand.

But even as Saul and his commanders plotted their plan of pursuit, a messenger arrived, filthy and exhausted from a long arduous journey. He had ridden ceaselessly from Kirjath-jearim with news that a Philistine army was invading the land and was even now encamped in the valley beside Aijalon.

Saul was unimpressed. "We shall complete the task at hand," he said. "We shall pursue David until we capture him and put him to death by the sword."

The messenger first looked confused, then distressed. In his agitation he seized his dirt-caked hair and tugged at it so hard that some of it came away in his hand. "But my lord, if the Philistines take Kirjath, they will command the roads north and south, and will have easy access . . ."

Saul spat on the ground at the feet of the messenger, who stopped speaking as abruptly as if a hand had been clapped over his mouth. "David is the greater enemy of Israel," said the king.

A subdued murmur of protest rose from the group of captains, but none dared voice open opposition.

Abner said quietly, "My nephew, you are mistaken."

He made no move as Saul's face swelled with fury, waited calmly until the king's speechless anger abated. Then he said, "If you desert your people Israel now, when they are menaced by the uncircumcised, it will be to your everlasting shame."

Saul asked, "Do you refuse to go after the traitor David as I have ordered?"

Abner let his eyelids close wearily for just one instant. Then he looked steadily at Saul and replied, "My nephew knows that I have never disobeyed even the slightest of his orders. Nor would I now. I have only spoken what is in my heart."

The king walked away from the group. As the messenger and the senior officers of Israel looked on, he paused beside one of the campfires, kicked at the smoldering embers, glanced up at the cave-riddled mountain. When he came back to the little clump of waiting men, his face was drawn and gray.

He said to the captains, "Inform your men that we shall march at once."

"In which direction, my lord?" Paltiel inquired respectfully.

"North to Kirjath-jearim, thence to Aijalon."

There were tears in both Saul's and Abner's eyes, but for quite different reasons.

So it was that the unwitting intercession of the Philistines saved David from certain capture.

We heard about this at Gibeah much later, after the Philistines had been turned back at Aijalon, and the army had returned to Gallim for a brief rest before setting out again after David.

But by this time, I already knew that David had been in the southern wilderness, and I had learned it from a totally unexpected source.

One morning while the Philistine campaign was still in progress, a rider entered the courtyard. We had seen him approaching from a distance, had noted the black cloak so weather-beaten it was fading to gray, the hood pulled up over his head, throwing his face into shadow.

He dismounted and put back the hood. Rizpah and I stared, unable to speak in the first shock of recognition. The unruly yellow hair was the same, but almost everything else about Jonathan had changed.

His face was lined and gaunt. Even muffled as it was by the cloak, his figure appeared thin and wasted. He had aged years in the four months he had been away from Gibeah. Physical erosion alone was not responsible for this. Jonathan's bearing was that of a man lost in deep sorrow.

He spoke pleasantly enough to Rizpah and me, and when Michal came running to greet him, he flashed her a semblance of his old quick smile. Then it was gone, and his face collapsed again into set, grieving lines.

Rizpah started to call for a servant to bring water, but Jonathan stopped her. "There is something I wish to tell all of you. I am married."

The announcement was hardly what we had anticipated, and delivered in such somber, weighty tones, it verged on the ludicrous. I exchanged a glance with Rizpah, and from her expression I knew she was also controlling a desire to laugh aloud.

It remained for Michal to mention the obvious, underlining it with her own peculiar twist of nature. She moistened her lips with her little pointed tongue and said, "It must be a remarkable woman that my brother has taken to wife, seeing that she has worn him so thin with her bridal exuberance."

Jonathan managed a desolate smile.

We all went into the house, and while he was eating, he told us something of his wife. He had been staying at the home of Abner, not wishing to be present at Gibeah when Saul marched off in search of David. Achsah was the daughter of a neighbor, related in some distant fashion to the house of Kish. Jonathan met her while paying a courtesy call on her father.

"Is she pretty?" asked Michal.

"She is a good girl."

Again Rizpah and I exchanged a glance, but of different import this time. Michal's question had been in the language of women, one of those many-thorned queries which catch and pull back shreds of truth.

And again it was Michal who pounced on the obvious, subjected it to scrutiny, translated it. "Jonathan . . . this girl . . . you did not . . ."

Now his laughter was genuine, overflowing from him like wine spilled at a feast. "No, my sister. I married Achsah because I wished to."

"Then why did you not bring her to us?"

The laughter stopped. His eyes grew murky, devious. "These are not times to bring a wife to Gibeah," he murmured. "She is safer with her family."

The lines of his face deepened. But rather than aging him now, they made him resemble a child about to cry.

Michal got up and went to her brother. With one of those rare gestures, so beautiful in spontaneity, she gathered his head to her breast. Her sleeve was pulled back, revealing the length of her bare arm: gently rounded, with delicate blue veins and a halo of soft golden down. It came to me suddenly: how desperately this woman desires a child. Woman, which I had never called her before. For as she clasped Jonathan's head to her, the sharp, sensual girl was lost in the mellowing aura of womanhood.

Jonathan remained with us for a week. I was sure more had happened to him in his absence than his marriage, but until the last evening of his visit I had no way of knowing what it was.

I was not overly surprised when he confided in me. His need to talk to someone was apparent. His sister would not have understood what he had to say, nor could he rely on her discretion. He was fond of Rizpah and under other circumstances would have trusted her, but her close alliance with Saul made this impossible now. That left me. I was available for confidences; I had always been sympathetic, and I was old.

The latter most of all. The young have an unflattering opinion of age. They pretend to accord us the deference our years have accumulated for us. But the never-mentioned fact is that they fear us, or rather, what we stand for. We are the living reminders of their own mortality. To the young we are the shells of pomegranates, drained of the juice of life, emptied of seed and substance. But, being hollow, we are safe repositories for the secrets of the young.

After the meal on his last night at Gibeah, Jonathan contrived to be alone with me. I watched his machinations with amusement, for he had no practice in guile. Rizpah left the table to go to her children, but Michal remained despite all Jonathan's efforts, obdurate, sensing with her female antennae something of what was happening, and resenting it. In the end I helped him by simply walking out into the garden and waiting. After a few moments Jonathan joined me.

It was difficult for him to begin. He fidgeted, regarded his sandaled foot with deep absorption, stripped some leaves from a marigold and crushed them between his fingers. Their pungent odor mingled with the pervasive perfume of jasmine and the evening smell of dew settling onto parched earth.

"I have seen David." He said it quickly, as though he wanted to get it out before he changed his mind.

I nodded but did not reply.

His account of the meeting took shape . . . via halting phrases, long silences, and finally whole sentences in which the words tumbled over each other.

After David's flight, Jonathan had been disconsolate. His anger against his father had burned out rapidly, leaving its residue of bitter ash. In private, he had asked Abner if he might have the freedom of his home. His great-uncle had of course agreed at once.

For a time Jonathan helped with the spring sowing, as he had assisted his father years before. There was pleasure and release in driving a plow through the unfurrowed soil.

But the nights passed slowly, and the day's work could not crack the shell of his loneliness. There were moments when he believed he had inherited his father's madness. Then in the silence before dawn he would know it was the burden of love he was carrying: his own, David's and Saul's. He could not remain forever aloof between the two people he cared for most in the world. If a man balances on the sharp edge of a wall, he must of his own volition come down on one side or the other. Otherwise he falls. And one who falls might find himself crippled for life.

Jonathan resolved to go to David. The friend he called brother was innocent. Jonathan would help David remain free of the king's pernicious grasp. Then, when his father's groundless hatred wore itself out, they would return, and together with Saul reclose the broken circle of their happiness.

He did not know where to find the fugitive. But his love for David was known, and Jonathan soon discovered there were many in the land who had fallen under the spell of his friend's charm.

Seeking word of David's whereabouts, he was recognized by a potter in the town of Etam, south of Beth-lehem. The man questioned him closely, then, without committing himself, sent Jonathan to a weaver in a village near Tekoa. The weaver fed him and sheltered him overnight, and in the morning sent him to a miller in Beth-anoth. In this fashion, moving ever southward, he was passed from town to town, village to village, house to house.

A stonemason in the town of Ziph broke the pattern by not giving him instructions for further travel. Instead, he woke Jonathan before it was light and walked with him out of the town in a southwesterly direction. The mason was a taciturn man with the great horny hands of his trade. He made no attempt to converse with Jonathan as they walked. Once he stopped and took from the pouch at his waist a loaf of bread, which he divided in two. They sat on the ground and ate as the sun came up.

At midmorning they reached the edge of a dense wood. The mason pointed directly into it, then turned around and started back toward Ziph.

Jonathan entered the forest. The trees were close together, and the foliage allowed only slivers of sunlight to filter through to the ground. He followed a more or less definite path. After a while his warrior's instinct told him he was being watched. He stopped, and when he heard a sound behind him, wheeled about. The soldier who rushed toward him, sword drawn, suddenly tripped over a root and sprawled headlong on the ground, losing his grip on the weapon. He got to his feet at once, crouching warily like a wrestler, circling in the direction of his sword. Jonathan laughed, recognizing Asahel, a young brother of Joab.

Asahel straightened up, looked sheepishly at Jonathan, sighed and said plaintively, "You won't tell David what happened?"

"If you had not tripped, I might not have had a choice."

"But you won't tell him."

"I shall say that he has the most murderous sentry in the whole history of warfare. David is well?"

"Well enough. But I do not believe he is happy."

"You have become an authority on happiness?"

"I have become an authority on the seasons of fear. Winter is a cold fear. Spring is a warm fear. Soon there will be summer, then autumn, then the cold fear all over again. There is no end to the fear of man but the grave."

"You've become a philosopher like your brother. But more gloomy."

"Joab knows only three things. Fighting, feeding and maiden-toppling. His philosophy is woven about these three threads."

They had been walking along the path, which was becoming better defined as they progressed. At length they entered a clearing which contained the camp of David's followers.

It resembled the camps Saul had maintained in the days before Michmas. There was no feeling of permanency. Each man had his weapons by him, constantly prepared for either combat or flight.

Some, seeing Jonathan, were on their feet at once, grasping swords and spears. Then one recognized him, and another, and soon he was the center of a noisy, joyous group, welcoming him, each seeking to touch him as they had in former times on the eve of battle.

He greeted them by name, bantering with the ones he knew best. But all the time his spirit was probing beyond the circle, searching through the clearing, knowing that very soon he would see David. Perhaps one of the great pleasures known to man is reunion with someone dear after prolonged separation. Not the instant of meeting itself, for this is often so overwhelming it creates a kind of numbness. I am speaking of the moment immediately before, that brief period when every fiber of the spirit opens out with the intense aliveness of anticipation.

The group of soldiers suddenly separated, and Jonathan was face to face with his friend. Their salutations were sparse and self-conscious. David said, "Welcome, my brother," and Jonathan replied, "It is good to look on you again."

Then they embraced, and the long shadows of separation melted away. They laughed and joked, cursed each other the way men who love each other will, with those black endearments as evil-sounding and yet as tender as the words a man whispers into a woman's ear.

But in the midst of the gaiety, the holiday atmosphere of the sun-dappled clearing, Jonathan shivered. His friend had changed. Not the externals: the red-brown hair, the green eyes sparkling with delight in Jonathan's company—these were still David. Nevertheless his friend had changed. In some intangible, chilling way.

Perhaps it was only the camp. He remembered again the bivouacs in which the men of Saul had eked out perilous existence in the early days. When Philistine patrols roamed the land with swords, spears, giant bows and needle-sharp arrows, seeking those who dared oppose the authority of the occupation. When no Israelite warrior knew if he would take his evening meal by the same fire where he broke his fast at dawn. If in fact he lived to eat his evening meal.

Perhaps then it was the camp. David was hunted now by Saul, as Saul had once been hunted by the Philistines. This took its toll of a man . . . of his heart and spirit, of the thoughts which moved behind his eyes.

"Would it please my brother David to go with me to a place where we can talk at our leisure? Or not talk, as we like."

David welcomed the suggestion. He sprang to his feet, lithe, quick, in perfect control of each movement.

Jonathan walked behind him as they penetrated deeper into the forest, finally stopping beside a small, gurgling stream.

The water flowing over the rocks gave off a peaceful sound. Here there was calmness between them, and Jonathan was able to feel that David was no different than he had ever been.

"How long will my brother Jonathan be able to remain?"

"Forever, if that is your wish."

"It would be my wish . . ."

He stopped. And now the rushing water took on a forbidding note, for David had held back, had applied conditions to the infinite.

Jonathan waited, for there would be something now his brother had to tell him, something which sat restless as tainted food in the belly of their love, something which had to be disgorged before health could return.

Then, without equivocation, David spoke of the blessing of Samuel, which he had not sought but had accepted, which had allowed him no peace since the day he had come to Elah and first laid eyes on Saul and Jonathan.

When he had finished speaking, they both sat quietly. And all about them was the rustle of the forest, timeless and comforting.

Then Jonathan said, "My brother will tell me . . ."

And again there was silence except for the murmuring of the stream and the whispering of the trees. David got up from the rock where he was sitting, broke a twig from one of the low-hanging branches and tossed it gently, almost reverently, into the water. Both young men craned their necks to follow its erratic downstream progress.

Jonathan asked tonelessly, "Does my brother aspire to the throne of Israel?"

He waited for David's reply as the hart pants for rain in the season of drought. But as the hart avoids danger even in the agony of his thirst, and will not go near the pool where the lion drinks, so Jonathan could not look at David's face. Surely the words he wished to hear, the soothing, erasing words, would be forthcoming.

But when they were not, when there was only the sound of the bubbling stream, Jonathan asked again, more brutally than he had intended, "Do you want to be king?"

And now at last he was forced to look into David's eyes. When he saw the torment of his brother's soul mirrored there, he could bear it no longer and took David's hands in his, saying, "There is nothing—the throne of Israel, even the judgment of God—which will keep my heart from cleaving to yours."

So spoke Jonathan the farmer, the blunt and inarticulate warrior. And David the lyrist, the composer of sweet songs, lapsed into earthy Judahite dialect and mumbled, "I wish I had stayed with my father's flocks." Yet it was better than if he had spoken in the most exquisitely fashioned figures of speech, for the words rang true. Then David said, "I once made a pledge, that as long as Saul and Jonathan live, only they will reign over Israel. I make that pledge again, my brother, in your presence, and in the presence of God."

Jonathan said, "You need not fear, for the hand of Saul my father will never find you. And you will be king over Israel, and I shall be next to your throne."

He was glad when David did not protest. He could not have endured falsehood from his friend at that moment.

Jonathan remained overnight in the camp of David. Both knew that in the morning he would have to leave, but each pretended there were endless days of comradeship stretching ahead.

As soon as it was light, Jonathan had retraced his path through the forest. David had walked with him until they reached the edge of the wood. Then, wordlessly, they had embraced and parted, and Jonathan had begun his journey north. . . .

He was silent now for so long I thought he had finished telling me what was in his heart. I was mistaken. "When I reached my uncle's house," he said, "I knew for the first time in my life what it was to be completely alone. The girl Achsah was gentle and kind. I found myself reaching out to her with desperate need. Perhaps in time I shall love her as I feel she loves me."

The last traces of dusk had fled from the garden. From the house came the faint sound of Rizpah's voice, singing to Armoni and Meribaal as she put them to bed. I touched Jonathan's shoulder. Sometimes a touch can mean more than words. In this case it was all I could do.

chapter eleven

DURING SAUL's absence from Gibeah, first searching for David, and later repulsing the Philistines at Aijalon, Rizpah never once forgot the plan she had initiated for dealing with Michal.

After Michal had assisted David in escaping from Saul, she showed signs of wishing to end the truce she and Rizpah had established. Rizpah had no intention of allowing this to happen. She continued to seek Michal's company; she ignored rebuffs and countered barbed words with sweetness; she brought all her charm to bear in retaining the status of their relationship as it was before David's flight.

And now that the army had returned to Gallim and Saul was home for a time, she was ready for the next stage of her scheme.

Because in a sense I am Rizpah's scribe, recording the events of her life as I know them, there is a temptation to weave elaborate justification for some of her actions. This I must strenuously resist. I have stated before that I intend to present a faithful chronicle of things as they happened. If on occasion the deeds of my principal subject become repellent, I have no apology to offer. I can only hope that out of the strengths and frailties, out of the welter of contradictions which comprise any person's make-up, there will emerge a portrait of Rizpah that is recognizable and understandable. And that this will depict neither demigoddess nor devil, but rather a woman both noble and corrupt, endearing and hateful . . . and above all, intensely human.

The crisis building around the person of Michal is a case in point. Saul's daughter had demonstrated that at times she was capable of warmth and generosity. She had more frequently shown herself to be arrogant, willful and deceitful. But the latter in no way excuses the fact that with her Rizpah was knowingly, calculatingly cruel.

Even before Saul returned to Gibeah, she would take every opportunity to bring Michal into close contact with Armoni and Meribaal.
The children were particularly appealing at the end of the day, when
they were just beginning to be sleepy. Rizpah would let Michal help
her put them to bed. I have also longed for children during my life,
and so I could appreciate the expression of yearning I would often see
on Michal's face as she bent over one of the cribs.

But it was after Saul's return that Rizpah began the most heartless
aspect of her campaign.

With some women, it would not have been effective. There is no
set rule by which one can predict sexual fidelity in a woman. I have
known trollops who, when they found a man they truly wanted, became models of faithfulness. I have also known those who have for
years been seemingly content with one man, and then, without warning, plunged into lives of spectacular promiscuity. And of course,
there are trollops who remain trollops, and one-man women who never
have need of anyone else. There are as many shadings to the question of woman's fidelity as there are women, and the only error one
can make in considering it is to become dogmatic.

There were several factors working for the success of Rizpah's
plan. Michal's nature, for one thing, which even under ordinary circumstances lent a certain desperate quality to her desire. Then the
possibility, which while Saul lived was a probability, that she would
not see David again. In addition to this, she was living in close asso-
ciation with Rizpah, who was obviously not deprived of her own man.
And to a sensual woman like Michal, probably one of the most potent
aphrodisiacs is being exposed to another woman's ritual of love.

Rizpah contrived to make her room a more or less set place of meeting for her and Michal. Often, when Michal would arrive, Rizpah
would apologize and say that Saul had sent for her, and that she would
have to leave in a few moments. But in the meantime, would Michal
sit and talk with her? Sometimes it would be true that she was going
to Saul, sometimes not. Rizpah would chat casually while she began
to make herself ready. With deliberate voluptuousness she applied perfumed oils to her face and arms. Then she would retire behind a
screen in the corner of the room. She would keep up her light chatter,
but with frequent interspersed pauses, thus allowing Michal the choice
of staying or leaving. She rarely left.

On occasion, after having arranged to meet Michal at a specific
hour, she would arrive late. She managed to create an impression not
only of being somewhat breathless from hurrying, but also of languor.

Again, she would apologize, intimating that she had just come from Saul.

The effect of all this low-key torture was soon obvious. Michal, already grown lean, with great dark rings beneath her eyes, became impossibly nervous. She could scarcely sit still for more than a few moments at a time. Everything her fingers touched—the arm of a chair, a wine goblet, a piece of cloth—she caressed with such pathetic longing that I sometimes had to turn away from her suffering. And her agony in public must have been only an iota compared with what she endured when she was alone.

Now, occasionally at first, then almost every evening, Paltiel began to appear at the king's table.

And now, finally, wondering how I could have been blind so long, I began to understand the simple, diabolical efficiency of Rizpah's scheme.

She would engage Paltiel in talk about military campaigns, carefully avoiding any mention of the army's search for David, referring only to battles against the Philistines or other nations. Paltiel was naturally reticent about speaking of his own role in the victories. Then, with great skill, Rizpah would draw Saul into the conversation. The king was fond of Paltiel. He would chide the young officer for being modest about his courage, and would elaborate at length on his exploits.

Once this pattern was established, Rizpah would throw it into sharper relief by flirtation with Paltiel. Nothing that would be obvious to either of the men, but conducted in a manner which said clearly to Michal and me: I find this man attractive.

I could see Michal responding to the treatment. She was already so savagely sensitized that I should not have been surprised if she had suddenly screamed and run madly out of the house to couple with the first man she met in the fields. Now Rizpah was focusing Michal's vision: slowly, with exceeding gentleness, but inexorably.

I began to wonder how much the girl could bear. Several times I almost spoke reproachfully to Rizpah. But I knew she would only look at me innocently and inquire what I meant. And even if I could prove any allegation I might make, I was sure there was not the slightest chance of dissuading her from what she was doing. The demon within Rizpah was in full control now, and it would not rest until she had brought the matter to a conclusion.

During the course of each meal, Michal would grow increasingly flushed; her eyes contained a hectic brilliance. She would usually ask to be excused before she had finished eating, and go directly from the table into the garden. Frequently, Rizpah would join her there, sometimes taking along a decanter of wine.

One evening, just before dinner, Rizpah took Paltiel aside. She told him that Michal was becoming very fond of him, and that only shyness prevented her from declaring her affection. This, of course, is one of the oldest devices known to matchmakers, but it is also one of the most effective.

Paltiel was first exuberant, then crestfallen. "She belongs to another man. How could I even think . . ."

"Can the king allow his daughter to languish as the wife of a traitor? Did I say wife? You have listened to Saul when he speaks of David. You have heard him say a hundred times, 'David is dead. We have only to find him and bury him.' "

The atmosphere at the table that night fairly crackled. Paltiel made no effort to avert his passionate gaze from Michal. She, poor child, could only grip the table and stare back at him, helplessness and desire alternating in her eyes. Only the king failed to notice anything out of the ordinary. Shortly after Michal left the table, stumbling in her haste, Saul went to his room.

Rizpah whispered to Paltiel, "Go to her. Now."

He got up and walked quickly out to the garden.

It was a lovely evening just past the height of midsummer. The trees and vines were heavy with fruit. Every flower exuded an overpowering fragrance. There could be no doubt of what would happen.

I was watching Rizpah. Her face had never seemed more beautiful. But her eyes were the eyes of Saul on the day he cast the spear at David.

She rose from the table, and after a glance toward the garden said, "I must speak to the king now."

Michal was given to Paltiel in marriage early the following week. The marks of weeping were upon her, and during the brief ceremony two tears rolled down her cheeks. But afterward, she pressed herself close to Paltiel and looked up at him with some of her former audacious sensuality.

Paltiel did not go with Saul when the king went forth again in search of David. The young officer was sent to establish and take command of a garrison on the border of Ammon.

Michal accompanied him.

chapter twelve

SAUL'S WARRIORS were seeking David in the wilderness of En-gedi.

Rizpah and I were traveling with the army now. In the two years since he had given Michal to Paltiel, Saul had been very little at Gibeah. The obsession to capture and kill David had deepened, and his lack of success in locating the rebels only served to increase the cold fury with which he tracked them. Rizpah wished to be with him, and she had obtained permission for me to accompany her. We had left Armoni and Meribaal at Gibeah with Helah.

En-gedi is a wicked stretch of wasteland on the western shore of the Dead Sea. The heat seldom abates and is intolerable even at midwinter. Great blisters of rock erupt from the desert floor to ring the sunken basin of the inland sea. In some places the rugged cliffs taper off before they reach the water's edge, and here there are slimy salt marshes which lie stinking under a stifling haze.

Saul searched the area painstakingly. He explored caves and crevasses, and the high promontories where wild goats challenged intruders. He even probed the drear and fetid marshes. All to no avail.

Although we had failed to catch a glimpse of David, there was no lack of word concerning his activities. He and his six hundred men had a certain procedure they followed upon entering any region. As soon as the camp was set up, David would send envoys to any prosperous farmers or owners of herds in the area. The message never varied. In return for suitable presents of food and clothing, David would protect the lands and herds of the donors. Those who were approached knew very well the doubtful benefit of protection offered by a fugitive. But they feared the consequences if they refused to give him at least some token gifts.

On one occasion a man did refuse, point-blank. And through his resistance David made a much more significant acquisition than loaves of bread or measures of dried corn.

Nabal was a wealthy landowner living near the wilderness of Maon. When David's young men came to him, requesting their usual donation, Nabal snarled in reply, "Who is this David, and who is the son of Jesse? Nowadays there are many servants who break away, each from his master."

When David heard this answer, he had no choice but to prepare to wipe out the household of Nabal. If such a churlish refusal went unpunished, word of the defiance would spread to every landowner in Judah. Accordingly, he took four hundred of his men and started toward the house of Nabal. He never arrived.

Nabal's wife was called Abigail. Upon learning of her husband's rejection of the envoys, she had her servants load pack animals with bread, wine, meat, corn and fruit. Then she set out for the place where she had been told David could be found.

The two groups met halfway between the outlaw camp and the border of Nabal's property. David was charmed by the woman's mature beauty, and by her humility. And she was smitten with him. He accepted her gifts and returned to his camp. She went back to the house of her husband.

That night Nabal tendered a feast to commemorate a successful sheepshearing season. He was accustomed to drink heavily, and on this evening he imbibed somewhat more than usual. During the feast Abigail said nothing to him of what she had done. But in the early hours of the morning, when the guests had departed, and Nabal was still sitting, sodden, with vacuous countenance, at the head of the banquet table, Abigail told him of her meeting with David.

He spoke no word, only looked at her out of eyes grown suddenly sober and baleful. He raised his arm to strike her, but when he tried to get up out of his chair, he found he could not move.

Ten days later Nabal died, and Abigail became David's wife.

We also learned he had taken a second wife: a young woman from the region of Esdraelon.

This was the remarkable thing. We were always able to learn where David had been, and what he had done. But our tidings were always late. By the time we reached the area of his latest reported activities, he was nowhere to be found.

From what Jonathan had told me I knew, and I am certain Abner suspected, that David had developed a network of supporters throughout the land. An outlaw is a romantic figure; he conjures up a vision of the precarious existence every man would like to lead, and yet is glad he is not forced to. As long as he does not commit excesses, a fugitive inspires sympathy, and a clever one can knit individual attitudes into groups dedicated to aiding him. Moreover, David operated mainly in Judah, and Saul, as a Benjaminite, could not expect too much assistance in the native territory of the shepherd.

Saul was not aware of this. His obsession blinded him to simple logic. He continued to accept each outdated report as proof of David's presence in an area, and he would search doggedly, day after day, week after week, until the next report reached him. Whereupon he would hasten to the new location and begin the search all over again.

However, in a chain as nebulous as the one David had forged there were bound to be weak links. Or no link at all, where David had assumed there was one.

The couple who entered Saul's camp at En-gedi caused a stir of excitement. Abner told me the girl's name was Sheerah, and the hunchback with her was her husband. Then I remembered having heard that it was she who, two years before, had informed Saul of the location of David's camp in Maon.

She was a very attractive young woman. Her skin had a rich, tawny color and was as soft-appearing as peach down. Her figure was almost as perfect as Rizpah's, tall and supple.

But her manner was sour and disagreeable. She obviously hated the man who was with her, taking every opportunity to show her contempt, even to laughing and rapping on his humped back as one would knock on a door. He dragged about after her, sometimes falling in his attempts to match her long stride, but always smiling bravely as he picked himself up and hurried to overtake his wife.

Sheerah demanded that she be taken to Saul. When she stood before him, she waited a moment without speaking, her mouth twisted in a sour smile. Then she said, "I suppose my lord the king is still interested in knowing where he can find the man David."

"I am."

"When I last delivered him and that filthy swine Joab into my lord's hand, he allowed them to escape."

This was too much for Saul. He rose to his feet and thundered, "I will brook no insolence! If you have information, speak!"

The hunchback's hands fluttered with fear, but Sheerah only smiled unpleasantly. "If my lord the king does not care to hear what I have to say, I can always return to Jeshimon. We can leave at once. My stalwart husband . . ." She rapped on his hump. ". . . my brave and beautiful man will protect me on the night journey should I be threatened by the beasts of the field." Again she prodded the hump. "Won't you, my love?"

The cripple said quietly, "I will protect you with my life, Sheerah."

She laughed. "Your life . . ." Then she turned to Saul and spoke earnestly, in a low voice. "My lord, when you find David, will you also kill Joab?"

Saul repressed his irritation and replied, "David and all who are with him will be brought down by the justice of the sword."

"The sword?" She was filled with dismay. "He will die so easily, so quickly?"

Saul's eyes narrowed. "Where is David?"

She hesitated, then leaned toward the king, beckoning him closer with a conspirator's gesture. "Listen, my lord. Do you know the hill of Hachilah near Jeshimon?"

"I know it."

"Beyond the hill begins a wood. In that wood is the camp of those you seek."

"They are there now?"

"I saw him yesterday before noon."

"You saw David?"

"David? I would not recognize him if I fell over him. It is Joab I speak of. I saw him emerge from the forest, look around, then turn back. I ran after him, but when I reached the wood, he had disappeared."

"You are sure it was Joab?"

The sour smile distorted her mouth. "I am sure."

Her husband spoke up. "The people of Jeshimon have also seen David's men. They must have arrived only in the past few days, because . . ."

Sheerah turned a withering glance on him. He stopped speaking abruptly. She said to Saul, "Perhaps, my lord, you have place in your army for another valiant warrior. My husband will acquit himself with courage and agility. You should see him wield a sword. And when he arches his body to cast a spear . . ." She choked with laughter.

Saul turned his back on Sheerah and spoke to her husband. "You have my deepest gratitude for coming."

"If we have been of service, my lord . . ."

"What is your work?"

"I am a baker, my lord."

"When we reach Jeshimon, we shall need bread. If yours is of good quality, we shall purchase all you have."

"It is of excellent quality."

"Then you shall bake for us while we remain in the region."

Saul put his arm around the man's shoulders and walked with him out of the tent, leaving Sheerah to trail along behind them.

We reached the hill of Hachilah the next evening at sundown, and set up camp at once. Five hundred cubits west of the hill began the forest. The fading light made the firs and pines glow with subdued golds and blues. A fresh spicy fragrance left over from the day's warmth still lingered among the trees. It drifted toward us to mingle with the odor of the campfires.

Rizpah and Saul strolled in the direction of the wood. Suddenly he stopped walking and looked keenly into the shadowy maze of branches. "David is in there," he said quietly. "Tomorrow night at this time he shall be dead."

She said, echoing her old chant of hatred, "His name shall be wiped out forever."

But into her heart crept an odd sadness she could not understand.

chapter thirteen

THE NEXT day Saul and his soldiers penetrated deep into the forest.

Once again, they found a freshly abandoned camp, but though they pressed forward as rapidly as unfamiliarity with the wood allowed, they saw no further sign of the rebels. But now Saul knew the trail was fresh, and excitement turned him into a whip of nervous energy. He had no thought but to go on until he found David.

As the sun began to set, Abner tried to dissuade him. "We should not spend a night in the forest, my lord, lest the few of David creep through the trees and fall on the many of us and make an end to the host of Israel."

"We shall lose the trail."

"What trail, my nephew? They have slipped away among the pines like wraiths and vanished. You know and I know they are here. But we could thrash about in a month of darkness and never see more than we see now. Tomorrow, my lord. Tomorrow when it is light again we shall surely find them."

Reluctantly Saul gave the order to return to the camp at Hachilah.

It was quite dark when they arrived. A priest from the town of Jeshimon was waiting to tell him news Rizpah and I had already heard.

The prophet Samuel was dead.

He had fallen ill of the sickness which cuts off the breathing and heats the body as the flames of a smelting furnace fire the metal in its innards. Two days later, in the great empty house at Ramah, the prophet had died.

Saul thanked the priest for bringing him this information and gave him silver for his trouble. The king spoke no word during the evening meal. When he had finished eating, he rose from the table and turned away.

Rizpah glanced quickly at Abner and me, and as we got up to leave she went to Saul.

He was weeping. But after a moment she could tell they were not the tears of madness.

He said, "Why should I weep for him? Should I not mourn the absence of my son Jonathan from my camp more than the death of Samuel?"

Abruptly he left the tent. Rizpah started after him, but thought better of it and paced about uneasily, waiting. After a while he returned, bringing with him a handful of dead ashes from one of the fires. Deliberately, he rubbed the gray dust over his hair and beard. Then he grasped the top of his tunic and ripped it until it lay open across his chest like a wound.

"I do mourn thee, prophet," he intoned. "I grieve for thy death in the manner in which Israel has been commanded to grieve. I mourn for the harshness between us, the anger and the conflict. I mourn for thy soul which, while thou didst live, touched mine as oil touches water, without mingling. I mourn for a wish of my heart, shriveled by the pride which murders feeling, the wish to call thee father. I mourn thee, Samuel, as I mourn unspoken truth and stillborn love."

He was silent then, but his tears continued, making greasy tracks through the ash smudges on his face.

Suddenly he said to Rizpah, "Why did he desert me? Why did Samuel remove his soul from mine?"

She started forward, trying to conceal her alarm. But there was still no madness in his eyes. He took her in his arms. "You have known my heart," he said. "You have known its darkness and its light. You have not flinched from the one, and you have given radiance to the other. Few men are so blessed."

"You are weary, my love."

"I am weary. Weary of hatred and bitterness. Weary of strife and battle." He looked at her and said softly, "And yet if I had peace, would I know now what to do with it?"

"Will you sleep?"

"I will sleep."

She placed a cruse of water at the head of the bed. Saul lay down and closed his eyes. She kissed him gently on the lips and was about to leave when he sat up and cried, "The spear . . . where is my spear?"

She brought it to his bedside. He held it for a moment, turning it in his hand so the lamplight shone on the scarred surface of the shaft. Then he set it gently on the floor beside the bed and lay down again. He was asleep before she left the tent.

The sentry outside bade her a good evening. She smiled a greeting to him and walked toward our tent. The red rim of a full moon was forging into the sky over the summit of Hachilah. Rizpah peered beyond the camp to where the forest spread itself out like a dark stain on the pure garment of the earth.

Now she also mourned Samuel, but no tears filled her eyes. "You will rest," she whispered. Then, "Is there also loneliness in Sheol?"

She was suddenly so tired she could hardly walk the few remaining steps to the tent. She flung herself on her bed and was asleep at once.

She was not sure what wakened her. She had been dreaming that Armoni had climbed to the top of the garden wall at Gibeah and had fallen. When she sat up his cry was still in her ears. Without knowing why, she rose from her bed and went out into the night.

The moon was high, but its brilliance was deceptive. Deep shadows shrouded the area where the warriors slept, so she could only barely make out their sprawled forms.

Suddenly she was filled with concern for Saul. She ran toward his tent, feeling her heart leap convulsively when she saw the sentry was not at his post.

The tent flap was open. Moonlight bathed the bed in which Saul lay. She knelt by his side, so fearful that she hardly dared look at his face. When she did, relief was nearly as overpowering as the fear had been. He was sleeping peacefully.

But there was something wrong. She could feel it, whatever it was, hanging heavy in the air.

Then she noticed that the water cruse was missing. And before she had time to turn over the significance of this in her mind, she realized she was kneeling close to the bed, in the exact spot where Saul had placed his spear. She looked down. It was gone.

Now danger was a person, real and tangible. Without rising, she let her glance drift around the tent to fathom the dark recesses where an assassin might be hiding. There was no one. She was sure of that.

A soft moan made her stiffen. At first she thought it was Saul. Then, when it was repeated, she knew it came from outside the tent.

She made her way stealthily through the doorway, looked around, smothered a cry as she saw the sentry lying on the ground by the side of the tent, partly concealed by the sloping overhang of its roof. She bent over him, saw that he was breathing, noticed the abrasion and the trickle of blood on his forehead near the left temple. She was about to rise when she heard a sound behind her. She turned her head slowly.

Then she saw David.

He was standing in a pool of moonlight a few paces from her. In one hand he held a water cruse, in the other a spear. He did not see her.

She breathed in, opened her mouth to cry out. But she could not. The breath left her in a soundless rush.

Truth came to her slowly, like heavy footsteps approaching up a flight of stairs. She did not want to raise the alarm. She could not see David destroyed. His life was as important to her as her own.

She felt engulfed, lost in a flood of bitter honesty which seethed in the quiet moonlight.

A figure moved out of the shadows to join David. It was Abishai, an older brother of Joab. She heard him whisper, "We should tarry no longer, my lord."

David started, struggling out of the depths of reverie. Then he clapped Abishai lightly on the shoulder and the two of them loped away into the night. David was still carrying the spear and water cruse.

Rizpah ran to our tent and fell into her bed, trembling. I awoke and called out to her, but she made no reply. I lay awake, wondering.

Then I heard the shout, riding clear into the camp from a distance. "Abner! Ab-ner!"

The soldiers of Saul heard it as well. Their voices rose sleepily, questioning.

"Ab-ner!"

I got up, threw a cloak about my shoulders and hurried from the tent, vaguely aware in the excitement of the moment that Rizpah was following me.

The warriors were getting to their feet, confused and a little fearful. Abner appeared through the doorway of his tent, looking around.

"Do you not hear me, Abner?"

The voice was coming from somewhere on the lower slopes of Hachilah. The syllables tumbled into the camp, echoing onto one another.

"Who calls me?"

"Are you a valiant man?" I had thought I recognized the voice. There was no mistaking its insolent tones now. "Who is like you in Israel? Why then have you not taken care of the king?"

Abner rushed toward Saul's tent, in time to meet the king coming out.

"Where is the king's spear, Abner? Where is the water cruse that was by his bed?"

Saul and Abner stared at each other foolishly. Then the king went back into the tent, and when he reappeared, his head was bowed.

The clear, mocking words continued to pour into the camp. "You should die, Abner. For you have not protected your lord Saul. Could I not have killed him as he slept?"

The echo had scarcely died away when Saul called, "Is this your voice, my son David?"

And the reply came. "It is my voice, my lord and king. Why do you continue to pursue me? What have I done? Has my hand wrought evil against you?"

By now the attention of the host was centered on Saul. He stood with his shoulders hunched forward, clearly visible in the moonlight. His head came up slowly, and he called in the direction of the hill, "Return, my son David. My soul was precious in your eyes this night. I have played the fool and have erred exceedingly. But I will do you no more harm. Only return to me!"

There was a long pause. A breeze rose and wandered through the distant treetops. Saul took a step forward, waiting, listening.

David's answer came, rolling down the slope of Hachilah and reverberating through the camp. "Behold the king's spear. Let one of the young men come over and fetch it."

Silence followed. Saul raised his arms and cried out once, sharply, "David . . . my son!"

When there was no reply, the king dropped his hands to his sides. After some moments he said to Abner, all emotion gone from his voice, "Send someone to fetch the spear." Then, "We return at dawn to Gibeah."

chapter fourteen

NONE OF US really wished to credit the rumor that reached Gibeah, was dismissed, then kept returning, persistent as a fly about the head of an ox.

But eventually there was confirmation. David and his men had joined the Philistines.

He had journeyed to Gath and approached Achish, the Seren of that city. I had known Achish's father, Moach, and I remembered the new Seren from the time of his boyhood. He had always been a clever lad, soft-spoken, with a thoughtful way of regarding you which said: My words are gentle, but do not make the mistake of testing their strength.

I could see him weighing the motives behind David's defection. He would have known, of course, of the feud which existed between the young man and Saul. He would have wondered if David's coming to him were a trick. But finally he must have decided to take a chance.

In return, David had consolidated Achish's tentative trust in him by taking his band out to battle the foes of Gath: the Geshurites, the Gezrites, the regrouped remnants of Amalek . . . in short, every city and nation that lifted a hand against Gath except Israel. Whereupon Achish rewarded David by giving him the ancient walled fortress of Ziklag as a permanent dwelling place.

After the episode at Hachilah, Saul had remained at Gibeah, resuming his duties as judge and administrator, only venturing forth now and again to observe the work of the deputies he had appointed in each territory to carry out his decisions.

His feeling against David did not disappear completely. During the winter following the expedition to Hachilah, Rizpah told me of several occasions when Saul's hostility had flared up. I myself saw him once in the common room, when he believed himself alone, tearing at his beard and muttering oaths against David. But the anger always died as quickly as it was born, and he made no move to go forth again in search of his erstwhile son-in-law.

But, again to be fair, David had no way of knowing if the respite would be enduring. He, more than any person besides Rizpah, had intimate knowledge of Saul's instability. For three years the king had hunted him throughout the land of Israel. On the one occasion at Maon, David had escaped capture by an uncomfortably narrow margin. The life of a fugitive must have palled, and he might very well have felt that leaving Israel was his only chance for peace.

A few nagging doubts, though. Why Philistia? Why not Moab, where his parents had already taken refuge? Also, future conflict between the Hebrews and Philistines was inevitable. Would David take up arms against Israel?

Like every attempt to analyze David's actions, this one ended in enigma.

As was to be expected, Saul received the news of David's desertion badly. For the first time in years he lapsed into the brooding reticence which had so often preceded his struggles with the demons. Rizpah attended him anxiously, battling the incipient madness with the twin weapons of her love and experience.

For several weeks none of us knew what the outcome would be. The servants avoided Saul when they could, remembering the unpleasantness of past episodes. He made the gentle Helah burst into tears simply by looking at her with his morose and piercing stare.

One afternoon, when he had not spoken since early morning, Saul said suddenly to Rizpah, "Bring the children to me."

She obeyed with some reluctance, resolving not to let them venture too close to the king.

Armoni was almost five now, a small, sturdy replica of Saul. Meribaal was three. He had Rizpah's coloring, and great innocent eyes which, one had the feeling, looked at everything and really saw little. He had been delicate since birth, and shied away from Armoni's rough games, but he possessed a smile of such sweetness that everyone who saw him wanted to gather him up and hold him close.

Rizpah brought the boys to Saul. He got up energetically and said, "I shall take them now. I have ordered the donkeys saddled."

Rizpah could not conceal her dismay, but there was nothing she could do. Saul had already tucked Meribaal under his arm, taken Armoni by the hand, and was walking from the room.

She followed, swallowing the fear which was rising in her. In the courtyard, two donkeys were waiting. Saul mounted one and placed Meribaal on the saddle in front of him. Armoni was already a competent rider. He scrambled up onto the other donkey and nudged its sides with his knees.

It was a dreary day in late winter, hardly the time of year for a pleasure ride. Rizpah watched Saul and the children disappear over the crest of a hill. She decided against going after them, for Saul had been pointed in withholding an invitation, and she knew he would be furious if he suspected she was spying.

She came to me in my room. I made a few attempts at conversation, then gave up, and we waited in silence.

They were gone for over two hours. Rizpah heard the sound of their return before I did. She leaped out of her chair and ran to the courtyard. I trailed along after her.

Armoni was wildly excited. He could hardly speak as he jumped down off the donkey. "Mother, Mother . . . Father took us all over our land. He showed me where the partridge nests in spring and where this year's wheat will be planted and how to tell if there will be rain . . ."

She smiled at him and turned her attention to Meribaal. The child was almost asleep. Saul's arm circled his waist, and Meribaal's tiny hand was holding onto his father's thumb.

The king lifted the boy from the saddle with tender care and said to Rizpah, "They are good sons."

That night at table I was able to amuse Saul with a tale I remembered from my childhood, about a goat who aspired to the love of a beautiful maiden, and who discouraged her suitors with his horns. When Rizpah and I heard his hoarse, sharp laughter, we felt finally that the danger was past.

All of Saul's family, however, did not regain their ease of mind so quickly.

A few days later Ishbaal rushed into the courtyard shouting, "He's coming, he's coming!"

Rizpah and I were baking date cakes in the kitchen. We went outside at the sound of Ishbaal's voice. He was seventeen now, a waspishly effeminate boy who spent much time by himself. He had given up his practice of torturing animals and insects, at least as far as we knew, but he retained his insatiable appetite for fruit, which he still smeared over most of his face.

He had developed a fierce affection for Rizpah, and would watch her covertly from behind trees and bushes, his sly foxlike face rapt with concentrated worship. It made my flesh crawl to see him doing this, but she did not seem to mind. She would often call him to her and run a damp cloth over his face, wiping off the fruit stains. Now and then she would speak sternly to him, and this seemed to send him into a kind of ecstasy. He would grasp her hand and keep stroking it until she would push him gently away.

With everyone else he was sullen and occasionally vicious. Saul paid no attention to him whatsoever.

Now, as we came out of the house, he cried again, "He's coming, Rizpah! He's coming! And he has someone with him. And her belly is big with child. Will she have it now, at once, in front of me?"

I felt a little sick, but Rizpah looked at him calmly and said, "Be quiet, Ishbaal."

He gave a little whinnying laugh and ran to hide in a corner of the courtyard.

We saw Jonathan riding toward the house, followed by a grave and placid girl, who was indeed big with child. I assumed this was Achsah, but had not time to wonder why Jonathan was allowing her to travel in her condition. I was much too shocked by his appearance.

The lines which had marred his features when he was at Gibeah two years before had settled in permanently. His expression held the same kind of torment which victimized Saul during his bouts of insanity, but there was none of this in his eyes. They were clear, contemplative, and filled with deep sadness.

Yet he embraced Rizpah and me with enthusiasm, and when he presented Achsah to us, his voice held true warmth. She greeted us shyly and sweetly, then stepped back to Jonathan's side, touching his hand and looking into his face. It was obvious that she loved him deeply and fully, and took great pride in her love.

Saul was in the common room when we all entered together. For a moment father and son looked at each other without speaking. In the air of the hall was the memory of anger, the doubts and renunciations of a three-year separation. Then Saul came forward, arms outstretched, and embraced Jonathan.

"You are home at last, my son."

"I am home."

"I shall have the servants open your room."

Jonathan regarded the king steadily. "I have come to tell you, father, that I shall be at your side when you need me."

Saul's brow furrowed with confusion. "You are not staying here at Gibeah?"

"Only tonight."

"Your wife . . ."

"Achsah asked to come along. I did not think it wise, but now I am glad she is with me."

He presented the girl to his father. She bowed as low as she was able, still holding onto her husband's hand. Her love for Jonathan transformed what might have been an awkward motion into something graceful and poignant.

Saul said, "I need you now, my son."

Jonathan hesitated before he replied. "Not now, my father. In time you will."

The name of David was not spoken that night. But his presence was felt by everyone.

chapter fifteen

THE PHILISTINE host was the greatest I had ever seen assembled under the banner of the five cities.

Their encampment stretched out endlessly. It was still visible where the tableland met the sky. Even at a distance we could see the tents of the Serens standing out proud and gaily colored, the tents of the lesser nobles clustered around them. I had heard that the sour and vengeful Kraseg had finally become Seren of Askelon. Surely he was pleased with what he saw this day.

Saul had mustered close to ten thousand men to repel the invasion. The Philistine ranks contained easily twice that number.

A river separated the two armies. The Israelites were encamped before the town of Jezreel. Behind us, its slate-covered slopes gleaming dully under the setting sun, towered Mount Gilboa. The legions of Philistia rested confidently at the edge of the Plain of Esdraelon, which opens out across the territories of Issachar and Zebulon.

We had arrived two hours before. Saul had stood for some time looking over at the camp of the enemy. Then he had shut himself in his tent and had not even permitted Rizpah to visit him. She had taken food to the entrance, but he had left it untouched.

It remained for Abner to engineer the deploying of troops, the placement of sentries, and all the hundreds of details which must be overseen when an army pitches its camp within sight of the foe. As usual, the general handled the intricate operation calmly and was unfailingly courteous with his subordinates. But there were indications that he was not as unruffled as he attempted to appear.

Only Jonathan seemed unimpressed by the display of Philistine might. He had joined Saul the night before we left Gibeah, and now that we could almost smell the forthcoming battle, a change took place in him. No longer was he the saddened, prematurely aged man of the year before, when he had come with Achsah to visit the house of Saul. Now he was once again the young warrior who had climbed the pass at Michmas, the beloved hero of the troops. As he moved among them, becoming as in former times their talisman of hope, the years seemed to drop away from him. His laughter was fresh and unforced, and wherever he went he left behind him men who responded to the brightness of his spirit.

Notwithstanding his efforts, the situation was serious, and everyone knew it. Tension mounted during the night. A cry from a nervous sentry brought half the camp to its feet, milling in confusion. Though the alarm was immediately found to be false, the warriors of Israel remained in a state of barely subdued turmoil.

Neither Rizpah nor I slept very much. We were awake long past midnight when Abner came to our tent. His eyes were bloodshot; his face sagged with weariness.

He wasted no time with preliminaries. "I have come to ask you," he said to Rizpah, "to return to Gibeah."

She was equally blunt. "I will remain here."

"There is grave danger."

A trace of the old contempt for him sprang into her eyes. "Does my lord Abner think he speaks to one who has never witnessed a battle?"

"All the more reason for you to be sensible."

He had used an unfortunate word. "Sensible?" Her voice rose on brittle laughter. "Am I some soft little maiden who trembles at the sight of danger and flees from the sound of fear? Am I a bride who lies by the side of her man when there is peace and slinks away when she hears the trumpet of war?" She looked at him insinuatingly. "For what reason do you ask me to desert Saul now?"

She had hurt him, and for once he retaliated. "Has your lord called you to his side? Saul has no need of you."

The anger went out of her. "I shall be here when he calls."

Abner regarded her with mingled admiration and concern. His hands moved outward in his gesture of resignation. He turned to me. "Have you no influence over her?"

"She is not a child."

"But you understand the risk."

I shrugged. "To walk in the sight of the gods at all involves risk. The day we are born the dice are cast for us in the first roll of chance. From then on there is no surety under the sun."

"Will you quote proverbs at me?"

"Will you attempt to move a mountain with a pigeon feather?"

"You are a pair of fools," he snapped. "A pair of stupid, idiotic fools!"

Rizpah and I began to laugh. In a moment he joined in. He was a warm, deeply compassionate man, with an understanding for the comedy of life which often brought him pain. My heart went out to him.

He stopped laughing. "May Jahveh be merciful to us all," he said simply.

Then he was gone.

Dawn crept toward us from across the plain. We could again see the Philistine host, appearing even more vast and formidable than on the evening before. Looking at the sea of warriors in the distance, I found myself wondering: is David among them? And as if in echo, Rizpah murmured at my side, "Is David among them?"

Neither of us speculated further.

Later in the morning two priests from the sanctuary at Shiloh came into the camp bearing *Urim* and *Thummim,* the sacred lot stones which were used to open a knowledge of the future. The priests remained in the tent with Saul for some time. When they reappeared, the elder of the two, whom I had marked for an overtalkative fellow, shook his head sadly and announced, "The stones will not speak for the king."

I looked at Rizpah. Her face bore the determined expression I had seen so often. I knew she intended to go to Saul. I made no attempt to stop her. If he had been my man, I would also have had no choice.

She found Zaccur and obtained permission to prepare special food for the king at one of the fires. I helped her cook a pot of lentils seasoned with aromatic spices. While the lentils were simmering, Zaccur himself went into the town of Jezreel. Most of the inhabitants had fled out of fear of the impending battle, but somehow Zaccur was able to find a quantity of new curds.

Rizpah took the food to the tent. Saul's armor-bearer, a fresh-faced lad from the forest country of Gilead, was standing guard at the entrance.

"The king will not eat," he said to Rizpah.

"I shall try to make him take some food."

"What I am trying to say, my lady, is that it would be better if you did not go in to him."

She smiled. "The king is fortunate to have such a tactful armor-bearer. Surely no harm will come to him while you are at his side."

The boy reddened with pleasure, then forced his expression into stern lines. "He moans. When the priests left, I heard him cry out as if he were hurt. When I went in to him, he bade me go away."

"I shall call you if I need you," said Rizpah, and she took the food into the tent.

Saul was kneeling beside the bed. He did not look up when she entered, but she felt he was aware of her presence. She placed the food on the table and approached him.

"Why are you here?" he asked. "I did not send for you."

She waited until he raised his head. Then she sighed with relief. His eyes were troubled but sane. "Does my lord send for his legs when he marches into battle? Does my lord have to summon his heart when he wakes in the morning?"

He got to his feet and stood beside her. "Last night I wished you were with me. But I was ashamed to call for you."

"Am I some casual acquaintance that shame should stand between us?"

He said miserably, "I am afraid, Rizpah."

"We have faced fear together before. It has always passed. It will pass now."

"The sacred lots will not speak for me."

"I have heard that," she said, keeping her voice unconcerned. She took a few steps toward the table. "Egrep and I have cooked some lentils. Zaccur has managed to find some beautiful curds." She turned, for he had not followed her.

"I sought the word of the Lord in a dream," he said. "And there was nothing but a great sword, flashing in the sunlight."

"Your sword," she said, returning to him. "The sword wielded by the lightning out of Benjamin, which will set the enemy in full flight, as it has done so often before."

"The enemy outnumbers us."

"Did they not at Michmas? And at Elah?"

She realized her mistake in mentioning Elah, but it was too late to do anything about it. Saul started and said, "At Elah there was David."

"The army which pursued the Philistines then was the army of Saul. It was his might that strengthened the hands of the warriors."

He looked at her sadly, and she knew again she had erred, this time by forgetting his honesty. "The Lord is not with me now!" His words ran together in a piteous wail. "I have spoken to him, and called upon his name, and there was no answer. No . . ." He stopped suddenly, and when he spoke again, his voice was surprisingly calm and strong. "I must know what will happen. Seek me a woman who can speak through a familiar spirit. I shall go to her, and inquire of her."

Rizpah turned away from him. Had he forgotten? And as if she had uttered the question aloud, he said, "I have not forgotten. But there is no decree that stands without violation. Seek me one of the soothsayers still abroad in the land."

She said, "I shall seek one, my lord," and left the tent.

When she told him what she wanted, Zaccur was appalled. His face went ashen, and he said, "Do you truly wish to destroy me, that you ask this of me? In a moment or an hour the king will forget his request, and remember only the decree and the penalty it carries."

"If he attempts to put you to death, he will also have to kill me."

"At the moment, vexed with you as I am, that might be some consolation. But not quite enough. There is wine I have not yet drunk, songs I have not sung, women—"

"It is true," she interrupted, smiling at him. "You are much too young to die."

They laughed, the way comrades will in the shadow of disaster, mocking death to put it to flight. The presence of the Philistine host had invaded their blood, lay heavily about each breath they drew.

Then Zaccur asked soberly, "Has he received no word from the Lord?"

"None."

He thought for an instant, then said, "Wait for me in your tent."

It was late afternoon when he returned. He came into the tent and sat down on a bench, sighing wearily. "It is no longer such a simple matter. However, across the valley from Mount Tabor is a village called Endor. In this village you will find the woman you seek."

"Will you take us there?"

"Us?"

She made no comment. He nodded curtly and said, "I will take you."

Saul did not object when Rizpah proposed accompanying him. He said only, "It will be necessary for you to dress as a man."

She smiled faintly. "It will not be the first time I have so disguised myself, my lord."

"I shall also put on other raiment so the woman will not fear to call up the spirit before me."

Rizpah sought me out and after some difficulty we were able to find for her the garb of a shepherd. Zaccur chuckled when he saw her. "Always if you wait long enough, you will see again what your eyes have seen before. I must say, though, that the shepherd of Gilboa is a whit more full-bodied than the warrior lad of Michmas." He pulled the hood of her cloak up over her hair. "There. I shall be able to travel in peace now, untroubled by your beauty." The smile left his face and he said, "This may end badly, you know."

She nodded. There was no need for a discussion of what was in both their hearts.

Saul joined them, swathed in a mantle like those worn by traveling merchants.

The donkeys were saddled and ready. They crossed the river in gathering dusk, skirting the base of the mountains to the north and east of Gilboa. They traveled as silently as possible, for at several points the path swung close to the Philistine outposts. However, they encountered no one and in time arrived at Endor.

Zaccur rode confidently ahead of them, along a street which wound among the mud-walled houses. He stopped at one at the end of the village.

When the woman opened the door, Rizpah was sure Zaccur had made a mistake. She was middle-aged, plump and genial, with a cheerful chirping voice. Her hands were white with flour. From the interior of the house floated the rich odor of baking bread.

Zaccur said, "May we come in?"

She smiled broadly. "Come in, come in, and dry the dew from your garments. The nights are still short, but they hold a breath of autumn." She kept chattering as she ushered them into the single room, wiped the flour from her hands and pushed forward benches so they could sit.

The room was warm with heat from the hearth oven. Rizpah wanted to remove her hood, but she did not dare. "All day," the woman was saying, "I have longed for someone to talk to. Now you have come. Are you journeying far?"

"Only as far as Endor," Zaccur said.

"And now you have found it," said the woman, innocently, but with the trace of a question in her voice. She looked sharply at all three of them, only for an instant, but long enough for Rizpah to discern the wariness behind her blandness. "Our village is poor, and not often visited by travelers."

"Unless they have a purpose," countered Zaccur.

"The purpose must be strong for three such illustrious gentlemen to brave the chill of night."

Rizpah could only see Saul's eyes, so closely had he drawn the hood of his own mantle about his head, but she could tell he was growing impatient with the devious approach to the point. "Tell her why we have come," he said to Zaccur.

The little man's expression grew pained. "I am telling her . . ." He checked himself just before saying "my lord," and in the pause that followed, Saul said to the woman, "Have you a familiar spirit?"

She opened her eyes wide and chirped, "Familiar spirit? The only thing familiar here is the calf tethered outside my door. And I shall soon have to take him to market, and he will be slaughtered and so become unfamiliar. That is, unfamiliar to himself, for he has never died, but familiar to those who have in the past been able to afford to eat the flesh of his ancestors." She stopped, drawing in her breath sharply. The heaviness of fear was in the room.

Saul said slowly, "I beg of you, divine for me by your familiar spirit, and bring up him whom I wish to see."

She plucked nervously at her sleeve. "Surely you know what Saul has decreed." Her bird voice was suddenly plaintive, bled of cheer. "How he has cut off those who have familiar spirits, and the wizards, out of the land. Why do you lay a snare for my life, to cause me to die?"

Saul's tone was quietly authoritative. "As the Lord lives, you shall not be punished for this thing."

The woman looked fearfully at him. "The spirit has not moved in me for many months." Saul did not reply. She whimpered a little and said, "Whom shall I bring up to you?"

"Bring up the person I wish to see."

She hesitated, then gathered the skirt of her robe about her and sat on the floor. For a moment she was absolutely still. Then she began rocking back and forth, gently at first, but with increasing tempo and fury. Her eyes went to slits, opened fully and narrowed again. She moaned, a meandering little singsong.

Rizpah grew conscious of something in the room . . . a presence, a force . . . something. The woman's moans grew louder. Rizpah looked at Saul. His eyes were burning as if he had a fever.

Suddenly the woman shrieked and was quiet. She opened her eyes and looked at Saul. Then she shrank from him, saying, "Why have you deceived me? You are Saul."

The king pulled the hood back from his face. The woman's eyes dilated. She tried to push herself away from him, making scrabbling motions with her hands on the earthen floor. Saul rose and went to her. "Do not be afraid," he said gently. "Tell me what you saw."

"I saw a godlike man ascending out of the earth."

"What form did he have?"

"An old man clothed in a stained mantle. An old man with the look of prophecy in his eyes."

"Bring him up again."

"My lord . . ."

"Bring him up again."

The fear was wild in her eyes, but she began to rock once more, and moan. Now her eyes went back into her head, so only the whites were visible. Suddenly the moaning ceased, and from lips that barely moved came an unmistakable, rasping voice. "Why have you disquieted me, to bring me up?"

Rizpah and Zaccur gasped at the same time. Saul fell to his knees and touched his head to the floor. "My father Samuel . . ." he whispered.

"Why have you brought me up from Sheol?"

Saul raised his head slowly from the floor. "I am sore distressed," he said. "The Philistines make war against me. And God is departed from me, and answers me no more, neither by prophets nor by dreams. Therefore I have called you, that you may make known to me what I shall do."

There was a silence, during which Rizpah could hear her own breathing and that of Zaccur. The voice spoke again. "Why then do you ask me, since you know the Lord has departed from you? For he has rent the kingdom out of your hand, and given it to your neighbor, even to David."

Zaccur moved convulsively, jarring the table next to the bench, sending a clay pot crashing to the floor.

"Because you did not obey the voice of the Lord and keep his commandments, therefore the Lord has done this thing to you."

Saul remained motionless on his knees, hands limp at his sides. Rizpah wanted to go to him, but knew she could not.

The voice continued, taking on a deep, sorrowful note. "Moreover, the Lord will also deliver Israel with you into the hand of the Philistines. And tomorrow you and your son will be with me."

The king fell forward and lay senseless on the floor. Now Rizpah and Zaccur sprang as one to his side. They attempted to revive him, chafing his wrists and slapping his face.

Only when he gave a shuddering sigh and opened his eyes did they remember the woman. She had risen and was standing above them, blinking like one emerging from sleep. "Now," she said in her former genial, chirping voice, "did he trip and fall? It must have been that terrible hole in the floor which I have been meaning to fill."

Rizpah glared at her. "You should not have said what you did."

"Said? I said nothing." Her eyes were innocent. Then, looking down at the prostrate Saul, they gathered fear. "He is the king."

"He promised no harm would come to you," said Zaccur soothingly.

"Was it bad?" she whispered. "Was it very bad?"

Zaccur nodded. "Is there water?"

She brought it, and Zaccur supported the king's head while Rizpah held the cruse to his lips. He groaned and sat up.

The woman knelt beside Saul and said feelingly, "My lord, I have obeyed you, and put my life in your hands. Now I beg of you, listen also to the voice of your handmaid and let me set a morsel of bread before you. And eat, so you may have strength when you go on your way."

Saul shook his head. "I have no wish to eat."

Zaccur said, "She is right, my lord. You will need your strength."

And Rizpah added, "You have eaten nothing since yesterday."

"There now," said the woman. "I shall kill the calf and you shall eat his meat together with fresh-baked bread."

The three of them helped Saul up, and he sat on the woman's bed. Zaccur helped her slaughter the calf, and she set the hindquarters to roast over coals in the fire. While they were waiting for the meat to be done, the woman turned to Rizpah with a shrewd smile. "It is warm in the room, dear," she said. "I think you can doff the hood now. Your voice gave you away some time ago. And even if it had not, I should have known." She laughed and looked down at Rizpah's sandaled feet protruding from under the cloak. "No shepherd in Israel has ankles like those."

Rizpah threw back the hood, liberating her hair to the firelight. The woman sighed richly. "Ah, but you are lovely, my lady. Is she not, my lords?"

And suddenly the terrible memory of Samuel's voice retreated, and there was joviality in the room. The meat sputtered on the spit and sent off savory odors to mingle with that of the bread.

After they had eaten, Zaccur drew the woman aside and offered her some silver. She refused vehemently. "Am I too poor a subject to entertain my king out of the fullness of my heart?"

"For your other services then," persisted Zaccur.

Her face clouded. "It was bad," she said. "You have told me it was bad. Shall I accept silver in return for calling forth blood?"

Saul came forward. "Take it," he said. "Not as payment, but as a mark of my respect for what you have done. And as a sign that no harm shall befall you for what has happened this night."

She accepted the silver then, and after bidding her farewell, they began the journey back to Gilboa. Rizpah watched Saul anxiously, peering at him through the darkness as they rode, but he showed no sign of being depressed. To the contrary, he seemed in excellent spirits.

They reached the camp of Israel two hours before dawn. Saul took

Rizpah by the hand and led her to his tent. He put his arms about her and kissed her tenderly. She drew away, frightened. "No, my lord. You will go forth in battle tomorrow. The law . . ."

"Did you not hear?" he asked quietly. "I have broken the law, many times over. If I am to die . . ."

Her voice rose. "You shall not die!"

He shrugged. "Did you not hear?" he asked again.

"I heard the words of a soothsayer. They do not speak the truth. In fact . . ."

Saul pressed her close to him, cutting off her words. Then he held her away, looking at her face with such tenderness that tears sprang to her eyes.

"Why do you weep?" He waited for her to reply. When she did not, he went on. "If I live, there is no cause for tears. And if I am to die, I shall weep in Sheol and you shall mourn me here in the land of the living. But now we are together, and I would tell you with my heart and body some of the things my lips have not been able to say."

He smiled. It was the second time in all their life together she had ever seen him smile.

"There is never time enough," he said, "but for us there is still a little."

chapter sixteen

FOR A time that morning, it did not appear that the battle would be joined.

The Philistine camp seemed the same as it had been at sundown the day before. The fires still smoked peacefully; there was none of the air of activity which usually precedes an attack. True, the warriors of Philistia were wearing armor, but so had they been since the arrival of Israel at Gilboa.

Abner, however, was taking no chances. At dawn he deployed his men in battle formation. The swordsmen and spear throwers were arrayed in their ranks; the archers stood easy, bows in hand, quivers filled with arrows riding high on their left shoulders. At the flanks were stationed the charioteers, seasoned and war-wise now, circling their chariots to test the fastenings of the knives attached to the wheels.

Rizpah and Saul had parted just before daybreak. He emerged from his tent now clad in full armor, pausing outside the entrance to glance speculatively over at the Philistine lines. Jonathan came toward him, and he walked out into the camp proper to meet him. He put his arm around his son's shoulder, and they stood talking quietly.

Abner and Zaccur came to fetch Rizpah and me. It was the general's intention to send us back from the lines, farther up the slope of Gilboa. Rizpah began to protest, and he turned on her. "There will be no contention about this."

She bristled and was about to speak again, but he stood in frosty silence, making it clear that she was to do what she was told.

As Zaccur led us away from the camp he said to me, "Have you managed to catch a glimpse of David or any of his band?"

I said I had not. But this would not necessarily mean they were absent from the camp across the river. "Six hundred men could not be picked out of a force that large, particularly if they have adorned their armor with Philistine insignia."

"I should know that little beast Joab anywhere," said Zaccur, "even if he wore the feathers of a dove. Still, I should not like to have him commanding a unit against me. Let alone the treason, he is as clever and bold as David. And he lacks David's recurrent seizures of conscience. Cold as the waters of the Jordan in the mountains of Dan, that one is."

We reached a ledge of rock high above the camp. It afforded us a clear view of the land below without exposing us to danger. Here Zaccur left us, but before he did, he turned to Rizpah. "Do you remember the day we first met, on the battlefield at Michmas, how for the longest time there was no talk between us, and yet we understood each other?"

She nodded.

"I had never until that day known much of the warmth and beauty of the human spirit. For this I thank you."

Then he was gone, his feet dislodging bits of slate as he hurried down the slope.

Rizpah began to tremble. I drew her close to me and held her until she stopped shaking.

The sun mounted in the heavens. We sat on the ledge, almost lulled to sleep by the silence and the warm, throbbing air.

Then it happened. I was looking idly across at the Philistine camp. Suddenly there was a flashing like the leap of myriads of silver fish from the sea. At first I could not understand what was taking place, but then I realized that there must have been some sort of signal, and what I had seen was the concerted donning of thousands of helmets.

There was a moment of apparently aimless milling about. Then, incredibly, the Philistine legions were in battle ranks, rolling toward the river like a great wave of molten metal.

The Israelite forces braced to meet the attack. Drifting up to us came the mournful wail of the ram's horn, followed by the first frenzied blood cries, the prelude to battle so similar in sound to the screams of hunting and hunted animals.

Then the horrendous, ground-shaking shock as the two armies met and closed in combat.

In the first moments of struggle it was not possible to distinguish between Hebrew and Philistine. Dust rose over the writhing, fury-ridden masses of men. Here and there the haze would thin for an instant, giving us a glimpse of an overturned chariot, a spear-impaled soldier's fall, an archer with his entrails ballooning at his side crawling forward, collapsing and crawling forward again.

Rizpah stood beside me, rigid, staring down at the field of battle. Her hand when I took it was icy.

Now, as the combat moved in widening eddies, I could pick out individuals. Abner led a small company of swordsmen into a tight-packed mass of Philistines, scattering them and felling half their number at first impact. Jonathan plunged out of another roiling group, stumbled, got to his feet and returned to the fray.

I scanned the spreading line of battle but could not see the king anywhere along its length.

The Philistine superiority of numbers was beginning to make itself felt. Slowly, fighting doggedly for every cubit of ground, the army of Israel was falling back. They would disperse, make an attempt at regrouping, then retreat a few more steps as the Philistines pressed in on them.

Jonathan was leading one of the bands of Israelites in a desperate counterattack. He raised his sword to ward off a thrust from a purple-plumed foe. Just then one of the Philistine chariots careened in from an angle. The merciless battle knives slashed into Jonathan's legs. One of the blades caught under the metal of his breastplate and he was dragged forward until the impetus of the wheel finally pulled the knives free. But not before he had been brutally mangled. He had lost his helmet, and his yellow hair was filthy with dust and blood. He lay limp and bedraggled on the ground.

Rizpah suddenly leaned over and vomited. I held her head, wondering how long I could keep my own stomach under control.

The heaps of dead and dying grew on the slope below us. As the battle swirled about the base of the mountain, more and more Israelites fell. The Philistines, gathering strength, began to form again into ranks and moved in on the remnants of the Hebrew army.

For some reason I happened to look out toward one of the flanks of the struggle. What I saw turned me faint with fear.

Saul was wounded. Part of his metal breastplate had been torn away, and an arrow was sticking out of his left shoulder. Next to him stood his armor-bearer, blood streaming from a cut on his forehead. Moving in toward them, carving their way through thinning ranks of Israelites, was a unit of Philistine swordsmen.

I hoped Rizpah would not see. I tried to move between her and what was taking place below.

I was too late. She looked up, pale from retching, and at once saw the king. For an instant she stood as if paralyzed. Then, shrieking, she lunged forward.

There was no time to seize her. I stuck out my foot and tripped her. She fell heavily, almost rolling off the ledge, and was immediately up again. But now I had a firm grip on her, one arm locked around hers, the other hand buried deep in her hair.

I did not know I still had so much strength. She twisted, bit, scratched and kicked. I held on grimly, but I knew that soon she would break free and rush down the slope to her death.

Then she clawed my face. The pain was so intense that I released her arm, but still managed to hold on to her hair.

All at once she stiffened. Her limbs shuddered, and she fell into my arms.

book four

ABNER

chapter one

I HELD her head in my lap, cushioning it against the jolting of the ox-cart. Across from us sat Abner, his head circled by a crusty, blood-stained bandage, his eyes looking past us with the hopeless stare of exhaustion.

Beside our cart stumbled the survivors of Gilboa: black with the filth of battle, silent before the enormity of their defeat.

The ox which pulled our cart was also a casualty of the conflict. Abner had found it lowing disconsolately at the edge of the battle-field, its eyes glazed with terror. It plodded ahead, barely keeping pace with the pitiful Israelite entourage. Occasionally Abner would reach out of the cart and give the beast a desultory prod with the broken haft of a spear; he had neither heart nor energy to urge it on more vigorously.

Twilight was coming in off the Ephraimite hills. Far ahead of us lay the Jordan. None of us looked back.

I felt the skin of my face drawing around the scratches Rizpah had inflicted. My whole body ached from the struggle with her. I wished for a stream where I could wash the dried blood and dust off myself, and bathe Rizpah's face and hands.

She stirred in my arms, and Abner's eyes came alive in immediate response. He leaned forward.

"She is reviving?"

His question, slightly stilted yet so full of solicitude and hope, coming out of his battered lips, moved me strangely. I wanted to weep, but I could not.

Rizpah opened her eyes. She looked up at me, then turned her head and saw Abner. Neither of us spoke to her. In a way, I suppose we were both dreading the beginning of talk as much as we desired it.

She tried to sit up. I helped her. This much she should know at once: that we were no longer beside Gilboa, that we were traveling, that Israel had lost the battle.

"Saul . . ."

It would come then. How could we shield her from it? Moreover, why should we? Why should we allow her to fight her way up to the light with pathetic expectation and wait until then to bludgeon her back into bitter darkness.

"Saul?"

She looked from one of us to the other. Abner's bruised face twitched. I blinked my burning eyes rapidly.

"Tell me . . ."

Tell you what, girl? That the collective might of Israel had bled itself white onto the soil of Gilboa? That love and hate, trust and regret lay tangled among the twisted limbs of thousands? That wives would weep and mothers run childless through the sterile corridors of grief? Who cared for thousands, and what solace lay in the endless intoning of the rolls of the dead?

"Tell me!"

Abner shivered and pulled his tattered cloak tighter about his shoulders. He freed one hand to make a small restraining gesture, as if to still what he knew would come when he answered.

"Saul is dead."

I saw she did not believe him. Nor would I have, for he had spoken as one who has no faith in his own words. But I had watched the king turning to his armor-bearer as the ring of Philistines pressed closer about them. I had seen him offer his sword to the boy with a gesture which spoke its meaning plainly. And though, at the distance, I had not been able to make out expressions, I had marked in the lad's body the horror with which he refused. There had been no palaver then, no ceremonious leave-taking. Saul had simply turned the extended sword in toward his breast and fallen on it. And the boy, with more silent eloquence than any funeral oration could ever contain, had knelt beside his king and placed a hand on his shoulder. After a moment he had risen, drawn his own sword and fallen upon it.

"Saul is dead," Abner said again, this time more firmly, as if to convince himself as well as Rizpah.

The expected outburst did not materialize. She nodded distractedly and turned to me, peering suddenly at the trail of scratch marks on my face. "You're hurt," she said.

Why at somber moments the irresistible compulsion to laughter? A mask for survival? Or deeper, some fierce rebellion against the inelastic pattern life draws for us, with its two fixed points of birth and death, and all the lines between of a mode ill-fashioned for freedom.

I did not break the pattern now. "It's nothing," I said smoothly. "Nothing a little water and a little more time cannot remove."

Abner said, glancing at the sky, "We shall stop for the night at the next stream or well. There would be no sense in trying to find the ford across the river in darkness."

"Where are we going?"

He raised his eyebrows at her show of interest. For myself, I would have been more pleased had she now been keening and wailing over the loss of Saul. Once before she had postponed grief. The soul is only so strong and the heart a vessel of limited capacity.

"We shall go to Mahanaim," Abner was saying.

"Mahanaim," she repeated, without knowledge, but in too bright a tone for my liking.

"It is a town of Gad. Somewhat dusty, certainly undistinguished, but safe."

"Will we have a garden?"

My sense of discomfort increased, but Abner said without hesitation, "Of course we shall have a garden."

"I am glad," she said. "Saul is fond of flowers, and I cannot live without them."

"Ishbaal is king now," said Abner.

I looked at him quickly, and knew from his expression that he was well aware of what he was doing. I gave him guarded encouragement with my eyes.

"Ishbaal?" she asked.

"Yes," he replied. "He is now king over Israel."

"Of course. Because Saul is dead. Then Jonathan also died."

"Jonathan was slain as well."

"Yes. I remember now. I saw him die." She turned to me. "We both did, did we not, Egrep?"

Her casual tone, verging cheerfulness, was too much for Abner. He had hoped to crack the shell about her heart and let the poison out.

Instead, he had only succeeded in intensifying his own grief. He turned away gloomily.

Shortly after this, we reached a clump of willows fringing a tiny stream. Abner stopped the cart and climbed wearily out of it, beginning to issue the necessary orders for setting up camp.

The stragglers were catching up with us now. As Rizpah and I were getting out of the cart, Zaccur came alongside. He was not wounded but obviously bone-tired. Rizpah straightened up and looked piercingly at him.

"What is it?" he asked disinterestedly.

"You're not dead?"

The question amused him, brought back the animation to his face. He felt his arms, punched his ribs. "I do hope not," he said. "If I am, I shall have words with the keeper of Sheol. I cannot believe I should still be burdened with all the weariness I earned on earth."

She laughed politely. This disconcerted me more than anything else. Rarely in all the time I had known her had she laughed without feeling. A small thing perhaps, but meaningful.

Despite Abner's attempts at organization, the men were too fatigued and depressed to make more than a token gesture at carrying out his orders. They collapsed by the side of the trail. Even those he assigned to sentry duty could only take a few steps toward their posts before they too lay down and went to sleep. After a while, Abner wisely gave up.

He was about to retire when Rizpah, seemingly for the first time, noticed his head wound. She insisted on changing the dressing. At any other time, he would have been consumed with joy. Now he could scarcely keep his eyes open. In fact, he was asleep where he sat before she had finished. Together we eased him onto the ground and wrapped his cloak firmly about him.

Then we were the only ones awake in the whole makeshift camp. I had been sleepy earlier, but now I was too concerned about Rizpah. I feared that any moment the fragile composure she was sustaining would be shattered. If once she wandered off into the night . . .

We did not speak for some time. The air grew cold. She kept looking about her with that brittle, too-bright interest she had been incubating since Abner told her Saul was dead. Only now, with darkness surrounding us, there was no object on which her gaze could settle, and it began to take on the vacancy of blindness.

She asked suddenly, "Where will Ishbaal meet us?"

"At Mahanaim. Abner has already sent a messenger to Gibeah."

"Then Armoni and Meribaal will come."

"Your children will be there."

"They are good sons," she said. And after a moment, "Do you remember the afternoon he rode with them around the land and I was so concerned about what would happen? That was what he said then: 'They are good sons.'"

Another silence. I felt myself beginning to doze off. The sound of her voice brought me back. I shook my head and mumbled stupidly, "What? . . ."

She whispered, "He *is* dead, isn't he?"

"He is dead."

She began to weep: copiously, silently, gratefully.

And holding her close, I was also able to shed tears now. For I too had loved Saul and Jonathan.

chapter two

IN THE court of Ishbaal at Mahanaim, the evening meal was served promptly, precisely one hour before twilight, by order of the king. Abner and the two captains of the decimated host of Israel, Rechab and Baanah by name, were required always to be present at table, unless they could present proof of being engaged in official business. There was a rigid seating plan. Ishbaal sat at the head of the table in a carved chair that was a replica of Saul's throne, wearing the golden circlet denoting his kingship. At his right was Rizpah, at his left Abner. The two captains and I occupied the other end of the table. Conversation began and ceased on command of the king and centered on subjects chosen by him.

In the house of Ishbaal, certain amenities were carefully observed. The officers of the guard reported at the end of each watch to Abner, who in turn presented himself before Ishbaal to assure the king that all was well. If one of the officers or men encountered Ishbaal anywhere in the house, he was obliged to kneel and wait with lowered eyes until the king passed. All except Rizpah and Abner were expected to address him by the full title: my lord the king over Israel.

There were still other prescriptions. A bowl of fruit was to be placed in each room of the house except the common room, where there were to be three bowls. All of them were replenished morning and evening. In season the fruit was to be fresh grapes or, as a second choice, figs or dates. Out of season, dried fruit could be substituted, but the servants soon came to know that this put the king in an ugly humor, so every effort was made to provide fresh-gathered fruit as often as possible.

Infractions of these and other rules were punished by a carefully codified catalogue of chastisement ranging from confinement in an airless room in the upper story of the house to a dictated number of strokes with the lash. The king himself heard each case and meted out the sentence.

To put it mildly, this was not quite the kind of life the survivors of Gilboa had hoped for as they traveled toward Mahanaim.

About five hundred of us had crossed the Jordan with Abner. At noon on the day after the battle we reached the bank of the swift-flowing river and forded it southeast of Beth-shan. The fragrant forests of Gad revived our spirits, and we should have been pleased to remain in one of the quiet towns near the river. But Abner felt such accessibility was dangerous, and we moved on in accordance with the original plan.

The green belt spans the eastern length of the Jordan from the Sea of Chinnereth almost down to the Dead Sea. However, it extends only a short distance from the river and rapidly thins into sparse brush and scattered watering places.

Mahanaim is situated in the midst of one of the larger of these oases. There are several wells, which give a good supply of water the year round. The combination of heat and plentiful moisture makes it possible to grow lovely gardens. But the encroachment of the surrounding desert is always apparent. Forget to water a plant for a single day and dusk will find it already beginning to wither and turn brown. Also, no amount of precaution can keep one free from the bane of dust. It is fine and siltlike, and possesses unbelievable penetrative qualities. It creeps in through shuttered windows, filters into cupboards and clothes chests. There is always a thick yellow coat of it on the foliage of the garden, and no matter how many layers of cloth one wraps around himself for protection, upon undressing he will find little gritty deposits in the folds of his skin.

Notwithstanding the disadvantages, the initial days at Mahanaim were most pleasant. Abner made arrangements, after a complex bargaining session involving the transfer of certain lands in Benjamin, for our possession of a large, tree-shaded house. The soldiers were quartered not far away, in a date grove near one of the wells.

We all needed rest, and the first few days passed uneventfully. Rizpah was still miserable, but the fact that she had been able to begin mourning so soon after Saul's death hastened the healing process. She had now accepted the loss, and her spirit was beginning the long, torturous course of restoration. Abner was attentive without being obtrusive; Zaccur had recovered his tough-minded good humor, and was able to make her laugh unrestrainedly, even the first day we arrived at Mahanaim.

When the children joined her a week later in the company of Ishbaal and the escort from Gibeah, her grief rose freshly to the surface. Armoni resembled Saul more than ever. He had Saul's mannerisms, even to hunching his shoulders forward and plunging without preamble into a description of something which caught his interest. He displayed the same gentleness, masked by the same bluff abruptness. More than once I saw Abner and Zaccur watching him with misty eyes.

Meribaal as always was a delight, with his open, wondering stare, his radiantly sweet smile, and his unspoken desire to be protected.

But, as can be imagined from what I have written earlier, Ishbaal's conduct was a source of immediate surprise and, later, of controlled dismay.

Having been warned of his arrival by a messenger who ran ahead of the party traveling from Gibeah, Abner summoned the entire complement of warriors and had them stand at stiff attention as the wagon containing Ishbaal rolled up to the house. Perhaps this was an error. If there had been a more prosaic welcome, perhaps Ishbaal's sense of self might not have undergone such rapid inflation.

I doubt it, though. We should have known what to expect from our first glimpse of him. He was lolling against mounds of cushions, nodding and smiling distantly to the soldiers who lined either side of the approach. I was tempted to laugh aloud, but something cautioned me against it, and in any event his appearance was too painfully reminiscent of the mad Saul of six years before, when we journeyed from Gilgal to the Valley of Elah.

The wagon came to a stop. Ishbaal made no effort to alight. We first thought he was waiting for the rest of the party, which was some distance behind. At length, after an embarrassing silence, Abner stepped forward, thinking perhaps that the boy was ill. Only then did he rise languidly and extend his hand to the startled general, obviously commanding Abner to help him from the wagon. The action was so imperious and unexpected that Abner did so.

Ishbaal looked around and snapped, "Where are the servants with water to bathe my feet?"

Abner, stammering and angry with himself for doing so, said, "There is water in the house, Ishbaal."

Ishbaal fairly squealed, "I am the king. I demand to be given proper royal courtesy. And I will have the proper royal address. I am the king!"

"You are the son of my nephew," said Abner evenly. "He was my king, and he was also my dearest friend. You are king only because of his death and the death of Jonathan."

They stared grimly at each other, the general and the sly-faced young man. I saw Rizpah turn and regard Abner quizzically.

Then Ishbaal saw her. He abandoned his newly acquired dignity and ran to her, shouting, "Rizpah, Rizpah, how happy I am to see you. Rizpah, make the servants bring some water so I can bathe my feet."

She said icily, "There is water in the house."

He giggled and grasped her hand. "All right, Rizpah. I shall go in. Are there any grapes? What a dusty den this is."

We all began to breathe somewhat easier. Too quickly, however.

As Ishbaal started to walk toward the house, one of the soldiers, who had been standing for more than an hour in the hot sun, wiped the perspiration off his forehead. Ishbaal turned on him, livid. "How dare you wipe off your foul sweat in my presence?"

The soldier blinked and said, "I am sorry, my lord."

"My lord the king over Israel." He waited, glaring. "Say it!"

"My lord the king over Israel," repeated the soldier glumly.

He probably should have been stopped then, at that very moment. But none of us really took him seriously, which was of course our mistake. By the time we did, it was too late. The ridiculous boy had become a vicious, demanding martinet. And since he was in truth the king, no one dared defy his orders.

Abner could have taken steps to curtail his autocracy. I think if Ishbaal had been unpleasant with Rizpah, the general might have acted. But the young man was obviously devoted to her. And she was still too distracted to be fully aware of what was happening. True, she would on occasion speak harshly to him, but her sternness had no direction, and the more he fawned on her, the more impossible he became with others.

In this manner, the pattern of Ishbaal's authority was established. Abner suffered his petty despotism out of reverence for Saul's memory, and also out of disinclination to create upheaval during Rizpah's most acute period of mourning. The remnants of the host bore the new king's outrageous conduct with amazing tolerance, mainly because of their love for Abner.

The court of Mahanaim had the smell of exile, the awkwardness of empty tribute. Ishbaal was king, but his influence barely extended beyond the limits of the town where he lived.

The Philistines were in firm control of the northern half of Israel. After the battle of Gilboa, they had found the bodies of Saul and Jonathan and had taken them to the city of Beth-shan in upper Ephraim. There they had impaled them on pikes above the walls as a symbol of their victory.

It was then that a moving incident took place. The men of Jabesh-Gilead, eternally grateful and loyal to Saul, heard of his death and the ignominious display of his body. Grieving deeply, they still had the courage and initiative to organize a raiding party which marched by night to Beth-shan. Fortune was with them. The Philistines, secure in the knowledge that they had crushed Israel, did not suspect that there would be any quick show of defiance. The bodies of Saul and his son were not guarded. And so the men of Jabesh were able to make off with them. They burned them under a tree before their own city, and after seven days of fasting, interred the remains with proper ceremony.

In the south, David finally emerged from his long-time ambivalent role to proclaim himself king of Judah and Simeon. Although he had been excused at the last moment from fighting on the Philistine side at Gilboa, he still maintained his cordial relationship with them. Now also, since Saul and Jonathan were dead, his pledge not to ascend the throne no longer bound him. With encouragement from the Philistines, who were happy to deal with a man who had lived among them in friendship, he established the seat of his kingdom at Hebron, a day's journey south of his birthplace, Beth-lehem.

This left Ishbaal with a shadow realm east of the Jordan, and an army of five hundred disheartened warriors to maintain him in his mock-kingly position.

Actually, the tiny band was augmented soon after we reached Mahanaim by the arrival of Paltiel and the three hundred men of the garrison he had been commanding.

Michal came with Paltiel. She had grown somewhat plump, but by no means fat, in the four years since we had last seen her. In fact, she was more pleasing to look at than in the days when she had been a bundle of imprisoned sexual energy. There was a softness about her; one had the feeling she was no longer tortured and driven by her voracious hungers. She was like a person who has been clinging for some time to a rope suspended from a cliff, holding on frantically to avoid dropping into an abyss. And gradually her grasp on the rope has weakened; her hands no longer possess the strength to maintain her grip. She lets go, expecting to be dashed to bits on the dark rocks below. To her amazement she finds she has fallen into a cushioning bed of flowers. The pleased surprise of the broken fall was on Michal's features, but there were also subtle lines of disappointment. One does not surrender to death and then escape it without feeling cheated as well as grateful.

She still had no children, but she had found sufficient diversion at the garrison to occupy her mind. She spoke much of cooking, and of the laziness of servants and the consequent difficulty in keeping her house spotless. She described in endless detail her visits with the wives of Paltiel's officers, sometimes repeating the last part of an anecdote if she felt Rizpah and I had been inattentive, or if she herself particularly relished it. She referred to Paltiel with complacent affection, dwelling at length on his likes and dislikes in food, his daily habits around which she had settled her own existence.

It seemed difficult to believe she had changed so radically in only four years. Yet beneath the placidity, under her almost flaccid exterior, I thought I detected some trace of the sensual little animal in whom restless desire had burned like a beacon torch. I wondered if she were ever aware of it, or if what I saw was merely a scar, the healed-over evidence of a disease which had once both ravaged and exhilarated her.

Paltiel had also changed. He had become just a trifle paunchy, a foreshadowing of what would eventually be middle-aged corpulence. He had the air of a man whose material wishes are catered to, who has only to request a special dish or a change of clothing to find it before him at once. His face had hardened; he had lost the look of benevolent simplicity which had made him so appealing. The flesh around his snub nose had thickened, lending him a slightly porcine appearance. But his eyes had undergone the greatest transformation. There was in them more than a hint of heavy-lidded cynicism, the weary glance that says clearly: we are all fools, but ah well, let us make the most of it.

However, there was none of this in his speech or manner. He was still an engaging young man. And if he had shuffled off some of his shyness, he had not replaced it with arrogance. He was still sincerely respectful, eager to please. His adoration for Michal had, if anything, increased. He hung on each word she spoke, listening with a rapt expression to her long, detailed stories, though it was obvious he must have heard them a hundred times over.

Abner welcomed him cordially. The young commander wanted to hear a full account of the events at Gilboa. He wept when Abner told him how Saul and Jonathan had died.

"But we shall avenge them," said the general. "I have begun planning action against the Philistines. Until now, my plans have been largely theoretical. You and your three hundred men will strengthen us considerably."

Paltiel looked thoughtful. "My men will need training. Garrison life has not kept them in condition for the rigors of battle. We have fought only once in four years, and that a minor skirmish with some drunken Ammonites. If my men are to help you at all, they must have time."

"It seems to me," Abner said mildly, "that you have had nothing but time."

"My lord, this is certainly true. But human beings are what they are. If a man knows that at the end of a day he is going home to his wife and children, and will sleep that night in his own bed, he will perhaps practice a bit at spear casting or swordplay. But his heart will not be in it as much as if he knows he is preparing for battle."

"Two or three weeks of rigorous work should make them ready."

Paltiel cleared his throat. "I was thinking more in terms of six months."

Abner looked at him sharply. Then he reached for the decanter on the table next to him and poured two bowls of wine. The two men were sitting in a corner of the common room. Abner glanced out through the open door into the garden, where Rizpah was walking with Meribaal. He handed Paltiel one of the bowls of wine. "Under your command," he said, "I am sure your men will be ready as quickly as we need them."

Paltiel shifted uneasily, looking down at the bowl in his hand.

"You already have two captains, my lord. Rechab and Baanah. They are experienced and competent."

"Neither as experienced nor as competent as you." He waited, then said slowly, "I have seen you perform feats of bravery that rivaled those of the king himself. I remember in Moab . . ."

"My lord Abner!" Paltiel's face was suddenly agonized.

"Is it possible," asked Abner quietly, "that the years of soft living have curdled the bravery of the king's most courageous captain? Is it possible he can no longer face an enemy charge, or mount an attack against those who defile his country?"

"If I did not have so much respect for my lord Abner," said Paltiel angrily, "I would thrust my sword through his gullet!"

"Then tell me," said Abner, unperturbed, "tell me why this reluctance to strike back against the foes of Israel."

"My lord, I should like nothing better than to help you lead our warriors forth to battle and bring them back singing psalms of victory."

"Only?"

"Only . . ." He stopped. "Will you force me to degrade myself?"

"I am entitled to an answer."

"My lord," whispered Paltiel, "I cannot leave her. Even for one night."

"I assume you are speaking of Michal." When Paltiel nodded, he said, "No man cares to be away from a wife he loves."

"It is not simply being away." He paused, struggling to find words. "My lord, I am afraid."

Abner sipped his wine and looked at the young man without speaking.

"Even when I go to inspect the outposts," Paltiel continued, "and I am absent no more than half a day, I ride back with my heart thumping louder than the hoofs of my horse. I wonder, will she be there when I return? I rush into the house. Sometimes she is not there. I know that she often goes to visit the wives of my officers, but I am almost in tears. I hurry from house to house, wild until I find her. I . . ."

He stopped abruptly, ashamed at having spoken so revealingly, and let his head fall forward on his chest.

Abner said, "Drink your wine. It has not the body of the vintages we grew in Benjamin, but it is the best Mahanaim has to offer."

Paltiel looked at the bowl in his hand as if he were surprised to see it there. Then he placed it to his lips and did not remove it until he had emptied it. "I am sorry, my lord. I have spoken like a weakling. But you do not know what it means to care for someone so deeply that without her your life would grow pallid and drab, that in truth there would be no living. . . ."

"Do I not?" Abner's voice contained just a touch of irony.

Paltiel blushed. There were few officers who had served with Saul who did not know at least a little of Abner's feeling for Rizpah. "I must humbly beg your pardon, my lord," he said in a low voice.

The general rose from his chair and placed his hand on Paltiel's shoulder. "Then, since you know I understand . . ."

"If I could fight a hundred battles during the day and come back to her at night . . ." He smiled, a lopsided, ingratiating grin. "I shall be glad to help with the training here at Mahanaim. And of course, if we are ever invaded, there is no question . . ."

"You are right. There is no question."

Paltiel regarded him inquiringly.

"You will help with the training," Abner said gently. "And if we are invaded, you will help command our defenses." He looked steadily at Paltiel. "You will also go forth with us, wherever the obligations of Israel may take us."

Anger burned bright in the younger man's eyes. He clenched his fists, opened his mouth, snapped it shut. Then he looked away, his anger gone. He sighed. "I will go, my lord. I only needed someone to force me to do what I knew I should."

So Paltiel and Michal joined the kingdom-in-exile at Mahanaim, and Paltiel began the task of readying his men for battle. The couple occupied a house of their own, despite Ishbaal's frenzied insistence that they live under his roof. But they did eat at the king's table at least three nights a week. I was surprised to see that Michal seemed to be afraid of Ishbaal. One night she said idly, as she had several times in the weeks since they took up residence in Mahanaim, "When my father was alive . . ."

Ishbaal leaped up from the table and shrilled at his sister, "Your father is not alive! I am king now! If I ever hear you use that expression again, I shall call a servant and have him take the lash to you!"

All of us, including Paltiel, sat motionless, too stunned to move. Ishbaal advanced threateningly toward Michal. In the old days she would have laughed and turned her back on him, or spoken scathingly to him. Now she cowered in her chair, watching her brother come toward her, his arm raised as if to strike her.

Rizpah said sharply, "Sit down, Ishbaal, and finish eating. Your face is dirty. Clean it."

He stopped and turned to her. His lips trembled. "Rizpah . . ." he said, and burst into tears. She got up, wet a napkin with water, and cleaned the grape stains from his face. Then she handed him the napkin. "Stop crying and blow your nose."

He clutched at her hand. "Yes, Rizpah."

She looked at him for a moment. Then she patted his shoulder and gave him a little shove toward the great carved chair.

Even though Rizpah could exert a salutary influence on Ishbaal, she quite understandably took no pleasure in being in his presence. In the gardens she found a measure of freedom. They were larger than the ones at Gibeah and contained many little areas of privacy: groves of trees, patches of tall lilies, arbors of climbing roses. Ishbaal seldom went to these secluded spots. Rizpah acquired the habit of taking the children to one of them as soon as she could escape from the king's table.

Abner would often join her. They talked at length of many things, but he would never speak of Saul unless she did first. Then they would recall and discuss some of the more impersonal incidents of his life. This was not easy. Saul had been an intensely personal man. There was too much pain for both of them in almost every memory. So they found themselves talking more and more of each other.

Rizpah's grief had left her with a residue of bitterness which on occasion made her say uncharacteristic things. "I was cheated," she said abruptly one evening. "Since I was very young, I have known little except violence and fear and sorrow."

Abner looked at her in silence. They were walking in one of the farthest corners of the garden. Nearby, Armoni, for once not noisily active, was picking apart a lily for Meribaal, telling his brother how the flower grew. Rizpah glanced fondly at the children, then said defiantly to Abner, "It's true!"

He replied, "I have never known you to pity yourself before."

"You and Egrep," she said disgustedly. "Twin thorns in my conscience."

"I cannot let you say what you did. Not when you have known love as deeply as you have."

"And where is that love now?"

"Would you rather not have known it?"

Tears filled her eyes. "You're being cruel. Do you want to torture me?"

He stopped walking and caught her hands in his. She made no effort to draw away. "I would rather," he said, "cut out my tongue than say anything that would hurt you. But I cannot bear to see grief and longing distilling poison in your heart, drop by bitter drop."

She smiled wanly. "Your words are almost as smooth as those of our erstwhile companion with the lyre. I didn't know you possessed a touch of the poet."

He was also smiling, but his tone was serious. "There are perhaps many things you do not know about me."

"Dear friend," she said. "Dear, dear friend."

He moved away from her irritably. "I am not your dear friend. And if you ever use that condescending manner with me again, I shall throttle you."

She laughed. "Then you must do it before the evening meal. At least then I shall be spared the dubious delight of hearing Ishbaal's opinions on the quality of Mahanaim fruit."

"He is Saul's son, Rizpah. He is the king."

"Fortunately he has very little to rule over."

"His kingdom will grow larger very soon."

"You will do this for Ishbaal?"

"Not for Ishbaal. For Israel."

"Abner," she said soberly, "I do not care so much now what happens to me. No, that's not true. Of course I care. But I am also concerned about you. Never let anything happen to you. Please . . ."

A light grew in his eyes, then faded. "You are lonely," he said. "This is why you speak as you do."

"Why did you have to say that?" she said, suddenly angry. "Why did you have to take a simple . . ." She turned away, making a harsh, ugly noise in her throat.

His hands started to climb upward and outward in their gesture of resignation. Then he laughed.

"Why are you laughing?" She was still annoyed.

"Because there is nothing else to do."

"I am sorry," she said. "And you are my dear friend. You always will be."

"Come," he said, his voice flat. "It's getting dark. We must find the children."

chapter three

THE ONSET of autumn made little difference to us in Mahanaim, aside from the fact that the days were growing shorter. There would be little rain in the winter, and the winds that swept in from the Great Sea would lose much of their cold and dampness before they reached the Jordan.

Abner was well pleased with the climate. The dry days meant that he could move ahead with his preparations for the recapture of Israelite territory. Training was going well. The veterans of Gilboa needed little practice in the handling of weapons. For them it was chiefly a matter of maintaining condition and morale. And Paltiel's company was composed almost entirely of blooded troops who had

marched with Saul against Ammon, Moab and Philistia. As Paltiel
had said, garrison life had softened them, but they were quickly regaining their former skill and fitness.

The inhabitants of Mahanaim enjoyed the presence of the soldiers
of Israel. True, there were the usual frictions between warriors and
civilian population, the usual altercations involving daughters and occasional property damage. However, generally speaking, those who
dwelled permanently in the region were delighted. The merchants
reaped their customary rich crop of profits from the exiles. But it was
among the farmers and shepherds that the men of Abner found their
most ardent admirers.

In the central sections of Israel, even the more isolated herdsmen
and tillers of the soil were cosmopolites compared with those around
Mahanaim. Judah and Ephraim and even northerly Dan were accustomed to the daily passage of caravans from far-off lands. There was
a feeling of activity, of ferment, that was missing from this semidesert
settlement.

Until the influx of the tiny army, Mahanaim had coursed through
the months of each year in endless monotony. Generations of its people proceeded from infancy to the grave without any appreciable alteration in existence. And as is often the case where men do not know
any other way of life, they had been content with what they had.

Now all that was changed. The narrow streets echoed with a variety
of accents strange to provincial ears. Laughter and song rolled out of
the army encampment long after dark, stirring up an odd restlessness
in the hearts of the residents.

The farmers and shepherds took to coming to town for the sole
purpose of watching the army go through its training maneuvers. They
would cluster at the edge of the date grove and stare openmouthed
at the spearmen and archers. They would cheer wildly during the
swordplay, shrieking and slapping their thighs excitedly as metal rang
against metal. For them it was pageant, festival and orgiastic revel,
all combined in a glorious afternoon of release. And it was there every
day, changing and still constant, waiting, whenever a man would steal
away from his flocks or vineyards.

In the course of time, the inevitable happened. The step from on-
looker to participant seemed an inviting one. They chose delegates
and sent them to Abner. The general received them courteously. Yes,
he told them, he could certainly use additions to his forces. Truly,
as they intimated, he had been impressed by the sinewy, agile appearance of the men of Mahanaim he had seen so far. But had they stopped
to consider the nature of war? Had they even imagined the mangling

terror of the chariot, the spear which tore gaping holes in a man's breast, the sword which spilled his entrails onto the ground? And had they thought of the slow death that often followed battle: the festering arrow wound, the smell of rotting flesh, the agonizing pain which went with the draining away of life through one, ten, a score of nights?

He might as well have been making an impassioned speech of recruitment. The more vividly he described the horrors of combat, the more inflamed with eagerness his listeners became, until one, more exuberant than the others, leaped high in the air and shouted, "Now, my lord! Take us now and let us go slaughter the Philistines!"

Abner smiled, then sighed, then assigned the new men to Rechab and Baanah for training.

Altogether, nearly two hundred farmers and shepherds from the region around Mahanaim swelled the ranks of Israel's army.

But even including these, there were still less than eleven hundred soldiers, not a quarter of the minimum required for any major assault on Philistine strongholds. While it was true that Saul had begun with fewer warriors, ill-trained and worse equipped, conditions were different now. In the early days of Saul's guerrilla warfare, his troops had been able to count on complete support from the people of Israel. With the exception of known collaborators, no inhabitant of Israel would have even thought of informing the Philistines of the whereabouts of the embryo army.

Now David was king of Judah. Those who would fight for the son of Saul were his enemies. And David had numbers of adherents even in the northern territories. Therefore, Abner could not lead his men on lengthy campaigns west of the Jordan, where they would have to live on the land, hide in caves and thickets, and exist in constant danger of betrayal.

He was able to make sporadic raids on border cities such as Bethshan. These forays were successful as far as they went. But Abner did not dare attempt them too frequently, for fear that the Philistines would send a massive reprisal force against Mahanaim. The attacks, such as they were, had to be confined to swift night assaults and equally swift withdrawals.

In time the men grew restless. None except the recruits from Mahanaim wanted to take excessive risks. But neither did they enjoy stagnating in a dusty desert town without any immediate hope that the monotony would be relieved.

Ishbaal did not help matters. He had commanded Abner to schedule a daily royal review of his troops, which would consist of their marching past him and executing complex maneuvers of his choice. Abner, with tact and amazing self-control, dissuaded the king from this pastime. But he could not keep the young man away from the training field.

At first Ishbaal only watched, looking on disdainfully as the new additions to the army went clumsily through their paces. It was not long before this ceased to amuse him. One day he interrupted Rechab and Baanah in the midst of instruction and lectured them windily on proper techniques of battle. The two captains were brothers, hardened survivors of a score of engagements. Rechab had a great scar running across his cheek from his left ear to his mouth. Otherwise they looked almost exactly alike: tight-lipped, thin-nosed men with cold watchful eyes.

The captains did not protest openly when the king disrupted their work. Instead they went at once to Abner.

The general was furious. Had it not been for the fact that Rizpah was with him when the brothers arrived, he might have taken the drastic and justifiable step of severing his relationship with Ishbaal.

Rizpah waited until the captains were gone. Then she said quietly, "Let me speak to him, my lord."

She found him in the courtyard, reprimanding a servant for failing to replenish the fruit bowl in one of the rooms. The terrified man was crouching against the courtyard wall, covering his face with his hands, while Ishbaal screamed at him and spat on his feet.

When the king saw Rizpah, he ran to her, took her by the hand and led her back to the servant. "This fellow has been negligent. I am about to punish him," he said proudly.

"I want to talk to you," she said.

He brightened. Turning to the man, who was furtively wiping the spittle off his sandals, he said with a lordly gesture, "Leave us. I shall deal with you presently."

The servant slunk away, and Rizpah said brusquely, "You have been at the army camp."

"They are idiots," he said. "How they ever expect to regain my kingdom for me with such a pack of fools . . ."

"From this day on, you will never again interfere in the affairs of the army."

"It is my army," he said plaintively. "I have a right to tell them anything I wish."

"You will never again interfere!"

The king's expression grew cunning and malevolent. "Who are you to command me? A woman . . . my father's concubine . . ."

She slapped him so hard that he stumbled and fell. He picked himself up, blinking back the tears, trembling before her fury.

"You hate me," he whined. "I thought you were my friend, but you hate me."

Rizpah felt suddenly weary and depressed. "No, Ishbaal, I don't hate you."

"Then you like me?" he said pleadingly. "Tell me you like me."

She evaded his eyes. "You heard what I said. Do not interfere, ever again, with the army."

"If it is your wish, Rizpah. Just tell me that you—"

"Come," she said, interrupting hastily. "I would like some fruit."

He was mollified at once. "The dates are the best I have ever seen," he said, skipping ahead of her delightedly. "For Mahanaim, that is. Fat and firm and sweet." He paused on the threshold and turned to her. "Do you remember the day of Michal's wedding?"

"I remember."

"I shall never forget it as long as I live. You were so good to me."

She had a vague recollection of having killed an insect he was torturing, of slapping him and making him cry, of being fearful and angry in his presence.

"You are the only one who never lied to me or made fun of me . . . except my mother." His eyes widened until they resembled two enormous dark pools. "I would die for you, Rizpah."

She escaped as quickly as she could and ran to her room. There she lay across the bed and wept. The last violence of her grief for Saul poured out that day.

Her admonition was effective. Within the house Ishbaal grew more demanding and implacable, but Abner was not troubled again by his interference in army matters.

And now the fortunes of Israel took a positive turn.

One morning, the captain of the house guard informed Abner that a man was waiting to see him in the common room. He descended and saw a figure in an austere white robe bending over a vase of flowers.

The man straightened up and turned to Abner. There was something familiar about him. The general studied the tall, spare frame, the piercing eyes in an otherwise saturnine face.

His visitor waited, then said, "Does my lord Abner not recall the march to Ammon, the near tragedy of the ambush outside Beth-nimrah?"

It came back. "You are from Jabesh-Gilead. Forgive me . . ."

"Man is a forgetful creature. His frailties demand no apology."

"Jabesh did not forget Saul. How ashamed I am that I did not have the courage to rescue the bodies of my nephew and his son from the walls of Beth-shan."

"You had fought a battle," said the man from Jabesh courteously. "The stench of death and defeat was still in your nostrils. We had not suffered at Gilboa. The least we could do was show our respect for the king we loved during all his lifetime."

"What can I do to reward you in the name of Saul?"

"The men of Jabesh do not seek payment. If we had wished that, we could have heeded the messengers David sent to us."

"David?"

"They blessed us, these messengers, with smooth tongues and glib promises of kindness. They made us see the face of David as benign and selfless. Then the adder's tongue appeared."

"I do not understand . . ."

"They made it clear, these messengers, that the house of Saul was destroyed, that the kingdom of David in Hebron was the only true power in the land. Their meaning was veiled but nonetheless palpable. We were being ordered to swear allegiance to the Judahite shepherd, to serve him. . . ." Anger flickered in his eyes. "No one makes demands of Jabesh. Saul taught us the courage of refusal in the days when Ammon clamored outside our gates."

Abner summoned a servant and requested that refreshment be brought the man from Jabesh. Then he said, "I am flattered by your presence in Mahanaim."

"It is no idle visit, as you are surely aware. At this moment, seven hundred men of my city are approaching this town. If you can make use of our services to regain the glory of Israel, we bring you our loyalty and our strength."

He bowed to Abner, then smiled as he saw the growing joy in the general's face.

Word of the action of the men of Jabesh spread quickly in Israel. It was a turning point. Now, individuals and whole bands from all the northern territories began to arrive in Mahanaim, asking to join Abner in rising against the Philistines. By midwinter, over four thousand men had assembled and were being shaped into a competent fighting force.

Now the time was ripe for a test.

On the evening before the army was to venture forth across the Jordan, Abner and Rizpah, as had become their custom, were strolling in the gardens back of the king's house. She was unusually quiet.

He said to her, "You are troubled."

"I wish you were not going."

"I shall return."

"How like a man," she said. "It is neither the going nor the returning I speak of."

"What lies between is necessary."

"For Ishbaal?"

"I told you once. For Israel."

"Has there not been enough violence? Enough blood poured on the ground? Enough wives made widows?"

"You believe there is a choice?"

"I believe nothing any more."

"Egrep wears cynicism well. It is her shield and ensign. But it ill becomes you."

"I spoke sincerely."

"That is why it ill becomes you."

She turned to him in the gathering gloom. "You will be careful?"

"Does it matter?"

"Would I have asked if it did not?"

"I would like to know."

"Do not question me any more. For whatever I answer I shall not know if I speak the truth. Only . . . promise me you will take no foolish chances."

"I promise."

She touched his shoulder lightly, fleetingly, then left him and hurried toward the house.

chapter four

As LONG as the remnants of Saul's army had seen fit to close themselves off from the world at Mahanaim, David showed little interest in them. After all, they were only a handful of weary men, paying court to an idiot king, perpetrating a travesty on the vigor and purpose that had vitalized the realm of Saul. They were led by an aging general who lived mainly in the past. And what of Abner's past? If it had not been for Saul, he would have remained a well-to-do farmer, at most taking part in the local councils of elders.

Could, then, a few hundred incompetents pose a threat to the king of Judah, whose star had risen so swiftly and brilliantly over Hebron?

The answer for some time was of course negative. But in dismissing Mahanaim from consideration, David had forgotten the insignificance of Saul's beginnings. He seemed also to ignore the fact that only a short time before he himself had commanded a nondescript band of dissidents.

Less than eight months after it had been defeated at Gilboa, Abner's army had again become a powerful, mobile force which was slowly but systematically ridding northern Israel of Philistine occupation.

No longer did they fear betrayal at the hands of those who sympathized with David. They marched in the open now, a proud, victorious host. One by one, they retook the cities of Israel and rolled the legions of the invader back toward the coast. Beth-shan, Shechem, Shiloh, then the whole territory of Ephraim. And after that, Benjamin, including Gibeah, where the Philistine governor who occupied the house of Saul was routed out of bed at midnight and executed in the courtyard. Then Issachar, Zebulon and Asher. It was not difficult at that point to retake Naphtali, Dan and Manasseh, where the Philistine grip was weakest. Finally the campaign was complete: Israel was restored to the house of Saul.

The nucleus of the liberating army was the contingent from Jabesh-Gilead. They were an unusual group. The pagan savagery of the desert was in their blood. They would march along singing the dark and sinister dirges of war born in the trackless wastes of the Ammonite wilderness. They worshiped Jahveh, but the shadow of the serpent-god and the one-horned bull hung over their devotions. They were given to taciturnity, but before battle they were likely to perform weird dances, during which they slashed their flesh and shrieked at the night sky. And in a fray, teeth bared, screaming like mountain lions, they struck terror in the hearts of the foe. They took a ferocious delight in close fighting, wielding their short, curved, razor-sharp swords with frightening accuracy and effect.

If Abner had been able to command a few thousand men from Jabesh instead of a few hundred, it is doubtful that he would ever have had to face the menace of David's army.

As it was, Joab, who now had full control of David's troops, was both cautious and clever. He avoided attacking any of Abner's units whenever he knew they included the men of Jabesh.

The active conflict between Judah and Israel began under cover of darkness and on a very small scale, with an attack on the camp of one of Abner's roving companies of a hundred. In fact, if one of Joab's men had not been wounded and left behind after the raid, it might have been considered just another Philistine counterattack. But the wounded man was unquestionably of Judah. Believing he was dying, he poured out an incoherent tale of plans for large-scale civil war. Though this sounded at first like the babbling of a man in fever, it turned out all too sadly to be true.

Thereafter, Abner had to consider not only the Philistine threat, but danger from the south as well. In the beginning, his men were reluctant to fight against those they considered brothers. But they soon learned that a spear cast by a man of David let as much blood as a Philistine sword. And because there is hardly anything more fierce than brotherly amity turned bitter, the strife between the two segments of the Hebrew nation became ruthless and unrelenting, with severe losses on both sides.

Abner's army laid waste to towns in Judah. The warriors of Joab swept into Benjamin, burning homes and pillaging. The northerners, so recently freed of the Philistine yoke, cried out in anguish at this new jeopardy to their security. In turn, the people of Judah protested vigorously against what they termed the atrocities of Abner. Yet neither army appeared willing to call off the hostilities which were gaining momentum with each passing week.

It seemed that the senseless and wasteful letting of blood could only resolve itself through some sort of crisis. This came in late summer, almost exactly two years after the battle of Gilboa.

Abner and a thousand soldiers of Israel were returning from a skirmish with the Philistines in the Valley of Aijalon, that oft-contested passageway to the coastal plain. They had repulsed a half-hearted Philistine thrust without suffering serious casualties, but they were hot and weary as they trudged eastward, beginning the long trek back to Mahanaim. Zaccur suggested that they make a slight detour and stop at the great pool outside the city of Gibeon. There they could eat and rest and wash the dust of battle from their bodies.

It was late afternoon when they sighted the pool in the distance. Abner ordered the marching pace picked up, and the captains of hundreds gladly passed on the order. When they were perhaps three hundred cubits away from the water, Abner suddenly blinked his eyes unbelievingly. Gathered on the far side of the pool were about eight or nine hundred men. And in the forefront, lounging at the water's edge, were the three brothers: Joab, Abishai and the young Asahel.

Abner held up his hand for a halt. Had they blundered into some kind of trap? But no, the men of David could not possibly have known they were passing. Besides, they were obviously taking their ease.

Weapons were scattered about on the ground, and some of the soldiers were stripping off their clothing, preparing to bathe in the pool.

While Abner was pondering whether to advance and launch an attack or simply bypass the pool and avoid a battle, Joab cupped his hands to his mouth and shouted, "Let the warriors of Abner come forward and rest on the opposite side of the pool, and bathe if they wish. Then they will go their way and we shall go ours, and there will be peace between us this day."

Abner hesitated. And as he did, a breeze ruffled the blue surface of the water and a flock of swallows rose from some nearby trees, soaring and swooping, twittering joyously.

The general felt dirty and sweaty. Dust from battlefield and road had made his mouth dry. His lips were swollen and cracked. He looked back at his men. Their eyes were weary, imploring. Beside him, Zaccur shrugged. "What can be the harm, my lord? If your skin itches as fiercely as mine . . ."

Abner smiled and raised his arm, beckoning the men forward. They advanced with scarcely contained delight, divesting themselves of helmets and garments as they ran. Soon they were splashing about like children in the cool water. Warriors of both sides, who had striven against each other in mortal enmity for many months, now met naked in the center of the pool and wrestled playfully, as they had often done in former years. Tension, suddenly released, came out in song, in shrill cries, in laughter that was close to tears.

But the fraternizing was short-lived. When they had bathed, the men of Abner and the men of Joab withdrew to their respective sides of the pool and rested, chatting quietly among themselves.

It was then that Joab broke out of a group of his warriors and called to Abner, "Should the show of friendship which has reunited us cease so abruptly? This is a festive occasion. Let twelve of your young men arise, and come to wrestle for sport against twelve I shall choose."

For a second time that day, Abner hesitated. He was thinking: if only there *could* be an end to strife and bloodshed. Now that Philistia was subdued, would it not be pleasant to live in peace, to bring the court of Ishbaal out of exile and dwell once again among the green hills of Benjamin? To bring Rizpah and the children at last to his home, to offer her the tranquillity she wanted and deserved. He remembered the words she had spoken and her touch on his shoulder the one evening several months ago. Since then, he had been seldom in Mahanaim, and when he was, there was no indication that she regarded him as anything other than a dear friend. Now perhaps if . . .

His reverie was shattered by Joab's voice calling again, "Surely

Abner will not refuse his young men the enjoyment of striving against mine in friendly contest. See, they only await the word of their general."

It was true. All around him men were getting up from the ground, laughing and flexing their muscles. Those from his own territory of Benjamin were particularly eager. They crowded around Abner, at least three score of them, each begging to be chosen as one of the twelve to wrestle against the select of Judah. Smiling and raising his hands to ward off their insistency, he shouted across to Joab, "Let it be done then. We shall gather at the end of the pool and hold the contest. Then we shall each go our separate ways."

Shouts of excitement from both sides greeted his words. The two bands of men funneled down the sides of the pool toward a flat, clear space at the end.

Abner chose twelve of the most stalwart from among his warriors, then sat down on the ground. He was not particularly concerned with either the contest or its outcome. But the prospect of peace warmed his blood. For the first time in months he could look around and enjoy the beauties of the land without thinking that such and such a crag might harbor an ambush and such and such a hill would create a likely cover for a flanking maneuver against the enemy.

The afternoon shadows were lengthening. The waters of the pool, having been stirred and thrown up to the sunlight by the men bathing in them, gave off a fresh and pleasing odor.

The wrestlers of Israel stripped to the waist and advanced to meet the young men of Judah, who did not come out against them at once. When they noticed this hanging back, the soldiers of Israel called out good-naturedly, "Are the striplings of David suddenly afraid then that they hold themselves aloof from the contest? Does the sight of the shoulders and limbs of our wrestlers fill them with fear?"

Finally the twelve Judahites came forward, still wearing their cloaks. This provoked Abner's men to hoots of laughter. "Our warriors are going forth against a flock of women whose modesty bids them cover themselves. Have a care, you naked wrestlers, lest your hands encounter something which will divert your zeal from the contest!"

To which Joab replied, "Our men of Judah are so confident that they need not even remove their cloaks to win the game. On with the match!"

Abner basked in the sounds of raillery. He recalled the days when all those at the pool of Gibeon, so lately divided, had stood as one against the foes of Israel, had marched, eaten, slept, and taken their leisure together. Now again the welcome noise of crude soldiery jests was replacing the cries of battle.

The twelve cloaked wrestlers of Judah moved cautiously into the center of the clear space. Abner glanced at them, then looked more sharply, puzzled by what he saw. The Judahites' faces were pale, their expressions grown suddenly grim, creating an odd contrast to the banter still flowing back and forth between the two groups of spectators.

And in this instant Zaccur spoke harshly in his ear. "My lord . . . look!"

Abner saw at once what he meant. The warriors of Israel had come unarmed to the end of the pool, leaving their weapons and armor scattered where they had dropped them prior to bathing. But Joab's soldiers were fully armed, each man's sword and spear lying beside him within easy reach.

As he looked, cursing himself for his stupidity, there was a grating cry of fear from the wrestling ring. The Judahites had thrown aside their cloaks and were advancing on their adversaries. Each was brandishing a sword which had been concealed under the garments. The wrestlers from Abner's ranks tried to escape, but it was too late. Each Judahite grasped one of them by the hair and plunged a sword into his side.

With which Joab's warriors leaped to their feet and charged across the open space toward the men of Israel.

There was no time for Abner to issue orders, no time for anything but flight. The Israelites ran in all directions, pursued by the shouting soldiers of Joab.

Abner was able, along with perhaps a hundred others, to reach the side of the pool where they had left their weapons. There they seized whatever came to hand, formed ragged ranks and tried to make a stand. But the sudden treachery had thrown them into such confusion that Abner realized this kind of resistance was useless. He called out to them to disband, and when he was certain they had managed to get away, he also turned and ran.

He had left his sword behind at the pool, but he was carrying a spear at his side, holding it in a loose grip as he sped toward the nearest hill, where there were rocks and brush which would offer some shelter.

His heart was pounding, his legs growing heavy with fatigue. Still he kept running, never looking back, never slackening his pace. He felt a sick anger at having allowed himself to trust Joab. If he had only been a little more wary, a little more ruthless, his men might have scored a victory instead of being dispersed like frightened sheep through the hills. No, he knew he could never have attacked Joab without warning. But he should have been on guard against deception. He would remember forever the sight of his twelve warriors, walking laughing and vulnerable into the wrestling ring, and their blood spurting out to stain the white sand on which they fell.

All this he thought as he ran, and it was only some stubborn sense of self-preservation that kept his legs moving, his feet rhythmically pounding the hard ground.

Then he heard the footsteps behind him. Thinking it was one of his own men, he glanced over his shoulder.

The warrior who was running after him was Asahel, the young brother of Joab.

Abner's sickness increased within him. He was fatigued, but he still possesssed enough strength to turn and smite the youth who pursued him. It would be so easy. The single quick glance had shown him that Asahel was running lightly, effortlessly, but he was holding his sword away from his body and thus leaving himself open for a sudden skillful blow. A hundred times in battle Abner had disarmed and slain men who had come toward him in just such a fashion.

He turned his head again and gasped over his shoulder, "Asahel . . . go back! Go back!" And his heart was echoing: Go back . . . why should I slay you? . . . how then could I hold up my head to your brother Joab for having killed one so young, so innocent?

Abner felt his energy flagging. The black spots which tokened exhaustion were beginning to dance before his eyes. He cried out again, "Asahel . . . go back!"

The footsteps behind him did not slacken. Now he knew he would have to stop and face his pursuer. And it would have to be done quickly, in one abrupt unwarning motion. He gripped his spear more tightly. If he could strike with the butt end, there was a chance he could knock the young man off his feet, take his sword away from him and send him on his way.

He waited until his warrior's instinct told him it was just the proper moment. Then he slowed down, and as the pounding steps came close, he wheeled and stood firm holding the spear hind end outthrust to catch Asahel's sword and flip it out of his hand.

But he had not reckoned with the youth's furious forward momentum, nor had he realized he was so near. He had a fleeting glimpse of the boy's sweat-streaked face, his angry eyes. Then there was a sickening jolt as Asahel ran directly onto the spear. Flesh gave; the handle shuddered as the spear end passed grindingly between Asahel's ribs.

The youth fell to the ground, still clutching his sword. Blood burst from the wound; a dark splotch appeared at the corner of his mouth. Abner knelt beside him. There was no life. Asahel had died instantly.

He pulled the spear out of the boy's body, feeling weak and spent. Asahel's eyes looked up at him, retaining the fear Abner had seen in them just before the spear struck. The perspiration was beginning to dry on the dead face.

Abner sighed and looked around. He had run a great distance. Death had pursued him in the person of Asahel, and then with the lightning irony of which it was capable, had felled the pursuer. Did Death really care?

The twilight sky was bright blue overhead, darkening to greens and soft grays near the horizon. A bright half-moon had risen. The between-light limned Asahel's motionless body, endowed the pallid face with a semblance of repose.

Somewhere far off he could hear men shouting. The sounds were gradually coming closer. He waited, listening, then recognized the bass voice of Abishai. The brothers of Asahel would be approaching, and would look on the death of one who had sprung from the same womb as they. He had destroyed part of the fruit of that womb. How many women had he made childless, how much suffering had he created with the battle might of his hands? And to what purpose?

Off to his right was a hill called Ammah. He had known it since boyhood. He plodded toward it now; the hill of Ammah would shelter him, let him lose identity among its thickets, provide him with a stream where he could cleanse the blood of Asahel from his hands.

He toiled up the incline, stopped short as he heard a twig snap. Shadowy forms were moving among the trees. He raised his spear. If you kill once, you must kill again, as surely as the heart beats in your own breast. And if it was death they demanded, he would weigh out good measure of payment before he acceded. Slowly he drew back the spear, directing the point toward the nearest shadow.

"My lord Abner . . ."

It was one of the men from Mahanaim. Abner let out his breath noisily and trudged toward him.

There were over a hundred of his soldiers in the clearing. Some lay wounded. Others sat kneading feet that had suffered cuts and bruises in the fury of flight. One young shepherd from Gad was stretched out full length on the ground, sobbing quietly.

From below came the sound of Joab's troops calling loudly, one to the other. Then there was sudden silence. They have found the body, he thought. A bereft animal cry split the stillness. With a sense of

wonderment and sorrow, Abner recognized the voice as Joab's. Again
the cry. Could this bold, conscienceless one feel grief then? Was there
space for it in his soul along with all the cunning and connivance?

Abner lifted up his voice and shouted, "Joab! Do you hear me,
Joab?"

His men looked at him in astonishment. The sobbing shepherd
scrambled to his feet and darted for cover among the trees. The man
from Mahanaim who had greeted him moved about uneasily, fingering the handle of his sword.

"Joab!"

"Who calls?" The voice of David's general, quivering with its burden of tears. "Abner?"

"I mourn for the death of your brother." And the reproach he could
not bring himself to speak: Had it not been for your own perfidy,
Asahel would live yet.

"Abner?" Even at a distance, the childlike tones of loss were evident
in the repeated question. "Abner?"

"Shall the sword devour forever? Now you must know that this can
only end bitterly. How long before you call back your men from following their brothers?"

There was a long pause. The men around Abner tensed, waiting.
One of the wounded groaned loudly, then was still.

Now Joab's voice came to them again, firmer, rich with feeling.

"As God lives, if you had not spoken, my men would have continued
to pursue you."

The sound of the ram's horn rose from the plain, and once more
Abner's warriors readied themselves to meet an assault. But after a
moment they realized the call was a summons, not the signal for a
charge.

Abner stepped out of the shelter of the thicket. The moonlight
showed him Joab's men gathering from afar about the prostrate form
of Asahel. Four of them picked up the body and bore it among them
back toward the pool of Gibeon. Abner could make out the figures of
Joab and Abishai following with bowed heads.

There was stillness now on the hill of Ammah. Abner turned to
his followers. "We shall assemble the living and number the dead.
Then we march at once to Mahanaim."

chapter five

I WATCHED them straggle into town. The unhurt and the walking wounded slogged along beside wagons containing the casualties. The scene was unpleasantly reminiscent of the retreat from Gilboa. Rizpah joined me at the courtyard gate, and we looked on in silence.

Abner was not at the head of the troops. Our eyes searched anxiously until we saw him walking next to one of the wagons. He bade the driver stop and came to us. His face lighted up as it always did when he saw Rizpah, but an underlying grimness drained away the joy. "Three hundred and sixty lost," he said cryptically, then in a few words told us of the encounter at Gibeon.

He jerked his head in the direction of the wagon and said to Rizpah, "Zaccur has been asking for you."

"Is he badly hurt?"

"He's dying," said Abner brutally, turning away.

He stopped some of the men from one of the marching companies and had them lift Zaccur from the wagon and carry him into the house. Rizpah gasped when she saw him. I felt my stomach move uneasily. Zaccur's arm had been severed just below the shoulder. The stump was a charred, festering mess.

"Our surgeon was killed," said Abner. "We did the best we could. Stopped the bleeding with a sword heated in fire. But we were not able to . . ." He broke off and called with unwonted anger to those carrying Zaccur, "Be careful. Do you think that's a felled tree you're jostling?"

Zaccur opened his eyes and smiled painfully. "It's a felled tree."

The little man's customary gray color had faded to a muddy white. We made him as comfortable as possible on a couch in the common room. There he seemed to gather strength, but the smell of death hung round him.

His eyes found Rizpah. "I said my farewell to you at Gilboa, so no more is necessary." Then, turning to me, "As for you, ancient one . . ." He grimaced. "Why do I have the feeling that my arm is still with me? I saw it lying under a tree near Gibeon. Do you think it will return to me in Sheol?" He was quiet for a moment, thinking, before he spoke to me again. "When I left my village to join the ranks of Saul, I put my little bit of land under the care of a kinsman, a man named Eliel. I want this chestnut-haired wench to have my land. If it will not bring forth fruit when she smiles on it, then it is doomed to lie fallow forever."

Rizpah said, "Zaccur . . ." and could not go on.

His eyes seemed to be growing clearer. "You are not going to be sentimental, are you, wench? Old comrades in arms like you and me, we save sentiment for looking on wine, or dancing, or telling lies to maids and men." A spasm of pain made him twist suddenly and try to sit up. Rizpah pushed him down gently. "I never thought I would be afraid, but I am. Talk to me, Rizpah. Talk to me and sing some of those ridiculous songs from Simeon. The ones which croon so tenderly of green pastures in a land where everything is brown. You too, wrinkled one. Tell me of the stars, about which you know nothing but always speak so charmingly."

We stayed by his side, talking, taking turns singing to him. Abner drifted disconsolately about the room. The servants came to set the table for the evening meal. Abner waved them away.

A little while later, Ishbaal entered, almost bursting with fury at the disruption of his prescribed daily schedule. Abner took him by the shoulders, turned him around and escorted him firmly from the room. I caught a glimpse of the king's face as he was being propelled toward the door, and I remember thinking: He will never forgive Abner for this.

Once Zaccur called for wine. Abner held the bowl to his lips, but he was unable to swallow. He was feverish now, drifting in and out of consciousness.

Just after midnight he died. Rizpah was singing when it happened. I know she saw that he was dead, but she continued her song to the end. Then we extinguished the torches which had been placed at the head and foot of the couch.

I retired to my room to be alone with the god and goddess and to pray for the spirit of Zaccur. Good friends are rare, and it matters not whom they worship, for death serves all gods.

Abner summoned the captain of the house guard and bade him care for the body of Zaccur. Then, when he and Rizpah were alone, he wept. The tears ran down his cheeks and fell to the stone floor. She went to him and took his head in her hands, holding him until his sobbing subsided.

He looked into her eyes. "You asked me once . . . will there be no end to violence? I ask it of myself now. And of God. How long, O Lord, will you continue to rob us of those we love?"

"You are alive," she said simply.

"Is it pity you feel?" he asked. "I could not bear pity from you."

"It is not pity."

"Then . . ."

"Must you always question?"

"I must know."

"And I am not able to tell you. Is it not enough that we are here together?"

He stared at her for a few moments. Then together they walked toward the stairs, their footsteps echoing in the empty chamber.

chapter six

SHE WAKENED early. The room, shuttered and dim, was unfamiliar. She turned her head and saw the form of the man at her side. Still drugged with sleep, she started to murmur the name of Saul, stopped herself just in time and came wide awake.

Abner stirred beside her, freed his arm from the covers and flung it across his chest. The gesture was so abandoned, so unlike him, that she smiled.

She had never known gentleness like his.

Before he returned from his last, catastrophic expedition across the Jordan, she had known they would be together. Whatever it was between them had grown and matured these past few months, so that from passive fondness she had come to wanting to give herself to him. But she had not believed it would happen so quickly. Zaccur's death and the resultant opening of sensibilities in both of them had been the catalyst. The little man would have enjoyed knowing that. It would have tickled his ribald sense of humor. And he had loved Abner and her with great warmth.

Yet she had been afraid the night before, and now in dawnlight she was still fearful. She had never loved anyone in the way she loved Saul, and though he had been dead two years, another man touching her body seemed some kind of betrayal.

It was not from this alone that her fear stemmed. She honestly did not know the nature of the feeling she had for Abner. For almost a decade he had been her friend and protector, and for a large part of that time she had treated him shabbily. Through it all, his love had never wavered, his understanding had never failed. And as her early contempt for what she considered his weakness had atrophied, she had found herself first respectful, then coolly affectionate.

And now?

She did not dare open her heart to now. That heart had belonged to Saul. He was dead and she was alive. If another possessed it, quickened it to tenderness, made her again vulnerable, and then he, too . . . She felt she could not survive another deprivation.

So she made excuses, called up the ghosts of long-past moments: Abner's too-rapid adoration, his refusal to defy her, his constant easy acquiescence to the will of Saul.

Still, even in the few hours since last evening, she knew her fondness was deepening. She had responded to his love-making with a fervor that confused her. And he had comforted, shielded her. He seemed to sense what went on in the very wellspring of her soul. He had understood her fears, her reticence, and this was in itself frightening.

Abner woke and looked over at her unbelievingly. He reached out his hand, drew it back, then put it forward again to touch her. She smiled.

He said, "What are you thinking?"

"Don't you know?"

"How could I?"

"I was beginning to have the feeling you knew everything I thought."

"I wish I did."

"I'm not sure you should wish such a thing."

"Would it be that bad?"

She took his hand. "Would you really like to know?"

He nodded soberly.

"I was thinking that you look no more than twenty years old."

"How charming of you to say it." He laughed richly. "And how happy I am for it not to be so."

"Has your life been so filled with regret?"

"Regret, no. There is much I wish I had done, much I wish I had not. But I have lived in the only way I knew. And until now, there has not been a single moment I would care to live again."

She was about to speak when a terrible cry resounded in the corridor just outside the door. It was so anguished, so inhuman, that for an instant Rizpah believed that a wild beast had somehow gained entry into the house.

Then the voice shaped itself into words—a mad torrent of incoherent phrases, oaths and obscenities.

Abner leaped out of bed and hastily threw on some clothes. He had scarcely finished dressing when the door burst open and Ishbaal dashed into the room, awkwardly brandishing a sword. He stopped short when he saw Rizpah; he ignored Abner and rushed to the bed. "The servant was right," he cried. "I beat him and called him a liar, but he was right." His face worked furiously. "Rizpah . . . how could you do this to me?"

She pulled the bedclothes up around her shoulders, aghast at this glimpse of a disordered and rotting mind, sickened by the implication of his words, ashamed and angry because she felt shame. "What right have you . . ."

He seized her hand and pressed his lips to it, making it damp with frenzied kisses. She pulled away, nausea surging within her.

Ishbaal turned to Abner, his face mottling with rage, clutching the sword so tightly that his knuckles were white.

"Why have you lain with my father's concubine? You shall die for this!"

Abner was beside him in two steps. Ishbaal swung the sword wildly. Abner ducked under the blow with easy grace and, grasping the king's arm, twisted it sharply. Ishbaal shrieked with pain; the sword clattered to the floor. Abner kicked it out into the corridor.

Ishbaal threw back his head and shrilled, "Guard! Guard, come at once! Kill this usurper!"

Furious as Rizpah had never seen him, Abner snarled, "Do you think they would obey you?"

"I am the king. You have stolen my property."

Rizpah cried out in anger and disgust. Abner went to her, and even enraged as he was, his hand on her shoulder was soothing. But the gesture further inflamed Ishbaal. "Do not touch her!" he screamed. "You have no right to put your hand on her. You shall be tried and executed!"

And Abner, his own anger rising again, said, "Am I a dog's head that you speak so to me? I have shown kindness to the house of Saul your father by protecting you from David. Whatever else I do is no concern of yours. Go! Leave my sight, before I forget my love for your father and tear the heart from your living body!"

Ishbaal backed away squealing, "I am the king!"

"From this day forth you are no longer king in my eyes. Now go!"

He took a threatening step toward Ishbaal, who turned and skittered out of the room like a frightened lizard.

Abner closed the door behind him. The sudden stillness was heavy in the room.

Both he and Rizpah were trembling. "I should have killed him," said Abner gloomily. "He has strewn filth about us and cast shame on beauty."

"Nothing he said will touch us."

He looked at her, a little relieved. "If this is the way you truly feel, then I am satisfied."

She could not bring herself to admit to him that Ishbaal had, in fact, brought shame with his intrusion.

"In any event," Abner was saying, "this has made me aware of something I should have known long ago. I was a fool to place him on the throne of Israel. Far from preserving the memory of Saul, he has mocked it."

"You yourself should have been king," she said softly.

"I?" He seemed to be considering this. "No," he said finally. "The crown is not for me."

"You are Saul's close kinsman."

"The Lord has not anointed me."

"Nor Ishbaal."

"This is something I should have remembered," he said with a wry smile. Then he spoke resolutely. "I must go to him."

"To whom?"

"David, of course."

She stared at him, incredulous. "Are you mad?"

"I was."

"You have reconquered all the land of Israel. You have risked your life again and again, not only against Philistia, but against the warriors of Judah. Was all this only so you could meekly surrender everything for which you have struggled?"

His hands moved. She watched the palms turn up in the gesture she hated. Then she rose and dressed in grim silence. He kept looking at her, a touch of hopelessness entering his eyes.

She said to him, "Very well, go to David if you must. But listen to me first. It does not matter if you become king or not. I have seen what the burden of kingship can do, and I blame no one for shunning it. But where there is a choice between that and . . ."

She stopped and waited. Abner said nothing. Rizpah muttered an exclamation and stalked from the room.

She did not see him again that day. When she inquired later in the morning, the captain of the house guard told her the general had left on a journey, but had informed no one of his destination. She could scarcely conceal her anger.

After the noon meal, when she took me aside, she was still fuming.

While she was telling me what had happened, I decided that under no circumstances would I venture an opinion.

She glared at me. "Well?"

I shrugged. "You have said everything. There is nothing I can add."

"You can agree with me."

"You mean I can support you."

"Say it any way you like. Do you?"

I was silent.

This infuriated her, as I might have known it would. "He is weak!" she cried. "If only he would act once in a way that could allow me to say: here is strength."

My lofty resolution not to interfere was slipping. "I thought you had grown and learned," I said, more heatedly than I intended. "I see I was mistaken."

"When Saul was alive, he deferred constantly to him. Now, when he has an opportunity to rise above the past, he can only run to David."

"And you see no strength in what he is doing?"

"I see only what is there. Weakness and indecision," she said stubbornly.

I was in it now. There was no turning back. "Then the death of Zaccur meant nothing to you. There is no feeling left in your heart."

She winced as if I had slapped her, but she had no intention of giving in. "The fate of Israel . . ." she began ponderously.

I cut her off. "The fate of Israel depends on peace. Do you think Abner fears David? Has he not shown that he will fight whenever he believes it will accomplish something?"

"Will surrendering to David accomplish anything?"

"Surrendering, no. But remember, David was chosen by Samuel to rule, and by now this is known throughout the land. He already controls Judah. Together with Abner he could unite the country and make it more powerful than it has ever been."

"You speak most convincingly," she said with considerable bitterness. "But these are only words. You still have not explained how this proves Abner's strength."

"If you are not able to see it for yourself, you had better stay away from him. You will only hurt him."

"Perhaps you're right," she said, suddenly morose. "I can never love anyone the way I loved Saul."

"You are old enough now to know that love takes many forms."

"This morning when I first awoke," she said, "there was a tenderness in my heart I had never thought I would feel again. After the unpleasantness with Ishbaal, I realized that feeling was false."

"You are using Ishbaal for an excuse."

She turned and walked away from me, her shoulders stiff with resentment. I let her go. I did not know if eventually she would say what she must, but I was sure that running after her would only postpone it.

We had been talking in the common room. She got as far as the door leading to the garden, where she leaned for a time against the jamb. When she came back, retracing her steps slowly across the room, she was crying.

"Old woman," she said miserably, "I do not want to love again."

chapter seven

THE FIRST day Abner was away Rechab and Baanah must have visited the house a dozen times to ask for him. They stood in the common room, shifting about uncomfortably, their garments exuding the wood-smoke odor of army campfires. They looked around, their narrow eyes taking in the quiet luxury of the big room, their thin noses sniffing the air with envious disdain.

I thought I felt an unusual restiveness in their attitude, but they were uncommunicative men and shrouded whatever lay in their minds with the stolid military politeness warriors affect in the presence of civilians.

Paltiel confirmed my suspicion that something was amiss. He and Michal came to the house for what was ostensibly a casual visit. Michal immediately began to talk about the difficulty of obtaining decent meat for her table. She and Paltiel no longer maintained their own flocks, and she was forced to buy animals in the market at Mahanaim. "The sheep are so thin and scraggly that they're nothing but bone by the time you take them off the spit," she said. "And the prices . . ." She clucked disapprovingly. "I thought my servant was lying, so yesterday I went myself. Three hours I haggled with that brigand. Three hours!" Her cheeks grew red with righteous indignation. "And in the end I had to pay twice as much as the animal was worth. I know it's only the wives of the army who are forced to pay so much. Now when we were at the garrison . . ."

And she launched into a long and detailed anecdote about one of the merchants in the garrison town where they had lived, praising him as the only honest man east of the Jordan. Paltiel, for the first time since I had seen him and Michal together in Mahanaim, was not listening. He cleaned his fingernails, he ran his hand repeatedly across his face, he stared with fierce attention at the spaces between the stones of the floor. As soon as Michal was comfortably settled in the body of her story, he signaled me, indicating that he wished to speak to me alone.

"Where is Abner?" he asked at once after I had walked with him into the courtyard.

"Away," I replied innocently.

"There is talk."

"There is always talk."

"Is it true that Ishbaal has kept to his room since yesterday?"

"The king is an unpredictable young man. Sometimes he stays by himself for days on end."

"But never at mealtime. The servants have said . . ."

"Servants gossip too much."

"Where is Abner?"

"I have told you . . ."

"Yes, I know," he said impatiently. "The camp is in ferment. There are all sorts of rumors. It is said that Ishbaal ordered Abner executed and he has fled. It is also said that Abner has denounced Ishbaal and told him he is no longer king. Also, we have heard that David is marching against Mahanaim . . ."

"Do you think the general would desert his troops if this were so?"

"Listen, Egrep." The lids came down like miniature hoods over his eyes, giving him the cynical expression that had characterized him so much of late. "It is obvious that you will tell me nothing. Very well. All I am trying to do is warn you and Rizpah. When men do not know what is happening, they become frightened. Their fear asserts itself in unrest. Rechab and Baanah are already asking many questions."

"What kind of questions?"

"They feel that something strange is going on. I agree with them, but I am content to wait and see what happens. They are impatient. They are talking among the men about the advisability of uniting our forces with those of David. If it were not for the men of Jabesh, who are in vigorous opposition, Rechab and Baanah would already be taking action. They maintain it is ridiculous for us to sit in this dusty hole for the sake of the fool Abner has made king. And whenever we do venture into our own land, we face the danger of being exterminated at the hands of Joab."

"Abner will be returning soon," I said, hoping fervently it was true.

"Will you promise to ask him to send for me as soon as he returns?"

I promised, not knowing then how unnecessary it would be to prompt Abner to do so.

The following morning Rizpah and I went to the market place. She said she was bored and thought she would be cheered up if she purchased some small bangle. I smiled to myself, careful not to let her realize how transparent I knew she was being.

She was in a beautiful state of subdued excitement. I had not seen her so happy since the days when Saul was alive and untroubled. The night after our conversation about Abner had been a sleepless one for her. But she was strong-minded and honest, and once she had faced truth she could only absorb it and make it part of herself. I could see there was no more doubt in her mind, and there remained only impatience for Abner's return.

We took Armoni and Meribaal with us. Of the three—mother and sons—Meribaal was the most sedate. He walked gravely beside me, holding my hand, surveying the narrow, dusty streets with his wondering stare. Armoni ranged ahead, now skipping, now running back to report some breathless observation to his mother. She did not skip, but she might as well have, her heart was obviously so light.

That is perhaps why she did not notice the forbidding atmosphere in the market.

We picked our way among peddlers hawking local pomegranates, figs and dates, olives brought from groves near the sea in Asher. We passed the enclosures confining sheep, goats and an occasional calf. The stalls where jewelry was sold were next to a space reserved for foreign merchants. Not many came to Mahanaim, and when they did, they usually brought spices or fine fabrics. Until the army of Israel established its headquarters here, there was little demand for such exotic wares. Now, however, competition had grown brisk over favored market locations. On this day the space was occupied by a squat Damascan rug seller, who called out the virtues of his merchandise in the oily accent of the north.

All around us, cutting under the strident voice of commerce, urgent whispered conversations were taking place. Little groups of merchants, their heads close together, nodded and gesticulated. As we crossed the market place, eyes came round to watch us: inquiring and surprised, faintly hostile.

The man from whom Rizpah bought the bracelet was obsequiously polite. He showed her one of the gaudy, crudely handsome copper pieces fashioned in the eastern desert, and when Rizpah expressed interest, he evinced no desire to bargain. She was able to buy it for only a little more than the first price she named.

As we were about to depart, the man said to her, "Would my lady tell me . . . is my lord the king well?"

Ordinarily, the question would have conveyed only a certain meaningless formality, part of the hand-rubbing formula of a sycophantic merchant. But there was something in the way he asked that contained an anxious insinuating note. Rizpah replied casually, "The king is well," but I looked at him sharply. He coughed and glanced nervously away.

I understood then. The rumors from the camp had spread to the business section of the town, had set the merchants on edge. Any threat of unsettled conditions within the court would understandably fill them with apprehension. Until then, I had felt that Paltiel's warning was prompted by the kind of internal gossip which runs constantly through encampments of warriors. Now I realized it was more serious and deep-reaching than I had supposed. Abner would have to act quickly and decisively when he returned. And if his absence extended much longer, rumor and reality could mix in dangerous proportions.

He arrived after dark the next evening, having traveled all day and most of the night before. It made me happy to see the way Rizpah greeted him, with an embrace that made of her touch both a question and a certainty.

It should have made Abner happy as well, but from the moment he entered the house, it was obvious he was preoccupied. There were deep lines of exhaustion in his face. He ate quickly and without appreciation of the food we set before him. When I stood up to leave, he raised his head and looked dully at me. "No, do not go. You will learn of this later in any case. I would like you to remain."

I sat down again, mystified. It was unlike Abner to deal in riddles. Rizpah and I flashed each other a glance past the back of his head. She knew no more than I.

Abner said suddenly, "Where is Ishbaal?"

"In his room, as far as I know," said Rizpah.

"He has not troubled you?"

"I have not seen him since your departure, my lord. The servants have taken him his meals."

The general nodded. He summoned the captain of the guard and asked him to bring Paltiel at once.

No one spoke while we waited. The torches in the common room flickered, fitfully lighting the far corners of the chamber. The transformation which had taken place in Abner amazed even me. He was no longer the gentle, too-understanding man who had supported Saul without question and worshiped Rizpah without hope of favor. This was a vigorous stranger I had sometimes seen on the battlefield, but in place of the blood lust which had invariably been a part of these moments there was a sad, stern firmness. Yet when Rizpah stirred uneasily beside him, he smiled at her with some of the warmth in which our liking for him was steeped.

Paltiel came in, believing he had been called through my offices. He nodded his thanks to me and immediately began to speak. "My lord, I shall waste no time. The situation is grave. There is dangerous sentiment abroad in the camp."

"And this sentiment is . . ."

"A substantial number of men have been coerced into saying they will join David."

A cheerless smile flitted across Abner's face. Paltiel edged forward. "My lord, you do not seem to understand."

"I understand well enough. How many of the men feel this way?"

"Nearly all, with the exception of the warriors from Jabesh."

"It is good."

Paltiel stared at Abner. His eyes bulged. He licked his lips. "My lord . . ."

"I have even now come from Hebron, where I conferred with David. There is no longer reason for the men of Israel and Judah to fear each other. From this day, we shall act as one, just as we did in former times. This is the first thing I wished to tell you."

Paltiel asked slowly, "And the second?" I believe he knew at that moment, even while Rizpah and I tarried far back in the maze of developing circumstances. He said again, "The second, my lord?"

Abner's eyes absorbed pain, let it go and became once more expressionless. "David has made it a condition of the alliance that his wife Michal be restored to him as quickly as possible."

I glanced quickly at Paltiel. His face was as waxen as those of casualties I had seen brought in from the battlefield.

"Has my lord Abner agreed to this request?"

"It is not a request. It is a condition."

Suddenly Paltiel burst out, "Why does he want her? He has other wives." His tone and words possessed the childish petulance that often accompanies deep despair. And I was aware that at this moment Rizpah was suffering almost as much as Paltiel.

He was gaining a measure of control. "When must she go?"

"Tomorrow morning."

"So soon?" His calm was deceptive. I had the feeling that if he fell to the floor he would shatter into a thousand pieces.

Abner wisely offered no words of condolence, and Paltiel started to leave. He turned back abruptly, his eyes filled with desperate hope. "If Michal does not wish to go . . ."

"She must," said Abner flatly.

"Would my lord deliberately flout the wish of the daughter of Saul?"

It was a clever move. Abner hesitated. He said, "Personal feelings cannot stand before the welfare of the land," but there was a note of uncertainty in his voice.

Paltiel hastily pressed his advantage. "Surely the heart of David has not grown so hard that he will force her to live in his house against her will."

Abner remained thoughtfully silent. After a time he said, "I can make no promises, but I will do this. If Michal desires to remain in your house, I shall journey again to David and present the matter in this light. The decision must then be his."

"I shall fetch her at once," said Paltiel. His jubilance was unbounded. He started for the door.

But Abner rose quickly and overtook him. "It will be better if we see her together."

For a moment Paltiel appeared crestfallen. Then he smiled confidently and said, "As you wish, my lord."

Abner called a guard and sent him to fetch Michal. She entered the room hesitantly, seeming to sense crisis in the air. Her glance darted from one of us to the other, divining, assessing. When she could learn nothing from our faces, she retreated to Paltiel's side.

"My love," he began, "Abner has just returned . . ."

"I shall speak to her," Abner said firmly. He turned to Michal. "I do not have to tell you there has been much bloodshed and bitterness between the houses of Israel and Judah."

Her dark eyes watched him, unwavering, speculating, but she said nothing.

"I also need not say that the act of setting your brother on the throne was a piece of dangerous folly on my part. We shall continue to protect him, but we shall remove from him the name of authority. An authority," he added, "that he only exercised to the detriment of himself and others. An authority that never rightfully belonged to him."

Now Michal looked sidewise at Paltiel. I do not think she understood yet all that was coming, but some vague comprehension was shaping in her mind.

"I have taken the first step toward a lasting cessation of hostilities," continued Abner. He was stammering slightly and was annoyed with himself for doing so. "Henceforth, the houses of Israel and Judah will be united."

An expression of dismay came over Michal's face. Paltiel, seeing it, could not conceal his joy, but he refrained from speaking.

"It is a condition of this venture," Abner said, "that you go to live in the house of David as his wife."

There was a sudden sob in the stillness. For a moment I did not realize it had come from Michal. Then her face lighted up with such radiance as I have seldom seen. It was only of an instant's duration, but even when it had departed, her lips and eyes retained the afterglow.

She took a long breath, and without looking at the man beside her, said, "Whatever my lord Paltiel says, this shall I do."

Abner said gently, "It is no longer a matter for Paltiel to decide, my child."

Michal reached blindly for the hand of the man with whom she had lived for over six years. Nor did he look at her. He was staring past all of us to the end of the room where the carved throne chair stood.

All at once Michal broke away from him and rushed to Rizpah. "Help me!" she cried. "Please help me. I'm so afraid . . ."

Rizpah held her close, stroking her hair with little stiff movements of her hand.

With great dignity Paltiel said to Michal, "Will you come home now?" It was a foolish question, one he regretted instantly. For Michal turned wide and tragic eyes on him, and in them he saw pity. He bowed his head and walked from the room. No one went after him. What good would it have done?

I took Michal to one of the upper bedchambers. We had never really liked each other, nor was there affection between us now. But she needed a woman with her, and Rizpah was too laden with guilt to be able to help. Only once did Michal speak. As she was climbing into bed she said, as much to herself as to me, "It hurts so to live again." Then, after a while, she slept.

When Rizpah and Abner were alone, she confessed to him the part she had played in bringing Paltiel and Michal together. It was a measure of his wisdom that he neither blamed nor excused her, but the few words he spoke signified his acceptance and understanding.

And the love she had been hoarding since the death of Saul burst free now, carrying into the open all the happiness and sorrow that love accumulates. And Abner knew at last some of the joy which had evaded him for so many years.

chapter eight

IT WAS a sad little caravan.

Twenty soldiers were to accompany Abner. They shuffled about the courtyard with downcast eyes, none of them daring to look at Paltiel, who stood motionless a little distance away. He had dressed himself in his finest white robe and had anointed his hair with oil so it glistened in the morning sunlight. He seemed calm, yet there was an air of madness about him. I would not have been surprised had he foamed at the mouth or howled like an animal.

Two camels were laden with Michal's possessions. She had not yet come out of the house. The donkey she was to ride was waiting, held by one of the warriors. Abner moved among the men, talking quietly, but obviously impatient to be gone.

A figure appeared in the doorway. The men tensed expectantly. It was not Michal, but Ishbaal. He drifted out into the courtyard, regarded those around him with an indifferent, slack-jawed gaze. Suddenly he gave a little cry and ran back into the common room. He appeared moments later, carrying a huge bunch of grapes which he began eating, stuffing them one after the other into his mouth until his cheeks bulged. He slithered toward a corner of the courtyard, where he remained watching, continuing his greedy consumption of the fruit.

At last Michal came out to join the group which was to escort her to Hebron. She looked cool and unperturbed, but overnight some of the plumpness she had gathered in the past several years seemed to have dropped away from her. There was a trace of hardness about her mouth. Her eyes held a feverish glitter.

She passed Paltiel without glancing at him, but her steps faltered and for an instant she appeared uncertain where she was. Then she shook her head and moved resolutely to the donkey, allowing the soldier to help her mount.

Abner immediately gave the signal to start. He had already said farewell to Rizpah, and as the procession moved through the gate into the dusty street, he only turned once to wave briefly.

Without warning, Paltiel broke from his motionless stance and ran after the departing group. His robe billowed out behind him, and his bare legs, impressive when he was wearing warrior's garb, now looked pathetic and defenseless. The sound of his wailing filled the court-yard. "Michal!" he called. "Come back, Michal!"

She looked steadfastly ahead. Paltiel ran alongside the donkey she was riding, weeping and reaching out frantically to grasp her hand. Three small boys standing in the street first looked on wide-eyed, then began to run behind Paltiel, aping his agonized cries. "Michal!" they shrilled. "Come back, Michal!" Paltiel did not even hear them, but some of the soldiers chased them away. With the cruel, accurate mim-icry of children they continued to shout from a safe distance, "Michal, come back!"

For a few moments Abner attempted to ignore the behavior of his grieving commander. But it was impossible to remain unconcerned in the presence of such heartbreak. Abner finally stopped the caravan, wheeled on Paltiel and snapped, "Go! Return!"

It was what was needed. Paltiel at once stopped weeping, straight-ened up and said simply to Michal, "Farewell, my love."

She did not look at him.

The procession started off again, and Paltiel came slowly back toward where we were standing. As he walked, the small boys approached him and trailed behind him, chanting over and over, "Michal, come back . . ." He stopped walking, and the smile he be-stowed on them was so bereft, so like a sightless stare, that they im-mediately ceased their hooting and scurried away.

Rizpah and I took Paltiel into the common room and poured him some wine. He seemed composed now, but his hands trembled as he drained three or four bowls in quick succession.

He began to talk. "I do not blame you," he said matter-of-factly to Rizpah. "You believed that as long as she remained at Gibeah she was a threat to Saul. I agree that she probably was. And certainly I had no objection to becoming the instrument for her removal."

It was the first we knew that he had even suspected the existence of Rizpah's plot.

"When we first went to the garrison, I would wake in the night and hear her weeping. I wanted to comfort her, but I knew this would only make matters worse. I thought: if I can be patient, she will learn to lean on my strength, and perhaps in time to love me. I was right about the first part. She depended on me, and this made me happy. It is possible that in a few more years she would have given me her love. I felt there were indications."

He held out his wine bowl to me. I refilled it.

"But I was always afraid," he continued. "And this I have learned— the greatest threat to love is fear. For six years I have lived with my own kind of mortal terror. And yet I have been content. Does this seem contradictory? I think not. She was with me. It was enough."

Paltiel finished his wine, got up abruptly and left the house.

Later that day, while walking in the streets of Mahanaim, I saw him. He was staggering drunk, and on his arm was one of the girls from the harlots' quarter. He caught sight of me and gave me one of his cynical, hooded glances, then turned back to the girl. She was dark and petite, with her eyes cleverly elongated with kohl, and a smile of liquid complaisance. As they passed me, he stiffened slightly, as if defying me to censure him.

This I had no intention of doing. I was not in the least surprised to see him with the prostitute. A harlot offers a man the comfort and release he needs. Harlots are like mirrors—better, for a mirror reflects the veritable image of the person who stands before it. Coat a harlot with silver and she will return the image of himself a man wishes to see. Empty relief perhaps, but in misery, solace is where one finds it.

The next day Paltiel disappeared, no one knew where. Some said he had returned to the home of his family near Gallim. Others stated that he had ridden into the desert in the company of a band of passing Bedouins. One of his servants was positive that Paltiel was journeying to Phoenicia. In any case, it was certain he had left Mahanaim.

The situation with the army was becoming hourly more tense. No longer did the warriors remain in their camp. They roamed the streets of the town, infecting them with the breath of violence. Drunkenness was rampant; there were frequent brawls. The merchants closed their stalls and hid their wares; the market place was turned into a vast, empty arena, populated only by the great black scavenger birds that came to pick at rotting scraps of produce.

Rizpah and I stayed in the house. It is doubtful that anything would have happened to us in Mahanaim, but we both knew the dangerous unpredictability of a restive army. Rechab and Baanah, far from being stabilizing influences, were themselves ringleaders of the discontent. They wished to march at once to Hebron and declare their allegiance to David. Paltiel might have calmed them, but Paltiel was gone. Only the fear of Abner's wrath and the knowledge that he was himself in Hebron kept them from defying orders and deserting en masse to Judah.

On the fourth evening after Abner's departure Rizpah and I took our dinner alone. Ishbaal, following his brief appearance when Michal was leaving, had again retired to his room.

It was a gloomy meal. Neither of us felt like eating or talking. Long before we had finished, Rizpah went to look after the children. I continued to sit at the table, staring at the ruins of our repast. Nothing is more depressing than sitting alone over hardly touched food, but I could not bring myself to do anything else.

The heat and dust were more oppressive than usual. From the streets came faint sounds of savage, pleasureless revelry. It seemed to me to have reached new heights of hysteria. Anarchy was in the air, and only the presence of Abner would restore some semblance of order.

Someone coughed behind me. I started so violently that the bench on which I was sitting screeched against the floor. The captain of the house guard was standing a few paces away. His calmness was reassuring. Could I come for a moment? Mattithiah wished to see me in the courtyard.

Mattithiah was a sober, horse-faced soldier from Ephraim, a veteran of all of Saul's campaigns. He had been one of the entourage accompanying Abner and Michal on the mission to Hebron.

I went quickly outside. Surely Abner had not returned, or he would have come himself, even before beginning the task of restoring order. More likely he was sending a message that he would be delayed. But why to me rather than to Rizpah, and why the secrecy?

I did not see Mattithiah at first. He was wearing a black cloak with the hood pulled up, and gathering darkness made him almost invisible in the shadow of the wall where he was standing.

He came forward, took me by the arm and urged me away from the shaft of light pouring out of the doorway. But not before I had seen that his dust-coated cloak was torn in several places.

"You have come from Abner?"

"I bring news," he said. He had a croaking voice which made even his simplest statements sound lugubrious.

"When will the general return?"

But Mattithiah was not to be hurried. He told me in detail of the trip to Hebron, of David's enthusiastic welcome when they arrived. Abner had wished to return at once to Mahanaim, but the king of Judah would not hear of it. With Michal and Abner as guests of

honor, they sat down to a feast the like of which they had not tasted
in all the days at Mahanaim. Only Joab was absent, being away with
a troop in the south.

"Then Abner is remaining to meet with Joab, and wishes us to
come to him."

Mattithiah held up his hand, bidding me be silent. I wished he
would remove the hood of his cloak. I could only see his eyes, and
the muffled, croaking voice was beginning to make me nervous.

"We left Hebron the next afternoon, all of us," he said, and before
I could question him further, he plunged ahead on another recitation
of endless detail. By dusk, he said, they had reached the well of Sirah,
where they paused to refresh themselves and to eat their meal of
cheese and dried figs before beginning the night journey toward
Mahanaim.

Just as they were setting out, two horsemen rode toward them, gal-
loping furiously up from the south. They came from Joab, they said,
and they begged Abner to return with them at once to Hebron on a
matter of some urgency. Abner demurred, but the messengers were
insistent. So the general had sighed and ordered Mattithiah to come
with him, leaving the rest of the soldiers at Sirah.

It was, of course, pitch-dark when they reached Hebron. The messengers who were escorting them brought them to the city gate and
left them. And standing among a small group of warriors they saw
Joab. David's general greeted Abner cordially, and took him aside. By
the light of a single small torch Mattithiah had seen them conferring
quietly. Then suddenly Joab drew his sword and plunged it into Abner's breast, crying, "This for Asahel, my brother whom you slew!"

At last Mattithiah was silent.

I said, my tongue having difficulty forming the words, "Abner is
dead?"

"He is dead. Joab followed the first thrust with others. Abner is
dead."

Mattithiah went on. He had fled from the gate of Hebron. In the
horror which succeeded the murder, paralyzing even Joab's men, he
had not been pursued. He stole a horse and, bypassing Sirah for fear
of capture, rode straight for Mahanaim. However, when he arrived
in the town and observed the mood of the soldiers, he had thought
it best to withhold the news from the army until morning. But he
felt that the lady Rizpah should know.

I managed to thank him and compliment him on his discretion.
After he had gone, I stood in the courtyard, trying to compose myself.

Then I went in search of Rizpah.

chapter nine

SHE WEPT, bitterly, for about an hour. Then she became remarkably calm, almost indifferent. It was not the self-deluding composure she displayed after Saul's death, to be followed by months of sorrowing half-life. She believed at once in the fact of Abner's death. I had the feeling that she accepted the tidings, absorbed them, and mourned intensely, all in the space of a few short moments.

I marveled at her easy grief. Perhaps I was even a little annoyed. Sorrow, guilt, pain . . . these are the human inescapables, obligations of living, with all their attendant ritual duties. We feel cheated when we think another person can, without visible effort, put off burdens which weigh heavily on us.

But then she came to me and took my hands briefly in hers. The gesture said as clearly as words: do not be deceived, old woman, and do not force me to do more than I have done.

The raucous unrest in the streets of Mahanaim continued far into the night. I was once again thankful to Mattithiah for his good sense in not spreading the word of Abner's death.

In the morning all seemed peaceful, which in a sense was as disquieting as the disturbance had been. Rizpah and I were wondering how we could obtain news of what was going on when a visitor arrived to see her.

It was Huri, the leader of the warriors from Jabesh-Gilead. He was wearing the austere, formal robe he had worn when he came to offer the services of his contingent to Abner. He bowed low to Rizpah and said, "I have come to bid you farewell, my lady."

"Farewell?"

"We are returning to our city." She was silent, and he regarded her thoughtfully for a moment, then continued. "Our loyalty to Saul is eternal. After his death, we gladly followed Abner. But now Saul is dead, and the king's uncle has gone after him to Sheol. There is nothing more here for us. We must go."

Rizpah said, "A son of Saul still lives as king."

The man from Jabesh smiled bleakly. "We were wholeheartedly devoted to Saul, but we are neither fools nor politicians. Abner repudiated Ishbaal before he died. We understand the reasons for his act, but they do not concern us. We were only waiting until there was a formal announcement of the alliance with David, when we would have left in any case. Now, with feeling the way it is . . ."

"What is the feeling among the troops, my lord from Jabesh?"

He outlined the situation as clearly as he could. It was not simple. Before word of Abner's murder, most of the army wanted to go at once and join David. Early that morning when Mattithiah passed on the bitter tidings of their general's death, there had been a flurry of sentiment in favor of revenge. This had passed quickly, for they realized that Judah was strong, and any attack they made at this time would be suicidal. "Now," he continued, "there is chaos. Speeches and counterspeeches. Some favor disbanding the army and returning to their homes. Rechab and Baanah strongly advocate going as a unit to David and placing the strength of Israel at his disposal. We from Jabesh will not oppose this course of action, but we cannot join those who will deliver themselves to David. The best we can do is what we have intended for some days—return to our city, from which we have already been too long absent. Unless . . ."

He paused, watching her carefully. Suddenly I had the feeling that if Rizpah were to declare herself queen regent of Israel and ask the support of Jabesh-Gilead, this grim-visaged man would kneel at once and vow fealty.

For one wild instant I wished she would do it. She would, in many ways, rule more capably than Saul or Abner. She was bright, resourceful and energetic. In the twelve years since I had first seen her come as a trembling virgin into the house of the Seren, she had gained experience and a great deal of maturity. Women had judged in Israel. Why could one not reign? It was probable that with her tact and ability she could effect a durable alliance with David. And with the power of Jabesh as a nucleus for her army . . .

Her visitor was still waiting. Rizpah rose from her chair and extended her hand regally to him, saying in a clear voice, "On behalf of the memory of my lord Saul and his servant Abner, I wish to thank you for the devotion you have shown to this house. Without your support, Israel would still lie under the cruel hand of Philistia. Go then in peace, and may peace attend your blessed city to eternity."

Huri sighed, and I was sure I had been right. He murmured, "May peace and prosperity follow my lady and her children all the days of their lives."

Then he looked around and said falteringly, "It was in this room that I offered the services of my city to Abner. We grew to love him in almost the same measure as we loved Saul. When we return to Jabesh, we shall dance the mourning dance to his memory, and pray that a portion of his spirit may descend on each of us."

A tiny spasm of pain touched her features, but her voice remained firm as she thanked him once again.

The man from Jabesh gathered his robe close about his spare frame and strode from the room without looking back.

He had been gone for no more than a few moments when there was a piercing cry from the upper corridor of the house. Ishbaal ran down the stairs and into the common room. "Rizpah!" he cried, coming to us across the stone floor. "Is it true? Is Abner really dead?"

She and I looked at each other. It had not occurred to either of us to tell him. We assumed that he would have heard from the servants long before now.

"Abner is dead," Rizpah said quietly.

The vulpine expression grew on his face. "Now that he is out of the way," he said, "we no longer need live in this filthy hole. I shall return to Gibeah, and you will come with me."

Her mouth tightened. I thought she would strike him, but her anger emerged only in the brittleness of her voice. "You will never go back to Gibeah," she said.

"I will go if I like. I am the king."

"You never were king, and you are not now. Whatever security you have in Mahanaim, you owe to Abner."

"I shall go to Gibeah," he repeated with childish persistence.

"Do you think David would ever allow you to live there?"

"David will not dare to touch. I reign over Israel, and my army will protect me."

"Your army," she said cruelly, "is even now preparing to join David's forces. And I do not know why I even discuss the matter with you. You can go where you like."

His lips trembled. "Rizpah . . ." He reached for her hand.

She swung away from him violently. "Don't put your slimy hands on me!"

He recoiled from her fury. "Rizpah . . ." he said again, despairingly.

She turned her back on him. He stood uncertainly for a moment, looking at her. Then tears began to pour out of his eyes and roll down his face. He hung his head and shuffled from the room.

Her anger abated gradually, leaving her listless and tired looking. The children came in from the garden, and as she talked and played with them, her spirits seemed to rise. By the end of the morning, she was feeling somewhat remorseful over her behavior. "There was no excuse for it," she said. "I shall go to him and ask him to join us at the noon meal."

But she did not go at once. First we heard the dirgelike marching song which signified the departure of the men of Jabesh. Then Meribaal asked Rizpah to sing a song, and after that Armoni also requested one. So it was some time later when she thought again of going up to Ishbaal.

All at once I began to feel that the house was abnormally quiet. At first I did not understand why, but then I realized that the soldiers of the guard were not making their customary rounds.

I had no opportunity to mention this to Rizpah, for by now she was on her way up the stairs. And here she also observed that there was no guard at the end of the corridor. However, being preoccupied with other thoughts, she did not attach any particular significance to the fact.

She rapped on the door of Ishbaal's chamber, and when she heard some odd thumping sounds from inside, she grew alarmed and entered.

The sight that greeted her turned her ill with horror. Ishbaal's decapitated body was lying on the floor, his feet entangled in a bloodsoaked satin bedspread. The tip of a ladder visible in the open window showed how the murderer had come in and escaped.

Without thinking she rushed to the window and looked out, then quickly drew back. For racing away from the house toward the far wall of the garden were Rechab and Baanah. Under his cloak Rechab was carrying a bulky object. It required no great imagination to know what it was.

She held back the panic that was closing in about her and descended unhurriedly to the common room. Taking me aside, she informed me of what had happened.

I left Rizpah with the children and made a hasty inspection of the house. It was as I had feared. Not only had the guards departed, but the servants as well. We were completely alone.

When I returned to the common room, Rizpah was standing close to Armoni and Meribaal. It was not necessary for either of us to say aloud what was in our minds. Ishbaal had been murdered by soldiers about to desert to David. They would be eager for approval from the king of Judah. If the opportunity presented itself, they would not be likely to stop at one killing to prove their new loyalty. No son of Saul could be safe now in Mahanaim. We must leave at once.

But this was not so simple. Departing in broad daylight would be inviting trouble. We decided to conceal the children in the stable until dark. Rizpah found a sword and stayed with them, while I made repeated trips into the silent main house, gathering as much food and clothing as we could conveniently carry in a small cart.

Until twilight we had no idea of where we might go. Then, on one of my trips through the common room, I found myself pausing before the couch in the corner where Zaccur had breathed his last. Neither Rizpah nor I had spoken of the bequest since the little man's death, but now suddenly it assumed great importance in my mind.

Rizpah agreed at once. Dan was far enough away to be reasonably safe. And where else could we go?

Meribaal was being his usual unperturbed, endearing self, with obviously no thought of danger. He was seldom loud or exuberant, so it was not even necessary for Rizpah to warn him not to raise his voice. Armoni, however, demanded to know what was happening. Rizpah hesitated, then told him the story, simplifying it somewhat and of course softening the more horrible aspects, of which there were more than enough. He seemed to understand at once all she said, nodding his head in the manner that was so like Saul. When she had finished, he did not speak for a time. Then he said, "When you are ready, I will harness the ox."

It was again so much Saul when he was being abrupt and decisive that both Rizpah and I turned away so Armoni would not see our eyes.

We left Mahanaim as soon as it was dark. As we came from the courtyard we could see the glow of the fires in the date grove where the army was encamped. There was shouting and wild laughter, and it appeared that soon they would be drunken again to the point of violence.

The stars were bright enough so we could be seen clearly, and the wheels of the cart squeaked with alarming loudness. But no one challenged us as we rolled eastward out of the town, then turned north.

chapter ten

As WE had left Mahanaim under cover of darkness, so we entered Ramoth-Dan by night. Actually, we had our first glimpse of it in daylight, but only at a distance.

Our northward journey took ten days. In the beginning we exercised considerable caution, seeking little-used tracks, traveling mainly between dusk and dawn. But after a time we felt secure enough to abandon the lonely, arid trails on the east side of the Jordan. We crossed the river and proceeded up the west shore of the Sea of Chinnereth.

Traversing the mountains north of Chinnereth was arduous, requiring many detours, but we did not find it altogether unpleasant.

And when, in late afternoon of the tenth day, we descended the last slope and saw the town gleaming jewellike at the end of a fertile valley, a kind of peace touched us all.

But it was dark and we were tired by the time our cart rolled into the streets of Ramoth-Dan.

It was a sizable town, not as large as Mahanaim, but certainly not to be classed as a village. Unlike the mud-and-straw brick houses of the south, the dwellings of Ramoth were constructed of round stones mortared together to form solid and durable buildings. The home of Eliel, we were told, lay some distance beyond the town, surrounded by the orchards he tended.

As we covered the last few hundred cubits of our journey, Rizpah and I began to feel acutely uncomfortable. During the whole northward trek, it had never occurred to us to doubt we would be received hospitably by Zaccur's kinsman. Now, confronted by the solidity and respectability of the countryside, apparent even in the moonlit darkness, and aware of our own travel-stained appearance, we were afflicted with sudden shyness.

"Who will speak to him?" asked Rizpah.

"It was you to whom Zaccur left the land," I said evasively.

"He will never believe a tale like that."

"Tale indeed," I said, working up a measure of truculence. "Zaccur's deathbed wish was a command."

"I would not blame him if he turned us away. After all, he has surely come to regard the land as his own."

"He will not turn us away without giving us a night's lodging," I said grimly, already full of resentment against Eliel.

"Perhaps he will not send us away at all," said Rizpah, switching about to defend him.

"Then we must decide who will speak to him first."

Armoni, who had been looking from one of us to the other as we went on with this nonsense, said importantly, "I will speak to him. He will not turn me away."

Rizpah laughed and patted his head, but curiously enough, the child's words made us feel better.

The ox, sensing that he would soon be able to rest, picked up his plodding pace. Rizpah pointed ahead. "This must be it." Armoni turned the ox through a gate into a walled courtyard fronting a substantial-looking stone house. We all got down out of the cart. Meribaal stared about him with his beautiful, open expression, and said, "It smells good."

Which, in fact, it did. Mingled with the pungent but fresh odor of clean, well-cared-for animals was the sweet and tantalizing fragrance of ripe apricots and the more subtle emanation of growing figs. And in the cool gentle breeze which brushed our faces was a fainter but still pervasive essence of spicy pine and cedar.

We were spared the decision of which of us would approach the door. A man appeared, holding a torch high above his head as he peered toward us. He was compactly built, not being overly tall, but possessing broad shoulders and a barrel chest. He had black curly hair and a short beard gracing a rugged, lined face.

He appraised us with a steady glance and asked, "Yes, what is it?" in a voice neither hostile nor friendly.

Rizpah stepped forward. "Eliel, son of Shallim?"

"Yes . . ." There was dignity in his manner, also the rooted suspicion of country people for residents of cities.

"We come from your kinsman Zaccur."

The torch dipped forward, momentarily hiding Eliel's face. Then he said, "Enter my dwelling," and stood aside for us. Meribaal, already sleepy, stumbled, and Eliel caught him about the waist and carried him into the house in our wake.

A fire was crackling in a great stone fireplace. The remains of a meal lay on a large scarred wooden table. Hunched close to the fire was a fragile crone, so motionless that she resembled a household image. After a moment she swung about slowly. The firelight played on her rheumy eyes and wrinkle-laced features. "Who?" she asked. "Who . . ."

"They come from Zaccur." Eliel turned to us. "My mother, Zaccur's aunt."

The old woman sighed like a rustling breeze and said again, "Who . . ."

Eliel touched her lightly on the shoulder. A tender smile worked its way across her face and was gone.

"Zaccur is well?" he asked us.

"He is dead," I replied, in a low voice so the ancient one would not hear me.

But her ears were uncannily sensitive, and she was suddenly alert. "Dead!" she wailed. She fixed us with a distrustful gaze. "How did he die?"

Eliel, visibly shaken, said with difficulty, "We shall hear in time. Our guests are tired. They must refresh themselves before we ask them to talk."

He left the house to stable the ox, and when he returned, began preparing us a meal, courteously refusing our help. His hands were big and callused and looked as if they would be clumsy, but he sliced the cold lamb into beautiful, delicate cuts and set it before us with bread, leeks and fruit.

The boys were delighted with the perfect golden apricots heaped in a wooden bowl. But now even Armoni, his energy uncoiling in the warmth of the room, was beginning to be sleepy. Eliel settled them on a bed in the corner and returned to sit down across the table from Rizpah and me, his expression inquiring but patient.

We told him of the events which followed Gilboa and of Zaccur's death after the treachery at the pool of Gibeon. He asked only a few questions, but they revealed a shrewd, keen mind. They also confirmed my original impression of a somewhat suspicious nature. Nonetheless I liked him. There was a fundamental warmth and generosity about him. He was not a man who would give his trust easily, I felt, but once he did, it would be virtually unshakable.

He told us something of himself. His land was not extensive, but coupled with Zaccur's, it made an appreciable holding, and in recent years the orchards had prospered. When he said that he lived alone with his mother and mentioned that he had never married, I perceived the fine matchmaking hand of Zaccur in arranging that we come here. He would have understood that Rizpah would not come to Dan unless she were herself alone. I could see the little man's puckish smile, could almost hear him saying to himself: I will throw them together, and we shall see.

And in truth, Eliel was regarding her with covert admiration. But then, so did many men, and she seemed no more than politely interested in him.

There was a lull in the conversation, and the old woman cried, "Why are they here? Why?"

Eliel said, "My mother has perhaps phrased the question more bluntly than I would have," and waited.

"We seek refuge," said Rizpah.

"And the land?"

"It does not belong to me."

"My cousin bequeathed it to you."

"You have only our word for that."

"I would hardly expect two ladies from the court of Saul to lie about a tiny plot of ground in a remote province." His voice grew unexpectedly harsh. "Nor would I expect you to journey all this distance unless you were interested. You are here. I shall respect my cousin's wish."

"But we do not want . . ."

"Then why have you come?"

"They want the land!" cried his mother.

The atmosphere had become suddenly tense. I could not understand it. Granted that he would be reluctant to give up the land he had tended for so long, there was something odd about the conflict that was developing: Rizpah disavowing any intention of taking the land, and he urging it on her.

She smiled patiently. "I have said we seek refuge. If you will only be kind enough to shelter us for a time . . ."

"I do not know what you mean. Shelter, yes. But refuge from what?"

"I have explained to you. Ishbaal was murdered by officers of his own army."

"I understand that."

"If they were capable of killing one of Saul's sons to impress David with their new loyalty—"

He cut her off angrily. "Surely you do not mean that grown men would stoop to killing two children . . ."

Rizpah and I looked at each other in disbelief. Was it possible that anyone could be so ingenuous?

Suddenly he laughed, and we glanced at him, startled. For it was the laughter of Zaccur that was filling the room: hearty and at the same time self-deprecating. "I can see by your eyes that you think I am mad."

"Not mad, naïve," said Rizpah bluntly.

He laughed again. "So my cousin was fond of telling me on his rare visits home. He would say, 'You are an unsophisticated peasant.' I suppose it is true. I know much of what goes on in the mountains of Dan and little else. I begin to appreciate now how little else. You have truly come for refuge?"

"They want the land!" interjected the old woman.

"No, Mother," said Eliel gently. "I do not believe they do. But it is theirs if they wish it." He turned back to us, still puzzled. "How much depravity there must be in the hearts of men who would seek the death of children."

"More ambition than depravity," I said. "Though often enough it is difficult to tell them apart."

He shook his head. It was evident that he did not yet believe us completely. And I was conscious for the first time in years of the rarefied atmosphere of intrigue in which our lives were steeped, a world where power is narcotic, a world where every word and gesture must be interpreted, sifted for motive, and translated into a bizarre, exclusive language. I sighed.

"You are weary," Eliel said.

"I think I must be."

"Then I shall not keep you from your bed. You will sleep here tonight. Tomorrow we shall put Zaccur's house in order for you. I have occasionally used it to lodge helpers during the harvest season. Otherwise it has remained empty, for I never knew when my cousin would return to claim it." His face saddened. "I shall miss him, even though for the past ten years I have seen little of him." He got up. "You shall have your refuge, for as long as you require it."

"We are deeply grateful," said Rizpah, "but there is one thing. Our identity must not become known."

"That will be simple," he said briskly. "You are Zaccur's widow. He was away long enough to have married and sired children the age of yours."

"But he returned to Ramoth-Dan from time to time. Will people not think it strange that he mentioned nothing of me?"

"He described you at great length to me," replied Eliel blandly.

I chuckled. "For a man who knows nothing of intrigue, you are beginning well."

And again the room was full of Zaccur's laughter. "I learn quickly. Peasants may be naïve, but they are not necessarily stupid."

"I heard an owl," said the old woman suddenly, turning from the fire.

"Yes, Mother, you probably did."

"He called three times in a row, quickly. That means he has been to the top of the mountain and has come back to tell us winter will arrive early."

"About things like this she is never wrong," he said to Rizpah and me, then added slowly, "You will be safe here."

book five

RIZPAH

chapter one

I FILLED the pitcher at the stream, and as almost always before turning back toward the house, I looked northward to the mountains. Lebanon reached upward on the left, and on the right, the heights of Hermon were shrouded in lacy cloud.

From the near orchard drifted the sound of voices. Eliel and Armoni were laboring side by side, cultivating the fig cuttings they had set out early in the spring.

The clouds eddying about the top of the mountain suddenly dissolved, revealing the craggy peak. Sometimes, I was told, Hermon retained its cap of snow the year round, but this summer had been warm, and the last white streaks had vanished from the high crevasses weeks before. It was almost noon. At dawn Hermon conveyed a sense of gentle mystery, in the evening, peace. At midday its emanation was uncompromising majesty.

For nearly a year I had watched its changing humors. I had seen the drabness of late autumn give way to the slashing winds of winter, had looked on Hermon and the land it guarded as spring torrents gushed off the heights into the valleys.

It had been a year of gradually assuaging tension. The reports from the south were garbled by the time they reached Ramoth-Dan, but

Rizpah and I were able to extract enough sense from them to piece together some assessment of events.

David had disavowed responsibility for Abner's death. He had publicly reprimanded Joab and had fasted ostentatiously following his speech of mourning at Abner's grave. Also, when Rechab and Baanah brought David the head of Ishbaal, he had ordered them executed and their bodies hung beside a pool which lies before Hebron. Then he had placed the head of Saul's son in the sepulcher where Abner was buried.

It appeared, therefore, that David considered his position secure enough not to take or welcome retribution against the house of Saul.

For a while after hearing this news we thought of returning to Benjamin, where Rizpah could claim and undoubtedly receive Saul's home at Gibeah. But the winter storms had already begun sweeping through the passes, and Eliel argued, quite correctly, that crossing the mountains at this time of year would be virtually impossible. We decided to wait until spring. When spring came, it seemed wise to wait a few weeks longer. Weeks stretched into months; the quiet of Dan settled about us, and now by tacit agreement no one spoke of leaving.

Just after the apricot trees shed their blossoms, Eliel's mother died. She walked out of the house one morning, hunched over her stick, and as was her custom, sat in the shade of an oak in the courtyard. She had developed the faculty of remaining motionless for such long periods of time that no one knew she was dead until Eliel returned to the house for the noon meal.

After the old woman's death, Eliel suggested that we move from Zaccur's house to his. Rizpah refused politely, but it seemed senseless for all of us not to eat together as a family. So, although we continued to live in separate dwellings, we had our meals in Eliel's house. He had been fending for himself and his mother quite adequately, but now he was happy to turn over the household tasks to Rizpah and me.

It was easy to see that he was greatly attracted to Rizpah. But with all his rugged outward assurance, he was a reticent man. He had never once approached her to plead his suit.

It was probably just as well. In truth, Rizpah worried me, increasingly as time went by. On the surface, she was tranquil and even cheerful. She pursued her daily tasks as if she enjoyed them: cooking, milking the several goats, making cheese and curds. Eliel spoke often of obtaining servants to take over the more menials jobs, but Rizpah discouraged him. "If we were not here," she would say, "you would have no need for servants. Let the matter rest. Give your orchards another year or two of prosperity."

To which he would reply, "It is not fitting for the widow of a king to be a milkmaid."

And she would laugh and say, "If I did not milk the goats, how would I be able to make cheese?"

Had I not known her so thoroughly, I might have believed in the peaceful front she presented. She often sang at her work, and on the occasions when we went into Ramoth-Dan, she was the image of a delighted child, exploring the tiny market place as if she had never seen anything more grand.

It was probably the very wholeheartedness of her seeming content that first made me doubt it. She was too easily pleased, too tractable. But there was no true glow about her, none of the inner happiness rising to her face as I had seen it do so often in the past. In fact, the serenity of her gaze was a little frightening. Seldom did I see any real feeling in her eyes now. Sometimes they softened a bit when she watched a sunset or looked at a flower, but even then her expression was like that of a worshiper who has ceased to believe, and comes to the temple out of habit or duty. Only when she was with the children did some of her former vibrancy emerge, but it was removed and withdrawn, a face viewed through a veil.

No longer did we spend long evenings talking. Her conversation during the day was lively enough, but through it she gave nothing of herself, and at night she would plead weariness and go as quickly as possible to her room.

When my man was alive in Askelon, a warrior-prince once came from Egypt and stayed in the Seren's house. He had traveled widely, and he entertained us with tales of the strange and mysterious things he had seen. I remember his telling us of the lush forests near the source of the Great River of Egypt, where there lived a clan of wizards who had a miraculous, sinister power. They would choose certain men and women and cast a spell over them, so that they would appear to be quite normal, pursuing ordinary lives as before, but the spirit was gone out of them and they would respond only to the will of the wizards. The people of Cush used a phrase to describe them which meant roughly: the-dead-who-walk-in-sunlight-with-their-spirit-lost-in-shadow.

It grieved me to see Rizpah like this, but Eliel, not having known her before, was only confused.

He was coming toward me now, having finished his work for the morning. Armoni, with the supreme dignity of a nine-year-old who has found a hero, walked soberly beside him, aping even Eliel's gait, though not even the new pattern of mannerisms could erase the imprint of Saul from the boy.

As they reached me, Armoni said gravely, "The cuttings will do well this year. In another two seasons they will begin to be useful trees."

And so will you, my small man, I thought, filled with the fondness and sadness the sight of a growing child can inspire. How swiftly the years rush by, bearing you to maturity and me closer to the grave.

Something of this must have been in my eyes, some lowering of my habitual guard, for Eliel gave me a rapid glance and then said to Armoni, "Run along and tell your mother the two farmers are ready for their noon meal."

When the boy had gone ahead and we were walking unhurriedly between the rows of ripening apricots, he said, "The children have been happy here." I nodded, and he inquired quickly, "And you?"

"I also."

He hesitated. "Rizpah . . ."

I said without expression, "She is content."

As I had feared, this did not satisfy him. He paused to inspect a branch of green fruit just beginning to take on golden lights. "I do not understand her, Egrep. Never have I seen a woman so beautiful, so endowed with wit and charm. And yet it appears to me that she is . . . how shall I express it?"

"A shell," I suggested wearily.

"Exactly." He was excited, as if I had concentrated the wisdom of the world in what I had said. "A shell," he repeated. "A beautiful, empty shell."

"She has suffered a great deal. When a tree has been blighted, as you know better than I, it may not bloom again for years. If in fact ever."

"There are men who understand trees, who can minister to their illness . . ."

"Trees are not women," I said, somewhat sharply.

"It was you who drew the metaphor," he answered, smiling.

"Then I will draw you another." I was a little resentful, showing the irritation of the aging against those who would make priests and intercessors of us. Nevertheless I felt I should warn him. "A wounded lioness may provoke compassion, but the wary hunter does not venture too close to her claws."

"I find that description most unkind."

"Kindness was not my intention," I said shortly.

He did not reply to this, and we walked on through the orchard in silence, but I was sure he was not convinced.

That evening, when Rizpah and I were walking to our house, I said to her, "Eliel will ask you to marry him."

She turned startled eyes on me, like those of a diver who has risen through murky waters and, upon reaching the surface, finds himself off an unfamiliar shore. "Marry?" she said, and the tone of her voice matched her glance. Then she shrugged, with a return of the equanimity and indifference I found so disturbing. "All I wish is to be left alone."

I knew she meant exactly what she said. And for Eliel's sake, I hoped he would heed the warning I had given him.

chapter two

HE WAS wise. He concentrated on being a friend to her and the children, and in this he was successful. But all the while he was waiting, biding his time, with the forbearance of those who have learned that living things sometimes grow slowly.

He once asked me, musingly, almost rhetorically, "Has no one ever hated her?"

I could have replied: many, among them even those who have loved her. But true though this was, like many truisms it would have had a pretentious ring. So I said only, "Some have hated her."

"But many more have loved and admired her."

"I have not kept count," I said tartly. Then, ashamed of my rudeness, I added, "A beautiful woman attracts many men."

"It is not only her beauty," he said slowly. "I have often thought that one must either love Rizpah or hate her. Her spirit will not permit indifference."

Eliel was certainly not indifferent to her. Yet he was content to wait. And who knows how effective his patience might have been if the chain of circumstance, slack for a time, had not again begun to tighten about our lives?

There was famine in a great part of Israel. It had started the first year we lived in Ramoth. Drought had pinched off the crops of Judah and Benjamin, and the harvest yielded only stunted sheaves and withered fruit. The next year had been even worse. There had been little moisture during the winter, and the expected spring rains were tantalizingly brief. Summer had turned the land into an oven. Rivers of flowing water dwindled to slime; streams dried up; cisterns were emptied, and only the deepest wells gave up water for drinking. Crops which had been hopefully sown barely managed to show a few green shoots before they were cut down by a sun that was like a devouring sword. Flocks and herds grew lean and died off. The rich were reduced to eating their stores of seed grain, the poor to scrounging for the more edible roots and bark, and later to boiling the saw-toothed grass which flourished in the wilderness.

Only northern Dan and the upper portion of Manasseh, isolated and protected by the mountains whose streams furnished ample water, were free of the scourge.

Everyone looked forward expectantly, desperately, to the third season. Surely such an affliction would not last another year.

The winter rains brought relief. They soaked the land and replenished the water beneath the land. There was rejoicing in the cities and dancing in the streets of villages.

Spring came. The olive trees sent forth tender shoots; the almond flowered, and the young grain burst from the earth. Life flowed back into the stricken country. The sound of laughter was heard again, and passing caravans were no longer quite so vigilant against raids by starving villagers.

The sun shone brightly, but gradually, unwillingly, the people became aware of an unpleasant fact. The gentle rains of spring, which had begun on schedule, and should have fallen at least once every week, had ceased. The days grew hotter. Farmers worked feverishly, carrying water from wells over great distances to pour on the new, still fragile, crops.

It was no use. By the first month of summer, the situation was as it had been in the two preceding years. Only now, with no reserves to give them hope and sustain their faith, the people themselves began to sicken and die. We heard stories of farmers who sat in their fields, surrounded by the brittle vestige of promising growth, and went mad, howling at the sun by day and screaming at the face of the moon.

All of this seemed very remote to us in Ramoth. Suffering communicates itself in an odd fashion. We can weep at the death of the gazelle who appears on our doorstep, its flesh torn by the fangs of wolves. But if we hear an account of the distress of a thousand humans, it often leaves us singularly unmoved. For misery in others is visual and must be witnessed. I sometimes feel the gods have shown wisdom in ordaining this, for if man were bowed down by all the wretchedness of which he heard, he would soon perish from the sheer weight of the burden.

So it was that the traveling merchants who passed through Ramoth brought news of what was happening, and we clucked our tongues and let our eyes rest on our ripening fruits and half stopped our ears, thus being able to hear but not to heed.

Until the day just before the zenith of summer when, abruptly, the mountain bulwark crumbled and the beauty round us turned to ash.

I had taken a basket of dried figs into town to trade for some cloth we needed. Both the children and Eliel required new cloaks, and I intended to make them before the cold weather set in.

I reached the market place, but I did not even begin to bargain with the cloth merchant.

What I heard sent me hurrying back to the oxcart. I prodded the beast, urging him to greater activity than he had known since our trip north to Mahanaim. Even so, he seemed to crawl along the road between Ramoth and the orchards of Eliel, turning now and again to question my urgency with his great pathetic eyes.

I found Rizpah in the kitchen-common room of Eliel's house, kneading dough for the next day's bread. Meribaal was with her, playing with some bright-colored stones on the floor near the fireplace. It was late afternoon, and the embers glowing beneath the hearth oven touched the child's face with tender radiance.

I was reluctant to speak in front of him. "There is news," I said brusquely to Rizpah.

She looked sharply at me, then, wiping the flour from her hands, went to Meribaal. "My son," she said gently—one always spoke gently to him—"do you remember the wood we cut yesterday, and left by the far shed?"

He nodded, looking up at her with such complete trust and love that I felt my heart turn over.

"Would you go pile it against the shed for me? And be sure to leave space between the logs so they will dry out properly."

Meribaal nodded again, happily. He gathered up his stones and left the house. I heard him calling to one of the goats as he crossed the courtyard.

She waited, brushing back a strand of hair from her heat-flushed face, then putting her hands on her hips and standing in silence.

Now that I was free to speak, I found it difficult to begin. "There was a trader," I said. "His home is between the wilderness of Shur and the point where it becomes the part of Egypt which is Goshen."

"It is important that I know this, of course."

Her voice was soft, but in her eyes was a trace of the cold, commanding expression I had rarely seen since the days in Askelon.

"You know it is not important," I said miserably, then with some anger, "Do you think I have no feeling about what I have heard? Do you think I enjoy having my tongue cleave to the roof of my mouth?"

She took a step toward me and stretched out her hand, imploring and soothing with a gesture that was Abner's. (How much of ourselves we owe to those we have loved, I thought, while my mind went on wrestling with what I knew I must say.) "Speak as you will, old woman," she said. "Whatever it is, it cannot be that terrible. And even if it is, with your help I shall be able to face it."

My story poured out then, the words dropping like tears into the stillness of the room.

The trader from Goshen had passed through Judah and Benjamin serveral weeks before. Conditions were frightful. Hunger coursed the land like a bitter hunter, and with him rode his twin brother, disease. Together they had ravaged Judah and brought Benjamin to its knees. There were even tales, which the trader piously hastened to say he doubted, of parents devouring their own children.

He had not tarried long in the south. His wares of bronze lamps and knives, reeds for writing, and cosmetics such as eye paint and lip rouge were not exactly in demand during these days.

"However, while I was there a momentous thing occurred," he had told his circle of listeners in the Ramoth market. "It so happens that I am a particular friend of the steward in the house of Joab, David's general—he, the steward that is, having been born in the same region as I."

The steward of Joab had whispered to him that if he wished to see a spectacle he should remain in the land for just a few more days. It seemed that the king had communed with his God as to the cause of the dreadful famine, and the Lord had answered that it was because of the sin the dead ruler Saul had committed against the Gibeonites.

David had immediately summoned the elders of the city of Gibeon and told them of the word of the Lord. "What shall I do for you?" he had asked them. "And how shall I make atonement for the crime which was perpetrated against you?"

Whereupon they had replied, according to what Joab's steward told the trader from Goshen, "We want neither gold nor silver. Only this we desire—that the seed of the man who wiped out so many of our young men shall in turn be destroyed and obliterated from the land of Israel."

And David had answered, "It shall be done."

"Now," the steward had said to the trader, "if you will but come with me to a certain high place, a table of rock which lies in the wild country between Gibeon and Ramah, you will truly see a thing."

The trader had gone with him, and had witnessed a sight, the memory of which even now brought up his gorge (though when he told it in the market place, there was a banquet light in his eyes). The five sons of Merab, daughter of Saul, were brought to this lonely spot in chains. The youngest could not have been more than seven, but each in turn was hanged from the branches of a tree until he was dead. David had knelt then before the elders and citizens of Gibeon and had proclaimed, "Thus does your servant David, King of Israel and Judah, in partial expiation of the sin of Saul."

I finished speaking. The words *in partial expiation* had come out with more emphasis than I intended. Rizpah turned pale, and for an instant I thought she would faint, but she recovered enough to reach a bench, where she sat down heavily.

"Then he does not feel as sure of the throne as we had hoped he would."

She spoke quietly, as if to herself, but her hands, fumbling with each other in her lap, betrayed her agitation.

I sat down beside her. Neither of us believed the tale as it had been reported. No doubt David had summoned the elders of Gibeon, and possibly he had told them of his communion with God. Then he would have hinted that he was prepared to eradicate the descendants of Saul in the name of their city. Only eleven years had passed since the massacre of the Gibeonites, and memory would still be strong among the bereaved. David was quick and eloquent. He could twist phrases and weave them into his discourse in such a manner that the Gibeonites would feel they had made the demand for blood and David had only complied.

But Rizpah and I had been too long schooled in the motives and methods of rulers to be deceived by the trappings of the story. Its meaning was simple, brutal and clear. David feared that the discontent of his people rising from the famine could coagulate into rebellion. By executing Saul's male descendants he would provide his subjects with release from tension in the form of a scapegoat. Equally important, he would destroy forever the possibility of one of Saul's sons wresting the crown from him. It was a bold, adroit move, and it placed Armoni and Meribaal in immediate peril.

Eliel and Armoni came in from their work, sweat-streaked and laughing. When Eliel saw our faces his laughter died, but he turned and in a normal tone told Armoni to fetch some extra water, since he wished to bathe that evening. The boy, seeing three full pitchers by the fireplace, looked puzzled but did as he was told, seizing a large clay jug and hefting it gracefully onto his shoulder. He had grown tall and strong in the two years we had lived in Ramoth. His face was burned deep brown from the sun; his arms were sinewy, his hands callused. He looked more than ever like Saul, which was most unfortunate at this particular time.

We waited until we were sure Armoni was well out of earshot. Meribaal, we knew, would remain by the shed where Rizpah had sent him, smiling dreamily and weaving some private fantasy, until someone called him.

I related the trader's story to Eliel. His face darkened when I described the death of Merab's children, but he said nothing. He remained silent for a time after I stopped speaking.

Then suddenly he smiled. "I do not believe it."

Rizpah sighed. "It is true."

"Is David then a monster?"

"He is the king."

"But not a monster. This is some figment of the trader's imagination, a tale concocted to draw customers to him. An old ruse of the market place."

"Are you a fool?" Rizpah asked irritably. Then, softening, "I am sorry. I did not mean that. But you do not understand. The trader could not have imagined this. There is little doubt that the sons of Merab have died. The only question is what we should do."

"You have no plans for leaving?"

"I have no plans. But David will be seeking my sons as well."

Eliel's eyes narrowed. "If he dares come after them here . . ."

She said in a low voice, "You are kind. But David will not come himself. He will send soldiers to scour the land, even as Saul once searched for him."

"I am no soldier, but I do not lack skill in the use of a knife. If they come . . ."

Now she smiled at him, but without derision. "You would be confronting veteran warriors with swords and javelins, seasoned in every trick of battle. If you killed one, or even two, the others would surely slay you."

"Perhaps you are right." He grinned ruefully. "I spoke like a boy, boasting of his prowess against the lion he has never seen." He was silent for another few moments, then, "You told me that no one knew of your destination when you left Mahanaim."

"No one."

"Then David will have no special reason to search for you here. Your identity is not known in the town. You will be as safe in Ramoth as anywhere in Israel. Safer in all likelihood."

His words made sense. In any event, there seemed to be no alternative at the moment.

But now the peace we had known in Dan was turning sour. Neither Rizpah nor I dared go into the town, and we were careful to keep the boys near us, away from the road. Now even the sounds of pastoral tranquillity were fraught with terror. A wagon rolling past the house at night became a chariot; two revelers returning from Ramoth, a troop of soldiers. We lived in fear of the instant when we would hear the cry at the door: Open in the name of King David.

Rizpah told me of a memory which kept recurring with startling clarity. When the prophet Samuel had been reminiscing to her during her visit to Ramah, recalling his days at the sanctuary of Shiloh, he had spoken of his fear before he understood the call of the Lord. He had described vividly the still halls of the temple in the hour before dawn, when he had lain shivering in his bed, waiting for he knew not what; when he had felt the Presence somewhere in the dark corridors, and in his mind's eye had witnessed the silent opening and closing of heavy doors. And yet when he rose and ventured forth from his chamber, he had seen no one. Not for many years did he realize that what he had felt was not fear, but rather its essence. Fear belongs to what a person can see or hear, what is known; the essence springs from the vastness of the unknown, the abyss without dimension, the aimless joining of time and space to form . . . nothing. A nothing which menaces because we do not know the answers to three vital questions: what, when, where.

Yet the days and nights went by, the time when it might have been wiser to flee. And when no further news came from the south, we relaxed a little, then a little more.

It was a mistake, of course. But those first few days and nights of terror had served a purpose. We had been close to hysteria then, and if the danger that finally arrived had come earlier, we might not have been able to meet it.

As it was, we were frightened but not paralyzed beyond action.

Eliel came into the house one evening, tense and shaken out of his usual calm. He had left after the meal, as he often did, to see to the animals and to walk about the courtyard in the gathering dusk. Now he closed the door quietly and carefully, dropping the heavy wooden bar into place. The boys were sitting by the fireplace, Meribaal serene as always, Armoni leaning forward wide-eyed now, sensing something amiss from Eliel's manner.

"Soldiers," said Eliel curtly.

I was proud of Rizpah. I knew she must be trembling inside, just as I was, but she asked with complete composure, "Are they coming here?"

"Not now, at any rate. They were moving north along the road."

"How many?" I asked.

"About twenty. All on foot except for the leader, who was driving a chariot. He passed so close to me I could see he only had one eye."

Rizpah and I exchanged a glance. There were probably other one-eyed officers in David's army, but somehow I was sure this would be Bela. From her expression I surmised that Rizpah thought as I did. Bela was not very bright, but he was thorough. If his orders were to find the sons of Saul, he would not rest until he had done so. There could be no hope of mercy from him. Orders were sacred, and he would still bear his grudge against Saul and Abner.

"We must leave at once," said Rizpah with deceptive casualness.

Eliel said, "But if they were traveling north . . ."

"Probably as far as the frontier," she said. "The officer will station some of his men on roads leading out of Israel to Aram. Then he and the others will work their way back from the border, searching houses along the way."

"You could hide in the forest until they have left the area."

She smiled wanly. "If this is the officer I think it is, he will not leave the area. He is dull-witted, but he is not entirely a fool. When he hears in Ramoth that the widow of Zaccur and her two children are living here in the company of an older woman, he will know at once. We must leave."

Eliel walked to the table, picked up a crumb of bread, mashed it between his fingers. "Where will you go? Phoenicia?"

"No," she said thoughtfully. "If the way to Aram is guarded, the roads to Phoenicia will be watched even more closely. The time for leaving the country is past. I suppose I did not truly wish to go, otherwise I should have." She took a deep breath. "I have thought about it. We shall go to Simeon."

I swung around, echoing inanely, "Simeon . . ."

"Why not?" Her eyes were filled with a strange light. "To the house of my father."

"But . . ." I began.

"We shall rebuild it," she said calmly, anticipating my objection. "There was even less when my great-grandfather came to the land."

It was madness. The journey would take at least a month, probably more, if in fact we completed it at all. And if we did arrive, there would be almost as many hardships as we would endure on the journey itself. Yet I found myself becoming intrigued with the idea. Certainly there was little chance of anyone searching for us there. And perhaps . . .

"You will need a man," Eliel was saying. "I will go with you."

Rizpah went to him. "Thank you," she said, "but we shall go alone. If we are captured, you would die because of me. I could not have that."

"Surely that decision is mine," he observed mildly.

"We must go alone!" Her voice was sharp and urgent.

Once when I had compared Rizpah to a wounded lioness, Eliel had objected. He could find no fault with my description now. The wild light had grown in her eyes. Her lips were drawn back a little from her teeth. Her bearing was defiant, savage.

"Are we truly leaving, Mother?" Armoni asked. I had forgotten that the cubs of the lioness were also present. "Now, tonight?"

The savagery left her face abruptly. "Tonight," she said. "The four of us."

She turned back to Eliel. "It is better this way. Please respect my wish."

He stood motionless for some moments, looking at her. She stared back, obdurate.

Then he said, almost inaudibly, "It shall be as you say."

chapter three

By DAWN we reached the upper edge of the swamp surrounding the Waters of Merom, the lake from which the Jordan plunges southward to the Sea of Chinnereth.

It had been an unnerving journey so far. The track was bumpy and ill-defined, the starlight uncertain. And during the last hours of darkness our progress was haunted by a bittern's booming call, which hung in the air like lingering thunder. I have always tried to ignore omens, but it disturbed me to hear the mating cry of a bird so long out of normal season.

However, the first light lifted our spirits. Faint rose and gold touched the clumps of long-stemmed papyrus, imparted a magical treasure-chest luster to drab marsh vegetation. Overhead a stork flapped its way toward the cedar-covered mountains, the ungainliness of its flight somehow cheering.

We could see our route clearly now. A narrow path, barely wide enough for the oxcart, wound along the border of the bog, adjusting itself to its irregularities.

Eliel had crammed the wagon full of supplies. In addition to the stores of dried fruit and grain, there were several cheeses wrapped in moist leaves and enough bread to last a week. He had also packed a mattock, a couple of spades, a hammer, a roll of leather thongs and a number of other household items. The wagon groaned as it jolted over the uneven trail, and the ox was obviously disgruntled by the heavy load.

Just before we departed, Eliel had handed Armoni a long, curved bronze knife, saying, "You will know how and when to use it if you must." The boy had nodded soberly and turned the knife this way and that, watching the gleam of torchlight on its blade. Then he had thrust it through a loop of his girdle. Rizpah had told him why we must flee again, believing it unwise and impractical to keep him in ignorance. He had already gathered most of the story from our conversation. He accepted the remainder of the details without any show of emotion. But as he leaped into the front of the wagon, he could not resist emitting a small whoop of excitement. He was at the age when childhood and manhood meet and produce strange turbulence, as when the rushing waters of the young Jordan enter Chinnereth and stir up the depths of the sea.

Our way south was to be necessarily circuitous. Since we thought the eastern side of the Jordan would not be as heavily traveled, we intended to cut through Manasseh, descend into Gad and the forests of Gilead, and from there enter the territory of Reuben. To that point the journey would be relatively simple. Even with the drought we should not have great difficulty finding drinking water, and the wooded hills would provide relief from the worst of the heat.

After traversing Reuben, we planned to make our way through Moab, Edom and the northern sliver of the land of Amalek, and from there upward to our destination.

The latter part of the trip, with its desert terrain and blistering sun, would naturally prove the most difficult. For a time I toyed with the idea of persuading Rizpah to seek refuge in Moab, but upon reflection I realized we should be no more secure there than we were in Mahanaim or Ramoth-Dan. Sooner or later someone would discover our identity and attempt to gain a reward from David by delivering the boys into his hand. No, harsh though the prospect seemed, our safety lay in attaining complete isolation.

The end of the third day brought us over the mountains into the region of Bashan, of which Manasseh is part. It is a pleasant land, sheltered by towering oaks and abounding in bird life. There were thousands of partridges, and Armoni was able with ease to snare several for each meal.

But the plentiful supply of food had its disadvantages. We had thought the area would be fairly free of people. Had we been a little more foresighted, we should have realized that the famine would force many from the central territories to leave their homes in search of sustenance. Bands of roaming families out of Ephraim and Issachar had crossed the river and were living on the abundance of game birds. With the onset of winter and the southward retreat of the birds, most of the wanderers would return to their own villages, but now we could scarcely have thrown a stone without hitting the tent of a farmer from Tabor or a miller from Beth-shan. We were forced to keep the hoods of our cloaks close about our faces and make extensive detours from the main trail to find secluded campsites.

So it was almost with a feeling of relief that we entered the arid hill country at the extreme south of Manasseh. The terrain was inhospitable, but we encountered far fewer people.

In fact, we hardly saw anyone for two days, aside from a clan of scabby Bedouins, whose numerous children gaped at us as we passed.

Toward noon on the third day out of Bashan we sighted two figures walking far ahead of us. Rizpah cautioned the boys to pull up their hoods about their faces, and we did the same. As we drew closer, we could see that one of the travelers was a woman. She was making her way with faltering steps, supported by the man. As we came abreast of them, the woman stumbled and collapsed in the road. Her companion looked at us with a helpless, imploring glance and knelt beside her. Rizpah and I questioned each other silently. Then she called to Armoni to stop the wagon.

The woman appeared to be in dreadful condition. Only the whites of her eyes showed in deep sockets. Her face was dust-streaked and covered with beads of greasy sweat. She alternated between retching and gasping for breath.

Her name, the man informed us at once, was Maacah. He was

called Shemed. He seemed about to burst into tears as he told us that they had left their home in the northeastern corner of Manasseh some days before to make a pilgrimage to the ancient sanctuary of Shiloh.

"Dear ladies," he said, as we proceeded to sponge his wife's face and give her water to drink, "dear ladies, you have no conception of what it means to live in our part of the country. Idolatry abounds. Every home has at least two or three household images to which they pray. If one tries to profess his love for Jahveh, he is laughed at and spat upon."

"Blessed be the name of the Lord," said the woman Maacah, beginning to revive. Her irises rolled down into a more normal position, and she blinked at us rapidly and uncomprehendingly. "For his mercy endureth forever."

"Poor soul," said Shemed in a low voice. "She has had a terrible experience."

He related how they were set upon by a group of Ammonite nomads. Their donkeys and provisions had been stolen. "We were fortunate to escape with our lives." Shemed lowered his voice still further. "Maacah was ravished."

Looking at her pasty, somewhat bloated face and her angular, bony figure, I spent a wry moment contemplating what must have been either the desperation or deplorable taste of the Ammonites. Still, as some anonymous warrior has written with sly and unmistakable double meaning, the raiding lance plunders what it finds, and when the eyes of the lancer are closed, all booty is the same. As if reading my irreverent thoughts, Shemed gazed at me reproachfully and said, "She suffered terribly."

And I muttered guiltily, "I am sure she did."

"The Lord provides and he also takes away," murmured Maacah with an air of patient resignation.

Despite the difficulties they had experienced, the couple had decided to complete their pilgrimage to Shiloh. As Shemed expressed it, "What a terrible opinion Jahveh would have of us if we were not willing to endure a little hardship in his name."

"Amen," said Maacah fervently, struggling to sit up.

"Dear ladies," said Shemed, his eyes filling with tears as he looked first at us, then meaningfully at the wagon.

Rizpah glanced at me. I shrugged. She turned away, considering, then finally said, "We are not crossing the Jordan and so could not take you all the way to Shiloh. But if you would care to ride with us as far as the river Jabbok, we shall make room for you."

Shemed fell forward and pressed his face to the ground. The woman seized Rizpah's hand and kissed it. I looked away. Excessive gratitude in any form has always repelled me.

But suddenly the elaborate protestations ceased. I heard Maacah gasp and turned quickly back, thinking she was about to be ill again.

Meribaal had thrown back his hood and was walking toward us, his eyes wide and inquiring. Rizpah started to call out to him, but realizing it was too late, watched the man and woman narrowly, trying to divine the reason behind their reaction.

She need not have worried. "The boy . . ." Shemed said in a strangled voice to Rizpah. "The boy is yours . . ."

"He is mine."

Shemed put his hand tenderly on Maacah's shoulder. She was looking at Meribaal's face, drinking in the sight avidly. Then without warning a torrent of tears burst from her eyes and rushed down her cheeks. She wailed in the pure, clear tones of a grieving Bedouin woman.

"Dear ladies," said Shemed, "forgive us." His expression was mournful, but his tears did not flow, remaining in his eyes and making them appear like overfilled pools. "We had a child . . . the same age as yours . . . with the same beautiful face. . . ."

Maacah caught her breath. Her wailing resumed, rising to a pitch two or three notes higher.

"Our child died last year," Shemed said flatly. "One morning he could not breathe except with great difficulty. By evening he was dead." He helped Maacah to her feet. They went to Meribaal and each placed a hand on his head. He smiled up at them, his slow, trusting smile of wonderment.

We got back into the wagon. Two additional people made the quarters most uncomfortable. When we stopped for the night, we decided to rearrange the load to give us a little more space. We removed sacks of grain and baskets of fruit, planning to reload them in the morning.

This upset Shemed. "Dear ladies," he said, "we have greatly incommoded you. I beg you, do not touch a thing. Tonight I am too weary, but in the morning I shall take care of everything."

He was so insistent that we ceased unloading. Shemed unyoked the ox and tethered it. I said to him, "You are a farmer then." When he looked at me in surprise, I laughed and explained, "The way you handle the ox."

"I have had experience with animals," he said shortly.

Something about the way he spoke made me curious. "Are you no longer a farmer?"

"I do not wish to burden you with the chronicle of our complaints."

"As you wish."

He looked at me meditatively, then said, "The death of the boy was only the beginning of our misfortune. Perhaps before we part I shall tell you the rest." He turned away.

Shemed and Maacah prayed long and loud before eating. Then they ate liberally, alternating apologies for their hunger with frenzied expressions of gratitude. At the end of the meal Shemed brought out a grubby packet of candied dates. "They are all we have left," he said mournfully, "and poor repayment for your hospitality. But please accept some as a symbol of our good intention, if nothing else."

Armoni and Meribaal greedily gobbled a couple of dates apiece. Rizpah and I shrank from the gooey mess Shemed was tendering us, but it was difficult to refuse. We were surprised at the excellent flavor of the fruit. "The date groves of Manasseh . . ." Shemed began, then clamped his lips shut. His eyes filled with tears. "I promised I would say nothing."

When Meribaal began to grow drowsy, Maacah whispered something to her husband. He approached Rizpah diffidently. "My wife wishes to know," he said, averting his eyes with a somewhat embarrassed air, "if she can hold the boy until he sleeps."

Rizpah nodded, and Maacah came to Meribaal in a transport of delight. She sat cross-legged on the ground, pillowing the child's head in her lap, crooning a soft melody I had never heard. Shemed sat next to her and kept looking from Meribaal to his wife. Suddenly he got up and strode to the fire, standing with his back to Maacah. His face was set in bitter lines, and now the tears flowed from his eyes.

I slept exceptionally soundly, and when I awoke the sun was already high above the hills. I sat up, conscious of a slight headache, and saw that Rizpah and the children were still asleep. Shemed and Maacah were nowhere to be seen.

Neither was the ox nor the wagon.

It took me some moments to realize we had been robbed. Everything—our food, supplies, extra clothing—everything was gone except two sacks of dried corn which Rizpah and I had used as pillows.

Chagrin sent the blood to my head. We had acted like a pair of gullible peasant women, falling prey to one of the oldest tricks of thievery. The feigned illness of Maacah (if that was indeed her name), the great show of religiosity, the tale of misfortune, the tears were all part of a role, a subterfuge employed by experts to fleece unwary travelers. It had all been carefully planned: the sighting of the victims, Maacah's collapse just as we reached her, the candied dates drugged just enough to make us sleep heavily.

Then, as I got dazedly to my feet, I saw something glittering on the ground. I walked over to it, picked it up and shook my head, wondering.

It was a polished metal amulet, one of those worn by Bedouin men to ward off the evil spirits of the desert. And scrawled in the dust in labored, crudely fashioned characters were the words: for the boy.

chapter four

THE FULL urgency of our situation did not become apparent until noon, when we walked along the unsheltered trail feeling the sun suck the moisture from our flesh, from the very marrow of our bones.

We had divided up the two sacks of grain among us for easier carrying. We knew we would not starve, but water was a problem. The thieves had taken our two waterskins. I could feel my tongue growing dry and swollen, and looking at Rizpah and Armoni, I knew they were no better off than I. But it was Meribaal who concerned me most. After only an hour of trudging in the heat his lips were cracked and scaly-looking. There was a bluish pallor to his skin; his forehead glistened with a thick film of perspiration. Still he walked along uncomplainingly, holding his mother's hand, staring wide-eyed at the scrub brush receding toward the yellow haze of the hills.

We came to a place where the north-south trail was joined by another, running off to the east. There were three possibilities now of obtaining water: veer back to the northwest and fight our way over evil terrain to the Sea of Chinnereth, strike out due west for the Jordan, or make for the town of Beth-arbel to the east. At Chinnereth or on the river we would have as much water as we could drink, but we had no vessel in which to carry a supply away, and following the course of the Jordan south would be both toilsome and risky. There would be less chance of our being seen by David's patrols in Betharbel. It was off the main track, and there also we could buy a waterskin. Even so, it would take us until nightfall to reach the town. We wondered, glancing anxiously at Meribaal, if evening would be soon enough, but there was little choice. We turned eastward.

The thin leather of our sandals afforded scant protection against the sharp stones of the trail. Our progress was slow. The sun seemed to hang directly overhead for hours. I had the feeling that we were suspended in time and space, and were doomed to eternal torturous wandering through the parched countryside.

A vulture flew past above us, circled and returned, was joined by another, and then by a third. The trio of loathsome birds drifted down, settled on a rock a short distance ahead of us and sat motionless, watching our approach. Armoni drew his knife and rushed at them, shouting angrily. They rose before his attack, circled, and lighted on another rock a little farther ahead. Armoni sank to his knees, sobbing bitterly. When we reached him, Rizpah said gently, "Do not waste your strength, my son."

"I hate them!"

"Hate will not help us."

He looked glumly at the knife. "If I ever find those two people, I shall cut their hearts out."

His expression was so fierce, yet so patently and comically frustrated, that Rizpah and I could not help exchanging a grim smile. "We shall not see them again, son," she said. "What is lost is lost."

"Will Jahveh not punish them?"

She looked hopelessly at him. "Jahveh . . ." she began, and stopped, shivering, as one of the vultures screamed quarrelsomely.

Meribaal looked up at her. "Will there be water soon, Mother?"

"Soon," she said, without glancing at him.

I helped Armoni to his feet and we walked on. The hills grew sandier and more arid as we pressed eastward. I began to be concerned that we would miss Beth-arbel and lose ourselves in the desert. But the track, though rough, was clear, stretching endlessly ahead.

The wind blew in our faces. I could smell the acrid odor of the dust as it entered my nostrils, could taste the grit and feel it grinding between my teeth.

"Mother . . ." said Armoni.

"Do not talk now, please, my son."

"Tell me what it will be like in Simeon."

The unchanging plea of the voyager. Tell me what it will be like where I am going. So the children of Israel must have spoken on their long journey from Egypt, addressing first Moses, then Joshua. So my own forefathers must have spoken to their leaders on the ships that sailed from Caphtor, seeking refuge from the ruinous invasions that had razed stately palaces standing in quiet groves. Tell me what it will be like.

"In Simeon," Rizpah was saying, "all is sweet and beautiful. There are green pastures beside still waters, fat herds and lovely vineyards, tender sheaves of grain raising their heads to a gentle sky. . . ."

"Like Dan then," Armoni quested eagerly. "Simeon is like Dan."

The light left her eyes. "I cannot lie to you, my son. Even now, for you will hate me when you see what is there. We shall find sand, and heat greater than this, and great black rocks thrusting themselves out of the parched land."

Armoni was silent for a few moments. Then he asked quietly, "Is there water?"

She smiled, a sad, transitory smile, perhaps remembering the day she and Saul had stood on the land of her childhood, and the soldier's shovel had grated into moist sand, uncovering the source of the buried pool. "There is water."

"Then we shall till the land and make it fruitful. With water it will live under our hands."

"Water . . ." echoed Meribaal in a harsh and hollow voice.

He was gasping for breath. His grip was tight on Rizpah's hand. We knew he should rest. So should we all, yet we dared not stop.

Meribaal stumbled. I took over Rizpah's portion of the food. She gathered the boy in her arms and staggered forward. Then Armoni carried him for a time on his back, hands under his brother's thighs, as he had carried him in their games at Gibeah and Mahanaim.

The sand ground under our sandals. The vultures circled, lighted, rose to circle again, plummeted earthward some distance ahead, crying their malicious triumph.

We saw what they had found: the carcass of a dog, not long dead, fresh-mangled by some beast of prey. The birds quarreled and shoved each other for the privilege of plucking out the eyes.

Was it a wild dog, one of those half-starved animals that course the fringes of the desert? Or had it traveled with some nomad clan, living a life as outcast as its masters? Or, I thought, seeking hope for ourselves out of the image of violent death, had it been a frequenter of the village which was our destination, a town dog who had wandered too far and too recklessly away from man its protector? How domesticated had been the brute that was now being torn to shreds by the claws and beaks of the carrion feeders?

Then, with startling suddenness, as we topped the next rise, the walls of Beth-arbel were before us, saffron in the rays of the setting sun.

But so deceptive are distances in the desert that it took us another hour to reach the gates. Twilight was beginning to shroud the town as we threaded our way through the maze of alleys leading to the square, where we had been told we would find the well.

We filled the clay water vessel again and again, knowing we should not drink so quickly, but unable to stop. Rizpah managed to restrain Meribaal, but Armoni gulped great quantities, spewed it out over the cobblestones as his stomach convulsed, and drank again, more cautiously.

The idlers in the square watched us with increasing curiosity. No doubt they were accustomed to the sight of thirst-driven wanderers descending on their well. But to see a young woman of unusual beauty, two children and an old woman traveling together without protection must have puzzled them.

One, grizzled and slack-mouthed, came over to us. We had sat down on the stones and were beginning to make a meal of our dried corn. The man leaned close to Rizpah, ogling her insinuatingly. Armoni stood up, grasping the handle of his knife, and glared at the intruder, who laughed self-consciously and withdrew a couple of steps. "You have come to see the holy man?"

We looked at him blankly.

"He will come soon. There has been word that he will visit us at twilight." The man looked at Meribaal. "I thought because he was sick you brought him to be cured."

Meribaal indeed looked ill. His breathing was rapid and shallow, his gaze listless, his face hot and flushed.

"I have seen the holy man work great wonders. He has restored sight to the blind and given withered limbs back their strength. Surely it will be a small matter for him to heal the boy."

Rizpah said to the man, "Can you tell me where we can buy a waterskin?"

He stared at her uncomprehendingly. "Waterskin?" Then a crafty expression crossed his face. "You have silver?"

Rizpah took a copper bracelet from her arm. "This for a new waterskin and some bread and fruit."

The man looked greedily at the bracelet, pursed his lips and spat onto the stones. "Not now," he said. "In the morning." He laughed soundlessly, showing the great cavern of his mouth. "Be here in the morning."

The square was beginning to fill with people, some carrying torches. They clustered in excited groups about a carefully preserved open space. A little apart from the others were the afflicted of Beth-arbel: the deformed, the crippled, the blind. They huddled together, shivering with anticipation. Those who could see looked over the heads of the crowd with intense, fearful glances. The blind turned their heads this way and that, sad flowers seeking the light of the sun.

A drum began to beat slowly, monotonously, somewhere in the gathering darkness.

We did not know where else to go, so we waited with the people of Beth-arbel, sitting on the stones close to one of the houses bordering the square. Meribaal was asleep, his head resting against Rizpah's arm.

The crowd quieted, rustled, parted. Along the path made for him, walking in sedate time to the beat of the drum, came the holy man. He was like many I had seen: emaciated, garments hanging in tatters, skin black with grime and long exposure to the weather, hair and beard incredibly long and matted, eyes burning with a bright demented fervor.

The holy man reached the space reserved for him in the center of the square. Torches set at the corners seemed to flicker in rhythm with the drumbeat, cast pulsating light and shadow against the sides of the houses. The little knot of supplicants surged forward: crawling, fumbling, dragging their disabled limbs. The holy man raised both hands, palms outthrust toward them. They stopped and trembled. Unintelligible sounds burst from his lips, a confusion of half-words and aimless guttural mumbling. Foam appeared at the corners of his mouth. His voice grew shrill; his eyes bulged.

I had a growing, uncomfortable feeling that I had seen this man before.

He waved his arms; his body moved back and forth in ceaseless, hypnotic motion. The crippled and the blind were chanting with him now, aping his strangled cries, moving as he moved. The drumbeat increased its tempo, imperceptibly at first, then more noticeably, until it became a frenzied tattoo.

One of the cripples, a man whose limbs appeared so useless that he could only drag them painfully behind him as he crawled like a snake over the stones, now rose suddenly and performed a grotesque, sickening dance, tottering, staggering, clawing for support at the shoulders of a blind man. The spectators roared their approval. They pressed close to the cripple, babbling and shouting. He seemed dazed but pleased by their show of attention.

The holy man was dancing now, leaping about in imitation of the cripple's gyrations of a few moments before, a travesty on travesty.

"More, great healer, more!" cried the crowd. "Heal more!" The afflicted pushed forward, beseeching in tremulous, bleating voices, "Help us heal us, help us heal us . . ." But the holy man gave a great final leap in the air and fell to the stones, lying face up and apparently senseless under the light of the torches. A sigh of disappointment swept through the crowd. They began to hurry out of the square, returning to their houses, where they would shutter the windows and bar the doors. The holy man had fallen into his trance. Evil was abroad in the square. No one must look unduly long on the prostrate healer, and no one must disturb him. In the morning he would be gone, and the offering of food set out in a prearranged spot outside the walls of the village would also have disappeared.

I could not move. The face in repose, even in the uncertain light, was becoming increasingly familiar. Beneath the mass of unkempt hair and tangled beard, the gaunt features . . .

Rizpah stirred beside me. Was she also troubled by elusive recollection? Where had we known him?

Then recognition flooded through me, alarming, unbelievable.

But before I could speak, Armoni had sprung to his feet, crying out, "Paltiel!" He ran toward the holy man, ignoring Rizpah's warning call. His voice echoed oddly through the empty square. "Paltiel!"

The boy stopped next to one of the torches, suddenly fearful before his own impulsiveness. But his voice must have reached deep into the holy man's soul. The bundle of rags, hair and beard quivered, twisted, achieved a sitting position.

It was indeed Paltiel.

Once I was sure, I could not understand how I had not known before.

He glanced around, blinking his eyes, let his gaze pass us, then return to where we sat. Slowly, like a man who has slept unprotected in intense cold, he rose and moved, stiff-limbed, in our direction.

My only thought then was to flee. It was Paltiel, but a suffering Paltiel, whose hurt had turned malevolent and menacing. There was no recognition in his expression, only a virulent hatred, undirected for the moment but terrifying in its potency.

He had almost reached us when Meribaal opened his eyes with a pathetic little cry. Paltiel stopped walking so abruptly he nearly fell. The sick boy and the demented man stared at each other. One of the torches hissed and went out. A strong smell of burned oil filled the square.

Meribaal said in a high, clear voice, "Paltiel?"

The one time commander of an army division shuddered. His teeth chattered. He clenched his fists, stared stupidly at them, then bit his knuckles until blood ran down the back of his hand.

His gaze shifted from Meribaal to Rizpah. Slowly, so as not to startle him, she stretched out her hand. He stared at it as if it were a scorpion. Then, suddenly, tears welled out of his eyes. He seized the hand she still held extended to him. "Rizpah," he said warmly. "My lady Rizpah."

"What has happened to you?"

I could see that she regretted her question as soon as she spoke, but Paltiel did not seem to be concerned. "The desert gave me back my life," he said. "Now I give life to others. I heal them." A mad glitter ascended into his eyes. "I heal . . ."

All at once he appeared to be peaceful. "She comes to me by night," he said. "She flies to me, across the desert, borne on the winds of darkness. She comes, and we are together. We will be together every night, forever."

He smiled. Several of his front teeth were missing. The others were broken and snaggled. "Forever," he said again, then in a mildly curious, quite rational tone, "Why are you here?" And before Rizpah could answer, "I know. There are many things I know."

Meribaal moaned.

Paltiel leaned forward, peering into each of our faces in turn. "The bones of a beloved one offer shelter," he whispered.

Armoni came up softly, knelt beside his mother. Paltiel's eyes found the boy's face, widened with fear. His hands flew up, fingers spread, palms outthrust. He backed away, gibbering to himself.

Then he opened his mouth in a wild shriek. "The king walks? The king! Sheol has burst its bonds!"

He turned and darted into one of the alleyways leading from the square.

We sat in silence, none of us able or wishing to move.

After a time Armoni began to sob softly. Rizpah put her arm about him and hugged Meribaal closer to her other side.

Somewhere in the depths of the town a dog howled once, loudly, and then all was still.

chapter five

I AWOKE to fear. I had been dreaming of Paltiel, vividly: Paltiel in the desert, growing slowly in stature until he was taller than the fierce, sharp-toothed mountains, until his tangled hair and flapping rags blotted them out . . . Paltiel walking toward me, advancing step after step in time with a drum which held silent for suspenseful eternity between beats . . . Paltiel seizing me by the shoulders . . .

Now I was awake and there was a hand on my shoulder. I opened my mouth to scream. Another hand pressed hard against my lips. I struggled until I realized that the restraining hands belonged to Rizpah.

The square was still dark. I could make out Armoni's huddled form, and Meribaal lying near him covered by Rizpah's cloak. The night wind whistled softly over the housetops.

Meribaal stirred and tried to sit up. Rizpah held him firmly. He began to babble, an outpouring of incoherent, frightening words, not unlike the sounds which had come from Paltiel's lips earlier in the night. He writhed under his mother's hand, but she did not release him until he subsided and his voice trailed away to an almost inaudible mutter.

"How long has he been doing that?"

Her eyes were troubled. "Most of the night. Feel his face."

He was burning with fever. "Why did you not call me before?"

"There was no point in both of us being awake." She sighed wearily. "But when I found myself dozing off . . ."

"I shall take care of him now."

"Thank you, old woman."

She was asleep at once. I moved close to Meribaal and held him during his seizures, wondering numbly how we could travel with the boy as ill as he was.

It looked as if we might have to remain in Beth-arbel until he recovered. This posed a number of problems. We had little food and no silver. We would have to approach the elders of the town for assistance. There would be questions, suspicions and possible betrayal. And as long as we stayed in the town we would be living in constant fear of the sight of one of David's patrols.

But there seemed to be little choice.

I discussed this with Rizpah when she awoke shortly after dawn. She nodded grimly and agreed. I went to the well for water.

When I returned she was sitting beside Meribaal, looking up at me elatedly.

Then I saw that the boy's eyes were open. They were clear. I felt his forehead. The fever was gone.

I sank down on the stones and wept with relief.

Armoni awoke and said at once, "I'm hungry." Meribaal smiled sweetly and repeated after his brother, "I'm hungry." Rizpah and I laughed and cried together. The whole world had suddenly turned bright.

Shortly after sunrise, the group of idlers who had been in the square the night before reappeared. The grizzled, slack-mouthed man sauntered toward us.

There was no friendliness in his tone. "Where is the bracelet?"

Rizpah replied coldly, "I said I would trade it to you for a waterskin and bread and fruit."

He feigned amazement. "My lady must take me for a wealthy man who has alms to spare for beggars."

"I am no beggar. The bracelet is worth many times what I ask, as you know very well."

"The bracelet . . ." He yawned and looked away, touching his gray locks, letting his hand slide down to finger his greasy beard. "Why is my lady in such urgent need of a waterskin? Can it be that our lovely city holds no interest for her? Must she then depart before she has properly seen all that Beth-arbel has to offer?"

"The waterskin . . ."

"Ah yes. The waterskin." He looked at Meribaal, who returned the stare with his beautiful equanimity. "I see the boy has recovered. I told you the holy man would cure him. Did you not witness how he healed Ibneiah of the affliction which has plagued him almost three years?" He yawned again. "Show me the bracelet."

She took it from her arm and held it up to the sunlight. It was one Abner had brought back to her after a raid on a Philistine fortress. The man's eyes sparkled briefly with greed. Then he resumed his air of careful indifference.

"Now if you will be so kind as to go and fetch four loaves of bread. And dates. A hundred shekels' weight will suffice, though I should ask more. And the waterskin."

"Go and fetch . . ." The man laughed soundlessly, pantomiming mirth as he glanced back at his companions on the other side of the square, as if the joke were too rich to enjoy alone. "Did I not tell you I would be here in the morning to trade with you? Do you think I would come unprepared?" From under his cloak he brought forth a shabby waterskin, cracks of age crisscrossing its surface, a crude patch sewn near the opening and reaching halfway down one side. He caressed it lovingly. "For my lady."

"Do you think I would accept that?"

"My lady is getting by far the best of the bargain. But I am a generous man."

Rizpah made an angry noise in her throat and turned aside. "Be on your way," she said. "I will buy what I need elsewhere."

"Elsewhere? The market time in Beth-arbel is the morning before the Sabbath. That will not be for five days."

"I will find a merchant. Or a tanner."

"Then I am at your service. My friends and I will speak to the merchants for you."

"I can speak for myself."

"Ah, but my lady is mistaken. The merchants of Beth-arbel listen most carefully to what my friends and I have to say. We have proved a number of times that our counsel is valuable, and that to disregard it can have most unfortunate consequences." He spat onto the stones and again caressed the ancient waterskin. "I do not think my lady will find a better skin than this anywhere within these walls."

I glanced across the square. The man's companions were lounging about, making a show of not looking at us. There were perhaps twelve of them, clothed in worn and stained garments. I had not paid any particular attention to them the evening before, nor evidently had Rizpah, else we should have known at once that we should stay clear of them. They were the sort of riffraff one can see in any town larger than a village throughout Israel and Philistia. In the more important cities they loiter outside the gates. The city guards will not allow them the freedom of the streets, for they are a nuisance, living by petty thievery and whatever opportunities for fraud and sly deception they can ferret out. They are neither as honest as beggars nor as enterprising as the hawkers of wares too seedy for the market place. And they have not the courage to become outright brigands. In smaller towns, where order is tenuously maintained by a few hired watchmen, their freedom is unrestricted, and often they are able to terrorize the more fearful among the citizenry, which group usually includes the merchants.

Rizpah looked hopelessly at me, annoyed at having allowed herself to fall into such an obvious trap. Her anger swept aside judgment. "I shall go to the elders of the town," she said. "They will help me."

"Perhaps," said the man. "Perhaps they will. We know them well. Particularly the chief elder. He is a most inquisitive man. And he does not possess my innate good breeding. No doubt he will wish to know the reason for the visit of my lady and her companions to Beth-arbel. You see," he added thoughtfully, "there are many fugitives from justice abroad in Israel these days. And my lady does appear exceptionally restless and anxious to travel on. But surely she will have no qualms about speaking of these matters to the chief elder."

The man's sly insinuations were a bluff. I was sure of this. But we were in no position to outface him. And since we could not, it was apparent that it would not be wise to remain in Beth-arbel even an hour longer. I would have felt easier if we could have allowed Meribaal to rest for another day, but fortunately he seemed well enough now to travel. However, it would be foolish to set out again without a waterskin, and the one the man was holding was better than none.

With a sigh she handed over the bracelet. He bowed low and gave her the waterskin, then retired to join his fellows. They watched me with great interest as I filled the skin at the well. I was surprised to find that it did not leak. It was more than we had a right to expect.

We traveled slowly. Meribaal seemed to have recovered, but the brief illness had sapped his strength. Rizpah and Armoni alternated carrying him on their backs, while I transported the waterskin and the bulk of the food. The first night out of Beth-arbel we slept by a well halfway to Camon.

We were fortunate. Near the watering place was a bearing date palm. Armoni climbed the tree to bring us the fruit. It was neither choice nor plentiful, the best probably having been stripped off by other travelers, but it augmented our diet of grain, of which we were growing quite weary.

That night I dreamed again of Paltiel. His image was not at all menacing now. He appeared in my dream more as the young commander we had known in the days at Gibeah. But he still wore the tattered garb of a holy man. He seemed to be trying to tell me something. I remember the word "bones" recurring in his speech, which was rapid, fluent and earnest, though I could make absolutely no sense of what he was saying.

The next day shortly before noon we reached the village of Camon. Rizpah and the boys rested some distance from the unwalled settlement while I trekked to the well to refill our waterskin. Two women were gossiping when I arrived, and when I heard the subject of their conversation I sat down beside the well with my back to them, pretending to nap. The husband of one of the women had just returned from the territory of Benjamin. Conditions were unbelievably bad. Famine still stalked the land. David had sent caravans to Egypt to buy grain, and had rationed it out carefully, but this scarcely improved the situation. There seemed little likelihood that the current harvest, already shriveled by drought, would offer additional relief.

Then they spoke of something which chilled me so that I found it impossible to move long after the women had left.

David had issued a public proclamation concerning Saul's sin against Gibeon, now generally believed to be the primary cause of the famine. The execution of Merab's children had, according to the king, not lessened the severity of Israel's predicament because other male descendants of Saul still lived. A reward was offered, the one woman said, the stilted language of the decree sounding odd and unnatural coming from her lips, for information leading to the capture of the two sons of Saul yet at large.

My heart was heavy as I labored toward the grove of tamarisks where Rizpah and the children were waiting. I took her aside and told her what I had heard.

Southwest of us, so near that we could see the tree-covered hills, lay the forests and towns of Gilead. There we would be able to travel more easily, sheltered from the wind and sun. And while water would be difficult to come by, it would still be more plentiful than in the parched land we had just traversed.

But now, knowing that David's proclamation would soon be widely circulated, we would have to avoid populous regions more conscientiously than ever. It would be necessary to travel directly south, over ground unenhanced by trails. The course we planned would take us well to the east of our old haven of Mahanaim, along the inhospitable border of Ammon. Food would become a problem before long, but we had enough left to enable us to reach Moab. There we might be able to obtain additional provisions. I had already resolved that if we found it necessary I would steal. The journey ahead was not one to afford anticipatory delight.

Meribaal was helpful. The child's courage and sweetness warmed me, raised the spirits of us all. He had never been a talkative boy, and now he was more locked off in his private world than ever. But he made it clear that he would no longer allow himself to be carried. In his eyes I saw for the first time some of Rizpah's stubbornness. And I felt that perhaps even we who loved him and did all we could to protect him from life's harshness had been underestimating his fortitude and understanding.

That night we were again fortunate. We had intended to make for the town of Ham. As I had done at Camon, I would leave the others at a safe distance from the town and go alone to obtain water. But just before sundown we saw a cluster of palms, and, approaching it, found one of those rarities, a dry-country well fed by a clear spring.

Then, next morning, something both Rizpah and I had been dreading happened.

We rose early, thinking to cover as much ground as possible before the heat of the day. Actually traveling by night would have been more comfortable, but we were entering country which abounded in beasts of prey: the mountain lion and the jackal, the swift cheetah which could run many times faster than a man. Even if we had been properly armed and possessed a warrior's skill with weapons, night travel would have been hazardous. Defenseless as we were, it was out of the question.

Daylight was just coating the hills as we ate our meager breakfast of corn and a few dates. I filled the skin with fresh water.

"Come," said Rizpah to the children.

Armoni lifted the sack of grain, settled it across his shoulder, and was ready.

Meribaal got to his feet and looked about him wildly. "Mother . . ." he said. Then he vomited, took a few stumbling steps and fell unconscious to the ground.

His heartbeat was fairly strong and his breathing was even, but we could not revive him.

We wrapped him in a cloak and sat down again. The calm which often grips people in moments of calamity took hold of us. Partly through fate, partly through our own unwariness and even stupidity, we had been plunged into an appalling and hopeless situation.

We watched the early light broaden into full morning. Each of us fastened his gaze on some fixed point—the base of a palm, an odd-shaped rock, the crest of a ridge with sunlight glinting off it—rather than look at one another.

My mind was empty. It was not unpleasant to think of absolutely nothing. I felt an unreasonable irritation when Rizpah broke the silence. "Here we have water," she said.

"And very little food," I snapped. And a sick child, I almost added, before I checked myself. Rizpah's expression was stricken enough without my wounding her more deeply.

I looked at Meribaal. His face was pinched, the skin so strangely translucent that it seemed I could see the bones through it. The bones of a beloved one offer shelter, I thought idly and wondered just as aimlessly where I had heard the expression. Was it written somewhere in the cryptic wisdom of Caphtor, immortalized in some forgotten scroll?

Then the words went through my brain again, racing this time. *The bones of a beloved one offer shelter*. I knew now where I had heard them. Paltiel's whispered message to Rizpah, ignored, then forgotten, in the shock of his appearing.

"Jabesh-Gilead," I said aloud.

Armoni turned his head at the sound of my voice. Rizpah stared at me dully.

"Saul is buried there," I said, excited now. "They loved him and they care little for David."

"Do you think I have not considered seeking shelter there?" Rizpah asked sadly. "Before we left Mahanaim it occurred to me. I thought of it again in Dan. The men of Jabesh would defend Saul's children with their lives."

She pronounced the last three words heavily, with weary emphasis. And she was right. Jabesh would gladly do battle to protect the family of Saul. But they were one city. David controlled Israel and Israel's army. It could only end in a tragic, futile struggle. And when it was over, Jabesh would be razed, its inhabitants slaughtered, and Saul's sons would still die.

"But," I said slowly, "we need not ask them for sanctuary. Surely they would be willing to give us a wagon, and supplies, and enough food to take us very nearly to Simeon."

Interest began to bring life back to her face, but her voice was still flat as she said, "I will not beg."

It was such a senseless rejoinder that I said sharply, forgetting Armoni's presence, "Then let the boy die."

Armoni stirred and said softly, "We must do it, Mother."

"Yes," she said.

Suddenly, energy seemed to flow into her. She got up from the ground. Now that she had made her decision, she was impatient to carry it out.

We agreed that I would remain at the well with the children while Rizpah walked to Jabesh-Gilead to present her plea. The city was no more than a day's journey away. If she were successful, she should return before the next dawn.

Meribaal's condition seemed unchanged. He did not even move when Rizpah knelt beside him and kissed him tenderly.

I watched her figure diminishing in the distance. When I could no longer see her, I left Armoni with his brother and walked a little way from the clump of palms.

There I faced the morning sun and prayed at length to the god and goddess.

chapter six

SHE HAD taken the waterskin, carrying it half-full, and thus, having no fear of thirst, was never troubled by it during the long hot morning. She was not sure of her precise direction; there was no track across the hills. So she simply walked westward, confident that she would sight some familiar landmark long before she reached the Jordan.

Just after noon she reached the top of a ridge and saw below her the serpentine path of a giant *wadi*, which she felt must be the one leading past the city of Jabesh. She made her way down the incline, carefully marking the point of descent in her mind against her return trip, and began to follow the *wadi*.

The nature of the terrain was changing; dry, crumbling ridges yielding to hills of softer contour, thickly carpeted with grass turned brown and brittle by drought.

Then, abruptly, she found herself among the treed slopes for which Gilead is noted. Great oaks dotted the ascents on either side of the *wadi*, dwarfing the terebinth and the sprinkling of pine. She climbed to seek the shade of one of the largest trees, where she ate the bit of grain she had brought with her and drank a few sips of water. After a short rest, she continued on her way.

The sun was beginning to set when she glimpsed the double-humped hill on which Jabesh-Gilead is located. The taller portion contained the fortress, thrusting its battlements grimly into the calm evening sky. On the lower hill, pressed close to the fortress like a bevy of fledgling doves about a mother, nestled the houses of the city.

She paused some distance from the gate and looked around carefully to see if the entrance to the city were being watched. David would surely keep Jabesh under surveillance against the possibility that she and her sons would seek refuge here. No encampment of soldiers was visible outside the walls, but this, of course, meant nothing. If one of David's detachments was in the vicinity, the warriors would have been instructed to keep well out of sight. Perhaps they would be disguised as beggars or hawkers, sitting before the gates and checking those who entered. But night was falling; the approaches to the city were comfortably deserted.

She pulled up the hood of her cloak and walked toward the gate, quickly because of apprehension, but slowly enough not to excite undue suspicion in the mind of any hidden observer.

When she passed the grove of tamarisk trees not far from the entrance, she saw out of the corner of her eye the pile of rocks and the stone tablet resting against it. Her heart leaped and she wanted to turn aside, for she knew that beneath these trees were the graves of Saul and Jonathan. But to tarry, even for a moment, might give her away. She moved steadily ahead, fighting back the tears that sprang to her eyes.

She walked through the gateway, breathing a sigh of relief. A soldier was descending from one of the turrets which dominated either side of the entrance. Rizpah recognized him as one of the men who had served with Huri at Mahanaim. She called out his name. He spun around and gazed at her curiously, then, as she uncovered her face, cried out, "My lady Rizpah!"

Some of the men were looking down from the towers now, but she did not care. She was safe. No one would molest her in the city which had so savagely preserved the memory of Saul.

At her request, the soldier took her to the home of Huri. Their way led through streets redolent of evening cooking. She sniffed the odors of vegetables frying in oil and was gripped by pangs of hunger so violent that they frightened her. The soldier saw her looking into a doorway, where a woman was stirring a pot simmering over a brazier. "We have also felt the effects of the famine," he said, "but not nearly as much as the people across the river." He looked sharply at her. "Your sons . . ."

"They are safe."

"David's proclamation . . . you have heard of it?"

"I have heard of it," she said evenly.

"Huri ordered it publicly burned the day it arrived. He was furious. I have seldom seen him so angry."

"David has sent no soldiers to watch Jabesh?"

"Soldiers?" He raised his eyebrows.

"No matter."

They reached the house of Huri. Her escort banged on the great wooden door with the handle of his sword. He instructed the servant who came to take Rizpah at once to his master.

The leader of Jabesh's warriors was about to eat his evening meal. She saw that he had grayed considerably in the two years since he had left Mahanaim. He looked at Rizpah without surprise as the servant showed her into the room and said, "Why have you not come before?"

He picked up a silver pitcher and himself poured out water so she could wash her face and hands. Then he bade her sit down and was silent while she ate. He maintained his silence until she spoke, telling him what had happened since Mahanaim and finally making her request.

"I will not hear of it," he said when she had finished.

She stared at him, feeling a return of the hopelessness she had known that morning as she sat by the unconscious Meribaal.

"You will bring your sons here," he said. "If Jabesh cannot continue to show its gratitude to Saul . . ."

"My lord Huri, you have shown your gratitude many times over."

"If Saul had not rescued us, I would not be sitting in this house tonight. Our city would be a heap of rubble covering only a memory of the pride of Jabesh."

"So will it be," she said softly, "if you defy the word of David."

He rose and stood above her, his spare figure quivering with anger and reminding her of the denunciatory fury of Samuel. "Is reverence a crippled bird?" he cried. "Is loyalty a caprice that comes and goes like a harlot's smile? Bring the children here. Let David stand ashamed before Jahveh and all the spirits of the desert!"

Her heart was raw with longing to accept his offer, but she said, "My lord Huri has his responsibilities and I have mine. We should each deal falsely with them if we yielded to emotion. Give me only what I ask, and I shall be grateful forever."

He continued to argue, grumbling more against fate than in opposition to her words. Finally he agreed that she was right and ordered a wagon stocked with provisions. Then they began to argue again, for Huri wanted to send an armed escort, to conduct her all the way to Simeon if she wished.

Once more she was firm in her rejection of his generosity. "An escort would do us more harm than good. Anything short of a full army could not protect us from David and would only attract attention. Our escape depends on our remaining as anonymous as possible." And again he bowed to her logic.

At his insistence she did sleep for a few hours, but shortly past midnight climbed onto the wagon, to which was harnessed a pair of mules. Huri rode beside her through the sleeping city. He called a curt order up to the turrets. Two soldiers came down and pushed the gates open.

There was no moon, but after a while she was able to see clearly enough. She drove down into the *wadi* and followed its winding course until she reached the spot where she thought she had entered it. Here she waited until dawn to be sure she was right.

I saw her come over the hill. The wagon with its sturdy mules looked more impressive to me than a golden chariot drawn by a team of blooded stallions. Armoni leaped about excitedly. Meribaal, who was conscious now, though very weak, opened his eyes wide and smiled as his mother stopped the wagon beside the well.

Rizpah opened one of the sacks and took out a loaf of bread and a fresh cheese. She watched us with obvious pleasure as we ate, then mixed some herbs Huri had given her with water and made Meribaal drink the concoction.

He was sipping from a clay vessel, pausing between each swallow in his grave, deliberate fashion, looking past us off toward the western hills.

"Drink it up, my son," Rizpah said. "Then we shall make you comfortable in the wagon and be on our way."

He raised the bowl to his lips, stiffened suddenly and dropped it.

We thought at first he was having another seizure. Then we heard the sound of the horses.

Coming down the slope toward us was a company of about thirty warriors, fully armed. As they drew near, I recognized their leader. It was Abishai, brother of Joab.

The horsemen surrounded us in a graceful, expertly executed maneuver. Abishai dismounted. He was a huge man with great pouches beneath his eyes and the lumbering gait of a tired bear.

"We waited a long time for you to reach Jabesh, my lady."

Rizpah was almost weeping with fear and frustration. "I saw no soldiers," she said. "I saw no one at all."

Abishai shook his head. It was apparent from his expression that he had no taste for this assignment. "Our camp was concealed many cubits away from the gates of the city."

"Then . . ."

"Even in Jabesh," he said with a touch of sadness, "there are those who prize silver above the memory of Saul."

Armoni drew his bronze knife and sprang at Abishai. The soldier scarcely looked at the boy. He side-stepped with surprising ease and struck Armoni's wrist sharply with the edge of his hand. The knife flew through the air, catching fire from the early sun, and clattered against a wheel of the wagon before it fell to the ground. Abishai lumbered over, picked it up and tossed it to one of the horsemen.

"Now let us go," he said gently to us. "We have a great distance to travel."

chapter seven

THE CITY of Gibeon was situated at the top of a steep, rock-strewn hill. In ancient days it had been one of the royal cities of Canaan. Its leaders, before making the truce with Joshua that was in effect shrewd capitulation, had been influential in the administrative network ruling the land. Now, though the people of Gibeon were assimilated by and large into their Hebrew surroundings, the city still displayed some of the garish aspects of pre-Israelite Canaan. The houses were austere, angular and generally primitive, except for the residences of the princely elders, which were even more luxurious than the houses of the richest Israelites. In the center of the market place stood the great gilded likeness of their god, a bull with long, twisted, needle-sharp horns. And in its shadow was the circular altar once used exclusively for human sacrifice, now garlanded with fresh flowers on the occasion of each festival.

The people themselves, having migrated in the deep past from the southern kingdom of Edom, still bore the bold, dark stamp of desert warriors. But as I have remarked earlier, they had grown peaceable to the point of passivity, and their warlike tradition had been sublimated to the interminable, argumentative discussion for which they were famous.

They were lining the streets, waiting, as Abishai and his company of horsemen escorted our wagon through the gates. On some of their faces, we could see the mark of implacable hostility, but the majority simply craned forward, jostling one another to catch a glimpse of the fugitives who had been so long and rigorously sought.

Our journey had been unpleasant and depressing. Several hours after we were captured, as our caravan rolled westward toward the river, Meribaal had again lost consciousness. Abishai, greatly concerned, ordered a canopy constructed for the wagon, which did keep off the direct rays of the sun, but the boy's fever returned and seemed to mount hourly.

Rizpah grew morose and lethargic, sitting with her chin sunk against her chest, scarcely speaking to anyone. And I blamed myself for our predicament, bitterly regretting having urged Rizpah to seek help in Jabesh.

Armoni alone seemed calm and unperturbed by what had happened. He made several efforts to break through Rizpah's gloomy reserve. "We tried, Mother," he said, and when she did not reply, he turned to me. "We did try, Egrep." Then he said nothing for a few moments, looking out at the impassive faces of the soldiers riding on either side of the wagon. Then, thoughtfully, "We can only wait and see." And he fixed his bright, curious attention on the country through which we were passing.

We crossed the Jordan just north of its confluence with the Jabbok, after winding among a series of spectacular gorges cut deep through shaly rock.

We forded at a break in the Ghor, that steep-walled valley which bounds the river channel. Once on the west bank, we began to see the causes and effects of persistent famine. Vineyards lay petrified and leafless under a merciless sun. The poverty of the fields was more harshly emphasized by a few hardy stalks which had somehow survived to rise with pathetic defiance out of the cracked earth.

The villages of Benjamin and southeastern Ephraim stank of neglect and decay. The inhabitants squatted on their haunches in the filth-bedecked streets, glancing up listlessly as we passed. One woman sat immovable in the center of the narrow thoroughfare and remained deaf to the shouts of the soldiers. Abishai ordered her removed, and two of the men picked her up and carried her to the side of the road. She did not once speak, nor did her expression change.

As we neared the border of Judah, we saw some of the most miserable sheep and goats I have ever looked on. Their bones showed through scraggly coats, and their eyes were rimmed with ulcerous sores. But they were guarded as if they were prize animals worthy of sacrifice in the sanctuary. The shepherds carried spears instead of the customary crooked staffs, and glared suspiciously at us as we rode by.

It took us five days to reach Gibeon. I would rather have spent those days in the Land of the Dead.

Our wagon pressed through the crowd of spectators thronging the market place and came to a stop near the statue of the god. The soldier who had been riding with us went to fetch water for the mules. Abishai disappeared, and when he came back, he was accompanied by two Gibeonite women. They looked at Meribaal with critical compassion.

"He will need a bath first," said the one. "A hot bath spiced with Gilead resin."

"Have you gone out of your head?" retorted the other scornfully.

"He must be plunged repeatedly into the coldest spring water we can find."

"Hot water," said the first.

"Cold," insisted the second.

"What do you know about treating illness?"

"Did I not save the life of Arat, son of Musaf?"

"So what did he suffer from? A little swelling on his arm the size of a grape."

"It was the size of a melon."

"All right, it was more like a peach. So what does it make you? A fruit vendor?"

"I saved his life. He says so himself."

"And look at him today. A wastrel, a criminal."

They argued on for some moments. To my horror Rizpah seemed neither to notice the controversy nor to recognize that Meribaal was about to be committed to the care of the two women. In fact, I was not sure she even knew where she was. Only when the soldiers fashioned a crude litter from a cloak and two spears, and lowered Meribaal onto it, did she stir and cry out: a small, childlike moan.

"I shall go with him," I said in a low voice. "I shall see that they take good care of him."

As I started after the little procession, shouldering my way past the gaping Gibeonites, two other soldiers took Armoni by the arms, lifted him from the wagon and marched away with him in another direction. Rizpah got down from the wagon and made as if to follow. Abishai restrained her, carefully but firmly. "You must come with me, my lady."

She went along meekly. They entered one of the palatial residences off the main square. Abishai led her through dim, cool corridors floored with polished cedar, and out into an enclosed courtyard.

A fountain, in disuse now because of the drought, dominated the courtyard. Two fig trees cast lacy shadows on a graveled walk.

Rizpah felt suddenly faint and allowed Abishai to take her to a stone bench. She sat down and put her head in her hands.

When she looked up again, Abishai was gone, and David stood before her.

His face had aged somewhat, but, if anything, there was more warmth and sensitivity than there had been ten years before, in the days when we had all lived at Gibeah. Yet the quality of ruthlessness, so carefully disguised then, was fully revealed now in his eyes and the set of his mouth. It was as though the two warring elements of his nature, having exhausted the battlefield of his soul, had at last emerged into the open, still locked in unresolved conflict.

Rizpah felt once again the strange affinity between them, essentially unchanged even after all these years.

But it was muted, oddly distant. For as they stared silently at each other, she was only conscious of a dull, rising hatred against him.

At length he spoke. "You must be very tired after your journey. I have arranged for you and Egrep to occupy an apartment in this house."

She said, looking away, "I want no favors from you."

He did not speak for so long that she felt her gaze drawn back to his face. In his eyes was a trace of the ironic deference with which he had always treated her. She half expected him to make his little mock bow.

"I can understand your feelings," he said. "But if you wish to remain in Gibeon, you will live where I tell you to live."

"And if I refuse?"

"The lady Rizpah is not a fool," he said sharply. Then his voice softened, took on the smoothness of his court manner. "Though she has always had something of the child in her make-up. I suppose every beautiful woman has."

"I am not interested in your opinion of me."

He shrugged. "As you like. I was about to philosophize on beauty in general. But you are right. Too much of my life has been wasted in empty philosophizing. It muddles the mind and blunts the name of action." He paused, reflecting. A twisted smile crept onto his face. "I did not mean that. If it were not for the ability to see behind the façade of life . . ." The smile broadened, became warm and appealing. "You have always had the power to make me say things I do not mean. It must be the childlike quality of beauty I mentioned before. Beauty is its own truth, a law unto itself. Its tragedy is that it inspires so much falsehood. Men are seldom themselves before a beautiful woman."

She felt her expression growing rigid. "What are you going to do with my children?"

The anguished look he flung in her direction was no pose. "Do not force me to parade pain in words . . ."

"You are going to execute them. Just as you killed Merab's sons."

He looked down at his feet. "Jahveh has ordained it."

Her sarcasm was heavy, brutal. "Has Jahveh given some deep and mysterious reason for commanding the death of two small boys?"

"For Saul's sin against Gibeon," he said miserably. "The wrong-doing of the father is transmitted to the sons."

"Then take me," she said in low, urgent tones. "The guilt for what happened to the Gibeonites is mine." She was breathing quickly now. Her eyes pleaded with him. "I am the one who should die. Take me and spare the children."

He shook his head. "Whatever you have done is between yourself and Jahveh. I cannot disobey the word of the Lord."

Her laughter was sudden, harsh. "The word of the Lord," she said bitterly. "The word of David, who is only a bit of ambitious flesh cast up onto the throne of Israel. Why do you not speak the truth? Why do you dress your fear and your lust for power in pious evasions? You must wipe out every male member of the house of Saul. You, the great monarch, tremble because two small children are still alive."

David sighed. He closed his eyes for a moment, and even through her anger Rizpah perceived something she had not realized before. David was weary, almost to the point of illness. He sighed again. "The lady Rizpah is no stranger to the ways of government. She knows the manner of human frailty, the slender loyalties which secure a kingdom, the clutching greed of those who covet. Will it give you satisfaction if I say aloud what we both already know in our hearts?"

"Then spare them. It is not necessary to kill them. Send them into exile. I will take them away myself. And I give you my solemn word that they will never set foot in any territory of Israel or Judah so long as they live."

"How I wish I could do what you ask."

"Is it so difficult? I have promised . . ."

"Your promise," he said slowly, "may be as sincere as your love for your children. But you are not the only one concerned." He looked away, then back at her. "The word of Jahveh must be obeyed."

She rose from the bench and spat full in his face.

For a moment she thought he would strike her. The veins in his forehead swelled; his eyes gave off fire.

But he said only, "Your apartment will be ready shortly."

He wiped the spittle from his face and walked out of the courtyard.

chapter eight

THOUGH WE never spoke of it then to each other, both Rizpah and I hoped Meribaal would die of his illness.

There was every indication that he would. He had regained consciousness, but his fever raged unabated, weakening him a little more each day. The room in which he lay was next to our apartment, and often I could hear him cry out in delirium.

Rizpah spent most of her time at Meribaal's bedside. She was only allowed to visit Armoni twice each day, morning and evening. He was confined to a room at the far end of the house, under heavy guard. When they took him out for exercise, eight soldiers accompanied him, and the sight of a small boy surrounded by such a show of armed might was indeed ludicrous. Armoni's spirits remained high. He rarely complained, and only once, when Rizpah was detained with Meribaal and did not visit him until half an hour later than her usual time, did he break down and weep.

I believe that Rizpah was more than once on the verge of killing the boys herself, rather than allow them to be executed. On one occasion before her evening visit to Armoni, I surprised her in the act of hiding a dagger beneath her cloak. She said nothing, nor did I make any comment. But before she left the apartment, she took out the knife and threw it angrily to the floor.

I do not think she really could have done it. Not that she lacked the courage or the will. But in spite of David's admission of motive and his refusal to spare the boys, Rizpah could not give up hope of a reprieve.

Nor could I. Of all human feelings, hope is the most tireless spinner of self-deception. In Dan, when I heard of the hanging of Merab's sons, I had believed it at once without question. Now, having seen David again, watching him move in flesh and blood instead of legend, seeing his weariness, his frequent gentleness and warmth, I could not believe that he would issue the final order, that he would one day raise his hand and give the last curt signal to the executioners.

However, the days went by, and there was no sign that his decision would be changed. In all other matters David was kind and considerate. He provided in every possible way for our physical comfort. He was unfailingly courteous to Rizpah, pretending not to notice her flagrant show of dislike. But not once did he speak to her of the boys.

As his pointed silence on the question continued, even the deluding comfort of our hope began to wane. And we began to wish fervently that Meribaal would die.

The two Gibeonite women, despite the unending arguments in which they engaged each other, were skillful and conscientious. They nursed Meribaal with untiring solicitude. They placed warm bricks in his bed, patiently pulled up the bedclothes each time he kicked them off, fed him massive doses of foul-smelling herb teas.

One night, a few hours after the evening meal, Rizpah came running into our apartment. "Come quickly!" she said, and at once turned and left without waiting for me. I followed her hastily, certain that the end had finally arrived for Meribaal.

The room where he lay was heavily curtained, so that scarcely a breath of air could enter. The atmosphere was thick, reeking of herbs, stale bodies and excrement.

Rizpah was already kneeling by the bedside. I looked down. Meribaal's face was covered with perspiration. His eyes were open, truly clear and aware for the first time since the morning in the square at Beth-arbel, over ten days before. And as he had done then, he gazed at Rizpah, smiled weakly and said, "I'm hungry."

I sank down beside Rizpah. We put our arms about each other and began to weep, half in relief, half in terror of what would now happen to the children.

The Gibeonite women paid no attention to us. They fussed about the boy, wiping the sweat from his forehead, plumping up the pillows and rearranging the bedclothes.

"I'll bring him some lentils," one said.

"Lentils!" sneered the other. "Do you want to kill him? Everyone knows the only food for such an illness is pickled leeks."

"I gave lentils to Hareb, son of Joseph, the instant his fever demon fled, and the next morning he was at work in his fields."

"And three years later he was dead. If you had given him pickled leeks, he would be alive and healthy to this day."

In the end they gave Meribaal a bowl of nourishing broth. And they remained with him, tender, efficient and unceasingly argumentative, until his convalescence was assured.

David stayed on in Gibeon, setting up a temporary court in the house adjoining the one in which we were lodging.

Joab came from Hebron, bringing with him an additional detachment of soldiers. The cunning of David's general had become almost mythical in the land; "as wily as Joab" was a common expression. He was known to be absolutely merciless in dealing with any threat to David's position. The treachery at the pool of Gibeon and the murder of Abner were only two among many of his violent, perfidious acts.

I experienced a certain sense of shock at his appearance when he alighted from his chariot and rushed to greet David. As a young man, his features had been coarse, his expression bold. Now, although he was still young, his hair was graying; his face had grown fine, almost delicate. He had the dreamy, withdrawn manner of an aesthete. It was only when he looked directly at you for any length of time that it was possible to catch a glimpse of veiled savagery. Then it was so unmistakable as to make you catch your breath. There was no doubt that he was a dangerous, relentless man. I was not happy to see him arrive in Gibeon.

Summer was almost over; the days of harvest (or what would have been harvest in the absence of drought) were fast approaching. David inquired each day, taking care to do so when Rizpah was not present, as to Meribaal's condition. It was growing increasingly evident that he considered the execution of the children a matter of vital importance, and also that he was delaying the event only until Meribaal was well. My spirit sickened before the calculated horror I was witnessing: a child being nursed back to health so he would be able to sit erect when the hangman placed the noose about his neck.

But about this time something happened to sharpen my awareness of the many facets of the situation, and to force me to view it in a somewhat different perspective.

David had assigned several servants to look after Rizpah's and my needs. Most of them were Gibeonites, but one was from the Benjaminite town of Beth-el. He was a quiet, dyspeptic man named Ahio, who had worked for many years in the house in which we were staying. Other than the most necessary discourse connected with his duties, he had hardly spoken to either Rizpah or me.

So, when he knocked at our door late one evening and, after entering, barred it and tiptoed toward us, we were sure he was drunk. Rizpah picked up a heavy clay jug and brandished it threateningly.

Ahio showed her a fleeting smile. "Do not be afraid, my lady. I bring you a message."

"From whom?"

"That, unfortunately, I cannot say." He came close to Rizpah and whispered, "The person who has sent me wishes to meet you in an hour's time, at the pool before Gibeon."

"Why?"

"This also I am not at liberty to reveal. But my lady must have faith in me. The matter has a direct bearing on the fate of her children."

Rizpah looked at me. I could give her no help. She said suspiciously, "The city gates are locked at this hour. How will I be able to go to the meeting place?"

Ahio smiled again. "Will my lady come?"

She hesitated only an instant, then snatched up a cloak and started for the door. Ahio intercepted her, said respectfully, "I must warn my lady. Absolute silence is essential. I know the way we must travel very well, and there should be no difficulty, but . . ."

She shrugged impatiently, cutting him off. The instant Ahio unbarred the door, his servant's manner disappeared. He moved quickly, decisively, looking out into the corridor, motioning to Rizpah with a brusque gesture.

They met no one in the halls of the house. Ahio walked ahead once they were outside, leading her stealthily around the perimeter of the deserted market place. The bull-god was silhouetted against the night sky, silent and menacing, crouching above the stone altar.

Ahio vanished into an alleyway; Rizpah darted after him. The passage ended abruptly against a section of the city wall. Rizpah felt a return of apprehension which persisted until she noticed a tiny door, almost invisible in the shadows. Ahio unbolted it, opened it cautiously, beckoned her to pass through.

They came out on the other side of the city from the main gate. The slope before them led precipitously down to the plain.

Ahio's foot dislodged a stone, which went rolling noisily down the hill. He drew her back against the wall, and they waited.

She saw his face contort in an agonized expression. Alarmed, she stretched out her hand to him. He shook his head violently, all the while screwing up his face most excruciatingly. And suddenly a deep, resounding belch came from his lips, startling her so that she jumped away from him.

"My stomach," he gasped. "Always when there is danger . . ."

He belched again, shaking his head disgustedly.

They waited awhile longer. Neither Ahio's clumsiness with the stone nor his gastric disturbance seemed to have attracted any attention, though Rizpah was sure the latter had been loud enough to rouse the city.

A half hour's walk brought them to the pool. Ahio asked her to remain beneath one of the oak trees near the edge while he went in search of the man she was to meet.

Steely light glinted off the surface of the water. She stood looking out across it, thinking: here my lord Abner was deceived by Joab; here the bitterness of blood cries out from the earth.

A figure approached the tree under which she was standing. She looked curiously at the man's face.

"Do you not recognize me?"

She peered more closely at him. He was heavily built, almost portly. There was a ponderous solemnity about his speech. She was sure she knew him, but she could not remember from where.

"Barzillai. I am the husband of Merab."

"Of course." She had only seen him two or three times, lastly on the occasion of Michal's marriage to David.

"I shall be brief. It is not wise for you to be gone too long from the city." He took a deep breath. "Your sons are under sentence of death, just as mine were. My sons are dead. My five sons are dead."

He sobbed. His thick body shuddered. And over his face came an expression of such naked, unbridled hatred that Rizpah moved involuntarily away from him. He hurriedly closed the gap between them. "I am sorry," he said. "Perhaps you do not know what it means to feel as I do." He clenched his fists and held them up at the sky. "I hate him with the blood of my body and the fiber of my soul. I hate . . ." He broke off. "I must be brief. I must remember . . ." Again he paused. "Are you willing to help us rescue your sons?"

She looked at him questioningly. "Us?"

"Are you?"

"I would have to know more . . ."

He was furious. "Are you a woman? Are you a mother?" A spray of spittle shot from his lips. "Can you be timid at a time like this? I am offering you the life of your children."

She drew herself up. "Tell me how."

"Listen." Barzillai leaned close. "Israel is restless. The famine will soon turn the discontent of the people white-hot. They hate the shepherd of Judah. They remember with longing the reign of Saul. If they could place one of the king's sons on the throne . . . I have heard that Armoni is the image of his father . . . Listen . . ."

He had a plan. Already, he said, there were hundreds in Israel who would rise against the rule of David. Soon there would be thousands, all prepared to rally to a son of Saul. True, Armoni was now only eleven years old, but a regency could rule until he was of age. With Rizpah's help, the boys could be rescued and kept safe until Israel gathered strength. The men of Jabesh-Gilead would protect her sons and train the young army in a desert retreat already selected.

Barzillai talked on, his manner still ponderous but growing more excited as he outlined the plan. He finished up by saying, "You will do it then?"

He was silent, waiting. The hatred glittered in his eyes. When she did not reply at once, he said, "If my sons were alive . . ."

She turned and walked to the edge of the water. To have her sons alive, to know that the bright vitality of Armoni, the slow gentleness of Meribaal would not perish . . .

She came haltingly back to Barzillai. He grasped her wrists and repeated, "You will do it then?"

"I must have time to think."

"Time? There is no time. Do you hate your children? Do you *want* to see them hanging from the same tree where they hanged my sons? Do you want to hear them strangle and see their faces turn blue?"

She broke away from him with a muffled cry.

"Listen," he said, his eyes gleaming with the satisfaction of having at last cracked her apparent calm. "Listen. Your sons are the last who can rule. Do you know about Jonathan's son?"

Rizpah shook her head. She had heard nothing about the child of Jonathan, except that the girl Achsah had given birth to a son.

"David is sparing his life."

She stared at Barzillai, confused.

"Do you not understand?" he said impatiently. "The boy is lame. Crippled. Unable to drag himself a hundred steps without sitting down to rest. He can never rule, and David knows it." He glared at her. "My sons are dead. Your son Armoni must be king. We must save him from David's hangman." He put his face close to hers. "We will!"

The acrid odor of his perspiration assailed her nostrils. He was waiting, quivering with anxiety.

"Let me think about it," she said in a broken voice.

He blew out his breath angrily. Phlegm rattled in his throat. "If only we did not need your help . . ." He made an impatient, furious gesture. "I cannot meet you tomorrow. Two nights from now. Here. You will think about it and tell me yes. You can only say yes."

He gave a low whistle. Ahio came running toward them. Barzillai said, "On the next Sabbath your sons will be free," and was gone.

Ahio guided Rizpah back to the city and into the house without mishap. I was waiting up for her, and we talked for the rest of the night.

We spoke of what it would mean to stir up war in the land, and there was a weary hopelessness in her voice. But it was impossible for her to turn away from the thought of saving her sons.

She could have spared herself the pain of dilemma.

In the morning Barzillai was found stabbed to death near the main gate of Gibeon. Ahio was discovered, his neck broken, lying on the altar in the market place.

That afternoon David inquired again after Meribaal. The Gibeonite women informed the king that the boy was still weak but improving rapidly.

An hour later David set the date for the execution. Rizpah's sons would be hanged the day before the next Sabbath.

chapter nine

MOST OF the inhabitants of Gibeon turned out for the occasion. The procession leaving the city stretched over several hundred cubits.

At the head of the column rode David and the Gibeonite elders, all dressed in the black robes of mourning.

Following them came the executioners, two sober-faced men of Gibeon, wearing gray cloaks and riding the dapple-gray horses which would be used in the hanging.

The cart bearing the two boys, Rizpah and me was heavily guarded. Joab's full complement of warriors patrolled both sides of the procession. Tension crackled in the air. The officers glanced anxiously and often toward the hills on either side of the trail. Two shepherds urging a flock of scrawny sheep across the line of march were unceremoniously routed, prodded with the butts of spears when they did not move quickly enough to suit the soldiers.

Rizpah had eaten little and slept only briefly in the five days since the time for the execution was set. Her skin was sickly yellow under the tan she had acquired during our desert flight.

When she had announced her intention of accompanying the boys, I had tried to dissuade her. She had not argued with me. I do not think she heard more than a few words of my lengthy and vigorous reasoning.

If I had had children, and this thing were happening to them, I knew full well where I would be. But my concern now was for her. She was a strong woman, physically and mentally, but I wondered if, having already endured so much, she would be capable of standing up to this.

David had given his consent for us to ride with the children. Now that we were under way, she sat between them, holding on to them firmly but not frantically. Meribaal, fortunately, did not quite seem to understand what was happening. He nuzzled his mother, smiled at one of the soldiers riding close by, then lost himself in contemplation of some scars on the worn wooden side of the cart. Armoni was all too well aware that he was being taken to his death. When we passed through the gates of the city, he had begun to weep copiously. Rizpah had held him close, but did not then speak to him, and after a while he had stopped, dried his tears, and stared straight ahead at the backs of the executioners. Now he was pale but composed.

Because most of the people of Gibeon were traveling on foot, and David and the elders adjusted their pace accordingly, we were over two hours reaching the place where the sons of Barzillai and Merab had been hanged earlier in the summer.

It was a desolate spot, but one long considered holy ground by the Gibeonites. An outcropping of rock resembling a huge table rose from an otherwise flat extent of plain. One end of the rock formation curved inward to create a kind of natural amphitheater. Roughly in the center of the indentation stood several trees, one of them a lightning-blasted oak, leafless but still sturdily rooted. The lowest branches were high enough off the ground to permit the easy underpassage of a man sitting upright on the back of a horse.

The sun's rays slammed down against the procession with the weight and ferocity of giant hammer blows. Dust rose round us in a filthy, enveloping cloud. By the time we arrived at our destination the black robes of David and the elders were almost as gray as those of the executioners.

Armoni began to cough. Some of the dust had gotten into his throat, and he doubled over in a sudden paroxysm of choking. He was unable to stop. Fear swept into his eyes, dominated his features. His face turned red, then blue. Rizpah put her arms around him and held him. "There, darling," she murmured.

He subsided, gasping for breath. "I will not cry, Mother," he whispered fiercely.

Meribaal looked up. His customary clear, wondering gaze was gone. In its place was an expression of calm, tragic knowledge. He said in a sad, unbelieving voice, "We are going to die, aren't we, Mother?"

I gripped the side of the cart so hard that my fingers lost feeling.

But Rizpah said to the boy, her steady tone betraying no emotion, "You must be brave, darling. I know you will."

Her face looked as if it had been fashioned from the rock which surrounded us. I cursed myself for having allowed her to come. I should have done anything to prevent her being here, given her a sleeping draught in her food, asked help from David's soldiers in locking her up, anything. But I knew she would never have forgiven me. And again I was forced to admit that she was right.

I began to weep. I could not help it. The tears poured from my eyes, rolled down my cheeks and dripped off the end of my chin. I had no strength to raise my hand and wipe them away. Rizpah did this for me. "Old woman, old woman," she whispered in my ear. Her face was still frozen in its expressionless mold, but her voice held the sorrow of the world. I took courage and comfort from her.

Through my own tears I could see Abishai, sitting on his horse at the head of his troop, crying unashamedly.

The band of spectators was silent. They had crowded into positions around the amphitheater and were watching wide-eyed as David conferred quietly with the elders of Gibeon.

Suddenly a woman sneezed, and as she struggled to suppress a second one, a ragged undertone of laughter started among the people and spread nervously, exploding in a great mirthful roar as the woman finally succumbed and sneezed again. Then once more there was silence: fearful, deadly, ashamed.

The chief elder of Gibeon stepped forward and spoke. "The sin against Gibeon is about to be expiated in full. The terrible drought which has so long plagued our land and caused both the people of Israel and Gibeon to suffer has been created by the evil Saul committed against us." He had a dismal droning voice, coupled with a speech defect. His pronunciation of both r's and l's as w's only intensified the horror of what he said next. "Because of the nature of the crime against Gibeon, it is hereby decreed that the bodies of the deceased will hang on the branches of this tree until the first rains fall, which will signify that the Lord of Israel again looks with favor on this land. Whosoever troubles or tampers with these bodies will do so on pain of his own death. On the day of the first rain, the bodies will be taken down and given proper burial."

Anger gripped me, so violent that I could not control my trembling. I wanted to shriek at him: you foul piece of excrement, you could at least have waited until the children were dead. But neither of the boys gave any sign that they had heard. I do not believe they had.

The executioners dismounted from their horses and removed the saddles. While they uncoiled ropes and flung them over the branches of the blasted oak, four soldiers came to fetch Armoni and Meribaal. Rizpah kissed each child lightly, almost casually, and patted them on the head, as though she were bidding them good night of an ordinary evening. After the soldiers had taken them away, I happened to look at her hands. The palms were red with blood where her nails had dug into them. But her eyes were dry, her mouth firm.

The soldiers lifted the boys onto the backs of the horses and guided the animals into position under the tree, where the executioners bound the hands of the children and placed the ropes around their necks. Both boys sat straight and proud, looking neither right nor left.

The men in gray cloaks looked questioningly toward David. He moved his hand in an almost imperceptible signal.

Suddenly Meribaal called out in a terrible, bereft voice, "Mother . . ." A woman sobbed loudly at the same time as the executioners, with co-ordinated motion, slapped the rumps of the horses. There was a flurry of hoofbeats as the frightened animals galloped away across the plain toward the distant blue hills, pursued by two of Joab's warriors.

A long sigh swept through the crowd. The sound was like a huge wave grating over the sands of some dark and lonely shore.

It was over.

Almost at once, the people began to depart, turning their faces toward Gibeon. Few looked back.

Rizpah climbed out of the wagon and started toward the tree. I scrambled after her, frantic to overtake her before she reached it. She turned just as I caught up with her. "I will stay, old woman," she said, in a voice so lifeless that I recoiled from it. "I will stay until the rains fall."

"Then I will also stay."

She shook her head. "This I must do alone. It is between Jahveh and my sons and me."

I knew there was nothing I could say to make her change her mind. I embraced her, but it was like touching an image in a temple grove. "I will bring you food," I said, but she did not hear me. I started back toward the cart.

When I had climbed into it, I looked back at Rizpah. She was standing beside the tree, her head bowed.

David rode slowly past her. His face was ashen, rigid with pain. He stopped, staring at Rizpah. Then abruptly, he moved on.

The horse's hoofs made soft thunder against the dry ground.

chapter ten

THE VULTURES did not come that first day, but the ravens did.

When I returned, I could see them even from a distance, hundreds of them, hovering above the blasted tree, screaming and flapping their wings.

I whipped up the mule. As I came closer, I saw Rizpah beating at them with a stick, occasionally bending down to pick up a stone and fling it into the thickest clot of birds.

Along with food and water and sackcloth I had brought a sword. I leaped from the wagon and rushed to Rizpah's aid. The sky seemed black with wheeling, excited birds. I took up a station next to Armoni's body, while Rizpah protected Meribaal. I killed three ravens in quick succession, kicking their carcasses as far away as I could. The others descended on them, squabbling for possession of the carrion, and after that they were more cautious in approaching the bodies of the children. Still, they remained close by, perching just out of reach among the branches of the tree, rising at intervals to blot out the sun with their beating wings.

I had a sickening remembrance of an evening long before in Askelon, when Rizpah had asked me to tell her of the future and I had suddenly envisioned something very like the scene in which we were now participants. The memory frightened me, as much by its implication as by its actually having come to pass. Is our fate then so completely in the hands of the gods that everything is preordained, leaving nothing to choice, prevention or change? If this is true, man is less fortunate than other animals, for they live life as it comes, untormented by some vain delusion that they control their destiny. I could not believe this, and I would not.

A raven descended recklessly, greedy mouth wide, light imparting a purple sheen to his black plumage. I swung viciously with the sword, only managing to graze his wing tip with the blade, dislodging a few feathers which drifted down to my feet. But with this last attempt, the birds departed, their hoarse squalling cries receding gradually in the distance.

Then I saw that dusk was beginning to settle around us. I spread the sackcloth on the rock for Rizpah, set down the vessels of food and water and built a small shelter of stones about them.

Rizpah came and touched my shoulder. Her hair was disheveled from fighting the birds and there was a large smudge of dirt on her forehead. "Thank you, old woman," she said, "but I must ask you to leave now."

"There may be no rain for a month," I said. "Please. Do not set yourself . . ."

I stopped, for she was already shaking her head. I handed her the sword. She accepted it listlessly, dropping it onto the sackcloth. She turned to look toward the bodies of her children. Darkness was closing in about them. I felt that I might weep again, but Rizpah seemed completely unmoved. There was a peculiar glaze to her eyes that disturbed me. I wondered how long her soul could retain the armor it had donned the moment her children were killed. Her spirit, never whole and free after the murder of Abner, was a forlorn and shriveled thing now, expiring somewhere deep inside her. But until it was finally able to die, it would never be born again. We cry out against the death of the spirit, but often it is more blessing than tragedy.

There was no point in trying to force my presence on Rizpah. She needed me, but she had asked me to leave, and I could only respect her wish. "I shall bring more food and water tomorrow," I said.

She patted my shoulder. It was an absent gesture, the kind one bestows on a favorite dog or horse, only with less feeling. But there had also been hopelessness in her touch, and any slight I might have felt turned sad long before it worked its way to the surface. I walked reluctantly toward the cart. She did not accompany me. When I looked back through the twilight, she was gathering stones, slowly picking them off the ground and piling them in a heap.

The next afternoon, as I was leaving the house preparatory to visiting Rizpah, I was intercepted by David. I thought he was going to tell me I must move out of the quarters Rizpah and I had been sharing. I was quite ready to do so.

That morning, Abishai had approached me diffidently and told me that when it became necessary, he could arrange accommodations for me with one of the less affluent Gibeonites, providing I would not mind working for my keep. I had looked gratefully at him. He kept shifting his great weight from one foot to the other, gazing at me out of his heavy, pouched eyes. I had the feeling that he would never recover from the effects of the role he had played in the apprehension and slaying of Saul's sons. I thanked him and he lumbered off, calling over his shoulder, "Whenever you wish . . ."

So I was sure that David's reason for coming to me had to do with this. Therefore, I was mildly surprised when he said, "You are planning to take food and water to Rizpah again." I nodded, waiting.

"Would you allow me to go in your place?"

His voice faltered over the words. I was more than ever conscious of the immense burden of weariness the man seemed to be carrying.

"I do not think she will be particularly anxious to see you." My tone was sharper than I had meant it to be. I saw him wince, but I was unable to soften my manner. "You may go if you wish. The king can go where he likes."

"That is not the point," he replied with a faint, enigmatic smile.

"Then you have my permission."

He stood looking at me, and I was at once ashamed of the heavy irony I had injected into my speech. I walked with him to the wagon and handed him the vessels of food and water I had intended to take. He called to a servant and ordered his horse saddled. I was touched somehow that he had not taken it for granted that I would agree to his going instead of me. But I could not help wondering why he wanted to go at all. Guilt, probably. However, this seemed too simple. And with David, nothing was ever simple.

The shadow of the rock table was reaching toward the tree when he arrived. A few birds, both ravens and vultures, were sitting on the highest branches. Rizpah stood before the two bodies, her cudgel held ready, looking grimly up at the birds.

She did not seem to hear his approach. He perceived one reason for this when he came closer to her. She was swaying with exhaustion, scarcely able to stand. David did not speak to her at first. He dismounted and set the provisions he had brought down on the sackcloth.

She turned slowly around to face him. Her eyes were wide and staring, her hair caked with grime and bird dirt.

"You have come to make me go away."

Her voice held a strained quality, as though it were rusty with disuse. David shook his head.

She moistened her lips gingerly, as if the lightest touch of her tongue against them gave her pain. "It would do no good. You cannot force me to leave."

He said, "If you would sleep for a time, I will stand guard."

She laughed, a sharp bitter sound resembling the cries of the birds she had been warding off. "You!" Again the harsh laughter.

He looked at her steadily, calmly. "If you do not sleep now, you will collapse after I leave. Then the animals will come . . ."

She nodded slowly, mumbling to herself as she shuffled over to the sackcloth. Then she wheeled about and snapped, "You will call me in an hour."

"In an hour," he repeated evenly.

She literally threw herself down on the rock and was immediately asleep.

The evening deepened while he stood guard, and out of the plain came the jackals, four of them, growling and circling, laughing hideously, converging on the tree. They remained just outside the amphitheater, snuffing loudly, seeming to consider the nature of the prey. When they began to close in, shambling, sidling toward the bodies, David drew his sword and advanced to meet them. They held their ground until he was almost upon them, then retreated, whimpering, to a spot about a hundred cubits from the tree. Here they sat, slavering, eyes fixed on the tree. Their stench was overpowering, all but obliterating the other sweetish, more subtle odor.

David had the good sense to do as Rizpah had asked. He only allowed her to sleep for an hour. He had built a fire by this time, and when he touched her shoulder, she was instantly awake and alert. She leaped to her feet and started for the tree.

"They are safe," David called, and she retraced her steps, coming back to him warily, as if half poised for flight. He picked up the bowl of dried corn he had brought and held it out to her. "Eat," he said, and when she hesitated, he repeated in a gruff, commanding tone, "Eat!"

She snatched the vessel from his hands and began to cram food into her mouth, her eyes never leaving his face. She ate all the corn and drank greedily from the jar of water.

David stood up. "Keep the fire going," he said. "I have found enough wood to last the night, but there is not a great deal more here. Tomorrow I shall bring a wagonload from the city."

He walked to where he had ground-tethered his horse. She stared after him, only turning her head when one of the jackals laughed evilly out of the darkness pressing in about the fire.

The next evening David brought the wood and also his lyre. After he had let Rizpah sleep, for about three hours this time, he woke her and again made her eat. Then he took the lyre from its wrapping of padded linen and began to play. He did not speak, except to say once, "How long it has been since I have drawn music from the night," and then it was mostly as if he were talking to himself.

After a time he stopped playing and they sat in silence.

The music had soothed Rizpah, helped to still some of her brutal, half-crazed frenzy. But in its place rose a cruel, detached lucidity. She was brightly, alarmingly aware of everything that was happening to her.

She said to David, "Why are you here?"

He shrugged and struck a chord on the lyre.

She flared at him suddenly, "Do you think you can erase your guilt this way?"

David said, "Guilt does not fly away so easily. I am an expert in such matters. This is not the reason I have come."

Her eyes narrowed. She leaned forward, peering suspiciously into his face. Just then, two of the jackals sidled into sight, snuffing and unusually bold.

He started to rise, but she said quietly, "I will deal with them. We understand each other now."

She walked slowly toward the animals, hands at her sides, then stopped and stood absolutely still. The jackals watched her, ears moving back and forth, nostrils quivering. Suddenly they turned and ran, yelping, into the night.

David did not leave until nearly dawn. When he returned the following evening, she had heard the sound of his horse and appeared to be waiting for him, frowning thoughtfully as he dismounted and came toward her.

It had been another day of unrelieved heat. The far-off hills were still throbbing with it. David regarded Rizpah, his gaze taking in her robe, torn now in several places, her grime-caked hair, her lips dry and cracked from unceasing exposure to sun and wind. He glanced toward the bare oak. "It is enough," he said. "I shall order the bodies of your children taken down and buried."

She looked at him for an instant without speaking, then sneered, "Will you defy the word of the Lord now?"

His mouth tightened. He did not reply, only motioned her to sleep. Toward the middle of the night, he wakened her and, as usual, made her eat. He heaped wood on the fire until it was burning brightly, then went to his horse. It seemed to Rizpah that she could hear the savage tattoo of hoofbeats long after he had departed. She did not expect to see him again.

The truth of the matter is that he almost did not make the trip the next day. He came to me and told me it would be better if I took Rizpah's food to her myself. I agreed at once, but as I started to walk away, David called me back. "I am sorry to have troubled you," he said. "I will go to her as usual."

From then on, he went each night. She would receive him without speaking, often not even looking at him. Sometimes she would be crouched near the tree, features twisted into a snarl, her eyes pools of madness. At other times she would move about, trancelike, completely ignoring him. However, she would sleep while David stood guard. Then she would eat, after which he would leave. It was a strange relationship, in which guilt and accusation flowed back and forth in the silence, like ebbing and flooding tides between two distant shores.

On the sixteenth afternoon of Rizpah's vigil, as David approached the rock, he saw the flock of birds wheeling and diving about the tree. During the past few days there had been very few of them. Now, for some reason, they had returned in force and were attacking not only the corpses but Rizpah as well.

She was fending them off ably enough, but it was obvious that she could not have lasted much longer. Her knees were sagging, and she could barely lift the cudgel to strike at the voracious creatures shrilling about her.

David galloped his horse up to the tree and without dismounting began to batter at the birds with his sword. They flew out of range at once, loosed a final vituperative chorus and soared away in the direction of the hills.

He caught Rizpah just as she fell and carried her to the rock, covering her with the sackcloth. He would have allowed her to sleep the entire night, but after only a few hours she started awake and ran to the tree. David went to her, led her back to the fire.

"I've brought some soup," he said. He took the pot from the fire and poured some in a bowl.

She drank it slowly, watching David all the while. When she had finished, she set the bowl on the ground and said to him in the voice of a child, "Why can I not hate you? I have tried, but I cannot."

They were the first words she had spoken to him for over a week. He smiled, but did not answer immediately. When he spoke, his tone was measured and reflective. "Once I thought I hated a man. The hatred was a long time consuming me, for my spirit had been filled with love for him. Only after he had tried to kill me, first by sending me on a dangerous mission, then by casting his spear at me, did my anger begin to brew . . . slowly but surely corroding, tarnishing the brightness of my love.

"He sought my life. He pursued me and sent me scrambling for mountain fastnesses. And on the nights when I lay shivering in some cave or crouching among the reeds of a swamp, my anger gathered itself together and in time became hatred."

David paused, and Rizpah remembered the long dreary days and nights of pursuit, when she and Saul had peered at the world out of the locked twin chambers of their obsession, when the sight of David's blood would have been the sole assuagement of their madness.

"I hated him then," David continued. "And I would think: if only the Lord would deliver him into my hands, I would kill him. Slowly, watching his life drain away before my eyes. And then the Lord answered my evil prayer. I had the man in my power." He laughed unpleasantly. "But I had forgotten about love. In all the days and nights of my hatred I had not reckoned with the sight of a dear face that close to mine. All my bitterness vanished, and I touched the hair of his head while my heart sang sadly: Saul my father. And the hatred still struggled within me and goaded me on. Kill him, it said, kill him now, or forever regret it. But I could not raise my hand against him. And my heart sang again: Saul my father . . ."

Rizpah stirred and said, "I saw you that night."

He was startled.

"I was kneeling beside the sentry you and Abishai had wounded. I saw you standing with Saul's spear and water cruse."

"And you did not cry out."

"I could not."

"Out of fear?"

She opened her mouth to answer, then clamped her lips shut. After a few moments she said stiffly, "I could not give the alarm."

She grew uncomfortable under his gaze.

Far out on the plain a jackal laughed. Another, closer, answered him.

David sighed. "I do not know if I could have fought against Saul at Gilboa. To this day I do not know. Achish of Gath trusted me, but the other Philistine nobles did not, and they sent me away from the battlefield. Achish had given me sanctuary. I felt he had saved my life. Yet it was with Saul, who for so long had sought to kill me, that my spirit lived that day. And Jonathan . . ." A shadow of pain grew in his eyes. "Death . . . we deal in death in order to live. When the tidings came . . ."

He shook his head slowly, then got up and went to the horse. It whinnied softly and he patted it, then took the lyre off the saddle. He detoured on his return trip to the fire, circling around to pass the bodies of the children, pausing to scan the rim of darkness. Then he sat down across from Rizpah.

He plucked the strings of the lyre, calling forth random chords, only gradually shaping them into one of the shepherd melodies Saul had loved. "Three days and nights I locked myself away after the tidings came," he said. "I had always prided myself on my facility for composition. If a song was wanted singing the praises of green fields or a warrior prince, I could combine words and melody while my brain was half busy with other matters. It is, after all, only a question of formula . . . building on what has already been played and sung. This time it was different. The words were in my heart, the melody in my soul, but neither would come out. Grief stood in the way. Do you know how long it was before I could make my own memorial to those I loved?"

Rizpah looked at him steadily, her head tilted to one side, saying nothing.

"The night Michal returned to me, and I learned that Abner had been slain. I wept then, and in the morning the song was with me."

He ran his fingers across the strings. The melody was plaintive, haunting and beautifully simple. And then David sang:

> *The beauty of Israel is slain*
> *Upon the high places.*
> *How are the mighty fallen.*
>
> *Tell it not in Gath,*
> *Publish it not in the streets of Askelon;*
> *Lest the daughters of the Philistines rejoice,*
> *Lest the daughters of the uncircumcised triumph.*
>
> *Ye mountains of Gilboa,*
> *Let there be no dew or rain on you,*
> *Nor fields of lovely fruits;*
> *For there the shield of the mighty*
> *Was vilely cast away,*
> *The shield of Saul,*
> *As though he had not been anointed.*
>
> *From the blood of the slain,*
> *From the flesh of the mighty*
> *The bow of Jonathan turned not back,*
> *And the sword of Saul returned not empty.*
> *Saul and Jonathan, how lovely*
> *And pleasant they were in their lives.*
> *In their death they were not divided.*
> *They were swifter than eagles,*
> *Stronger than lions.*

Ye daughters of Israel,
Weep over Saul,
Who clothed you in scarlet,
And gave you other delights,
Who decked your apparel
With ornaments of gold.
How are the mighty fallen
In the midst of the battle.

There were tears in David's eyes. Rizpah watched him wonderingly. His face held grief, but from it also shone a love such as she had never beheld, a sweetness which banished all trace of care and guile and ruthlessness.

O Jonathan, thou wast slain
Upon the high places.
I am distressed for thee,
My brother Jonathan.
Very pleasant hast thou been to me,
Thy love was wonderful to me,
Passing the love of women.
How are the mighty fallen,
And the weapons of war perished.

The notes of the lyre died away. Again the jackal called and received a reply. Their voices were close and seemed to contain a strange undertone, expressing fear more than hunger. David rose and heaped wood on the fire.

He said musingly, "How strange the communion between life and death and love. It took the return of Michal and the death of Abner to release my grief for Saul and Jonathan. Abner, who I knew had loved Saul with his life. And Michal, whom I thought I had loved and learned I did not."

The mood which had possessed him while he had sung the lament was gone. His mouth was set, giving him the worldly, weary expression Rizpah had noted when she met him in the quiet courtyard in Gibeon.

"How anxiously I waited for her. And when I knew that she was coming to Hebron, that she had preserved her love during all the years of separation, I was beside myself with joy. I pitied Paltiel. We sing of love as generous and open, but it is really niggardly and jealous, and from all its riches it can only spare the falsest of emotions, pity.

"Then when she arrived and I saw her, my heart expanded and filled with warmth, for she was even more beautiful than I had remembered."

A jackal laughed. David smiled sardonically.

"We had not been together an hour before my heart, so warm before, grew small and cold. I perceived that she was indeed the girl I had taken for my bride. She had not changed in word, gesture or spirit. All the little expressions and mannerisms that had once enchanted me were still there. But through her I saw how much I had changed. Grown perhaps, tempered in enthusiasm, broadened in understanding. Or perhaps merely turned cynical and weary. Who knows the truth about things like this? I held in my arms the body of a mature woman housing the spirit of a provincial girl. Now I know how unwise it was of me to expect more. And so I have hurt her. She could never return to Paltiel, and I cannot give her the love which should be hers."

He was silent then. In the stillness Rizpah felt her anger rising against him. And because she could not understand its meaning, it frightened her, and the fear in turn further fed the flames of anger.

"Go!" she said. "Leave here at once!"

David looked at her in astonishment.

She jumped to her feet, ran to the rock and seized the sword which lay there. "Go!" she screamed.

He started to protest, then shrugged and walked to his horse.

When he had gone, she sank to the ground. It was the first time feeling had stirred in her since the death of the children, and it sapped her strength. In another moment she would have wept. Instead she fell asleep.

What wakened her she was never sure. Perhaps it was the hysterical laughter of the jackal, so close that its voice seemed to be shrilling in her ear. The fire had burned down to embers. She snatched up the sword and rose from the ground, rushed toward the tree.

She thought the yellowish form moving out of the shadows was an exceptionally large jackal, or perhaps a hyena. Then, before she even noticed the mane, she saw the twitching of the tail with its ridiculous tuft of hair.

The lion moved to the foot of the oak tree.

A chorus of laughter dinned in from the outer darkness, nervous, respectful. The lion padded forward, looked up toward the branches and sniffed.

Rizpah screamed and sprang at the beast, swinging the sword wildly. She felt it bite into flesh, heard the roar and smelled the fetid breath, all in what seemed a single instant.

Pain streaked out of the night, burst into myriad flashes of light, exploded.

chapter eleven

THE FIRST thing she knew upon reviving was that it was morning. Barely morning. Dawn.

Then she was aware that she was sitting up, supported by a pair of knees against her arm. Her robe was in shreds from shoulders to waist.

David was carefully removing the tattered garment from her body. The cloth stuck to her skin. The pain was almost unbearable, on her back, her left arm. She looked at the arm. There were three gashes in the soft under part, just below the elbow.

"It could have been worse," said David laconically. "You must have wounded him so badly that he lost anger in the face of fear. There's a trail of blood . . ." He began to pull the last bits of cloth from her back. She cried out, and he grasped her right hand and squeezed it hard. She held on grimly. "I had almost arrived back in Gibeon," he said, "and I felt I had to know why . . ."

Pain made her faint before she heard the rest of the sentence. When she came to again, he was plastering a mud poultice over her wounds. Then he took off his cloak and wrapped it around her. "That will do for now. We shall get healing oil and bandages when we arrive in Gibeon."

She said, "I am not going to Gibeon. I am staying here."

"You are stubborn," he said exasperatedly. "Stubborn and a fool."

"I am staying until the rains come."

"I could take you away by force."

"But you will not."

He looked at her for a long time.

"No," he said, "I will not."

chapter twelve

ALTHOUGH SHE refused to leave the bodies of her children, the nature of Rizpah's vigil underwent a decided change.

For one thing, she could no longer be alone. By agreement, David stood guard by night, and I stayed with her now during the day.

Most of the danger from carrion seekers was past. Sun and dry air had done their terrible, merciful work, and while the burden of the oak was as fearsome as ever—perhaps more so—the poor relics were not nearly so likely to be molested now.

As soon as I arrived, I set about shrouding the bodies in sackcloth. It was hardly a pleasant task, but one I considered necessary. Rizpah made a feeble effort at protest, then watched me apathetically.

Her wounds were painful, but not too severe. The lion's claws had lacerated more extensively than deeply, and a great deal of the discomfort had eased by the second day after the attack.

"There were scars on your back," David said musingly to her one night. "Old scars."

She had told him then of her attempt, years before, to help the Israelite prisoner escape from the Philistine camp. And this led to her speaking of Torash, and of the sojourn in Askelon, and of her life before in Simeon.

They talked late that night. David spoke to her of his early life as a shepherd and of the day of Samuel's visit to his father's house, and also of the time of flight, the moment when he had decided to seek refuge from Saul in Philistia.

She was more than a little disturbed to realize how close they had drawn to each other. On her part, it was a feeling she did not understand completely, but she could not deny its existence.

And to increase her sense of uneasiness, he was asking, "The night the lion came . . . just before, when you sent me away with such fury. Do you know why?"

He waited, and when she did not reply he said, "There was something . . . even my first day in the camp of Israel, when you entered the tent where I was playing for Saul. And there were other times. The night by the river in the Valley of Elah, when we spoke of Saul and the kingdom . . ."

She said, suddenly angry, "I do not want to remember anything about that."

"Rizpah," David said with a faint smile, "I believe I understand the depth of your love, and its purity. You have no need to defend it."

A chill wind blew across the plain and troubled the fire.

"It will soon be dawn," he said. "You must sleep now."

When I came in the morning and David returned to Gibeon for the day, Rizpah said, "I dreamed last night that it rained."

I looked out across the shimmering flatland to the parched hills. "I hope your dream comes true."

And indeed, shortly after noon, clouds grew on the horizon and began passing overhead: great gray monsters, heavy with moisture, coiling and uncoiling like angry serpents.

But not a drop of rain fell.

chapter thirteen

TWILIGHT CAME early. The wind blew fiercely, whipping up curtains of dust, obscuring our view of the hills. "Surely it will rain tomorrow," I said.

David rode into the somber amphitheater. "Surely it will rain tomorrow," he said as he got down off the horse.

I climbed into the wagon, waved to Rizpah, and started back for Gibeon.

Twenty-six days had passed since the execution of the children. Soon now the tragic, macabre episode would be over. I would not be sorry to see it relegated to memory.

Beside the rock, David began building the fire for the night. Rizpah helped him arrange the wood. He struck flint against metal, sending out a spark which ignited the dry grass and twigs beneath the larger sticks.

They stood together watching the flames grow and leap toward the darkening sky. "Tonight," she said hesitantly, "I would like to be alone here."

David nodded, still looking into the fire. "Then I shall say now what I intended to say later."

He glanced out toward the plain. The wind was dying, leaving a heaviness in the air. They could feel the oppressiveness of the clouds they could no longer see.

"I shall be returning to Hebron," he said, "but I shall not remain there long. For a number of years I have sought a city in which I could build a permanent capital. I have considered several locations. Shiloh, Shechem . . . cities with the pride of tradition. The tribes of Israel would be pleased if I selected a site so far north . . . to be blunt, so far from Judah. But for many reasons, none of these cities would be a practical choice."

He turned a little away from her. His face in the firelight was hard. She had seen David the shepherd, David the sweet singer of songs, David the warrior. In each of these there had been an element of ambivalence, a conflict of natures. Now there was none. Here stood David the king.

"I have selected a city," he said. "A place of beauty and strength, a place where I can set my name. It is called Jerusalem, the city of Zion. Those who live there now, the Jebusites . . ."

He broke off and looked at her. Suddenly he smiled warmly. "What kind of dull oaf am I, to speak to you now of conquest and capitals and eternal cities? But I will also do you no disrespect by wooing you with honeyed words and double-tongued flattery."

He took her hand. "We are alike, Rizpah. We think alike; we have often acted alike. Neither of us has any illusions about the other, so there can never be disillusionment. I know your beauty and I know the stone and softness beneath it. You know what there is to know of me. Between us now there is not yet love. But in time, whatever drew us together in the beginning could grow and ripen, and perhaps turn to love."

She looked at him in silence.

"Must I make it more plain? I am asking you to become my chief wife, my queen. To rule the land with me. To live with me to the end of our days."

Still she did not speak.

He hesitated, then said gently, "Perhaps I should have waited. It was tactless and inconsiderate of me to speak to you here. I . . ."

She placed her fingers against his lips. "It was here that I began to know you," she said. "Let my lord David not regret having spoken."

"But you do not wish to answer tonight."

"I cannot."

He looked up at the blackness of the sky. "Tomorrow," he said. "Tomorrow I shall wait for you."

He stretched out his hands. She put hers into them, and they remained motionless for a few moments. Then he turned away.

She waited, listening, until she could no longer hear the sound of his horse's hoofs.

Far off on the plain a jackal cried.

Rizpah walked to the oak tree and stood for a long time before the shrouded bodies of her children.

chapter fourteen

IT DID not rain until midmorning.

But since shortly past dawn the little group had been waiting on the plain. David talked quietly with the elders of Gibeon. I stood apart from them, looking toward the amphitheater.

By tacit agreement, no one approached it. I could see Rizpah pacing slowly back and forth before the tree, now and again glancing at the sky.

The clouds were heavy and black-rimmed. It seemed that they could not hold their moisture another moment. Yet, like spiteful demons, they roiled about, jostling one another, mocking us with unfulfilled promise.

I did not believe it when I felt the first drop. Nor, apparently, did the others. The assembled men, somber portraits of dignity in their black robes, began lifting their heads like startled deer and gazing about wide-eyed, one at the other.

Then the heavens opened.

The chief elder gave a sign, and the cart in which the boys' bodies were to be placed started through the downpour.

The rest of us waited. David walked a few paces forward, then stood without moving, the rain pelting down on his bared head.

When the cart reached the blasted tree, the two black-clad elders who were guiding it performed the task for which they had come.

Rizpah followed the cart as it returned.

She came to David and stopped. For a few long moments they stood an arm's length apart, looking at each other, as the rain drummed about them on the hard ground.

Then she walked past him.

epilogue

THE LAND around Gibeah is awakening. All about the house where Saul once lived the green is tender on the earth. Anemones spot the hills with brilliant red and shaded pink, and daffodils wave their lovely grave heads in the spring breeze.

For a time I was not sure it was a good idea for us to come here. Too many memories live in these rooms. Too much pain and joy mingles in the shadow of the hills. Let the dead be dead, I thought.

Now I see how mistaken I was, how wise Rizpah had been to accept David's offer of the house for as long as we wished to remain.

We were lonely at first. Lonely and desolate. Rizpah would sit day after day in the common room, not speaking, looking out over the dead winter countryside. Or she would drift through the cheerless halls, eyes blank, shoulders bowed.

But little by little her spirit began to come alive again. First in sorrow. In a flood of tears and even in shrieking and battering her fists against the wall. It was hard for me not to go to her then, but I knew this was a battle she must win alone.

Then one day, when she had come back to the house after a long walk in the hills, I saw a glimmer of life in her eyes, the first faint hint of a smile.

She took me by the hands and said, "I have been selfish, Egrep. I have thought only of myself for longer than I care to remember. I do not ask you to forgive me. And I will not thank you for being with me, except in my heart. But I am glad you were here."

And then just a few days ago, when a fine spring drizzle was falling and the trees glistened outside the window, she turned to me. Her voice was low and reflective. "I do not know where," she said, "or when, or with whom. But I think, old woman, that now I will be able to find peace."

I have no doubt she will.

about the author

CHARLES E. ISRAEL *was born in Evansville, Indiana, in 1920, brought up in Baltimore, Maryland, and he attended schools in North Carolina and Ohio. He served in the Merchant Marine during World War II in the Atlantic, Pacific and Mediterranean theaters of war. At the war's end he returned to Europe to work with displaced persons as a member of the UNRRA staff and of other international organizations, and it was during an assignment in Germany that he met his wife, the former Verna Sweezey.*

In 1950, en route to India, the Israels visited Hollywood, California, and remained for three years while he wrote for radio and television (they still haven't been to India). Four scripts which he wrote at that time for the Ford Foundation series The Ways of Mankind were produced in Canada, and this resulted in a move to that country, where he has been residing ever since (except for trips to Holland, Ghana and the United Kingdom).

Today Mr. Israel is one of Canada's best-known writers and is a frequent contributor to Canadian television. His novel The Mark was published in 1958. Rizpah, two years in the writing, was inspired by his studies at Hebrew Union College in Cincinnati and his continuing interest in Biblical lore and literature.